Maggie O'Farrell is the author of six nov[...]
Lover's Lover, The Distance Between Us, wl[...]
Maugham Award, The Vanishing Act of Esme Lennox, The Hand That
First Held Mine, which won the Costa Novel Award, and Instructions
For a Heatwave. She lives in Edinburgh.

Praise for Maggie O'Farrell:

'Spellbinding' Barbara Trapido

'Unputdownable' Ali Smith, Scotland on Sunday

'Thoroughly engrossing and suspenseful . . . O'Farrell, in this
beautifully written tale, gets the psychological nuances just right'
Anita Shreve

'Genuinely unputdownable . . . evidence of her place as one of
Britain's most engaging contemporary novelists' Literary Review

'Another stunning novel' Grazia

'Here is an author whose depth and insight hover just below the
surface of an apparently effortless lightness' Joanna Briscoe, Guardian

'A traditional, old-fashioned storytelling striptease, seductively
unveiling layer after layer of revelatory secrets' New York Times Book
Review

'A writer of rare insight and intellect with a feel for language
that renders her love story both tender and tragic' Financial Times

'O'Farrell has a gift for storytelling which makes the reader long
for her next effort' Erica Wagner, The Times

By Maggie O'Farrell

After You'd Gone
My Lover's Lover
The Distance Between Us
The Vanishing Act of Esme Lennox
The Hand That First Held Mine
Instructions for a Heatwave

my lover's lover

and

the distance
between us

Maggie O'Farrell

TINDER
PRESS

My Lover's Lover Copyright © 2002 Maggie O'Farrell
The Distance Between Us Copyright © 2004 Maggie O'Farrell

The right of Maggie O'Farrell to be identified as the Author of
the Work has been asserted by her in accordance with the
Copyright, Designs and Patents Act 1988.

An extract of *The Distance Between Us* first appeared in *New Writing* 12

My Lover's Lover first published in Great Britain in 2002
by REVIEW
An imprint of HEADLINE PUBLISHING GROUP

The Distance Between Us first published in Great Britain in 2004
by REVIEW
An imprint of HEADLINE PUBLISHING GROUP

First published in this omnibus edition in 2013 by
TINDER PRESS
An imprint of HEADLINE PUBLISHING GROUP

1

Cataloguing in Publication Data is available from the British Library

ISBN 978 1 4722 1250 4

Typeset in Perpetua by Palimpsest Book Production Ltd, Falkirk, Stirlingshire

Printed and bound in Great Britain by Clays Ltd, St Ives plc

Headline's policy is to use papers that are natural, renewable and recyclable
products and made from wood grown in sustainable forests. The logging and
manufacturing processes are expected to conform to the environmental
regulations of the country of origin.

HEADLINE PUBLISHING GROUP
An Hachette UK Company
338 Euston Road
London NW1 3BH

www.headline.co.uk
www.hachette.co.uk

my lover's lover

For Catherine and Bridget,
with all my love

ACKNOWLEDGEMENTS

My thanks to: William Sutcliffe, Ruth Metzstein, Flora Gathorne-Hardy, Victoria Hobbs, Mary-Anne Harrington and Geraldine Cooke

now that I'm nearly gone, I'm more here than I ever was

ALI SMITH

good lovers make great enemies

BEN HARPER

part | one

As I was going up the stair,
I met a man who wasn't there.
He wasn't there again today;
I wish that man would go away.

ANON

She steps from the taxi, pushing at the metal weight of the door, clutching cigarettes, change and the thorned stems of roses. Sarah says something to her over the taxi roof and she half turns. She's aware too late of her foot catching on the granite curve of the kerb, and the next moment she is airborne, falling upwards.

Lily sees the world swivel on its axis, her hair, lighter than her, flowing past her face, her fingers shedding roses and spinning discs of coins. As she arches through space she sees, walking along the pavement towards her, a man. It seems odd somehow that he should be alone because he strikes her, in that split-second shutter-snap moment, as the kind of person who is rarely without others. He walks with a peculiar emphasis, as if trying to leave an imprint of himself on the air. Then concrete and grit smack against her body, and the skin is flayed from her hands.

At the touch of fingers, tight as ivy on her sleeve, she looks up. His eyes are a surprising, unambiguous blue. The flowers are crushed beneath her, seeping yellow pigment into her clothes. He is helping her upright, speaking to her, asking her are you all right, are you hurt. Her hands feel

3

scalded, raw, and when she looks at them she sees beads of blood springing from the skin in neat rows. Then Sarah has made it round from the other side of the taxi and is holding her arm, pressing tissues to her grazes, thanking the man. When Lily looks round, he's vanished.

'My God,' Sarah says, peering at her. 'Are you OK?'

'Yeah,' she says, laughing now, embarrassed, 'I'm fine. Don't know what happened there.' And they walk through the night air, towards the party. A repetitive, thrumming pulse of music is stretching at the walls of the building.

Inside, the rooms and corridors are crushed with people and hung with heavy nimbuses of smoke. It's the exhibition launch of a friend of Sarah's, but no one's looking at the art – photo-realistic paintings of people and animals being consumed by fire. Lily has the sensation of wanting to stretch up to the ceiling where there might be more air. Her injured hands feel sensitised, peeled like eggs.

She leaves Sarah in the main room, talking to a girl in a turquoise dress. The dress is rimmed with silky, frail fur, strands of which cling to the moistness of the girl's skin like seaweed. The people all seem to be of a type, or wearing some kind of uniform. The girls are small and gamine with cropped hair and dark-kohled eyes. The men are brash, filling their clothes complacently, gripping cigarettes between meaty fingers. Maybe it's the fall, or the pain in her hands, but she can't get over how distant everyone seems, as if she's looking at them down the wrong end of a telescope.

At the drinks table, she picks up a fragile-feeling plastic cup filled with acidic pale wine. Next to her, a woman is

4

fanning herself vigorously with the exhibition catalogue, her cup-rim stained with a simulacrum of her violent crimson lips. Holding her drink above her head, Lily starts pushing her way through groups of people and cross-currents of conversation, towards the back and shoulders of a man she knows. She hears the rub of her black corduroy trousers as her legs move under her – a sound of secret, velvet friction. She had a lover who'd been obsessed with these trousers. '*Cor-du-roy*,' he would say as he eased them off her, separating each syllable in a fake French accent, 'cord of kings.'

A hand darts through the crowd and seizes her arm. It's brown-skinned, crooked-fingered, with silver nails. She stares down at it, surprised, then leans around the back of a thickset woman with bristly hair to see Phoebe, Sarah's friend who works at the gallery. 'Hi,' she says. 'How are you?''

'Come and talk to us.' Phoebe tugs at her. The abrasions on her palms and wrists ache, threatening to split apart. 'This is my cousin, Marky Mark.' Phoebe moves to one side and Lily sees the man who'd picked her up off the pavement. Phoebe holds out her hand, flat, palm up. 'This is Lily.'

Lily steps forward. He looks different in the light. His shirt, hectically patterned, is rolled up at the sleeves, one higher than the other so that she can see the line of his tan. The curve of his bicep is a pale, milky white, his forearms a deep brown. His fingers are stained with green ink and he has the heel of his right shoe balanced on the toe of his left.

'Marky Mark?' she repeats, when she is close enough for him to hear her. 'That's a funny name.'

'It's Marcus,' he murmurs, lifting his glittering blue gaze

to hers. He scans her face for a second or two, then smiles. 'How are your hands?'

Lily holds his gaze. She refuses to be intimidated by flirtatious men. 'All right, thanks.'

'What's wrong with your hands?' Phoebe is saying, but neither of them replies.

'Can I see?' he asks.

She holds out her wrist. He transfers his beer can into his other hand and reaches out for her arm, curling his fingers around it. His touch is surprisingly hot. Around the pressure points of his fingertips, her skin empties of blood.

'Hmm,' he says, leaning close, 'nasty. You should get it cleaned up properly.'

Lily retracts her arm. 'I'm sure I'll live.'

Again, he smiles. 'I'm sure you will.'

'What happened? What happened?' Phoebe twitters.

'Lily fell,' Marcus replies, still looking at Lily. 'Outside. Tell me, do you make a habit of falling –'

'Not really,' she cuts across him.

'– at people's feet?'

There is a pause.

'No,' she says again. 'No, I don't.'

'Marcus,' Phoebe begins, in a strident, bossy voice, obviously put out, 'I want to hear about you.'

Lily raises her eyebrows at Marcus, but then becomes aware of a shift between the three of them. Marcus looks at Phoebe quickly, moving his mouth as if about to speak. Phoebe is gazing at him intently and he is staring back at his cousin with a strange, wry, almost pained expression, one hand pressed, oddly, to the centre of his thorax.

'How are you doing?' Phoebe's voice is nearly a whisper. Something private, hidden, is being referred to. Lily looks from one to the other, suddenly wanting to be away from them both. Whatever this is, it has nothing to do with her.

'Well, I—' He stops. Slowly, he rubs his nose with his knuckle, managing to keep his beer can upright at the same time. Someone passes in the corridor beyond the kitchen door, saying, 'And she never knew, never found out.' Marcus sniffs in a deep breath, seems to be examining the lino on the floor. Lily sees in horror that he might cry. But then he grins and says, 'I think I need a new flatmate.'

He and Phoebe collapse into sudden hysterics. Phoebe hoots with laughter, leans on Marcus while the two of them giggle and snort and hiccup and wipe their eyes. Lily smiles at them both and turns towards the wall of people and sound. As she walks away, she hears Phoebe, behind her, ask: 'What on earth happened?'

Last night, the radio he'd thought long broken sputtered into life. Suddenly, a woman's voice, in the cracked vowels of a language he couldn't fathom, was sliding down the spiral staircase of his ear.

Aidan flicks over a page of the magazine, and takes a tentative sip of his tongue-flayingly hot coffee. He'd lain there for a while, listening to the sound of a distant radio station, broadcasting from somewhere, surfacing in his room. He hadn't been able to get back to sleep and half an hour later he'd been sitting on the edge of his mattress, screwdriver in hand, the radio in pieces around him, trying to find the loose connection.

The magazine is one he found in the café. It's about 'lifestyle choices', it tells him, and is full of soap stars he's never heard of in their underwear. He spends a few minutes doing a ridiculous questionnaire entitled 'So you think you're immune to love?', and scores dismally low, putting him at highly infectious. He does it again, fiddling his answers, until he gets cross with himself and turns instead to an article about a testicle festival in Montana.

He's been to see a movie and he knows he won't sleep for a while, so has found this late-night coffee bar. He had to go out, had to leave the flat, had to pretend he'd had other plans all along. He's supposed to be at Phoebe's exhibition launch, but just couldn't face it.

He sits on a high stool with an iron rung for his feet and a mirror in front of him. He avoids his own eye and looks instead at the room behind him. The people under the white strip-lights look pallid and vitamin-less. Cigarettes balance between fingers or in ashtrays, legs are crossed, feet dangling in the air, napkins are concertina-folded against the table surface. No one talks much. The Italian men behind the counter mutter monosyllabically to each other and gaze at the large TV screen where two teams zigzag up and down a lurid green pitch. Outside, late-night crowds drift past the glass door.

Without warning, a huge yawn overtakes him, and his jaw hinge cracks – a startling, inappropriate noise that from inside his head sounds like a gunshot. He suppresses an urge to laugh, and glances about him to see if anyone else has heard it. What would he say? Sorry to have disturbed you, that was just my malfunctioning mandibular joint. A man brushes past him, putting on his coat. The waiter flaps a tablecloth free of crumbs at the door. Someone standing in the corner lets a cup of coffee slip from their fingers and it shatter-smashes, a hot, dark lake of coffee spreading over the neat chess-squares of lino.

Lily slips into the back stairs of the gallery, in search of another bathroom. There's a toilet on the ground floor, but a long queue of people is snaked around its door. The sweat she's broken out in from being crammed in a room with too many people cools on her skin. As she climbs the flight of stairs she imagines she's leaving a swirl of water molecules in her wake.

The gallery is in one of those Victorian terraced houses that stretch in rows all over the city. They are all roughly the same layout, but where the bathroom usually is – at the back of the house on the first floor – Lily finds a small office smelling faintly of wet coffee granules.

She leans on the spiralling banister and looks down. From this distance, the mass of voices sound like frogs, high-pitched and regular. Then she hears something else – heavy footsteps of someone descending the staircase.

The floor judders as Marcus comes down from the upper floor. She straightens up, turning towards him in the half-light. But he moves nearer and, without speaking, slides one arm around her shoulders and the other around her waist. The length of his body rests against hers. He bends his head and presses his lips to the dip just below her cheekbone.

Lily is so shocked she does nothing. She stands in the

cage of his arms, breathing in the scent of his hair, his skin, the wool of his sweater, the wine on his breath. His face feels damp, as if he's just washed it.

Then she feels something else entirely. A movement of air, tiny, imperceptible, a slight disturbance in the atmosphere. Someone else is there. Someone else is with them, watching them. She pulls away from him, twisting her head round. No one there. She cranes her head past him. No one there either.

She looks back at him, slightly thrown. It's in her mind to ask him a question, but she can't quite form what it is. The moment see-saws between them, and it's one of a peculiar, febrile clarity: she can hear the blood-throb of his heart, the static shift of her shoe-soles against the carpet. There are textures everywhere: he scratches his head and hair-shaft crackles against scalp, nails against follicles. Their clothes, moving on their bodies, are bonfires of silk against cotton, wool against denim.

He is rooting for something in his back pocket. 'I've got something to show you.' He makes an elaborate circling movement with his hands, like an illusionist revealing the final apparition of a trick. He opens his palm, flat, and holds it out to her. In its centre is a slip of paper. 'It's a piece of paper,' he says.

Lily reaches up and touches the place where his lips had been. 'I can see that.'

'Do you want it?'

They look at it together, a tiny runway on his outstretched hand. She keeps her face serious. 'Not really.'

'How about if I write my phone number on it?'

Lily laughs.

'Well?' he says.

'No,' she says, an inexplicable belligerence taking hold of her, 'still don't want it.'

'That's very rude,' he says. He stretches the paper between his hands and snaps it against the air. 'Didn't your mother ever teach you any manners?' Leaning on the banister, he scribbles on it with the narrow lead of a propelling pencil. 'Here,' he says, pushing it into her pocket. 'Promise you'll call me.' He keeps his hand in her pocket, pulling her to him. 'Promise?'

And because she doesn't want to give him what he wants, or at least not yet, doesn't want to let him have things his way, she asks, 'Are you really looking for a new flatmate?'

He blinks. The hand in her pocket moves, tenses, then withdraws. 'Maybe. Why?'

'I know someone who's looking.'

'Who?'

'Me. I've been living at my mother's for two months and it's driving me mad.'

He studies her face with such intensity that she knows he's thinking about something else. 'You,' he says, as if weighing the word on his tongue. Then he swallows. 'Yes,' he says, 'yes I am. You have to call me now,' he shouts, as he thunders down the stairs.

Seconds pass. Lily stares up at the shut, opaque windows, waiting. Nothing.

'Marcus!' she calls again, scanning the brickwork, as if expecting it to register some kind of reaction. The narrow-mouthed courtyard, surrounded on three sides by wide-windowed warehouses, swallows the impact of her voice, leaching it of decibels. She sighs and glances at the scrap of notepaper to check the street number he'd given her, before stepping up to the door again. There are four separate bells and beside the top one is written 'Sinead + Marcus'. The bell didn't work, he'd said; she'd have to shout up, he'd said. He'd come straight down.

She steps back, away from the door, shading her eyes against the dull glare of the sky. The top windows look blank, impervious, throwing back reflections of their counterparts opposite. She looks out beyond the mouth of the courtyard and down the street. Two elderly people in beige mackintoshes are crossing the street at a painfully slow pace, followed by an arthritic-looking terrier in a tartan coat. She could just go. She could just walk away, get on the tube, go home, take off her makeup and tights, which are cutting into her middle, and sit under the flickering blue gaze of the television. She could just forget the whole thing and go. She jiggles keys inside her pocket, considering this idea.

But then she inhales deeply, imagining her alveoli filling out, darkening with oxygen. 'MARCUS!' she bellows. It comes out much louder than expected, and she giggles in surprise and a kind of private pleasure at the noise she's capable of making. His name bounces off the wet cobbles, the polished panes, the windscreens of the cars hunched along the pavements. Then, above her, a window swings open and a man appears. It's not Marcus. He's got black hair. He's also frowning. They examine each other for a moment.

'He's not here,' he calls down, leaning with one hand on the sill, the other holding his hair out of his eyes. He looks as if he's been interrupted from a deep sleep.

'Oh,' Lily says. 'Do you know when he'll be back?'

The man shakes his head and shrugs.

'I was meant to meet him here at seven.'

The man looks at his watch. Lily doesn't look at hers. She knows it's about ten past.

'No idea.' He gazes down at her. Lily waits. 'Maybe you'd better come in.'

'Thanks,' she mutters.

Moments later, the heavy grey door opens on to the street. It swings outwards, the man pushing it with his foot. Lily has to duck in under his arm. 'Thanks,' she says.

He is examining her curiously, unsmilingly; she beams back at him. Sulky people always make her want to do this – annoy and irritate them out of their glumness. Then he lets the door slam closed and they are plunged into complete darkness. Lily starts and puts up her hand to feel for a wall, a surface. She would never admit it to anyone, but she's never liked the dark. She is locked into the foyer of a large warehouse in darkness with a man she's never met. She has a dim memory of seeing some stairs climbing up and turning a corner, but are they to her left or to her right?

'Dark, isn't it?' she hears herself say to the grumpy bloke, but her voice sounds high and thin.

There is no response. Lily shuffles her feet towards where she thinks the stairs might be, holding her arm outstretched. The floor surface feels grainy. Something crunches underfoot.

'This way.'

The voice is very close to her ear, and on the other side of her head. He must have moved around her and she didn't even notice.

'Is there a light?' she says, turning her face towards the direction of his voice.

'There's one up here.'

His voice is further away now, higher up. He must have started climbing the stairs. An inexplicable fear infiltrates her like a chemical, her head hot, her breathing fast. She is telling herself off for being stupid, but salted water is prickling at her eyelids when there is a burst of light like a flashbulb going off: the front door opens, and someone – Lily is too blinded to see who – comes in. The door slams shut and a light is snapped on, and in front of her, holding a bicycle helmet under his arm, is Marcus. His hair is wet, velvet-short, holding webs of drizzle.

'I'm so sorry,' he says. 'I'm late, aren't I?' He pushes back the cuff of his jacket to see his watch. 'I am. I'm really sorry. I got held up by this idiot person I work with and I couldn't get away and . . .' He comes close to her, so close that she can smell the rain off him, seizes her arm, and pulls her towards the stairs. 'Let's go up. We mustn't waste another second. Did Aidan let you in? Where did he go to anyway? How come he left you standing in the dark?'

She follows the backs of his shoes – different from the ones he'd been wearing at the party – up the stairs. The stairs are rickety, narrow and steep: thin, bendable boards and a wooden handrail slippery with cheap paint. They go up two floors, three, four, and on the fourth is a door left ajar. Marcus pushes it, and holds it open for her.

'There you go, Lily.'

'Thanks,' she says, and they inadvertently catch each other's eyes as she passes close by him in the doorway.

But she isn't thinking about that because she's looking around the room she's been shown into. She would never have imagined that such a worn, dirty building could contain something like this vast, echoing space. Scrubbed, polished floorboards stretch away from where she is standing to a kitchen in one corner, a big table in another, to huge windows at the other end. Red lampshades hang from the double height of the ceiling; the wall from the door where she is standing to the kitchen is painted a pale green; the rest is white, with shelves and shelves of books.

Marcus has walked in, and is taking off his coat, slinging his bag into a chair. Lily advances across the boards, her shoes clacking on the polished wood.

'Lily's come about the room,' Marcus says.

Aidan, standing at the long kitchen counter, drops something. 'The room?' he snaps, his head jutting out as if Marcus has said something obscene. 'What do you mean?'

His anger pulls her up short like a dog that's reached the end of its leash. She looks at Aidan and then Marcus.

Marcus says nothing, levelly regarding the other man. Then he shrugs. 'Well, you know, we need someone to help pay bills and stuff.'

'Oh.' Aidan picks up an ice tray and cracks it between his hands. It steams as he slams it against the rim of a pint glass of water. Lily hears the ice cubes splinter on contact. 'Do we.'

Marcus seems unconcerned by the venom in Aidan's voice, rubbing his palm over his head. They watch as Aidan snatches up the glass and strides across the centre of the room. He then opens some heavy double doors and disappears like a magician's assistant into a box.

'Don't mind him,' Marcus says, searching for something in a drawer.

'Where's he gone?' she asks.

'Gone?'

'Yes, gone.' She points. 'Through those doors.'

'Oh,' he laughs, 'that's the lift shaft. It's his room.'

'The lift shaft?'

'Yeah. It's quite big. About twelve by fourteen.'

'Oh, right.' She has no idea what size that is.

'Have you never been in a warehouse before?'

'No. Seen pictures of them, but never anything like this.'

'When we found it,' he has moved into the kitchen area now, and is putting the ice tray back into the steel-fronted fridge, 'it was just a shell.'

Lily leans against the other side of the counter. 'A shell? Really? None of this,' she waves her arm, taking in the kitchen, the lights, a small area boxed in by glass bricks that she assumes is a bathroom and, down past Aidan's lift shaft, near the windows, two doors leading off the main space, 'was here. You built all this?'

'Yeah.'

'You and Aidan?'

'No.' His voice drops, diving down to sound low in his body, making her look up. There is a pause. Marcus runs his finger along the side of the counter, his head bowed. 'Me and my girlfriend.'

The words make Lily feel as though she is standing on a floor made of rice paper. He has a girlfriend. He has a girlfriend. The fact turns over and over in her head, and, aware that he is looking at her, she has to smile and nod when she actually feels as if she is missing a skin. 'Sinead?' she asks, and the word feels odd in her mouth. She's never said it before, she realises, her lips and tongue have never conspired together to perform this series of shapes.

Marcus looks at her and the blue of his eyes is like the thickest, coldest block of ice. 'Yes. How did you—'

'It's on the bell.'

'Oh. Oh, yes. So it is,' Marcus says, his voice still unsteady. Lily feels confusion swarm at the back of her head. He stands up straighter, seems to push something off his shoulders. 'Why don't I show you the room?'

She walks after him, deeper into the flat, and as she does so she builds an image in her head. She'd be Irish with a name like that, so Lily gives her flowing skeins of burnished red hair and quick, green eyes. She is small, neat and petite, and her skin is the colour of buttermilk, with a snowstorm of freckles. She has a soft, full, voluptuous body. She says his name with a soft, drawn-out R. Lily is trying to assemble these elements in her head but somehow the image won't meld, won't coalesce.

When he stops at a door right at the other end of the warehouse, Lily sees that a partition has been built, floor to ceiling, across what would have been an alcove. She turns her head and sees that there is another room, built in exactly the same way, directly opposite the one they are about to enter.

'You've done a lot of work, haven't you?' she says.

'Yeah, we did. But it's not too difficult for me,' says Marcus, 'I'm sort of . . . in that line of business.'

'You're a builder?'

He shakes his head. 'An architect.'

She is working up to asking what Sinead does, but she steps into the room and for a moment she can't say anything. It is rectangular and the ceiling seems even higher in this enclosed space. The outer side is dominated by an expanse of glass. The curtains are drawn right back; and across the courtyard, Lily can see into a room where a woman in a lilac dress is leaning on a computer, talking to a man with his back to them.

But it's not the space or the dimension or the aspect or the deep indigo blue of the walls that stuns her, but that this room is obviously still very much lived-in: there's a half-open wardrobe from which a tangle of clothes – female, from what Lily can see of their texture and shape – is strewn on the floor. The desk is covered in a tumble of loose sheets of paper and piles of books; nail-varnish bottles are lined up on the window-sill, their iridescent colours of blue, orange, purple, green, deep red glinting like cats' eyes. The bed looks as if whoever it is has just got up, the sheet whipped up into peaks, the duvet flung back, the pillows with rounded indents, crumpled tissues scattered across the mattress. Up on the walls are black and white prints of Marcus running with his arms outstretched along a beach, of an older woman with a hissing tabby cat tucked under her arm, of Marcus again, this time balancing on one foot on the roof of what could be this building. A glass of water stands by the bed, and a book with a pen stuck in to mark the reader's place. It seems as if someone has just left it for a moment, to fetch something from the kitchen or to answer the telephone. Lily feels uncomfortable, as if this person will at any moment return and find them standing there and ask, 'What are you doing in my room?'

Marcus moves, and Lily sees him take two steps into the room. He stops by the desk and takes a leaf of a succulent plant between his finger and thumb. The tendons in the back of his neck arch up through his skin.

'I don't understand,' Lily bursts out. 'Is this the room? I mean the room you want to rent?'

He nods.

'Then why – Whose is all this stuff? Whose room is this?'

Marcus goes to fold his arms, but he seems rather to wrap them round himself, his hands tucked under his arms, his fingers clutching at his own ribcage. 'It's . . . it was . . .' his voice is barely audible '. . . it was Sinead's.'

'Sinead's?' Lily repeats, before she can stop herself, before she realises the import of his words. 'Oh,' she says, thrown, 'I—'

'I'm sorry . . . all this,' he gestures around him, 'is still here. I intended . . . I thought it would be . . . cleared away by now. But . . .' He trails away, touches the plant again.

'She . . . she . . .' Lily attempts to take hold of the situation, to steer the conversation away, but her throat is blocked. Part of her wants to touch him, and the other part wants to get the hell out of here and never come back. Whatever it was that had made this girl leave in such a hurry could not have been good.

'What?' he says, and his face seems weirdly altered in the bright light from the bulb.

'She . . . er . . . she painted the room a good colour.'

'Yes.' Marcus presses his hand to the vertical, vibrant blue slats. 'She did.'

They shut the door behind them with the pressure of both their weight, and as it clicks into its frame, they move closer to each other.

'So, you like it?' He touches her shoulder, but doesn't draw her near, the space between them the width and length of a third body.

'The room?' She presses her lips together. It disturbs her, unsettles her; she wants to ask what happened, why did she go, when did she go. What on earth could make someone leave in such an evident tempest? What could end a relationship so quickly that you don't even take your clothes with you? The room feels to her like the scene of an accident – perversely compelling to look at, but not something you'd ever want to be a part of. His face, close to hers, is tense, waiting for her answer, and his hands, pressing hot on her arms, confuse her. Something is telling her to leave, leave now, walk away down the stairs, through the mouth of the courtyard and never come back. 'I love it,' she hears herself say.

'Then you'll move in?' he says, a smile breaking across his features. 'You'll come and live here?'

'Yes,' she says, nodding, more for herself than for him, 'I will.'

He leans his forehead to hers. They don't kiss, but their hands move over each other, slow and tentative, like skaters unsure of the ice.

When Aidan was a child, he stopped speaking for a year. Not for any reason – he just wanted to see if he could. One morning he woke up and decided that this was how it was going to be, his lips shut over his teeth, his tongue flat and still, a white, pure silence around him, and the clamour in his head just his, private, shuttered up.

His parents turned like litmus paper from exasperation to anger to concern. He wrote them notes in blue pencil on a notepad held together with a metal spiral. He was sent to a psychiatrist who asked him to write down what personalities he thought colours had. The children in his class at school called him 'spaz' and 'mongol' until his sister Jodie gripped fistfuls of their hair and rattled their heads like maracas. And when the year was up – he remembered the date, but nobody else did – he sat at the breakfast table and felt the words rising up in him like the thin thread of mercury in a thermometer.

Aidan sits in a chair, one leg resting on the other, one hand supporting his temple. He is regretting not taking off his jacket like the man suggested: he always forgets that the air-conditioning in this country isn't as fierce as it is in the States. The chair is soft, with hard plastic arms, and is digging into the space between his shoulder-blades. He can't find a way to be comfortable in it. Which is ridiculous, he reflects, because an orthopaedic specialist probably spent months working on the optimum ergonomic design for this swivel-based, seat-adjustable, back-supporting contraption.

Wardour Street hums, six floors below. He is sitting in the personnel office of the company for which he'll be working. In front of him a man on the other side of a desk is talking. The human brain is capable of decoding up to forty-five different speech sound units per second. Maybe, Aidan thinks, this man is talking at twice the normal speed because he's not hearing anything he's saying; his voice is reaching Aidan as a low, incomprehensible drone. The man is trying to persuade him to sign the contract between them on the desk. He has got Aidan to drop in here discuss this. But Aidan isn't going to sign it. Don't you have anything better to do? he wants to ask him: take off your suit, go out, meet some people, have some fun.

Instead he makes an elaborate looking-at-my-watch gesture, and is surprised. He's meeting his sister in fifteen minutes for lunch. The movement has caused a clink of metal against metal in his pocket. The keys. He'd almost forgotten.

'I really must be going,' Aidan says gently, edging forward in the uncomfortable chair.

The man looks alarmed. 'Well,' he says. 'Thank you for coming in at . . . at such short notice.' He picks up a pen and proffers it hopefully.

Aidan smiles and shakes his head. 'When you've made the changes,' he gestures at the pages filled with tightly spaced type, 'I've marked them in pencil, we'll talk again.'

'Oh.' The man looks crushed, fingering the silky nap of his tie. 'Oh. OK. I'll let them know.'

Aidan nods. 'Thanks.' And he walks away, out through the sprung-hinged metal door, taking the stairs down to the street.

Lily is processing photographer payments at the agency where she works. A pile of unfolded papers sits next to her left wrist. She picks them up, one by one, types a number in a column, hits the return key and waits as the sluggish hard drive turns over. In one hand she fiddles with a paperclip, unwinding it from its tightly set form. Across the office, a woman wrenches open and slams shut the photocopier doors, swearing.

Lily doesn't believe in careers. She had a 'proper job', as her mother referred to it, or the beginnings of one a few years ago, working as an interpreter, translating the strange desires, beliefs and objections of diplomats and politicians. But – and she hadn't admitted this to anyone – she'd found that after a few weeks she'd become unable to switch off the translating synapse in her brain. Like a tap left running somewhere, it became the constant background noise to her life. Having conversations with her friends, watching TV, listening to the radio, some small, inaccessible, ungovernable part of her mind would persist in translating whatever she heard into French. And when the translating devil within her began to give a running commentary on each and every tiny act in her life (*Ouvres ton porte-monnaie, prends les pièces – tu as la monnaie? oui – et mets les l'une après l'autre dans la machine, appuies sur le bouton, et maintenant ou vas-tu encore?* it would crow at her as she stood in front of the ticket machine in the Underground station) she decided she had to take some drastic action. These days, she has it largely under control; only occasionally does her inner interpreter start whispering to her about herself in French.

So she has three jobs – none of which she cares about and none of which invades and colonises her mind when she's away from it – which she does from nine until six, six days a week. Monday to Thursday she performs various administrative and organisational tasks for a group of actors' agents; Friday she has charge of a mostly silent toddler, Laurence, from Stoke Newington so that his mother can attend her yogacise and pottery classes. Lily is supposed to be teaching him French, but there is a limited amount of conversation to be had with an eighteen-month-old, French or otherwise. On Saturdays she works as a bra fitter in the lingerie section of a big department store with Sarah, who is supplementing her weekday incarnation as an art student.

Lily tells her mother that she's saving to do an MA. Sometimes, she tells herself she is saving to go travelling. Or for her own place. Or for a computer. Or for some course that will train her to do something brilliant and interesting. She's saving for something, she knows that, some indistinct future as yet unformed in her mind. When whatever it is presents itself to her, she tells herself, she'll have the resources to do it. And, besides, the jobs have a way of soaking up time, giving life a structure, a momentum.

Lily's phone rings, making her jump.

'Hi, it's Reception. There's a man here to see you. He says he's got a key for you.'

Marcus. It's Marcus. Lily sits still for a moment, her pulse thudding past her ears. Then she saves her work and gets up. In the smoked glass of the office wall she is bleached black, walking in the opposite direction to herself, moving towards a head-on collision with a darkened doppelganger.

At the front desk, under the candid stare of the receptionist, stands Aidan, a large bag on the floor next to him. Lily stops where she is. 'Hi,' she says. Aidan seems taller, broader than she remembered him. He's not skinny, as the image she held of him in her head, but well-built, with shoulders that obscure a large section of the room behind him.

'All right,' he says, raising his chin in a kind of nod.

The receptionist taps a biro against her nails, grins at Lily and winks. Lily ignores her.

Aidan holds out his hand, palm up. 'I brought these for you.' Hooked around his middle finger is a ring of keys.

Lily moves towards him and slides them off. 'Thanks.'

'The big one's for the outside door. The silver one's for the top lock. And the other's for the . . . well, the other.'

'OK. Great. Thanks a lot.'

He shrugs, reaching for the bag.

'So . . . where are you off to?' she asks, hoping to stall him. It seems odd for him to leave just like that. They are going to be living together, after all.

'Japan.'

'Oh.'

'For work.'

'Right.' She is gripped suddenly by an urge to laugh and has to pretend to cough, putting her hand over her mouth so that he doesn't see her smile. She is aware that for some reason, this man has taken a dislike to her, and she wants him to know she knows. And that she doesn't care. She decides to keep asking him questions, to prolong his agony. 'What do you do?'

'I'm an animator.'

'What do you animate?'

'Er . . . adverts.'

'Yes?'

'Music videos.'

'Oh?'

'And some films.'

'That must be great.'

'It's . . . well, yeah . . . it's all right.'

Lily smiles at him effusively. He looks away, at his feet, at the pavement outside, at the veneer of the reception desk. She decides to let him off the hook. He's suffered enough. 'Well,' she passes the keys from one hand to the other, 'I suppose I'll be seeing you when you get back.'

'Uh, yeah. See you then.' He backs away and out of the door, his bag held awkwardly over his shoulder.

''Bye!' She waves at him until he disappears from view.

As she returns to her desk, she is accosted by Sonia, the woman who had been swearing at the malfunctioning photocopier. 'Who's the GLM?' she demands, hands on hips, blocking Lily's path.

Lily suppresses a sigh. Sonia has an irritating habit of

giving everything an acronym. GLM meant Good Looking Man.

'Who *was* that?' another woman shouts from her desk. 'He is *gorgeous*.'

Lily laughs and sits down in her chair. She glances to where she and Aidan had been standing, as if she might see some after-image of him there. 'He's my new flatmate.'

'Nice,' Sonia says, shuffling pages around, dropping some to the floor, 'very nice. Can I come round for dinner?'

'Sure,' Lily says, picking up her next payment form. 'But he's not a GLM. He's an RPITA.'

Sonia looks up. 'A what?'

'A right pain in the arse.'

She must have moved, jerked her arm or shifted in her seat or something, because the keys suddenly fall from the desk to the carpet. Lily bends to pick them up and for the first time she wonders if they were once Sinead's.

Aidan walks away, the white level light of the low winter sun obscuring his view of the street ahead. The air is still today, unmoving, cold, amplifying the sound of his footsteps, the crack of a car engine further down the street, the staccato shout from a window above. He shivers inside his clothes.

Outside a shop, he thinks he might go up to the men's department to buy a shirt. He stands in front of a display of identical shirts in twelve different colours and finds he is unable to make a decision. A wordless version of a pop song trickles from speakers hidden in the suspended ceiling. He circles a stand of ties and touches a pair of socks. Then he takes the escalator down, surrounded by tourists and rich, jobless women with expressionless faces.

The warehouse is empty when Lily arrives. She struggles up the narrow stairs, a rucksack on her back, heaving at the handrail, the suitcase banging against her leg. Her mother, Diane, had offered to drive her there and help her 'settle in' but Lily couldn't think of anything worse. After the flat she'd been renting had flooded, she'd been forced to move back into her mother's, shrinking herself down to fit the life she'd had as a teenager, living in the house in which she'd been born – 'Right there in that bed,' Diane was fond of saying to almost anyone who would listen. Her father had left them, in what Lily always considered a flagrant disregard for male cliché, for his secretary, years ago.

She's forgotten, or failed to pay any attention to, Aidan's lesson on the keys, so spends ages at the door, fiddling with locks and latches.

Inside, it seems unnaturally quiet and still. The fridge trembles, notes pinned to its outer skin. A mercuried bead of water collects on the kitchen tap. The red lanterns overhead cast the room in a hellish, kiln-like glow. Her footsteps on the boards make a crashing, echoing sound as she walks towards the room that is now hers. She pulls at the handle, but nothing happens; she tugs harder. The wood seems to have swollen into the frame. She puts the keys in her pocket and pulls with both hands. Then she is falling back on to the floor, landing hard on the base of her back. Lily sits for a moment in agony, rubbing her back, cursing.

Then she stops, because she can see through into the room. Slowly, without taking her eyes from what she sees beyond the doorframe, she slides her rucksack off her shoulders and staggers forward into the doorway, clutching with one hand at her injured back.

Everything is stripped bare. It could be a different room. The blue walls are empty, the desk is gone, the nail varnish and books from the shelf, even the bed has gone. In the place of the big, rumpled-sheeted mattress is a new bed, still in its clear plastic wrapping. Just beside it, near the corner, is a small hole in the wall – a dent, as if something has been pulled out of the plaster, a distracting flaw in the wall's perfect block of colour. Lily sits down on the bed, the polythene crinkling beneath her. The bareness makes her jumpy, wary, as if in all the emptiness there is space for something else, something other than her.

Sinead must have met someone else, she decides. Maybe it had been going on for a while, Marcus had found out and kicked her out. Why else would she leave so suddenly? She wonders who came and packed everything into boxes to take away and whether Marcus was there, whether he and Sinead did the packing together, whether they argued or silently avoided each other, and whether the other man was there. Lily pictures him outside on the pavement, jiggling his keys impatiently, looking up at the windows, his car boot open, ready and empty, waiting to receive the boxes and take them to another room, another flat, another life. How could Sinead have done that to Marcus, when it was obvious to anyone that he'd loved her? What kind of a woman could she be?

Lily gets up and drags in her bags from outside. She unfastens the catches of the suitcase and up-ends it. Clothes tumble out: socks, knickers, jumpers, trousers, shirts. She steps over them all and pulls open the door of the wardrobe. Empty hangers clatter against each other, but in the middle of the rail is something that makes her flinch in a kind of fear: a dress, strung by narrow straps, swaying slightly from the movement of the doors. She watches it until it is once more still. Then she puts out a hand and runs her fingers down its length. The material is cool and moves like liquid. It is dark blue, darker than the walls, and if it is pulled one way, the colour bleeds into black.

Lily curls her hand around the hanger, lifts it over the rail and draws it towards her. In the mirror inside the wardrobe door, she holds the dress against herself. Sinead is slim, Lily can see, thin even. Lily morphs the image she has of her in her head. Why, out of everything, has it been left? Did she want Marcus to see it? Was it some kind of message, a private sign?

She presses the material with the flat of her hand to her body, and moves closer to the mirror. A floorboard behind her creaks as her weight shifts and she gets that crawling feeling where her hair meets her neck that someone is watching her. Her head jerks round, as if she is expecting to find Marcus standing there, looking at her with Sinead's dress. But there's nothing there.

As if it might burn her, Lily places the dress on the rail so quickly that it slips off the hanger to the floor. She leaves it there, slumped in a puddle of material like a discarded skin, and walks out of the room, fast. It's another hour or so before she can bring herself to go into it again.

Marcus returns just as she is putting sheets on the bed. The swathe of polythene lies crushed into the corner, rustling and uncurling. The acoustics of the place distort and deaden sound, and she doesn't hear him until he's knocking on her open door.

'Hello?' he says, leaning into the room.

'Hi!' Lily leaps across to slam the wardrobe door shut. She has shoved the dress to one side and crammed her clothes in alongside it. 'Hi.'

They stand a few feet apart.

'So how's it going?' he says, looking about. 'All un-packed?'

'Almost. I'm sure I've forgotten everything.' She is going to mention the dress to him, she really is, but she sees that his face looks exhausted and white, and it somehow doesn't seem the right time. 'But I can always go back and get stuff I need.'

He nods. She finds she wants to look at him for a long time, memorise the set of his jaw, the way his shirt sits on his chest, how he grips his thumb in his opposite hand, as if she's going to have to sit a test on him. She had forgotten the way his hair parts just to the left of his crown and how he presses his teeth into his bottom lip. She is surprised at how pleased she is to see him, at how strong the pull of her attraction for him is. And she is surprised at herself. She always thinks of herself – prides herself almost – as having no illusions about men or the reasons for her need of them. She has them sometimes, and other times she doesn't. But this one seems to have got round her cynicism somehow, circumnavigated it, short-circuited it. She feels self-conscious suddenly, gripped by an irrational fear that she may, in that second, have become transparent, as if he can look at her and see her veins, spread out like webs, and her heart, pulsing, caught in the branches of her ribs.

He smiles at her. Has he read her thoughts? He suddenly seems a lot closer than he did, as if the room has shrunk around them. She has to bend down, pick up a book from the floor and place it on the bed so that he doesn't see the rather inane grin that has spread over her face. 'So,' she says assertively, then realises she has no idea what she is about to say. 'Um . . . thanks very much for having me,' she improvises.

'It's a pleasure,' he says quickly, and touches her arm. 'It's really good to have you here.'

'Oh,' she says, her hand moving involuntarily to meet his, 'well, thanks.' Their fingertips bump, his thumbnail touching the healing grazes on her palm.

Marcus breathes in deeply, passes his hand through his hair. 'Do you want a cup of tea?'

'That would be great.'

He disappears out of the door. Lily slumps to the bed. This is ridiculous. How long is it going to be until they sleep together? About two hours, by the way things are going. Sarah had been dubious about her moving in with Blond Man, as she called him. Sex with flatmates was never a good idea, she'd said on the phone yesterday, don't shit where you eat, Lily.

Not yet, Lily is saying to herself, as she walks towards the kitchen. At least, not tonight.

'I'm working on site this week,' he says, as he fills a kettle at the sink. 'The builders are really messing things up, and I've got to be there to sort it out. I've been away working on this building in New York, you see, so I'm getting all the shitty, tying-up-ends jobs until they put me on to something big again.'

He takes two mugs down from a shelf and shoves a tea-bag into each. She watches the way he does this – his thumbs flicking open the lid of the chrome tea caddy, his hands gripping the tea-bag like tweezers before he drops it, the two cups next to each other on the counter.

'I don't even know what you do, Lily.'

'I . . . er . . .' She laces her hands into each other. 'I do a few different things.'

'Really?'

'Yeah. I'm . . . I don't really know what I want to do yet.'

He hands her a mug of tea. It is too brown and steeped for her liking. She chases the bloated tea-bag around with her spoon, trying to hook it out.

He crosses the room and sits on the sofa. 'Do you have any ideas?' he asks.

'Well,' she says, 'you know, it's a bit of a thing with me—'

'What?' he interrupts. 'Jobs?'

'Yeah. People are always saying "What are you going to do with your life?" and I hate that. It doesn't mean anything to me. What about what life is going to do with you?' She takes a sip of her scalding tea. 'Have you ever—'

She stops. Across the room, Marcus has pulled out from under a cushion a single black leather glove. A woman's. It has taken on the shape of its owner's hand, its fingers curled slightly, its thumb almost touching the middle finger. He holds it up in front of him by its narrow wrist. His face is strained, set, but somehow unreadable. As she watches, he places the glove on the arm of the sofa beside him, smoothing the leather flat.

Lily puts down her mug on the counter, walks through the room and sits down next to him.

'What happened?' The words have slid out of her before she can check them or stop herself or decide if indeed she should really ask. 'Something happened, I know. Did she meet someone else? Is that it?'

Marcus shakes his head, then inhales and holds his breath, rubbing his fingers over and over his forehead. 'She . . .' His face is stiff, pulled, as if he's trying to prevent any expression making its mark. 'She's no longer . . . here.' He speaks the words with great effort and attention, as if there are many, many more inside him that he's holding back. 'She . . .' he hesitates, as if unable to decide how to put it '. . . she's no longer with us,' he finishes.

Lily's heart is giving long, drawn-out thuds. She feels as if she may very easily stop breathing. The euphemism sounds odd to her. It feels like something she's either never heard or hears every day. She can't quite remember what it's supposed to mean. He pronounces it with a heavy, almost ironic emphasis. She stares at him, baffled, her brain resisting whatever it is he is trying to tell her. His mouth is twisted into what might, under other circumstances, pass as a smile, and she is experiencing a variety of impulses: to shout, 'What on earth do you mean?', to place her hand comfortingly on his arm, to laugh. Somewhere behind them a bluebottle rattles, butting its head again and again against a pane.

Marcus raises his eyes to hers. It's then that she knows, and horror crawls over her skin like ants.

'How did she . . . ?' Her voice sounds strange to her, as if someone else is speaking through her. 'How?' she whispers, as if sound itself might hurt him, injure him.

But Marcus cannot speak. Lily hears herself saying she is sorry, she is so so sorry, and presses his hand between both of hers. To touch any other part of him at that moment would have seemed inappropriate, a trespass.

Lily pushes through the ticket barrier at Warren Street. A fine drizzle hangs in the air, suspended. She can't be bothered to walk down to the pedestrian crossing so she dodges the traffic, weaving between the cars that slough past her, slicked with rain.

Sarah's art school is a grey building arranged round three sides of a square. As Lily walks across it, the spiked green casings of conkers split and crack under her feet, revealing swirled, polished brown. She bends and breaks them from their impossibly white pods. There is something about their weight, their firm temperaturelessness, the way they fit exactly into the curve of her palm that pleases her. She fills her pockets, aware of them as she climbs the stairs, shifting and resettling inside her clothes.

The corridors remind her of her primary school – the high, white-timbered windows, the wide grey worn concrete floors, the scent of paper and paint and chemical-heavy cleaning fluids. When she reaches Sarah's studio, she peers through the marbled glass of the door, and spots her, bending over a pot on the floor, stirring energetically. The rest of the room is empty.

'Hi,' she says as she unlatches the door.

Sarah turns. 'What are you doing here?'

'Laurence has a cold,' Lily says, 'and his mother's convinced it's pneumonia, which means . . . I get the day off.' She holds up a carrier-bag. 'I brought some food. Have you had lunch?'

'You,' Sarah says, 'are a psychic marvel. I'm starving. But I've got to do this first. The plaster'll dry out otherwise.'

Sarah is making a body cast. She's been talking about it for weeks. Next to her, Lily now sees as she moves towards the window, is the framework, dangling on a string – a female form in frail, twisted wire, its hands resting on its hips. With the light directly in her eyes, it had been invisible. Lily places the conkers in a row on the window-sill, watching as Sarah soaks gauze strips in the wet plaster and wraps them, carefully, concentratedly, around the curves and planes of the framework. She works quickly, chewing the inside of her cheek, her fingers moving over her creation, deft and capable.

Lily unpacks some of the food, and feeds Sarah torn strips of bread. Some other students pass through, pausing briefly to watch, then moving on down the long, thin room. Sarah is older than most of the other people on her course, a mature student, although she prefers to refer to everyone else as 'immature students'. Lily drinks from a water bottle, rubs a conker into the dip of her hand and watches as the woman emerges, feet first, like a lone parachutist, waiting for the earth to come up and meet her.

'Gypsophila,' Sarah says at one point. 'Great word.' Lily pokes at the wet, creamy tub of plaster with a fingernail. It is the consistency of cake mix or mud. Sarah tells Lily about a lecture she went to that morning about male nudes, and about two people on her course who are going out together and insist on holding hands throughout the tutorials.

'How's Laurence's French coming along?' she asks.

Lily grins. '*Très bon, naturellement.*' She shakes her head, thinking of Laurence's mother, a tall, anxious woman with prematurely whitening hair and not enough to do. 'That woman is mad, really mad. How is it you need a licence for a dog but anyone can have a baby? It shouldn't be allowed.'

'And how's the new flat?'

Lily concentrates on peeling the tight, pungent skin of a clementine in one long, coiling strip. 'It's fine.'

She feels Sarah looking at her. The possibility of telling her about Sinead opens somewhere, like a window in another room. But something is blocking her. Some kind of loyalty to Marcus, maybe, or a reluctance to reduce it to small-talk, or to make real these nebulous fears she's been having. It seems too new, too undigested in her own mind, to speak of it easily.

She swallows a clementine segment, neat and contained as a goldfish. 'It's fine,' she says again.

'And have you bedded the landlord yet?'

She removes the white web of pith from her clementine, frowning. 'There's been a bit of a new development on that front.'

'Oh, yes?'

This all seems wrong. Sarah's using the flippant voice with which they do all their chit-chat. How can she sit here, munching her way through a clementine, discussing the death of a woman as if it means nothing at all?

'Um,' Lily begins, wondering how to go on. Then it comes out in a jumbled rush. 'You know the girlfriend I told you he had? The one whose room I've got? Well, she died.'

There is a short, shocked silence. When she looks up, she sees Sarah on a chair, standing beside a perfect white replica, her hands dyed the same colour. 'Are you serious?' Sarah steps down with a thud. 'My God. How come? I mean, how did she die?'

'I don't know. He couldn't really . . . talk about it'

'When did he tell you?'

'Last night.'

'My God,' she says again. 'How long ago was this?'

'Not sure. I think pretty recent.'

'Jesus, the poor guy.' Sarah picks a dot of dried plaster from her shirt and crumbles it between her fingers. 'You've got to be careful, Lily.'

Lily doesn't say anything.

'I mean, that's a big situation you've got there.' Sarah holds her arms wide, as if measuring it. 'You need to think carefully about whether you want to . . . take it all on.'

She comes in to find him watching a film on TV. They don't say much to each other and she sits down next to him, pressing her shoulders against the sofa, and discovers that there is no way of sitting so that their bodies aren't touching. The film is an old black and white one. An orchestral score surges as a woman is creeping along a corridor towards a big ornate door, the tempo of the music becoming more and more frantic.

Lily tips back her head and looks around the huge room. Rusted steel girders transect the ceiling, and by the window hangs an old, ropeless pulley. It seems peculiar to her suddenly that they should be living in this space: a hundred years ago it would have been a garment factory, where immigrants from eastern Europe stitched fabric into human shapes and practised getting their tongues around the muted diphthongs of English. This is what Lily loves about London, that every building, street, common and square has had different uses, that everything was once something else, that the present is only the past amended.

She swallows a yawn. Marcus's thighs are encased in jeans. She imagines that if she were to let her hand drop on to them, they would feel taut and warm, the muscles close under the material. It would be so easy: all she'd have to do would be to let her arm relax, and it would fall naturally, her hand coming to nestle close to his groin. She then realises that Marcus is looking at her, saying something. 'Sorry?' she says.

'He had more money for this one.'

'Pardon?'

'He had more money. He went to the States.'

Lily has no idea what he's talking about. 'Really?'

'Yeah,' he says, and turns back to the screen. 'It was his first Hollywood-backed film. Have you seen it before?'

'No.'

'Oh. Well, I won't spoil it for you then.'

A few minutes pass. The young woman is descending

a staircase in a frothy white dress and a big hat. An aristocratic man in a tuxedo stands at the bottom with his back to her.

'How was your day?' Lily asks after a while.

He glances at her. 'Good, actually.' He nods. 'I've got moved on to a new job. Project Architect.'

'Oh.'

'It's means being in charge of everything,' he explains, his eyes fixed on the screen.

'Right. That's great.'

'I suppose so.'

'What do you mean, you suppose so? It is great. Really great.' She touches his arm, wanting to press her point home.

'Mmm.' He shifts around so that he is facing her, and sighs. 'You're right.'

'Is it not a good project?' she asks, confused by his lack of enthusiasm.

'No, no, it's a great project. Really interesting – a bus terminus. It'll be . . . it'll be . . .' he rubs his forehead '. . . great.'

She looks at him, puzzled. They are sitting close together in this huge room, knees touching.

'I don't know,' he says, and gives a funny little laugh. Lily sees that he is trembling, his jaw muscles clenched. 'Life's just hanging on me a bit heavily at the moment. I don't know . . . I don't know what I can do to make myself feel better.'

'Do you . . . would it help at all to talk about it?'

'I don't think so, no.' He gets up and walks away quickly,

closing his studio door behind him. Lily sits where she is, her hands tucked between her knees.

The film still plays in the corner. An evil-looking woman seems to be trying to persuade the girl to jump out of a window. Lily wonders if she should switch it off.

It's Sunday afternoon. Lily is having a hibernation day. She has to do this about once a month. It's the only way, she tells herself, that anyone can remain sane in this city – lock the doors, put on the answerphone, don't leave the house, don't even think about going on public transport, just surround yourself with silence and do nothing.

At this precise moment, she is lying on her bed the wrong way round, her head tipped over its end, her legs crooked at the knees. She teases knots out of her hair with her fingers; she peels away loose jags from around her nails; she presses her eyes, then shuts them to see technicolour sparks behind her lids.

She sits up. Her head swims with the quick movement. She has no idea what time it is. Hunger tears like paper in her stomach. She should probably return the message Sarah left her earlier but can't quite make the move to do so. The day is ebbing away, the sky that blank, whitish, shut colour.

Lily stands, wanders to the window to look down into the street, and reaches up her hand to unfasten the latch. She encounters not cold metal but a dry crackle. She stands up on tiptoe to see a folded piece of lined paper, jammed into

44

the join. Lily tugs it out and opens it. It's a list of things: *hairgrips* is first. Then:

> *notebook*
> *stamps*
> *hair serum*

In a different column, with slightly neater, more thought-out handwriting, as if the person had shifted position or moved to a table or readjusted the pen:

> *pick up photos*
> *call I*
> *shoes?*

Shoes. Question mark. Was she going to buy shoes or not? Had she seen a pair she liked but wasn't sure about, and maybe needed to try on? Or did she need some and was just reminding herself to have a look? The writing is spiked, sloping. The bottom of the *g* a deft, straight line. No loops, the dot of the *i* pulled into a dash in her haste, her *es* missing a space in their top half, the taller letters dwarfing the smaller. Who is 'I'? 'Call I' seems strange, as if it had been a reminder to place a telephone call to herself. What kind of hair needed grips and serum?

The paper feels crisp and brittle. Lily holds it to her face and sniffs. The floor beneath her shakes, as if a washing-machine is on somewhere else in the building. There is a rumbling sound in the next-door room like a radiator digesting heat.

45

She wrenches open the window and, without thinking about it, lets the paper fall from her fingers. It floats down in a straight line, and she thinks suddenly of the paper fish her father used to make her by looping a strip of paper into itself. He would stand her on a chair and hand her the delicate curl of paper: Lily would hold her arm up above her head and release it; there was always a moment when you could see it twist and spore like a sycamore helicopter into a fish shape before it hit the ground and became just a loop of paper again.

She leans out of the window, wanting to catch that moment when it meets the ground but as she does so, the window-ledge seems suddenly lower; her body swings far further forward than she intended, her feet sliding on the boards. Her heart convulses, blood cooling her chest, and she has to grab for the window-frame to steady herself, her nails scraping against the woodwork, her fingers scrabbling for a hold. The courtyard, street, cars, Tarmac, cobblestones wheel and tip beneath her, looking at once far away and sickeningly close. Her mind seems to split away from her body and she seems to see herself or maybe someone else fall, limbs flailing, hair arching behind her, hitting the ground with a crunching thud. She imagines that final, immovable, hard kiss of stone as she is moving back into the room, into safety, into balance. Then she grips the window-frame with both hands, standing up very straight. She doesn't shut the window, but keeps the breath of the street moving around her. She is aware of the swell of the room at her back and the rush of the drop in front of her, and she stands there for a while, thinking.

That evening, Lily sits at the table, her dinner in front of her, half reading a book. Her eyes keep straying from the tight blocks of printed text, floating upwards to rest on Marcus. Across the room, he is murmuring into the telephone, his face turned to the wall. Another black and white film plays out, unwatched, on the TV.

Lily turns a page. Marcus dials a number, hangs up, dials again, hangs up, redials, speaks inaudibly into the receiver before dragging the phone on its extension lead into his room. The white cord rattles after him like a snake.

With one hand, she winds strings of tepid spaghetti around a fork. Marcus's film, freeze-framed to a moment where a man in too-short trousers is vaulting over a low wall, continues to flicker in the corner. She puts the fork back on the plate and starts clearing the table of her dinner things, stacking the plates on each other, balancing her mug on top of them. As she walks around the table towards the sink, she sees, she is sure she sees, out of the corner of her eye, something in the bathroom – a movement, a flicker, the greenish glass bricks refracting and splintering it.

And then suddenly it is gone and the space behind the glass is empty and clear. She'd blinked or looked straight at it and it had vanished. Lily slides the stack of plates on to the counter and moves towards the bathroom. The light is on and the window wide open. Rain flecks the curtain and the sill. There is the faint, sickly scent of jasmine in the air. The hinge is stiff as she tries to shut the window; she pulls hard on the catch and the curtain billows and reaches for her, the dampness clutching at her. It must have been what she saw, moving in the wind.

But she inspects the shower. It is dry, pristine, unused for hours and hours.

The next day, Marcus is out of the flat before she even wakes. As she's leaving her room, her bag on her shoulder, struggling with one arm in and one arm out of her coat, hooking her foot into her shoe, she sees on a chair outside Marcus's room the patterned shirt he was wearing when she first met him. It is draped, its material creased and rucked, the geometry of its pattern interrupted, one arm flung across the chair back, the other dangling to the floor. The top three buttons are undone, as if he pulled it over his head in a haste to be undressed.

Lily stands a few feet from it. She takes a step forward, but a movement at the corner of her eye makes her stop almost guiltily and flick her head towards the rest of the flat. It's empty. Of course. Who does she think might be there?

She covers the last two steps in a rush and seizes the shirt in both hands, as if someone is about to snatch it from her. As she does so, there is a sense of something being spilt inside her. She presses the shirt to her nose and mouth, trying to adjust. It is an unaccountable feeling, like the sting of sunburn you weren't aware of happening.

She's in love with him. This is not good. She doesn't want this.

Lily thrusts the shirt from her, looks away, out of the window, and sees for the first time that the green cones of shoots are pushing up out of the black soil in the window-boxes. She frowns. It's far too early, or perhaps even too late, for them. How come they're growing now, just as winter is beginning? Lily steps to the window, staring down at their green tips – waxy, speared and determined. Beneath them, she knows, are the paper-dry cortexes of bulbs, and inside them, the germ of flowers, folded and folded into themselves. Sinead planted these bulbs, she thinks. There's no way Marcus or Aidan would have. Sinead packed in their parchment bundles with powdery peat, watering them, placing the boxes here where no one has touched them since. How long can she have been dead? Two months? Three? How long ago did she plant these bulbs and would it have crossed her mind that she wouldn't see them flower?

She turns away. The flat seems sticky with Sinead's fingerprints. She doesn't know what to do.

She arrives at work late. Natasha, the lingerie supervisor, who Lily knows for a fact wears padded bras, gives her a narrow-eyed glare as Lily tries to skulk into the back room, unnoticed.

Sarah bursts in as she is stripping off her jeans.

'Shit,' Sarah says, flinging off her coat and struggling out of her sweater. 'I overslept. Through two alarm clocks. Can you believe it?'

'Natasha's on the rampage.' Lily yanks her shirt over her head. 'Did she see you?'

'Don't know.'

As they struggle into the green nylon skirts of their uniform, bumping into each other in the hot proximity of the tiny windowless room, Lily says, 'I have a question.' She stops, unsure of how Sarah might take this, then decides just to launch in. 'If you wanted to find out how somebody died, how would you go about it?'

'*What?*' Sarah straightens up from lacing her shoe. 'Who on earth—?' Her face clears. 'You mean the girlfriend. Whatshername. Lily, you can't be serious.'

'I just want to know.' She shrugs. 'That's all. Satisfy my curiosity.'

'But you can't go poking around behind his back! Lily, that's – that's devious and dishonest. It's stalker territory. If you want to know, you have to ask him.'

'I can't.'

'Just ask him. It's not an unreasonable demand. He tells you, he cries on your shoulder, you fall into each other's arms, you live happily ever after. Simple.'

Lily drags a brush through her hair. 'I don't feel I can. He's so . . . wrapped up in his grief. Most of the time he seems fine, and normal, but when she's mentioned, he just clams up. Won't say another word – about anything. And it's not exactly hard to imagine why, is it? I'd feel like some horrible ambulance chaser if I forced the issue. It's much easier this way – on everybody.'

'Can't you ask the other guy? The flatmate film man?'

Lily snorts. 'Yeah, he talks to me a lot.'

'So what are you going to do?'

'Don't know. Go to the Public Records Office? I've no idea how you go about these things.' She meets Sarah's exasperated gaze. 'Look, this is something I have to do. Once I know I'll be able to—'

'What?' Sarah demands. 'Sleep easy at night? Know what you're dealing with? What?'

Lily doesn't answer.

'Just what are you hoping to gain from this?' she persists.

Lily scrapes her hair back into a band, avoiding Sarah's eye.

'I don't understand you!' Sarah cries, still cross, crushing her clothes into a tight bundle. 'Why can't you just let it lie? Leave the poor woman alone.'

There is a tense pause. Lily pushes stray strands behind her ears and straightens her skirt. Then Sarah sighs: 'OK,' she relents. 'I shouldn't do this. I really shouldn't do this. But I have this friend. An investigative journalist on a tabloid. A real door-stepping, garbage-sifting rat. Nice guy, though, otherwise. He'll know what to do.'

Lily grabs her hand and squeezes it.

'Don't,' Sarah says, snatching it away. 'I'm only doing this to shut you up. This doesn't mean I agree with it.'

'I know.' Lily grins.

Sarah shakes her head. 'Just . . . give me her name.'

'Wilson,' Lily says. 'Sinead Wilson.'

Aidan is drifting, his mind running over thoughts like

water over stones. If he does buy a flat in Kentish Town should he spend a bit more for the one with a garden? Does he have time for gardening? He can't quite picture himself digging and planting things somehow. He'd have to start visiting those funny places . . . what are they called? They smell of peat and compost, and have rows of plants with roots bursting out of black plastic containers. Garden centres. Would having a garden involve the purchase of a wheelbarrow? Then he has the alternative vision – alternative to the one of him in wellies in the pissing London rain shovelling clods of manure around – of him in a deck-chair in summer. Behind him, someone is tending a barbecue, and music floats from his open ground-floor windows . . . He must remember to get that CD Jodie wanted. What was it called? He has it written down in a notebook back at his hotel. Something FunkMasters. Or FunkMasters Something. And he must call Sam when he gets back. What else is on that list? Something about—

At the sound of his name, Aidan jerks his swivel chair round from the window and the Tokyo skyline, its monoliths gleaming in the sun, and looks at the row of faces around the table, all angled at him expectantly. The man next to him is clearing his throat with a discreet, scraping sound. Was it him who'd been talking? Or someone else? Who'd just said his name? And what had been said during his little zone-out? He tries to arrange his face into a thoughtful, rather than panicked expression, busying himself with stabbing a drink carton with the sharp end of a straw.

'So,' he says, in what he hopes is an unruffled voice, looking round the table, 'shall we just run through that once more?' He leans back in his chair, raises the carton to take a drink, and misses his mouth with the straw.

Lily is balanced on a display pedestal, embracing an armless dummy. She can't get the bra fastener done up behind it. She wrestles with the two strips of elastic, her knees aching, her face pressed against the steel-hard fake tits, but the hooks refuse to connect with the eyes.

She yanks the bra off the dummy and examines the label. She's brought the wrong size up from the storeroom: a 30B, for God's sake. What was she thinking? Shop dummies are always a 32C. Temper tightens like a coil inside her. She doesn't like knowing things like that, doesn't like the fact that this job is, no matter how much she tries to resist, filling her head with useless, pointless crap. The average width of stocking tops. The number of bras British women buy per year. Which manufacturer caters for which type of figure. How to recognise those figures at a glance. The pros and cons of underwiring, adjustable straps, front fasteners, seams.

Lily climbs down from the display, leaving the dummy naked, and stamps over to the storeroom, the 30B hooked around her wrist like a catapult. Minutes later, she emerges with the same but ever so slightly bigger bra, this time stretched between both hands. This sour, furious mood, she's aware, is fuelled by an impatience for information about Sinead. The desire for it moves within her like a pulse.

She hitches up her skirt and climbs on to the display again, pins gripped between her lips, just in case. The bra slides easily over the dummy's shoulders, but she has to struggle with the back fastener again. She has just managed to hook it together and is straightening the cups over the hard swell of the fibreglass breasts when she notices a man watching her, his head on one side. He is wearing a tailored woollen coat and suit, and has a long, furled umbrella clamped under one arm. He smiles and arches his eyebrows when she catches his eye. She is pulling back her lips in a snarl and, as she does so, forgets all about him and all about the bra and the dummy and all about the humiliation prickling at her because she is suddenly struck with a thought. A thought so obvious and so thrilling she doesn't know why it hasn't occurred to her before.

She runs most of the way from the tube. By the time she pounds up the stairs, her legs feel like liquid and her lungs like fire. When she throws open the front door, the flat is dark and Lily almost cheers. She needs the place to herself.

She knows exactly what she's looking for. She scans the bookshelves first – art books, novels, random magazines, CDs. Nothing. She opens the long, thin doors of the cupboards opposite the kitchen, and finds shoes, coats, a dismantled desk, boxes of tools, a tent in a bag. She's going to have to do what she was hoping she wouldn't.

She stands on the threshold of Marcus's room. It's exactly like her own, but reversed, like the reflection of a room in a mirror. Two plan chests sit in the corner, with architectural models, sheets of cardboard, tins of paints, pens and cutting tools heaped on top. The walls are a bright magnesium white. Bits of paper, plans, diagrams, sections, maps, are stuck around the area where he works. It has a slightly temporary, unlived-in feel: an unshaded bulb, hangs from the ceiling; clothes are stacked in boxes; electrical flexes criss-cross the floor like tripwires. He lies on that bed every night, she thinks. Then she recognises it as the bed that used to be next door, in Sinead's room. Shoving that thought aside, she strides across the room and sits at his desk. Surprisingly comfortable chair. Slightly splintered edge to the desk.

She cocks her head, listening out for any tell-tale noise, then leans over, pulls open the drawers and begins sifting through the contents with bent, anxious fingers: staplers, pens, stanley knives, screws, batteries, rulers, set squares, glue, erasers, bills, postcards, letters addressed to Marcus Emerson (Lily can't bring herself to open these, but peers briefly into their folded, inked depths before putting them back). Files containing A3 sheets of drawings. Folders stuffed with tracing paper, bits of newspaper articles, contracts, official-looking letters. At the bottom of one drawer, she finds among paperclips and pencil shavings, face-down, a business card: 'Sinead Wilson, Lecturer, Department of English Literature'. She holds it between her fingers. It's light, flimsy card, the letters raised. If Lily pressed hard enough she could push them back into themselves. But she doesn't. She looks up, looks round the room, and sees her own face outlined in the grey of Marcus's shut-down computer screen. Then she turns towards the shelves, and sees what she's been looking for – the gold and red spines of photograph albums, five of them, arranged in a row.

Lily pulls down the first. It's one of those flip ones where you slot photos into little plastic sleeves. She opens it, starts flicking through it. Her initial apprehension melds into disappointment: buildings. It's just buildings, one after another after another. She skims through them, faster and faster. Gutters, windows, flooring, staircases, doorhandles, paving slabs, marble walls, light fittings, ceilings. A large, undulating, silver building, all waves and shimmering expanses. A low, white, angular one with a gap in the middle as if a bite's been taken out of it. She shuffles through them, perplexed. Then something makes her stop, go back two to a black and grey building with wide steel girders on its exterior. At the building's base, near the entrance, very small and very far away, legs blurred as if she was walking too fast for the camera's shutter, face angled towards the camera – or its owner – a rucksack on her back, her hands pushed into her pockets is a thin, tall woman with dark hair. The black dots of her eyes stare out at Lily, fixed, inquisitive.

She replaces the album, takes down the next. It's more buildings. She puts it back, tries the next. More buildings. She replaces it and opens the last and as she does she gasps and has to clutch the album so as not to drop it. The top photograph is the woman from the other photograph at the bottom of the building, the woman who used to live in this flat, the woman who helped create this flat, the woman who wore the blue-black dress that is now hanging among Lily's clothes, the woman who is now dead.

She and Marcus are on a pavement somewhere. A city that isn't London. It's evening-time; angled rhombuses of sunlight lie over the street and gutter. Cars pass them, frozen into blurs. She has her arm curled round his neck, her fingers in his hair, her nails a dark red. The person behind the camera has just said something funny because she is facing the lens, eyes wide, laughing, the coils of her hair swinging into her face so that it's partially obscured. Wherever it is must be hot because she is wearing a red dress with thin straps over her shoulders. It has beads sewn into the material filled out by her breasts. Her lips, painted the same red, are parted to show sharp, precise teeth. Sinead was beautiful. Lily sees this, sees the length and turn of her neck, the dark, rather wide-set eyes, the narrowness of the waist, the long, long legs that end in shoes that tie around the ankle. Marcus is side-on to the camera, slightly behind and to one side of her, his hand is held flat against her solar plexus, as if he is holding her upright, as if he is holding her to him. He is looking at her, ignoring the camera, ignoring the photographer, ignoring everything else going on around them. His face, unlike hers, is solemn, intense.

Lily shuts the album, pushes it back into its space on the shelf. Terror, inarticulate and obscure, is surrounding her like a force field. She bolts from the room, through the flat, out of the door, down the stairs and out into the darkening streets. She twists round to look up at the flat as she leaves, and its windows look blank, innocuous.

She gets back late. She's been sitting at a corner table in the pub down the road, tearing beer mats into the tiny, identical squares of confetti. When she opens the door, Marcus is walking from the kitchen past Aidan's door.

'Hi,' he says, 'good day?'

'No. Shit actually.'

'Oh. Well. You're back now, at least. Don't bring the office home with you – that's what Sinead always said.'

Lily, caught in the act of taking off her coat, panics. She's never heard him refer to her voluntarily. Does he know what she's been doing? Has he sensed it? Did she leave signs? She can't have done – she remembers replacing the album, shutting the drawers, pushing the chair back under the desk. She did. She knows she did.

Marcus, also, seems taken aback, confused, blinking rapidly as if he can't quite believe what he just said. They stare at each other in mutual shock. Lily looks at his hands, resting on his hips and she suddenly sees, suddenly understands, their sinewed strength, their flex and power. As she looks, she finds she is wondering at their stretch and capability.

She goes into the bathroom and picks up her toothbrush. Her arm is shaking slightly. Her face looks out at her from the mirror – porcelain white beneath the remnants of her summer freckles. She makes herself pick up the toothpaste, keeping things normal, keeping herself calm, and squeezes out a length on to her brush and starts scrubbing at the flattened tops of her molars. She rinses her mouth, spits, rinses and spits again. The splashing of the tap echoes round the boxed-in room. It's all gleaming metal and reflectiveness, like an operating theatre. Or a morgue. Nothing would leave a mark in here that couldn't be washed or sponged away. Stainless steel lines the walls, seamless concrete covers the floor. Male things are lined up on the shelf – shaving foam, deodorant, razors. Half of it is noticeably empty. Lily wonders what happens to the cosmetics of the dead.

She is about to go back into her room when she stops, turns and presses open Marcus's door. He is sitting at his desk, writing something on a pad of paper and he looks up, surprised.

'You know,' Lily begins uncertainly, 'my grandfather died two years ago.'

He looks startled. 'Oh,' he says, and crosses his legs. 'I'm sorry . . . I'm sorry to hear that.'

'Yes.' She waits. Marcus looks at her. She looks back. What is he thinking? What does he keep wound up behind that brilliant, fathomless blue gaze?

'I'm sorry,' he says again.

'It's OK. I didn't . . . it wasn't as upsetting as . . .' She tails off expectantly.

Marcus doesn't seem to know what to say. His hand moves slightly on the paper.

Lily sighs. She's never been any good at the softly-softly approach, never been one for pussy-footed game-playing. 'Look,' she says, 'I just wanted to say that if you ever wanted to talk to me about Sinead, you can. I . . . I'd be happy to listen. Or to help. If I can.'

The pen drops from his hand and rolls away from him on the sleek surface of the desk. He makes a grab for it, managing to catch it just as it is falling to the floor. When he is holding it fast, trapped by four curled fingers, he looks at her again. 'What do you know about Sinead?' His voice is steady, toneless.

'Not much, but—'

'Well, there you are, then.'

Lily turns on the pivot of her heel. 'Fine,' she says. 'OK.

See you later.' Her foot strikes a box of nylon-tipped pens on the floor, their coloured casings skittering away over the boards, but she doesn't stop. As she is reaching for the handle she thinks she hears him say: 'Don't go.'

Two words. Just like that. So quiet that Lily is convinced she imagined them. But her hand hovers over the door-handle, and without looking round she tries to gauge the silence behind her. It stretches, elongates and swells. Lily presses the cold metal of the door-knob into her fingers. He said nothing, he said nothing. She imagined it. Must have done. But she half turns. He is looking at her, uncertain, almost shy.

'Did you . . . did you say something?'

'I said don't go. I don't want you to go. I'm sorry,' he says. 'I don't mean to be . . .'

Lily has left the door and is crossing the floor towards him. He pushes the letter he is writing into a drawer. *You always*— Lily catches sight of before he closes the drawer and stands up. He puts his hands around her neck, his fingers in her hair. His breath is hot on her face. He lifts her arm and presses his mouth to the blue river delta of veins at her wrist.

They reach the bed quickly, her hands finding their way through his clothes to the hard smoothness of his back, his mouth against her neck, her cheeks, her hair, her eyelids, her throat. There is the sweet burning, the confusion of limbs and fabric before the relief of skin upon skin. He feels his way about her, his face intent, concentrated. She shuts her eyes against the glare of the electric light, lifts herself from the mattress to allow the layers of clothes to be peeled away.

The weight of him on her is a relief, a release. As he arches the upper part of his body away from her to pull off his T-shirt, Lily opens her eyes to take the shortest glimpse of him, to store the snapshot into her memory. What she sees, though, makes the blood stop in her veins.

Standing beside the bed, near enough so that Lily could reach out and touch her, is a girl with black Medusa curls and an angular white face. She is looking straight at Lily.

Lily jolts as if electrocuted, and she screams, the noise stretching at the walls of the room. It seems easy to push Marcus off her and to turn away and leap in one fluid movement from the bed. The thing is behind her then, as far away from her as possible and she can't see it and she never wants to lay eyes on it ever again.

'What the hell . . . ?' She hears Marcus say and she looks back at him. She doesn't want to, she wants to keep her gaze and her face and her body – naked and cold now the warmth of Marcus's is leaving her – averted, but she cannot ignore his voice and the sound of it drags her eyes to him. Marcus is kneeling on the bed, staring at her, dishevelled, perplexed. Beneath him, between his thighs, is the imprint of her body. She's left a kind of negative space behind her, a vacancy where, if she'd kept her eyes closed she'd still be lying. The room is empty apart from the two of them.

'What's the matter?' he says, his face flushed. 'Are you OK?'

Lily blinks, looks down at the crumpled outline in the sheets below him. There is just Marcus in front of her, the air behind him blank, clear, hollow. It was nothing. She imagined it. It was nothing. 'I saw . . . I thought I saw . . .'

He reaches out to her. 'What?'

At that moment, there is a swift knock at the door and someone outside saying, 'Marcus?'

Marcus struggles over the bed to get to the door. But Aidan opens it before he reaches it.

'Marcus, I—' Aidan stops short on the threshold and stares at them – semi-clad, clothes strewn about the room, the thrashed-about bed. Lily bends to gather up her things, holding them to her front. Aidan says nothing and doesn't move, just turns his head to look Marcus full in the face.

'How was Japan?' Marcus says.

There is a pause. The two men's eyes are locked on each other. Lily walks towards the door.

'Excuse me,' she says.

Aidan steps aside and she passes through into her room. She gropes for the lamp on the desk and switches it on. It sparks blue, the bulb filament exploding with a hollow pop, pain streaking up the fibres of her arm. Through the dark air of the room she can make out the black outline of her reflection in the mirror. She stares at it wildly: in it she has no face, no features, no dimension. She moves and it moves with her. She feels a bit crazed, light-headed, and struggles with a desire to burst into giggles. This is ridiculous! What *was* that? Did she really just see Marcus's dead girlfriend? During sex? Or did she imagine it? Was it real? And what does 'real' mean, in terms of a dead girl?

At a noise behind her, she leaps into the bed, scrambling beneath the covers, pinning them to her with her fists. Her mind gallops, falling over itself. I don't even believe in ghosts, she wants to shout.

Aidan presses his forehead to the cold, slick glass, and peers into the distance at the four pale columns of Battersea Power Station rising above the low city skyline. It's weird, unaccountable and bizarre. He's known this city all his life and suddenly everything looks rejigged, Battersea Power Station north of the river, Harrow-on-the-Hill in Leytonstone. Someone has clearly moved the river.

He's in a glass capsule of the London Eye, a huge white wheel that circles slowly next to the Thames. He'd had an hour to kill before meeting his friend Sam and, curious about this strange structure that's appeared since he was last here, bought a ticket and climbed on.

People line the sides of the oval capsule, taking photos, unfolding maps. The wheel is surprisingly silent and slow. He'd been expecting a faster, more fairground ride, not this rather sedate amble through the skies of London. As they approach the apex, two American girls leap up from where they were seated and indulge in a frenzy of photographing each other. They approach him with their camera and he takes it, trapping them together in the viewfinder, clicking the shutter.

Aidan looks out at Canary Wharf tower, glinting like mica in the sun. When he'd left London, three years ago, it had been alone on the skyline, a tall, shimmering blip in the levels of buildings. But now other structures, half built, are crowding in next to it, blurring its outline. A friend of his died in the bombing there a few years ago. Sam, who'd also known him, said recently that he sometimes still forgets he's dead, still gets the urge to call him, to tell him things. Ridiculous, he said, isn't it?

Aidan turns northwards again and, as the city rises to meet him, thinks about how he nearly slipped from a high-level footbridge as a child. His father caught him by the straps of his dungarees just in time, and he saw his feet swing out over lanes of traffic, parks with children on climbing frames, roofs of houses, fishponds in back gardens, people shopping on a busy street.

Shuffling out of the capsule and back through the barriers, he sees Sam waving at him. Next to him stands a woman whose eyes are still searching the crowd. Lisa. Sam's been seeing her for almost a year, but Aidan's never met her before.

When Sam introduces them, with a mock-formal flourish, Lisa grips his hand in hers and says, 'At last, the elusive Aidan.' They talk about where to go, what to eat, the geographical dislocation you get from being in the Eye, how cold it's suddenly become.

As they are walking to the nearest pub, Sam asks: 'How's Marcus?'

Aidan sees Lisa glance up at him quickly, then look away. Sam's told her, he sees. Not that he minds. He just forgets sometimes that couples, like body cells, have a kind of permeable barrier between them.

'Don't ask,' says Aidan.

'And I said to him,' Diane, Lily's mother, is saying, 'I said, Graham I really don't think it's on if I'm here for the evening and she calls up and you spend three-quarters of an hour on the phone to her. I mean, it's not that I'm jealous because I'm not the jealous type, am I, but I think basically that it's just not on.'

Lily holds the phone to her ear with one hand and, with the other, twirls a length of hair around her index finger. The office is empty, the agents out at lunch. She's supposed to be sending out a stack of letters to casting directors, but has phoned her mother instead for a chat.

'. . . and he replied that I shouldn't feel threatened. That it's not an issue for him any more . . .'

Lily is being calm today. Very, very calm. All this shit about ghouls and ghosties is just nonsense. Nonsense. She knows that. It was just a product of an overwrought mind – she was having sex with Marcus for the first time, she'd just looked at those photographs (and how stupid was that, she can't believe she did that, what an idiot), the whole affair with Marcus has that discombobulating feeling of turning into something big, and so on and so on. Nothing to worry about. It won't happen again.

She stares at the hair wound around her finger. Her nail is filling with blood, turning a bright pink. She releases her hair and it unravels quickly, settling back into place. What is it that makes hair curl anyway? Isn't it something to do with the follicles?

'Did you ever see your father after he died?' She hears herself interrupt her mother's monologue.

There is a short silence.

'What?'

'Um . . . Grandad,' Lily says. 'I mean, do you think ghosts . . . er. Nothing. Forget it.'

'Ghosts?'

'It's nothing. I didn't mean it.'

'Why are you asking me that?'

'No reason. Sorry. Carry on with . . . with what you were saying.'

'Well,' Diane doesn't need a great deal of encouragement, 'anyway, so after that he decided to buy an answerphone. And I said . . .'

Lily zones out again. Lights hum above her head; phones ring in rooms down the hall; outside, cars wait in line for the lights to turn.

She walks fast, her feet skimming the pavement, her lungs filling and emptying. When she'd reached the turning into the courtyard, the flat was obviously empty, its windows dark and hooded. Something failed her. She couldn't go in, she just couldn't. She'd stood there for a while, tussling with herself. This was ridiculous. She was being stupid. There's nothing there. It's all in her imagination. All this alarmist shit about ghosts and apparitions. She needs some time out, a holiday maybe. She doesn't really believe she saw anything. Does she? Before she was even aware of deciding to do it, she had turned on her heel and run back down the street.

Cars pass, lifting her hair with their backdraught. At the end of the road, she turns in the opposite direction to the tube station. She passes a Victorian iron bridge that drips cold, slimed water into her hair, a milliner's shop with hats poised on featureless, smooth dummy heads, a closed flower stall, the ground strewn with severed stalks, a church with its façade illuminated in greenish light and 'Ever thought about what might happen after death?' emblazoned on a sign outside. She finds it hard to understand how small turn-of-the-century terraces, industrial warehouses, huge powering roads and bars filled with boys with mobile phones can all exist together in one space.

She returns clutching a carton of milk against her jacket. A triangle of light is slanting out from the warehouse window. Marcus must be back. Relief opens out around her like wings.

Before letting the front door close, Lily is careful to turn on the light. It lasts just long enough for her to make it up the narrow staircase to the first-floor landing where she turns on the next. As she is climbing the flight of stairs that leads to their door, she hears, or she thinks she hears, something behind her. Later she'll go over and over it in her mind, trying to identify it, reclaim it, clarify what it was. But at the time, she stops on the stairs and turns her head. And as she does so, it's as if a very fine mist is brushing over her face, leaving the surface of her skin cool and moist.

I am not afraid, she tells herself, I am not. But her

legs move under her like pistons and she hurls herself at the door.

Aidan had heard the footsteps pounding up the stairs, but the door crashing open still makes him jump. Lily bursts into the room as if she's been pushed, losing her footing, stumbling to her knees. Aidan stares at her, astonished. A second ago he'd been deep in his book and now there's a woman sprawled across the flooboards in front of him.

'Are you all right?' he says, after a moment. He wonders if he should go over and help her up, but he hardly knows her for heaven's sake.

'Yeah,' she says, getting up and dusting down her skirt. 'Sorry about that. I must've . . . er . . . I must've tripped or something.'

'Right.'

She brandishes a milk carton at him in the manner of a terrorist with a hand grenade. 'Do you want something to drink?' she asks, her chest still heaving from her run up the stairs, the words jerking out between breaths. 'Hot chocolate?' she demands.

He hesitates. 'Um . . .' This girl really is quite odd.

'I'm having some.'

'OK.' He nods. 'Why not? Thanks.'

He hears her banging through the cupboard of pans, then the milk gulping out of the carton. He steals a surreptitious sidelong glance just as she is striking a match against its box – one, two, three times. When the flame catches, she puts her thumb quickly into her mouth, wincing. It must have burnt her.

She stands above the cooker, absorbed in watching the simmering milk, blowing her fringe away from her eyes. Her attraction, Aidan decides, as he watches her across the room, lies in her embodiment of opposites. The way her fragile, slight frame and her apparently meek silence are belied by that restive, elf-like glimmer in her eyes. She may not say much, but Aidan reckons she keeps an awful lot to herself; he's seen her with Marcus, listening to whatever he's saying, her lips shut and expressionless, but her eyes veiled, moving about his face, her mind churning over, thinking, thinking, always thinking.

Suddenly she's there beside him, handing him a mug with oiled, coloured bubbles at the rim. He takes it, looks up to thank her, and as he does so sees that she's young, can be no more than twenty-two, twenty-three. He gives a minute shake of his head as she takes a seat opposite him.

'Aidan?' Lily says. She is aware of the air around them, like a kind of soundless buzzing, but she doesn't care. She has to ask. This division in herself, between the rational and the irrational, has to end. She has to put a stop to it. And the only way to do that is with hard, immutable facts.

'Yes?'

'What happened . . . with Sinead?'

His head jerks up from his book. He looks at her for a moment, then starts blowing on the surface of his drink.

'How much do you know?' he says quietly.

'Nothing.'

'Then that's something you'll have to talk to Marcus about.'

'I don't feel I can. Can't you—'

'Lily,' and his voice is sharp-edged, 'I don't . . . I hardly know you. It's really none of my business.'

She looks at him. His eyes are so dark that his pupils are lost in the liquid ebony of the irises.

'What was she like?' She can't help herself.

Aidan sighs. His fingers work at a dog-ear on his book's cover, his nail flicking at the white-creased triangle. He's not going to tell me, she thinks, then something is released in his face. His fingers stop flicking. He gets up, shoving a bookmark into the pages.

'She . . .' He places the book on the table, carefully, as if it's a fragile artefact, and pushes his hands into the back pockets of his trousers. 'The kind of woman people fall in love with. Just like that.' He pauses, then adds: 'The kind of woman who collects broken hearts.'

Lily doesn't know what to say. Jealousy clots inside her like frog spawn, and she is surprised by it, discomforted.

He gives a little expellation of air, like laughter, yet not. 'Look,' he says, 'what I will say is this. If you have any sense you'll stay well away from Marcus.'

Later, Aidan and Marcus stand in the pooled light of the kitchen, Marcus stirring something on the cooker, Aidan clattering dishes around. Lily sits at the table, a newspaper spread before her, her fingerprints stained with its ink. Her mind clings to what Aidan said and images of those hearts keep appearing in her head. She imagines them, small, damp and pulsating, lying at the bottom of a handbag, or skewered together in rows on a kebab stick. Lined up on a windowsill like pot plants. Packed into the glovebox of a car.

'So if you wanted to render it in 3D, you'd have to — what? — use Quark?' Marcus is saying.

'Nah,' Aidan replies in a monotone. 'Quark wouldn't do it.'

There is a silence.

'So what would?' Marcus prompts.

'You could design it in Quark, if you wanted to. But CAD is what you need.'

'CAD and what else?'

'An animation package. But if you're going to download that — which you can off the internet — you're going to have to get a memory upgrade. It'll just keep crashing otherwise and you can't have that while you're render-ing because it'll just get fucked and pixellated every five mintues.'

'How much will that be?'

'Couple of hundred quid. Maybe more. It depends.'

'Lily,' Marcus says suddenly. She is deep in an article about a woman who disappeared the previous month, so that when she looks at him she feels disconnected and distracted. 'Have you eaten?'

'Not yet, but I'll cook when you've finished.'

'Have some of this. There's plenty. I've made far too much for just me.' He gives a short, mirthless laugh. 'Can't seem to get used to cooking for one person,' he mutters, more to himself than either her or Aidan.

'Well . . . if you're sure.'

'I am. It's curry. Do you like curry?' He is looking at

her, eyebrows raised, the muscles in his arm clenched from his stirring.

'Lovely. Curry. Yes. Thanks very much.'

Aidan swills water over a plate in the sink. Their terse and incomprehensible conversation seems to have come to a standstill. Marcus walks from the fridge to the table and holds out a green bottle. 'Beer?'

She raises her eyes to his. His mouth is curved into a half-smile. As she looks, it splits into a full, expansive grin. She looks away, smiling herself, and sees two things happening simultaneously: Aidan seeing them and his face contracting in something like disgust, dropping the plate into the sink; and, in the reflection in a chrome bowl on the table, an elongated shape, behind her.

Marcus nudges the rim of the fridge-cold bottle into the flesh of her upper arm. 'Beer? Lily?'

'Um.' She is twisting around, despite herself, to see behind her. Where is it? Where does it go when it's not here, when she can't see it? Does it lurk behind doors or – the idea horrifies Lily – in other rooms, waiting for her? 'Beer. Er, yes. Please.'

Aidan passes them, heading for his room. The walls of the huge space boom and resound as he slams his doors shut.

Marcus heaps rice then yellow curry on to two plates. He is talking – something about the curry and a place in Kerala, but she is finding it hard to concentrate on what he's saying. The room around them seems live, dangerous with possibility, like a severed electrical flex. As she is raising her first forkful to her mouth, she feels his thigh against hers and she lurches back, food falling off the fork.

Marcus laughs, 'You're very nervy, aren't you?' And he moves in closer, his voice dropping to a whisper. 'Are you afraid of me?'

There are curry-stained grains of rice scattered around Lily's plate. She plucks at them. 'Afraid? Of you?' From here she only has a vista of the end of the warehouse, half of the kitchen and the door to the bathroom. There's a whole mass of air behind her, stretching to the long windows and the bedrooms, that she can't see. She casts a quick look over her shoulder. 'Afraid?' she repeats. 'No. Of course not. Don't be ridiculous.'

'What went wrong, then?' His voice is a murmur now, and his hand is pressing down on her thigh.

'Um, well.' Lily does a swift all-round check. Still nothing. 'I thought I saw . . . I thought I saw something.'

'What?'

'Er. Well, I'm not sure.' She looks again over her shoulder. The end of the room is in darkness. It's the black void that frightens her. There could be anything in it.

'Marcus.' She turns back to him. His face is inches from hers. He is looking at where her shirt opens at her throat. This has to stop, she tells herself, you have to know the truth. 'Can I ask you a question?'

Something alters in his expression. Tiny muscles round his eyes tighten. Lines appear at the side of his mouth. 'Sure,' he says, leaning back, 'ask away.'

'Well.' Lily swallows. The roof of her mouth feels dry. Her fingertips clutch at the cold, wet column of her glass. 'You see, I was wondering—'

Two feet away, the phone rings. They look at each other. She closes her mouth.

''Scuse me,' Marcus says and gets up, walks away from the table, lifts the receiver. She hears him say, 'Hi. How's it going?'

Lily lifts the food to her mouth and chews. Then, with that kind of sentience where information is elided with knowledge, when even without any proof or warning you just know something to be true, she realises that Sinead is sitting in the chair next to her. Lily swallows, the lump of food scraping at the soft part of her throat. There is a strange, collapsed feeling at the front of her face, like tears or hayfever. Her hand, grasping a fork, shivers in mid-air. She has never felt colder. She glares down at her plate, lecturing herself fiercely and rapidly with words like gunfire: This is nothing, get a grip, come on, Lily, this is nonsense, you know it is.

She slides her eyes inside their sockets. Sinead is there at the table, opposite Marcus's abandoned plate. She is staring, with great concentration and intent, into Lily's face, one hand covering her mouth.

Then Marcus is pulling back his chair with an atonal scrape against the floor. 'Sorry,' he is saying, 'it was some guy at the office who's having a problem. They've got this big hand-in and they're all gearing up for an all-nighter and—' He breaks off. 'What's wrong?' he says. He leans towards her, his face creased in concern, putting his hand over hers. 'You look . . . What is it?'

Lily looks from Sinead to him and back again. Sinead has removed her hand and her lips are moving, as if she's speaking, as if she's trying to tell her something. Marcus can't see her. *He can't see her.* He doesn't know she's there. How can she tell him that sitting opposite him is—

'Nothing,' she says, with an attempt at a smile. He mustn't know. He mustn't ever know. 'I'm fine.'

Lily stands at the basin. Marcus has disappeared into his study to take another call from the office, and Aidan has stayed in his lift-shaft room since dinner. She has listened for him coming out to make a cup of tea or to go to the toilet even. But nothing. What on earth is he doing in there, and what is it animators do anyway? And why would he say that about Marcus? Marcus is supposed to be his best friend.

She has a length of waxed cotton wound round each finger and she is sawing it through the gaps in her teeth. She makes herself hum fragments of a song she heard earlier in the day on the radio at the office. Without warning, something falls from the top of the bathroom cabinet, striking her on the head. The floss jerks up to cut into her gum. Red soaks quickly into the white string. Lily looks down. In the basin is a a medicinal-looking foil-covered strip with the word 'Femodene' emblazoned across it, days of the week connected by tiny black arrows. She picks it up. The strip's purple foil crackles in her hand. Tiny round pills rattle inside their sealed foil holders. About a third of them have been punctured from their casing.

Anger swarms at the back of her head, unexpected and potent. 'Right, that's it!' she shouts. 'I've had enough of you!'

She flicks the blood-stained floss into the toilet bowl and, with both hands, twists the foil strip until it cracks. Pills pop out and bounce around the basin's curves, disappearing down the eye of the plug. She pushes any remaining pills out of their cases and turns on the taps full so that the basin is flooded with icy water. She imagines the tiny white pills dissolving into milkiness as they are flushed far, far away. Then she crumples the strip into itself, piercing her palm as she does so, and flings it into the bin.

'See that?' she cries to the empty room. 'See that? I'm not afraid of you! I'm not! So just – just piss off!'

Her voice sounds reedy and weak to her, the high ceiling above her swallowing her words. The shower curtain moves slightly.

Lily pushes out through the door, not wanting to look back into the room, not wanting to see the mirror – she has this fear that the reflection thrown back might not be her own. She marches down the dark warehouse and through Marcus's door. In the semi-light she can see that he's lying on his back in bed, his face turned away.

'Marcus,' she whispers, climbing into the bed and wrapping herself around his warmth. He's naked and she is wondering if he always sleeps naked, if he never gets cold in this unheated crypt of a flat, if he always slept naked with—

And she is keeping her eyes shut tight because she doesn't care if she's there, she doesn't want to see, because this way even if she is there she is winning because she's not going to open her eyes to see.

'Hang on a sec,' he says, and leaves the bed, and the surprise makes her eyes lift and she sees the darkened room and it seems to be tilted slightly but maybe it's only because her head is tipped back on the pillow, and there is only her on the bed and Marcus leaning over a drawer in his desk. She turns her head fractionally and before she can clamp her eyes shut again she sees a minuscule draught run along the wall, lifting the papers stuck there, one by one. But he is back, and she is going to do this, she will do this, this will happen. And then he is inside her very suddenly, it seems all the way, and the shock makes her gasp and before she realises it her mouth and her eyes are stretched wide open and she can't shut them again because everything is happening at once, and right beside her, crouched down next to the bed, is Sinead, her head angled to look right into Lily's face, her features as clear as if she were real and alive and flesh.

Lily has to clamp her mouth shut and press her face into Marcus's shoulder, which is damp with salt and moving over her. It's as if she's split into two separate existences, one that can only feel and the other that can only listen to the other's breathing and think of the thing crouching right next to her. But she is in the grip of determination to do this thing, to get it done, to have it out of the way and behind her. Somewhere in her mind is the conviction that, after the first time, she'll go, she'll leave them alone, she'll vanish and never come back, that the very act of Marcus sleeping with another woman will make her disappear.

When it is finished she waits until she feels back in herself before she opens her eyes. It takes a while for her to be able to see anything through the thick, pitchy dark that surrounds her. Then objects start sinking into grey – the chair in front of the desk, the window frame, Marcus's form next to her, asleep. Nothing else.

Because she's not sure if she should stay, she returns to her room. She puts her hand to the wall next to her bed. The paint feels ridged, unreadable as Braille. Sinead painted these walls. Those imperceptible ridges were made by the fibres of her brush dragging through the paint. At some point, Sinead stood on this very spot and daubed wet, vibrant blue colour on to these walls, utterly unaware that Lily would ever sleep within them.

Lily would like to scratch them with her nails, over and over, scraping off the paint, paring them back to the bare, colourless plaster.

When she returns to the flat the next evening, six or seven people are sitting around the table. Plumes of blue smoke rise to the ceiling and low, throbbing music plays in the corner. Marcus turns. 'Hi,' he says. 'This is Lily,' he tells them all, 'our new flatmate.'

They nod or say, 'Hi' or 'Nice to meet you.' Lily nods from the door then walks around them to the kitchen.

She pulls two slices of bread from a bag, their texture damp and spongy, and slots them into the toaster, eyeing the group. A woman with a short red bob and black hipster trousers is saying: 'Frankly, Tim, I think they should be paying you at least five grand more. I mean, you got your Part Three – what was it, two years ago? You want to know what I think? I think you've long outgrown their design strategy.'

Lily smears butter on to her toast. The knife edge rasps against the crisp surface. Bob-haired woman glances her way.

'Has anyone seen the new Parks and Simpson building in Manchester?' says a man in a grey army fatigue shirt. 'Designed by some year-off students, apparently, and signed off by one of the partners.'

'And you can tell,' says Marcus, standing with a wine bottle gripped between his legs, pulling at the cork with a slim, steel handle. 'Looks like a self-build scheme.'

Everyone laughs. Lily swallows down clods of toast, watching as the gathering breaks up into smaller conversations. From the other side of the room is a shrill, insistent ringing. The phone.

'I'll get it,' she says, putting down her plate. Marcus glances up at her and smiles. As she walks towards it, she hears the grey-shirted man ask him, 'How are things?'

Marcus's back is towards her so she can't make out his reply. She hears him say, 'Well,' but the rest is lost: she can make out 'she' and 'me', then 'she' again, and 'each other'.

She lifts the receiver. 'Hello?'

'Lily, it's Sarah.'

'Hi, how are you doing?' The connection crashes and wanes. 'Sarah? Are you still there?'

'Yeah. Can you hear me now? I can't talk long, I'm about to go into a film. But I spoke to that friend of mine.'

'What friend?'

'The journalist.'

'Oh.' Lily glances back at Marcus, but he's standing up, cutting up something on the table with a long silver knife in each hand.

'He says there's nothing on her. Nothing at all.'

'Really?' She turns back to face the wall, whispering now. 'Are you sure? You got the name right?'

'Yeah. Wilson, Sinead. He couldn't find any deaths registered under that name. He went back two years.'

Lily bites her lip, pressing the phone to her ear.

'Lily? Are you there?'

'Yes,' she says, 'I'm here.'

'He says that it could mean she died abroad or . . .'

'Or?'

She hears Sarah sigh. 'Or that her death might be unresolved.'

'Unresolved?'

'If the coroner's still investigating it. Or the police. Or if they haven't got a body yet, in the case of disappearance or . . . or murder.'

Lily stares at the framed picture in front of her. It's made up of rows and rows of people's faces, all grinning for the camera. So many teeth, strung across their faces like necklaces. 'Right,' she says. 'I see.'

'Listen, I have to go. You'll call me later, won't you?'

'OK.'

'Promise?'

'Yup.'

Lily wakes to feel Marcus's hand on her breast, his mouth on hers. She turns over, the sheet tightening around her. She is aware of being very hot. Things seem to be quite far on: Marcus is naked and so is she. She can't quite work out in the dark the orientation of his body in relation to hers. Bits of him float and collide, disembodied, against hers, and her hands flail like webbed feet against the sheet, searching for a hold on him.

She hears his breath next to her ear and she forgets, in her vague and bleared state, that she has to close her eyes.

But there's nothing there. Her room is empty. The walls, the ceiling, the door, the windows all look blissfully as they should. Her mind is a sheer, measureless blank as she comes; he holds her to him very tightly, cradling her head in his hand, as if comforting her.

She sits bolt upright suddenly, decisive, determined. Marcus is stumbling about the room, trying to locate some clothes, muttering about needing the toilet.

'Marcus,' she says, 'I have to ask you this. What happened to Sinead?'

The name makes him flinch as if she's slapped him, and he freezes. 'Why do you ask?'

'Why do I ask?' she repeats, her impatience leaking out. 'Marcus, for God's sake, we're living together,' she gestures around the room, 'sleeping together and . . . I mean, this was a huge thing that happened in your life and I know nothing about it. Nothing at all.'

He ties the dressing-gown cord slowly, and she sees that his hands are trembling. 'Well,' he says, 'the thing is . . .' In one movement he reaches his palm towards the bed and lowers himself on to a corner of it. She can see only his profile, etched against the glow of the streetlight outside the window. 'It's quite difficult to talk about.' His voice is even, level, reined in. He doesn't look at her, but winds the cord round and round his wrist. 'When something like that happens it's hard to . . . to organise it . . . in your own thoughts so that you comprehend it, let alone trying to put it into words so that somebody else can. I'm sorry.' He shakes his head as if he has water trapped in his ears. 'Do you know what I mean?'

'Sort of.'

'I will . . . I will tell you . . . at some point. I promise. Just not at the moment. If that's OK with you.' He grips her ankle through the duvet. 'Is that OK with you?'

'Yes,' she says, struggling to sound kind and understand-ing, when what she really wants to do is yell, no of course it bloody isn't, just tell me. 'Of course.' She pulls her face into a strained smile.

He gets up, stopping in the doorway. 'I'll be back in a sec,' he whispers.

She looks up. He is framed by light, half his face illuminated, half invisible in dark. Behind him, at the window where the building falls away to the pavement, a black-haired girl hovers, moving, shifting, crackling, agitation simmering in her face, her hands pressed to the xylophone bones of her chest.

Aidan waits in line, a newspaper in one hand and the money to pay for it in the other. A man at the front of the queue is paying by credit card, and making very heavy weather of finding a pen to sign his name. People around Aidan tut and sigh and shift from foot to foot.

From his back pocket his phone gives a single, plaintive cheep. Aidan pours the coins into the hand clutching the newspaper and pulls it out. He has a deep love, combined with a certain admiration and gratitude, for the items of technology in his life that he would never admit to anyone. He believes the person who designed his phone a genius: sleek but durable aluminium casing, tiny aerial, curved but unslippery buttons, and a blue light that comes on when he touches the keypad. The tiny screen tells him that he's got a text message from Marcus.

Aidan looks around the cramped shop. An undergrown teenager with hair shaved down to his skull is standing by a stand of CDs, staring straight ahead of him. There is something oddly fixed and static about him. Then Aidan sees that with one hand, he is shovelling CDs into his coat. Their eyes meet for a second: the boy's arm hesitates, then reaches to button his coat. Aidan looks away, looks back at his phone. The boy flits past him and out of the door. Aidan hits the erase button on Marcus's message.

'There's a bar that's just opened, done by someone I really like. I'm going there now to have a look.' Marcus is pulling on his jacket. 'D'you want to come?'

In her room, she kicks off her shoes and slides her feet into a different pair. She pulls off her sweater, which smells of the Underground and traffic fumes and air-conditioning, and puts on a cardigan from a pile beside her bed. It's just been washed so she has to stretch and resettle it to the shape of her torso. Her hair crackles with static as she walks back towards Marcus, standing by the door.

She is heading for the road to the tube, but Marcus reaches for her hand. 'Let's get a cab,' he says, nodding towards the main road.

The bar has a floor made of glass bricks, lit by bulbs from the basement. The expanse of light underneath her and no discernible floor makes Lily feel giddy and malcoordinated. She has to suppress a desire to cling gecko-like to the grey walls, has to force herself to balance on this skinless block of light.

They sit at a table in the corner and she touches the angled join where the walls meet. Marcus has placed in front of her a tall glass filled with pink liquid. Cubes of ice shift and jostle in its depths. She puts her lips to its surface and her teeth and tongue fill with the bitter tinge of citrus fruit, then the afterkick of vodka. Marcus is drinking beer from a bottle, its neck foaming around a sliver of lime.

He has met someone he knows. A man with very tight green trousers. The corner of his mouth drools a cigarette. His ash falls in flecks to the surface of Lily's drink until she moves it out of his way. At her eye level is his exposed navel. A very neat line of black hair, so neat it could have been drawn on with a marker pen, runs from his belly button to disappear into the waistband of his trousers.

'I've never been to Dallas,' Marcus is saying.

'You must go,' the man says, with a kind of religious fervour, and, as if to emphasise Dallas's wondrousness, touches Marcus on the shoulder with his cigarette hand. A snake of grey ash is left on Marcus's sleeve. He doesn't notice.

Dallas. Funny word. Backwards, it spells 'salad'. Almost. She takes in another mouthful of her drink and looks at Marcus. His brow is creased and he is holding himself slightly away from this man. He doesn't like him, she sees.

'But have you seen the one in Reykjavik?' Marcus asks.

Reykjavik? He's been to Reykjavik? When did you go to Reykjavik? she wants to shout. Her mind is filled with an image of him and Sinead swimming naked, hair slicked to their heads, in a steaming, sulphurous pool. She thinks: I don't know anything about you.

'Sorry about that.' Marcus turns back to her when the man finally leaves.

'Who was he?'

'Oh, some bloke.' He flicks his hand in the man's direction. 'He goes out with someone I used to work with.'

'When did you go to Reykjavik?'

'Reykjavik?' He has to think. 'Two years ago? Something like that.'

'Right.' She nods. 'How old are you?'

'What?'

'I said, how old are you?'

Marcus laughs. 'Why? What is all this?'

'I just realised I hardly know anything about you. So I thought I'd ask.'

'Oh.' He smiles. 'Well, I'm thirty.'

'Where were you born?'

'France.'

'Any brothers or sister?'

'A sister.'

'Younger?'

'Older.' Marcus laughs again. 'Anything else?'

How did your girlfriend die? Lily thinks. 'When did you decide to become an architect?' she asks instead.

'When I was nine.' He up-ends his bottle, taking another swig. 'I was ill, off school, lying on a sofa. My mum had, you know, brought down the duvet while I watched TV. I had chicken pox. Anyway, I saw this Open University programme about architecture, and that's when I decided.'

'I envy you,' Lily says.

'Do you?' He is surprised. 'Why?'

'You've got a vocation.'

'But doesn't everyone? I mean, on some level?'

'No.' She shakes her head emphatically. 'Not at all.'

He looks confused, as if he wants to ask more but is unsure what. Lily doesn't want to talk about it, so she says, 'Do you like this place, then?'

Marcus looks up at the ceiling, his throat whitening with the tilt of his head, then at the wall ahead of them. 'It's very fashionable, all this brutal, utility stuff. And I do like it. But this place,' he rubs the underside of his wrist with his fingers, 'is too contrived. It's a bit formulaic.'

'Is it?'

'Well, it's like they've got a list of all the elements a trendy bar should have and ticked them off one by one. Exposed pipes, distressed concrete walls, iron banisters, back-lit bar, glass brick floor, aluminium furniture. You know?'

'Yes,' Lily looks around again, 'yes. I see what you mean. What are your buildings like then?'

Marcus laughs. 'My buildings? Non-existent. I haven't built anything yet, only bits of buildings. That's how it works. The one I was working on in New York – I designed the staircase and the ceiling.'

'Right.'

'You need to set up on your own if you want to build your own stuff, but I'm not really ready to do that yet. Got to put in a few more years in other offices first and do competitions in my spare time.'

Lily plucks a peanut from the bowl on the table between them and drops it into her mouth. 'Tell me about Aidan,' she says, then coughs. The peanut is covered in a kind of dusty coating.

'Aidan?' His eyes flick over her face quickly. 'What's he got to do with your interrogation?'

'Nothing,' she croaks, still coughing. 'I'm just interested.'

'Well, what do you want to know?'

She tries to swallow, but she keeps on coughing. Marcus

asks her if she's OK. The peanut bounces around the inside of her mouth. She takes a swig of her drink. When she's gulped it down, the peanut has disappeared. She's so relieved she grins at him. 'How long have you known him?' she asks, with her new, empty mouth.

'Years. We were at school together.'

'Are you good friends?'

'Me and Aidan?' Marcus shifts in his seat, picks at the label on his bottle. 'Yeah. He's my best friend.'

Without warning, a violent cough erupts from her oesophagus. She hacks and splutters, water springing into her eyes, her hand clamped over her lips, her lungs labouring for air.

'Are you all right?' she hears him ask, concerned. 'Do you want me to bang you on the back?'

'Nh-nh,' she manages, shaking her head. The peanut seems to have reappeared in her mouth. She pushes it with the end of her tongue between two teeth and crunches it into powder. She breathes in deeply, then says, as if nothing has happened, 'How long has he lived with you?'

'Not long. A couple of months. He'll be moving out soon. He's been living all over the place for years – the States, Japan, Germany – and now he's moved back here permanently, and he's bought a flat. He's only staying with me until he gets the keys for his new place.'

'Oh. I find him . . .' She pauses. 'He's a bit . . . unapproachable, isn't he?'

'You think?' He considers this. 'Perhaps. He's . . . he's been slightly . . . going through a funny time recently.

Moving back here and . . . and everything. He's a very talented man, you know, our Aidan.'

'Is he? What does he do exactly?'

'He's an animator.'

'I know, but what does that mean? What does he do all day? Draw cartoons and stuff?'

'Well, a bit of that. But he works on films mainly. Animated feature films. That kind of thing.' Marcus drains his bottle swiftly. 'Another drink?' he asks, getting up.

In the cab on the way back, he reaches over, takes her hand and folds it into his. She stares at her hand in his lap as if it is no longer connected to her. How did it get there and what is it doing there? He leans over and his lips brush her face. Tarmac rumbles beneath them. The taxi dips in and out of cones of orange light. In the rear-view mirror, Lily sees the eyes of the driver swivel towards them, then away. Marcus lifts her hair and presses his mouth to her neck. It's an expansive gesture, and there is something about it that makes her uneasy. The ends of her hair fall back into his face too soon. His hand travels up too far into empty air. She thinks: My hair is too short for that. She thinks: that gesture belongs to Sinead.

At the flat, he pulls her into his room and takes off her clothes one by one, dropping them to the floor.

'Let's turn the light off,' she says.

In the morning she is waiting for Lily, sitting on the washing machine. Lily nearly cries out, but clamps shut her mouth just in time. Her throat is prickly with thirst after the alcohol last night, but she cannot bring herself to go near her. The kitchen taps are only a short reach from the washing-machine, and to get to the bathroom, she'd have to pass through the gap between the counter and the machine. What if she reached for her, touched her, grasped her?

Lily brings her clothes into the big room and dumps them on the floor, getting dressed with Sinead sitting just ten feet away. Lily stares at her and she stares at Lily as Lily slides on her underwear, yanks a sweater over her head, pulls up the side zip of her skirt. Dressing in the bedroom while this is out here would be worse. At least she knows where it is if she keeps her eyes on it. One foot dangles over the washing-machine's convex, eye-like door, the other is tucked underneath her. Her fingers rest in her lap, twisting, curling, knotting into each other.

After that, it gets worse.

Lily wakes with a jolt, knowing somehow that she's been standing there for some time. She is lying in the sarcophagus hollow made by Sinead's body in the mattress. Marcus sleeps next to her, the covers pulled up round his shoulders.

Sinead is standing, pressed in between the bed and the wall. Lily's leg lies alongside her. She is dressed only in a vest and knickers. Her arms and legs are pale and smooth as soap. Lily's breath rattles in her throat. She's been staring at them while they slept. Her face is drawn, the texture of candle-wax, a small V between her brows. Lily cannot look at it for long, but she sees more misery there than she can ever imagine.

The moment stretches. The room is jagged with the dark mounds of furniture; a vase looms on the table, the lamp's face is angled towards her. Sinead seems to be breathing, the blunted peaks of her breasts rising and falling beneath the vest.

'Please, please, please.' The muttered words break from Lily's lips. 'What is it that you want?' She clenches her eyes shut, her fingers gripping Marcus's shoulder. He sighs and turns towards her. Everything is icy: her hands, her hair, her limbs. The heat from Marcus fizzles out as it reaches her skin. She can feel, metres and metres below the infrastructure of the building and the streets, the shaking of the first Underground trains of the morning.

When she opens her eyes again, she sees that Sinead is creeping in slowed-down, mesmeric steps, as if walking through water, towards the door.

Lily moves her dry tongue over her lips. Her teeth are

banging against each other with the cold, trapping wedges of her mouth. There is a swelling pressure in her bladder, but nothing, nothing would persuade her to leave this bed.

Then she is everywhere: leaning against the fridge, behind doors, reflected in the windows, standing at the basin, crouched in the wardrobe in the morning, hanging around the flat door, sitting straight-backed on the sofa. She is always watching Lily, fixing her with a look that seems to veer between sadness and a kind of soft frown, almost like confusion or concern.

And it seems to Lily that the flat itself is conspiring against her. Doors swing back in her face. Locks stick around her key. Plugs spark under her touch. The refrigerator refuses to open, then yields easily to Aidan's hand. The hot-water taps give only cold water then scalding, skin-peeling jets. Stacked arrangements of tins crumble and clatter if she so much as passes. The blue flame of the cooker ring gutters out, leaving wreaths of sour gas hanging in the air. The phone rings then cuts dead. A bike in the hallway crashes to its side. Her clothes slip their hangers and lie in creased, lifeless heaps at the bottom of the wardrobe. Stair-edges seem to shift and multiply beneath her feet, tripping her, leaving a grey-mauve line along her forehead. Table corners leap out at her. The kettle boils but won't switch itself off, filling the kitchen with burning billows of steam that condense in a transparent slick on the walls that makes Marcus tut and run his finger down it.

It's as if she seethes from every door lock, every cupboard hinge, every lightbulb, every nail, every brick, the putty holding in the windows, the water that circulates in the radiators.

Sleep eludes Lily. Waking hours gnaw at those she spends unconscious. Violet shadows leak into the hollows under her eyes. She tears at her nails until the skin is pale, peeled and raw, her fingertips tender, her fingerprints blurred. Headaches pincer her temples by the afternoon. She dozes on buses, misses her stop, and trips as she stumbles off to the pavement. She finds she has begun forgetting words: in the middle of a sentence, she'll be pulled up short by a blank in her mind. She'll know the shape of the word, she'll be able to envisage the object, but its syllables aren't where she usually finds them.

She is sitting on her bed one morning, getting ready to pick up Laurence, bending over to tie her trainers when her nose catches a scent: faint, sensual. Jasmine? But she knows it — it clings to the room she lives in, to certain cushions on the sofa, to a shelf in the bathroom. She doesn't move, but crouches over her shoes, waiting. The air around her seems to thicken and curdle. The scent becomes stronger. She feels it scorching a path along her nose and the back of her mouth until she can almost taste it, feel it smarting at her eyelids. She blinks, water rimming the edges of her vision. In front of her there seems to be a shadow. Or less of a shadow than a shape, as if oxygen is densifying, its molecules buzzing faster and closer and closer together. She can't see it if she looks straight at it, but if she blinks at it askance, the elements in the atmosphere seem to be pulling themselves into a shape. A definite shape. The shape of a pair of feet, standing on the boards before her.

Lily gulps at the air, but the scent is so strong she almost chokes. She wants to shut up her lips and nostrils like a seal under water. She can't look up, can't raise her head to see what she knows will be towering above her. Her fingers fumble with her laces, which have become as slippery as liquorice between her frozen knuckles. She doesn't wait but makes a run for the door, laces snagging at her feet.

'Relax,' Jodie commands, her body curved like a comma over the steering wheel.

'I am relaxed,' Aidan replies and, as if to prove it, spreads his fingers out on his thighs. 'I'm calm.' He pulls his face into a fixed, false grin. 'I am enjoying myself,' he says, in the robot voice they invented as children.

His sister shoots him a look. She is clearly trying to come up with a retort.

'Eyes on the road, please,' he incants, in the same voice.

'You are so—' Jodie begins, and the car veers towards the line of parked vehicles at the side of the road. Aidan puts out his hand and nudges the wheel.

'Get off!' she shrieks. 'I'm driving!'

'I know you are. I just don't want you to take all those wing mirrors with you.'

'Like scalps,' she says, with relish.

'Er, perhaps. Hang a left here, would you?'

'*Hang* a left?' she repeats, mocking. 'You've spent too much time in America.'

'I'd never deny it,' he says quickly, then: 'Handbrake.

Into neutral. OK. First gear. Foot off the clutch.' The car leapfrogs forward then judders to a halt. Someone behind blasts their horn, three perfect semi-quavers.

'You impatient bloody bastard boy racer!' Jodie yells at the rear-view mirror, yanking at the handbrake, then mutters to herself about the restarting procedure.

'Road rage,' he warns.

'Shut up.'

'Foot off the clutch slowly,' Aidan says, 'slowly, slowly. That's it.' The car glides forward in a steady curve. 'Perfect.'

Jodie pulls the gearstick back into second. 'I have to pass this time, I have to,' she moans softly.

'You will.'

'I have to,' she repeats. 'I'll never get promoted otherwise. And I really don't want to be one of those women who can't drive. You know the ones.' She sighs and slumps down in the driving seat. 'Oh, God. I'm never going to be able to drive.'

'Stop being such a doom queen,' he says, eyeing a beige Mercedes approaching down the middle of the road. 'Cut your speed for Mr Swanky up ahead.' Jodie presses the brake. 'You're going to be fine. Is Rory taking you out much for practice runs?'

'Ha,' she barks.

'What do you mean, "ha"?'

'Ha.' She shrugs. 'Just ha. You know.'

'No, I don't.'

They pull up rather abruptly at a zebra crossing. Her face, when he looks across at her, turns from orange to pale and back again in the flashing Belisha-beacon light.

'Oh,' she shrugs again, 'I just didn't think it would do our relationship much good, him teaching me to drive.'

'Mmm.' Aidan puts his head on one side, watching her. 'I can see that.'

People stream in front of the bonnet, pushing prams, bikes, scooters.

'He's being a bit . . .' she scratches at the raised red parabola of an insect bite on her upper arm '. . . wearing at the moment.'

'In what way?'

'I don't know.' Her fingernails scrabble at her arm. 'Too attentive,' she says at last.

'Too attentive?'

'Yeah.'

'How?'

She considers this while she moves the car over the zebra crossing and out into a river-like expanse of empty Tarmac. 'The other day, for example . . . you know I've just moved into my new flat?'

'Uh-huh.'

'Well, he goes out and buys me an Ordnance Survey map of the area from 1884 or something.' She looks over at him, pointedly. 'And the house is on it.'

Aidan frowns, puzzled. 'Yeah?'

'Well,' she sighs, exasperated, as if he's just said something really stupid, 'don't you think that's just a little bit . . . too much?'

'It sounds nice.'

'Nice!' She pounces on the word like an aggravated

cat. 'Nice! Exactly! That's exactly my point.' She sits back, satisfied.

'But, Jodie—' He stops. They are pulling up behind a car at a large junction. A building site looms up on one side of them; a park sweeps away from them on the other. Coming out of the green, curlicued gates of the park is a figure that makes his words evaporate, dissipate into his lungs. A familiar figure is walking along the pavement, arms crossed over a bag held in front of her. The low, cold wind blows her hair flat against her head. Aidan watches as she waits for the pedestrian crossing lights to change.

She passes within six feet of the car. He is nervous, afraid that she might turn her head and see him, sitting, hands idle, in the passenger seat of his own car. And as she comes closer to them he sees that her lips are animated, moving slightly, almost imperceptibly. For a moment he thinks she must be listening to her headphones and mouthing the words to a song only she can hear. But he sees her hair, stretched sleek behind her ears. No headphones. She looks white, gaunt, ill even. Her lips conduct a secret conversation with something or someone, her eyes fixed to the paving stones in front of her.

'Co-pilot Nash,' Jodie is shouting, 'calling co-pilot Nash.'

Aidan turns, blinking, towards his sister. 'Sorry,' he says.

'What's up with you? You look like you've seen a ghost. Who is that woman?' Jodie demands, leaning forward to look after her.

'Oh,' he says. 'No one.' He claps his hands together,

rousing himself. 'Green light,' he points up through the windscreen. 'Let's go.'

As the car pulls away, he looks into the side-view mirror and sees Lily's back receding into the distance, moving away from him. He feels somehow ashamed at having seen her here, as if in some way he's violated her privacy, her secret self. Then the car moves around a corner and she is gone.

Lily's lost her. She'd been right there, right beside her, just a few seconds ago, saying something about how her sister has torn the ligaments in her ankle. But now Lily has found herself suddenly alone in the crowd, a man with a toddler on his shoulders to her right where Sarah should have been, and in front of her a woman with a large wicker basket hooked over her arm.

Lily hefts the weighty terracotta pot holding the lemon geranium from one hip to the other and strains up on tiptoe in search of Sarah's red-hatted head. They are in a Sunday-morning flower market near the flat. The pavements are lined with stalls, plants, shrubs, star-faced flowers, trays of herbs, ferns, bunches of holly. People seethe along the road in groups and currents, holding foliage and blooms aloft. Music pumps from one stall and a young boy thrusts a cluster of pink petals into her face. 'Gladioli!' he yells. 'Four for a pound!'

She turns round, turns back, then heads for the pavement, which is lined by the bare wooden backs of the stalls, where the crowds are thinned out. Sarah's lemon geranium is covered in fine, invisible hairs, which prickle and itch at her. She walks the length of the market, then back, along the other side of the street. No sign of Sarah. The sun strains through the piled, grey cloud and beneath her feet there are stray, blackened flowers, flattened to the pavement. When she reaches the place where she'd last seen her, irritation overtakes her. She stamps down the pot and sets her fists on her hips. This is ridiculous. She'll never find her again. She'll take the bloody geranium and go back to the flat and hope that Sarah follows her there.

She lifts it again and starts forcing a path through the people, sidestepping bodies, turning sideways to get through. And suddenly she sees her, standing beside a stall crammed with lurid, sharp purple flowers.

'Where were you? I lost you,' Lily says when she reaches her. 'Here, take this,' she hands her the geranium pot, 'it weighs a bloody tonne. Where did you . . .' she falters, then stops. Sarah is gazing at her, frowning. 'What's the matter?' Lily asks.

Sarah sighs, looks up the road, twiddling her hair, then back at Lily. 'What's the matter with me?' she says. 'Nothing. Absolutely nothing. Apart from the fact that my closest friend never tells me anything.'

Lily is taken aback. 'What do you mean?'

'You. I mean you.'

'What about me? What haven't I told you?'

'You haven't told me anything!' Sarah cries.

Lily is baffled. 'About what? I don't—'

'I want to know,' she cuts across her.

'Want to know what?'

'What's wrong.'

'Nothing,' Lily shoves her hands in her pockets crossly. 'Nothing's wrong. Why are you being so weird?'

'*I*'m not being weird.'

'Neither am I!'

The two girls glare at each other. Sarah crosses her arms and then, just as quickly, points her finger at Lily's face. 'Something's going on with you,' she says.

Lily swallows. 'This is ridiculous. Come on,' she turns round, 'let's go.'

Sarah holds her ground. 'There is,' she asserts. 'Something's going on. I know it.'

'Know what?'

'I know it,' she says, 'because I know you. I was standing here and I saw you before you saw me, and I was watching you come along the road. And you looked . . .' She hesitates.

'I looked what?' Lily scoffs.

'Hollow,' Sarah says, quiet now.

'Hollow?'

'Yes. Hollow.'

'That's bullshit. Hollow? You can't look hollow.'

'You did. You looked . . . empty and . . . and worn out and . . . you looked hollow, I'm telling you. Like a part of you was gone or missing or something.'

'Oh, for heaven's sake, it's too cold to stand around having a stupid conversation. Let's just go.'

Sarah seizes her wrist. 'What is it, Lily?' Lily tries to withdraw, but Sarah holds her tighter. 'Is it Marcus?'

Lily pulls her wrist free. 'No.' She looks down at her feet. 'No, it's not.'

'What then?' Sarah sighs. 'Look, Lily, for weeks now you've been . . . all funny and preoccupied. And you look like death warmed up. And I can't take it any more. What is it?'

Lily shrugs, silent.

'It's Marcus, isn't it? It must be.'

'No,' Lily says, 'it isn't him, it's . . .'

Sarah leans closer to her. 'What? It's what?'

'Well . . .'

'Yes?'

Lily closes her eyes. 'It's his girlfriend.'

'Sinead?' Sarah says.

Lily nods.

Sarah takes her arm. 'Let's get a coffee.'

They sit on a wooden bench in a narrow alleyway filled with hard-edged winter sunlight. Sarah has bought coffee and rolls from a small kiosk in the brick wall behind them.

'But, Lily,' she is saying, 'everyone has a past.'

'I know that,' Lily says.

'And the people who haven't aren't interesting enough to bother with.'

'I know, I know.'

'Then what is it? That you still don't know what happened to her? Is that still bothering you?'

'No,' Lily says, then: 'Yes. I don't know. I suppose,' she leans her head on the back of the bench, 'I suppose it's that it doesn't feel like she is past.'

Sarah looks at her. 'You mean you don't think he's over her?'

Lily flicks crumbs from her lap. 'Mmm.'

'Well, she did die, for God's sake. I mean—' Sarah stops. 'What I mean is, it's not a situation . . . I mean, it's unusual. However she died, it's unusually difficult . . . not difficult . . . heavy. It's an unusually heavy situation for . . . him to be in. For you to be in.' She fiddles with the zip of her coat, agitating it up and down its track. 'What I mean is,' she says again, 'that you shouldn't worry.'

'I shouldn't worry?'

'You shouldn't worry that you worry.'

Despite herself, Lily smiles.

'It's a big, huge thing. Bigger than anything you or I have ever faced. And of course he's going to take time to . . . to get right.' Sarah drains her cup and regards her friend. 'And he's worth it, isn't he?'

'Worth what?'

'The wait. Worth allowing him a bit of time. I mean, you like him a lot, don't you?' She zips her coat all the way up to her throat. 'I've never seen you like this about anyone. You're in deep.'

Lily shakes her head. 'Nah.'

'Yes, you are,' Sarah says, accusing, turning on her.

'I'm not,' Lily protests.

'Yes you are.'

'No, I'm not.'

Sarah leaps to her feet and strides off down the alley. 'Are too,' she throws over her shoulder.

Lily gets up and, struggling with the pot, shouts, 'Am not!'

'Are too.'

'Am not.'

They run through the crowds, shouting to each other

and, at the edge of the market, Sarah has to stop, breathless and laughing.

A note on the table:

> *Dear Lily and Aidan,*
>   *I've had to go away for a couple of days – maybe more. Work stuff, mainly. The project's going to tender and I've got things to sort out and it looks like I'm going to have to be on site. See you both next week.*
>   *Take care of yourselves, M x*

She picks it up. On the back is an architectural drawing, or part of one; a slip torn from a larger sheet. It's a bathroom from above. She is amazed at the detail: the oval sweep of the bath, the sunken dip of the sink. Taps, shower-head, plug-holes, door handles. Two toilets. Two? Why would anyone need two toilets in one room? Then she realises that one is a bidet. She wonders if Marcus did this drawing. If this arrangement of bathroom appliances is his design. If he laboured over every measurement, every angle, every inch of the flooring.

Turning over the piece of paper, she runs the words around her head. Tender. Going to tender. On site. Work stuff. Mainly. Things to sort out. Take care. She lets it drop back to the table surface and looks about her, letting her coat slide off her back. The buttons clunking on the metal of the chair makes her jump. The air movement caused by the coat pushes the note off the edge of the table and down to the floor. She bends over and it's only after she's put it back on the table that she notices a long coil of black hair attached to its corner.

She holds up the hair between fingerpad and thumbnail at arm's length. She moves towards the kitchen where she gropes on the surface for matches, never taking her eyes away from that sinuous black spiral. She strikes the match and holds the flame to the hair. On contact, it sparks and sputters upwards into nothing, leaving only a bitter scent in the air.

She seizes the broom by its neck and sweeps each floorboard in long, skating movements. The brush-head clunks like a croquet mallet against the skirting boards. What she collects in the metal dustpan – an aerated clot of dust and hair and indefinable fluff, from the quick glance she allows herself – she empties into the steel sink and drops in a lit match. The flames flare blue, briefly. From under the sink she gets a bucket and a tall, squeezable bottle of fluid. She squirts a thin, green stream into the ridged bottom of the bucket and directs a jet of hot water after it. Foam froths and masses around the top. She pulls on a pair of pink rubber gloves, their insides furred like moleskin, and she cleans. She scrubs the table, the counter surface, the sink area, the front of the washing-machine, the cooker hob, all the door-handles, the shower, the toilet seat, the bathroom mirror, the shelves, the window-sills, and then gets a mop and, starting from one corner and backing towards the opposite one in the way her mother always taught her, cleans the floor in wide, damp sweeps of the string-headed mop.

When she's finished, she perches on the arm of the sofa, her feet buried in the cushions, watching the floorboards lighten in unexpected patches.

She is tired out by love, tired of love.

He's hot in the sun, which is pouring in through the large frosted-glass window. He'd quite like to move out of it, into the shade, but there are no other chairs. The solicitor who's dealing with Aidan's house-purchase has disappeared with a sheaf of paper, leaving Aidan sitting there with nothing to do but fiddle with the cap of his pen, and think – follow trails of thought like a dog does smells. It's like trying to keep a virus at bay, he decides, trying not to think about it and what happened. If you feel the warning signs of an infection filtering through your body, you take drugs, stay in bed, keep warm. But this is like a more virulent disease than anything else Aidan's ever experienced.

At the back of the solicitor's office two men are baiting another, younger man. The victim, still in his late teens, is sitting at his desk, eyes fixed on his screen, giving the impression that he is working so hard he hasn't noticed what the other two are saying. A deep red stain rising from his collar to his cheeks betrays him. Aidan sees that if they carry on much longer he might burst into tears.

'Why haven't you got a girlfriend, Matthew?' one of the men with an even fuzz of sand-coloured hair covering his head is demanding. 'Just tell us, Matthew. We're interested. Is it because you're boring? Is it because you're ugly?'

'Or is it because you're gay?' the other one joins in, flexing a ruler between his thin, white hands.

'Are you gay, Matthew? Are you? Just tell us, Matthew. We want to know.'

Aidan shrugs himself out of his sweater and shoves it into his bag, which is lying at his feet. Tell them to fuck off, Matthew, he wills him, tell them to fuck right off. Matthew, shrunk into his keyboard, mutters something soundlessly, his hair stuck into sweaty strips across his forehead.

'What was that, Matthew?' The one with the ruler. 'We can't hear you.'

Aidan gets up quickly, unable to stand any more. The two men, sensing a movement in the room, shift and turn towards him, their faces wary, defensive. Aidan holds their gaze for longer than necessary, until they look away, until one of them puts down the ruler. Then Aidan walks very slowly and deliberately across the carpet to the water cooler. He pulls a paper cup from the holder and fills it, silver bubbles streaming up into the inverted bottle. He drinks. The three men watch.

Aidan's solicitor bursts back into the room, shirtsleeves rolled back, shuffling pages in his hands. 'Sorry about that, Mr Nash,' he says, as he passes him. 'I think we're all set now.' He stops midway to his desk, looks back at the men. 'Have you boys got no work to do?' he demands.

Aidan sits again on the hot plastic of the seat in the sun, watching as his solicitor collates pages and staples them together. It is ridiculous, he decides: he tries all the time not to think about it, not to dwell on it, not to be always ruminating on the 'if I had' or 'if he hadn't'. But even today, when he's completing on his new flat, when he can finally move out of that accursed warehouse, when he should be the happiest man in London, he can't shake the unease that's rooted itself within him.

Lily is watering Marcus's plants, which are lined up in rows along the kitchen shelves. She knows they probably aren't his at all, but is choosing to call them Marcus's plants all the same. She found a little, sharp-snouted watering-can at the back of a cupboard behind cloths, old newspapers and cleaning-fluid bottles, and every few days she gets it out and drips water into the dried-out soil.

She is standing at the sink, the CD-player turned up loud, refilling the watering-can when, suddenly and without warning, the flat is plunged into darkness and silence.

Lily freezes, her hands under the tumbling water of the tap. It's as if she's fallen down a hole. The dark is so black and so dense that she can't tell if her eyes are open or not. She feels for the tap and twists it off, trying to ignore the adrenaline kicking at her ribs. It's the key, she tells herself, the blue electricity key that Marcus showed her when she first moved in. It needs to be taken to the garage down the road and recharged every couple of weeks or so. That's why the electricity has cut out. It must have run out. No other reason.

No other reason, she mutters to herself, turning in the black, fathomless space, no other reason at all. She is, she estimates, facing the length of the room now. All she has to do is walk through the kitchen, between the counter and the units, past the table, through the living area and down to the electricity meter, which is in a small, high-up cupboard on the wall outside Marcus's studio. That's all. Simple. She knows the flat. She could do it with her eyes closed.

Putting out her hand, she touches the counter top more quickly than she imagined, and she snatches back her hand in shock. She rubs her palm against her hip, feeling its definite fleshiness, its corporeal realness. It was just the counter, that's all, it just means she is further to the right than she thought.

Lily shuffles her feet and shunts forward a few inches. She battles silently with herself about putting her hand out in front of her. She doesn't want to *touch* something there, to feel anything brush up against her palm. But, then, she doesn't want to walk face first into anything either. She dithers, rubbing the edges of her shoes against each other then stretches out her arm into the black beyond and edges forward, the other hand resting on the counter edge.

At the end of the counter she lets go of it. To her right now should be a dining chair with her coat over the back. She gropes towards it, just to feel the cool solidity of its metal spar. Nothing. Her hand flails in a black void. Panic jags at her chest. To her left should be the fridge and she pushes her hand towards it, and almost falls sideways when she comes into contact with nothing, a vacuum.

Her breathing is fast and shallow now and she steps back, hoping to regain her bearings by finding the counter end and starting again from there. But she steps back and back and back again and there is nothing behind her. Just space and more space.

Lily whirls round and then whirls back, not wanting to lose the way she was facing, the way to the electricity cupboard, the way to light and release, but she is so disoriented now that she can't remember which way she's facing and which way she should be going. She's experiencing a kind of inverted, negated perception. Usually, it's her environment and the people in it that seem firm and immutable, while she just passes through it, wraith-like. But now it feels as though the flat has dissolved into a black miasma and she is the only live, complete element in it.

She stands on one leg and moves the other in a semi-circle around her, to see if it comes into contact with anything. Nothing. Her heart is beating so fast and hard that she feels dizzy and breathless. She tries clearing her throat, tries humming the song that had been playing, but can't remember it and what comes out of her mouth sounds so disjointed and echoes around this sightless space so much that it, too, frightens her.

She shakes her head, presses her hand against her leaping heart in an attempt to calm it. All she has to do is walk in one direction and she'll come across something that will tell her where she is. It's simple. It's easy. She does live here, after all. It's only electricity.

She strikes out in the direction to her left. She expects any second to encounter the fridge or the bookshelves. But nothing happens. She keeps moving, one hand held in front of her, knees bent. She thinks about how ridiculous she must look. Then the idea that she is being watched plants itself in her head, spreading deep, gnarled roots. Watched by something that can see in the dark. Or something that doesn't need light, is beyond light.

Still nothing, and she continues to shuffle in her chosen direction, a small whimpering noise escaping into the air every few seconds, and, knowing it's coming from her, she chooses to ignore it.

Then her fingers meet something. She flattens her palm against it. A cold, smooth, hard surface. Glass. Which means she's reached a window or the mirror near the door. She doesn't get the chance to move her hand up or down to find a window latch or a mirror edge because there is a tingling, stinging feeling at the centre of her face. The very back of her nose. A familiar, dreadful scent is itching at her.

Lily has never experienced pure fear. She thought she had, but realises now that it was some weaker, poorer relation of what she is feeling now. Pure fear is clean, flawless and contourless, almost tipping you over into the sensation of nothing at all. It doesn't so much take over your whole body as deprive you of one.

The scent gathers in the air around her. Lily screws up her eyes, trying to see something, anything ahead of her. Nothing. She can see nothing and all the time the smell is getting stronger, closer. It's as if her heart has stopped beating now and Lily wonders if she's going to die, if that is what this has all been leading up to, what it's all been about. Maybe she should dart aside, run, struggle, fight it, but her mind seems to be divorced, elsewhere. She wants to say the name aloud, just so it knows that Lily knows it's there, just to hear it, just so both of them hear it together. Lily is drawing in breath, her mouth ready to form the strange word when something light and damp seems to wreathe her ankles. Balance, then body tension desert her; her hand slides down the cold skin of the glass and her last thought is that her head is cracking against what, for a micro-second, she believes is the wall but is in fact the floor; and everything doesn't go black but blank – formless and infinite.

Something is touching her stomach and Lily leaps the rest of the way to consciousness.

Aidan is leaning over her, his hand flat on her front, his other hand holding a torch, which he is directing not at her but near enough to her for them both to be in a capsule of yellow light. His face is shocked, concerned. Lily tries to sit up but her vision merges everything together.

'Don't,' Aidan says gently, his hand pressing her down, 'just stay still for a bit. Lie flat.'

He puts the torch down on the floor next to them and pulls himself out of his leather jacket, which he spreads over Lily. The heat left in it warms her hands and she moves them under it.

'Are you all right?' he asks, picking up the torch again. 'What happened?'

'I – I – the electricity key ran out and . . .'

He is shaking his head. 'No, the whole street's out. Didn't you notice? There are no streetlights. They're digging up the pavement down the road and they cut through the electricity cables by mistake.' He laughs but it's shaky – pent-up and relieved at the same time. 'You scared the life out of me, Lily. I'd been in here for a bit, looking for the torch before I found you. I thought you were . . .' He bites his lip. 'Can you sit up?'

He helps her upright against the wall, his hand around her arm. Then he rests his thumb and index finger across her cheek and peers into one of her eyes, then the other. Lily has never seen him at such close range and finds she wants to study his face.

'Well, I don't think you're concussed. But did you just faint or did you hit your head?'

His hands are exploring her skull, gently moving her hair aside as his fingers search and press different sections of her head. His touch is so assured, so tender and so unexpected that it seems to hit some exposed spot in her. Her throat closes and liquid swims into her eyes.

'Oh, no,' he is ducking down to look into her face, 'I didn't hurt you, did I?'

'No, no, not at all.' She rubs her hand over her face. 'I'm fine. I really am.'

He leans back on his heels. 'Well, there are no lumps. But I think you might have a big bruise here tomorrow.' His thumb brushes her cheekbone.

'Yeah. I think . . . I think I just passed out. Fainted, I mean.'

'Right.' He nods, frowning, then asks: 'Do you faint much?'

'Er . . . no. Don't think so. Can't remember having fainted before.'

'My sister does.' He moves off into the kitchen, the cone

of his light bobbing over the walls and ceiling. 'She faints all the time.'

Lily follows the jittering beam of light. Relief is ebbing through her. She is indeed in front of the mirror behind the door, and she can't believe that the flat is all still here, still intact, still existing. 'Does she?'

'Yeah. Always has done. Always will probably. She has low blood pressure.' He wedges the torch on top of the fridge between a pile of magazines and a jam jar. 'It takes an hour or so to fix,' he is saying, as he moves about, opening drawers and rattling boxes of matches, 'or so they said.'

'What will?' Her brain is disordered: she seems unable to follow the thread of the conversation. Does he mean his sister?

'The electricity. Idiots,' he mutters, as he stands two half-melted candles on the table and holds a match to them. The wicks catch and vertical shadows reach up and touch the ceiling. He comes back over to where she is propped up. 'You know, you ought to go to the doctor. Get yourself checked out. Just to be sure.'

Lily moves her feet, preparing to stand. Aidan leans down and, grasping her by both forearms, pulls her up. She sways, her legs feeling frail. But he catches her round the waist and, his arm supporting her, walks with her to the sofa. When she sinks into it, he remains above her, standing. 'You must go to the doctor,' he says again, looking her over, 'tomorrow. You really must. You're white as a sheet.'

'I will,' she lies. 'I promise. But I'm sure it's nothing.'

'Yeah, well, let the doctor be the judge of that.' He

turns and goes to his doors. 'Right. I'm going to pack, but if you need anything just shout.'

'Pack? Are you going away?' she asks, hearing the dismay in her voice and hating it.

'Not exactly.' He pats his trouser pocket and a metallic clink answers. He smiles. 'I got the keys to my new flat today. At last.'

She watches as he walks to and fro in the quivering candlelight, piling up by the door suitcases, bags of books, and boxes of computer screens, leads, hard drives, scanners, CD-ROMs. A cup of tea appears at her elbow, heavily sugared, and, feeling guiltily better, she gets up, laying his jacket carefully over the arm of the chair.

'Do you want a hand with anything?' she calls.

'No. I've just about finished.'

Keeping the bathroom door open to catch the flickering of the candles, she washes her face, examining the faint mark on her cheek. As she comes out of the bathroom the lights rise up to meet her as if she's just walked on stage. Aidan is standing at the table, hands shoved into his back pockets. Behind him, the CD clicks and whirs in the machine, and then loud, inappropriate trip-hop fills the space between them. For some reason, they both laugh.

'Let there be light,' he says.

'Power to the people,' she returns quickly.

'If music be the food of light,' he says, just as quickly.

'And so put on the light.'

'It's lighter than air.'

'Here's some light relief.'

'*Eine kleine lichtmusik.*'

That makes Lily giggle. 'Er . . .' she can't think of one. 'Let them eat cake!' she blurts wildly.

Aidan laughs. 'I win,' he says. Then: 'Look, I'll . . . I won't go tonight. I'll take my stuff over to the flat in the morning.'

'Oh.' She is suddenly sober, knowing she should protest, that he should go, but she can't find the words, for him leaving now seems like the worst thing that could ever happen to her. 'Thank you,' she says meekly, 'thank you so much.'

'No, it's fine.' He scratches his head. 'Marcus'll be back soon. So you'll be . . . fine.'

The next morning their awkwardness is back. Aidan stands at the door with a cardboard box.

'I hope . . . you'll be all right,' he says, holding out his hand. She is set off balance by the formality of this gesture but she takes it anyway, presses it in hers, knowing that she should say something. He drops his eyes, easing his hand out of hers, turning away.

Lily realises that she'll probably never see him again. She wants to ask him for a phone number, or an address, whether he'll be happy now. But she doesn't.

'Good luck with . . .' she can't think how to end the sentence '. . . your new flat,' she adds in a moment of inspiration.

'Thanks,' he says, and without looking back, ''bye, then.'

The instant the door closes, she whips round to face the

room. The tap drips, water tap-tapping into the well of the sink. Underfoot, a central-heating pipe sighs and shudders. At the far window, a breeze fills a shirt with her shape.

She stares at it for a second then jerks herself into action, running towards her room, fear tightening her scalp. She seizes her bag from the floor and starts snatching up objects to shove into it: tube pass, purse, book, keys. Where are her keys? She storms about, lifting clothes, magazines, books and hurling them in to the air. No sign of them. She leans around her door. The flat looks impossibly long from this perspective, the bathroom and kitchen stretching away into the distance. She makes a sudden dash across the floorboards, her footsteps crashing and bouncing off the walls. Keys, keys, keys, she is intoning to herself. Where the hell are they? Not on the table, not on the sofa, not by the door. Keep looking, Lily, she tells herself, they've got to be somewhere, can't be far away.

In another part of her mind, a terrible thought is growing. She is struggling to ignore it, keeping her mind on the search, but it's getting louder and louder. If she can't find her keys, she can't open the door, which is fitted with a stupid self-locking mechanism. If she can't open the door, she can't leave. If she can't leave, she'll be stuck in here all day. And all night. And all the next day. And the next. Until Marcus gets back.

And around her the room is suddenly quiet and still, the kind of stillness she has come to hate. The tap is silent, the sink dry. Her shirt is pressed flat at the window. She darts a glance at the door, six feet away. Maybe it won't be locked after all. Maybe, just maybe, it didn't lock after Aidan. She almost tries it, just to make sure, just on the off-chance that the mechanism hadn't worked for once. But the idea of her tugging in vain at an unyielding handle isn't a good one. She runs briefly through other means of escape – the lift shaft, the windows – and then a very cold focus descends on her brain: I have to get out of here. I have to find my keys.

She scatters objects from the table to the floor – unopened mail, Marcus's note, newspaper supplements. She wrenches open the kitchen drawers and ransacks their contents. She runs her hand along the shelf where the plants sit in a neat row. She empties out the chrome bowl on the counter and matchboxes, elastic bands, corkscrews, a tiny silver earring, some hairgrips scatter over the Formica and on to the floor.

'Come on!' she shouts to the air. 'Where have you put them?' Then mutters, 'Bitch,' as she strides to the bathroom and pulls open the cabinet. By the sound system, she pulls CDs from their shelves. She hurls the sofa cushions to the floor. She lifts up the corners of the rugs. Then she walks slowly and deliberately to the large windows at the end of the flat, where the bulbs are pushing up through the soil.

On the sill is a mug. Lily has seen it before but never really thought about it. It has a black 'S' printed on its side. She pushes her fingers into its cold porcelain mouth and lifts out her keys.

Laurence has found a stone and is bashing it against the hollow iron leg of the swing. He takes his steadying hand away from the swing for a moment to look back at her, delighted.

Lily smiles at him and waves. 'That's a good noise, Laurence.'

He turns back to his labours and the dull, metallic thud rings out again over the misty park. A mother in a pink bobble-hat, bouncing a miserable-looking child on a see-saw, glances at her disapprovingly. Lily is tempted to stick out her tongue.

She feels light-headed and edgy, and a heavy knot of dread is tensing her stomach, like the feeling before an exam. What is she going to do? She can't go back to the flat, and she can't very well move out either. How would she explain it to Marcus?

Laurence is coming over the grass towards her, with the emphatic, solid stagger of a toddler, grinning. His mother has dressed him in so many clothes that he is quite spherical.

'Hi,' Lily says, 'what happened to your wonderful stone?'

His fists grip the material of her coat. He extends the index finger of his hand towards the bench she's sitting on and looks up at her enquiringly. He's going through what his mother refers to his 'acquiring verbalism stage'.

'Bench,' says Lily.

He points again.

'Bench.'

He points up.

'Sky.'

And behind her.

'Tree,' Lily says. 'Tree. You try.'

He points instead at the mother beside the see-saw who is involved in a struggle with her child. It is weeping piteously and trying in vain to get off the see-saw.

'Horrid lady,' Lily says.

He points again.

'Silly hat.'

Laurence jiggles at her leg. 'Up,' he commands, in his throaty growl. 'Up.'

Lily scoops him off the ground and on to her knee. 'Shall we go home?' she asks him. 'Are you cold yet? No, probably not. You're dressed for a Himalayan expedition, aren't you?'

He twists round in her arms to gaze at her. She sees his slate-grey eyes fix on the bruise that has bloomed on the side of her face.

'What do you think will happen?' she asks him, straightening his hat on his soft, blond hair. 'Eh? What's your view? What am I going to see next? And the million-dollar question: am I losing my marbles?'

Laurence extends his finger towards the bruise, frowning.

'Wouldn't you like to know?' she says, pressing her face into the silky skin of his neck. He wriggles, laughing his emphysemic old-man laugh. 'You ask too many questions, that's your problem.'

'How much does he earn?' Diane says, attempting to hold up a burgundy shirt against Lily. Lily pushes it away from her. She is regretting telling her mother about Marcus. She's spent the night back in Ealing and, in a weak moment, Diane had extracted a promise from her to be a shopping companion the next day.

'I don't know. I haven't asked him, have I?'

Shoppers flow around them, bumping bags and umbrellas and elbows. Diane places the shirt back on the rack. 'Must be considerable. An architect.' Diane rolls the word around her mouth, giving it about five syllables. 'It's wonderful, Lily. I'm so pleased.'

'It's not . . . like that, really.'

'Not like what?' Diane demands. 'Serious, you mean? Lily, nothing is serious at first.'

Diane makes her way through the racks and carousels of clothing with the weaving gait of an expert department-store shopper, leaving Lily stranded among the cardigans. Nearby another mother and daughter study a blue angora twinset with religious intensity. 'Is it me?' the daughter asks.

'Well,' her mother replies, 'it could be.'

'I hope you're taking care of yourself, Lily,' Diane shouts, from the sock and hosiery department. Lily starts to calculate whether she can get to her mother's side quickly enough to stop her continuing in that vein. 'You are taking precautions, aren't you?' she bellows. 'What are you using?'

'Mum,' Lily hisses, stumbling to her side, plastic bags flapping from her arms like angel wings, 'for God's sake. Do you have to? Everyone can hear you.'

'Who?'

'Everyone.' Lily gesticulates around the shop.

'Well, it's important. I have to ask. You don't have to give me any details if you don't want to. Just tell me, put my mind at rest, are you being careful?'

Lily closes her eyes. 'Yes. Of course. Of course I am.'

Half-way through the morning they have coffee. Lily stacks up her mother's bags on a spare chair. Diane swirls white cream from a tiny carton into the black of her decaff, agitating the surface with a spoon. Lily watches the colour sink into brown.

'You don't look well,' Diane announces, peering into her daughter's face. 'What is it? PMT?'

'No.'

'When's your period due?'

Lily stares at her mother. 'Why are you so annoying?' She glances at the surrounding tables, but everyone is engrossed in shopper's conversations. 'It's . . . I don't know . . . two weeks or something.'

Diane flattens her fingers against Lily's brow. 'Are you

off-colour? Do you feel ill? What's that mark on your cheek from?'

Lily ducks away, 'It's nothing. I . . . I fell, that's all. Tripped. I'm fine.'

'You don't look it. You look like you've got tuberculosis.'

'Thanks.' She sips at the slick black surface of her coffee. 'He had a girlfriend,' she says.

'Really?' Diane is immediately there, listening. 'A serious one?'

'Yeah. I think so. They lived together.'

'How long for?'

'Four years? Five, maybe. Don't know.'

'How long ago?'

'Don't know.'

'Well, haven't you asked?'

'She died.'

'Oh.' Diane frowns as if this information is irksome to her. 'When?'

'I'm not sure. Quite recently I think. She's still . . . sort of . . . around the flat.'

'Around the flat? In what way?'

'Er,' Lily breaks the Danish pastry on her plate into smaller and smaller crumbs. 'Um. Well, all her stuff was still in my room . . . when I first saw it.'

'I see.' Diane considers this, displeased. 'What did she die of?'

Lily sees paving slabs, regular and neat as fields seen from an aeroplane. She closes her eyes. 'Don't know.'

'For heaven's sake, Lily,' Diane takes an exasperated

swig from her cup. 'Don't you and this Marcus ever talk to each other? Hold a conversation?'

Lily eats her Danish slowly, dipping it into her coffee until her mother tells her to stop that, it's disgusting. A waitress comes, an orange pencil gripped between her teeth, and slides the crockery on to a tray. Diane starts looking at her watch.

'She was really beautiful,' Lily says.

'Who?' Diane is searching in her handbag for something.

'The girlfriend. Marcus's girlfriend.'

'Ex-girlfriend,' Diane corrects her.

'Can you be an ex if you died?'

'Of course,' Diane snaps. 'You're his girlfriend now . . .'

'Well—'

'. . . so that makes her his ex.'

'Mmm,' Lily picks at a loose thread in the seam of her shirt, 'maybe.'

'Look, Lily,' Diane leans across the table and takes hold of her daughter's hand, 'don't worry about this, this . . . girl.'

'Sinead.'

'Sinead? What kind of a name's that?'

'Dunno. Irish, I think.'

'Well. Anyway. Don't worry about her. Put her out of your mind. She's gone. He's yours now. He's a good catch.'

'I wish you wouldn't talk about him as if he was a fish.'

Lily weaves in and out of the crowds on Oxford Street. Diane has gone home. Three hours' shopping is 'just her limit'. Lily's bought a blue shirt of sheer, flimsy fabric. She folds it up into a small, square parcel and crams it into her bag.

She walks down Charing Cross Road and, turning left, wanders through Covent Garden. It begins to drizzle and Lily realises she's forgotten her umbrella. At a pharmacy on a corner she stops and peers through the window at a woman having a makeover. She's tilted back in a chair like a dentist's, her hair pulled into a grey, clinical band. A woman in a grey overall and orange foundation is standing over her smearing something white and foamy on to her face. She's wearing a badge that says, 'Ask me about options for lips.'

Suddenly, something beyond the woman having a make-over, something through the window that faces out over the perpendicular street makes the depth of focus in Lily's eye flicker and stretch. Then her stomach drops to the pavement she's standing on.

Sinead passes the window without looking her way, a hood obscuring most of her face. Then the window is blank again, veils of grey drizzle sweeping across its greenish glass.

Lily edges to the corner and peers round. Is this how it's going to be now? That she's going to follow her everywhere? That Lily will see her everywhere – outside, in shops, at work, on the tube? Is this how it's going to be?

The figure is walking at a steady pace away from Lily. She has a rucksack on her back. A smaller woman with blonde hair is walking beside her. The blonde woman is saying something to her and now Sinead is nodding, unfolding her arms and turning her face towards her friend, her right palm upturned in a gesture of affirmation to whatever it is she's saying. They stop at a zebra crossing. They are still talking. The friend is shaking her head. Lily finds that her feet are moving under her and the scene where Sinead and Sinead's friend are standing waiting to cross the road is getting closer. Lily feels incredibly calm, as if somehow she had always known this would happen, had always seen this coming.

They cross the road. Sinead adjusts her hood, pulling it further over her face against the steady rain. Lily is five maybe four paces behind them. Sinead's jacket rustles as her body moves inside it. At the tube station they stop and face each other on the pavement.

'. . . but I should be back by Thursday,' the friend is saying. 'I can't believe it will take longer than that.'

Sinead nods. The two women embrace.

'So I'll give you a call, then. OK?'

Sinead says something Lily can't hear.

''Bye,' the friend calls from the station entrance, 'see you soon.'

Sinead watches her go through the ticket barrier, waves, then turns away. She walks fast when she's on her own, Lily discovers, weaving in and out of the Saturday crowds. She turns unexpectedly and quickly into a bookshop, and Lily leaps through the doorway so fast she almost falls into her.

The windows are steamed up. Umbrellas stand by the door, dripping pools of rainwater on to the black-tiled floor. Sinead wanders over to the fiction stands, pulls off her gloves, shrugs back her hood and gives her hair a shake, freeing it from the neck of her jacket.

Lily pushes her way through the groups of bent-necked people. And from somewhere a memory twitches then opens out in front of her – a day trip she took with her parents when they still had her baby brother Mark, before Lily found him in his cot, blue and cold as marble. Her father held him in a papoose on his chest and the family walked through a field of long grass. She doesn't know where it was exactly, but she can see it all clearly. It must have been a field near a cliff-edge because she remembers the sensation of a steep, sheer drop that she couldn't see to her left. It was sunny and the grass was washed in yellow-green. She had on open-toed sandals and in her hand was a green plastic dinosaur, which had come in a kit, in two hollow halves. Her father had glued it together, pushing the gummed edges against each other until they set. There was a ridge of bubbled, hard glue along the dinosaur's back, through its blank-eyed face, through the swell of its belly and along its tail. It was most comfortable to hold it by its upper tail. They all walked through the field, her parent's voices criss-crossing over Lily's head, the faraway sea – was there sea? there was definitely sea – throwing pebbles up on to the beach far below them, Mark breathing breathing in his papoose, the soft creases of his nose and mouth pressed to her father's sternum, and the grass swooshing, sussurating, cleaving open to her steps. Part of her was frightened. The grass came up to her neck. What if she was swallowed up and her parents couldn't find her again in this endless, rippling green sea? She held up the dinosaur until her arm ached. If she didn't allow the grass to touch it, everything would be all right. When she looked down, she saw the dense brown roots, clinging to the sods of dried earth, falling open for her, shrinking back at the pressure of her sandal; and in front of her opened a path through the field.

And this is how it seems again in the bookshop. As if surrounded by a negative magnetic field, people fall away from her, step out of her path. And she carries on walking through them, right up to Sinead.

She stands near her and breathes in. She can catch her scent – inky, musky, with a hint of hair wax, soap, rain and that perfume. Sinead trails her index finger along the shelf, draws down a book, flicks over the title pages and reads the front page. She shifts her weight from one foot to the other.

Lily circles her, stands on the other side of the shelf, peering through the books. Sinead's eyes flick from side to side on the page. Lily sees her swallow, cough, and swallow again. She rubs the heel of her palm against her head. Lily comes round to Sinead's side of the shelf, picks up a book, puts it down. Touches the cover of another. 'Sinead?' she says.

She turns, the book still in her hands. She keeps her thumbnail in the page she'd reached. Her eyes scan Lily's face, moving from her eyes to her mouth, over her hair and back to her eyes. Sinead is taller than Lily. Lily's brow reaches her shoulder. Her expression is open but perplexed.

'You're Sinead?'

'Yes,' she nods, 'I am.'

There is a pause. She's not Irish, after all. Her voice is modulated, accentless, placeless.

'Sorry,' Sinead shakes her head, 'I don't—'

'No, no. You don't know me. I mean, we've never met. Not properly. Well, we've never actually met at all.'

'Oh. So how do you—'

'My name's Lily. I'm—'

Sinead recoils as if she's been blasted by cold air. 'I know exactly who you are.'

Before Lily can absorb this, Sinead has twisted on her heel and walked off. Very fast. Lily sets off after her.

'Sinead, wait.'

She turns a corner, Lily pursuing her. Sinead has her hands around her head as if protecting it.

'Please, Sinead. I just want to . . .'

'What?' Sinead turns on her suddenly. Lily jumps back, striking the edge of her wrist on a bookstand. Several people turn round and stare at them. Sinead towers over Lily. 'You just want to what?' She is crying now, silver tears dripping into the raindrops on her coat. 'Leave me alone, for God's sake. What's wrong with you?'

That Lily has caused these tears appals her. She feels about in her pocket for a tissue. 'Don't cry,' she says, putting out a hand to touch her sleeve. 'Please don't cry.'

Sinead pulls away from her and for a moment in front of Lily there is just the space where Sinead had been. Lily steps through the door after her into the cold air of the street. Again there is that sensation of Sinead – on the pavement again, sobbing now with uncontrolled, deep, wrenching gasps, sobbing with her hands around her eyes – getting closer to her, not the other way round.

'I'm sorry,' Lily says, 'I'm so sorry. I didn't mean—'

Sinead wipes at her wet cheeks with the edges of her fingers. 'Go away,' she hisses, 'leave me alone.'

Lily stands there, outside the bookshop as Sinead lurches away from her. She watches as she makes her way through the crowd, and even after she can no longer see the shape of that head, she stares at the spot it disappeared from for a long time, just in case it might return.

He's back. The lights are on in his room. Lily hurtles up the stairs and into the flat, flinging aside coat, bag and keys, bursting into his room, breathless and loud. 'She didn't die, did she?'

Marcus starts, the wheels on his chair jerking backwards, and looks up from his computer, blinking as if he can't see her properly. 'Hello to you too,' he says, with a nonplussed smile. 'Who didn't die?'

'Sinead.'

His smile shrivels like burning paper. '*Die?*' He passes his tongue between his lips. 'No. Of course not.'

She sighs in exasperation, surprised to find she is close to tears. 'But you told me she did!' she screams.

Marcus stares at her, his face scrunched into itself. 'No, I didn't.' He shakes his head slowly.

'You did!' She is furious, spitting with outrage. 'You did! You—'

'Lily, why would I tell you—'

'You said . . .' She stops, thinks back, fists clenched at her sides.

'What did I say?'

'You said . . . you said . . .' She grapples with her memory, re-enacting in her mind that moment on the sofa with the glove stretched out beside them. She asked him what happened, and he said . . . Then she remembers: 'You said she was no longer with us,' she shouts, accusing. 'Those were your exact words. No longer with us.'

He is still staring at her, disbelieving. Then he clears his throat and crosses his legs. 'Lily,' he begins, 'I may have—'

'What?' she demands. 'You may have what?'

He shrugs, helpless. 'I may have used those words but—'

'You did!' she insists. 'You did use them!'

He holds his hands up, fingers spread, as if calming an excited horse. 'All right, all right,' he says, thinking. 'But I must have used them euphemistically. No one uses that phrase for what it really means any more. I meant it as . . . a figure of speech. A joke. I never thought—'

'A joke?' she yells. 'A joke? You think this is funny?'

'No,' he says. 'Not at all. But . . .' he sighs '. . . you . . . we obviously misunderstood each other. I certainly never meant to—'

'Well, what did happen, then?' she demands.

He seems to shrink a few inches. He looks away from her. His hands move from his keyboard up to his eyes then his forehead. He supports his bowed head, his back bent over like an arthritic man. 'She . . .' Lily waits. He looks out of the window, grips his fingers in his hair, inhales. 'She . . . she left.'

Lily steps forward into the room. 'Why?'

'I don't know.' He has to force the words out, as if they choke him. 'She . . . just left. She left me.' He says it as if he's trying to make himself believe it. 'God, Lily, I don't know.'

'But she must have said why. You must know.'

'I don't, I swear it.' He tugs at his shirtsleeve. 'She just . . . walked out. One morning. Wouldn't talk about it, and . . .'

'What?'

He shrugs. 'I really don't know.'

'But . . . was there someone else? Did she leave you for—'

'Lily, please!' he says sharply. They are silent for a moment, Lily staring at him closely, as if the reason might be inked there on his skin. Eventually, he looks at her again, rubbing his jawline, taking a deep breath like a man about to go under water. 'Things can change,' he begins, his hand circling in the air. 'People move on. And sometimes it's hard to nail down the reason for it. Sometimes there really isn't one. I never got a clear idea of why she . . . why she wanted to go. And I probably never will.' He stands and comes towards her. 'That's all I can tell you, I'm afraid.' He reaches her and he touches the ends of her hair. His face looks sad and distant for a moment, then he smiles. 'Now, is there anything else we need to clear up?'

Lily is silent for a moment, looking up at him. Then she says, 'No. No, I don't think so.'

But later, on the bed, with his head weighing down her shoulder, she thinks about Sinead's hands as they covered her head, and how the bones and veins and tendons made an intricate latticework beneath the white, pellucid skin.

At lunchtime, Lily wanders beyond the hinterland of the office. She's alive, she's alive and in this city. It makes Lily look differently at the streets she walks through: she could meet her at any moment, catch a glimpse of her, could be walking on paving stones that Sinead walked on last week or yesterday, today, this morning. London feels different all of a sudden – pulsating with a kind of stirring possibility. Street corners she passes every day look unfamiliar. Every dark-haired woman makes Lily's heart vault in her chest, half in dread, half in hope.

Back in the Covent Garden bookshop, Lily stands at the bookshelf, plants her feet where she estimates Sinead's shoes might have have been less than twenty-four hours ago, reaches for the book Sinead had been looking at. Lily opens it, her eyes sliding over the words, and looks up. Repeats the action. Opens the book, looks up at the gap through to the other side of the shelves. Then looks to her right. That's what she saw. This view is what Sinead saw yesterday – the corridor through to the children's section, the posters dangling in the air-conditioned draughts, people milling through the tables, the glossy display stand for thrillers.

This is all exactly what she saw when I said her name —
except with my face in the middle.

Lily comes out of her room, magazine in hand, heading for
the TV. But there is a distinct and recognisable change in
the atmosphere — a kind of chilled stasis. She stops dead
in her tracks, her teeth rattling against each other, scanning
the flat. She can't believe it, she really can't.

Something flits and twitches in the unlit recess beside
the front door. Lily treads slowly over the boards, rolling
the magazine into a truncheon. She can glimpse a restless,
ceaseless motion. Something is moving in the dark.

She feels for the light switch and snaps it on. Sinead is
pacing from the door to the bathroom's glass wall and back
again. When she reaches the wall she does a half-circle,
then walks back with stiff, urgent steps to the door. At the
door she puts out her hand as if to open it, but hesitates,
withdraws it, then turns away and walks to the bathroom.
Round and round she goes, as if on tracks. It makes Lily
think of a cheetah she saw once in a zoo, circling back and
back on itself as it trod the same section of cage, over and
over again.

Lily slams the magazine against the wall. 'You're not
real!' she screams. 'You're not!'

Sinead seems to glance her way, falter in her rhythmic
steps. She pauses for a moment, poised. Then she turns and
walks towards her.

Lily is crying now, sobs racking up from her chest. She
stares at the apparition coming towards her, and batters
her face and head with her fists. 'You're losing it,' she

whispers to herself, 'you're really losing it.' Sinead is close enough now for Lily to reach out and touch her. Lily starts backwards, hitting her head against the wall. 'Oh, God,' she sobs, trapped, 'please leave me alone, please. You're not real. I know you're not. You're not even dead,' she yells, 'so just go away! Please! GO AWAY!'

When she peels her fingers away from her eyes, Sinead is still there. Lily stares at the face of the woman in front of her. She is talking, fast and insistent. But no sound comes out. Lily watches, transfixed. Sinead's lips move soundlessly, and she scans Lily's face, as if anxious for her to understand.

'I can't hear you!' Lily sobs. 'What are you saying?'

Sinead pauses, glances around them and leans closer, as if she doesn't want to be overheard. Her mouth is moving even faster, a secret flood of words pouring out. Lily bangs her ears in frustration. There is one word she forms over and over again. Lily watches her lips carefully: don't, she is saying, don't.

'Don't what?' Lily cries. 'Don't what? I don't under-stand! I can't hear you!'

Then she can stand it no more. With a strange, low cry, she steps sideways and darts past Sinead. Her whole body is shaking and her legs barely hold her. She seizes a chair and slides into it, crying and coughing.

When she looks round, Sinead is gone. The room feels as it should. Lily sits at the table. She wipes the tear tracks from her face, listens to her breathing slowing down. She knows what she has to do.

She can't believe how easy it was. She stands at the crossroads holding the piece of paper, still amazed. All she'd had to do was look in the phone book: and there it was, in black cramped letters on thin, grey paper. She doesn't know why it shouldn't have been there, but somehow, when she'd been running her fingers down through the columns of all the other places beginning with 'uni', she'd thought there'd be a blank or it would be missed out or it wouldn't exist. All she'd had to do was dial the number and an efficient-sounding woman answered and told her the address straight off, and the number she should ring for a 'lecture schedule'. It had been the easiest thing in the world. Two phone calls, a lie to the agents about feeling ill, and here she was.

Tall, neatly terraced houses surround her, most with a brass plate by the side of the door. To her left is a large bookshop. People mill around the pavements, talking, folders and books clutched in their arms.

Lily checks her watch and checks the piece of paper. Then reads the street sign again. This is the right place.

She takes a seat at the back, near the door, sliding into

the polished wooden bench. The room is huge, with long tiered benches full of people and, at the bottom, a lectern and a blackboard. Everyone is talking, banging open folders, fiddling with tape-recorders or waving at someone in a different row. The girl next to her is saying to her friend: 'And he got this squid and chopped it up. Just like that. Lengthways and, you know –' she gestures, bringing down her hand in a sheer cutting movement '– sideways. It got *everywhere.*'

Lily experiences a sudden surge of nerves. What is she doing here? All she wants to do is find her and talk to her, but why is she sitting here? She must be mad, thinking she can just walk in here. She should be back at work. She should leave.

The door next to her opens, and there she is, striding past Lily and down the central steps. She is wearing a grey skirt, split to the thigh, long black boots that zip close to her ankles and a soft, diaphanous sweater with horizonal ribbing. Her hair is up, coiled on her head and speared with what looks like a silver knife. At the front, she lays out her papers then looks up and surveys them all. Lily ducks down.

'Right.' Sinead announces, and silence falls over the room. '*Gawain and the Green Knight.* If you have the parallel text with you, you might want to open it at page seventy-three.' A scuffling motion passes over the room like a Mexican wave. 'Or, for the braver among you, you can follow from page fifty-eight in the original.'

Lily has nothing – no book, no paper, no pen. What was she thinking of? She must stand out a mile. She looks around, fear crawling up her neck, and inadvertently catches the eye of the girl next to her. She is pretty, with very straight brown hair parted down the middle. She gives Lily a half-smile and pushes her opened book towards her so that it rests on the bench between them.

'Thanks,' Lily whispers, and the girl smiles and glances back towards Sinead. Lily looks down at the book and sees a sea of incomprehensible words, some that look like English and some with letters that don't appear in any alphabet she knows. On the page opposite are stacked lines of text – in recognisable English. '*And I shall stand and take a blow from him, unflinching, provided I have the right to deal him another when I claim it,*' she reads.

'There is no clear evidence as to the identity of the person who is known only as the Gawain Poet,' Sinead is saying. 'A number of people believe the Pearl Poet is also the Gawain Poet. Now, I'm not going to speculate here about the whos, whys and wherefores because, to be honest, I don't really care. It got written. By someone. That's all. But what I do believe is that the so-called Gawain Poet was a woman. Which might explain why she wanted to remain anonymous, her kind not being taken very seriously in those days. Now,' she says again and, lifting the book, reads: '*I declare he was the biggest of men, and the handsomest . . . for although his torso, back and chest were thick-set, his stomach and waist were attractively slender.*' A stutter of laughter circles the room. 'What self-respecting bloke is going to write that?'

Lily crosses and recrosses her ankles underneath the bench, pushing each hand up the opposite sleeve. Around and in front of her, rows and rows of heads are bent over notes, arms jerk with quick note-taking; one or two people are whispering something in their neighbour's ear. Lily is amazed by the rapt concentration in the room, how everyone is listening to the words that flow from Sinead's mouth, how this one woman is the vortex of everyone's attention, the reason they're all here. People are concentrating and transcribing her every word in a notebook, or trapping the rises, falls and modulations of her voice on a tape-recorder. This is not how she remembers university.

'What we have to realise,' Sinead reaches up to pull down one half of the blackboard, and the sweater lifts to reveal the bottom rung of her ribcage, 'is that Gawain is caught in the workings of a social machine that is beyond his ken. And doesn't even know it. What he ignores, or doesn't have the nous to take notice of is in fact the clue, the key to the whole plot in which he is ensnared. What appears to be the periphery is in fact the centre.'

Lily leans, her hands flat on the glass, against the big bookshop window. Daylight is sinking into violet. The sky is lighter than the buildings. The clocks will be going back soon: in a few days' time, this hour of the day will be gloomy, orange-lit and cold. She sinks down and rests on her heels, making sure she is still tucked into a doorway, just in case. A group of men with briefcases, tight shoes and well-cut hair pass her. The hem of one of their raincoats brushes against her knee. 'Hello, darling,' one says and they laugh, but Lily doesn't react. Her eyes are fixed on the building opposite.

There is something about this woman that strains and tugs at some vital part of her, as if her heart, connected to Marcus's, is connected to Sinead. And at her very core is an unease of things not quite fitting into each other. Questions, small and insistent, whisper to her from corners of her mind. How does Sinead know about her? Can it be possible that Marcus really doesn't know why she left? What is she – or the thing that looks like her – trying to tell her? What can be so bad to make a live woman haunt another?

She's going to stop her, that's what she's going to do. She's going to just stop her in the street and ask her straight out. No messing about. Why did you leave? That's all. Simple. Tell me why you left. And Sinead will tell her. And then she'll know.

Students she recognises from the lecture leave, bunching outside the door to pore over maps or to chat or to look up at the sky. Two men in caretaker uniforms wander out and down the street, a few lone academic-types. But not the person Lily is looking for. Lights are switched off in an upper floor. An elderly man stands by the now-locked doors, gazing at passers-by – a woman with a double-seated pushchair, a couple in matching fleeces, a man trailing an empty dog-lead. Then, just as Lily's legs are becoming numb with cold and inactivity, Sinead appears.

Lily leaps upright. Something in the hinge of her knee catches and twangs, but she ignores it and moves swiftly over the pavement, never taking her eyes off the figure on the other side of the road. Sinead is carrying a bright red and purple woven plastic bag in the crook of her elbow. She walks fast, and Lily's knee sends arrows of pain up her thigh. Sinead crosses Gower Street at the lights, but Lily misses them and has to wait in agony, watching Sinead's back recede into the distance. As soon as the lights glow amber she is running over the tarmac and along the road in a kind of stumbling jog, her breath steaming out in front of her, careful not to get too close. By the time they reach Tottenham Court Road, Lily is ten yards behind her.

To her horror, Sinead suddenly breaks into a run, dodging cars, across the road. Has she seen her? Lily staggers after her, blood surging through her head. Sinead swings herself up into the back of a bus. Lily pushes herself into a sprint. Sinead is climbing the stairs to the top floor. Lily hears the ding of the bell and she stretches out her arm, making a lunge for the rail. Grasps it, thumb meeting fingers. Feels the bus powering away from her. Her feet scrabble for the platform. Her left foot makes contact and she hauls herself up.

'Good exercise, eh?' the conductor says, and winks.

She manages a smile, then, steadying herself like a sailor against the swell and roll of the bus, cautiously climbs the winding stairs.

It's quite busy, people sat singly on most of the seats. Sinead is next to a man in a baseball hat on the front seat, the one Lily doesn't like sitting in, the road eddying and rushing underneath her, and that teeth-smashing bar across the window against which she could be thrown at any moment.

She sits near the back, in an empty double seat. Leaning towards the window, she can spy Sinead's profile through all the other heads. She is reading something, her bag propped on her knee. Lily is suddenly aware of the loud labouring of her breathing. A few rows ahead, a teenager chirps into a mobile phone and a red-haired man opposite is muttering to his girlfriend, who is staring fixedly out of the window. Otherwise, silence.

Lily swipes a sleeve through the condensation and a fan-shaped segment of the street appears – computer shops, a big stationer's, a window full of futons. Her breathing is returning to normal when the bus judders to a halt. Feet thud on the boards. People clomp down the stairs. The baseball-cap man stands. Sinead moves her knees aside to let him pass. Lily folds her body in half, her face almost buried in her lap, her finger plucking at the heel of her shoe.

The bus jolts forward and swings left into Euston Road. Lily peers up over the top of the seat. Sinead has moved next to the window and is looking out. There are four other people. The bus has picked up speed and is rushing along Marylebone Road. For the first time, Lily wonders where they are going.

She could speak to her now. It would be so easy. Too easy. All she'd have to do is stand, walk a few paces and slide into the seat behind her and say – say what? Remember me? Hi, how are you doing? Great lecture, by the way.

Lily turns her head away and gazes out of the window. Huge corporate buildings skim past. Thin darts of horizontal rain fleck the glass. Her own reflection – large-eyed, wild-haired, staring straight at her – makes her start.

At Bayswater, Sinead shunts herself along the seat and stands. Lily bends, fiddles with her shoe, her tights, her buttons until she hears her descend the stairs. Then she gets up.

They stand on the landing board together. Sinead leans right out, one hand holding the pole, hair and drizzle whipping across her face. Lily could push her. She could peel those fingers away from the pole and release her into the blasting flow of traffic. The thought, which appeared unbidden in her head, shocks Lily so much that she almost forgets to jump off after her.

Sinead strides up a side-street, tugging her coat around her, shifting her bag on to the other arm. Then she turns into a doorway. Lily hesitates outside. There are double glass and dark wood swing doors, with a kind of wooden kiosk beyond, where Sinead is paying and being handed something large and white. Above the doors, in twisted, unilluminated neon, are the words 'The Spa'.

Lily pushes at one side of the door and steps in. She hands over the money to a large, florid-cheeked woman, who slides two towels across the counter towards her. Holding them to her, she goes through the second doors.

Everything is very still and very cool. She is in a huge, high-vaulted room. People lie on rows of reclining chairs, draped in towels. No one speaks. The walls are gilt and stained-wood panelled, with lamps throwing circles of dusky yellow upwards. Reflections of water oscillate on the ceiling. The centre of the room is missing and people stand at the crater's edge, looking down into the floor below. As she walks through the room, people turn their eyes to her then look away.

Sinead is standing in a corner, stepping out of her skirt. Her hair is loose to her shoulders and her spine stands out from her back like beads on a thread. She folds her clothes into a narrow metal locker, wraps herself in a towel and descends the stairs. On the other side of the room, Lily does the same, the building opening out to her as she drops below street level.

There are women everywhere, naked. Milling from hot-room to showers to loungers to a steel drinking fountain to a small kidney-shaped blue pool, they step on crinkled, bare soles over the damp tiles, hair twisted to necks. Everyone is graceful and slow. Sinead slides between the vertical, heavy plastic slats of a doorway and is swallowed by steam. Lily follows.

The air is whited-out and heavy with the medicinal tang of eucalyptus. The hot, wet smell stings the edges of her lips. Through the mist she can make out figures, lying or sitting, and wooden benches running around the walls. Lily moves through the steam and lowers herself down. She peers around. Sinead, barely visible and recognisable only by the mass of her hair, is sitting at right-angles to her, her feet on the floor, hands on knees, her head tilted back on the china tiles. Lily is mermaid-wet, the towel soaked. Hot drips fall on to her face and hair from the ceiling. Every muscle seems to flex and droop, her limbs socketless, her head weighted on her neck. The pain in her knee fades. The steam machine hisses and sighs somewhere near the floor. Two people in the corner murmur to one another; the woman next to Lily rubs her hand over her skin in long, methodical strokes. Sinead hitches one heel on to the bench and leans her arms on her knee, her hair falling over her face.

Suddenly the heat is too much – sealed in around Lily's nose and mouth. Every breath seems to take in only more heat, and when she moves her eyes they scald her lids. She stands and pads over the floor, through the plastic slats, and gulps at the cold, still air in the shower room.

She walks around: echoing, empty hot-rooms linked to a further, hotter twin; another steam room; showers with three jets; the small, seething box of a sauna; a belching, spitting jacuzzi; an icy plunge pool with a glassy surface. She finds it strange that just above this warren of heat and cleanliness is a road where cars and lorries and taxis power to and from Westway, the city's arched concrete spine. When she returns to the first steam room, she almost walks straight into Sinead.

She is coming out between the slats, her cheeks pinked by blood, her body gleaming with sweat and moisture. She walks up some steps and around a corner. Lily raises her eyes over the small, surrounding wall just in time to see her lower herself into the freezing plunge pool. Feet first, her body disappears into the turquoise water like a woman swallowed by quicksand – calves, legs, buttocks, waist, back, torso, neck, head. For a moment, all that remains on the surface are the ends of her hair; then they, too, are pulled down. Lily waits. And waits. Counts to five, anxiety brimming. Counts past seven, then eight, then nine.

Sinead explodes up through the surface, an emphatic column of flesh, gasping and shivering. She reaches for a towel and rubs roughly at her stippled skin. Lily looks at her, a delicate white all over; she looks at the small, tilted breasts, the dark arrowhead of hair, the thin, muscular arms, the twelve, evenly spaced ribs. She pictures Marcus's hands and how they might fit in the dip of the waist, or curve over the buttocks, or how his fingers might slot between each of the ribs. There is a scar pleating the flesh of her upper arm. Lily imagines it would feel like braille under your lips.

Upstairs, she watches in a mirror as, across the room, Sinead, dry and in a robe now, settles herself back on a lounger, picks up a book, opens it, places the bookmark inside the back cover. And she watches as she tries to read it, tries to go over the same paragraph, again and again. She watches as something keeps tugging at her attention and as she lets the book fall closed. When the tears come, they don't surprise her. They don't fall like Lily always thought tears did – out of the corners of the eyes and one by one. Sinead's all seem to come at once and from every pore, flowing down her cheeks and nose and chin as if her whole body is crying, as if they will never stop.

It is dark. Her wrists are pinned to the bed. Something is travelling over her, something cold and inquisitive, sucking and sniffing at her so vigorously she feels as though she's being vacuumed.

'What do you smell of?' Marcus is demanding, pressing his nose to her arms, shoulders, the cleft between her breasts, her stomach.

'Nothing,' she says, trying to turn away from him.

He places his hands on her shoulders, buries his nose in her neck, inhaling. 'What is it?' His hands are strong and insistent on her limbs. She wriggles, turning this way and that, trying to get away from him, but he holds her fast.

'Marcus,' she says, cross now, 'get off. You're hurting me.'

Suddenly he stops, his hands disappear from her skin.

She opens her eyes, uncurls her neck. He is above her, staring at her, his brows drawn together. 'It's eucalyptus,' he whispers, his voice low and barely audible. 'Why do you smell of eucalyptus?'

Lily thinks of an avenue of eucalyptus trees she once drove through in Portugal, the wind turning their leaves silver. 'I don't know.' She turns her back to him, pretending to be asleep.

But for the rest of the night she lies on her side watching the dark soak into grey, while Marcus, next to her, thrashes around as if he can't find a way to get comfortable.

'What you have to recognise,' Sinead says, one hand raised to waist-height and turned upwards, 'is that they are two halves of the same personality.' She pauses and walks to the other end of the platform as if to allow time for the furious scribbling around her. 'She represents all that Jane has been forced to suppress.' Her eyes travel the room, veer close to Lily, pass over her, and – is it Lily's imagination? – return, linger, then move on. Sinead turns on her spike heel, walks the other way, and moves the tip of her tongue across her lips. 'And as for him . . .' she continues.

Sinead has stopped on a corner, looked up and down the street and checked her watch. Is she waiting for someone? Lily leans against the wall of the doorway she is concealed in. She's going to approach her tonight, definitely. No more messing around. She just has to wait for the right moment, that's all.

Sinead folds her arms, as if she's cold, takes out her phone and starts pressing at the buttons. At the sound of someone approaching, she looks up quickly but when she sees a woman in a red mac looks back down at the phone.

Soho seems empty tonight, the café doors closed against the cold and the windows steamed over. People don't loiter at this time of year, but hurry along the usually thronged pavements, coats hunched up around their ears. Lily feels her feet begin to numb and she tries to curl her toes inside her shoes. Sinead is also cold, Lily sees. She stamps her feet against the concrete, pulls her scarf more tightly around her face.

Suddenly her head snaps round and her whole body flexes expectantly. She smiles. 'What time do you call this, then?' she shouts. A man in a leather jacket, tall, big, with dark hair, is running towards her down the middle of the road.

'I'm so sorry, I'm so sorry,' he is saying over and over again. 'The tube stopped in a tunnel for about three years.'

Sinead steps off the pavement and they meet near the kerb, Sinead saying something Lily can't hear and the man bends over to kiss her cheek. Sinead brings her hand up to curl round his shoulder and he presses his hand to her back like a tango dancer. It's only when he pulls away that Lily recognises him. The shock is like the shock of infidelity. She has to put out her hand to steady herself against the wall.

Aidan. It's Aidan. Running towards her, late. Kissing her on the cheek. How come Aidan is meeting up with her? Does this happen a lot? And does Marcus know?

They are moving off now. He is pulling something from his pocket and showing it to her, and their heads are bent over it together as they walk. Lily hurries after them, watches them stroll along pavements, skirt puddles and parking meters, cross roads, exchange sentences, brush against each other, hand a magazine back and forth between them. Outrage floods through Lily, and she isn't quite sure why. They stop at a cinema and wait in line to buy a ticket, standing close together as they talk. There is nothing serious in their demeanour. Sinead is talking, animated, in a long spurt, Aidan listening intently. The noise in the foyer means she has to lean on his shoulder and speak into his ear. He bends down to hear her, his hair falling into his eyes, and then he throws back his head and laughs, clutching at the arm she'd laid on him.

They reach the counter, buy a ticket then disappear down the stairs. Lily is left standing on the street outside, still unable to believe it. Seeing them together seems incongruous, ridiculous. She wants to go up to them and demand an explanation.

After saying goodbye to Aidan at the cinema doors, Sinead walks quickly through the city. Lily keeps about fifteen paces behind her, the city moving beneath them. The high, narrow streets of Soho give way to shops and boutiques, and by the time they reach Leicester Square, Lily is wondering how long they'll be walking. But there's no stopping. They pass the crowds outside the Hippodrome, the people streaming out of the theatres, the National Portrait Gallery, and take a left towards Charing Cross Station. Sinead turns in her direction once before she crosses the road and once more when she stops at a shop window and glances up the street. Both times, a cold fear closes around Lily's heart and she looks down, hiding her face in her scarf.

Sinead walks on past the station and down the side road towards Embankment. Lily can smell the river now, over the chalkiness of a building site and the doughy odour of a streetside pizza place – that fetid, dank heaviness of air. They pass through the tube station, and on the other side, Sinead inexplicably speeds up, the rucksack bouncing off her back as she weaves through the crowds. She must be late for something. People tut and sigh as Lily shoves her way past them, desperate not to lose sight of the tall figure ahead.

Sinead starts up the metal steps to Hungerford Bridge. By the time Lily reaches them, a large group of people is coming down, five abreast. She darts from one side of the staircase to the other but, drunk and unhurried, they don't let her through.

'Excuse me, excuse me,' Lily says. The people mill and sidestep, chatting and calling to each other; Lily stumbles through them and, as she turns to go up the second flight, she looks up.

Sinead is standing on the bridge, looking down.

Lily doesn't move, poised like a cat. Sinead turns and disappears from view. Lily leaps up the stairs two at a time. Did she see her? Was she looking at her? Did she imagine it?

When she reaches the bridge, it is busy, people ambling, holding hands, roller-blading, pushing bikes and buggies. There's no sign of Sinead. She's lost her. Lily shoves her way through the crowds, searching for the woman now so familiar to her.

Then, without warning, she's there, bearing down on Lily, her eyes flashing fire. 'Why are you following me?' With every word, Sinead gives Lily a shove until she's pressed up against the barrier, the metal pushing into Lily's back.

'I—'

'What is your fucking problem?' Sinead towers over her. 'Leave. Me. Alone. Do you hear me? And tell . . .' she falters '. . . tell your boyfriend as well.'

'Marcus?' Lily says, the word coming out more loudly than she'd planned.

'Yeah. *Marcus*. Every time I turn around it's either you or him. Is stalking a thing for both of you?' Her bravura cracks. Lily sees her face collapse, tears spring down her cheeks. 'Leave me alone,' she whispers. 'I want nothing to do with either of you.'

There is a kind of ringing, like tinnitus, in Lily's head. 'Do you mean Marcus has been . . . in touch with you?'

'In touch?' Sinead repeats hysterically. '*In touch?*' She holds the barrier for support. 'Christ! He— he phones me twelve times a day. He follows me to work. He follows me from work. I'm surprised you haven't bumped into each other.'

There is a pause. Sinead presses her hands to her eyes. 'Look,' she says, more quietly, 'I don't know what you want from me, but . . . but I really have nothing to say to you.' She walks off.

'Wait!' Lily goes after her. 'I just want to know what happened. I thought you were—'

A train thunders past them, overhead wires crackling, lighted windows throwing bluish light on to Sinead's wet and furious face, its roar swallowing Lily's words.

'What?' Sinead yells.

'I thought you were DEAD.'

'Dead?'

'Yes!'

The train rattles past, receding into the night. Sinead is incredulous, disgusted. 'Is that what he told you?' Her hands are shaking, Lily sees, as they tug at imaginary folds in her jacket. Below them the Thames twists black in the dark.

'No . . . he . . . no.'

'Then why on earth would you think that?'

'I . . . I . . .' Lily stammers '. . . he . . . I don't know.'

'Well, I'm not,' she says. 'Sorry to inconvenience you,' and she moves away again.

'Sinead,' Lily catches up with her, 'please tell me what happened. Please. You have to.'

'No, I don't.'

'Please. I just . . . I need to know.'

Sinead stops and gives a short laugh. 'You *need* to know?' she repeats. 'Well, why don't you ask him?' She spits out the last word as if it tastes bad. 'Why haunt me?'

Lily blinks and a part of her almost laughs. 'I'm . . . he doesn't . . . he won't talk about it.'

'Well, that's really not my problem.' She is walking faster now, sidestepping people. Lily hurries after her, the butt of blows from people's shoulders and bags.

'I know,' she says, breathless, 'I know it's not. But, *please*. What happened? Just tell me what happened.'

Sinead stops, her teeth set against each other. Fury seems to have flared again within her. 'Look,' she almost shouts, 'I refuse to have this conversation. This is nothing to do with me. You are nothing to do with me. I don't want . . . I don't want to . . . to see you ever again. *I want you to leave me alone.* Just . . . just go away! OK?' Without waiting for an answer, she dives into the crowd.

Lily follows, blind now, and seizes a fistful of her jacket sleeve. 'Listen—'

'Get off!' Sinead splutters, appalled, trying to wrench her arm free. Lily sees a kind of panicked astonishment in her still-wet eyes, feels the hardening of sinew and muscle beneath her grip. 'Let go of me!'

'No!' Lily grips her arm with all her strength, aware that this is her last and only chance. 'I want you to tell me. Please!'

A sob tears from Sinead's mouth, her fist batters Lily's hand, then scrabbles, trying to peel away her fingers. 'Why are you doing this?' she whispers hoarsely. 'You're *mad.*'

Lily feels the fabric of Sinead's sleeve slipping from her grasp. Sinead gives one final, vicious wrench to her arm: she comes free and reels backwards, colliding heavily with the rail. There is a dull clunk as the side of her pelvis impacts with the metal. She gives a small, bewildered, 'Oh', bends away from the pain, her hair swinging over her face, then tries to straighten herself, one hand pressed over her back, and limps away.

Lily watches, shoulders slumped, tears aching in her throat. 'Sinead!' she calls after her.

She doesn't look round, doesn't falter.

'He told me you walked out on him!'

She takes two more strides. Then another. Then her left foot slows, hesitates, and comes to rest next to her right. Lily moves forward. When she reaches her, Sinead is turning slowly towards her. Lily waits. Her eyes lock with Lily's, flick from one to the other. She frowns slightly, appears to be thinking.

'He told me that one day . . . you just went,' Lily says quickly, the words tagged to each other. 'That he didn't know why.'

Sinead swallows. She looks down at the river for a moment, then back. 'He said that?'

'Yes. That you . . . just walked out.'

'I just walked out?'

'Uh-huh.'

'He said I just walked out?'

Lily nods.

Sinead touches her forehead with her first two fingers, stretching the skin next to her hairline. 'So . . . you have no idea why he and I . . . why I left?'

'No.'

'None at all?'

'He won't talk about you. Not to me anyway. He just told me you left him. That's all.'

Sinead stares again at the river. 'If I tell you,' she begins, and Lily's pulse quickens with something between excitement and triumph, 'will you promise never to come anywhere near me ever again?'

'Yes.'

'Or to any of my lectures?'

'Yes.'

'Do you promise?'

'I promise.'

'All right.' Sinead nods. Twice. 'I'll tell you.'

part | two

If I told you the whole story it would never end . . . What's happened to me has happened to a thousand women

FEDERICO GARCIA LORCA, *Doña Rosita*

The shower-head gasps as she turns it off and the silence of the empty flat rushes in on her. She grips handfuls of wet hair and squeezes rivulets of water down her body, shaking herself like a dog, misting the glass bricks with spray. Then she steps out of the steam and, winding a towel around her, leaves wet soleprints marking out her route, which are already evaporating by the time she reaches the bedroom.

Sinead towels herself roughly, tugging a comb through her hair, grimacing as the teeth snag on knots. Then she pulls open her desk drawer and rummages about for a pair of scissors.

The new dress hangs on the outside of the wardrobe. She bought it weeks ago when, numbed by the idea that she was not yet half-way through the allotted two months of their separation, she'd gone on a shopping spree. She'd returned to the flat with that heady feeling of glee and guilt that comes after a major spend to find Aidan and his friend Sam cooking huge amounts of food in the kitchen. They'd taken an amused interest in the contents of her various plastic bags, and made her hold up her purchases one by one as they sat at the table and ate their way through their labours. 'God, I'm so glad I'm not a girl,' Aidan had said after a while. 'It's so *complicated*.'

With the scissors, she clips off the price label and flings it into the bin behind her. Humming now, she pulls the dress over her head, drawing the zip up through the fabric. Then she wanders through the flat, turning the CD-player up to volume ten, filling the air with sound.

Her bloodstream is full of bubbles, tiny pockets of pure oxygen hammering round her system. Marcus is coming back.

My birthday fell almost exactly half-way between the Christmas and Easter vacations, when post-grad students like me had a break from the carousel of giving lectures and tutorials, and had a chance to catch up on the supposed real matter in hand – the thesis. February in that city was the worst time, the fog rolling for miles over the flat, ditched fields to collect in the hollow where the city cowers. Icy moisture hung in the air. It rained constantly, the streets wet and polished like sealskins, the sky getting dark at half past four. I lost my gloves and my bare hands would ossify round my bicycle handlebars in the freezing damp air as I cycled from my house to seminars, tutorials, the faculty. I had to insulate my books in layers of plastic bags to keep them dry on my rides to the library. When I arrived, I headed for an out-of-the-way wing, piled my books into a towering ziggurat beside me and risked chilblains by resting my wet feet on the tepid, vibrating pipes. As I flexed my back up from the desk, I could see my face thrown back at me in the window opposite, teeth biting the inside of my cheek, left index finger twirling my hair.

I was, at this time, bored with my life. I was teaching two days a week, giving three lecture courses, and I was, on and off and usually more off than on, seeing an art historian called Antony who lugged great A3 illustrated books around everywhere he went, and refused to cycle because he couldn't buy a bicycle basket big enough to fit them in. It was the second year of my Ph.D. I'd given up the freedom, and the mind-crushing tedium, of an underpaid job to come to this insular city to study. At that very moment I couldn't think beyond or around the five-thousand-word chapter I had to write by the beginning of March. Thesis hand-in, in two and a half to three years' time, seemed like a distant, mystical grail. This annoyed me. I wanted to be able to project myself beyond these lodestones, which sucked all my thoughts towards them and repelled any others from my head.

I wasn't sure about this city, about this university, about this library, about the people who taught me or the ones I taught, about being here among stacks and stacks of spine-indexed, recorded, catalogued books that smelt of mice and rotting leaves. Could I see myself here for another two years, maybe more? Was this what I wanted when I'd vaulted that blind hurdle of my thesis?

I didn't know. All I knew was that when I read the late-medieval texts I was studying for my Ph.D., my mind latched on to something: it caught and sent a fly-wheel spinning somewhere, which then cranked another movement, slow at first, then bigger and bigger until it filled all space with noise and momentum until there was no space left at all, until when I looked up again at the window it was pitchy black outside and my face, puzzled and unfamiliar, was suspended out there in the dusky branches of the trees surrounding the library.

Three weeks before my birthday, I was sitting with my hands curled round an empty blue china teacup in the library café with my two housemates, Kate and Ingrid. Ingrid was slumped over, her forehead resting on the table's chipped surface.

'Get me out of this place,' she groaned.

Kate and I didn't respond, both staring into space, Kate jiggling her foot up and down on the spar underneath the table.

'Hello?' Ingrid said, raising her head. 'Are either of you two listening to me?'

Kate's attention zoned in on her. 'Huh? What did you say?'

Ingrid scrumpled up her chocolate wrapper viciously, and flicked it towards the bin. She missed, but didn't go and pick it up. 'Nothing. Sorry to interrupt your reverie. I was only attempting some, you know, conversation.'

'Do you know what I think?' I said suddenly.

Kate sat up, stopped jiggling; the cups, knives and tea-spoons were still once more. She looked at me, expectant.

'I think we should have a party.'

Kate and Ingrid were silent. They turned to look at each other, then back at me.

'Now that,' Ingrid said, 'is a fantastic idea. When?'

'My birthday.'

'Oh, yes,' Kate breathed, in her oddly feverish way, 'a party. Oh, yes.'

'God, that's such a good idea. Let's get everyone down from London. We need a really good—' Ingrid broke off, staring at something over my head. 'Hey,' she said, 'don't look now, but lover boy's just come in.'

I ducked down and rested my chin on my hands, folded on the table. 'Has he?'

'Yup. It's all off again, I take it?'

'Um. Kind of.'

'Well, I'm not surprised if he's taken to wearing those in public.' Ingrid pointed and, despite myself, I turned round. Antony the art historian was standing with his back to us and was wearing a pair of dungarees.

'Oh, my God.' I swung round again.

'He probably bought them in a spate of lovelorn grief over you. Think about it. You're sleeping with a man whose choice of garment is dungarees. What does this say about you? Oooh, he's coming over.'

'I quite like them,' Kate said.

'You would,' muttered Ingrid, then trilled, 'Hi!'

Antony dropped his books down on the table with a thud. 'Hello. Kate. Ingrid,' he nodded at us in turn. 'Sinead.'

'Hi.' I turned up my face to look at him. 'Are you going to sit down?'

He hesitated.

'Don't worry,' Ingrid said, 'we're off. Come on, Kate.' Ingrid seized a fistful of Kate's jumper and dragged her up off the seat. 'See you later, Sinead.' They disappeared, Kate protesting mildly at Ingrid's manhandling.

'So,' Antony said, 'how are you doing?'

'Not too bad.'

'How's medieval romance?'

'All right.'

'Have you got any further with it after that critical essay you were telling me about?'

I shifted impatiently in my seat. I had a policy of not talking about work during my tea breaks.

'We're having a party,' I said, hoping to distract him.

'Really? When?'

'My birthday. '

'I didn't know it was your birthday.'

'Well, it is.'

He emptied a small packet of sugar into his murky cup, releasing a fine spray of tiny crystals all over the table. 'You didn't tell me,' he said, looking down as he stirred his tea.

'I'm telling you now.'

'I see.'

For something to do, I flipped open one of the covers of his art books and pretended to be reading the frontispiece.

'Do you want to come?' I said, and realised the book was upside-down. I turned it round.

'To what?'

I glared at him. 'The party.'

He glared back. 'Do you want me to come?'

'Do you want to come?' I batted the question back at him like a forcefully aimed ping-pong ball.

'I want to come if you want me to come,' he said quickly, a smile beginning to curl his mouth. He was good at this, I remembered. I sighed and shut the book. This could go on all afternoon. I had work to do.

'All right.' I gave in. For now. 'I'd like you to come.'

'Great.' He smiled and, under the table, I felt his knee brushing mine. 'I'll come then.'

Sinead crams a carton of juice into the fridge door and a vodka bottle into the freezer, the ends of her hair brushing the layer of white, steaming ice. Then she slumps down on a chair at the table. She wonders where Aidan is and if he'll be in tonight. She thinks, idly, that she's hardly seen him since he came back from New York. He must be busy with his new job.

She lays out on the table a sheaf of student essays, some pens, and a volume of poems she needs to read for a seminar she's giving next week. She looks at her watch. Only seven fifteen. His flight doesn't even land until seven thirty.

She fiddles with the chair, getting a cushion from the sofa and settling it behind her back, shifting the chair towards the table and then back again by increments. She leans her elbows on the tabletop. Is she supposed to bend slightly or have a straight back? She can't remember and spends several minutes trying to conjure up those X-ray pictures that show bad positions for the spine. She picks up a pen and tests it several times on the back of an envelope by writing her name over and over again in a variety of different handwriting styles.

Then she gets cross with herself and slams down an essay in front of her, pen poised. '*Aphra Behn wrote in a time when women didn't write, about things that women didn't write about,*' she reads. Sinead frowns, shuffles the essay to the back of the pile, and looks at the next. *'What one must always be asking oneself is whether one's sexuality can be read and understood by one's'* – Her eyes slide away from the page and, putting down her pen, she examines her bare feet, her beetle-green toenails. Looks at her watch again. Rolls a mango from the fruit bowl beneath her hand. Jumps up again. Changes the CD.

I was standing in the hallway. This was the only reason. In the years in which I will look back at this moment and trace back why it happened and how it happened like it did, I will think: I answered the door, not because it was my party, but because I was standing in the hall. I won't be able to remember why I was standing in the hall. I just was. There are always points of collision – moments at which it is possible to say, yes, if I had done that differently or I had been standing slightly to the right or I had left the house two minutes earlier or if I hadn't crossed the road just then my life would have taken a completely different course.

So I was – for whatever forgotten reason, or maybe for no reason at all – moving through the hallway of the house I shared with Kate and Ingrid during the party celebrating my twenty-fifth birthday when the doorbell rang. And I moved towards it, ignorant of the effect it would have on my life.

I unlatched the lock and swung back the door. What I saw: two blokes, shivering in the fog-laden air, blinking in the light cast by my hall lamp. One was taller than the other, hanging back. Dark eyes with dark hair hanging over them. The other had short but soft-looking yellow hair, blue eyes, a duffel coat, and cans of lager under his arm.

'Yes?' I said. I had one hand on my hip and the other on the door jamb as if at any minute I might slam it shut.

The men shifted uneasily. The short-haired one transferred the cans to the other hand, then back again.

'Hi. We're friends of . . . of Sinead.'

I looked them over again, just for effect. 'Are you now?'

'Yes.' He nodded, gaining confidence. Even grinned.

'Well, I'm Sinead,' I said, 'and I've never met either of you before in my life.'

Their faces wilted. But I smiled. 'It's all right, you can come in.' I stepped back into the hall to let them in, they passed me, the cold from their bodies brushing my skin. 'Who are you anyway?' I called after them over the music.

'This is Aidan,' the short-haired one said, pointing at his friend, 'and I'm Marcus.'

She decides to do the washing-up, her hands disappearing beneath hot frothy suds, the glasses and plates knocking against each other under the surface. Water and stray bubbles slide from drying crockery down the draining-board and back into the sink.

Lying on her back on the floor, she calls Ingrid, leaves a message on her answerphone, and then calls her brother. 'Michael Wilson,' she says, 'it's me.'

'Hi,' he says, sounding surprised, as he always does. 'Wait a sec. I'll turn the music down.'

She hears the receiver drop to the table and his feet

slapping over the room and the music dim, as if it's been sucked into the distance.

'So,' his voice is back, close to her ear, 'how are you?'

'OK. I was trying to work but I appear to have the concentration of a goldfish, so I thought I'd call you instead.'

'Oh. Thanks. So I shouldn't be alarmed if you suddenly forget who I am and what you're doing on the phone to me?' There is a sudden cracking, crunching noise, followed by the sound of loud chewing. 'Anyway,' Michael says with his mouth full, 'I thought—'

'Are you eating?' Sinead shouts. 'How many times have I told you not to do that when you're on the phone?'

He laughs, chewing again. 'I know, I know. I only ever do it with you.'

'Is that supposed to comfort me? Or flatter me? It's foul. I feel like . . . I feel like you're filling my ear with saliva.'

'OK,' he swallows, 'sorry.'

She balances the soles of her feet against the wall, and they speak of their grandmother's operation, of when Michael will go home next, of a film Sinead saw last week, of meeting up for coffee on Saturday. And Michael tells Sinead how his girlfriend had a scan today and how the baby was lying in an invisible hammock, its thumb between its jawbuds, and how they could see the small, electronic flicker of its heartbeat.

There were walls of pounding music surrounding everyone and everything. I wanted to slice through the sound with a knife, pull its edges apart and step through into the silent beyond. The kitchen was crammed with bodies and flesh.

Kate had wrapped the lampshade in blue tissue paper, and people were swimming through the slow, aquarium room, holding drinks aloft, mouthing words, the music blanking out any sense of what they were.

On my razor-blade shoes, I slid round the walls, the skin of my bare back to the grain of the wallpaper. I'd put my glass down somewhere but had no idea where — I recalled the feeling of its hard curves leaving my palm, but couldn't dredge up where that happened or why or who I was with. I could also remember the sensation of the crackling, membrane-thin paper of a joint between my fingers. But that had gone too now.

Suddenly Antony was next to me, smoke wisping from his mouth and nostrils into the blue light surrounding his head. Then his lips were making a moist crescent shape on my neck, his fingers dragging through my hair. I slithered out from underneath him and through the doors into the garden.

It was cold. Mist hung just above my head. The back lawn, enclosed on all sides by an uneven brick wall, was full of people holding sparklers. The fizzing, crackling fires scorched trails of light on to my retinas, and I blinked, still seeing the streams behind my eyelids.

Holding up my dress, I climbed on to the wall and, holding out my arms, I stepped, one foot at a time, along the length of the wall, my heels digging into the loose plaster. The air felt clearer up here, I seemed to be above the mist and closer to the stars. Below me, people shrieked and laughed and the sparklers jittered through the dark like fireflies. I peeled my feet off the wall one by one and placed them in front of me; and I progressed gradually the length of our ramshackle and weed-choked garden. I'm twenty-five, I thought, twenty-five, I have existed in this world for a quarter of a century. When I reached the intersection with the back wall I heard a voice below me: 'Jump.'

I snapped my head around, and lost my balance: suddenly stars and tree branches and sparklers were swerving before me, and I didn't know which way I was facing or if I was falling. My arms whirled in the air around me. The scene stilled. Balance returned. I was amazed to find myself still on the wall. Below me was the man who had gatecrashed the party. The one with the blue eyes. Arms outstretched. Duffel coat open to reveal a slippery red lining.

'Jump,' he said again.

'No.'

'Go on.'

'Why?'

'Because I said so,' he said.

'That's not a good enough reason.'

'Because I want you to.'

'Neither's that,' I said.

'What?'

'A good enough reason.'

'Why do you need one?' he asked.

I was silent, flummoxed.

'Go on,' he urged again. 'Jump.'

He narrowed his arms to about the width of my waist, and then I was passing through the air, under the stars but above the sparklers and I felt the impact of his hands on my ribcage and my arms were about his neck and before I was even aware of it happening he was swinging me round and round.

I would remember this when, sometime in the dead hours of the next morning, I woke with Antony's arm heavy across me and the light grey behind the curtain. Antony's frame was holding the covers away from me, and there was a channel of freezing air between us. I got up, put on layers of clothes from my drawer, padded to the bathroom through the party debris and drank from the tap, holding the ends of my hair out of the flow. Looking into the mirror at my smudged face, I recalled not an image but a sensation of the gatecrasher's body imprinted on my front, and his fingers pressed into the spaces between each of my vertebrae.

When she puts the phone down from Michael, the roots of her hair are still damp so she opens the window in the bedroom, and leans with her elbows on the wide, stone sill, looking down into the street. Through the open door of the pub down the road, she sees the barman laying out mats on the tables and lifting down upturned chairs.

A group of people who live a few doors down pass below her. One of them jumps from paving slab to paving slab, avoiding the cracks, singing a song Sinead recognises. The rest laugh. She looks up, up over the roofs of the buildings opposite, over the dome of the Hawksmoor church two streets away and up into the sky where planes are circling over the city, pulling lines of vapour though the ether.

I walked down the aisle of a supermarket, pushing a trolley with wayward wheels. Antony trailed me, three or four paces behind.

'The thing is, Dr Jarvis just isn't a Vermeer expert at all,' he was saying, 'and that's the kind of person I need. I don't need some bloody cowboy like Jarvis. Do you know what he said to me the other day? Tony, he said, because remember I told you he always calls me Tony . . .'

I came to an abrupt stop in front of the pulses. Antony nearly fell into me, then wandered towards the cereals, still talking. To quell an urge to ram the trolley into his ankles, I snatched up a packet of red lentils and pretended to be reading the instructions.

'I wouldn't bother with those if I were you.'

I turned. My instant reaction was the thought that there was the most beautiful line between his lips; undulating, curved up at the ends. When he smiled, the pointed tips of his incisors showed – something I have always found peversely sexy.

'Why not?'

Marcus shrugged. 'Too much effort for too little taste.'

His face altered after he said that. His eyes slipped from mine. He seemed nervous and cleared his throat, as if about to say something yet afraid to.

'It's nice to see you again,' I said.

'Yes. I was thinking—'

But a proprietorial hand on the small of my back interrupted us.

'Hello, Marcus.'

I was appalled to find Antony next to me, leaning on the handle of my trolley, letting fall a box of cereal into its chrome meshing.

'Oh.' Marcus made no effort to hide his surprise. The beam of his vision swung from me to him to me again to our joined bodies, comprehension percolating through his face. 'Hi, Antony. How are you doing?'

'Not bad. Yourself?'

'Er.' He glanced at me again. 'All right.'

Antony didn't say anything further. I moved away from his hand, but it followed me across the new space between us. The three of us stared at each other, then Antony turned round and shoved at the trolley.

'Well, we must be off. See you.'

'Yeah, see you later. 'Bye Sinead.'

As we walked away, I asked, 'How do you know him?'

'He's an architect. Part Three, I think, or maybe diploma year. They're in the same faculty building as us. He thinks he's pretty hot shit. Doesn't deign to mix much with us *hoi polloi*. He lives in some derelict factory in London somewhere and commutes in when he needs to.'

At the end of the aisle, I turned, hoping to see him still standing there. But he must have walked away fast, because it was empty, the metres and metres of shiny grey lino stretching out underneath the strip-lighting.

I turned back to Antony, saw the way his hair grew away from the whorled flesh of his ear, saw his hands curled round the trolley handles, saw his lips moving over his teeth. Later that afternoon, in his high-windowed room, I told him our affair was over.

Sinead closes the window. Night air is settling over the city like a sheet of damp muslin. Further down the street, she sees a teenager lighting a sparkler, which spits sharp white darts into the gathering dark. He spins around, shrieking, a fiery dervish, his friend watching, a lit match in his fingers. The window sticks so she has to reopen and slam it closed three times.

She waters her plants, gives the floor a sweep, straightens the rug. She leans over the fridge and the cupboards, and takes out things she'll cook with later: a purple-black auber-gine, hollow-centred and taut-skinned, onions, a limp sheaf of basil, a china mortar with a chipped pestle, a chopping knife with a thin, lithe blade.

If you lived for any length of time in that city, you knew that if you bumped into someone once, you'd bump into them again. But Marcus disappeared. I didn't go out of my way to find him: I could have looked him up on the post-grad directory, could have asked for him at the architecture faculty, could have reached him over the internal e-mail. But I didn't. That wasn't the way I did things; my pride prevented me. But that didn't mean I didn't look for his shape in the library or on pavements as I passed on my bicycle, or for the gleam of his hair in bars when I sat at night round tables with my friends. By April I'd given up hope of seeing him again; by May I'd banished him from my thoughts.

I was cycling along the main street. It was car-free so I could weave about in the middle. It was, I'd decided that morning, the first day of summer: my side-split skirt rippled and tugged like a kite around my legs as I rode; the students were all in post-exam frenzies so I could spend the day back at work on my thesis. I was heading for the library, which would be cool and silent and empty.

I was about to turn off into a cobbled laneway when I felt a restrictive tightness round my thighs. Then it was as if I'd hit a brick wall: my bike wheels screeched to a sudden halt, I nearly fell over the handlebars, my front wheel veering to the right. I had to slam my foot on the ground to stop myself toppling over. For a moment I thought I'd hit a fissure in the cobbles, but then I bent over to look down at the bike.

'Shit.'

The panel of my skirt had tangled itself up in the back wheel, winding its length round and round the hub. Not only was the bike now immovable but I was tied to it.

'Shitshitshit,' I cursed, through gritted teeth, as I lifted as much of the bike as I could, dragging it towards the kerb. Holding the handlebars with one hand, I tugged ineffectually at my skirt, but the material just tightened, pulling at the spokes.

I straightened up, assessing my options. Bicycles crunched past me, chrome glinting in the sunlight. The pavements were full of shambling groups of tourists, dressed in leisurewear, clutching maps and cameras. I calculated in my head the distance to the nearest cycle shop and whether I could prevail on any passer-by.

'Excuse me,' I wailed, in the general direction of the people on the pavement. A small man with a neatly clipped moustache and a blue cloth hat hesitated. 'Excuse me?' I repeated, hopefully, trying not to lean over and seize his arm. '*Excusez-moi? Français? Non?*'

The man frowned.

'*Deutsch?*' I hazarded.

He nodded, unsmiling; relief swept through me, then I trawled my mind for German phrases I hadn't spoken since I was sixteen. 'Um . . . *meine bicyclette* . . .' No, that was French. '*mein Fahrrad ist . . . ist kaput.*'

The man and his tight-lipped wife lowered their eyes to my bicycle, then looked back at me.

'I . . . er . . . *ich brauche* . . .' I felt sweat beginning to moisten my back. 'I NEED HELP!' I shouted, suddenly losing patience. Wasn't it obvious what had happened? '*Hilfe!* PLEASE!'

The Germans flinched, stepped back, then began sidling away.

'Wait!' I yelled after them. 'Don't go! Please! *Bitte!*'

Then, first wandering into my peripheral vision and now standing smack bang in front of me, was Marcus. He was wearing shorts and a grey shirt, holding a folder under one arm, sunglasses hiding his eyes, a half-eaten apple in his hand. All the blood in my body seemed to heat and rise to the surface of my skin.

'Hello,' he said, in a conversational tone, 'how are you?'

My relief and pleasure transmuted into irritation. 'How am I?' I shouted heatedly. 'How am I? Well, I'm great. Never better. How are you?'

He nodded, flinging the apple into a bin. 'Pretty good.'

Stepping forward, he lifted a book from the basket on the front of my bike and flipped it over in his hand. '*Maidens and Sorceresses: the Representation of Women in Medieval Poetry,*' he read, and grimaced. 'Is that what you spend your time doing?'

I snatched it back and slammed it into the basket. 'Much as I would like to discuss my work with you, right now isn't a good time.'

Marcus stepped up close to me, pushing back his sunglasses to rest on his cropped hair. 'Why not?'

'*Why not?*' I shrieked. 'Look at my fucking bike! I'm trapped! I can't move! I may never walk again!'

He considered me from our very close proximity. He had smooth, even-toned, blemishless skin. I'd forgotten about the curve of his lips. I felt the heat rising again to my neck and face, but was too cross to acknowledge it.

'Which one are you?' he said.

'What?'

'Maiden or sorceress. Which one are you?'

I ran through my head the pros and cons of slapping him: it would make me feel an awful lot better but he might run away without assisting me. I decided, on balance, against it. 'I need your help,' I said instead.

'What's happened to that boyfriend of yours, then?'

'What are you talking about?' I snapped, taken aback by the direction the conversation had taken.

'I haven't seen you for ages,' he changed tack again, ignoring his earlier question and my lack of answer, 'where've you been?'

'Here. I've been here. Where've *you* been?'

'Here too.'

'Look.' Flustered and completely wrongfooted, I attempted to take command of the situation: 'Marcus, will you please help me, please?'

He stepped back, surveyed the bike, my tangled skirt, the jammed wheel, then shoved his folder into my basket. 'Wait here,' he said – unnecessarily, I felt, as I clearly wasn't going anywhere. 'I'll be back in a sec.'

I stood, tethered to my bike, watching him go. If there had been a heat-sensitive camera on me at that point, you could have seen a plume of fiery red flaring up from the top of my head.

When Marcus returned, he was deft, serious and efficient – and clutching a monkey wrench. I tried to take it from him. 'It's all right, I can do it.'

'Don't be stupid,' Marcus said. 'It's easier if I do it.'

We fought over it, tug-of-war style, like toddlers over a doll.

'I can't let you.'

'Why?'

I struggled to formulate an answer. 'Feminist guilt,' I said eventually.

'Bollocks to your feminist guilt. Just stand still and shut up.'

Marcus pulled it from my grip and, squatting down, wrestled it against the wheel.

'So,' I said, not looking at him, 'have you finished for the summer?'

'No. I've finished for good.'

'For good?'

'Yep. That's it. Eight years of architecture training in the bag. Thank the Lord.'

Marcus rolled the wheel away from the bike and, lowering the back end, started unravelling the twisted, oil-smeared cloth of my skirt. It was concertinaed into black folds. There were translucent tears in its crosshatched fabric like stretchmarks. I plucked at it. 'Oh, God, look at the state of that. You don't have a penknife, do you?'

He dug into his shorts pocket and dropped into my hand a bunch of keys, attached to which was a red-cased penknife. The keys were warm, almost hot. The physics of it: the heat from the surface blood in his groin had heated the metal of the keys in his pocket, which in turn were now warming my palm. A chain of heat-agitated atoms.

He was reattaching the wheel to my bicycle, breathing hard as he turned the wrench. I examined the back of his neck and shoulders as I used the blade of his penknife to slice through the material of my skirt above my knee. 'There!' I exclaimed, balling up the ruined excess and chucking it into the bin.

He looked up, the wheel in place, and a rush of red fired his face. 'Oh,' he said, 'right. Looks OK. I mean it looks better like that, I think. I mean, I liked it before and everything but, you know, it's good. Yeah. It's great.'

I took the weight of the bike from him, balancing it against my leg. 'Thank you so much for helping me. You were brilliant.'

He was sheepish, looking down at his feet, which

he was shifting around on the pavement. 'That's fine. Anytime.'

There was a pause. Marcus scratched the back of his neck. I examined the plastic rimming of my bicycle seat.

'So,' I said eventually, 'er . . . what are your plans for the summer?'

He pushed something up to my face and for a moment I didn't recognise it.

'Didn't you have a look at this while I was gone?' he was saying. It was the folder he'd left in my basket.

'Er. No. What is it?'

He put it into my hands. I read the label on the front: 'The Beaufort Chinese Architecture Grant'.

'I'm off to Beijing tomorrow.'

'Beijing?' I repeated.

'Yeah,' his face was confused, almost apologetic, 'I got this grant to go to China. To study . . .' He was staring at me and seemed to lose his thread. I waited. He rubbed his thumb across his nose.

'To study . . . ?' I prompted.

'To study the processes of developing Chinese architecture. For three months. Initially. But then . . .' he trailed off again, but rallied himself '. . . it could be extended. I don't know.'

'China,' I declared loudly, as if preparing for a lecture on the subject. I swung my leg over the crossbar of my bike. 'China,' I repeated. 'I see. Well.' I was furious. I knew that. But I didn't quite know why. All I did know was that I had to leave. Fast. Or I might do something embarrassing. Something I'd regret. 'WellImustbeoffnow'bye,' I gabbled and leaned my weight on the pedal. The bike ground into movement agonisingly slowly.

'Sinead,' Marcus said, apparently alarmed that I was leaving, 'wait a sec.'

The bike picked up momentum. I waved in what I hoped was a cheery, carefree manner as I swept away. ''Bye! Have the time of your life!'

By the time I reached the library, the bones of my fingers were hot and sweat itched at my hair.

Four, or maybe five days later the phone rang late at night. I wasn't asleep but lying on my front on my bedroom floor reading a book I shouldn't have been reading – a contemporary novel. Nothing to do with post-feminist readings of medieval literature. The phone rang, four, five, six, seven times. I propped myself up on my elbow and peered at my watch. Eleven forty-eight. I returned to my book. The phone carried on ringing. Where the hell were Kate and Ingrid? It was bound to be Kate's boyfriend – an emaciated medic from Birmingham with a sparse goatee. After the fifteenth ring, I hauled myself to my feet, my finger still hooked into my place in the novel's spine, and pulled open my door.

'Bloody bastard phone, won't be for me anyway, who rings this late anyway, bastard,' I grumbled to myself, as I stomped down the stairs, slipping slightly in my socked feet. 'Yes,' I barked into the receiver.

'Can I speak to Sinead, please?'

I frowned. Didn't recognise the voice. The line blizzarded with static and distance. 'Yes. Speaking.'

'Oh. Hi. Sinead, it's Marcus.'

I clutched my novel so hard my finger popped out of my page. I looked down at it in annoyance – I'd never find my place again now.

'What?' I said, bizarrely, then tried again: 'Marcus. Where are you?'

'I'm sitting in a small glass booth in the Friendship Store.'

'The . . . ?' I shook my head, as if to try to understand what was going on. 'I thought you were in Beijing.'

'I am.'

'But . . .'

'The Friendship Store in Beijing.'

'Oh. OK.'

'It's like a supermarket for foreigners.'

'Right.'

There was a silence. I panicked, ran through the limited things I knew about China to think of a question to ask.

'Sinead?' said Marcus's voice, from a huge distance.

'Yes?'

'I realised I never asked you what you were doing this summer.'

'Huh? Oh. Staying here mostly. I've got work to do. You know – meetings to go to. Courses to prepare. That kind of thing.'

'Well, I was wondering . . . I mean, you can say no if you want. You hardly know me and everything – I mean you don't really know me at all. But,' Marcus said with emphasis, as if gathering courage, 'I just thought I'd call and see if you wanted to come out here to meet me.'

'To China?' I said. 'You're asking me to come to China?'

'Er. Yes.'

I would later try to convince myself – and all my friends, and all my family – that I thought it over, that I considered it, that I understood and assessed and came to terms with all the problems of abandoning my life and plans to go travelling in a developing country with a man I hardly knew. But I didn't.

'Yes,' I said instantly, 'yes, I will.'

She leaps on to a chair and by the time he's opening the door, she's standing on the table. The door opens and there he is. Her initial impression is his tan – his skin has been turned a warm, even colour by the American sun – and he's smiling. She wants to close her eyes, to still this moment, not let it pass, to let them wait there before they get their hands on each other.

He is laughing now at the sight on her on the table, slinging his backpack to the floor and coming towards her.

'Wait!' she cries. Marcus stops immediately. 'I have something to show you.'

He smiles. 'Do you want me to close my eyes?'

'No.'

Slowly, slowly Sinead raises the hem of her dress. Centimetre by centimetre it creeps up over her thighs, the tops of her legs, her mound of Venus, her hipbones. She is wearing new black lace knickers. He watches, eyes fixed on her hem. Neither of them breathes. Finally, she stands with her belly button exposed.

They stare at each other. He puts out one foot, then another and another, coming towards her slowly across the floor. 'You know what I think?'

'What?'

He is in touching distance now. If he raised his arm, his fingertips would brush her skin. 'I think that they look great, but there is one slight problem.'

She is covering her mouth with one hand now, suppressed laughter jamming up her throat. She knows what comes next. He is standing right in front of her now, looking up, his head on one side.

'I'm not entirely sure that they fit you very well.'

'Really?' she says in mock-concern. 'Do you think so?'

'Yeah. I'm actually very worried. In fact,' and he unfolds his arms and puts out his hand, 'I think I may need to check.' Very, very slowly, he puts his hand under the skirt at the back and rubs his palm over her left buttock.

'Hmm.' He frowns, puts out his other hand and runs both over her backside. The palms of his hands feel roughened and create a static frisson on the material. Sinead is holding her breath now. This is almost more than she can bear. 'Well, they fit OK at the back, but what I'm more worried about is round the front. If I could just . . .' He brings his hand up over her hipbone and it inches down. 'It's here that really worries me. I'm just not sure if they fit here,' and he plunges his fingers between the tops of her legs. Sinead gives a piercing shriek, Marcus buries his head between her legs, she leaps down on top of him, he grabs her round the waist. Entwined and paralysed with laughter, they crash backwards into the kitchen cabinet.

'Ow,' says Sinead, as their combined weight glances off her backbone, but it doesn't really hurt because they are kissing and kissing and pulling at each other's clothes. She has her legs wrapped round his waist and she is pulling at his hair and he is ripping down the straps on her dress and laughing and they are very good at this, very practised, their lips meet exactly and she remembers this even before she remembers remembering it. And all the time they are talking and the words come out a bit like this:

'Oh, God . . . how was . . . the flight . . . hey, it's so good . . . did you miss me . . . so good . . . this much . . . so good . . . I'm so glad . . . so good to see you . . . glad . . . those pants . . . you're back . . . where did you . . . your hair . . . get them . . . it's fab, I love it . . . it's great, it suits . . . and the dress, are they . . . you . . . new . . . Sinead, oh, Sinead . . . you don't look . . . are you hungry, are you . . . any different . . . jetlagged . . . God, I've missed . . . you smell the . . . you all the time . . . same, just the same . . . really? . . . my love, my love . . . you're back . . . I'm back . . . you're back . . . how was it . . . show me, tell . . . in New York . . . me everything you've done . . . did you take . . . since I went away . . . any photos . . . can't believe you're really . . . some, I'll show you . . . back . . . later.'

I stepped off the boat on to the small, rotted wooden jetty. It swayed and buckled, and I had to bend my knees so as not to stumble. I wanted to take my rucksack off my back. The muscles in my neck and shoulders were stretched like cello strings, but I was too afraid to put it down.

Behind and ahead of me were other people who'd been on the boat with me: men carrying woven baskets filled with hens, a pig on a leash, women with bright bundles strapped to their back and babies with faces like pansy flowers, a boy with a tyre, women balancing on their shoulders poles weighted with water, vegetables, bales of cotton.

Everyone was shouting and pushing. And staring at me. On the boat, four women had sat themselves round me in a circle on the floor as if I was about to tell them a story. But instead they were contented just to stare – not aggressively. They smiled if I smiled at them. I tried looking out of the window, getting out my book, fiddling with the straps on my rucksack. But everything I did was of interest to them. Their curiosity was entirely open and, it seemed, insatiable. The language wasn't as I had expected: it was soft, undulating, melodic, with lots of *sh* sounds and falling scales.

What I felt: tall. Sick from the boat. Afraid. Wet. Ungainly. Sweat down my back under my rucksack. A scratching in my throat as if I wanted to cough. Rich. Alone. My hair plastered to my head like seaweed.

What I could smell: riverwater. Boat diesel fumes. Animals. Feathers. Leather from my wet shoes. A milky, baby smell from the child in front of me. Woodsmoke. Damp soil.

Above me were towering columns of bamboo, creaking and bending in the wind, their ridged trunks the width of a man's thigh. Ahead of me, beyond the muddle of people who'd got off the boat, was a dirt path. Beyond that, I could see the village – grey buildings and a paved, wide street. Marcus. Marcus was in that village.

I elbowed my way through the small crowd, shifting the weight of my rucksack further up on my shoulders.

I didn't want to understand what the woman behind the blue-topped counter was saying.

'*Meyoh.*' She shrugged.

'Emerson,' I said clearly, 'Marcus Emerson. Are you sure he's not here?'

'*Meyoh-la.* No here.' She was wearing high-heeled turquoise wellingtons, I noticed, and a man's suit jacket.

I looked down at the piece of paper I was clutching. 'Traveller's Guest House,' I had written, 'Yangshuo.' I had written that just over two weeks ago while on the phone to Marcus. Only two weeks. 'Fly to Beijing, then Guilin. Boat to Yangshuo.' Confident, straight arrows between the words. 'M will be checked into TGH.' That meant Traveller's Guest House. Where I was right now. And this woman was telling me he wasn't here. I cleared my throat, felt again under my clothes for the pouch containing my money, passport and tickets. I had carried this scrap of paper all the way from the phone in my house.

'Could I have a room anyway, please?'

I sat on the side of one of the double beds – the room, for some reason, had two. It sagged under my weight. It was a few moments before I remembered the weight on my shoulders, and eased off the straps, letting the bag fall backwards on to the bed. I stared around the room. Chicken wire covering a small space above the door. A red flask standing in an enamel basin decorated with orange fish. A small shadeless bulb beside the bed. Mosquito nets bunched up above the mattresses like great grey puffball mushrooms. The window smeary. The mountains beyond. The mountains. I hadn't been able to believe what I was seeing as the boat wove up the river: vast, toppling, lumped rocks rearing up from the water, hung with mist. I'd always thought those Chinese silk paintings were of fanciful, mystical landscapes from the imagination of some artist. But they actually existed – weird, looming, almost top-heavy, planted into flat, river-threaded plains. Karst topography – the phrase, appearing unbidden in my head, thrown up from some distance geography lesson, surprised me. I smiled for a moment, then: he's not here, I thought, he's not here. Shit.

I woke with a start, sitting bolt upright. The cone of a muslin mosquito net surrounded me. It gave the room the kind of dim, nostalgic haze old romantic films had.

China.

I was in Yangshuo, China.

It was hot.

Marcus had promised he'd be here.

He wasn't.

It was hot. Very, very hot.

I kicked off the heavy quilted bedcover, rushed to the window and yanked it open, gulping for air. But the air that met me was the same as that in the room – heavy, heated, moisture-filled. I was wearing just pants, I was vaguely surprised to notice. Had I pulled off my T-shirt in my sleep? Around the room were scattered the clothes I'd had on yesterday – jeans, trainers, socks, hooded jacket, vest. I was wearing those when I left my house, I thought.

I picked up my clock. Three twenty. I peered at it. Three twenty? *Three twenty?* Confused, I looked out of the window. Definitely daytime.

I stood in the centre of my doubly double-bedded room in my pants, uncertain, disorientated. I thought: I've travelled non-stop for thirty-eight hours. I thought: Antony gave me these pants. I thought: I've taken a break from my Ph.D. I thought: I've come all the way to China to meet a man I hardly know. I thought: He hasn't turned up, maybe—

Then, without warning, a wave of exuberance sent me skipping across the bare boards. I'm in China! *China*, for God's sake! Who gives a shit about some unreliable man? I riffled through my bag, packed so carefully in Britain, tipping its contents out on to the floor, selecting a pair of shorts and a clean T-shirt. Must go out. Can't lie about in here all day. He might arrive at any moment. Don't want him to think I've been hanging around the hotel waiting for him.

I walked the streets of Yangshuo. Bicycles, tractors and things like big motorised lawn-mowers with seats slewed up and down the streets. I passed open-fronted shops crammed with tailored clothes, kettles, bright plastic buckets, farm tools, the pale globes of pomelos, electrical fuses, the hard, flinty green shapes of jade, stacks of red flip-flops, silk dresses. The women were ruddy-cheeked and dark-eyed, hair pinned up with coloured slides, dressed in navy Mao suits and high heels. The men didn't look like they deserved them – sitting in glum groups, smoking and drinking tea from jam jars. Everywhere I went people stared and pointed or shouted, 'Hello!' or '*Laowai, laowai!*'

I scanned the groups of white westerners sitting around café tables. But no one even resembled him. Approaching the guest house, I had to slow my walk because moisture was crawling down my body like insects. But the room was empty, the bed undisturbed, my clothes still in arcs where I'd left them.

I couldn't sleep so later I went out again into the unlit streets, shiny after a quick rainstorm. I couldn't remember the way to the river but followed the scent of its fecund dampness on the air. Down at the water's edge the top of the thick vegetation shifted in the hot breeze. I rested on the backs of my heels, arms folded over my knees. I watched as narrow rafts of lashed-together bamboo came gliding over the surface of the blackened water. Three of them. A man stood at the back of each with a long pole like a gondolier's; at the front sat a large woven basket. And around them, sleek-throated cormorants dipped in and out of the water.

The second day, I woke late again and lay for a while plucking at loose threads in the quilt, watching geckos dart across the ceiling. I ate in a café where I met two men from New Zealand. The three of us then went to a fan-maker's and watched a boy of about sixteen paint blossom on to the sanded surface of the fan slats. I told them about the fishermen and they explained that the cormorants have rings around their throats to stop them swallowing the fish.

They were going to Xian next, they told me, to see an army of terracotta soldiers, each with a different face. Did I want to come? I shook my head. I can't, I said, I'm waiting for someone. They nodded. As we parted, the taller one turned round to see me go.

The third day, I woke and my watch said only nine. I'd been dreaming about university and seminar preparation and the writing of my thesis. I got up immediately. I hired a bike, cycled out of the town along the dust road, which meandered between the bulk of the mountains, through glassy-surfaced paddy-fields, herds of crescent-horned water-buffalo, tiny villages where people would shout after me, amazed by this lone white woman on a bicycle. Away from the tourist zone of the town, people were living in shacks with animals, children worked in the fields, and ancient women hobbled on twisted, broken feet, carrying bundles of firewood.

The fourth day I was glum. I sat in a café. On the table in front of me was a mug full of shavings of ginger and scalding water, and an exercise book. On the first page, I had written 'Fact: he is not coming. Fact: you haven't got enough money for this on your own.' I had crossed out 'on your own' and written 'trip' instead. I had five mosquito bites the size of ten-pence pieces on my leg. They progressed up my shin in a meandering line like a child's dot-to-dot drawing. The New Zealanders arrived and started teaching me the Chinese numbers and the hand-signs that went with them: '*yee, er, san, si, wu, lui, chi, bah, jiu, xi.*' The broad palms and cracked fingers of the New Zealander curved, crossed and straightened. I copied them, repeating the words.

'What you writing?' one asked, nodding towards my book.

'Nothing,' I said, flipping the cover closed.

After they'd gone, I rested my head on my cupped hand. *Yee*, *er*, *san*, *si*, *wu*. He wasn't coming. *Lui*, *chi*, *bah*, *jiu*, *xi*. What was I going to do?

A week ago I'd been to see my supervisor, Dr Hilton. He was a tall, ungainly man with over-large hands and a barely audible voice. When I had described my Ph.D. to him he had murmured, 'I'm very excited indeed.' But on this day I sat in front of him and said, 'I've decided to go away. To China.'

His forehead had creased, his hands darting to the edge of his knitted waistcoat. 'China?' he'd whispered, as if it was a swear word. 'What for?'

'For . . .' I picked my words '. . . a break.'

'I see.'

There had been a pause. Dr Hilton had adjusted and readjusted the height of his chair. 'Sinead,' he'd said, then stopped. 'You are going to come back, aren't you?'

'Of course,' I'd said quickly. Was that too quickly?

'You must,' he'd said, 'your work is . . . very important. Very important indeed.'

I scratched at a mosquito bite with the ineffectual, heat-softened curve of a fingernail. I'd spent my living allocation for next term in coming here. A girl in a red tracksuit passed, waving at me. I uncurled my fingers in reply. I drew a line in green biro up my leg, connecting my reddened bites. The New Zealanders were away down the street, in conversation with a man with a cart piled high with striped melons. I recognised the bartering gestures. *Yee*, *er*, *san*, *si* . . . I carried on staring down the street. A man with sun-whitened hair was walking quickly up the hill, a rucksack on his back. In his hand he held a camera and a piece of paper. I uncrossed and recrossed my legs, knocking my ankle on the table. Then I stood up. Called his name. Watched him coming over the square towards me.

'Where in God's name have you been?' I shouted.

'Sorrysorrysososorry,' he was saying. Then his arms were around me and his mouth was next to my ear, the strap of his camera knocking against the green graph-line on my shin.

They topple on to the sofa. Marcus half falls on to the floor and Sinead holds him fast and he has his face stuck in her neck and she is grappling with the belt on his trousers when she realises she wants to look into his face. She wriggles backwards, making her back twinge a little because all their limbs are tangled up, and grabbing his head between her hands, pulls him away from her so she can look at his face.

His eyelashes part, Marcus opens his eyes and looks into hers. She wants to examine every feature, every contour, every millimetre of him. It's him, it's really him, she wants to gaze at his face for a very, very long time until she's had enough and can turn her eyes away again. His face is beautiful to her, but a strange, shifting kind of beauty. It moves across him like clouds over a landscape. The French have a word for it – *joli-laid*. Marcus has always had a protean quality about him: sometimes he can look quite different from one moment to the next, just the subtlest alteration in his facial muscles switching his features from a serene, absorbed beauty to a harder near-ugliness. It's never an unattractive ugliness, merely a recast version of his face. She's always found that—

Then he is arched between her legs, his hands behind her head. Her breathing sounds far off to her, as if in another room. She holds him to her, her hand in the dip of his back and his spine labours and flexes under her palm. Laughter bubbles somewhere inside her, which comes out into the air as shortened, staccato gasps.

Suddenly his back is still, straight, taut as a sprung trap. He rests on his elbows, motionless, his torso held over her. She waits, peers up, but can see only his neck, grizzled with stubble, and the wishbone curve of his jaw. She twists her head to try to see his face, but his elbow is leaning on her hair and she is trapped there. An image of Gulliver is flitting across her mind, making her smile, when he says something and she feels him shrinking inside her. He says the something again.

'Huh?' she says.

'Sinead, we need . . . we need . . .' He rears up above her, straightening his arms. 'We need to talk.'

This is not what Sinead was expecting. 'Do we?'

He nods.

'OK,' she says, 'but later, all right,' and goes to pull him towards her.

'No.' He adjusts his balance, and she feels him pulling away from her. 'Now, I think.'

Sinead sits up, puzzled, straightening her dress. Marcus, his back to her, pulls up his trousers, fastens his flies and belt, and walks about the room for a few seconds, his hands crossed behind his head. Then he slumps down in a chair opposite her.

'The thing is . . .' he begins, and stops. 'Have you seen Aidan?'

Sinead laughs at this strange non sequitur. 'The thing is have I seen Aidan? What – ever? Today? This week? What are you on about?'

There is a pause. Sinead tucks her legs up under her, waiting. Marcus has tipped back his head and is staring at the ceiling. She drums her fingernails on the soles of her feet. What is all this?

'Marcus—'

'The thing is,' he says again quickly, 'the thing is, I wasn't exactly faithful to you in New York.'

I didn't know how to pitch things when we got back to the room. Should I leave him to unpack, shower? Should I pretend we were just here as friends? Or should I just seduce him and get it out of the way?

Marcus stood at the window, one hand resting on his hip, the other behind his neck. I kicked the loose clothes on the floor into a rough heap. Sat down on the bed. Stood up. Sat down again. I was being pulled in the directions of two opposing impulses: to remove all my clothes or to suggest we go for a brisk, edifying walk. *Femme fatale* versus Brown Owl.

I tucked my hands underneath my legs to prevent myself acting on either. Marcus's back was towards me. The backs of his legs, his neck, his arms were brown, his boots muddied.

A shuffling sound. The soles of his boots swivelling on the wooden floor, leaving dusty, whitish compass marks on the boards. His boots creaked slightly, I noticed, as he walked towards me. Leather that had been wet, had expanded and then contracted. The toes had a grey tidemark on them.

'How was Beijing?' I was horrified to hear my voice braying. Brown Owl appeared to be winning.

Marcus crouched in front of me. Rested his fingertips on my knees to steady himself. 'I can't tell you,' he began, his voice low, 'how glad I am that you're here.'

There was a pause.

'You can't tell me?' I said. 'Why not?'

Marcus shrugged. 'I don't know. Just can't.'

'Well, how am I meant to know, then? I mean, just how am I supposed to guess that's how you feel?'

'Other things.'

'What other things?'

Marcus leaned forward on to his knees, brushing against my legs. Outside a band of mist drifted off a limestone peak. A woman called for her child in the street below.

'This, for example.' He put his hand on my waist, thumbs at the front, fingers around the back of my pelvis. Then he leaned forward and pressed his mouth to where my neck met my shoulder. He didn't lean back again, just stayed there, breathing into my hair. 'I've wanted to do that ever since I first saw you.'

'Is that right?'

'You've got an amazing neck.'

'Have I?'

My first kiss missed his mouth, catching him below his

cheekbone. But for the second he had his hand cupped round the back of my head and our lips met just as I was inhaling. We were both shuddering, bodies vibrating with each blood-beat.

I always love the first time you sleep with someone. No matter what happens later, there is always that clarity, that amazement, that steep learning curve – how to deal with someone else's body, how it likes to be touched, how it wants to fit into yours, how it responds to the things you do. There are always surprises, always idiosyncrasies, always things that differentiate it from other, similar acts. I believe you could sleep with a hundred people and still be surprised.

Scale enlarges and distance shrinks. What I can never get over is that change: how, before, you know them at a certain range – in clothes, over the other side of tables, with no further touch than perhaps a brush on the arm or a momentary kiss on the cheek. But then suddenly you are pressing your lips to theirs, their eyes blurringly close, touching their teeth, their palate, their gums with the tip of your tongue. You are looking into the one blind eye of their penis, seeing the lie of their body-hair, the creases of their skin, tasting their sweat, their saliva, their tears, their semen. You are knowing them more closely than even they do.

What I would always remember about my first time with Marcus: that we giggled over which bed to use. That he pressed his cheek to mine. That he was tenderer, gentler than I'd expected. The rasp of his stubble on the skin of my inner thigh. The first, unpeeled, round, silk push of him. That I knew, half-way through, or maybe not half-way but somewhere in the middle or near the end or maybe not near it at all but right after the start, that it was going to be good, very good, in that way that things that are right feel already familiar, that I knew what to do before I knew I was doing it, and that this was just the beginning, that they would get better, and keep on getting better and would be better, perhaps for a long time.

The room stops like a lift.

Sinead stares at Marcus. It is a sentence that will return to her over and over again – for months, for years. It will echo round her head. She'll hear it again during the many, many sleepless nights ahead of her. Right now, though, she is attempting to process it. The sentence seems to have lots of different bits: the thing is; in New York; exactly faithful; I wasn't. That weird negative understatement bothers her: I wasn't exactly faithful. Exactly faithful. What does that mean? Why 'exactly'? Does it mean he wasn't faithful or that he was unfaithful? And what's the difference?

The answer pops up in her head like a price total displayed on a cash register: it means something between the two. It means he kissed someone somewhere. Maybe he was drunk. He kissed someone. That's all, and he thinks he should tell me. But Sinead continues to stare at his face. He drops his eyes and that's when she knows. This isn't just about a random, drunken encounter. This is more. Much more. I wasn't exactly faithful. To you. In New York.

'Are we talking just one,' she is astonished at how calm and even her voice sounds, 'or lots?'

Marcus shakes his head and shrugs simultaneously. 'Lots,' he says.

Sinead has never been surprised like this by anything before. If someone had said to her, what's the most unlikely thing for Marcus to do, she might have come up with this, but probably would have felt it was so unlikely as to be off the scale of things Marcus would do. She looks down at the way her body is arranged – legs curled under her, one hand resting on her feet, the other laid across her front. She hardly recognises it. She can't remember how long ago it was that she sat herself down in this position.

She feels hollow, but something flutters around the space inside her: her lover has metamorphosed into some strange, cruel being. Marcus has gone mad. Or this is some tanned imposter, a destructive double. Or he's possessed by some evil spirit. She looks at him closely. He looks the same. A little tired, maybe. A little deadened around the eyes. But how can this be Marcus, her Marcus?

'Why?' she hears herself ask. '*Why?*'

He slumps further into the chair, as if she's physically assaulting him. Sinead is getting up, standing, spinning away from him across the floor like a gyroscope, hair and dress whirling round her. She reaches the kitchen and doesn't know what to do there, so she turns again and looks at him, her mind returning to the sentence: why didn't he come out and say it properly, instead of that cowardly negated, roundabout way, why didn't he just say it: Sinead, I've been unfaithful to you.

And then she is remembering a time at the beginning of their relationship when she'd been considering ending it. She'd arranged to meet him in a pub and when she arrived, he was sitting with some people he knew, playing a game involving sticking cigarette papers on their foreheads. She had sat on a stool, hands folded in her lap, staring at him in disbelief as he talked too loudly and laughed and made jokes she'd never heard before. It was as if she'd never met him, never had anything to do with him, as if she'd just spent weeks in China with someone else entirely. He was a different person, not the Marcus she knew and was starting to love. This one – whoever he was – was louder, brasher, cockier. She looked around at the rest of the table and slowly began to realise that what he was doing was being like them. He had just morphed himself to fit in with these people. It reminded her of a species of bird she'd read about once that had no predators because it could mimic the calls of whichever birds were around it, surviving by dint of imitation. As soon as they were alone again, walking to catch a bus, he switched back instantly to the person she knew. But she was unable to look at him, unable to let him take her hand, unable to touch him. It appalled her that there was such a lack of solidity, of permanence, in his sense of himself that he could be so easily swayed. He hadn't understood, was hurt and angry, and they'd stayed awake until dawn, arguing. She'd got used to his plasticity, in time, but it never ceased to shock her. And as she stands in the kitchen in her new dress, she finds herself wondering what kind of people he must have been spending time with for him to do this.

'I don't understand,' she says, quiet and still now. 'I don't understand. Why have you done this?'

Across the yards of space between them, she sees him flex his shoulders as if shrugging something off. He scratches his head and says with an odd, worldly bravura that doesn't sit well on him, that looks as though it's a gesture he's borrowed from someone recently: 'It's hard to say.' He shrugs, turning his palms up to the ceiling. 'It was a bit of a strange time. You were so far away and everything here seemed so distant and y—' He glances at her, his mouth open, half-way into forming the next word. But something in her face must have made him falter, because the word vanishes into the air between them like steam. He stares at his hands, mutely, moves his lips as if he's about to say something else, but changes his mind. 'You see, I . . .' he begins uncertainly, sitting forward, then stops. 'These things happen,' he mutters.

She is filled with fury – pure, molten, towering fury. 'Do they?' she shouts. 'Do they really? They just happen. Just like that. One minute you're walking along and the next, before you even know it, my God, you're shagging someone. What – they slipped and fell on your dick? Is that what you're telling me?'

Her mouth is suddenly full of rushing, sweet-tasting saliva. She's going to be sick. She darts to the sink and waits, but nothing happens. The nausea subsides. She realises that she hasn't eaten since lunchtime, and is wondering why, when she remembers that she was going to cook a meal for her and Marcus. Artichoke hearts. They are still sheaved into themselves, hard petal against hard petal, at the bottom of the fridge. Then she feels a hand pressed into her back.

'Sinead, are you—'

She whips round, smashing the side of her fist into

his arm. 'Don't touch me,' she hisses. 'Don't even lay a finger on me.'

She sees him flinch with pain, covering the place where she'd hit him with his other hand, and something pulls at her. How could she hurt him like this? How could she strike him? But then the knowledge that the hand, the body she knows like her own, has touched another woman's is agony.

There is a noise on the stair outside – the measured footfalls of someone walking up the stairs, the tinkle of keys. Aidan. They both look at each other and, despite everything, Sinead is surprised to see panic in his eyes.

'What do we do?' he whispers.

Sinead sidesteps him, runs towards their bedroom. 'Do what you want. You always do anyway.'

I was listening to Marcus's story of why he was four days late. It involved a long queue for tickets, a thirty-eight-hour bus journey, a man with a goat, and a minor traffic accident.

'I heard a squeal of brakes and I woke up to find myself, and all the bus – goat included – flying forward through the air. The bus's front wheels had got stuck in a muddy ditch like this.' He demonstrated with his hands. 'I thwacked my thigh on a bus seat when I landed.' He showed me a blackened, purple patch at the top of his leg, uneven and adrift in the white of his skin like a continent that had been shifted by tectonic plates. I'd seen it earlier, but hadn't asked.

'I was terrified I'd missed you,' he said, and his hand on my arm twitched tighter. 'That you'd have gone before I got here, disappeared into China without trace.'

My head was resting on the joint between his shoulder and his arm, my eye facing the aureole of his nipple. I was listening, not to his voice, but its reverberation through his body, my ear pressed to his ribcage.

I turned over on to my front, the rucked sheet catching at my elbows and hips. Marcus turned with me, his hand coming to rest in the hollow of my back.

I reached for his passport on the bedside table, flicked it open.

This night is the saddest. Or so it seems. What she doesn't know yet is that there will be a long, long string of sad nights, some of a different kind, some worse. What she doesn't yet know is that ending a relationship cannot be done in one conversation over one evening, that such extrication takes days and months and sometimes years.

When she reaches the bedroom, she doesn't know what to do. She stands in the middle of the floor, arms crossed behind her body. She feels confused, divided, unreal, as if her actual everyday life has been stopped somehow and she is being forced to act out this strange scene belonging to someone else. It's as if she's mouthing along to a script she doesn't understand and wants no part in. She wants to return to her other life, to step back into it, but doesn't know how.

She hears Aidan come in, close the door behind him; Marcus's voice saying hello and then a rumbling, inaudible exchange between them. Feet over the floorboards, the slam of Aidan's doors. More feet. Her door opening. Someone stepping into the room.

There is silence between them for a while. Marcus sits at the desk by the window, Sinead on the bed. He runs his thumbnail along the edge of the desk. She cannot stop swallowing, as though she has eaten something she cannot digest. She draws her knees up to her chest, pulls the duvet around her: a shivering chill has settled into her bones. Some corner of her mind tells her that she must talk, find things out, to cross somehow this crevasse that has opened up between them, but she can't think of anything to say.

She clears her throat, tries to focus her thoughts. Lots, he said. There were lots. In New York. 'When did you,' she begins, unsure of how the sentence will end, unsure of what it is she's asking, 'when was the first one?'

'Um.' Marcus thinks. 'Just after I'd arrived,' he almost whispers.

'And did . . . how long did . . . it . . . go on?'

'The . . . the whole time.'

Sinead thinks about all the letters and the postcards that dropped through the door, the e-mails that she'd picked up at the end of her working day, the phone calls that came twice, sometimes three times a week, sometimes in the middle of the night. Were they ever there when he was talking to her? Did he ever call her from their apartments? Did they listen in the background? Did they read the letters she sent back? Did he ever call after—?

'The whole time?' she repeats, as if for herself. 'The whole time you were away?'

'What's the G for?'

He raised his head lazily, running his finger down the knuckles of my backbone. 'Huh?'

'The G.' I flapped the passport at him. A picture of him, sealed under plastic, younger, with that soft-edged look that teenagers try in vain to rid themselves of, flicked past. 'Marcus G. Emerson,' I read.

'Promise not to laugh?'

I smiled. 'No.'

'I can't tell you, then.'

'Go on. It can't be that bad. What is it? Gerald? Geoffrey?'

'Gabriel.'

I laughed. 'Gabriel? Are you serious?'

'Unfortunately, yes. My mother has a bit of a New Testament thing.'

I dropped the passport back on to the table, that picture of him, longer-haired then, winking at me. I pulled myself over the bed towards him and laid myself along the length of his back, my head in the curve of his neck. His heartbeat was slower than mine.

'Do you know what?' he said, and his voice rumbled through the mattress. 'There's this artist who did a whole study into the physiognomy of angels. He did research into flying creatures – birds, bats, you know – and worked out that if angels were to fly, they'd have to have a breastbone one metre thick for their wings to support their body weight. At the end of it, he painted a physiognomically correct version of the Sistine Chapel ceiling, with these weird, stocky, deformed-looking creatures winging their way about the celestial skies.

'Imagine it,' and he turned over. I slid off his back.

Sweat had pooled between us where our bodies touched, transpiring against each other. 'One metre thick.' And he held his hand out from his body to demonstrate. I narrowed my eyes, tried to visualise it, but couldn't make the leap, couldn't imagine him any different.

She is staring at him, and he looks unfamiliar to her, as if she's never met him before, as if she's seeing him for the first time. Her imagination wriggles out from under her control, and begins to flash her a series of single-frame images: him thrusting into a woman on a bed, him with a different woman up against a desk, a woman on top of him, a woman bending over him, his hands on another woman's waist, his head resting in the neck of a faceless female, him on—

It all disappears when, suddenly, it hits her that, a few minutes ago, they were . . . that he was . . . on the sofa . . . they were . . .

'How could you?' she blurts, and her voice cracks, choked by shock and disbelief. 'How could you sleep with me after that? How could you *do* that?' She hears her words rise to a wail and her limbs twist and convulse in bodily horror at the recollection of him on her and in her, as if daubing her, smearing her with traces of those other women. '*How could you?*' she shouts again, looking around her, as if for something to hurl at him. She wants to hurt him, to mark him.

'I . . . I didn't . . .' he stutters, 'I didn't mean to . . . it just—'

'Happened?' she yells over him. 'Is that what you were going to say?'

He darts a look at her then at the door. 'Hush,' he says. 'Aidan will hear.'

'Aidan?' she splutters, struggling off the bed. 'Do you think I give a shit if Aidan hears?' Her feet move under her as she paces around the boards and the walls of the room constructed for the life she used to have veer around her giddily.

'Sinead,' he reaches out for her as she passes him, but she swings away from him and his hand closes around empty air, 'please don't shout,' he begs. 'This has all,' he presses his fists into his eyes, 'come out wrong. Let's just . . . let's just talk about this.'

'Talk?' she says. 'You want to talk? OK. Let's talk. Why don't you tell me what it was like, and whether it was any good, and whether you feel like a big brave man now, and was it better than it is with me, and how you could come back from that and sleep with me before you had the decency to tell me, and . . . and why you didn't tell me.' Strength and words ebb out of her. Silence, after the tumble of her speech, pulses between them. 'Why didn't you tell me?' she whispers.

He rubs his fingers across his forehead, not looking at her but at the walls, his feet, the desk.

'Why, Marcus? Why leave me all that time, thinking that everything was the same?'

'Everything is the same,' he says quickly.

She gives an incredulous laugh, then looks at him, trying to see if he's joking, if he really means what he just said. His eyes, a deep navy blue in this light, look back at her, unwavering.

'Nothing has changed,' he insists. 'Nothing. I promise you. All that didn't mean a thing. It had nothing to do with you and me. Nothing. I love you. You know that. I always will.' He is crushing her hand in his, the ring he gave her a year ago pressing painfully into the flesh of adjacent fingers.

'Marcus,' she flounders, unnerved, 'that's ridiculous, I—'

'No, it's not ridiculous. It's not ridiculous at all. You and I couldn't live without each other. You know that. Nothing could ever come between us, or change how we feel about each other.'

Cross now, she wrests her hand from his grasp. 'Really? Is that what you think? That you can behave exactly as you like and I'll just accept it? That you can go off and screw your way around New York City and I'll just be here when you get back saying, "Oh, Marcus, do what you like because I'll love you no matter what?"'

He is still looking at her with that unblinking, wide-eyed stare, but there is now a hint of desperation in his voice. 'I missed you so much,' he says softly.

'Fuck you,' she spits out. 'How dare you say that to me?'

He stroked the tips of my hair with the fingers of both his hands. I was impressed that he knew straight away how to touch it: some men were overawed by it and never went near it; others tried manfully to run their hands through it, which was impossible, not to mention painful. I had one man who wanted to brush it. I think he thought it would be a romantic gesture. I tried to explain that you couldn't brush my hair, that I never did, that it wouldn't work, that it was too difficult and the results too horrific. He went on and on about it and, close to the end of our affair, I seized a brush and showed him why, dragging the nylon bristles through the ravelled curls, transforming my head into a huge, crackling, electrified tumbleweed.

But Marcus, that first afternoon, just explored its properties, didn't force it when one spiral refused to part from its neighbour, didn't try to run his fingers from root to end. He held it to the light, where I knew that he'd be looking at it sparking brown and gold. He spent ages playing with one ringlet, stretching it out to its fullest length down my back before letting it ping back.

'Wow,' he murmured eventually. He elongated it. I felt the ends whisper on my back.

'Imagine if you could harness the energy in your hair.' He released it and it sprang back to nestle among the rest. 'If there was some way of wiring it up to the National Grid you could power the whole country.'

He pulled it straight again.

'Who were they?' she says, standing in front of him, hands behind her back.

'It doesn't matter.' He reaches out for her. She steps back.

'It does matter. It mattered to you at the time. Tell me.'

'Why?'

'Because I want to know.'

'Sinead, it's not important. Believe me, it doesn't matter. They don't matter.'

'They mattered enough for you to fuck them. Just tell me. Were they people you were working with?'

'No.'

'Do I know any of them?'

He hesitates, looks away.

'Do I?' she persists.

'Sinead—'

'Tell me. Do I know any of them?'

'No. I don't think so.'

'But you're not sure.'

'I . . .' he waves a hand around his head '. . . I thought for a minute you might have met . . . one of them, but then I remembered you . . . you weren't at that particular party.'

'So one of them you knew from London.'

'No.'

'But she was in London.'

'Yes,' he says, impatient. 'She was here briefly a few months ago for . . . something . . . work, maybe, or friends, or something.'

'And you planned to sleep with her when you saw her then?'

'No, I did not.'

'So where did you find the others?'

He puts his hands to his head. 'I really don't think—'

'Where, Marcus? In bars? In clubs? Where do you go if you want to find women?' Something occurs to her. 'I take it they were women?'

He looks at her, outraged. 'Of course they were.'

'Well,' she gives a bitter laugh, 'I just wondered if you had any other bombshells you wanted to drop.'

She does another circuit around the room. Anger leaves her and settles on her within seconds. 'Did you plan to do this before you went?' she asks, bewildered.

'Um . . . I . . .'

'Did you? Were you planning this before you left?'

'I don't think so.'

'You don't think so?'

'No, I wasn't.'

'Then when did you decide?'

'When I was there . . . when I . . . I don't know . . . it wasn't something . . . I mean, it isn't like I decided to do it, not like I made a decision or anything.' He suddenly bows his head, as if overcome, burying his face in his hands. 'Sinead,' he cries, his voice breaking, 'this is awful. Awful. None of this is coming out right. I never meant . . . I didn't think you'd react this way. I—'

She gives a short bark of laughter. 'Why? How did you think I'd react? That I'd welcome you back with open and forgiving arms?'

He stares at her for a second, his face wild and miserable. 'I've no idea,' he whispers hoarsely. 'I don't think I'd . . . thought it through properly.'

'You haven't thought any of this through, have you? That's always been your biggest problem. You know that? You have this incredible inability to understand causality. You can never make the connection that if you do A then B will happen. You have this . . .' she has that feeling of having hit her stride now, as she does at the midway point in her lectures, words and ideas pumping together like blood and oxygen '. . . this pathological blindness to the most basic mechanisms of human nature. You're always so focused on the realisation of your own bloody desires that you can't stop and think about what the results might be. You didn't stop, did you, when you were climbing into bed with some woman in New York, you didn't pause for a moment and think, I wonder what Sinead will say when I tell her about this, I wonder what effect this might have on my five-year relationship?' She stops, breathless, suddenly struck by the weirdness of talking about her own life in this way, and not just some text. 'Did you?'

He doesn't move.

'Did you?' she shouts.

He gives a minute shake of his head.

She strides to the window, stares out unseeing, then strides back. Something is preventing her keeping still. Between the bed and the wardrobe, she stops and turns back. 'Were you always going to tell me?'

'What?'

'Were. You,' she says, with sarcastic slowness. 'Always. Going—'

'Yes!' he exclaims, with an unconvincing vehemence, not meeting her eye.

She feels oddly calm and somehow unsurprised by this new discovery. 'You weren't, were you?'

He doesn't reply.

'That's why you haven't thought it through. Because this was never part of the plan.' In a flare of fury, she kicks the base of the bed. But everything she does somehow feels divorced from her, has a tinge of forced theatricality to it, as if she's just following directions, behaving in the way you're supposed to behave when you find out about infidelity. 'You shit,' she says slowly, 'you utter, utter shit. You were going to just come back and pretend nothing had happened. What made you change your mind, Marcus? Last-minute nerves? A sudden pang of conscience? Or were you scared I might find out anyway and thought the best thing was just to come clean?'

He's still silent.

'Hmm?' she persists, then suddenly pulls away from the subject, abandoning it, tiring of it, knowing she'll never get an answer. 'Just how many are we talking about?' she asks, quiet now.

He sighs unsteadily. 'I don't remember.'

'Come on. You must remember.'

'I don't. I don't want to think about it.'

'It's a bit late for that,' she snaps. 'Come on. Think. More than ten? Less than twenty?'

Marcus hesitates. Scratches the back of his neck. 'I can't remember. A lot.'

She sinks down to the edge of the bed, scuffing the woodgrain in the floorboards with her bare feet. Marcus hasn't moved from his seat at her desk. His back, usually straight, is curved, and he rests his elbows on her desk, his face averted. He looks tired – jet-lagged and pale under his tan. She is overcome with an urge to press her palm to the dip between his shoulder-blades, to curl her fingers around his shoulders. But she can't. She can't ever again.

'Why?' she says, very quietly. 'Why did you do it?'

We peeled ourselves from the sheets, forced out of bed by hunger and the airlessness of the room. When I stood up, my head stuttered and blurred, as if filled with fluid. Our clothes lay together on the bare boards, the arm of his shirt across my crumpled shorts.

'It's not that bad.' I protested, as I ransacked my things for a towel. 'I don't spend my life sitting about discussing the finer points of Chaucerian English, you know. And anyway,' I said, flapping a skirt in the air to shake it of its creases, 'I love my job.'

'But aren't all your friends academics as well?' His voice came from the far side of the room, where he was unpacking his bag.

'No,' I lied, with my back to him. 'Not at all. I know lots of people who . . . who do ordinary, normal jobs in the real world.'

'But don't you wish you lived in London?'

'No,' I lied again. 'I like it there. It's . . . small and . . . and friendly.'

'I don't know how you stand it. Everything closes down at eleven o'clock. You can walk across it in twenty minutes. You never meet anyone who isn't attached to the university. It's just a campus that's built like a town.'

'You can't say that!' I turned round. 'You've never even spent any time there.'

'Maybe I will now,' he said, his voice suddenly serious.

I faltered when I tried to look at him. It was far too early for that kind of talk.

It's a question she can't let alone. 'But why?' she says again. 'I don't understand why you've done this. Are you not happy with me any more?'

'No. I mean yes, of course I am.'

'Was it a way of ending things with me?'

'No! Absolutely not.'

'Were you bored with our sex life?'

'No. No,' he appeals to her, holding out his arms. 'No. Sinead, how can you say that?'

She stays where she is, on the bed, ignoring his gesture. 'Then what? What went so wrong that you . . . that you couldn't talk to me about it?'

He lets his arms fall to his sides. 'I . . . I . . . Nothing,' he says firmly. 'Nothing went wrong.'

'What do you mean?' she demands. 'Something must have gone wrong for you to do this.'

'No, no, it didn't.'

She gives an exasperated click with her tongue, gets up, walks around the bed once, then turns back to him. 'Then *why*? If nothing went wrong and you're still happy with me, why did you do it?'

'I don't know,' he says, with a strange, almost surprised look on his face. 'I really don't know why I did it.'

Outside, it was raining – a heavy, sudden downpour with drops like coins – but the air didn't feel any lighter.

'I love tropical rain,' Marcus said, as we stood at the window together, looking out. 'It's so serious. It makes British weather look really weedy and half-hearted.'

In the street below, umbrellas bobbed along the pavements. The bicycles wore bright plastic ponchos. When we ran to the shower-room, a grey, boxed-in building behind the hotel, we were soaked in seconds.

We showered. Everything seemed slow. Cockroaches scudded over the floor, disappearing into crevices. Marcus turned the thin streams of water down to tepid, and then he washed me, carefully and solicitously, soaping my legs and arms, rubbing shampoo into my hair, scooping up water to rinse off the strings of bubbles that spiralled down the drain. I was suprised again by his gentleness. My nipples creased into themselves as he washed my breasts. As the rain rattled the tin roof, I braced myself against the wall, grainy and cold, one foot holding shut the door.

A thought occurs to her, making her sit up straight, making her wonder why she hadn't thought of it before.

'Have you ever done this before?'

He looks puzzled, seeming not to understand.

'Marcus, we've been together for five years – have you ever, in that time—'

He stands and comes across the room, towards the bed. He seems taller, bigger somehow in this room she's slept in alone for two months.

'Don't,' she orders, holding up her hands, 'don't come anywhere near me.'

But she hears the lack of conviction in her voice, and realises she is cold with the craving for physical contact. He crawls over the bed towards her, pulls her to him and as she registers the familiar breadth and smell and weight of him, she feels the first tears come. They surprise her – rapid and hot, they wrench up from her stomach and spill down her face.

'No,' Marcus is saying, as he holds her head to his chest, 'never, Sinead, never.'

'But how do I know?' she sobs against him. 'How do I know you've not been doing this all the way along? You might have been shagging left, right and centre the whole time.'

'I haven't. I promise you I haven't.'

'But how can I believe you?'

'Because I wouldn't do that to you.'

She shoves him away from her so hard he falls back on the bed. 'You just have,' she says.

Washed and dressed in clothes that still smelt of my house in England, I sat opposite him in a café. He hadn't eaten for a whole day, and ordered amazing amounts of food from the menu. Steamed dumplings in bamboo pots kept arriving, their tops pursed together like pale lips. I was feeling a bit peculiar, disjointed: my hunger had vanished and I seemed to be having difficulty in catching up with my life. Every time I glanced around me, and saw buffalo-drawn carts, a whole family on a single bicycle, a man dragging a goat on a string, I'd get a slight shock; I'd look at him, and think for a split second, who are you, and what I am doing here?

He pulled from his pocket a pair of metal chopsticks; with one hand he levered torn strips of dumpling into his mouth, with the other he sketched a diagram of a teacher-training college he'd seen in Beijing.

'The roof isn't fluted,' he was saying, 'like a pagoda, but slanted like this.'

I shifted in my seat, drawing up one leg under the other. It was late afternoon but we'd just emerged from bed. A secret ache pulled at the insides of my thighs. I felt a strange urge for cigarettes I'd given up four years previously.

Things have degenerated into cyclical exhaustion and worn tracks of unsatisfied anger. She is sobbing. Pain is bleeding across her forehead into her temples. The bed is covered in wet tissues. Marcus is lying on his front, his head propped up between his hands. They are both shouting.

'Are you telling me,' he is demanding, 'you've never, not once, in all the years we've been together, thought about sleeping with someone else?'

'No. Of course I'm not saying that. The point is—'

'Who?' he says sharply. 'Who have you wanted to sleep with?'

'Oh, for God's sake, Marcus, listen to me—'

'Tell me. Who?'

'Shut *up*. Just—'

'I want to know. Which men, out of all the ones we know—'

'All I'm saying is—'

'Why won't you tell me?'

'Because you're being stupid and jealous and because it's not important and because—'

'Look,' he says, slamming the sides of his hands into their mattress, 'if we split up—'

'If?' Sinead interjects. '*If?*' And before she's even aware of having made the decision, she says: 'Marcus, I'm walking out of here tomorrow morning.'

There is a silence. The air is filled with the noise of their panting breath. There's no traffic on the road outside. They stare at each other in shock.

'No,' he says, 'you can't. Sinead, you can't.'

She nods, miserable, tears sliding down her face to soak into her clothes and the bed and him. Pain and exhaustion and grief overwhelm her and she curls into herself as if with stomach cramps. She kicks her legs off the bed and lets her bodyweight carry her to the floor. Marcus leaps for the door, putting out his hand to keep it shut. She feels as if she might fall, but he holds her to him and suddenly she is face to face with him, the length of her against him.

'No,' he whispers, 'you can't leave. You mustn't. How can you say that? You mustn't ever leave.'

And she has to close her eyes to keep on nodding because she can't look at him at that proximity. He seizes her head between his hands, desperate, and turns her nodding into shaking, and she lets him, but as soon as his hands fall away, she starts nodding again.

When he leaned back in his chair to catch the eye of the waiter, I saw his loose-limbed easiness, the calm well-being that permeated his whole form. It gave me a kind of anxiety. I wanted to ask him: what would you have done if I hadn't come, or if I'd gone by the time you got here? I wanted to say: why did you ask me to come? And: what do you see for us, where will it all go?

But I didn't. When he said, 'Shall we go?' I nodded and started gathering up my things.

And then she is tired and his body close to hers is painful and familiar. She moves away, towards the window. Dawn is greying the light behind the blind. Consciousness of the streets, the people and the city beyond those glass panes filters back to her. The blue walls look black still, but morning is only a few hours away. She has to work tomorrow. She has to give a lecture in four hours.

'I have to sleep,' she says, and her voice sounds flat and deadened.

Behind her, Marcus steps towards her, but she draws away. The sudden movement from the bed has made the blood curdle in her head and she presses her hand to the wall for balance.

'I'm going to bed now,' she says.

'OK,' he says, and sits down on the bed, bringing up his foot as if to start untying his shoelaces.

'Marcus!' she says sharply. 'What are you doing?'

His head jerks up. 'Taking my shoes off.'

She stares at him, incredulous. 'You're not sleeping in here.'

Guilt and confusion criss-cross his face like car lights across a room at night. He gets up slowly and shuffles to the door. Stops. Turns. 'Sinead . . .'

She is getting undressed. She doesn't care. She just wants to be in bed, under the covers, her face pressed into the pillow. She lifts the dress over her head, lets it fall to the floor, unsnaps her bra, slides it off each arm. Eases the pants down her legs and kicks them into the corner. Climbs into bed.

He is still in the doorway. He hasn't finished his sentence. She doesn't care. He has watched her. She doesn't care. She pulls the covers up over her head. He leaves, closing the door behind him.

Sinead cries again almost immediately. She doesn't sleep, but pleats the cotton of the duvet into itself, winds her fingers into her hair, worries at a dent in the plaster with a pair of tweezers until, as the dawn light bleaches the room, there is a cone of dust on the mattress next to her.

We climbed a hill with a spherical hole through its centre. Marcus wanted to reach the top before sunset. The heat of the day had passed, scorching stones until they cracked open; but here, on a path next to a twisting, orange-bedded stream, under the dense vegetation, the air was dank and cool. There was the heavy smell of things rotting and regenerating. Monkeys chattered and shrieked overhead. A woman with a pole balanced on her shoulders and two round-eyed toddlers in buckets, fingers curled over the rims, jounced past us. *Ni hao, ni hao, ni hao*, we said.

At the top, Marcus pulled a paper bag full of lychees from his backpack and passed them to me, one by one, juggling their pitted, pinkish skin between his palms. I sat with my back against a tree. The sun swung across the hole in the hill. A virulently green beetle landed on my arm, its antennae extended and reeling in the air. I shook my wrist and it fell to the ground, legs scrabbling frantically. I flipped it over with a twig and it flew off, drunk with relief, wings invisible with movement.

The lychees had tough skin that could be pierced with a thumbnail, then peeled off like the shell of a boiled egg. Underneath was grey-white flesh, viscous, wet, the texture of eyeballs. In your mouth, they felt huge, almost choking, until your tongue split the sweet slipperiness and found the smooth, mahogany-coloured stone.

'Sinead,' Marcus said, his head in the crook between my thigh and stomach, 'if I ask you something do you promise to tell me the truth?'

I held a coil of lychee skin between my fingers. Its inside was already dry in the heat. When he'd arrived he'd had three-day-old stubble. He'd shaved after the shower and his face looked younger and softer now. His head was heavy. My innards shifted and resettled under the weight of it.

'That depends on what it is.'

Marcus opened his eyes, but focused on the tree branches and not me. 'What was someone like you doing with someone like Antony?'

I laughed and looked at how the paddy-fields below us were pulling down fragments of the silver-blue sky. 'I don't know,' I said. 'Why do you ask?'

'I was just wondering how he managed it. What's his secret?'

I laughed again. 'He's not that bad,' I said.

'No. Believe me, he is. He's an idiot. And smug into the bargain. After we'd all met that day in the supermarket, he used to talk about you to me all the time.'

I looked down at him. 'Did he?'

'Yeah. Every time I bumped into him at the department, it was Sinead and me this, Sinead and me that.' He closes his eyes and smiles. 'I wish he could see us now.'

'Now who's being smug?' I broke a twig into pieces with one hand. 'He's not that bad,' I said again. 'And you have to admit he's nice-looking.' Marcus grunted. 'But I suppose, if I'm honest, I'd say that there's not a great deal of choice in a place like that.'

Marcus smiled again. 'I thought so.'

When the bedside clock has unwound to seven thirty, Sinead gets up. She pulls out from under the bed a bag. She keeps her thoughts very practical: pants. I'll need pants. Bras. She lines the bottom of the bag with underwear. Trousers. Socks. Address book. Where is address book? In desk drawer. Pen? Also in drawer. Comb. By bed. Alarm clock. Next to comb. Toothbrush. In bathroom. Will get later. Also get cleanser, moisturiser, shampoo, pill packet—

She stops, hurries her thoughts along. OK, won't be needing pill packet, what else, what else? Tops! My God, can't go with only trousers. Red blouse. Green T-shirt and blue shirt. Blue sweater – oh, no, is in wash. Tears are falling now on to the blue shirt at the top of the bag. She scrubs at her face angrily. Panics. Starts dragging out the clothes she'll have to leave for now and come back for, but when, and how, and how can she leave all this and where is she going? Um, um, take that vest top and need my diary and – and – and—

I'm leaving.
I'm leaving.

Marcus is already in the kitchen by the time she comes out of the bedroom. She walks down the length of the room on her bare feet. He doesn't hear her and she can observe him as he rinses a glass at the sink, his neck curved, his shoulders hunched over, until he lifts the glass to the draining rack and his body uncurls, opens out, his back straightening. She wants to say: do you know how much I missed you, do you know how I longed for you all that time, do you know that I ticked off the weeks until your return like a traveller counting down the strung-out telegraph poles to home?

But she doesn't. She drops the bag to the floor. He jumps and looks up.

'OK. My turn,' I said. 'When did you decide you liked me?'

He crumbled a shard of lychee peeling between his fingers. 'The first moment I met you. When you opened your front door.'

'Really?' I was impressed.

'Sinead, I—' He sees the bag at her feet, and stops. She waits. He says nothing, so she goes into the bathroom and starts collecting her things. Toothbrush. In a mug with Aidan's and—

Toothpaste? No. Wherever she goes will have toothpaste. Face cream. By the bath. Razor – no, will get later. Later? Another time. Whenever. Makeup remover. Open cabinet, avoiding reflection, which looks puffed and swollen

and old: cotton wool, vitamin pills, hair serum, conditioner.
These things she piles into her arms. Her pill packet she
hurls, with a flick of her wrist, to the top of the cabinet.

Back in the kitchen, Marcus is sitting at the table. She
walks across the room and empties what she is holding
into the open, waiting mouth of the bag. Zips it up.
Ready to go.

'I made you breakfast,' he says.

'Why didn't you come and find me sooner?'

'Because . . .' Marcus blinked into the sun, thinking
'. . . because I didn't think you were interested. I mean, I
thought you might be, but I wasn't sure. You're quite hard
to read, you know.'

'So it wasn't the fact that I happened to be with
someone else?'

'Oh, God, no.' He grinned. 'I wouldn't let a little
thing like that stand in my way. Especially if it was only
Antony.'

Sinead sits opposite him at the table. She doesn't look at him
but looks down. Two slices of toast are on a plate in front of
her. A yellow slab of butter. A jar of marmalade, twists of
stippled peel suspended in orange jelly. A thin, blunt-bladed
knife with a bone handle. Water in a glass. Is it the same one
he was washing a minute ago? No, there it is, still drying on
the rack. It's the same type – a thick bottom like a lens, and
octagonal sides. She's always liked the solid, geometric-ness
of them. They bought them together in—

'I know you're not really going,' she hears him say.

She is surprised. And doesn't know what to say. So she says nothing. He scrapes the blade of his knife over the surface of the toast. *Skkklllrrrufff*. Reaches the end of it into the marmalade pot.

At that moment, Aidan appears out of his room. Marcus lets his knife fall into the pot and turns quickly, almost nervously. 'Aidan! Hi!'

Aidan grunts. Sinead doesn't look up, but sees his feet pace towards the kitchen, hesitate, then move towards her. He is bending over her, very close, close enough for her to catch a wave of him – soap, washing-powder, leather from the jacket he's holding. She turns to him involuntarily and sees that he is looking right into her face. His hand is outstretched for the car keys on the table next to her. His fingers curl round them, then he is dropping them into his pocket, struggling into his jacket, crossing to the door, through it, and gone.

Sinead stands, pulls a cardigan around her, pushes her feet into her shoes, and goes over to her bag. She can't find a way to hold it that's comfortable: gripped in her hand it knocks against her leg; over her shoulder it pulls too much on her neck. Stupid design for a bag. Where did she get it anyway? She settles for it hooked over her forearm and makes for the door.

'Why did you agree to come?'

'I don't know,' I said.

'Not good enough,' he retorted. 'Try again.'

'Um,' I writhed under his head, shifting my legs, readjusting the curve of my body, 'I . . . er . . . Well,' I said, suddenly cross, 'you just disappeared. One minute

I couldn't even go shopping without you appearing to tell me what and what not to buy and then suddenly you fell off the end of the earth. And . . . I . . . well . . . I don't know.'

Marcus rolled up on to his knees and kissed me, his tongue cool, sweetened with lychee juice.

Marcus reaches the door before she does. 'Sinead, don't go,' he pleads, in a low, panicked voice. 'Please don't go. I'm so . . . so sorry. What I did was so fucking stupid. *Stupid.*' He bites down on his fingers. His face is wild, afraid. 'I don't know what came over me. Please. I can't . . . I can't bear the thought of losing you. Please don't go. Please.'

'I'm going,' she says simply.

'But just for a few days. OK? Then we'll talk. You can't just leave. Not like this. We need to talk about this more.' He clutches her arm.

'No.' She shakes him off. 'I'm going.'

'Well, where? Where are you going?'

'I don't know yet.'

'Sinead,' he says, 'for God's sake. You can't just walk out on me like this. You can't. OK, I did a stupid thing – a really stupid thing – but you can't just leave. After five years, for Chrissake, you can't just drop me like this. Please.'

She pulls open the door and she can hardly see the staircase in front of her, which leads down into the depths of the building, and before she heads off down it she turns and slides her arm around Marcus's neck and presses her mouth to his because now she is leaving and not coming back and because it will be the last time, and it feels strange because she is crying and they are both shaking and her face is soaked and slippery and it doesn't feel like it should and she pulls away in case it starts to and before his arms can imprison her and pull her to him as she knows they will.

Suddenly she is alone and walking down the stairs and she can hear him calling her name, over and over, and the strap of the bag is cutting into her shoulder and she concentrates on this – and how she wishes she couldn't hear him shout – and putting one foot down below the other until she is out in the street.

'Why don't you come and live with me in London?'

I was appalled. It was said in exactly the same, conversationally curious voice as his other enquiries. I looked at him and this time his blue eyes were directed right to the retinas of mine.

'What?' I said, nervous. Maybe I'd misheard him. He couldn't have just asked me to move in with him. Could he?

'I've got this space,' he said. 'My parents are going to lend me the money. To do it up. It's my first ever project.'

'Space?' I repeated stupidly.

'Yeah, you know, a warehouse. It's an old Victorian garment factory. Top floor.'

'Victorian?'

'Well, thereabouts. Early Victorian, I think. Big.' He holds wide his arms, then drops them. 'It's in a bit of a state right now. It's a bit like camping, living there. There's no bathroom, or kitchen, or anything. But it could be beautiful – will be beautiful. It's near—'

'Look,' I shouted, pushing him away and staggering to my feet, 'you can't just . . . just go around doing this all the time.'

'Doing what?'

'You know what I mean.' I was standing with my hands on my hips. I almost started wagging my finger at him. 'This . . . this . . . upping the ante all the time. Saying things . . . like that.'

'But I'm in love with you.'

'There!' I shrieked, putting my hands over my ears. 'That's precisely the kind of thing I mean! You can't say that!'

'Why not?'

'Because — because we've spent exactly one afternoon together . . . and . . . and you hardly know me.'

'I don't care. I do love you. You know that.'

'No, I don't,' I blurted childishly.

'Yes, you do. I would hardly have asked you to come out to China otherwise, would I? You knew that when I called you from the Friendship Store.'

I was silent, ruminating.

'And you know what else?' he said.

'What?'

'You wouldn't have come unless you loved me.'

That was too much. Temper fizzed in my sternum, kindled by incredulity and outrage. I snatched up the bag of lychees and began pelting him with the hard, pink orbs.

'You arrogant swine,' I shouted. 'I've never met anybody so . . . fucking cocksure in all my life.'

The lychees were bouncing off his face and head. He

lunged at me, catching me round the waist. I battered his back and shoulders with my fists. 'Get off me! Let go!'

Straightening up, he grasped my flailing wrists in his hands and, with one of his feet, hooked out my feet from under me. Suddenly the sky was wheeling above my head and the ground came up to meet me. I didn't land hard on my back – he was holding on to me, breaking my fall – but as soon as I reached the ground, he had me pinned down. Astonished and infuriated, I wrestled and fought under his grip, but he remained effortlessly above me, laughing.

'Temper, temper,' he said. 'I misspent lots of my youth in judo classes. You might want to remember that. For future reference.'

I tussled and snarled, twisting my head round, trying to bite his wrist. 'I'd never live with you!' I spat. 'Never!'

'Really?'

'And I don't love you – I hate you!'

'Is that right? Well, I love you.'

'Fuck you! Let – me – go.'

'No. Not until you promise to move in with me.'

'I'd never live in your poxy, stinking warehouse – especially not with you.'

'Not even if I paid you?'

I laughed. I couldn't help it. Sweat was soaking into my hair and into the T-shirt, which was clinging to my ribs. I stopped struggling, exhaustion simmering down my fury. 'How much?'

'I don't know. What's the going rate for a concubine these days?'

'How about a tenner an hour and extra for sex?'

'You drive a hard bargain, Sinead Wilson.' He sat back on his heels, pretending to think. 'But your rates seem reasonable.' He nodded. 'It's a deal.'

'OK.'

'You promise?'

'I promise,' I said meekly.

He released his hold from around my wrists. Sensation surged back into my hands. I got up and began brushing grit, twigs and small stones from my back. Marcus picked bits of leaves from my hair.

'You know what?' I said, slowly and quietly.

'What?'

I raised my hand to his face and held it before his eyes. The second finger was crossed over the first.

'Looks like you'll be very lonely in your Victorian warehouse.'

He snatched at my arm, but I was too quick for him, darting from his reach and setting off down the winding path, my boots pounding the stone steps. I heard him thundering after me. Laughter tore up from my throat and my heart sent spurts of blood shooting round my system.

Further down the path, he'd catch up with me and I'd shove him into the stream. He'd be so wet he'd have to take off his clothes and then we'd both disappear for a while into the thick undergrowth where no one could see us.

But for now we were chasing at speed down a twisting path on a hill in south-west China, the light of the day draining out of the sky above us.

Sinead is waiting on the platform for the train that will take her to Michael's house. She hasn't called him to say she's coming: she didn't know how to explain it, how to phrase it in words.

Minutes flick by on the station clock above her head. Blackened pigeons roo-coo in the metal beams of the roof arch. A man opposite her stares with brute curiosity as she cries, tears soaking her coat front and gloves.

It is very simple. Yesterday you had a boyfriend; today you don't. Yesterday you had a flat where you lived; today you're homeless.

She would have been going to Phoebe's launch tonight. She imagines that, in some parallel universe, the person she was yesterday afternoon still exists, that somehow her identity has bifurcated and somehow somewhere she – or someone who looks and sounds like her – is holding hands with Marcus as they walk through the streets to Phoebe's gallery. She can see this Sinead: she is dressed in a tight-seamed skirt, black-tongued boots and a coat with ostrich feathers curled into the neck. She is holding a bottle of wine under her arm. She and Marcus are talking about Phoebe's funny friends, about Phoebe's gallery; they are saying that they won't stay long, that they'll go for a bit then they'll walk back, get a mini-cab, maybe, from a small, lighted room at the side of a road, and when they get back home they'll unwrap each other like gifts.

part | three

We live our lives, for ever taking leave

RAINER MARIA RILKE

Lily pushes the ends of her fingers, nail deep, into a slit between the planks of the table top. The wood is crusted with the delicate fractals of frost, but somehow doesn't feel as cold as it should.

Sinead has stopped. Her breath leaves her body in grey-white streams. She is shaking, either from the cold or from the effort of not crying, Lily can't tell which. She sits turned away from her, legs straddling the bench. Behind her, the Thames slips through the city, a black ribbon splintered with light. Ink-dark clouds race over their heads.

It seems peculiar to be sitting on the South Bank at a picnic table on a winter night. They are surrounded by other, identical tables, all deserted and whitened by frost. A strange muffled silence stretches between the river and the high concrete wall of the Royal Festival Hall. When people pass, giving them no more than a quick glance, their footsteps make no sound.

When they'd sat down together like this, Lily's head had been filled with the protocols of other meetings – you buy a coffee, a drink, discuss where to sit, engage in chat about how you are, what you've been up to. But with this there was nothing – no drink on the table between them, no preamble. There was only one purpose, and Sinead launched straight in.

Lily clears her throat. Sinead looks up, as if she'd forgotten she was there.

'So you left,' Lily says. She finds she cannot look into her eyes. Sinead must feel the same because as she talked she stared dead ahead of her. When their eyes do meet, it feels too acute, almost dangerous.

'Yes.'

'The next day?'

'The next morning.'

Lily rubs her chilled fingertips against her sleeve. 'And you haven't been back?'

Sinead shrugs. 'I came back to get my stuff.'

Lily nods, remembering. 'But after five years,' she struggles to control her incredulity, 'and that's it? One conversation and then you went?'

Sinead presses her teeth into her lip. 'There was . . . I didn't exactly have much choice.'

Lily senses their conversation is over. Part of her has a weird impulse to reciprocate, to tell Sinead something – a secret, a story, anything. To stop herself, she stands up, 'I must go.'

'Lily,' Sinead says her name quickly, in a new, thin voice.

'Yes?'

'Would you mind . . .' she begins unsteadily, her teeth gritted, as if the words are being dragged from her against her will. 'Can I ask you a question?'

'Sure.'

Sinead breathes in. 'When did you meet Marcus? I mean, when did things between you and him start?'

Lily feels in her pockets for her gloves, somehow knowing that whatever she says won't be the right answer. 'It was at a party. At a gallery.'

Sinead stares her straight in the eye. 'Phoebe's exhibition launch,' she murmurs.

Lily nods, shifting from one foot to the other. 'Well, I must be off,' she says awkwardly. 'Thanks.'

As soon as the word leaves her lips, she regrets it, wants to snatch it back from the air. Sinead gives a short laugh. 'For what?' she says. 'For Marcus?'

'No. I meant—'

'You're welcome to him,' she snaps.

Lily scratches her head. 'Goodbye, then.'

Sinead doesn't reply.

She climbs the worn metal steps of Hungerford Bridge two at a time, resting a hand on her knee for balance. At the top she stops, reaches into her pockets and drops what change she has into the battered polystyrene cup of a boy wrapped in a sleeping-bag. 'Thanks,' he calls after her, then returns to his mantra: 'Spare some change, please, spare some change.'

Half-way across she stops, leans on the metal barrier, and looks back to the Royal Festival Hall. The glass front of the building glows with yellow-orange light and people stream out of its doors. Sinead is still sitting at the wooden table, hunched against the cold. As Lily watches, she sees her stand, step clear of the bench, sling her bag on to her shoulder, and walk away towards Waterloo.

These things happen.

Sinead's words are only now beginning to sink in. As they sat together, all Lily could think was, there she is, right in front of her, talking, telling her. But it's only now, as distance stretches between them again, that Lily can start to turn over in her head what she'd said.

She looks down into the water. Boats glide, lit up and vibrating with music, under the bridge. She remembers, years ago, a story in a newspaper about two students – law students, were they? – who got into a fight on this bridge and were thrown over, their bodies washed up by the Thames Barrier days later. She wonders if Sinead had been watching her.

By the time she gets back, Marcus is asleep, the flat dark. She pushes at his door and peers into the gloom. He is lying on his back, one arm flung above his head.

Exactly. I wasn't exactly.

She kneels on the mattress. Marcus sighs and turns his head, his neck flashing white in the dark. But his eyes are still closed. Lily, scanning the room quickly, stretches out beside him, fully clothed.

Her hand moves out to touch his face, her fingertips meeting the ceraceous, heated skin of his cheek. She leans over him, watching his eyes flicker beneath the lids. Her hand moves up towards the fragile, membranous pale of his temple where the bone of the head is at its thinnest. She pictures his skull, grey-white, minutely pitted, fused along meandering lines. Just beneath her fingers cells swell, pulsate and quiver.

Lily has never had a secret before. Not a big one. At breakfast the next morning she feels it curled inside her, hot and breathing. Marcus has an architectural magazine propped up against the teapot, folded vertically, the pages furled. His eyes zoom from one side of the column of words to the next. Then he is talking, saying something to her about a job he's working on, a film he wants to see, a person he spoke to yesterday. With one hand, he stirs milk into his cereal with a spoon. The other rests on the table top, the nails blunt and clipped. Lily pours tea into her mug but lets the heat ebb out of it.

She breathes in through her mouth, feeling the air rushing past her teeth, and holds it. There are sentences crammed into her throat, waiting. Marcus has stopped speaking. He is transfixed by an invisible point midway between the sofa and the fridge, his jaw held in a crooked, concentrated set, mid-chew, his spoon still, resting on the side of his bowl. He is thinking about Sinead. Lily sees this and the secret twitches and vibrates inside her, the sentences twisting helix-like into confusion. She exhales, allowing the air to pass out through her nostrils. It makes a louder rushing sound than she intended and Marcus is roused from his reverie. He blinks, glances towards her, then down at his breakfast. His spoon hand resumes.

'I'm off now.' She walks towards the door. She hasn't eaten any breakfast. There is a kind of ascetic pleasure in her light-headedness, her hollow abdomen.

Aidan stands in the middle of the skeletal structure of his new, semi-erected bed. Metal struts lie scattered like jack straws all over the floor. In his left hand he holds an Allen key – ridiculously small, he feels, for the magnitude of this operation. In his right is an unfolded sheet of instructions. So-called instructions. He doesn't have the right kind of brain for this sort of thing, or doesn't speak the right language. He's not the right species with the right set of adapted physical features. If survival of the fittest depended on furniture construction from flat-packs, the Aidan Nashs of this world would have died out long ago. He only has to glance at the instruction sheet – large, white, with complex, incomprehensible diagrams of unidentified parts of furniture fitting effortlessly into other equally unidentifiable parts – and his mind just melts into a horrible, stultifying mix of boredom and frustration.

'Jodie,' he calls.

There is no answer. He can hear her and Rory, who appears to have a temporary reprieve, unpacking crockery in the kitchen, the click of china against china that takes him back to his teenage years, in his bedroom, listening out for when dinner would be ready.

'Jodie!'

His sister appears round the door, her arms folded. 'Hey, flat-pack king, how's it going?'

'I am not the flat-pack king. If flat-packing were a feudal system, I'd be the lowliest serf in history. I wouldn't even be a swineherd,' he mutters, looking around for something called 'axel B'. 'I'd be the swineherd's . . . au pair.'

Jodie laughs. 'Why are you putting the table up in the bedroom, Aide?'

'Very funny.' He is forced to take small, mincing steps through the heap of metal struts and packaging material towards her. 'Hilarious, in fact. Now, can you help me find axel B? It looks like this.' He stabs the instruction sheet with his finger. 'Do you see anything like that here?' He waves wildly at the heap of metal and wooden objects. 'Anything at all? No. Do you know why? Because you don't actually need it. Why would any bed need anything that resembles a small egg whisk? It's all a conspiracy to make you think it's worth spending an extortionate amount of money on a heap of junk.'

'Stop being silly,' she snatches the paper out of his hand, 'and give it to me. Honestly, sometimes I really think—'

The doorbell sounds, shrill and unfamiliar. They look up, surprised.

'Shall I get it?' Rory calls from the kitchen.

'No, I'll go.' Aidan dashes from the room. 'It'll be Sinead.'

He hardly has any time even to lay eyes on her before

she is over the threshold and pressing her glass-cold cheek to his. Then she is off down the hallway, hanging up her coat with the others on the pegs, and into the front room.

'God, Aidan, it's such a nice street,' she is saying, 'really close to the tube. And that amazing ivy all over the front of the house.' She turns to him and smiles. The light in the empty room, filtered through the ivy leaves, seems to oscillate around her, green and cool as river water. 'Can I have a guided tour?'

She is silent in every room: the hall, the kitchen, the lounge. She walks the perimeters, looking up, looking down, looking from side to side – everywhere but at him. Anxiety begins to pulse at his temples. On the stairs, she presses her palm to the wallpaper of dark, twisted, sinuous fronds and branches growing up the stairwell, then moves on. At the top, she turns.

'Aidan, it's beautiful. Really beautiful.' Her voice is serious, modulated, her eyes rapt.

His heart opens like a book and he climbs the last two steps to reach her. 'You think?' He has to be looking at the stretch of the banister, back down to the front door, as if checking it for straightness.

'Yes. Absolutely beautiful.' She enunciates each syllable. He can almost taste them on the air between them.

'Come and see the bedroom, and meet Jodie.'

His sister appears around the door. Sometimes their twinness strikes him as an odd impossibility: he looks at her and cannot imagine their bodies pocketed together in the same womb. And sometimes – often when he is alone – he feels an absence in the air around him, a chill down one side of his body that makes him shiver. Their mother told them that, in the final days, Jodie's foot had been pressed against Aidan's right ear, folded like an envelope against his head; and that when he was born it stuck straight out. They had to bind it back with 'the gentlest Sellotape'. He touches it now, his right ear, as Jodie leans forward and takes Sinead's hand in hers. He wants these two to be friends so much he almost can't bear them to meet.

'Aidan's making a right mess of putting his bed together,' Jodie is saying. Rory hovers just behind her, doing that united-front thing that couples always do when they're introduced to someone. 'Are you any good with flat-packs?'

'Let's have a look.'

Aidan stands in the doorway as Sinead inverts a long, wooden panel and stands it on its end.

'No,' she says to Jodie, 'wait. This must be part of that.'

Jodie stops, and the two of them bend over the instructions.

'You're right.' They look about them, hands on hips. 'If that fits in there, then that means—'

'That this one goes here.'

They laugh at their own ingenuity. Rory, by the window, looks over at Aidan and shrugs. 'I'm going out to get some wine,' he says.

All the surrounding rooms are still and empty; this room, the kitchen, vibrates with food and talk and people and candles. My flat, Aidan thinks, and leans back in his chair. Sinead has soaked a napkin in melted candle wax and is poking the flame with its edges, the light flaring up to pool on the ceiling.

'That's not the point, though, is it?' Rory says.

'It is!' Jodie exclaims.

'It's exactly the point,' Sinead chimes in, hooking her feet around the chair legs so that she seems to levitate out of her seat.

A week ago, in a restaurant, Sinead had told him that her favourite food at the moment was rocket. 'A highly incongruous name, don't you think?' she'd said, as she held up a fragile, limp, serrated leaf. He'd bought it for her tonight, but most of it lies untouched on her plate. Her clavicle is more pronounced than last week, he notices. Unless you knew, he thinks, she does a pretty good job of pretending. Unless you knew, you'd never be able to guess that underneath all that – the smile, the hair, the chat, the careful makeup, the exact clothes – was a broken heart. He imagines it as a fractured china cup in a paper bag, with sharp, snagged edges that could rip open its casing with one slight move.

'But the problem with those kind of trousers,' Jodie says, 'is that everyone can tell what kind of pants you're wearing. I think that's more information than most of my colleagues need.'

Sinead laughs, 'Yeah, but have you seen those high-cut maxi-briefs?' She shakes her head. 'Not pretty.'

Women are amazing. Within two hours of meeting, they're discussing underwear. Aidan stacks up plates and carries them to the as yet unused draining-board. Rory lifts his wineglass from the debris on the table and wanders into the front room. Aidan turns the tap, feeling the pleasure of doing something for the first time that you know you'll be doing over and over again. Water drums into the aluminium sink. A reverberating bass suddenly sounds from the other room and he realises Rory must have got the stereo up and running. There is a slow run of notes, a shift in tempo, then a woman's voice – high and pure – floats out over the top.

His body acts faster than his mind. He is letting the plate he is washing slide back into the water and turning towards her while his thought processes are still catching up: why does this music give him a strange feeling and where has he heard it before and who does it remind him of and someone, who is it, plays this track over and over.

The effect on Sinead is faster and more dramatic. She crumples into herself, her face sliding into horror and fear. She starts up, stumbles across the kitchen, clamping her hands over her mouth and nose as a kind of coughing sob tears out of her. 'Oh, Christ,' they hear her say, and she is scrabbling at the clasp of the windowed doors and then is out into the garden, swallowed up by the gloom.

'Shit,' says Jodie.

'Get Rory to turn that off,' Aidan says, as he pushes through the doors after her.

The garden is cold and not yet familiar enough for him to navigate with confidence in the dark. He is striding through the dew-soaked grass when the black shape of a tree looms up in front of him. He stops, rests his hand against knotted bark. Listens. Distant traffic. The spiralling threads of the music still going inexorably on. Stifled sobbing coming from – where? He dips his head, leans closer to the tree. The far wall. Near the crappy ornamental fountain. He edges closer.

'Sinead?' he half whispers.

He comes upon her more quickly than he thought. She has both hands over her mouth and is bending over as if in physical pain. The sound she is making is not inhuman, but it's like nothing he's heard before – high, ululating, childlike. He hesitates, wondering what kind of sound it would be if she took her hands away and let rip, how loud it would be, how many gardens it would travel. He puts a hand on her shoulder. 'Sinead.' He can't think of what he wants to say. 'Please,' is what comes out. 'Please don't. Please.'

She straightens up, still with her head averted, still with her hands over her mouth. Then he has his arms around her, tight, and her body is shuddering against his.

'I'm sorry, I'm sorry, I'm so sorry,' she is saying between sobs, and he is telling her to hush, his chin against her hair, and her fingers gripping the wool of his jumper, her face crushed into his chest.

'Sssh,' he says, 'it's all right now, it's all right.'

The music is abruptly silenced and they are surrounded by dark and stillness and quiet. Her sobbing is slower now, less high-pitched and frantic. He feels her shift in his arms and he wonders if she wants him to let her go, if she wants to step away, and he loosens his hold on her, but she is just moving her face, letting her head fall into the curve of his neck. Aidan puts his arms around her again.

'It's all right,' he murmurs. 'You're going to be all right.'

It's never usually possible to pinpoint when a friendship

begins, the moment when a casual acquaintance moves up a gear. It's usually a gradual, incremental process that takes place over many evenings, or many drinks or many chats on the phone; a slow attrition of differences or a slow discovery of similarities. But with Sinead it's easy. Aidan can narrow it down to the day, the hour, the minute: when she phoned him on the morning she'd left Marcus. He'd been in the office, working at something on screen and had picked up his phone, unthinking, to hear her voice: 'You knew, didn't you?' He had sat up straight, knocking his mouse to the floor. 'All that time, you knew. Sinead—' he'd begun, scrabbling to retrieve his mouse, already knowing he could never lie to her.

'God,' she says, pulling away. 'I'm so sorry, Aidan. It's ridiculous.' She half laughs, wiping at her face, 'I can't go two hours these days without this happening.'

'That's OK,' he says. The sudden distance between them, filled with chilled autumn air, makes it seem more difficult to comfort her.

'I'm really sorry,' she mutters, her breathing still unsteady, as she turns to go back up the garden. 'It's stupid. It really is.'

He follows her. Her tears have soaked into his neck. Later that night, when he undresses, he'll find mascara-black trails where they ran down his body.

Aidan was quite good with jet-lag. He'd had to get used to it in a job that could send him half-way round the world without a day's notice. So when he arrived in New York he'd been surprised to feel it – a slight nausea, a thickening of the head, leaden limbs – while he was sitting on the bus taking him to Manhattan Island, bag on knee, passport still clutched in his hand.

By the time he reached his hotel, it was worse. He stumbled into his room, tripping on the rug, and closed the door. He'd intended to unpack his laptop, lay out his notes in preparation for the next day's meeting. But he reckoned later that he must have fallen asleep before he actually hit the mattress because his last recollection was crawling over what seemed like metres and metres of crinkly, haemorrhage-red counterpane.

When he woke, sensations filtered through to his consciousness like images on to photographic paper. The light outside was a liquid indigo. He was lying on his back, diagonally across the bed. Incredible thirst. Cold from the air-con. Light too bright. Tongue dry and swollen. Traffic and sirens from the street below.

He turned on to his side, his vision swimming with nausea and exhaustion. He sat up, and tentatively shook his head. Was he drunk? Hung-over? Ill, perhaps? He hadn't yet worked out where he was and what he was doing here. But this was nothing too unusual: he hadn't 'lived' anywhere for the past three years, spending months in Japan, then New York, then LA, then Berlin, then London and then back again. Hotel rooms. Temporary apartments. But that had all changed. He was now going to be based permanently in London. He was buying a flat. His own flat.

Aidan flopped back on to the pillow. It was all coming back to him now: he had accepted a contract with the UK-based branch of an American firm. He was staying at

Marcus's place. With Sinead. While he waited for everything to be sorted with his flat. While Marcus was working in New York. Which was here, in fact. Where Aidan was right now. A hotel in New York. To finalise the designs on an animated music video.

A red light was flashing on the phone next to his head. He turned, stabbed at it with his index finger, and listened blearily to a recorded electronic voice. A message from Marcus to meet him at eight at the corner of Broadway and 57th. He brought his left arm up in front of his face and stared at his watch as if he'd never seen it before. Its round face, reinforced with black plastic, a neat circle of tiny numbers. The lurid, pointing hands, split like protractors. He'd heard about a woman who, in the days when they used uranium for glow-in-the-dark watches, used to lick the tip of her brush before painting the luminous clock face. Ingested all that carcinogenic poison over years and years. Died of leukaemia in the end.

Aidan squeezed his eyes shut then popped them open again and, with effort, squinted at his watch. Small hand – seven. Large hand – three. Or between three and four. Which meant? Seven twenty. Shit.

He leaped off the bed and waited until he regained his balance. His clothes felt stale and stiff, but there was no time to change. He slapped his pockets: wallet, hotel keys and the crinkle of paper in his breast pocket. Aidan pushed his fingers into it and felt hard, sealed edges. Envelope. He remembered: Sinead's letter for Marcus that she'd given him this morning. He'd seen her fold the tightly written pages into three, slide it into an envelope, lick its edges and press them down. Yesterday morning. Whenever.

The bones in his legs felt jointless and malleable as he walked down Central Park West. Joggers and rollerbladers lashed past him. He wondered about hailing a cab, but decided the air would do him good. To his left, the trees of the park rustled and swayed; two men were throwing a baseball between them, the orange sphere ricochetting through the darkening air. His neck and shoulders were crunched up, his forehead stretched with the beginnings of a headache, and as he walked he tried rolling his arms inside their sockets to relieve the pulling on his neck.

At the intersection of Broadway and 57th was a Duane Reade chemist's shop. The apartment Marcus was renting until the job finished was further west towards the Hudson River. After checking up the street to see if he was coming, Aidan ducked into the shop to buy some painkillers. He hadn't seen Marcus for six months, having moved into the flat after he'd already left for New York, and didn't want to be dragged down by a headache.

He stumbled up and down the aisles. Nail varnish. Moisturisers. Shampoos. Toothbrushes. Chocolate. Potato chips. A song came on the store's intercom, a hit from about fifteen years ago; a song that at one point he and Marcus used to listen to when they were at school, on Marcus's Walkman with two headsets. He hoped that Marcus would arrive before it ended, so that he could drag him into this strip-lit shop to listen. Razors. Vitamins. Suntan lotion. His body clock thought it was one in the morning. Toiletry bags. Hair accessories. Leg waxers. Sanitary towels. Slimming powders. Deodorants. Pharmaceuticals. At last.

He stood by the display of coloured, striped, logoed boxes, mesmerised. Throat sweets. Hayfever sprays. Antiseptic cream. Painkillers. There were twenty or so varieties. Did he want Tylenol, Motrin, Advil, Excedrin or Anacin? Soluble or insoluble? Aidan rubbed his palm over his face, smelling sweat and fatigue, stale air and travel. Coated or non? Capsules or pills? Caffeinated or not? Bottled or foil-wrapped?

Then there was a hand pulling at his shoulder and Marcus's voice, oddly American in intonation: 'Hey, Aide, how are you doing?'

He was grinning, tanned and dressed in his architect uniform, sunglasses hanging, folded, from his grey shirt pocket. A jumper was tied by its arms round his waist. Aidan moved forward with a slight lurching movement, pleased to see him yet confused, unable to remember how he and Marcus usually greeted each other, whether they hugged or shook hands or nodded or did nothing.

'You look rough,' Marcus said, as he closed his fingers briefly around Aidan's. 'When did you get in?'

'Couple of hours ago.'

'New jacket?'

'Yeah. You like it?'

'No.'

They smiled at each other, their right arms falling to their sides in unison.

'So, have you had to touch base yet?' Marcus said.

'*Touch base?*' Aidan repeated, one eyebrow raised (an

ability of his that Marcus had always envied). 'Where are you from? California?'

'Yeah, very funny. Listen, what do you fancy doing tonight?'

'I'm not sure. I'm feeling a bit wrecked to tell you the truth, so—'

'Oh, don't be such a wuss. We have to go out. You're only here for . . . how long is it?'

'Five days.'

'Exactly. So I think we should head down to SoHo and—'

Marcus broke off. Two American-Chinese women were coming down the aisle towards them, chatting, wire baskets bumping against their legs. Aidan didn't really look at them, but noticed at this point that one had cropped, spiked hair, and the other a long, silky ponytail and an impossibly short suede dress. Aidan stepped aside to let them past, still waiting for Marcus to finish his sentence. But Marcus was holding his ground, hands on hips. He was widening his eyes and grimacing, and for a second Aidan didn't know what he was doing, pulling a strange face like that, and was wondering if there was anything wrong, when he saw that he was grinning at the two women, who were staring at them, then looking at each other, then laughing and looking back at them. 'Hi,' the short-haired one said as they passed.

What happened next happened fast: the women walked on, one glancing over her shoulder, towards the end of the aisle. Marcus touched Aidan's sleeve, said, 'Hang on,' and went after them. 'Hi. Hi. Hello,' he heard him saying to them, stepping between them, 'how are you?'

They giggled. The long-haired one hoisted her basket on to the other arm. 'Are you British?' he heard her say.

And Aidan just watched. Either jet-lag or surprise or disbelief or all three kept his mental deductions at bay. When his friend disappeared around the corner with the two women, Aidan found himself actually turning back to the pharmaceutical display and selecting a blue box of Advil. Then he walked into the next aisle and picked up a small bottle of mineral water. As he approached the till, he glanced around for Marcus but, not seeing him, stood in line and waited.

Just as he was handing over his purchases and feeling around for his wallet, something came through the air, whizzing past his ear, to crash-land on the counter in front of him. Aidan jumped back in surprise, then saw what it was. A box of condoms. Three. Trojans. Spermicidally lubricated.

Marcus appeared next to him, delving in his pockets and bringing out a ten-dollar bill. 'Right. OK. We're sorted,' he said, 'Thanks,' he said to the cashier, as she gave him his change, and, handing Aidan his things, pushed the condoms into his back pocket. 'They're heading for a club over in TriBeCa,' he began, in a low voice, as they walked towards the door, 'but not till later. We could meet them there or we could all go for a drink first. What do you think?'

Aidan's brain was picking up the momentum of what was happening. He stopped just outside the door so abruptly that Marcus fell into him.

'What are you doing?' he said.

Marcus blinked. 'What do you mean?'

'What do I mean? I mean what are you playing at?'

He gestured at the women, standing a few yards off on the sidewalk – who, he now noticed, were probably still teenagers – and back at Marcus's pocket where the condoms were. He watched, incredulous, as a weary smile insinuated itself into Marcus's features.

'Aidan, you're not going to come over all pious on me, are you?'

Fury flared in Aidan's chest, adrenaline arrowing through his system, banishing all traces of exhaustion. 'Pious?' he repeated. '*Pious?* This has absolutely fuck all to do with piety. Does the word "Sinead" mean anything to you? Anything at all?'

At the mention of her name, something flickered in Marcus's face. Something recognisable, identifiable. Then it was gone, as quickly as it had come. 'Look,' he said, 'I think we should go for a drink with these two. Are you up for that or not?'

Aidan stared at him, aghast. 'No. I'm not.'

'So what do you want to do?'

'Marcus—' he began, then stopped. 'I just think—' Vocabulary eluded him. 'Do what you want.' He waved his hand at him. 'We – we can't talk about this now.'

Marcus didn't answer, but stood where he was, his face turned towards the girls, one foot balanced, jiggling, on top of the other. 'I can't desert you like that,' he muttered, still not looking at him. Aidan watched him, wary, curious as to which way he would go.

'You're really jet-lagged, are you? You're just going to go to bed?' Marcus said, turning his face back to Aidan. 'So give me a call tomorrow at the office, OK?' Aidan was silent. 'All right,' Marcus said, ignoring the fact that he'd had no reply. 'I'll speak to you then.'

Aidan watched as his friend walked off, flanked by the two women, down Broadway. He went to rub one hand against the other and discovered that he was holding a plastic bag containing the Advil and the water, and remembered his headache. He felt as if he was peering out of a mask of pain, his head throbbing, his eyes smarting in his skull.

Aidan had spent the day arguing over the anthropomorphisation of a penguin. Corners of his brain still twitched with images of the video footage they'd been watching on a big conference screen: penguins sliding down glaciers, penguins sleek-swimming in barely liquid Arctic waters, penguins shuffling over their eggs.

Walking back to his hotel, he scrolled through his mobile messages. He'd diverted five calls from Marcus, telling himself he was too busy, that it was rude to answer his phone when in a meeting, that he'd call him back later.

As he was walking across his hotel lobby – a monstrosity of curtain-glass walls, plastic ivy plants and explosions of fairy lights – towards the lifts, he saw him, sprawled across a seat in the bar, one leg hooked over the side of the chair, reading a folded-up paper. Aidan hesitated, looked at the lift doors, the illuminated descending arrows, then back at his friend. He walked over to him. 'Hello,' he said, when he got within two feet of him.

Marcus leaped up, standing to attention as if Aidan were a teacher and Marcus a pupil wishing to ingratiate himself: 'Hi!'

Aidan readjusted his bag, where the strap was cutting into his shoulder. He felt as if the weight of it was driving him into the deep pile of the carpet, that if he stayed standing there any longer he might never move again.

'So,' Marcus said, rolling the paper into a funnel in his hands, 'how are you?'

'OK.'

'Have you finished for the day?'

'Yeah.'

'Do you want to go and get something to eat?'

Aidan shifted his feet. Static from the carpet sparked under his shoe soles. 'OK.'

The taxi driver had a radio pumping out heavy gangsta rap so, as they sped past Central Park, they were able to sit without their silence becoming embarrassing. Even when they got out of the taxi, slamming their separate doors and fussing over who was paying, they didn't talk much. The sidewalks were so crowded that all the sidestepping and weaving made conversation difficult. Then they were queuing in a line for a Chinese restaurant, which was huge, on three floors. The waiters wore headphones and could radio each other. 'Sending two up to you now,' the tall, ponytailed waiter muttered into his mouthpiece, gesticulating to Aidan and Marcus as they reached the front of the queue, 'a couple of guys.'

The stairs were polished, smoked glass, edged with steel. When Aidan sat down at their small, white-clothed table, it felt like hours since they'd set out. A man behind them was arguing with his wife about crackers, and Marcus was saying something about king prawns and soup. They fiddled with the different menus, folding them and unfolding them, gave their order to a woman with dark lipstick, unsheathed chopsticks, upturned their bowls, poured tea into their tiny china cups, said that, yes, this place was good, very nice, and how long had it been open. Aidan noticed that every time he turned his head there was a rushing sound, like someone crumpling paper.

'Well,' Marcus said, and Aidan suddenly saw that he was nervous, one hand plucking at his shirt cuff, the other picking at its nails. There was a pause. Aidan filled his mouth with beer, let it effervesce on his tongue, then swallowed.

'It's . . . it's good to see you,' Marcus tried again.

Aidan nodded.

'The other day,' Marcus began, forcing a lightness of tone into his voice, 'someone told me that the funny thing about being a Brit in New York is that you never know—'

'Marcus. Cut the crap.' Aidan needlessly readjusted his beer bottle to the other side of his plate. 'Just tell me what's going on.'

Marcus hesitated. Aidan could see he was trying to decide whether or not to pretend that he didn't know what Aidan meant. Aidan studied the features of this man he'd known since he was eleven, and it was as if he barely recognised him. Did he really know him? Did he really know him any better than he knew the man behind him? Or the waitress? Or the people he'd spent the day working with? He had the strange sensation that they'd only just met and that they should be talking about where they grew up, what music they liked, where they'd been travelling, what jobs they did, not some ridiculous personality crisis that Marcus seemed to be going through.

'What do you mean?'

He'd decided to pretend. Aidan sighed and looked away. The waitress was swaying between the tables towards them with steaming plates. Aidan looked down as she placed a plate of thin, frazzled noodles in front of him. The image of a penguin fluttered, inappropriate and unbidden, in a corner of his mind. He picked up a strand between his chopsticks, and blew on it.

'I mean last night,' he said. 'Those girls.' He pushed the noodle into his mouth. It tasted of soy sauce and peanut oil, and coated his tongue with grease. 'I mean your new game of hitting on random women in drugstores.'

'What's got into you?' Marcus said, flushed. 'Why are you being so judgemental? It's not as if you've never . . . I mean, how come there's one rule for me and another for you?'

'I don't have a long-term girlfriend, Marcus,' Aidan pointed out calmly. 'Slight but crucial difference.'

'So that's what this is about.' Marcus rubbed his hand over his brow. 'Look. All I'm doing is . . . getting out there. That's all.'

Aidan tapped the ends of his chopsticks against his incisors, as if considering this statement.

'It's a whole realm of human experience,' Marcus continued when he saw that Aidan wasn't going to speak, 'that everybody should have. I'm in New York City, for God's sake. Do you really think I should be staying at home every night?'

Aidan was silent, didn't move, didn't blink, but held Marcus's gaze.

'And it's not as if . . . I mean, I love Sinead,' Marcus said, filling the silence. 'She is the only one for me, I know that and I've always known that, right from the moment I first saw her. Without her, I'm nothing. Nothing. None of this has anything to do with her.' He sat back in his chair, expecting Aidan's comment.

Aidan took a mouthful of beer, set down the bottle and surveyed his friend. He kept his face blank, impassive for a moment, then inflected his brow, indicating that Marcus should go on. Which he did.

'I've never done this. Ever since I was nineteen, twenty, I've been from one big, monogamous relationship to another, pretty much back to back. Never had the chance to . . . It's something I just wanted to get out of the way, I suppose. So the thought of it wouldn't . . . distract me any more. Everybody should have done it at some time or another — you know, given in to their desires.'

He stopped. Aidan felt him readjusting his feet under the table; the tablecloth tugged at the table corner; a toe of his shoe nudged Aidan's shin.

'And I really think you need to have a period of . . . of exploration before you . . .' He scuffed his feet again, uncrossing and recrossing his ankles. 'I mean, we're going to get married, Aide. We talked about it before I left. And I know this isn't perhaps the most . . . I don't know . . .' he appeared to search for the word in the air '. . . *honourable* way to go about things. But just for myself, I felt I needed to . . . you know . . .'

'Shop around?' Aidan suggested.

'Exactly.' Relief flooded Marcus's face. His lips parted in a smile. 'Shop around. That's it. I knew you'd understand. That's it exactly. And now I do know. I really do. All this is kind of good and nice and easy.' He paused. 'It's amazingly easy. But she's what I want. I think I know that now.'

'You think?'

'I know. I think I know. I mean, I know I know. I've always known, really.' He picked up his chopsticks and started pushing food into his mouth. He seemed happier now, relaxed, pouring tea, gulping down his beer. He looked back at Aidan. 'Well, are you going to say something, or are you going to just sit there staring at me all night like a moron?'

Aidan placed his chopsticks on the side of his plate. His food had cooled and coagulated while Marcus was talking; a tangled mess of cold, MSG-coated threads. 'There's nothing to say.'

Marcus frowned, puzzled.

'What do you want me to say? Congratulations? Well done? You've sown your wild oats. Bully for you.'

There was a long silence. Marcus chewed, his jaw working, his eyes scanning Aidan's face. A waitress hovered on the periphery of Aidan's vision.

'I get it.' Marcus started nodding, smirking slightly.

'Get what?'

'Nothing.'

'What?'

'Nothing,' Marcus said again, grinning now.

Aidan glared at him. 'Marcus—'

'You're jealous.'

A tiny muscle under Aidan's eye started up an invisible, convulsive twitching, as if connected to a distant electrical current. 'Jealous?'

'Yeah.'

'Of you and Sinead? That's—'

'No,' Marcus cut across him, shaking his head. 'No, no. Of this. Of what I've been up to. The time I've been having.'

Aidan gave a bark of laughter. 'You think I'm jealous of you? You think—' He gulped with incredulity. 'Yeah, you're right. I am jealous. I'd love to have sex with teenagers I find on the street. It must be great. Really fantastic. And I'm sure Sinead will agree.'

'Will you stop banging on about Sinead?' Marcus snapped, aggressive, his chin jutted out, his fists curled. 'This has nothing to do with her – I told you.' He stared at Aidan for longer than was comfortable. 'What is all this sudden concern for my girlfriend, anyway?' he said, in a new, steely voice.

'*Concern?* Well, how do you think she's going to react?' Aidan retorted, pushing back his chair. 'What do you think she's going to say? Have you thought about that?'

Marcus threw down his chopstick, rolling his eyes up to the ceiling. 'Jesus Christ, she's not going to say anything, of course.'

Aidan stared at his friend across the table. This time Marcus held his gaze, exasperation and impatience creasing his features. Aidan suddenly remembered a day when they were teenagers, when they were walking through the park in the town where they'd grown up: it was early summer and they were too young for that to mean exams. Marcus was wearing his school tie around his head like a sweatband, both of them had their shirts untucked, and they were flinging a frisbee between them as they walked, fifteen metres apart, still carrying on a conversation. It was one of those rare, isolated moments in adolescence when everything is pure and keen, when you glimpse an adulthood ahead of you that seems unfettered and gifted and worth the wait. The disc of the frisbee spun between them, fast and flawless as an electron.

'You don't think she'll work it out?' he said eventually.

'How would she?' Marcus shrugged.

'She's not stupid.'

'No. But,' and he smiled, 'we haven't seen each other for so long that she's not exactly going to stop to sniff my underwear, is she?'

'*Shut up.*' Aidan spat out. 'Just shut the fuck up. I don't want to hear any more of this shit. You're – you're –' articulacy deserted him, '– you're . . . What the fuck has happened to you?'

'Liberation.' Marcus smiled, folding his napkin on the table with a flourish. 'Liberation is what's happened to me, my friend. The truth of the matter is that everyone would do this. If they could. Very, very few people would hesitate, given the right circumstances. Nobody could resist. And here, in New York, it's completely foolproof. I'm thousands of miles away. The whole Atlantic Ocean lies between us. No one I've slept with knows her. She'll never find out. There's no one to tell her. No one she knows knows.'

'The perfect murder.'

Marcus frowned. 'Hardly.'

There was another pause. Marcus stabbed at a spring roll, mashing it into a pool of soy sauce.

'There is one person,' Aidan said.

Marcus looked at him sharply. 'Who?'

'Have you had some kind of lobotomy?'

'Who?' he demanded.

'Me. Remember? I live with her. In your flat. You remember your flat? Nice place? Big? Architect-designed?'

The anxiety evaporated from Marcus's eyes. 'Yeah, right,' he said, looking around as if for the waitress. Then, as if something had suddenly occurred to him, his head twisted back to Aidan and their eyes locked. And it was as if Aidan could feel their friendship slipping and skidding out from underneath them like feet on black ice.

He stood, letting his napkin drop from his hands on to the table. He suddenly felt incredibly tired, felt the weighted pull of jet lag on his limbs. Marcus stood too. Aidan flung down a couple of notes and lifted his chair to push it back under the table.

'Are you threatening me?' Marcus came fast around the side of the table, almost squaring up to him, shoving his face into his. 'I can't believe this. You're supposed to be my best mate.'

Aidan looked him full in the face. Again, that sensation of unfamiliarity, of disparity, that they were strangers.

'You're not going to tell her, are you?' Fear bubbled beneath Marcus's clenched-fist aggression. 'Are you?'

'Do you realise the position you're putting me in?' Aidan said.

'Position?' Marcus said quickly. 'What do you mean? You don't have a position. There is no position.'

'I live with her,' Aidan said. 'In the same flat. I'll be going back and seeing her every morning and every evening in . . . in three days' time. She'll be asking me how you are, what we did, what you're up to, how you're looking. Don't you see?'

'What? See what?'

'You're making me lie to her. Collude. You're forcing me to be your accomplice.'

'And that's beneath you, is it, Mr Morality?'

Aidan turned, yanking his arm away from Marcus's grip and walked across the yards and yards of dimly lit carpet and down the stairs and out into the pollution-heavy night. Outside the restaurant he passed a man carrying an albino child in a hooded blue anorak on his shoulders, his hands gripped around her socked ankles. The child's skin gleamed like pearls in the streetlights. She had fine white hair that hung out of her hood and a knowing, searching, oddly prescient gaze. She stared at Aidan from the fringes of her colourless eyelashes until he felt ashamed and looked away.

For the next four days, Aidan worked. He watched more videos of arctic wastelands, of creaking blue ice floes, of the small black birds skimming down through the surface of the petrifying waters. Small simulacrum penguins began to emerge in the margins of his notes, at first static, two-dimensional sketches, then proper creatures with depth, dimension and perspective. These were scanned into his laptop. They disappeared from his screen for a day to the software designers, and his creations returned to him, duplicated twelve times, each clone in a different pose. By the end of the last day, a penguin was mouthing something at him silently from the other side of his screen.

At night he ate alone, slept, worked some more, then walked the streets, past illuminated bars, past stilled fountains, through streets overhung with skyscrapers, and past the bright windows of late-night nail bars, where Korean girls bent over the hands of vacant-faced women, filing, clipping, cleaning and painting nails in luscious, glittering colours.

It was only when he got to the airport that, searching in the pockets of his bag for his passport or his ticket or maybe some chewing-gum, his fingers came into contact with the crackle of paper. Gripping it between index and middle finger, he drew out Sinead's letter to Marcus: sealed; a cream envelope with a raised grain; his name on the front with a firm, deft underline. The recognition gave him a shock like the contact of his skin with cold water. He turned it over in his hands and, to his shame, held it up to the light. The double folds of paper created unreadable palimpsests of slanted writing. It struck him as strange that a letter could be creased and worn yet unopened.

Sinead has left. Rory is driving her to the tube station. She kissed them all lightly, one by one. 'I'm sorry about the histrionics,' she said, hovering in the doorway, half in and half out of the light.

'Yeah, we're really angry,' Jodie said.

Sinead had smiled, raised her hand in a small wave, then was gone.

The table is littered with after-dinner debris: wine corks, ruined candles, bits of food, ash, circle-stains of wine and balls of wax sculpted with fingerprints. Jodie puts a cigarette between her lips and presses down on the Zippo lighter Aidan bought her in the States.

'So,' she says.

Aidan is moving plates around futilely, from table to draining-board to sink. 'What?'

'Are you going to tell her?'

He half turns. 'Tell who what?'

Jodie draws on her filter tip, the smoke making a slight kissing sound as it explodes into her mouth, and fixes him with an assessing stare. 'Tell Sinead you're in love with her.'

He turns his face back to the blue tiles in front of him, rests the heels of his palms on the Formica. The tiling distorts his features like a hall of mirrors – lengthening his nose and upper lip and making his eyes disappear into small raisin-sized hollows under a huge dome of forehead. He looks down, sees his thumb picking at the side of his finger's cuticle. He leafs through possibilities: pretend, laugh it off, lie. But this is Jodie. It would never work. Desperation and denial grapple within him. He doesn't want to talk about this, doesn't want to vocalise it because until he does he can convince himself that it's all an illusion, a trick his heart is playing on him, that it will pass, that it's not something he or anyone else need take seriously. He can keep it sealed up inside himself and no one need ever know. He doesn't want to besmirch this secret by opening it to oxygen, to sunlight, to scrutiny. He wants to keep it folded up somewhere deep and dark so that no one need ever know. But this thing – whatever it is – has taken root without him really noticing, and is spreading its lithe, choking branches to every corner of his being.

'Don't,' he says quietly. He moves a plate from the draining-board into the sink and picks up a glass. Behind him, he hears her suck again on her cigarette. Wait. Exhale. He turns, glass in hand. She isn't looking at him but out through the doors into the black garden. It's only two steps to the table, where he sits. Places the glass on it. Rests his elbows on the table top. Pushes his hands through his hair. 'I don't know what I'm going to do,' he says.

She balances her cigarette on the bevelled lip of the ashtray and slides her hand into one of his.

'I never meant for this to happen,' he says. 'I really didn't. I never even saw it coming.'

'You rarely do, though, do you? It's not as if anyone can ever plan these things.'

'Yeah, but there are slightly better situations.'

'Are there?'

He looks up, exasperated. 'How many women are there in London?'

'I dunno. Six million?'

'OK, let's say six million. Out of all of them, I had to fall for her.'

Jodie smirks. 'Of all the gin joints in all the towns—'

'Shut up,' he says, but starts to laugh. 'OK. Out of all the women in all the gin joints in all the city, I

271

had to walk into the girlfriend of my best friend. Which is—'

'Ex-girlfriend,' she interrupts. 'Ex-best friend.'

'Whatever. Which isn't, of course, the only problem.'

'What is?'

'Jodie,' he says impatiently, 'you didn't notice anything slightly amiss tonight? Anything at all? Floods of tears? Extreme misery? No?'

'All right, all right,' she says, 'so she's in possession of a broken heart, which—'

'Which is a rather major stumbling block.'

'Hmm. But that's the *only* stumbling block,' she tells him sternly. 'Who cares about that fuckwit? You mustn't even think about letting him stand in your way.'

'Jodie—' he tries to interject, but, insistent, leaning forward, stabbing the air with the burning tip of her cigarette, she talks over him: 'Aide, you don't owe him anything. Ever since you were both children, you have always looked out for him, always helped him, always picked up his pieces, always sorted out his various cock-ups. You're his bloody stunt man. Yes, he's basically an all right guy but he's messed up too badly this time to get away with it. He treated her like something he'd scraped off the bottom of his shoe and you just have to take one look at her to realise what a fool he is. He's a feckless emotional retard. You owe him nothing. *Nada. Niente.* And neither does she. I'll be livid with you if you don't follow your heart because of any kind of vestigial loyalty you might have to him.' Jodie flicks her ash viciously into the ashtray.

'You like her, then?' he says eventually.

She rolls her eyes in exasperation. 'Aide, she's wonderful. She's clever and funny. And gorgeous. In fact,' she says, 'I hate her.' She grips his hand in hers, hard. 'You have to tell her.'

'I can't.'

'You have to. She has a right to know, apart from anything else.'

'Look, you saw her. The woman's in no fit state for anything. How could I tell her? How do you think it would go down? I'd just come across as some opportunistic bastard, and she'd never want to see me ever again. The last thing she needs right now is more emotional shit dumped on her.'

Jodie sighs, fiddles with the lid of her Zippo. 'Maybe,' she says. 'But you will tell her, won't you? At some point? You're not just going to let this lie?'

Aidan grunts and attempts to press a ball of cold, rigid wax into a perfect cuboid shape with the blood-heat of his hands. Jodie comes to stand behind him, hugging him. Aidan feels the thud of his sister's heart along his back.

'Poor Aide,' she murmurs.

'Hardly,' he says, flinging the wax aside. 'Poor Sinead I'd say.'

'I could kill that fuckface Marcus Emerson.'

'No, I could.'

'No. *I* could.'

'No, no, no. I think you'll find that—'

'We both could,' she concedes.

'OK. When?'

Lily and Sarah sit on a row of three tilting metal chairs, holding a newspaper between them. Sarah is reading the job adverts and Lily is half pretending to do the same, but her mind feels swollen, overblown: things sink into it, as if into wet concrete, never to be seen again.

One of her feet swings over the cold floor of the tube station. The sole of her shoe squeaks ever so slightly on the floor at the nadir of each swing. Back, scuff, forth, scuff. It's reached that point now where the movement has created its own momentum, the pendular sweep powered by its own self-perpetuating physics.

Sarah met her from work and they've been to a café with red leather seats and steamed-up windows, where they ate ribbons of pasta from oval plates and eavesdropped on the first-date conversation going on behind them. They were going to go to a film but they've had one of those London nights where nothing comes together, when the city seems to conspire against you: the film they wanted to see was sold out, and by the time they'd found that out they'd missed the other screening of it across town; the bar they liked was full, the rather smug bouncer on the door told them; walking to another it had started to rain, and then hail, sharp pellets of ice bouncing off the pavement, into their hair and down their collars. They'd given up, beaten a retreat to the tube.

Lily glances up at the box suspended from the arched ceiling, where destinations and times of tube trains are displayed in ever-changing combinations of tiny orange lightbulbs. This movement of her head, which pulls on the muscles and tendons down her back, spine, ribcage and pelvis, combined with the distracting, unbalancing effect of a man in a wide, insulation-stuffed coat walking too closely by them, makes the movement of her leg falter, stutter and lose rhythm. Lily stills her foot, crosses her legs, and glances up at the board again. Still blank. '1,' it announces proudly, 'High Barnet,' but next to it, where the number of minutes in which the train is due should be, is a dense black blank.

'What about a sushi chef?' Sarah says. 'I could do that.'

Lily leans over to look at the advert. 'Must speak Japanese,' she reads.

Sarah peers more closely. 'Damn,' she exclaims. 'That's discrimination, that is. Just because I can't speak Japanese doesn't mean I can't make sushi.'

'But would you really want to spend hours rolling bits of raw fish into balls?'

Sarah sighs. 'I don't know. It'd be better than cleaning toilets or chambermaiding or flipping burgers.' She crushes the paper shut. 'I have to get a job,' she moans. 'Woman cannot live on art alone.' She opens the pages again. 'OK,' she says, smoothing the adverts flat on her lap. 'What can you do in the evenings that's not too strenuous or depressing that earns you loads of cash?'

'Be a hooker?'

'Very funny,' she mutters. 'And you shouldn't joke. It may still come to that.'

Lily smiles, leans her head back on the wall and closes her eyes. And as soon as she does, her mind is swarmed with the thoughts Sarah's presence has been holding at bay. Indecision is not something she's ever really experienced before. It's a strange feeling: cloying, unaccountable, gluing everything together. It frustrates and angers her. All day, no matter what she is doing, an internal debate is running in her head, questions and doubts wrestling and fighting each other. She can't switch it off, even when she wants to sleep. Sometimes she wonders if she's spoken it aloud. She's thought about telling Sarah everything, the whole story, and has been on the brink of doing so several times tonight. But somehow she needs to sort it out in her own head first.

She opens her eyes again. Sarah is talking about the pros and cons of dot.com businesses. A man with the polished, slick box of a briefcase in one hand and a red tartan scarf in the other keeps twisting round to glare at the still-blank board. When he turns away, he lets a short sigh snap his tongue against the back of his teeth. It makes Lily think of the momentary suspended click of an alarm clock reaching its assigned hour before its mechanics connect up to the bleep. A woman in the kind of stack-heeled, thin-soled boots that would make the jigsaw bones of her feet ache and strain is marching up and down the yellow-lined edge of the platform. Six paces – the heels of her boots hitting a cloc-cloc sound off the porcelain tunnel walls – stop, a swizzling turn that makes her skirt swirl around her, then six paces back.

In the days since Sinead told her, nothing she does or thinks or feels is separate any more, but connected to and dragged down by another reason or effect and then another and then another, until everything in her head and everything around her seems to sink into an obscure haze of doubt and uncertainty. She's not used to this, doesn't know how to deal with it, can't organise her thoughts. She's always just known how she felt or what she thought, just as she knew her own name. But now, at whatever point she starts, her thoughts go round and round like beads on a rosary.

If she loves Marcus – does she love Marcus? – then she should tell him what she knows. She should be honest. But then he might be angry. Why? Because he did something wrong. But if she thinks it was wrong then why does she love him – does she love him? – why is she still with him? And if she still loves him knowing what he did, is that wrong of her?

The woman's shoes cloc-cloc one way and, when she turns, her hair swoops around her head. A man she'd met once in a theatre bar told Lily that human hair clogs the walls of these tunnels, that cleaners clear tonnes of it away from the tracks every year. The idea fascinates her – those great clots of soot-brushed, matted hair.

How does she know she's telling the truth? But why would she lie? To get Marcus back. How could he do that to someone he loved? She can't imagine him doing anything like that. It doesn't seem like him, but then maybe he didn't, maybe she's lying.

'For God's sake,' Sarah says loudly, looking up at the

board, 'you'd think they'd give us an announcement to tell us how long we're going to be sitting here.'

She should just ask him. Just come out and say it, say, Marcus, is this what happened, and what made you do it. There must be some explanation. There has to be. She's only heard one side of the story, after all. But if he'd wanted her to know he would have told her. So he doesn't, and maybe it's none of her business anyway.

If she told him she knew he'd want to know how she knew, how she found her, how she recognised her. She'd have to tell him. Couldn't tell him that. Couldn't ever tell him that. Couldn't tell him she sees her still in his flat, behind him, next to him, in front of him. Does he still love her, does she still love him, does he love her, should she leave?

There is something about him that binds her to him, and Lily can't quite see clearly what it is. It's as if many narrow strands of wire, twisted together, link her to him; individually, they're inexplicable and frail, but together they are indissoluable, cannot be hacked through. She doesn't understand it, this strength of feeling. It follows her around like a dog on a lead. If she looked at this objectively, she wouldn't love him, maybe even like him. But somehow this transmutes into a sensation of inseparability, of longing, of need. His unhappiness causes a collapse in her chest, as if it has somehow spread to her like a virus. How could she leave him? But disquiet silts up her veins.

'What about a swimming-pool attendant?' Sarah is saying. 'I could do that.'

Carpe diem, she tells herself, as a disturbance in the atmosphere – minuscule at first, but unmistakable – heralds a far-off train rattling along mercury-smooth rails. Seize the carp, she thinks, a screeching of brakes and wheels filling the tunnel, and almost laughs.

The lights are on, and his coat is slung over a chair.

'Marcus?' Lily calls, hesitating on the threshold. No reply. 'Marcus!' Nothing, and then, a plink-plink-plink sound and a kind of swishing. She extracts her keys from the lock and walks into the flat. Again, that plink-plink sound. 'Marcus?' she says again. 'Are you there?'

On the floor, in a trail through the kitchen, are items of his clothes, as if he undressed on the move, as if in a hurry to get stripped. Shirt, shoes, trousers, socks, underpants, scrumpled and collapsed on the boards. Lily walks by them, examining them like a visitor in an art gallery. She cocks her head, listening out for the sound of running water – the shower or the bath. But nothing. Then she hears a noise like a sigh or a gasp.

Coming round the bathroom door, she sees him: the bath is full, water tipping over the sides. He is face-down, naked, his shoulders and buttocks breaking through the surface. The rest of his body shimmers pale under water. His hair trails from his head like seaweed, his feet rest up against the rim of the bath. There is a black tube jutting up through the water, through which comes the sound of his breath.

'Marcus,' Lily says. She reaches out and touches his shoulder. He rears up out of the water, his face encased in a black mask, his feet slipping, and for a moment he flails, limbs thrashing. A tidal wave flops out over Lily's shoes. He laughs, water streaming from his face and hair.

She looks at him, her head on one side. 'What are you doing?'

He takes the snorkel out of his mouth before answering: 'Testing my new gear.' He replaces it and puts his face back in the water, his hands braced on the sides of the bath. 'I think it's watertight.' His words come out of the snorkel tube distorted, consonants fusing into long vowel stretches. 'The man in the shop said to check it straight away and if it leaked I could take it back.'

'Oh.' She lowers the toilet seat and sits down, arms folded. The bathroom is cold, the windows opaque with condensation, whirls of steam rising from the water. 'Are you going snorkelling, then?'

'No,' and then he says a word that comes out as 'die-wing'.

'What?'

He says the word again.

'Die-wing?' she repeats, mystified.

He resurfaces, removing the tube from his mouth. 'Diving. Scuba diving.' He pulls off the mask and starts fiddling with the strap. There is a red weal in a perfect oval around his face. 'It's something I've always wanted to do. And this guy I work with was booking himself a holiday today. Two weeks in Thailand. So I decided to go with him. The diving course takes a week, so I'll have another week to travel about.'

'It's just the two of you?'

'Well, I asked Aidan if he wanted to come, but . . .' He trails off, frowning at his mask strap.

'But what?'

'He said no,' he says quickly. 'So, yeah, it's just the two of us.' He looks at her. 'You don't mind, do you?'

'Mind? No, not at all. It sounds great.'

'I know. I can't wait.' He snaps the mask back into place on his face and dives under the water again.

Beyond the door, something flickers at the periphery of her vision. Her pulse stutters and she tells herself, it's nothing, it isn't real, she wasn't there, she isn't dead. But when she brings herself to look, just to be sure, she's there, standing by the window, her hand resting on the kitchen counter, looking straight in their direction. How can she still be here?

Lily looks back at the bath. Marcus has submerged the end of the snorkel tube. Saucer-shaped bubbles rise to the surface in a steady stream. Then he moves and the tube rises again like a submarine periscope and she hears him drawing in air. Some water has got trapped in the tube, which rattles when he exhales. She resists the urge to block up the end of the tube with her hand.

Lily stands and walks away, through the door, past the kitchen, giving Sinead a little wave, and into the bedroom. She lets the door slam closed behind her. It's only as she's removing the clothes she's been wearing all day, heavy with smoke from the café and damp from the hailstorm, that the idea comes to her. At first, it's slight, a notion, almost nothing, but as she lifts her shirt over her head, it solidifies, calming her mind with resolve. Quick as a flash, she hurls her clothes to the floor, opens the wardrobe, and starts leafing through the hangers. Where is it, must be here somewhere, where did she put it?

Her fingers close on its material before she sees it. There is a sighing sound almost like music as it falls over her skin. She swings the mirror round until she is caught in its frame. The material seems dark and measureless, sucking all light into its depths. It hangs from her shoulders, coating her hips, thighs, pooling around her legs. It was expensive, she can see in the way the seams meet, in the caress of the fabric, in its effortless, fluid drape. It would have been shorter on Sinead.

Lily opens the door and steps out. The dress moves around her like liquid tar, warmed now by her flesh. Marcus is standing by the table, reading a postcard, wearing just a towel, his hair dark with water, standing up in spikes. She glances around. No sign of Sinead. She must have decided to leave them to it.

'Have you eaten?' he says, without looking up. 'Do you want to go out for something?'

'No. I ate with Sarah.'

'Oh. Maybe I'll phone for a takeaway, then.' He moves towards the pinboard, riffling through the menus stuck to it. 'Don't know what I fancy.' And turning round, says, 'Are you sure you don't want anything?' He blinks slowly. His eyes travel down her body to her feet and up again.

She holds his gaze. 'No thanks.'

'Sure?' he says again, turning back to the menus in his hand. 'Maybe I should have Thai. To get myself in the mood.' He sits down at the table and pulls the telephone towards him. 'You know, I can't believe I'm finally going diving. Apparently, you have to sit an exam. Can you imagine? Going on holiday to do an exam. I never thought . . .'

His head turns back to her. She breathes in, the material tightening around her.

'Is that new?' he says, his hand poised to dial.

'What?'

He points. 'The dress.'

'No.'

'Oh.' His face is distracted, slightly perplexed. 'I don't think I've seen it before.'

'Do you like it?'

'Yes.' He nods. 'It's . . . it's beautiful.' Then, drawing his hand across his eyes, he dials the number. 'Hello? I'd like to order a takeaway.'

Aidan turns from the window and picks up the ringing phone. 'Aidan Nash.'

There is an explosion of laughter. 'God, you sound so *serious*. What are you doing? Solving world peace?'

His heart punches his ribs. He's been thinking about her so intensely he is finding it hard to believe it is actually her on the phone, calling him, not just some projection of his imagination.

'Hi. Sorry. I was . . . er . . . I was miles away.'

He had been thinking about when he and Marcus first met her. How he'd been up helping Marcus with some designs. How they'd taken a break, early afternoon. How they'd met someone in a queue for a sandwich in a delicatessen. Someone Marcus knew. And this guy had known someone else who knew about a party and why didn't they come along. Tonight. East, beyond the park. Just say they were friends of Sinead. There'd be no problem. Sinead? Yeah,

Sinead. Tall girl, curly hair. There'd be no problem, he'd said again.

And about the day she'd called him and said, you knew, didn't you, and the way he'd held the receiver clamped to his ear, trawling his mind for explanations, excuses, but found only questions: where are you staying, do you need anything, where are you, we can't talk about this now, tell me where you are and I'll come and find you.

'. . . never thought you'd be at work so late, but I just wondered if we were still on for tomorrow.' Her words puncture his reverie.

'Tomorrow?' He snatches upon the word. Had they arranged to see each other? What day is tomorrow? What had they planned to do? 'Fine.' He gropes around his desk for his diary, encountering memos, computer discs, pens, staplers, then, mercifully, the hard edges of his diary, under a sheaf of film stills. He grabs it and flips it open. Tomorrow. Saturday. The oblong of the day on the page is completely white. 'That would be great.' In the lineless space he writes the word 'sinead' in red ink. 'What sort of time?'

'About midday?'

'Fine.'

'So what are we doing?'

'Um . . . it's a surprise,' he improvises. He'll think of something.

It's quiet for a Saturday morning. Lily is leaning alone on the counter at the front of the cubicles, surrounded by lingerie, frilled like sea creatures. There are only two customers in, and other people are seeing to them. Christmas music spirals from the ceiling. She can see herself in the reflection of a picture frame opposite, containing an advert for 'natural, stick-on, peel-off implants'. She is practising: I'm leaving you, her mouth is telling her silently. Too melodramatic. I'm going. No. I think I should go? Lily sighs and squints more closely at the image of her mouth. What do you want, it asks her, why—

The phone in front of her rings, making her jump. She flings aside the bra and string set she's holding, lifts the receiver to her ear and before she can even say the department how-may-I-help-you spiel, she hears the fuzzing line of a mobile phone and: 'Lily? It's me.' Marcus.

'Hi,' she says. 'how—'

'Guess where I am,' he says over her.

Lily hates games like these. 'Don't know.'

'Go on. Guess.'

'The flat?'

'No.'

'Your office?'

'No.'

Just tell me, she wants to shriek. 'Istanbul?' she says, exasperated.

'No. Do you give up?'

'Yes.'

'Your shop.'

'What?'

'I'm near your shop. About ten minutes away. Do you want to have lunch?'

Aidan sees her before she sees him. He is waiting in the traffic, engine churning over, while she is standing on the corner they'd decided on. Her mobile phone is clamped to her ear. He can tell she's agitated – walking in tight, controlled circles, her free hand jerking in the air then raking through her hair. Who is she talking to? He leans briefly on the horn as his car eases forward and she looks his way, recognises the car, but doesn't break off her conversation.

As he pulls over to the kerb, she is there, opening the door and climbing in. Tears are streaking down her face and the finger she holds to her lips, warning him not to speak, is shaking.

'No . . . no . . . I don't care . . .' she is saying into the phone in a strangled voice. 'I'm going now. No . . . that's none of your business . . . no . . . I don't want to talk about it any more . . . Goodbye . . . . I'm not interested in anything you have to say . . . Goodbye.' She drops the phone into her lap and clenches her hands around her face.

'Was that who I think it was?' The words are barely out of Aidan's mouth when the phone in Sinead's lap trills into life.

'Shit,' she says, and looks down at it. Then she stabs the divert-call button. There is a moment's silence and the phone trills once more. 'Bastard,' she shouts, and slams her hand into the button again. This ritual repeats itself over and over again.

'Give it here a sec,' Aidan says, and she hands it to him. 'You can bar calls from his phone, you know,' he says, as he fiddles with the unfamiliar buttons at a traffic light.

'Can you?'

'It's really easy, look.' Aidan shows her how to enter Marcus's number, press a button and get the message 'Call Barred' appearing in tiny, squared-off letters on the screen.

Sinead stares at it. 'Wow,' she says. 'That's fantastic.'

'Well, he may get wise to it and call from somewhere else, so be careful.'

Sinead is scuffling about in her pockets for a tissue, mopping her face and peering at her reflection in the mirror above her seat. 'He's driving me mad,' she mutters.

'What was it about this time?'

'The usual, to begin with. Whingeing on and on about would I come back, and why not and how he made a mistake, blah blah blah. And so I confronted him about Lily.'

'Lily?' Aidan is thrown. 'I didn't know you knew about Lily.'

She gives a short laugh. 'That's exactly what he said.'

'But how . . . I mean, who told you?'

'No one.'

'Then . . .'

She sighs as if she doesn't want to go over it, doesn't want to think about it. 'I called the flat once and hung up when I heard a woman answer. Then . . .' she sighs again '. . . when Marcus called me I asked him about it – stupidly – and he told me this girl had moved into my . . . the room. And, you know, I could just tell. I could just tell from the way he said her name, that kind of falling intonation he has when he's talking about something he's not particularly proud of . . .'

Aidan, changing gear, nods.

'. . . I could just tell he was fucking her.' She clears her throat. 'Then I met her.'

'*You met her?*' The car swings into the wrong lane. Someone behind hoots and gesticulates in the oblong of his rear-view mirror.

'Yeah.'

'Are you serious? You met Lily? What do you mean? When? Where?'

She is staring fiercely out of the window, her hands gripped around her knees. 'Aide, I'd rather not . . .' she begins unsteadily. 'I'm sorry . . . I don't want to talk about it . . . if that's OK with you.'

'Of course.'

Then she is turning her head; Aidan turns his quickly and their eyes meet for a second.

'So where are we going today, then?' she says shakily, pulling her face into a lopsided, unconvincing smile.

They walk along the black iron railings of Lincoln's Inn

Fields. Lily drags a gloved finger over their even rhythm. Next to her, Marcus is holding a bag of crisps between them and, with her other hand, she puts them into her mouth. It feels strange to have one bare hand and one gloved.

She is having one of those days where everybody looks like somebody else. This morning on the bus she thought she saw her aunt who lives in Devon, a boy she knew from chemistry lessons at school, and a newsagent from Ealing. Each time, she'd been convinced, for a split second, maybe more. Then they'd moved or the bus had swung round into a differently angled light, and their familiarity had shifted and slipped away. Just now, she's walked past someone she could have sworn was a man she'd been in love with at university. But when they got close he looked nothing like him – hair another colour, nose too long, face too wide, an inaccurate version of him.

Marcus is taking her to the John Soane Museum. She's been before, years ago with her mother, but doesn't say. The house is cool, dark and tomb-still. A group of Americans, large in coloured jackets, keep appearing and disappearing from view through the many doorways and windows in the Chinese-box structure of the rooms. A green-suited attendant, sitting on a slender-legged chair, cleans his nails with a piece of card. They walk through a dark carpeted drawing room, through a narrow wooden passageway, past small gardens with sanguine-faced statues, through rooms filled with broken bits of classical buildings, pots, paintings, velvet-covered furniture.

'He placed mirrors in odd places,' Marcus tells her. 'In

alcoves. Panels. False window-frames. To give the impression of distance and space where there wasn't any.'

These mirrors disconcert her: she keeps glimpsing slivers of a woman who looks disturbingly like her before her brain catches up and tells her, it's only you. In some obscure way, these reflections frighten her: she's not expecting them, they don't look the way she thinks she does, the women in the mirrors seem trapped, shocked and cold behind the glass. She'll glance sideways and see herself turning away from herself. 'Are you all right?' Marcus asks her at one point and, in a fragmented portico above their heads, twelve Lilys nod back at him.

In a small, high-ceilinged room, he hooks out of the wallpaper a brass handle and tugs at it. The wall seems to come away in his hand, swinging out into the room on a hinge, unfolding like a book to reveal panels hung with strange, faded, meticulous drawings of Grecian buildings, one after another after another. They make her mistrust the building, these traps set into its architecture. She doesn't want to touch anything in case it gives and she is swallowed up in its hidden mechanisms. She walks carefully down the corridors, not touching the walls, thinking of that children's story where a kitten gets trapped behind the wainscot and captured by a grinning, thin-tailed rat.

At a railing, they stand and look down into the room below, and into the hollow of an Egyptian sarcophagus.

'It's beautiful, isn't it?' says Marcus softly. 'Alabaster. Makes it seem almost worthwhile dying, don't you think, if you get to lie in that?'

'Yes, but . . .' She's not sure why it makes her feel ill

at ease. Why is it here? She imagines John Soane packing it tightly into a crate with deft, acquisitive fingers and lowering it on to a ship. Who was buried in it and what did Soane do with the body?

'But what?'

'Well, it shouldn't really be here.'

'Why? Where should it be?'

'Egypt, of course. I mean, don't you think it seems, I don't know, inappropriate here?'

'I hadn't thought of it like that.'

Then Lily sees, walking below them, around the sarcophagus and across the room, a curly-haired, tall woman. Her hands grip the rail. She can't see her face properly. Is it her? And if it is, is it really her or the other her? She turns her head and looks at Marcus. Did he see it? Can he see it? She wants to blindfold him, shield his eyes from the possibility of her. But he is talking about the hieroglyphics inscribed in the alabaster and, when Lily looks down again, the room is empty.

'It says here,' Sinead says, 'that these frogs hold enough poison in their sacs to, and I quote, "fell an average man".'

Aidan peers into the murky tank at a frog the size of a pencil sharpener, green-black with a lurid blue mark on its back, symmetric as an early Christian cross.

'What is an average man, do you think?' she continues. 'Do they exist?'

Aidan adjusts the focus of his vision and sees, in the reflection in the tank, that two men are staring at Sinead. 'Maybe only in Brazil,' he says.

'Brazil?'

'Where the frogs come from.' He touches her lightly on the shoulder. 'Come on, let's go upstairs.'

They pass through the aquarium room, with groups of people huddled round tanks, set like bright, lit windows into the wall. Aidan glimpses, for a second, in the side of a huge tank containing shoals of flitting angel fish, an image of him and Sinead, walking side by side. His brain snaps shut on it, wanting to hoard and preserve it – her next to him, holding up the leaflet about Kew Gardens to show him something. It occurs to him for the first time that when they are together like this people must just take them for a couple.

The stairs, winding like those in a castle, lead to the biggest palm house with arched white struts like the ribcage of a dinosaur. Large spread-leaved plants strain up and out towards the light. The air is as humid and heavy as Tokyo. He tells Sinead this and she looks at him for a moment then asks him questions: how he liked being there, did he mind the travelling, was Japan beautiful, had he ever been to the mountains there, did he ever get lonely, could he speak Japanese, did he prefer working with Japanese or Americans, would he feel trapped now he was based in London.

They wander out of the narrow, white doors of the palm house, and walk past oblong flower-beds, lakes sprouting fountains, a line of very vocal pink-footed geese, a sound garden (which Sinead pronounces a 'load of new-age shite'), a bank full of prickling, thorned cactuses, a high pagoda, a winding pathway through dense foliage, bouffant rhododendron bushes, and giant lilypads a metre in diameter that make her lean over the barrier and pull them up from the water to see what they look like underneath.

He notices that her hair has curled tighter in the humidity of the palm houses, that she bites her lip when she's thinking, that she touches the leaves of the plants she likes, that she walks faster than most people, that one of her shoe soles is slightly more worn down than the other, that she wears a gold ring on the smallest finger of her right hand, that her ear-lobes have been pierced three times but she doesn't wear any earrings, that she carries four books in her bag, along with several lipsticks, a notebook, a pair of retractable scissors, a picture of her brother aged four, and a cowrie shell.

As the light drains from the sky, they sit on a bench, hands tucked into their coats for warmth, at the edge of the gardens. Sinead brings a polished aluminium flask from her bag and they pass a cup of hot chocolate between them that tastes slightly metallic but burns a path down Aidan's chest. Above their heads, planes come into land at Heathrow, stitching the sky with threads of white. They talk about jobs and Aidan's flat and her lectures and her friends and, eventually, Marcus. She doesn't weep, and tips back her head to look at the planes when she says, 'I think if someone rejects you like that, it means they're not right for you, doesn't it?'

When he doesn't reply, she looks over at him and asks: 'Do you think it was out of character?'

Aidan swirls the dregs of chocolate around the base of the cup. A dark slurry of grains has coagulated there, bleeding into the liquid. He knows that it's been inevitable that they would have this conversation at some point. And he knows she wants him to say yes, that she wants to be vindicated for loving him.

'I think,' he begins carefully, 'I think that he's always been rather . . . focused on his own needs.'

She looks away, starts playing with the laces of her boots, untying them and retying them, her face confused and miserable. He can bear anything but that. It makes him want to comfort her, touch her, take her in his arms – and that he really shouldn't do. He puts down the cup and takes a deep breath. 'OK,' he says, 'two things about Marcus. First, he's very impulsive. Agreed?'

She nods.

'Which can be a good thing,' Aidan continues, 'a very good thing. But it can also be annoying. He always has to satisfy his urges immediately, have you noticed? He can't wait. If he's hungry, he has to eat right there and then, no matter what. He can't think about anything else until he has whatever it is he wants. He was the same when he met you. And I think that has relevance to . . . what happened in New York.'

She isn't looking at him, but he can tell she's listening.

'Second,' he says, 'he has this spooky ability to completely compartmentalise his life. I've had loads of arguments with him about this, over the years, and I'm sure you have too. If there's something upsetting him or making him unhappy, he can just switch it off. Just like that. And get on with his life as if nothing at all has happened. I don't know anybody else who has that capacity. I've always found it very disturbing, that he can just put things in a box and shut the lid. And I think . . .' He trails off, suddenly wondering if she really wants to hear this.

'. . . that's what he did with me,' she finishes for him.

Aidan nods. 'Yes.' He picks up the cup again, swirling it around in his hand. 'I also think that what he did is a bit like the Ancient Mariner shooting the albatross.'

She turns her eyes on him.

'That he just did it. It was an action empty of reason. He did it because he did it. And that he – and you – will never really know why.'

She doesn't speak for a long time, and when she does, it is to tell him how, when she was a little girl, she always used to climb up this one tree, a sycamore tree it was, when she was in trouble. And how her parents used to stand at the bottom, shouting at her to come down, but she never would. One day, after she'd been up there for hours, her father had gone to the garage, ripped the chainsaw into action, climbed the tree and lopped off the top half with one swipe. It looked dreadful for years, she says, that half-tree.

Lily's cheek is pressed to his, her head drooping. She is staring at the ridged, whorled flesh of his ear, inches from her mouth. She could strain forward and touch it, brush her lips against it, take its lobe between her teeth. Whisper something – anything – into that small, black hollow. The message would reach him instantly.

Beneath her, his lungs inflate and deflate, raising her ever so slightly up, then letting her down. The water-weight of her breasts is flattened against the dense, fleshless hard of his chest, his hair leaving menhir swirls on her skin.

What would she say? She flexes her tongue between the cage of her teeth. One of his hands is pressed against her lower back. The other lies limp on the mattress beside them. If she elongates her foot, ballet-style, she could touch the round, hard bone of his ankle. He swallows, the muscles at the side of his head tensing.

I know what you did.

It would be so easy. The words are there, ready to be carried out on the carbon dioxide she's returning to the air. Her heart makes flailing punches at him through the arched tent of her ribcage. His eyes open and flutter, his lashes scything at her neck.

I see her. I see her everywhere.

Lily rolls away, sees his ear and his face pull out into distant focus. The sheet beneath her feels cold, starch-sharp.

'You must be Aidan.'

He looks up. Standing in front of him is a petite, untidy-looking blonde woman in a blue coat.

'Yes,' he says, 'I am.'

'I'm Ingrid.' She offers a red-gloved hand, and when Aidan takes it, the wool feels rough and cold to the touch. 'Sinead told me to look out for you.'

They are in a café off Tottenham Court Road. Aidan is waiting for Sinead, who is late. Ingrid strips off her gloves, unbuttons her coat, drops her bag on the floor next to her chair, goes to the counter and orders a coffee, then sits down.

'It's nice to meet you,' he says. 'Sinead's told me all about—'

'We've met before,' Ingrid interrupts him, rather accusingly.

'Have we?'

'Yes. A long time ago. At a birthday party.'

'You mean—' He stops.

'I do mean.' Ingrid nods. 'That party. The one where she met him. Thingy. Whathisname.'

'Shitface,' supplies Aidan.

She smiles, at last. 'Yes,' she says, with relish. 'Shitface. How is Shitface these days?'

'I wouldn't know.'

She raises her eyebrows. 'I thought you and he were best buddies.'

'We were.'

'I see. It's like that, is it? You've taken her side?'

'Um. Kind of.' Aidan is anxious to change the conversation. 'So you were at that party?'

'I lived in the house. I was Sinead's housemate. Well, one of them.'

'I'm not sure if I remember you.'

'I had long hair then,' she says, her grey eyes moving restlessly over his face, as if collating information in order to assess him at a later date. 'We met again, at Shitface's place, a few years ago. You were with your friend.'

'Was I?'

'Josh? No . . . John,' she says, pointing a finger at him as if daring him to correct her. Her hair is so blonde that it's almost white at the temples, where the hairs starts flecking out from the skin. He wonders if she's Scandinavian by origin. Could be with a name like that. He considers asking her, then rejects the idea.

'You've got a good memory,' he says instead.

'You and him and Shitface were all sitting around the table and Sinead and I came in. We'd been out shopping, I think. Your friend John had made lots of paper animals – what do you call them? origami – out of some newspaper and was talking about some girl he'd just fallen for, and agonising about the fact she wasn't Jewish. Or something.'

Aidan nods slowly.

'We were all giving him advice – probably not very useful advice.'

Aidan clears his throat. 'I remember.' He nods again. 'You did have very long hair. Sinead had bought a juicer thing and kept squeezing oranges for us all.'

The waiter places Ingrid's coffee in front of her and removes Aidan's cup. She keeps her hands flat on the table, her head on one side, considering him.

'So,' he says, uncomfortable under her scrutiny, 'you're an academic.'

'And you're a bit of a mystery,' she returns.

'Am I?' He is taken aback. 'Why?'

'The tall, dark and mysterious friend. Always talked about. Never there. Always away. Has some vaguely glamorous job in film.'

'It really isn't glamorous at all.'

'I bet it's more glamorous than what I do.'

'What do you do?'

'I'm an academic.'

'I know that. I meant what's your subject?'

'History.'

'Where?'

'North London.'

'Do you like it?'

'Yes. D'you like your job?'

'Yes.'

For some reason they smile at each other. Ingrid lets a

heaped spoonful of sugar slide into her cup. Aidan feels as though he's passed some obscure test.

'So how do you think she is?' she asks, stirring her coffee vigorously.

'She . . . Very up and down. But on the whole, I'd say . . . pretty bad. Like someone who's had a section of themselves removed.'

'Do you think they'll get back together?'

'What?' For a moment he can't think who she means. 'Sinead and Marcus?'

Ingrid frowns. 'Who's Marcus?'

'Sorry,' he is distracted by the thought, unable to formulate an answer, 'I mean Shitface. Well . . . I don't know. I doubt it. I mean . . . I don't think she'd have him, would she? Why? Why do you ask? Do you think they will?'

'I don't know.' She shrugs, blows on her coffee. 'I really don't know. I obviously would never speak to her again, but he can be very persuasive.'

'She'd never do it,' he says. 'Surely.'

'I hope you're right. Though I wouldn't bank on it. She still loves him. It takes more than behaving like an oversexed imbecile to change that. And *amore* does occasionally *vincit omnia*.' Ingrid puts down her cup and starts folding a napkin into pleats. 'You've heard the latest, I suppose? His little consort's been stalking her as well?'

'You mean Lily?'

'Whatever,' says Ingrid, dismissively, then looks at him with narrowed eyes. 'Of course,' she says, 'you must know her.'

'Well, I wouldn't exactly say know her. She moved in while I was still living there. That's all.'

'Hmm.' She ruminates on this for a moment, still raking him with her gaze.

'Anyway, what do you mean, stalking?'

'Well, apparently he—' she breaks off, staring through the window. Aidan follows her gaze. In the distance, it is just possible to make out a figure running along the pavement towards them. Sinead. The evening is darkening and something she is holding flutters white against her clothes. 'Here comes Wilson,' Ingrid says, getting up, 'and it looks like she may have some news for us.'

'News?' Aidan says. There is something in Sinead's euphoric expression, and the paper she's holding that makes his pulse quicken with a kind of dread. 'What news?'

'Did you get it?' Ingrid shouts, hands cupped around her mouth. The waiter glances over, peeved.

'Get what?' Aidan asks.

Sinead bounces up the steps of the café, beaming, and wrenches open the door.

'You got it?' shrieks Ingrid.

Sinead nods. Ingrid flings her arms around her, laughing and shouting congratulations, I knew you would, I knew it.

'Got what?' Aidan asks again.

'She got it, she got it!' Ingrid is chanting.

'I just heard,' Sinead is babbling, 'I checked my e-mail before I left, just in case. I didn't really think it would be there, but it was! I can't believe it! I printed it out for you, look.'

Ingrid grabs the paper and scans it quickly. Sinead laughs, watching her, and claps her hands.

Aidan catches her by the elbow. 'Sinead, what is it? What have you got?'

'Oh, Aide,' she wraps her arms around his neck and smacks a kiss on to his cheek, 'the post I applied for. Didn't I tell you? Maybe I didn't. It's in Sydney. Literature and Gender. Teaching and research.'

'Sydney? As in Australia?'

'It's not exactly my field, but—'

'How long for?'

'A year. Two years. Who knows? It all depends on whether or not . . .' She trails away, staring at his obviously blank face. 'Aidan, I'm sorry I didn't tell you. It all happened so fast. The person they had pulled out last weekend and they called me and asked if I'd be interested, and it seemed like just what I needed. I just have to get out of London, what with . . . everything. You know. I'm sorry. You're not angry, are you?'

'Angry? No, no, not at all.'

Ingrid thrusts the paper into his hands and hugs Sinead again. 'I'm so pleased! I'm so proud of you! It'll be fantastic.'

'You will come and stay, won't you?' Sinead is saying. She is clutching both of their hands, her fingers curled into his palm. He is reading the lines of the e-mail, but is unable to get beyond the first lines. Dear Dr Wilson. Dear Dr Wilson. We are delighted to inform you. Delighted. Dr Wilson. We are delighted.

'I've never been to Australia,' she is saying. She turns

to him and as she does so, her hand slides from his grasp.
'Have you?'

Lily has bought herself a new lipstick. In the loos, she swivels
it in and out of its metal case, its glistening column of colour
rising and retracting. The walls are covered in tiny pale green
mosaic tiles. She stares at them, wondering who would have
been patient enough to line up these minute squares in such
neat, regular rows. Then she leans in to the mirror and
applies the lipstick, smoothing the colour to the edges. She
rips sheets from a loo roll and dabs at her lips, leaving tissues
with dark purple mouths strewn along the shelf. They look
too personal, too strange to leave there, so she sweeps them
into her bag and zips it up.

She's wearing new, sleek boots with steep, slender heels.
Her feet seem narrower and longer, and her ankles ache
as she climbs the stairs back to the main room. She's at
the opening of an architectural exhibition. Why? She's
not sure. Sometimes, when she tries to explain herself
to herself, there is a gap, a crevasse before which her
comprehension falters.

She sees Marcus at the far end of the room, talking to
an Asian man with an exaggerated, spiked hairdo and thick,
black-framed glasses. The drawings on the wall confuse her:
a swarm of lines, axes, angles, measurements. Some bleed
into smudgy, sketchy impressions of buildings that look dark
and gloomy to her. But the models, on long tables down
the middle of the room amaze her: tiny replicas, like dolls'
houses, built in white card, complete with stairs, doors and
acetate windows. Leaning over them, she feels the glee of

perfection run through her; she can bend over and peer into their white, empty, people-less rooms, run her finger down the roofs and, if she wanted, crush them with one blow of her fist.

The room is littered with people. None of them look at the exhibits. The man who opened the show earlier with a short speech that Lily, standing at the back, couldn't hear is in the centre of a group of people, flushed, drink in hand, the other hand whirling in the air as he relates some complex thing to his listeners.

Marcus is still some distance away, one hand shoved into his back pocket, still talking to the spectacled man. A woman with blonde hair falling straight down her back has joined them. She has her forearm resting on Marcus's shoulder in a way that Lily can't decide is matey or possessive, and is bent at the waist, her head close to Speccy's, saying something into his ear.

Lily feels a weariness in her arms and shoulders. It suddenly seems a long time since this morning, since she left the house. She's going to go to Marcus and tell him she's going home, but there are so many people between them it's going to take an extra push of effort to get to him. Then she realises that because the room is really two rooms knocked into one, she can disappear through one door, walk along the corridor, and reappear next to him through the other.

She slips through the door into the stilled hush of the corridor. Papers and notices on a pinboard rise and stir as she passes. As she reaches the door she hears Marcus's voice, and the mention of her name makes her stop.

'Do you know what Lily said when she saw that building in the *AJ*?'

'No. What?' The blonde woman.

'She said, "It looks like a sauna."'

Marcus gives her a high-pitched, squeaky voice, almost a whine. They all laugh. Lily hears a slapping, as if someone has thwacked their palm against their leg.

'A sauna!' Marcus is repeating his punchline again, and everyone laughs back: hegh hegh hegh hegh, says the speccy man, hee hee hee, says the woman, ha ha ha, says Marcus.

'The lay-woman,' Blonde says, each word savoured in her mouth like a taste.

There is a pause. Lily realises she is on the opposite side of the wall to them, their mirror image. She is just putting up her hand to touch the width and mass of the bricks and mortar separating them, when she hears the speccy man: 'Now don't be unkind. That's not all you use her for, is it, Marcus?'

Again, there is a heartbeat of silence. Then her skull is filled with their laughter: great whooping jerks, high giggles, low coughs, and in among it the broad sound of Marcus's ha ha.

She stands there, stupid in her new shoes, her nails just touching the plaster of the wall enough so that when she turns to go there is the roughened, emery-board sensation of them scraping along the paint, before her hand falls back to her side.

When she arrives in Ealing later, her mother's hall light is on. The pavements have a thin sheen of ice and she has to walk carefully down the path. When Diane opens the door, her face for a second looks troubled and worn before she sees who it is.

'Hi,' Lily says, and her mother takes her by the hand.

'I was just about to get the Christmas decorations down from the loft,' she says, as they walk through the hall. 'You can help me if you like.'

They stand in the sitting-room together. The house feels cold, Lily notices, and the sofa has been moved.

'Are you staying over?' her mother asks, her head on one side.

Lily nods. 'If that's all right.'

She calls in sick, sits in her room, stares out at the swollen grey sky that threatens snow. She goes for a walk on the common with Sarah, who whips twigs against the stacks of wet, disintegrating leaves and shouts, 'Lay-woman, my arse!' at the trees. She cooks dinner for her mother, dusts the house, paints the downstairs toilet, stews apples from the garden in saucepans with cinnamon and raisins. In the room that used to be her father's study, a long time ago, she lets the globe spin under her hand, countries, oceans, mountain ranges, continents, islands, latitude lines skimming past her fingertips.

She clears out the garden shed, mends her mother's bike chain. She covers a chest of drawers in woodworm repellent, a thick, tawny mixture the consistency of treacle. She plays a new game with the globe – letting it spin and then stopping it and seeing where her index finger is. She hoovers.

After a while, she creeps back up the rickety stairs in the middle of the day when she knows he'll be at work. Everything is the same, which somehow amazes her. It's only been a few days, not even a week, since she was here, but already it seems like a different lifetime. Sunlight stretches along the floor and over the furniture; the tap drips in the sink. The plants droop, yellowing and curling.

There is a low, regular murmur coming from somewhere. She turns her head, glances about. The phone extension cord runs the length of the space and disappears under Marcus's door. She approaches on the balls of her feet and presses her ear to the wood of the door. 'No. Please,' she hears. 'Just listen. What I did was stupid, so . . . so fucking stupid and I am sorry. I'm so, so sorry. Don't take this job. Please. I couldn't bear it. Just give me another chance. I know I don't deserve it, but please. What can I do to make you come back?'

As a child, the boldest thing she'd ever done was, one day after baby Mark had died, she'd gone to the triangular cupboard under the stairs where they kept their coats. It was dark and smelt of old, pungent wood. She'd taken her stiff woollen coat off the brass peg that was hers and was screwed into the wood at her height, except that was last year and she had grown by now, buttoned it up and walked to the front door. She'd stood in the porch for a moment, then yanked at the front door, which had blurry glass shot through with a wire mesh. She'd first seen Mark through this glass, a hazy bundle with – the surprise – red hair, as she stood in the hall waiting for her mother to bring her new brother in from the car. She walked away down the front path fast, thinking, I'm leaving, I'm leaving, the words turning over in her head like wet clothes in a washing-machine. She got as far as the first road, where she was hesitating because she knew she wasn't supposed to cross it on her own, before Diane caught up with her. Her mother snatched her off the pavement and pressed her to her, saying her name over and over. Don't go, her mother said, in tears, don't ever go. Lily could never get over that her mother had somehow known that she was running away, that she didn't just think Lily was going for a walk.

She takes her hand off the door-handle and tiptoes away. In her room, she looks about: books, shoes, papers, makeup. These she shovels into bags, quickly and quietly. Her clothes she drapes over one arm. She leaves Sinead's dress, just as she found it.

She walks back through the flat. Marcus is crying now, heaving deep sobs down the phoneline. At the door, she turns. ''Bye,' she says, to the empty air. She looks around. Nothing. The windows, at either end, are open-eyed to each other. A mass of cloud passes, slow as a ship. ''Bye,' she says again. A lampshade moves at the other end of the room. Without thinking about it, Lily moves towards the phone point, a white box low on the wall. Her fingers close over the small plastic plug and flick it out of its socket. She straightens up and waits. Marcus's voice blunders on, unchecked, oblivious, into the silence. She steps out over the threshold, closes the door and drops the keys back through. She listens for metal hitting wood, then withdraws her hand from the jaw of the letterbox.

She is surprised at how easy it is to dismantle her life. She leaves a message on the agents' voicemail saying she's not coming back. She writes a letter to the shop. She visits Laurence and his mother, and hugs him goodbye. He squirms in her arms, affronted by this sudden display of emotion. She inserts her card into an auto-teller to find her bank balance. She calls up a number she finds among adverts in a newspaper and buys a flight out of Heathrow. She buys a rucksack and guidebooks. She changes money into foreign currency and finds the notes are too long for her wallet. She and Diane sit hunched on the floor over a world map. Sarah comes round and gives her a length of string: 'You always need string,' she says. Diane buys her travel wash, mosquito repellent and diarrhoea tablets. Lily packs and unpacks her rucksack three times.

On her last morning in London, finding she's done everything she needs to do and having several hours of dead time to kill, she goes swimming, rolling her costume tight into the length of a towel, and taking a bus to the pool. She used to like swimming. Her father would take her when she was a child, sliding the armbands on to her arm before blowing them up, his teeth around the transparent nozzle. 'They're uncomfy to put on when they're blown up, aren't they?' he would say. In the water, her feet would pedal wildly beneath her, excitement making her shiver. Before long, her father no longer brought the armbands. He kept his palm under her abdomen and the water swung underneath her as she moved her legs in measured, symmetrical flexes. 'The water will always support your weight, Lily,' he said then, 'remember that.' When she was tired she was allowed to rest the curves of her feet on his leg. He would crouch in the water and she would stand, waist-deep, feeling like those women on the prows of pirate ships. But later, at school, there were girls with speed-racing bathing suits and taut glossy skin who could do strokes that churned the water into white froth, and she lost interest.

At the pool, she shuts her eyes and jumps through the surface into a wide, long, mercury-ceilinged room that sways with trapezoids of light. Whitened, bleached bodies flail through the slow blue. She pushes up and, breaking into the echoey heat, does backstroke, a tiny replica of herself in the glass ceiling following her up and down the lane. When she gets out, she finds that water has got trapped in her ear.

Half-deaf, she goes home and packs up her last things. When she catches the train to the airport, her mother runs beside it as far as she can, saying something Lily can't hear, her face distorted with fierce grief, her hand, clutching a shopping list, waving or flailing in the air.

As the plane rises and falls through the night, Lily's ears block and unblock, but always in her left ear is the muted, secret roar of water. She shakes her head, pulls at the soft nub of her ear-lobe, tilts her neck and, in the toilet, hops up and down with her head on one side. But nothing. She bundles up her cardigan and sleeps against it, hoping to wake to a clarity in her left hemisphere. When she arrives and stumbles down the metal stairs, she has to lean in close to hear the immigration officer over the shifting swell of chlorinated water.

Later, she's found a hotel, left her bag, and is walking down a hill through the city's heat. People in bright clothing on motorbikes swish past her and wave. Her rubber-soled shoes feel soft against the melting tarmac. She buys a prickly pear from a streetside seller, who cleaves it with a blade, revealing the wet orange flesh for her.

As she walks away, pear held gingerly in her palm, there is a sudden break, a release, then a hot rush: water from a London swimming pool drops to the curve of her breast, where it quickly evaporates in the heat of the afternoon.

After checking the number, Aidan turns in at the gate and walks down the unfamiliar garden path, tiles loosened from the concrete plinking under his shoes. He tries to ignore his heart, which is sending blood around his system at a rate that is far too fast. Stop it, he tells it, stop it now. You're not helping.

He rings the doorbell, his heart openly and brazenly defying him. I'll talk to you later, he is saying to it when a man opens the door.

'You must be Aidan,' he says. 'Hi. I'm Michael. This is Lindsay.' He points to a heavily pregnant woman behind him, who smiles as she buttons up her coat.

'We're off out,' she says. 'Sinead's through there.'

Aidan passes quite close to Michael. There is very little of his sister in him: the line of the nose, perhaps, and the slightly fragile chin, but otherwise nothing.

'See you,' he says, as he closes the door after him.

''Bye,' says Aidan, 'nice to meet you.' He stands for a moment in the hallway. His pulse is so quick and light he wonders if he's about to faint. That would be just great. Perfect. How to win women and influence lives. He hears them whispering to each other on the doorstep and Lindsay exclaim, 'He's delectable! Why don't you have friends like that?' and Michael, laughing, telling her to shush, he'll hear you.

'Sinead?' he calls.

'In here.'

Aidan walks down the corridor and into the first door-way. It is a small basement flat. Sinead is sitting crosslegged like a tailor in the middle of the floor, surrounded by heaps of clothes. She holds up two jumpers.

'What do you think?' she asks.

'About what?'

'Should I take this one or this one?'

Aidan sits on a sofa. 'Can't you take both?'

'No! I'm going to Australia, for heaven's sake. You don't need more than one jumper in Sydney.'

Aidan looks around. They are in a small sitting room. White linen blinds cover the windows. A cat lies curled like a lifebuoy on a patchwork cushion. There is a pile of boxes in the corner labelled things like 'Sinead's books', 'Sinead's crockery', 'Sinead's winter clothes'.

'Are those going too?' He points at the boxes.

'No. Michael's going to store them for me.' She flings down the clothes she's holding, gets up and, bending over at the waist, gives him a brief hug. 'How are you? It's nice to see you.'

'Yeah, I'm . . . pretty good.'

'Do you want tea? Wine? A whisky?'

'Whatever you're having.'

She wanders from the room and a few moments later he hears clashing glasses, a fridge door opening, liquid glugging out of a bottle neck. He gets up, paces the rug. He has to do it. He's going to do it. He's going to do it now. When she gets back from the kitchen. He knows what he's going to say. He has it all laid out in his head. He rehearsed it in the car. Now he's here, though, it's doesn't quite hang together. She seems preoccupied, distracted. And the words he'd selected so carefully in the car now sound hollow and trite. But he has to do it. He has to. She'll be on a plane to Sydney this time tomorrow.

'Is this where you've been sleeping?' he calls, trying to ignore the waver in his voice.

'No. Michael's got a spare room.' She appears in the doorway, a glass in each hand. 'Well, it'll be the baby's room when it arrives. So it's about time I was out of here.'

He takes the wine and sits down in a chair next to a table. A bouquet of red roses is spilling out of its wrapping. They are limp and wilting under the cellophane. She sees him looking at them.

'I should put them in water, shouldn't I?' she murmurs, stroking the velvet of their petals with her thumb. Then she tilts the glass to her mouth, swallows, walks over to her heaps of clothes, picks up a pink T-shirt, and lets it fall. 'Do you think I'm doing the right thing?'

Aidan wets his finger and runs it around the rim of the glass. 'In going to Australia?'

'No . . .' She hesitates. 'I mean . . . I mean . . .'

'Marcus?'

'Yes.'

'I . . .' the glass beneath Aidan's thumb begins to hum and vibrate, making her look up, '. . . I really can't say.'

She nods, her mouth pressed shut.

'Are you . . .' he begins, '. . . do you think you'll take him back?' His heart hurls itself against its cage. He is sure she'll be able to hear it.

She sighs. 'I don't know,' she admits. 'I just don't know. Sometimes I can't envisage a future without him. Sometimes it seems . . . inevitable . . . that he and I will be together again. Like I can't see a way around it. But I don't know, Aidan. What he did was so . . . well, it was so unnecessary and . . . and so painful.'

Aidan says nothing. The glass murmurs and cries in his hand.

'But I just have this feeling that I can't get around him. I was talking to someone about it the other day,' she continues, 'and they said, "Well, you need to weigh up whether you'll be happier with him or without him." And that if I thought I'd be happier with him I should try to get over it and forgive him.' She shakes her head, tugging at one of the ends of her hair.

He puts down the glass, his fingers brushing against the flowers. He stands and crosses the room to the window where he can see slices of the street between the blinds. He is foolish and deluded, coming here thinking he could say those things to her. He must be mad. What kind of a response did he expect? He is ridiculous, but still wants to say to her, it's not inevitable, if you take him back he will only do something worse, can't you see he doesn't value you, and what am I to do when you are gone, what shall I do with this weight in my heart and why did you have to infiltrate me like this.

'I should go,' he says instead, turning back from the window.

'Already?' She is looking up at him, surprised.

In the hallway, he puts his arms around her, he knows for the last time. She won't come back and even if she does it won't be for him. He touches her hair, pressing her forehead to his shoulder, then pulls away, reaching for the door lock, because starting up in him is a pain so deep, so profound that he feels it will never leave him.

''Bye,' she calls after him. ''Bye!'

He doesn't look back, but climbs the spiralling concrete steps to the pavement. He walks past his car, past the end of the street, and on. And he feels as though she is holding on to the end of one of his essential fibres and that every step he takes away from her is, bit by bit, unravelling him.

part | four

*To know and love one other human being is
the root of all wisdom*

Evelyn Waugh

The earth was red here, sodden clay that sucked and pulled at the soles of her feet as she walked to the side of the road. The colour had ingrained itself everywhere – her hair, her backpack, her trouser bottoms, and the grooves of her palms, where scarlet rivers flowed from her wrist to the base of her fingers.

Yesterday there had been sand, and wind that flung and sprayed the minute particles into her eyes and mouth. Lily had sat at the front of the truck, a scarf swathing her head, sunglasses jammed down on to her face, teeth gritty against each other, her skin grained with the surface of the desert that was rolling past.

The other people were jumping down from the truck, their feet thudding on the soft ground. The driver sat on his heels beside his open door, flexing his shoulders, a cigarette poised between his fingers. Lily peeled off her hat, soaked her scarf with water from her bottle and held it against her face and neck as she wandered off the flattened dirt track into the uneven scrub. The soles of her sandals clacked against her heels. A small, sweet-voiced bird swung overhead on a high thermal draught. She could see so far she was sure she could almost make out the curve of the earth.

She shaded her eyes, her gaze travelling along the vanishing point of the track. In the far distance there was a black, heat-haloed spot or fleck. It shimmered and wavered on the horizon. The light glanced off it, and staring at it brought salty water to sting at her eyes, her lashes forming coloured prisms around her vision. She blinked, pressing her eyes shut then opening them again. Light flooded her retinas, putting everything in negative, the scene before her dancing with hundreds of white spots. The fleck, when she located it, had got larger, and was swirling with dust and speed. A truck.

The water held in the fabric of her scarf had warmed to air temperature. She glanced back to her own truck at the side of the road. The driver was standing up and waving at her to come back, to get on. The other travellers were staring and pointing in the direction of the oncoming vehicle. Lily moved back towards the road, the red earth caking her shoe soles. At the side of the truck, a Belgian man offered the cradle of his entwined hands; she put her foot into them and felt the ground fall away and her rising past the wooden side of the truck. She gripped it, her feet finding the foothold of the wheel, and swung herself into the back of the truck, which was littered with backpacks, people, water-bottles, tents, sacks of food.

The other truck ground towards them. Lily leaned out over the side to watch it. It was moving fast, its wheels kicking up dirt, its glinting radiator grinning like teeth. It was newer and faster than theirs, a gleaming blue, and was close enough now for her to see the faces of the two drivers and a leather doll that was suspended as if on a gibbet from their rear-view mirror. The noise of its engine clapped like thunder around her ears. Twenty yards or so from them it slowed suddenly as they realised the narrowness of the track. Her own driver stood out on the road, watching, his arms folded. The blue truck rumbled on to the opposite side of the track and began easing itself past them. She saw the drivers eyeing the narrow gap between the vehicles and then the people in the back were sliding past her, as if on a slow conveyor belt.

What Lily saw next was an image that would be sealed up inside her for ever like the packed pod of an unborn twin. She would never speak of it to anyone, never refer to it, and would only think about it when she was alone. It had been a long time – months, perhaps over a year, she couldn't remember. Long enough for it to seem like something she'd read or seen in a film, or something that had happened to someone else. But as the truck jolted past her in the desert, it was as if that time had been telescoped shut into itself. Just in front of her, close enough for her to reach out and touch her, was Sinead.

She was standing in profile, looking out over the top of the cabin to the road ahead, one hand gripping a spar of the tarpaulin roof above her. The air around Lily seemed suddenly hot, too hot to breathe in. Her eyes travelled again over the long neck, the thin arms, the coils of hair. It was a sight so familiar that it tipped over into strangeness. It seemed at once the most natural thing to see in the middle of the desert and the most preposterous. Lily stared, put her fingers up to press her cheek. Was she really seeing this, or not? Sinead half-turned, her gaze taking in the other truck, the people she was passing. Her lips curved slightly. If she had turned her neck just an inch more, she would have seen Lily standing there.

Lily watched as she turned back to the road, watched as she saw something, and as she exclaimed, pointed, and reached her hand behind her, like a relay runner stretching back to grasp the baton. Lily knew even before she looked at the man she'd failed to notice before. He withdrew his hand gently from Sinead's and passed it instead around her waist, pulling her towards him, looking out to whatever it was she was pointing at. Just before they slipped out of sight, Lily saw that she was saying something to him and that Aidan was turning, laughing, looking Sinead full in the face.

The truck vanished in an eddy of dust and fumes. Lily didn't lean out to watch it go. The air around her settled back to its still, simmering heat. The woman next to her was spreading sun lotion over her arms and relating an elaborate story about a hotel manager. The Belgian man was offering round a packet of dried apricots. Lily took one and bit into its dense orange flesh. Beneath her, the truck quivered into life, the engine straining and pulling against the brakes.

The scenery slid into motion. There was no wind, just a vertical sun, and miles of red, red earth, the trees writhing up from the ground, bone-white, like petrified forks of lightning. Lily shaded her eyes against the glare. Far away into the distance, a large-eared dog-like creature was standing on the crest of a rock, nose high, reading the air for her scent.

the distance between us

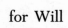for Will

I do know that lives can change overnight, though it usually takes much longer than that to comprehend what has happened, to sense that we have changed direction
                                            Jay McInerney

I came to these places . . . to claim kin with them, to be guided by them

                                            Geoff Dyer

She was my liegeman, my alter ego, my double; we could not do without one another

                                            Simone de Beauvoir,
                                            on her sister

part | one

He wakes to find himself splayed like a starfish across the bed, his mind running at full tilt. On the other side of the room, the fan turns towards him then turns away, as if offended. Somewhere beside him, the pages of a book flutter, reel and divide. The apartment is filled with an inky light and flashes of neon scissor the ceiling. Late evening.

'Shit,' he says, and raises his head with a jerk. Something soft yet integral between his shoulder blades stretches and tears like wet paper. Swearing and reaching round to feel for the point of pain, Jake stumbles to his feet and skates in his socks over the wooden tiles to the bathroom.

His face in the mirror is a shock. The creases and pleats of the bedsheet have left reddened lines over his cheek and temple, giving his skin a peculiar, raw look. His hair stands up as if he's been electrocuted, and appears to have grown. How had he managed to fall asleep? He'd been reading, head propped up on his hands, and the last thing he remembered was the man in his book descending a rope ladder into a disused well. Jake glances at his watch. Ten past ten. He's already late.

A moth blunders into his face, then ricochets into the

mirror, the faint powder on its wings leaving a mottled mark, a ghost of itself, on the glass. Jake stands back for a moment, watching it, tracking its course through the air, then snaps his cupped palms at it. Misses. The moth, sensing danger, spirals upwards towards the light but Jake aims again and this time he gets it, its delicate, confused body knocking at the cage of his hands.

He nudges the lever with his elbow and pushes at the window. The roar of the street, nineteen floors below, rises up to meet him. Jake leans out over the strings of washing and, opening his hands, tosses the moth upwards. It falls for a second, turning over, disoriented, then recovers and, catching a hot thermal draught from an air-conditioning unit down below, flitters into invisibility.

Jake slams the window shut. He rattles through the flat, collecting wallet, keys, jacket, pulling on his shoes, left in a heap by the door. The lift takes an age to come and when it does, it stinks of sweat and stale air. In the entrance hall, the janitor is sitting on a stool beside the door. Above him are the frilled red and gold decorations of Chinese New Year – a fat-cheeked child with tar-black hair rides astride a pink pig.

'*Gung hei fat choi,*' Jake says, as he passes.

The man's face cracks into a gap-toothed grin. '*Gung hei fat choi,* Jik-ah!' He slaps Jake on the shoulder, making his skin prickle and sting like sunburn.

Outside, taxis splinter the light of the road's puddles and an underground train shakes the pavement. Jake tilts his head to look up at the building tops. The year is turning from ox to tiger. When he was a child, he used to imagine the year at the stroke of midnight as a strange mutant creature, caught in half-metamorphosis.

He moves away from his building, almost crashing into a diminutive elderly woman pushing at the handle of a cart laden with collapsed cardboard boxes. Jake sidesteps her and heads south, past the basketball courts, a small red kerbside shrine with a bouquet of spent joss sticks, past men sitting in a *yum chai* shop, mah-jong tiles clicking on the tables between them, past serried rows of draped motorbikes, intricate webs of bamboo scaffolding, past restaurant tanks where doomed fish are stretching out their gills, searching for oxygen in the cloudy water.

But Jake doesn't see any of this. He is looking up at the darkening clouds, humming as he walks, his thin-soled sneakers moving over the pavement. The air swings with incense, firecracker smoke, and the amniotic salinity of the harbour.

The bus isn't coming. Stella pulls her scarf closer round her throat and stands on tiptoe to gaze down the line of traffic. Cars, cars, taxis, motorbikes, the odd cyclist, cars, more cars. But no bus. She looks up at the screen that is supposed to tell her how long she has to wait. It's blank.

She separates her coat sleeve from her glove to check her watch. She's on an afternoon shift today and she's going to be late if she waits any longer. Stella stands for a moment, thinking. Is it better to stay and wait for a bus that will come eventually or to start walking and get there just a little bit late? She could get the Tube but that's a ten-minute walk from here and might be delayed as well. She'll walk. It's probably the quickest way, now.

With a brief glance over her shoulder to make sure the bus still isn't coming, Stella sets off. The street is cold, unusually cold for this time of year, the ground sharp, gilded with frost that cracks underfoot. The sky is an uncertain grey, crazy-paved with leafless branches.

She's back in London for several weeks – no more than that, she hopes – working on a late-night radio show. She has a flat here, a bedsit on the edge of Kennington, but usually rents it out while she goes off to different places. A month in Paris, a stint in Moscow, half a year in Helsinki. She's not sure where she'll go next – Rome, maybe, Madrid, Copenhagen. Stella doesn't like staying in one place.

She marches north, towards the Thames, her breath steaming, her body inappropriately warm inside the layers of clothing. As she takes her first steps on Waterloo Bridge, the city begins to split in two, the river opening out to her. The bridge was built entirely by women, she read somewhere once, during the Second World War. It's deserted today. Cars swoop past, heading north, but on both sides the pavements stretch out, empty.

At the crossroads, Jake leaps on to the backboard of a rattling tram just as it's pulling away. The downstairs, murky and dim, is crammed – people filling the seats and clinging to the ceiling rails. An old man in a vest and faded trousers is nearest Jake, a birdcage held on his lap. From its pendulum perch, the bird regards Jake sideways with the tiny black beads of its eyes. The heads of the two Westerners on the tram sway above those of the Chinese.

Jake thunders up the wooden stairs. He takes the seat right at the front, leaning his head out of the window, facing into the speeding breeze, and watches the cluttered, neon-scribbled buildings of Wanchai slide into the slick concrete-and-mirror edifice of the huge shopping complex.

Jake's hair is dark and his skin can turn to almost the same shade as his friend Hing Tai's if he stays in the sun long enough, but his eyes are the colour of deep water. He has a British passport, a British mother and, somewhere, a British father. But Jake has never seen Britain, or his father, and has never been anywhere near Europe.

Stella sees a solitary figure, far away, at the other end of the bridge, heading towards her. A man. Shrunk down by distance. She could raise her hand and encircle him with a finger and thumb. As if pulled towards each other by a string, they walk and walk and walk. He becomes more defined: tall, hulking, wearing a green jacket.

Stella looks out over the river, where the huge wheel is sequined with lights and people small as insects swarm along the South Bank. She swings the beam of her vision back to the bridge, to where she's heading, and the shock is so great she almost stumbles. She has to grip the wall with her hand to stop herself falling and her heart trips and stutters, as if unsure how to continue.

Stella stares down at the brown, twisting water of the river, then back at the man. He is closer again and Stella wonders if he will just carry on getting bigger and bigger until he is looming over her, vast and terrible as a brockenspectre. He is looking straight at her now, his hands jammed into his pockets.

She cannot believe it, she really cannot. He has that swollen, white-pink skin, the same dense fuzz of red hair, and the eyes pitted deep into the flesh of the face.

It's as if time has buckled back on itself, as if the years have swallowed themselves. Stella can feel the clammy give that skin would have beneath her grip, and the peculiar, damp animal smell of his hair. The man is coming towards her now, close, so close she could touch him, and a scream hovers somewhere at the base of her throat.

'You all right, doll?'

Her gloved fingers tighten on the rail. He is Scottish. Just as she had known he would be. Stella nods, still looking at the river, its surface muscled like the backs of serpents.

'You sure?' He is standing just out of view. Stella can't breathe, seems unable to stretch open her lungs for air. 'You don't look it.'

She nods again. She doesn't want him to hear her speak, to hear her voice. She has to get away. Without looking at him, she starts to move off, pulling herself along by the railing. She has to pass quite close to him and she can feel the movement of his breath on her hair as he says, 'If you're sure, then,' and it makes her shake, makes her flesh shrink around her. ''Bye for now,' he says.

Stella swivels her head to see him go. That same lumbering gait, his feet splayed, the massive shoulders hunched. He turns round once. Pauses for a second. Then carries on. 'Bye for now.

Two trucks thunder past in quick succession, making the air churn. She breaks into a stumbling run, her coat flapping and tugging behind her, the city buildings veering ahead. A sharp, dragging ache has started up in her chest, as if something with teeth and claws is trying to fight its way out of her. She trips, her palms and knees meeting the pavement, and before she scrambles up, she looks behind her.

He's vanished. The bridge stretches away from her, domed, curving and deserted.

She drags herself to her feet. Grit and dirt smudge her palms. Her hair is wet with tears and sticks to her face in the cutting February wind. She looks up and down the street, unsure of what she is seeking.

Coming towards her on the other side of the road, she sees the lighted oblong of a taxi sign. She darts into the traffic, one arm raised above her head. A car screeches and swerves. 'Please stop,' she mutters to herself, her eyes fixed on the light speeding towards her, 'please.'

The taxi slows and pulls up. Stella runs towards it, opens the door and climbs inside.

Jake clatters down the stairs as the tram does its double-corner-swing into Central. He likes feeling the swooping, shuttling change of direction beneath him, likes to be standing for that bit when you have to brace yourself against the contrary motion. He drops down to the road in front of the weighty, jagged structure of the bank and cuts through, under the black glass of the building where empty escalators are humming, churning round, transporting nobody up and down.

He toils up the steep incline of Lan Kwai Fong, threading his way through the already thick crowd. The cobbled road is lined with bars and clubs, all filled with Westerners who work in the legal offices, newspapers, schools, radio stations, IT departments of Hong Kong Island, and return each night by ferry to their flats on Lamma or Lantau, stopping off here to tank down some alcohol and meet their friends. Jake never usually comes here, but Mel and her crowd like it.

Jake often thinks of Hong Kong as a kind of overflow pipe for Europe. The people who come here have left their homes and their families for a reason, and not usually one they ever disclose. They're all in varying degrees of separation, or running away from something, or in search of an elusive element that might complete them. Or at least hoping the feeling that something is missing from their lives won't pursue them over the ocean. If you go far enough you might never catch up with yourself.

At the top of the hill, Jake turns left into the Iso-Bar. It is filled with icy, over-conditioned air and hordes of people, drinks in hand, packed close together. He scans the crowds, searching for Mel. Suddenly she is there, right in front of him. Their eyes haven't yet met but she is printing a kiss on his face in lipstick and turning her head towards her friends. 'I told you he'd be late, didn't I? Didn't I say he'd be late?' Her face swims before him in the murky gloom. She has her light, fine, almost colourless hair pulled into a ponytail high on the back of her head and her hands are fastened behind his back.

'I'm sorry, I fell asleep,' Jake yells over the music. 'I don't know how. One minute I was reading and the next I—'

'You must have been tired.' She smiles up at him.

'Yes.'

He extracts himself from her embrace to say hello to the others. They nod and smile at him, raising their glasses, and Lucy, Mel's best friend, gives him a brief, distracted kiss before turning back to the man she's talking to. Someone gives Jake a tall glass, slippery with condensation.

'We're going to Lantau tomorrow,' Mel is shouting over the noise, leaning towards one of her colleagues, her fingers hooked into Jake's arm, 'to see the Buddha. Jake wants to go hiking in the hills.'

'Are you going with him?' the colleague asks, amused.

'Yes.' Mel nods and glances his way. 'If he'll have me.' She squeezes his arm. 'I thought I should give it a go, you know.'

'But you hate that kind of thing!'

Nina places the phone on the floor next to her and dials the code for London, then the number. There is a short pause before the pulsing purr of a distant ringing.

She waits, frowning, picking apart one of the sandwiches Richard made for her that morning, extracting the silvery half-moons of onion. He knows she doesn't eat raw onion. Then there's the gasp of electronic ether before the hiss of a voicemail recording: *Hi, you've reached Stella Gilmore in Production. I'm either away from my desk or on another—*

Nina hangs up, reassembles her sandwich and puts a corner of it into her mouth.

'Twelve minutes to go!' Lucy exclaims, peering at her watch. 'And we all turn from chickens to pigs!'

Mel turns to Jake, a slight anxiety on her face. 'Is that right, Jake?'

'Ox to tiger,' he murmurs, 'and it's not really us it's—'

'Let's go to that bar down the road!' Lucy is saying. 'The one with the DJ. Come on, let's go!'

They toss back their drinks and head for the door. Outside, the air is tepid and a thin, fine veil of drizzle brushes their faces. The street is packed, a sea of heads bobbing and rippling between them and the buildings opposite. Jake has to flatten himself against the wall to let a group of Japanese boys go past. Lucy stumbles on the raised kerb, falling against him. On his other side, Mel grips his hand. Across the street, a gang of Brits are singing 'Auld Lang Syne'.

In an office in London, a mobile phone starts to ring. The sound is muffled, as if the phone is underneath a coat or a folder or a bag. It makes several people in cubicles around it turn their heads, listening, wondering. Then they realise it isn't theirs and turn away again.

The girl who shares an office with Stella pulls the headphones down from her ears and looks across at Stella's desk. The chair is tilted away from the computer. Where Stella should be there is just a view through to the uneven chimneys and blackened, rain-polished roofs of Regent Street.

Should she answer it? Stella quite often forgets to take it home with her. It's rung several times in the past hour or so. Someone must be anxious to get hold of her. The phone stops, as abruptly as it began. The girl pulls the headphones back into place. She'll tell Stella when she gets in.

The noise of the street rises, as if someone's turned up the volume. People are shouting and laughing and yelling. A man just in front of Jake is brandishing a small, fragile paper dragon, its teeth bared, its nostrils trailing fire. Jake starts pushing his way through the throng of bodies, in the direction of the bar, Mel just behind him, in his wake, Lucy behind her. The others have melted into the swell. More and more people are streaming out of doors to join the thick current of people. Jake is hit and buffeted by shoulders, elbows, hips, feet. He twists his head and looks up the street. Is it any less crowded there? No. Heads are appearing, flowing in from adjoining lanes, and D'Aguilar Street is blocked half-way down by a police barrier. He feels his heart accelerating inside him, falling over itself, and he clutches Mel's fingers.

Everyone is shoving and pushing. Jake forgets how selfish people become in a situation like this. Three men all wearing red party hats elbow their way past, one treading on his foot, grinding the bones against the pavement. More and more bodies are pouring like water into the street. Jake feels very warm all of a sudden. He turns one way and then the other, unable to decide what they should do, which way they should go. Mel is saying something to him and as he turns to hear her, he stumbles and nearly goes down. He grabs for the nearest thing – the coat of a woman standing to his left – and drags himself up again. The woman gives him a quick, panicked glare but turns away silently when Jake apologises. The crowd is pressing nearer, closing in on his ribcage.

'I don't like this,' Mel says. 'Jake, I don't like it.'

'I know,' he says. 'Let's try—'

His words are snatched away from him because several things happen at once, and very fast.

Behind them, a man carrying several bottles of beer trips and falls forward. The bottles burst from his fingers and drop to the ground. The glass explodes and beer fans out over the cobbles, a frothing, dark, slippery stain. Jake pushes back into the dense pack of bodies on the pavement, dragging Mel with him. There is a sudden wild surge from up the hill. Jake sees the beer-bottle man go under. Then Lucy slips, pulling away from them, vanishing, the crowd closing over her head.

Francesca is in the garden, bending over the echium she bought in a nursery in Arran, which, she's just noticed, is beginning to be blackened by frost. Francesca hates frost, hates it more than the sticky-footed greenfly which in summer swarm up her roses, more than the orange-frilled slugs that tear their way through her nasturtiums. She can't ever kill slugs, though. The thought of poisoning them with noxious chemicals or sprinkling them with salt is too much, too cruel.

She shivers and pulls Archie's cardigan more tightly round her. The Edinburgh sky above her droops, low and soft as the belly of a goose. The cold today has the metallic tang of snow.

Her body responds to the electronic trilling before her mind. She's straightened up and turned towards the house before she's realised what it is. The telephone. The new telephone that Stella bought her.

She picks it up and presses a button at random, but the trilling doesn't stop. Francesca sighs, reaches for her glasses, looped around her neck on a chain, and peers at the buttons more closely. There is one with a minute picture of a telephone receiver on it. Maybe that was it.

'Hello?' she says tentatively, expectantly.

'Have you still not worked out how to answer that phone?'

It's Nina, she's pretty sure. They sound quite similar on the phone and neither of them ever seems to think they need to identify themselves. 'Of course I have,' Francesca lies, playing for time. They'd be offended if she got the wrong one. 'I was in the garden, that's all.'

'Oh.' There's a pause in which Francesca hears the suck and drag of a cigarette. Definitely Nina, then. 'How are you, anyway?'

'Oh, fine. You know, busy. Your dad's gone to Munich.'

'What for?'

'I'm not sure. A conference, I think.'

'Look,' Nina announces, 'I can't talk now. I've got an appointment in five minutes. I was just wondering if you'd spoken to Stella today.'

'Stella?' Francesca repeats, thinking. Stella is the one she doesn't have to worry about. 'No.'

'When did you last speak to her?'

'Last week. I think. Or maybe the week before.'

'But not today?'

'No. Why?'

'No reason. I just can't get hold of her. I've left messages and she hasn't called me back.' Nina takes another drag of her cigarette. 'She's disappeared.'

Francesca often feels at a slight disadvantage when faced with the relationship between her two daughters. It's always seemed too private, too elliptical for her to comprehend. She brightens with an idea. 'Maybe she's taken the day off or—'

'She would have told me,' Nina interjects.

Francesca doesn't know what to say. But diversionary tactics have always worked best with Nina so she asks, 'Why don't you come over later? There might be a good film on TV. I'll make you dinner.'

'OK,' Nina concedes. 'Perhaps.'

Mel is screaming Lucy's name over and over, and fighting against Jake's grasp. The crowd seethes with yells and sweat and the hot stench of beer. Jake struggles to keep hold of Mel while pushing forward to find Lucy. Then there is another great heave and surge, and Jake feels the ground drop away from his feet, and they are carried by a current of bodies away from Lucy, towards the window of a bar where people are dancing to music only they can hear. Jake is jostled up against the cold grain of a wall. Mel has been snatched away from him. He fights his way round, pushing his elbows into surrounding flesh to create space to breathe, kicking his feet against the wall. His lungs feel red hot, airless and compressed.

'Mel!' he shouts. 'Melanie!' But he can't even hear his own voice over the noise. A blond man with a beard is pressed up against his back and a Filipina girl is clinging to his jacket sleeve, sobbing rhythmically. 'Mel!' he yells again, trying to twist round.

The crowd rushes again, in a different direction, down-hill, sweeping him along, and Jake feels something beneath his shoes, something soft and yielding. A body? A sharp jag of panic crosses his chest and he tries to look down but he is wedged between a screaming teenager with hennaed hair and a woman with wide, staring eyes. Jake looks into them and sees the black stretch of the pupils, the way her head is lolling on her neck, the slackened jaw.

Jake thrashes his legs beneath him and tilts his head back, gasping to draw breath. Drizzle feathers his face. High above, the sky domes over them, black, depthless and impassive, brittled with silver. He can hear the thin wail of sirens, far away. He can hear the tearing screams of the teenager next to him, tailing off to a whimper. The blurred, metallic words of someone somewhere over a Tannoy, telling them in two languages to keep calm, stop pushing, keep calm. Different currents of music from the bars around them. The distant crackle of the harbour fireworks. The rushing, thudding trip-trip of his blood against his ears. The terrible silence of the woman with the staring eyes.

By four thirty, the girl who shares the office with Stella is annoyed. She and Stella still have to sort out a guest for next week's show; one of them is supposed to have read a book, or part of a book, and written the interview questions for James; PRs keep on phoning, pushing their clients for appearances on the show, and the girl, Maxine, doesn't have the time to edit this week's interview while answering the calls. Where the hell is she?

The production phone rings. She snatches it up. 'Hello, *James Karl Show*, this is—'

'Maxine,' a quiet but offhand voice, 'sorry, it's—'

'Nina,' Maxine cuts in, even more annoyed now. Stella's sister. She'd recognise that voice anywhere. She rings about twenty times a day, and usually about absolutely nothing. Maxine and another woman who works on the show have a joke that Stella's sister can't make a cup of tea without asking Stella first. 'She's not here,' Maxine snaps.

'I gathered that,' Nina snaps back. 'Do you know where she is?'

'I wish I did. She was supposed to be in by one, but she hasn't turned up.'

'Where was she this morning?'

'I don't know.'

'Was she meeting anyone?'

'I've no idea.'

'What time did she leave last night?'

Maxine sighs. The last thing she needs right now is Stella's loopy sister giving her the third degree. 'Nina, I'm actually really up against it here and—'

'What time did she leave?' Nina repeats.

'For God's sake,' Maxine mutters. 'I don't know . . . twelve thirty. One a.m. maybe. It would have been after the show finished.'

Maxine hears the flick of Nina's lighter.

'Can I take a message?' Maxine enquires, twirling a pen round and round her fingers. She has to get back to that interview – James will go mad if it's not finished by five. She waves to another woman through the glass partition in another office. The woman is motioning drinking, asking her if she wants a coffee. Maxine signals yes and gives her a thumbs-up.

'No,' Nina is saying, 'no message,' and hangs up.

'Goodbye to you too,' Maxine mutters to the empty cubicle.

He is caught in a surge again, carried this time uphill, the pressure around him increasing until he can no longer draw breath. The scene in front of him dissolves and blurs, and a deep pain is spreading from his shoulder down his back. The important thing is not to fall, he is telling himself, over and over, to stay upright, not to go under. His ribcage creaks and strains, there seems to be no oxygen getting to any of his body, his limbs are numb and prickling, and Jake feels sure that this is it, his time is now, that nothing and no one could withstand this, and his mind is flat and calm and heavy as molten lead.

Suddenly he is cannoned into the back of a man who turns round angrily. 'Oi, do you mind?'

The man turns back to his companions. Jake stares at them. They are drinking and chatting. He has come up against a section of the crowd who don't know, who are still caught up in the change to the Year of the Tiger.

The man with whom he collided is saying, 'I mean, what would you do if a client took you to one of those places with flattened pigs' heads in the window?'

The woman beside him cackles, throwing back her head. 'When in Rome!' she shrieks, and they all laugh.

Around him, he feels a sudden release. Bodies fall away from him. It's as if a membrane has been punctured: the currents of people start draining away. His legs buckle like melted plastic, and the cobbles come up to meet him. He crouches there, gagging and coughing for breath, trying to suck air down into his bruised lungs, aware of people standing around him, staring, murmuring. It seems very quiet all of a sudden.

Jake raises his head and looks down the street.

Nina drops into Richard's surgery on her way home over the Meadows, striding past his row of patients, past the receptionist (who never speaks to Nina because Nina once accidentally called her a fat cow at the annual surgery party), and up to his door.

Richard is putting some funny equipment made of steel and black tubing back into its box. 'Hello, beautiful,' he says, when he sees her, and kisses her forehead, which Nina hates but doesn't want to have a row about now. 'What are you doing here?'

'Came to see you.' Nina sits herself down on the examination couch and crosses her legs.

'How nice,' he says, but she catches him throwing a swift glance towards the clock.

'I'm worried about Stella,' she says.

'Oh?' He is shuffling pages together on his desk, looking at something on his computer screen.

'She's gone AWOL.'

He is writing something on one of the papers. 'AWOL?' he repeats – his trick to reassure her that he's listening. 'But she's always doing that, isn't she? It's an integral part of the . . . the Stella package.'

'What is?'

'The vanishing act.' Richard glances up. Nina sees him put down his pen, sees him reminding himself to tread carefully when talking about her sister. In the early days of their relationship – years ago now – she'd hurled a tin-opener at his head when he'd asked if she didn't think Stella was just a little bit flighty.

'But she always tells me first. I . . .' she shrugs uneasily '. . . I've just got this feeling that something's happened.'

Richard comes towards her. 'I'm sure she's fine,' he says, stroking her cheek. 'When was it you last heard from her?'

'Last night,' Nina says, then regrets it. She sees his mouth twitch, sees the diagnosis 'hysterical' crossing his mind. 'But I've left her loads of messages since then.'

'She'll turn up,' he says soothingly. 'She's probably just busy, don't you think?'

Nina doesn't answer. She reclines on the examination couch, her spike heels snagging in the paper cover. Richard's palm lands on her hip. She can feel the heat of it through the thin material of her skirt.

'Maybe you need an examination,' he says, his fingers beginning to hitch up her hem, the callus on his thumb snagging on her stockings.

Nina stares at the ceiling above her, listens to the rustle of the paper that covers the couch, the leaping second hand of the clock on the wall, Richard's breathing.

'No,' she says, sitting up and pulling down her skirt. 'I have to find Stella.'

Jake stands next to a melamine desk, his right hand clutching his left arm. The ache in his shoulder is overwhelming, drilling, rooted, and the arm dangles at an angle, turned away from him, as if it belongs to somebody else. Something is bleeding at the side of his face. He has to keep wiping it away, tiger-striping his sleeve. Nurses, orderlies and paramedics swirl around him, busy, electrified.

Jake leans over the desk again. 'Melanie Harker,' he says to the receptionist. 'Is she here?'

'Please take a seat,' she says, without looking at him. 'The doctor will see you soon.'

'I don't want a doctor,' he says, 'I have to find her.' The white light from the overhead strips is making his eyes smart. 'How about Lucy Riddell? Is she here?'

The receptionist fixes him with a glare. 'Please take a seat.'

If he moves his head too quickly, the walls and corridors see-saw around him. He grips the peeling edge of the desk for balance. His hand is shaking like an old man's. He is still struck by the ease with which his lungs swell and deflate, swell and deflate. He feels he will never get over this.

The white flash of a doctor flits past the double doors into a perpendicular corridor. Jake moves after him, propping himself up on the wall as he walks.

'Excuse me,' he says, stumbling down the corridor, sliding along the shiny pale green paint, 'excuse me.'

The doctor gives him a quick side-glance but hurries on.

'*M'goi, m'goi*,' Jake switches to Cantonese, '*gau meng ah*. I'm trying to find Melanie Harker. Is she here?'

The doctor stops in his tracks and stares at him, attentive now, shocked, as people always are, by a *gweilo* speaking Cantonese. 'Melanie Harker,' the doctor repeats, still staring at him. 'Yes. She's here. I saw her earlier. She is . . .' He stops. 'Are you a relative?'

'No . . . yes . . .' Jake attempts to formulate an explanation. He fills the seemingly massive capacity of his lungs from the endless supply of air around them. 'She's my . . . my girlfriend. Her family are in Britain,' he manages. 'Norfolk,' he adds, without knowing why.

The doctor, a man with grey circles of fatigue under his eyes, looks him over. 'Have you been seen?'

'No,' Jake shakes his head impatiently, 'but I'm fine. I need to know—'

'You don't look fine,' the doctor says, fishes a slender torch from his coat pocket and shines it into Jake's eyes. When he touches his left arm, Jake flinches, hot pain arrowing down his arm. 'You'll need an X-ray for that,' the doctor says. 'It's broken. And you're in shock. You'll stay here tonight. *Neihih ming m ming ah?*'

'*Ngor ming*. But when can I—'

'Melanie Harker,' the doctor interrupts, 'is in a critical condition. She's in Intensive Care.'

Jakes stares at a light fixed to the wall. A fly has got

23

trapped inside it and is battering against the white, opaque glass. It feels as if the movement and the noise are inside his head. He opens his mouth to ask a question, but can't quite think what it is.

'I'll see if you can visit her,' the doctor says, more gently.

Stella sits on the floor, her back against the door of the flat, her coat still wrapped round her. Everything in this room seems unfamiliar. Did she buy that picture on the wall, the vase, those books? Do they belong to her? Is this her life, or someone else's? Was it her who spent a whole weekend stripping and waxing these floorboards, a mask over her face? Why had she done that? What was it for?

Beyond the thick green stalk of an amaryllis, Stella catches sight of herself in the mirror. Her face seems bloodless, and it stands out, stark, from her hair. She has the long-boned hands of her father, the green eyes and dark hair of her mother, and, she was surprised to discover recently when she found an ancient, browning photograph in her grandparents' flat, the face of a great-great-aunt from Isernia. A mish-mash, a collision of genes.

The phone rings again, making her jump, making her look away from herself. She plucks at the interlocked stitches of her gloves. It rings four, five, six times, then the answerphone clicks on and she hears her sister's voice, unspooling into the silence.

Stella bows her head, covers her ears.

Mel seems drained of colour. Her skin is so pale that she sinks, like some camouflaging animal, into the magnesium-white sheets and walls. Machines sigh and blip around her. Somewhere overhead the air-conditioning hums.

'Mel?' Jake curls his fingers around hers. They feel dry and cold, a loose collection of bones. On her other hand is a grey plastic clip, like crocodile jaws. 'Mel, it's me,' he whispers.

Her eyes slide under their lids, marbled with violet, then her lashes part. It takes her a while to focus on him. Her mouth opens, but nothing comes out. He sees her inhale and swallow. Everything seems to take her so long and so much effort. He wants to tell her that it doesn't matter, that she doesn't need to speak, but she is saying his name on an outward breath and her hand twitches beneath his. Then she is mouthing something he cannot hear.

'What was that?' he whispers, leaning closer. She doesn't smell as she usually does. Underneath the starched antiseptic tang of the hospital there is a sour, queer scent, like something left too long in the dark.

'Lucy,' Mel whispers. 'Lucy.'

Jake looks away as he says, 'She's not here.' He finds lying hard, has never been very good at it. He's always afraid that the truth is obvious, that it's readable on his face, as if projected on to it. Lucy is lying in the morgue, several floors below Mel's bed. 'She was taken to another hospital,' he invents quickly. 'Queen Mary. In Happy Valley.'

Mel's eyes travel over him, over the plaster cast on his

arm, the sling on his shoulder, the vivid bruises blooming on his face. 'Are you OK?' The words come out jerkily, separated, as if in different sentences.

'Fine.' He nods. 'It's just a fracture. And a dislocated shoulder. But it's fine. How are you feeling?'

Her head moves on the pillow and she sighs, misting the oxygen mask. Jake sees tears spreading into river deltas at the corners of her eyes. Her mouth moves again.

He bends over her and touches his lips to her cheek, smoothing damp hair away from her forehead. 'What was that?' he says.

'I'm scared,' he hears. He is leaning over her, so close that he can see her tongue forming the words. 'Jake, I don't want to . . .' Her eyes swivel until they find his. 'I don't want to die –'

'You're not going to,' he gets out, before he realises that she hasn't finished, that she is saying:

'– without having married you.'

Jake, crouched around her on a bed in Intensive Care, blinks. He is about to say, 'What?' but stops himself. He heard her. It's such a bizarre thing for her to come out with that a very distant part of him wants to laugh. Surely she can't mean that. 'Mel,' he begins, unsure of what he wants to say, what he should say. What do you say to something like that? To a girl you've only known for four months?

'I don't want . . . I can't bear the thought,' her voice rises like a leaf on the wind, 'of dying without being . . . tied to you.' She is sobbing now, and people are running around them, feet hurrying against the tiles. 'I can't bear it without . . .'

A nurse is readjusting the mask over Mel's face. Mel is struggling against her, trying to speak more, but the doctor is there, fiddling with a machine, telling her to shush, to please lie back.

'Maybe . . .' Jake tries again but he can't seem to order his thoughts. He would give anything just to be able to lie down for a minute, to shut his eyes against the violence of the lights, to stretch out on some starched sheets, for one of these nurses to tell him what he should do. 'Maybe we should see how you are tomorrow,' he says. He is aware of how lame these words sound and he catches her look of dismay.

'You know, she isn't going to last the night,' the doctor, standing to Jake's right, says in Cantonese, gentle but emphatic.

Jake turns to look at him. The pain in his arm and shoulder judders and twists. It suddenly seems incredibly hot in here. He looks back at Mel. Her eyes blaze and glitter behind the mask.

'I'm sorry,' the doctor says.

Stella is shivering cold, her flesh studded with bumps, her teeth chattering. The heating's not on. Earlier, she'd leant across and snapped on the light. Above her, the bulb burns yellow. She has no idea what time it is. The building and, indeed, the whole city seem to have disappeared, dissolved around her, receded into the night. The phone rang twice more, and fell silent. The people next door had their television up very loud. But that's stopped too now. It's as if the lit box of this room hovers, alone and solitary, in dark space.

Stella shuts her eyes, tight. There must be some way to stop this dominating her existence. How many times has this happened to her? How often does she glimpse him in the face of a stranger, on the street, in a train, in a bar, in a lift, across a shop? These sightings mar her life like sinkholes, the ground around them eroding, precarious.

Stella stands up quickly. Her vision blurs and wanes from the sudden movement, her joints aching. A small, winged creature flutters round her head briefly, then circles up to the light. She stands watching it for a moment and it's then that the idea appears in her head. It reaches her from some external place, like lightning hitting a conductor, and as soon as she thinks it, she's made the decision.

She jerks into action, an over-wound toy, moving through her flat, collecting things: clothes, a jacket, a map, her compass, wallet, some books. She pulls a bag from the top of a cupboard and shoves the heap of things into it, yanking the zip closed.

The priest is someone who knows Hing Tai. He greets Jake as Jik-ah, tells him he is sorry for his troubles. An unsmiling nurse with a white cone hat perched on top of her thick black perm acts as a witness. As the first light of the Year of the Tiger soaks into the little room, Jake lays one hand on Mel's and another on the black leather of a book he doesn't believe in and says I will, I will, I do, I will.

A frost is forming as she unlocks her car. She has to sit

for several minutes, hot air blasting through the dashboard, until the starbursts of ice have dissolved from her
windscreen.

The keys to the flat she slides into an envelope, addressed
to a friend. As she drives out of the fringes of London, she
pulls up near a postbox and pushes the envelope into its
wide red mouth.

She is surprised by how many cars are out on the
streets in the middle of the night. At a motorway sign
saying 'Scotland, The North' she pushes her foot down on
the accelerator and almost smiles.

part | two

Stella is sliding a knife along the seal of an envelope. The paper, a heavy-grade cream, gives and separates, the edges fraying like lint. As she inserts her fingers, easing out the letter, the building shudders around her.

She looks up. A pair of precisely laced hiking boots is descending the stairs. Stella watches them for a moment, then drops the letter, slips off the chair and wedges herself behind a tall, spike-leafed plant balanced on its own special stand. She's served breakfast, cleaned up the kitchen, taken two booking enquiries already this morning, and she doesn't really feel like getting into idle conversation with a guest.

The man from room four lopes through Reception, dressed as if about to take part in a polar expedition, a pair of binoculars swinging from his neck. When he reaches the front door he extends his head out, tortoise-like, holding up his palm to check the weather. His other hand, Stella sees, is busy scratching one of his buttocks. She wrinkles her nose and a strangled giggle escapes her, which bounces around the deserted hotel reception like a ping-pong ball.

The man stops scratching and looks round. Stella holds her breath, her mind racing through possible explanations of what she might be doing crammed behind a pot plant. He doesn't see her. Her neck is beginning to ache from being crunched like this but she can't exactly reappear now.

When she hears the slam of the front door, Stella unfolds her body and stretches, her arms held long above her head, her vertebrae shifting and clicking all the way down her back. She sits down in the chair again and picks up the letter, smoothing it against the desk with the heel of her hand, flattening the loops and dashes of her mother's handwriting.

Her mother's always written with a fountain pen. Stella knows where she keeps it – in the smallest drawer on the right-hand side of the bureau – and she knows exactly what her mother would have looked like as she dipped the moulded, fragile nib into the wet mouth of the ink bottle. She can picture her as surely as seeing her own face in a mirror: blutting out the air pocket from the rubber pipette in a stream of bubbles, drawing ink up into the pen like blood into a syringe. Francesca would then cross her ankles under her, set a sheet of paper on the blotter, which lay squarely in the middle of the desk under the bay window, and making a peculiar motioning gesture, like a conductor silencing an orchestra, she'd have leant forward, pressed her pen to the blemishless white and begun: *Dearest Stella*.

Stella glances down the pages: *your father and I*, she sees. Then: *trying hard to understand why you've done this*. She skips a few lines . . . *don't see how anyone could just throw in a job, a very good job, in London* . . . she turns over . . . *such a strange thing to do* . . .

Stella looks up, away from the pages, and through the

window. It's possible to see right across the valley from here – through the trees, which toss and stir in the breeze, along where the burn winds its way through patches of marsh, patches of peat, and to the cluttered houses of the village beyond. The day is bright, the sky scudding with fast-moving clouds. The reflective surface of the loch is pleated, made restless in the wind. Behind the hotel, the terrain gets rockier, wilder, the ground lifting and steepening towards the mountains, fast-moving rivers cutting their way through rock. Stella doesn't look out of those windows much.

She turns back to the staircase, lined with gilt-framed oil paintings in soupy, dark colours. A man with abundant side-whiskers glowers at her, a shut-eyed hare slung by its heels over his shoulder. A cross-eyed child of indeterminate gender in a tam-o'-shanter poses next to a harp. The moth-eaten deer's head at the top of the stairs, Stella notices, is slightly skewed.

The letter is still held between her fingers. *All best and love*, it ends. Then the flattened loops of her mother's signature. *All best and love.*

Stella scuffs her sandals together, the buckles snagging. Her fingers are tucked beneath her thighs. She chews the final, greasy mouthful of sausage and gulps it down. Her plate is empty now, apart from the beans. Everything else gone. She's eaten round them very carefully, banking them up on the rim, making sure that nothing else touched them.

At a right-angle to her, around the four-sided table, her grandmother is leaning on her elbows and saying something about side-plates. Opposite, Nina slices her food into equal, geometric shapes, her eyes lowered. Whenever their mother has to work during the week, their grandmother – their Scottish grandmother, their father's mother – comes to look after them. 'Who else would cook your dinner?' she asks, in the kind of question that Stella knows doesn't require an answer. Under the table, the cat weaves invisibly through ankles and chair legs, fur sleeking against their shins.

Stella puts her knife and fork together, a mismatched pair, as stealthily and noiselessly as she can. The fork end makes a minuscule click against the china, but maybe no one heard it, maybe no one will notice.

'But, Archie, surely there are colleagues who can help you with . . .' Stella hears her grandmother's voice trail into silence. She keeps her eyes trained on the repetitive pleats of her school skirt. She is aware of the height of her grandmother towering next to her and she's aware that she's looking at her. Or, more specifically, her plate.

'Are you not eating your broad beans, dear?' Her grandmother's voice is melodious, studiedly offhand.

Stella's father grows the beans in the vegetable patch so disapproved of by the other people in their tenement, who prefer roses and cyclamen. Stella loves to pick them, to disentangle and pull the swollen lengths of the pods from the mass of wreathing leaves; she loves to split them open and find the perfect rows of beans bedded down in the silvery fur. But boiled by Granny Gilmore for a good twenty minutes and spooned on to a plate, they have metamorphosed: a puckered, toughened hide clings close to twin halves that squeak against your teeth. The taste is sickly, cloying and dry. She cannot eat them, she cannot, she really cannot.

'I don't want them,' Stella says.

'Pardon?' Granny Gilmore says, still achingly polite.

'Maybe—' her father interrupts, low, but Stella sees a quick gesture from her that silences him.

'Come on,' Granny Gilmore leans across, picks up her fork and nudges three of the green shapes on to it, 'just try them. You might like them.'

Stella presses her lips together and leans back into her chair as the fork looms towards her.

'Open your mouth.'

The waxy, compost smell of them is reaching her nose. She shakes her head.

'Stella, open your mouth.'

She stares fixedly at the three beans before her. Could she? But she imagines the feel of their chill solidity on the damp warmth of her tongue, the sore ache of the salivary glands in the back corners of her mouth working to digest them: her throat closes just as her stomach heaves up. She gags, coughing. Her grandmother must have seized the opportunity of her lips opening because metal is clashing against her teeth and her mouth is jammed full of rubbery, green shapes.

Stella retches, her mouth swilling with acrid liquid, and the beans shoot out on to the tablecloth. She sobs and clamps her hands like a portcullis over her face.

'Well,' her grandmother puts down the fork with a clash, 'I'm not prepared to have a battle about this. You're to sit there until you've eaten what's on your plate.' She scoops the regurgitated beans back on to Stella's plate. 'And those as well. All of it.'

Stella hears her father mutter something.

'Archie,' her grandmother warns, 'she has to learn.'

Through the slits in her fingers, Stella sees her grand-mother clear away the plates, her father pouring more water into Nina's glass. After it gets dark, their mother will come back from the café, smelling of cigarettes and suds and coffee, bringing a carton of *gelato di cioccolata* for her and *gelato di fragola* for Nina. It's getting hot behind the shield of her hands and her arms are aching but she won't take them down. She watches them leave the table, one by one. Nina gives her a swift, unreadable glance as she goes.

Stella peels her hands away from her face. The house is quiet around her. She can see her grandmother, sitting on a chair in the garden, reading a paper. A radio is playing somewhere. Footsteps in the room above. Everyone feels very far away. The striped back of the cat faces her from the window-sill. No use. The cat won't eat beans. She doesn't look at her plate. She has no intention of eating them.

Then, behind her, a door sighs open. Stella doesn't turn round. She is wondering if it's Granny Gilmore. Back to save her? Or back to scold her? But it's Nina, tiptoeing across the carpet on shoeless feet. Stella gazes at her, her face stiff with dried tears. Her sister holds a finger, as straight and definite as an exclamation mark, against her lips.

Nina leans forward, stretching out her hand, and picks up the fork. She stabs the beans, one by one, right through their hearts. She opens her mouth and the fork disappears into it. Stella sees it come out again, clean and silver. Nina chews, quickly and concentratedly, and swallows. Once.

Twice. Then she grins, puts down the fork and flits away, out of the room.

Before there was anything, there was Nina. Stella is sure her face is the first thing she ever saw, or ever remembers seeing. Their mother tells them that Nina spent all day hanging over the bars of Stella's cot.

For a long time, Stella couldn't tell the difference between them. She thought Nina was her or that she was Nina or that they were one person, one being. For years, she believed the blood that pumped through their veins was in some way connected, that if she cut herself she might very easily see crimson seeping from a part of Nina's body.

But she has a clear memory of, one day, Nina lifting her up to the mirror in the bedroom they shared until Stella left home – even though she was younger, she left first. It was a hot day. They were both in shorts, so it must have been summer. Festival time, maybe. She has an idea that she could hear the droning hum of faraway aeroplanes, streaking the skies above the city, and the gentle murmur of a crowd at some event on the Meadows. But she might have imagined that since.

Nina hooked her hands under Stella's armpits and clutched Stella to her. Her skin against Stella's hurt, like the wring of a Chinese burn. It took Nina a great deal of effort to lift her from the ground – even then Stella was catching up on her in height – and Nina had to strain and heave.

Stella saw the curve of a second forehead rise into the silver square of the mirror and suddenly there were two faces in the glassy, reversed world ahead of her. It was a shock. They were almost the same, but not quite. Nina's was narrower, sharper, her hair, in the forked tongue of summer sun slanting in from the high window, ever so slightly fox-coloured.

There is no sky here. Just a depthless, grey-white miasma. Jake stares up into it for a while, at the black cut-outs of birds streaking through it. Then he wheels round, the wind plastering his hair into his eyes, and looks towards the village, indistinct with mist as if dissolving into air. The clustered buildings, stuccoed with brown-black pebbles, are huddled together against the low, persistent wind, the tall cone of the windmill standing above them, its immense sails stuck into a giant black X, as if warning him away.

He shivers in his borrowed clothes. Ever since he arrived in this country he's been unable to get warm.

A restless tea-coloured wave turns and turns back on itself on the brown shingle. A bird with a curved beak scuttles up the beach, wings folded to its body. Further out to sea, a piece of flotsam heaves up and down on an invisible swell. He stares out at the horizon, barely discernible: grey sky, grey sea. This place feels to him like the edge of the world.

He thrusts his hands deep into his pockets, turns and walks back up the beach, through the scrubby marsh and the tall, restless reeds. As he passes underneath the mill sails, they are vibrating in the wind with the high-pitched whine of a mosquito.

He vaults over the garden fence, remembering too late that the wet grass always soaks through his shoes. Why do they bother to have fences, ostensibly to keep people out, which are so low a child could climb over them? He makes his way down the side passage of the house, past the trees, which are being slowly espaliered, branches pulled and trained back with wire frames. He can't look at those trees without feeling a kind of sympathetic ache in his shoulders.

His shoes are sodden and squelching by the time he reaches the kitchen. He bends over, yanks them off and hurls them towards the big, boiling stove thing in the corner. What's it called again? It looks like a steam engine. It's a funny word. Aga. That's it. Aga.

He pulls open the tiny freezer compartment and crams cracking, steaming oblongs of ice into a glass, which he then fills with water. He reaches up to a shelf for a bowl and pours cereal into it.

Barefoot, he climbs the stairs, the tray held in front of him. Florence bloody Nightingale. He should get himself a lamp. In the bedroom, light glows like a furnace behind the flowered curtains. He puts the tray down on the bedside table. The duvet is pulled up high, covering the pillow, covering the chrysalis form of a body.

Jake sits on the edge of the bed, the mattress bouncing from his weight. Nothing. No movement. No acknowledgement. He leans forward and tweaks down the top of the duvet. 'Hey,' he murmurs. 'You awake?'

Her hands, pressed together as if for prayer, are slid between her face and the pillow. Is she still asleep? No. Her eyes open slowly and she looks up at him.

'I brought you breakfast.'

He helps her to sit up, arranging pillows behind her, placing the tray on her lap.

'You're so good to me.' She smiles at him, high spots of colour in her cheeks. From the heat of the room? Or does she have a temperature? Perhaps he should check. 'I don't know what I'd do without you.'

Her hand rests on his for a moment before Jake stands and moves to the window. He pulls back the curtains and peers out.

'Jake,' her voice is low, teasing, 'have you put ice in the water again?'

He turns. 'Oh. I might have.'

She shakes her head. 'We don't need ice, now that we're in a place with a normal climate.'

'Sorry.' He folds his arms. 'Force of habit.'

Mel stirs the cereal, then lifts a minuscule amount to her mouth.

'How did you sleep?' he asks.

'Not great.' She pulls a face. 'But I'm OK.'

He doesn't say that he lay awake most of the night, listening to the way she breathes when asleep, with a tiny, shrill whistle on each exhalation. *Wife*, his mind hisses at him, *this is your wife*. He turns back to the window and grips the sill, staring out at the row of cottages, the wind-bent trees, the coiling wet road, the undulating sea, the flat estuarial mud, as if he's never seen them before. What is he doing here? How did he get here? Between them, the ice shrinks in its glass.

Jake knows the story backwards, and sometimes used to tell it to himself that way when he was a child, beginning with the fact of his own existence and working back, like a genealogist.

His mother, Caroline, decided to leave Britain and join the wave of people dropping out of their lives and going on the road to travel east. London was grey, wet and cold, and when the man who shared her bed listed the attractions of India, there wasn't a great deal her room's damp-scarred walls and temperamental gas fire seemed to have going for them. Her parents hadn't spoken to her for months, but she phoned her brother to tell him of her plans and he said the family would consider her dead if she went. After putting down the phone, she called the man to say, yes, she was coming, so please save a place for her.

It amazes Jake how young she was – much younger than he is now – when she packed up her entire life and left in a VW camper-van with three men and another woman. They drove into Europe, through France, through Turkey, through Iran, into Afghanistan. In Herat, they shed the other woman, one of the men, and gained a German, a cat and a parrot. In Kabul, they shed Caroline. 'Irreconcilable differences,' she used to sigh when Jake asked her why. She carried on alone, hitching her way into Pakistan.

In Islamabad she was sitting beside a road with her pack and 'the biggest bunch of bananas you've ever seen'. A man on a motorbike stopped and offered her a ride. 'He had black hair,' Caroline would tell him, smiling, 'tied back in a ponytail,' she would let her fingers stray through Jake's hair, 'lovely blue eyes – just like yours – and a beautiful deep voice. Scottish. It was the accent that did it for me.'

He was called Tom, that much she could tell him, but she never knew his last name – 'You didn't really ask questions like that then' – and as they chugged their way through

Pakistan, into India, through Amritsar and up to Dharmsala he told her about the commune he'd started, somewhere in the Highlands, near Aviemore, in a place called Kildoune. 'It worked really well, apparently – not like a lot of them. He loved it so much he talked about it all the time.'

They separated in Delhi. They had spent three weeks together. 'Tom wanted to go into an ashram and I didn't – I was headed for Nepal.' Two days after she'd waved goodbye and watched him being swallowed into a seething crowd in a Delhi street, she realised she was pregnant. At this point in the story, she would look guilty and say, in a kind of singsong, rhyming chant: 'By Kathmandu I knew I was having you.'

She washed up in Hong Kong, a place she'd never imagined for herself, seven months pregnant, with six US dollars sheaved into themselves in her back pocket. She told herself she'd stay for three months – enough time to have the baby, earn some cash and buy a ticket out of there. She had this image in her head, of her wandering out into the world with a baby on her hip.

She found a job teaching English, and somewhere to live: a one-bedroomed apartment on the nineteenth floor in the middle of the red-light district in Wanchai. 'As many floors as my age,' she would say, 'which was a sign that something was right.' She braided her hair into a plait, slid her feet into her only pair of shoes and took the escalator to Mid Levels to teach the well-fed children of ex-pats. She discovered that she was good at teaching, that she liked it: 'I'd never been good at anything before.'

When the baby was born, she called him Jake Kildoune,

after the only concrete thing she knew about his father. She wanted to give him a new name, a name no one else had. Calling him after a place would, she decided, tether him to the world and not to people, would free him for ever from the stranglehold of family.

She told herself that she'd stay for a few months longer, earn a bit more cash, let the baby settle, at least until he was weaned. Mrs Yee on the floor below minded Jake during the day: this they had worked out in the lobby while waiting for the lift to descend, with hand gestures and a Cantonese–English phrasebook. Mrs Yee had a son, Hing Tai, the same age as Jake; she said two was no different from one and, besides, the coloured eyes and white-soft skin of this baby fascinated her. Also – and this she hadn't told Caroline – she'd felt terribly sorry for this lonely *gweilo* with her long, floaty clothes and her long, floaty hair and a tiny baby strapped to her back.

There seemed nothing to return to the UK for. Caroline's family held true to their word. She wrote aerogrammes, letters, cards, but nothing ever came back. She decided she'd stay for a bit longer, then a bit longer, then perhaps a little more, just until she'd saved some money, and one day she turned round and Jake was sixteen, feet propped up on the kitchen table, reading a book, the radio on full volume, cracking the striped pods of sunflower seeds and scattering them to the floor. She would eventually leave five years later, when she hooked up with a man closer to Jake's age than her own and moved to New Zealand with him. Jake would carry on living in the flat he was born in. It would take him months to get used to the space.

Everything in Jake's world had two names, an English one and a Cantonese one, even himself: he was Jake to his mother and the white people he knew, and something that sounded like Jik-ah to the Chinese. Mrs Yee always spoke Cantonese with him, his mother English, so he grew up thinking it was normal for the world to have a double meaning.

The Hong Kong Chinese have a name for those who have become too assimilated with the pale-skinned colonialists: a banana, they'll spit, yellow on the outside, white on the inside. Jake has never known what this meant for him, born and raised in Hong Kong, speaking English and Cantonese, educated in the school for rich European children where his mother taught, but going back down the hill each night to a narrow apartment block. His classmates called him Chinky, laughed at the Chinese comics they found in his bag, pulled the corners of their eyes into slits when they saw him coming. He spent hours in his childhood trying to think of something that was white on the outside but yellow in the middle. What was the opposite of a banana?

He went to his mother who was lying under the ceiling fan, writing a letter. 'What's white on the outside but yellow on the inside?' he asked, damp fingers clutching the bedsheet.

She looked up, smiling, as if it was the first line of a riddle or a joke and she was ready for the punchline. Jake watched her smile fade like cloth left too long in the sun. She thought rapidly and concentratedly, biting her lip. They remained like that for some time, her silent and him standing beside the bed, waiting.

'An egg,' she said eventually. 'A boiled egg.'

He ate boiled eggs for his dinner for a whole week. His mother never said anything. Every night she would ask, 'What would you like for tea, Jakey?' and he would say, 'A boiled egg.' 'OK,' she would reply and go into the kitchen and place two in a pan of water. She ran them under the tap afterwards so that they would be cool enough for him to dissect, pick off every bit of shell, cup in his palm the slippery grey-white flesh, dense and hard as an eyeball. The crystallised yolk was always perfectly circular, might sometimes still be warm, still liquid, a soft yellow heart.

Sometimes he hears people who don't know him mutter, '*Gweilo*,' behind his back – foreign devil, walking ghost. If he's in the mood, he'll turn and give them a reply in flawless, tone-perfect Cantonese. Other times he won't.

They were filming a scene on one of the winding, hidden stone staircases that run like spines up the centres of buildings. A beautiful but lonely female assassin was finally meeting her biggest rival – a beautiful but lonely male assassin. Jake cast his eyes over the set. Everything was ready: the lighting, cameras, crew, makeup, actors, continuity, the director. The leading woman was just touching the end of her cigarette with a sputtering yellow match-flame when the peculiar, muffled sound of an electronic voice started up behind a wall somewhere, grinding and continuous.

The director, Chen, shouted, 'Cut,' the actors shifted impatiently from their marks, and the crew raised their eyes to the slanted ceiling, the sweating walls, listening.

'Where's it coming from?' Chen snatched off his cap.

Everyone turned their heads, first one way then the other, trying to locate the sound.

'What is it?' Chen shouted, and turned, as he did in all moments of crisis, to Jake.

Jake put down his clipboard. 'I'll go and find out.' He pushed his way through the fire door and stepped from the hot, graffitied dark of the stairwell into a tiled corridor. The strip-lighting in the corridor hummed as he walked, his head cocked to one side, listening. Everything else was silent – no TVs, no radios, no gasps and exclamations of distant sex, no rumbles of conversation came from behind the row of closed doors. Jake ran his hands over the speckled concrete walls, pressing his ear to them like a doctor in search of a heartbeat. A security camera winked from the ceiling.

The corridor bent away from itself and Jake arrived in a cul-de-sac with two lifts, their steel doors shut. In a square black screen above them, flickering red numbers rose and fell, rose and fell. The noise was louder here.

Jake leant towards one of the apartment doors. The noise subsided. He stepped towards the other: the noise was clearer and sank into distinct words. He listened for a moment. A recorded voice saying something about a cat who walks alone. Jake frowned, then smiled. He recognised the words from a story his mother used to read him. Who on earth stays at home listening to recordings of English children's stories in the middle of the afternoon?

He reached his hand through the metal door grille, pressed the buzzer and waited, turning to watch the lift numbers flicker and settle. Behind him, the door sucked open and he turned again to see a white woman holding a small Chinese boy by the hand.

They looked at him, the boy with wide eyes and the girl from under her fringe.

'I'm really sorry to bother you,' Jake began. Why was she staring at him like that? Had he met her before? No, he didn't think so. 'I'm with a film crew, we're filming in the stairwell, and we were just wondering if you could possibly turn off your tape-recorder – just for half an hour or so.' He shrugged awkwardly. 'Maybe more. Would you mind?'

The woman's gaze flicked from one side of his face to the other, as if she couldn't decide which to settle on. 'My tape-recorder?'

'Yes.' He nodded. 'We can hear it through the wall, you see.'

'Oh.' She pushed at her hair. Jake was surprised to see the red stain of a blush creeping up from the neck of her shirt. 'Well . . . I'm giving a lesson,' she indicated the boy. 'It won't be long though. Another ten minutes.'

'Ten minutes? OK. That should be fine. Sorry again for disturbing you.'

'Miss Mel,' the boy whispered, pulling at her arm. 'Miss Mel?'

'Be quiet a moment,' she said, still looking at Jake, 'please.'

'You be good for your teacher,' Jake said to him, in Cantonese. 'Thanks,' he said to Mel. ''Bye.'

They both stared after him as he left.

She came out into the stairwell twice that day to put out rubbish. The next day, when they were filming in the lobby,

49

she walked past four times in an hour. On the third day, she phoned the film company and left two very hesitant messages on his voicemail – the receptionist said, giggling, that she'd asked for 'the guy with the blue eyes'. The fourth day, the entire crew was teasing him about his persistent admirer: 'Hey, it's your stalker, Jik-ah,' the soundman shouted, whenever she happened to walk past. When they finished that evening, he waited for her outside the building, more to try to stop her turning up on set than anything else. He was also curious about this woman who made her desire so clear, who seemed so unswervable in pursuing what she wanted. He took her in the vertiginous tram up to the Peak, where they watched the Star Ferry stitching the black water of the harbour with light.

Francesca is planting bulbs, her knees pressing dents into the damp lawn edge. The soil in the new garden is thick and dark. It has rained and rained for weeks, and the ground feels sodden between her fingers. Each of her nails is crescented with black. She presses a dense root tangle into the hole, then packs earth on top of it. She has to do this quickly: her mother will be here in half an hour and if she sees her bending over in the garden she'll shriek her head off about the *poverina bambina*. She's been in this country for forty years, but still hasn't mastered the language. Francesca has always had to be the linguistic filter between her parents and the world – writing letters, making phonecalls, translating rent demands, tax forms, bills, prescriptions.

The tight drum-curve of her belly rests on her thighs, the feet of the child pressed up against her lungs. This baby is different from the first. It can go for hours in utter, almost eerie stillness without moving a hand or a limb, then something will wake it – a noise, a peristaltic gurgle, the rumbling echo of a cough, Francesca never knows – and it flips into manic, vehement action, somersaulting, punching, flailing, as if grappling with an invisible assailant. With her first baby, Francesca felt all along that she knew her, that she almost recognised her when she was handed to her, bloodied and dripping and compressed, but with this one she has no idea what she's getting. It could be anyone.

Somewhere behind her is Nina. Francesca can hear her panting, the shuffle of her small unformed feet through the grass. A hot hand grips Francesca's shoulder and a strand of her hair, and Nina appears, flushed and purposeful, a doll dangled by its foot in her hand.

'Hello.' Francesca circles her daughter with an arm and presses a kiss into the creases of her neck. Nina staggers backwards in surprise, thrown off-balance by this sudden rush of affection. 'What are you up to?'

Nina frowns. 'Messy,' she admonishes, pointing at Francesca's hands, stained with the garden.

'It's only mud,' she says, 'look, it feels nice,' and tries to press Nina's fingers to her own. She doesn't want her to grow up fastidious, fussy.

Nina snatches away her hand. 'No-no-no-no-no,' she wails, 'messy.'

'OK, OK. I'm sorry.' The sight of her daughter's affronted, indignant face makes her want to laugh, but she bites her lip. 'Sorry,' she says again, more seriously.

Nina is surveying her, assessing, critical, her wide green

eyes travelling over Francesca's face, hair, shoulders and neck, coming to rest on the swelling beneath her shirt. Francesca doesn't breathe, but waits, tense and ready. She hasn't mentioned the pregnancy to Nina yet: a child-psychologist friend of Archie's told her to wait until Nina asks. Is she going to ask? Is she? Oh, please, ask.

Nina's eyes flick to her mother's face, then back again. 'What's that?' Nina enquires, in her high, reedy voice.

Francesca's spine straightens and lengthens towards the spring sun above them, as if an invisible thread is pulling her upright. She's had this rehearsed for months and is now so excited the words are tumbling around her mouth like bubbles in champagne. She breathes in through her nose and out through her mouth, like they teach her in antenatal classes.

'It's a baby,' she says, beginning the first words of the speech she has down pat, because she wants these sisters to be happy, to love each other, more than anything she has ever wanted in her whole life, and because she knows that whatever she says in the next few seconds will impact through Nina's and this unborn child's life for ever. 'For Nina,' she adds.

Nina leans closer, her hand gripping the collar of Francesca's shirt. Francesca feels the baby shudder and flex, arching its back as if waking from a long sleep.

'For Nina?' Nina repeats.

'Yes.' Francesca swallows, nervous. She presses the back of her hand to her cheek. Pregnancy makes her feel hot and full. 'For you. It's going to be your sister. When she's born she's going to be very small, like this.' Francesca holds her hands apart like a fisherman measuring a fantasy catch. She speaks slowly, watching Nina's face. 'And we're going to have to look after her, you and me, because she's not going to know how to do anything. She won't know how to feed herself, or dress herself or—'

'A sister,' Nina says, and Francesca realises she's never said the word before. 'For Nina.'

Francesca nods, takes Nina's hand in hers and presses it to the hard, dense dome of her stomach. 'Let's see if we can feel her moving.'

They wait. A lawnmower roars and belches in the garden over the wall. The tune of an ice-cream van unwinds somewhere out on the road. Nina looks unconvinced. Come on, Francesca wills the baby, just this once. She pictures it as she saw it first in the grey, soupy fuzz of the scanning screen, floating upside-down, a trapeze artist in freefall. There is a flash of movement, a twist, a snake shrugging off a skin.

Nina's face is stretched, disbelieving, like a traveller who's just been told that the earth is flat after all.

Stella lies on her front, resting her chin on her knuckles. If she narrows her eyes to a certain point, the sun makes prisms of her eyelashes, lining the edges of her vision with jewels. At the top of the garden her mother sits with Evie on a rug. Evie is her mother's friend. They talk together in low, laughy voices, drink wine and sometimes Evie combs out her mother's hair with her fingers. With just one word, Evie can make her mother throw back her head and laugh so that her throat is long and tears wet her face.

Evie has hair the colour of gold – 'Dyed, of course,' her father says, in a way Stella always thinks shows he doesn't like Evie very much. Her fingernails, like candied hard petals, can be lilac, pink, frosted white or glaring scarlet. She wears lacy cardigans with buttons that strain over her breasts, lots of clanking necklaces and high red shoes that she lets Stella try on sometimes and shuffle around the kitchen. 'A child after my own heart,' she announces, when Stella does this. Stella pictures Evie's heart as pulsing, dense as a pincushion, covered in thick, plush velvet. She can't imagine why she might be after it or want it, or what she would do with it if she got it.

Evie has her own words for everything. She calls her mother 'Cesca'. Stella and Nina are 'darling' or 'Franette One' and 'Franette Two'. Cigarettes are 'ciggies', wine 'drinkies'. Stella's father is 'Himself'. Definitely with a capital H.

She is Nina's godmother and every year on her birthday, Nina receives a package with spangling paper and ribbon curled in ringlets, which means it was wrapped up in a shop, not at home. Inside is a pair of shoes or a feather-adorned hairslide or a necklace or a bag crusted with glass beads. If it's a dress, Stella will get to wear it, eventually, a year or two later (Evie always buys big – 'I never know what size children are, darling!'), bleached by washing, but still beautiful, still desirable, still Evie's.

Right now, Evie is leaning against Francesca on the blanket while they watch Nina, who is dressed in a leotard with sequins like the interlapped scales on a fish – an Evie present that Stella is waiting for. Nina, who has recently been told by her ballet teacher that she is double-jointed, is performing the splits, her legs folding out from under her like the struts on a deck-chair. Francesca doesn't usually let Nina perform in front of visitors – 'Not now, Nina' – but for some reason Evie is an exception.

'Darling,' Evie's voice floats down the garden, 'it looks like *agony*. Can you do it the other way, I wonder?'

Evie is English, her mother told her, when Stella asked why her voice was funny.

'She's so like you, Cesca, it's *eerie*.'

Eerie. Eerie. Agony. Eerie. Stella likes Evie's words. She likes the shapes they push her mouth into, the weight of them on her tongue.

'Where is Franette Two?' Evie calls. 'Can she entertain us with contortionist gymnastics as well?'

The air is swirled full of airborne seeds, slow as moths, and the tang of Evie's Turkish cigarettes. Stella is aware of the soil beneath her, the hardness of it, the way it presses up into her body, holding her there on the crust of the earth.

'No,' Stella hears her mother answer quickly, 'but she's good at other things. Aren't you, Stella?' she calls.

There is a pause in which Stella senses Evie sensing her mistake.

'Of course she is.'

At the other end of the garden, she sees Evie pass her cigarette into her other hand and hold out her arm. 'Darling Stella, come and give Evie a cuddle. You are very good at cuddling, I know.'

Jake trudges along the road, laden with shopping bags. Mel's mother, Annabel – a woman with the same mild grey eyes as Mel – asked him if he would mind going to the shop, and Jake had jumped at the chance. One of the worst things about this insane situation he's got himself into is that he has nothing to do. No purpose in life. No definite idea about how he's supposed to spend his time. Other than to dance attendance on Mel.

Jake shudders inside Mel's father's coat. This is mad. He has to do something about it. It cannot go on. He feels as if he's been buried alive.

He doesn't like the word 'homesick', doesn't feel it does justice to what it's supposed to describe. He prefers the long, pulling, mournful vowels of the German word, *Heimweh*. For him, it's not just a mild case of nausea – he feels flattened, steamrollered, horrified, miserable, disjointed, desperate. It's as if he's the wrong species for this place: there's not enough sun, the air doesn't have the right ratios of gases, everything is too spread out, too sprawling, and he can barely understand what people are saying to him. He never realised how much he thought in Cantonese. Maybe it's because he's never been to Britain before, but he's never felt so cut off, so far away from Hong Kong and everything he knows and everything he likes and everything that makes up his life and him.

What really disquiets him is that this is the country his mother is from – and his father, for that matter – the country stamped on the outside of his own passport, and he has never felt so alien. He cannot get over that everyone here is *white*. He has never in his life been in a crowd of people where all the faces are pale. He cannot understand why people here don't stare at him, why they don't give him more than a cursory glance when he passes them in the street, why they don't stand stock-still and gape at him, because he feels like an extraterrestrial. The idea that he looks just like them shocks him more than anything else.

He has found that he cannot think about the apartment he's lived in all his life. He cannot think about the feel of the hot wooden tiles under his feet, the rattle of the faulty air-conditioning unit, the aluminium window-frame, which doesn't quite fit, the buzz of the electric mosquito repeller, the discoloured patch on the ceiling above his bed, where the people in the floor above him had a leaking shower. Sometimes, still, he wakes and wonders for a split second where he is.

He stops on the corner outside the church to swap round the bags. He's packed them badly and one is heavier than the other, making him lopsided. An immense car the colour of forests swoops past him, spraying grit against his trousers. In the churchyard, a large black and white bird hops from gravestone to gravestone. Jake watches it, the shopping at his feet.

He is going to have to talk to Mel at some point. Why not now? This cannot go on. He presses his fingertips into the sides of his skull. It seems to him a problem so unusual, so unaccountable, that there is nothing to relate it to, to explain it. Is it worse to talk to Mel now, when her health is still fragile, or to wait until she's better? Jake doesn't know – doesn't have any idea. He spends endless nights awake, cogitating his way around this question, while a tickertape machine somewhere in his head prints the same words over and over again: I never loved you, I have to leave, I never loved you.

Jake is seventeen and walking through a wet market in Wanchai when Leah spots him. The paleness of his skin and his height draw her eye from a long way off: she looks all the way through the low red lamps, the banks of star fruit, the crowds of raven-haired people, the wooden stalls stacked with oozing carcasses and slit-bodied fish – and fixes him at the centre of her gaze.

She watches him buy a slab of beancurd at one stall, a dangerously spiked durian at another. The Chinese boy with him chats constantly, gesticulating. The white boy doesn't say much back, she notices, just nods. He moves with a kind of grace, a loping, even stride.

As they near her, she runs a finger over an eyebrow, pulls her blouse straight and steps into the aisle, blocking their way. They both pull up short. The Chinese boy is wary, she sees, but the other scans her face as if wondering whether he knows her. 'Maybe,' she says, addressing them in English, 'you could help me.'

They glance at each other. The white boy shifts the leaking skin of the beancurd into his other hand. 'Sure,' he says, frowning.

Leah suppresses a smile. She loves boys at this age – fresh from their mothers, untainted, not cynical, not worldly. They are like molluscs without their shells. The sickly, opiate scent of the durian spirals towards her.

'I want to buy some fruit,' she gesticulates at the stall behind them, 'but am having a few language difficulties.'

She hopes he'll ask his local friend to help and then she'll be able to talk to him. But she is astonished when the blue-eyed white boy speaks to the toothless stallholder in the jerked, hacking sounds of their language. The friend adds a few monosyllabic rejoinders. Mangoes and papayas and lychees are produced, wrapped in unreadable newspaper parcels.

Outside on the pavement, the light is white and level, the heat almost audible – Leah imagines it would make a hissing sound, like air escaping from a tyre. She stands with her arms weighed down by the fruit she didn't really want. Sweat is crawling down her back like ants. The boy is in front of her, about to leave, his friend lurking behind him.

Leah is thirty-three, a film producer from LA, with one minor hit, three flops and two divorces on her resumé, in Hong Kong for several months working on a co-production. She always wears co-ordinating underwear, lipgloss and a ring on each finger. She likes piercing the seal on new jars of coffee with the end of a spoon, and the smell of the underside of men's wrists. She is very good at packing suitcases, matching colours, soothing difficult actresses, and persuading financiers – especially male – to sign large cheques. She likes the way her hair grows away from her brow in a peak. She doesn't eat carbohydrate, squid or processed sugar. She has a manicure once a week and a hair colour once a month. She once stole a jazz album from a friend she didn't like.

She holds out her business card. 'You should call me. Come for a swim in my hotel pool.'

The boy blushes furiously as he takes it. Part of her is certain he will call, part is certain he won't.

Mel's medication is laid out on the kitchen table. Jake picks up the bottles one by one, extracting the pills and dropping them into his palm. He's going to talk to her. Right now. After she's taken her pills. He can't put it off any longer. He is turning to make his way down the hall when Mel's parents appear on the threshold. 'Hi,' Jake says, realising they are all standing disconcertingly close, crammed between the table and the door.

'Jake.' Annabel moves towards him as if she is going to embrace him, her arms outstretched, but at the last moment she seems to change her mind. Her arms fall back to her sides and she stands before him. 'Andrew and I,' she begins, taking his hand in both of hers, 'wanted to talk to you.'

'Right,' Jake says, and forces himself to smile at them. He can feel the pills warming up in his other hand.

'In private.'

'OK.'

'We wanted,' Annabel exchanges a pleased glance with her husband, 'to give Melanie a present.'

'A present?'

'A surprise,' Andrew says.

'A wedding,' Annabel says.

Jake is speechless. Mel's pills are melting in his grasp and her parents are both beaming at him, as if they expect him to hug them.

'But . . .' He gropes for something between what he

should say and what he wants to say. 'But . . . but we're already married,' is what comes out of him.

'We know that.' Annabel laughs. 'But we thought it would be nice if . . . that you might like to do it properly. Now that you're back.'

'We feel,' Andrew begins, clearing his throat, 'that it might be something for Melanie to,' his hand circles in the air, 'look forward to. Work towards.'

'Something to get better for,' Annabel explains, peering at his face. 'She doesn't know anything about this yet.'

'We were wondering if you'd like to ask her,' Andrew says.

There is a pause.

'Or tell her,' Annabel amends.

There is another pause. Jakes stares at them blankly. They appear to be waiting for him to say something. Did they ask him a question? He can't remember.

'It is a present from us,' Annabel says hastily, clutching at his arm. 'From Andrew and me.'

'We'd be paying for everything.' Andrew leans towards him as he says this. 'Don't you worry about that.'

Jake realises he has to say something. 'That's very kind of you.' His voice sounds thin and unrecognisable. 'I think perhaps . . . maybe I should . . . we should . . .' He tries again: 'I might need to have a think about it.'

'Of course,' Andrew says.

'Naturally,' Annabel agrees.

Leah's hotel was the oldest and most famous in Hong Kong. Jake had never been inside it. He'd seen it, of course, from the outside – it was hard to miss, sitting as it did in colonial, chiselled-stone assurance on the waterfront in Tsim Sha Tsui. He'd heard his schoolmates talking about it: how it had two helipads on the roof, how for afternoon tea you got an immense tier of cakes, that a live orchestra played in the lobby, that it made its own chocolates, that there was a barman who had been taught how to make a certain cocktail by Clark Gable himself.

Jake hid himself behind a pillar in the gold-ceilinged entrance hall, fingering the clammy leaves of a pot plant. This was a side of the city he didn't know about: marble floors, chandeliers, white women in hats drinking tea from bone china, uniformed lackeys opening the door. A boy of about his age in a bellboy's suit passed by and gave him a suspicious, sidelong look.

'Are you going to stand there all day or are you going to sit down and have some coffee?'

He turned. Leah was sitting at a table five feet away, a cigarette held in the V of her fingers, thighs crossed, a waiter pouring dark liquid into her cup. She motioned towards the chair next to her.

He told her about the school he went to on the Peak, about Hing Tai, about how he had never been to America but that he'd always wanted to go to New York. She said she thought he would love New York because everybody did. LA, she said, was more of an acquired taste. He told her about his mother travelling the world and how he didn't know his father. 'Your mother,' she said, drawing smoke into her lungs, 'sounds like a very brave lady.'

They went swimming in the pool on the hotel roof. He

could see all the way over the harbour, beyond Wanchai to the Peak and, in the other direction, all the way to the immense, mist-hung mountains of the New Territories. Jake showed her how he could dive backwards and she, sitting on a sun-lounger, her face hidden behind dark glasses, laughed for the first time. Her teeth were small and pointed. He did it again for her and watched her image refract and distort as he rose to the surface of the water. He couldn't look at the way the circles on the pattern of her bikini stretched into ovals across her breasts.

By the time they got to the door of her room, he was shaking. He wondered if he should run or stay, but the idea of getting into the lift with the uniformed boy asking him, 'Which floor, sir?' scared him more than what might be expected of him inside the room.

But Leah took him by the arm and steered him in. As she leant against the door to shut it, she pulled him towards her by the collar of his shirt. She tasted of coffee and cigarettes and sadness. Jake had kissed girls before, after school, in the breathing dark of a cinema, but it had felt nothing like this. Her body was sinewy, febrile and insistent beneath his.

'My beautiful English boy,' she whispered, as she pushed him into a chair, unbuttoning his trousers, bending her head over him.

Leah is not something Jake talks about much – at the time, only Hing Tai knew. At first, Hing Tai flatly refused to believe it. Then he laughed hysterically. Then he pressed Jake for a detailed description of everything they had done.

The affair lasted for most of Jake's final year at school

– eight, maybe nine months. He would bolt from the school gates, catch the Star Ferry across the harbour to wait in her suite. The doormen got to know him and, although they were obsequiously polite to his face, he was sure they sniggered about him behind his back. But he didn't care. Leah's suite was three times the size of his mother's apartment, had floor-to-ceiling windows, a Jacuzzi, the biggest bed he'd ever seen, and room service. Jake would sit at the desk in the bedroom and, as the light drained from the bowl of the harbour and the neon across the water came on, he would study for his A levels. When Leah appeared, she would pull off his school uniform, item by item.

'You know,' she said to him once, after the third time that evening, 'women don't reach their sexual peak until their thirties, whereas men reach theirs at eighteen. We match perfectly.'

He didn't tell his mother, and Caroline didn't ask where he was disappearing off to each evening. The only time he managed to shock Leah was when he let slip that Caroline was only four years older than her.

'Jesus fucking Christ,' she said, dropping ash over his bare chest.

Leah didn't think what she was doing was wrong but she knew it wasn't something of which she was proud. She'd never intended it to become a lasting arrangement – she'd thought of it as something that might happen once or twice. It had been years since she'd slept with a teenager; she was curious. But she loved him, envied him his youth. Her second husband, the last man she'd slept with, had been forty-nine: she was fascinated by the beauty, the flawlessness of the young, the way the muscles still clung close to the bones, the way the skin fitted the frame. She hoped that some of it might rub off on her, like pollen on a sleeve.

'I'm not taking you for ever,' she said to Jake over and over again, 'just for now.'

She told herself she was helping him. Men needed to be taught, especially young men. She was good for him in other ways too: she made him study, made sure he was prepared for his exams, nagged him about his revision, read over his applications to British universities and tossed them back to him, covered in her rounded handwriting.

When his exams finished, she got him a summer job as a runner with a new Hong Kong director, Chen. By the time his results came out and he found he had a place to study languages in London, he'd decided he wasn't going to university after all. Despite the cajolings of both Caroline and Leah, he refused to leave Hong Kong, and Chen.

Leah went back to LA at the end of the year. Jake went to the airport with her, even though she told him not to. 'I detest airport farewells,' she snapped. When she walked away from him, through the barrier, she didn't look back.

Years later, when none of it matters any more, he will start to tell the whole thing to Caroline, while they stand in her garden in Auckland.

'Oh, yeah,' his mother will say, flapping her hand dismissively, 'I knew about all that.'

'Did you?' Jake will be appalled. 'How?'

'I have my spies.' Caroline smiles. 'We met, you know.'

'You and Leah?'

'Mmm. We had lunch together once.' His mother will

continue walking down her rows of beans, which are coiling themselves round and round criss-crossed bamboo poles. 'I liked her a lot.'

Stella slams the caravan door, releasing a shower of drops from the roof on to her hair and face. The caravan is behind the hotel, hidden by firs on the fringes of the Rothiemurchas Forest. The smell of the trees around her is thick and pungent after the rainstorm, the earth soft, marshy and yielding under her boots. She ties a cagoule – a find from the hotel – by its arms round her hips and sets off up the winding, climbing driveway.

The road is empty, the intermittent white line swooping and curving before her. She walks along it, feeling the raised grainy surface of the paint through the thin rubber soles of her boots. A watery sun is straining through the clouds. A ginger, crescent-horned cow, scratching the underside of its chin on a five-bar gate, stops still and looks at her with soulful brown eyes as she walks by. A lone car passes, wheel-treads crunching on the Tarmac. She picks a tall frond of grass from the verge and strips it of its seeds, scattering them into a hedge. The conifer trees give way to tall, restless-topped beeches.

At the crossroads, she turns and, as she reaches the crest of the incline, suddenly it rises up before her – Loch Insh, a huge, silvery expanse of water, poured into the lowest dip in the valley. It's mirror-flat today, throwing back fragmented images of the trees, the mountains, the scattered houses of Kincraig.

Stella follows the road round. The loch disappears for

a while behind a bank of dense-growing pines, but she can smell it on the air – that damp, fecund scent. At the church, she cuts off the road, past the new trees growing out of the wet, blackened stumps of dead ones, along the pebbled shore. The hotel boat is tethered to a rock. She slips off the knot and wades into the water, the boat rocking expectantly. Then, placing a hand on each side to steady it, she scrambles in.

Stella pulls at the oars, leaning back against the weight of the water, the prow of the boat cutting through its glassy surface, the wet wooden poles squealing in the oarlocks. Close up, the loch is less inscrutable – a rocky, lunar terrain slides below the curve of the boat. The water is clear but dark; peat has been picked up by the Spey river, which passes through the loch like thread through a bead. Beyond where Stella is rowing, through the low, narrow bridge to Kincraig, the river re-forms, pulling itself together again from the wide embrace of the loch.

She steers herself away from the shore, pulling on her right oar while the left hovers, drip-dripping, above the water. When she's half-way between both banks, she lifts the oars, swings them forward to rest in the boat and shuffles herself off the seat-plank, lying back among the lifejackets and tarpaulin. The scenery vanishes from view and clouds hang above her, held separate by snatches of blue. She listens to her pulse slowing down and the whir-whir of birds streaking over the loch.

A crackle comes from the pocket of her jeans. Stella reaches in and pulls out a card from her sister – forgotten and unread. She holds it in front of her face for a moment, gazing at the familiar writing. But her hands are still wet from the oars, and the ink dissolves and blurs, printing her fingers with lost meaning.

Francesca's parents, Valeria and Domenico Iannelli, came from a village in a high, wooded, mountainous area of Italy. If the country had been a booted leg, their village was where the ankle is at its slenderest, where the bone narrows down above the spread tendons of the foot. A stream flowed down from the mountains and in the main piazza of their village, where people congregated at night for *la passeggiata* and to talk over the day, there was a double-arched bridge where it split into two, one half flowing to the Adriatic, the other towards the Tyrrhenian.

Fifty years on, Valeria could still spot someone from her region, a skill that never failed to impress Stella. 'Agnone,' she would whisper to Stella, as a woman entered the café, 'definitely. Either that or Vastogirardi.' Stella would peer up over the counter at the middle-aged woman, headscarfed, cardiganed and looking for all the world like any other woman in Musselburgh, then glance back at her grandmother who would be leaning forward and greeting her in hopeful Italian.

Valeria married Domenico in the church in the square where the stream split itself in two. She wore her mother's dress and her cousin's shoes. Her father, who owned the chemist's shop in the village, didn't smile once throughout the ceremony. He didn't want his daughter marrying a *contadino*, a man whose family had worked the land for generations. This Domenico had got himself work with a *padrone* overseas, and would be vanishing off to some place called Edinburgh in two days' time. Why any child of his would volunteer herself to be a *vedove bianche*, a woman abandoned by her husband for him to serve ice-cream to godless people, was beyond him.

After Domenico had gone, Valeria sat in her father's house, trying to learn the hard consonants of English from a book with pages fragile as onion skins, knitting shawls and cardigans and socks and gloves. People said Scotland was cold, as cold as it got here in the middle depths of winter when snow massed up on the mountains, but all year round.

'How do you do?' she intoned to the fireplace, the window frame, the shut door. 'My name is Valeria, Valeria Iannelli.' She paused to check her book, then returned to her mantra – knit one, purl one, knit one, purl one – as the body of her first child formed in her belly.

Every month, Domenico sent her money, which she tied into the silk scarf he'd given her when he'd asked her to marry him, as they stood under the canopy of his brother's olive trees. His letters, at first, were a disappointment. Valeria wanted, needed, love letters. She wanted pages of inked passion, adoration, descriptions of what he could see from his window, of the city she was saving to buy her way to, of how much he missed her, how much he longed for her, how he was desperate to see the face of his baby son.

Instead, Domenico told her that he worked a seventeen-hour day, that the *padrone* often lost his temper with him and the other man in the ice-cream parlour, that the people who came in were sometimes rude and called them 'darkies'. He almost had enough for their own café, where he would cook and she would serve – almost, almost. The *padrone* had agreed to let him buy one in a place by the sea called Musselburgh. When they'd made enough money, they could help bring out his younger brothers and cousins and anyone else from their village who needed to come. '*Campanilismo*,' he wrote, at the end of one letter, 'it's the way the whole world seems to work.'

Valeria waited two years, three years, the money for her passage straining at the frail fabric of her knotted silk scarf. When she finally shuffled down the gangplank of the ship after days and days at sea, her son clamped to her hip, she was gripped by a sudden fear that she might not recognise him, that she might walk straight past him and be stranded in this country of foreigners with nowhere to go. But when she saw him fighting his way towards them through the heaving throngs of people on the quayside, stretching out his hand to her, she almost laughed. She had remembered his face so exactly it was as if it had been her own.

Stella has never been able to give a simple answer when people ask her where she's from. She's unable to say just 'Edinburgh' or 'Scotland', but always has to add a qualifier, a codicil: '. . . but my mother's Italian' or '. . . but I'm half Italian'.

She doesn't know when she realised she was different from other people in this way. Maybe she always knew, maybe it was something she imbibed with the *fagioli*, *tortelloni*, *pollo al cacciatore* and *calzone* her mother fed them on. Other people were called Kirsty or Claire, spoke only

English, and ate fish fingers, mashed potato, baked beans. She had stories from her grandfather about wolves in the woods around his farm, how they had to give half of everything to the landowner, how they had to eat horse-chestnuts when food was scarce; and stories from her mother about living in one room over the café, about having to pick up English at school, and how Domenico had been sent to prison during the war for being an 'enemy alien'. Stella never knew where this left her, a child who slept in a bunk-bed in a heated flat in Marchmont.

She was aware there was something about her that wasn't quite right: the way she looked, maybe, the darker hue of her skin, how she spoke or behaved, the things she said. She couldn't for the life of her pin down what it was. But when teachers and friends' parents asked her, curiously, loftily, 'What are you?' she knew the answer they were looking for: 'I'm Scottish-Italian,' she would say obediently.

Stella always thought that the two words didn't seem to go together, the hard sibilants of the first repelling the softer vowels of the second, like magnets set together. But it was a good phrase, a useful phrase, and she and Nina clung to it like a charm or a password. It explained, or at least gave a name to, their ever-present feeling of being not quite right, not quite convincing, not quite like everyone else.

Stella rested her chin in her hands, leaning on the counter, thinking about the homework she had to finish by tomorrow. The café was quiet today, the freezing, sleety weather keeping everyone at home. Their mother had said that maybe when the races finished they might get some customers.

Near the window, Nina was slicing potatoes into chip-sized pieces, scowling, her shoulders bent. Nina hated chopping chips. She complained that the knife slipped on the wet, uneven planes of the peeled potatoes, and she didn't like the feel of vegetable debris under her nails. Francesca had told her not to be silly and that she and Stella could swap if they wanted to. But Nina hated serving even more. 'I just can't be polite to people,' she said.

Francesca was sitting on the high stool at the till, going through the books, uncoiling the roll of receipts, a pen balanced behind her ear. In five minutes, possibly ten, Stella estimated, she could clear table six – a family with three horrible whiny children who had sprayed crumbs and soda stains all over the floor. Surely they'd be leaving soon. Stella sighed and began pleating a tea-towel into a fan.

'Hey,' Nina said.

'What?'

'By five o'clock we'll have earned . . .' Nina paused and did some calculations on her fingers '. . . six pounds each.'

Stella thought about this. 'Nine pounds,' she corrected.

'Six.'

'No, it's nine. Because we'll have done a total of—'

'OK, OK, whatever,' Nina said, lining up the knife with the centre of a potato. 'Nine pounds.' She grinned and lopped the potato in two. 'Which means I have enough for that coat.'

'Which coat?'

'You know, the one we saw ages ago. The fake fur one.'

'Where?'

'In—'

'Stella,' Francesca's voice cut across them, 'table three, sweetheart.'

Stella put down the tea-towel and walked round the counter, hitching up her trousers. They were men's suit trousers that had got separated from their upper half. A serious, heavy, grey material. She'd bought them in a charity shop. The hems dragged on the ground below her shoes but she liked them.

Half-way across the lino of the café floor she stopped. Her hands flew to her neck. A kind of tense, crushing feeling had closed about her. She suddenly couldn't breathe, as if her apron was tied too tightly, as if her clothes were suffocating her. The clink of crockery and cutlery around her seemed deafening, booming.

At the table near the door sat a man. Stella looked at him for no longer than she needed to. He was alone, he was tall and burly, his frame folded down to fit into the booth, he had violently red hair.

She swivelled round. Her mother was looking up at her, questioningly, but her sister's head was still bent over her chopping. Stella walked back to the counter and placed her hand upon it. There was a sound like crashing water in her ears and she had the sensation that if she didn't watch where she walked, she might trip over a large drop.

'Did you get the order?' her mother asked.

Stella looked down at her shoes, at the hems of her trousers that had trailed through all the silty puddles of Edinburgh. 'No.'

'Why not?'

Stella moved round so that she was behind the counter. She wanted something between her and the man, something solid, something he couldn't see through. She held one elbow with the opposite hand. Her skin felt cold and slippery, like marble.

'What's the matter?' Francesca said, puzzled.

Stella saw Nina raise her head, saw her look at her, look at the man, then back at her.

Nina slammed down the knife. 'I'll do it.'

'What?' Their mother was really exasperated now. 'But Nina, I need you preparing the chips. If Stella's serving, she's serving. I can't have you both swapping over and swapping back, it's much easier if—'

But Nina was reaching into the pocket of Stella's apron and pulling out the pad. When Stella looked up, Nina was walking over the lino towards the red-headed man.

If there's one thing Irene Draper knows about it's running a hotel. When she found this place, twenty-five years ago, it was half derelict, decayed by neglect. The old man, the final relic of a line of lairds, was living in only two rooms on the ground floor, the rest of the house shuttered up. The staircase, when she took to it in her good leather shoes, was splintering and rotted, mushrooms were pushing their way out from between the treads.

The rooms on the upper floor were damp and mildewed, carpets curling, beds wet and sagging, the wallpaper peeling away from the crumbling plaster. There was no electricity – rusted gas-lamps dripped orange-brown stains down the walls. In a small corner room, Irene found a bath filled with what looked like old curtains, and an irate, spitting cat, guarding her litter of squirming, pink-footed kittens. Downstairs, the rooms in which the man lived gave off an airless, close, mammalian fog. From under the parquet floor of what would once have been a ballroom, the roots of the rampant laurel hedge had burst up into the light, thick, pale, fibrous and somehow obscene.

The estate agent had glanced at her as they stepped out again into the bright, sharp light outside and cleared his throat. 'It needs some work,' he began.

Irene ignored him, partly because he was annoying her just by being there, and partly because she didn't want to let on how excited she was. She knew a bargain when she saw one. This place smelt . . . well, of rot and damp and lichen and filth . . . but it also smelt of Potential. And Potential is something Irene has a good nose for.

All kinds of wastrels and undesirables were living in the outhouses and the gate-lodge. The first thing she did was serve them yellow-backed eviction notices. She stood over them with two policemen from Kingussie as they left on the final day of the demand, slinging their bags into the back of a rusting van. They made an emphatic rude gesture at her as they drove off. But Irene hadn't cared. She wasn't the type to let that rattle her. She had turned back to the building and begun rolling up her sleeves.

She'd been proved right, of course. It was a thriving, successful country-lodge hotel, these days. *A two-hundred-year-old crenellated, turreted, grey-stone country house, surrounded by acres of woodland and parkland*, the brochure reads. *Unparalleled service and luxury*. She'd installed power showers in the

1980s, whirlpool baths in the 1990s – she had a go in one once, when the honeymoon suite was empty for the night, but didn't think much of it. She's not sure of her next move. That's the secret of good hoteliering: improve, renovate, innovate. Always stay ahead of the game. It will come to her, whatever it is, she's sure of that.

Irene crosses her legs under her desk, enjoying the rasp of nylon against nylon. She has her own office, these days, in a former dressing room, with views out over the wood. She turns her head and looks out of the window. Something is moving among the emerging spring green of the trees. A figure, walking along the path. Stella.

That's another thing Irene had been right about. Stella Gilmore had arrived mid-morning on a day back in February, a day so cold that each leaf had encased itself in brittle white frost. Irene had had fires lit in the bedrooms and the heating on full, radiators rumbling and shuddering in every room. The cost had been hideous. And this girl had appeared in Reception, all of a sudden, asking for work.

February is slump-time for the hotel trade and Irene doesn't take anybody on in February. But, coming down to tell this person so, she changed her mind. As she stepped down her lovingly restored stair treads, she took it all in: the scarlet coat, the cropped dark hair, the bag at her feet. She heard the vowels of the Edinburgh voice. She saw the slightly wild eyes, the white, pinched look to the face. She saw the car outside, engine whirring from a long drive.

By the time Irene's court shoes had come into contact with the hall carpet, she had the situation assessed, and had already decided to give her a job. This girl would be worth it in the long run, Irene was sure. She'd recoup the extra outlay over the slack weeks with this one, as long as she stayed until after the spring. She heard the girl explain that she'd been working in broadcasting, which she knew didn't have much to do with hotel work, but she used to waitress when she was a teenager and she really needed a job for a while.

Irene didn't ask a thing. Sometimes, she knows, people just have to exit their lives. You get all types in the hotel trade. It attracts runaways like this. A husband, a lover, Irene guessed, with this one. Something like that. This girl was the type to incite passion and foolishness in men – those green eyes, that shut, expressive mouth, that coat. But Irene hadn't asked. She was no fool, and she was a business woman. If a well-spoken, easy-on-the-eye young woman turns up at your hotel in search of work, you don't turn her down. Who cares who or what she's on the run from? She'll be good for business.

As Irene sits in her office, watching the distant figure of her general assistant move along the path, she remembers something. She stands, unlatches the window and heaves it up. 'Stella!' she calls.

Stella stops in her tracks and wheels round. For a moment she can't locate where the voice is coming from, and she scans the building's façade. Irene waves her handkerchief in the air. 'Over here!' she calls. 'Yoo-hoo!'

'Oh.' Stella shades her eyes. 'Hi.'

'I have a telephone message for you.' Irene looks again at the slip of paper she'd written it down on. 'Nina called.'

Stella doesn't move. Irene waits to be told who Nina is. But Stella is silent.

'About half an hour ago,' Irene persists. 'She said that you should call her. It sounded quite urgent.'

From a long way off, over the grass and between the trees, Stella nods. 'Right,' she says.

'You can use the phone in my office, if you like,' Irene offers graciously. Then adds: 'If you need privacy.'

'Er, no,' Stella shakes her head, 'thanks.'

Irene shuts the window, thwarted, peeved.

Francesca stands in the middle of her home. Out of the front window she can see the street, which is full of children – the boys riding bikes in circles, the girls on rollerskates or ducking in turn under a big skipping-rope. Some of the children she recognises as their neighbours or from the school; others she's never seen before.

She turns the other way and looks out of the back door, which she leaves open in summer. She likes the heat, the fresh, pollen-heavy air to drift in. Her daughters have spent all morning constructing a den with sheets and cushions, tying a rope from railing to railing and draping the sheet over it, weighting down the edges with stones. They have disappeared into it, their luminous cave, with books and crayons, the cat, jigsaws, drinks of milk. Nina came into the house half an hour ago, her face shining with exertion and pleasure, to ask if they could have their lunch in there, and Francesca had said, of course, what would you like?

Francesca glances out again at the gangs of neighbourhood children, then back at the billowing white sheets shielding her daughters. Somewhere, she knows, something has gone wrong. She doesn't know why her daughters aren't out there, as they should be, playing with the other girls, doesn't know why they spend all their time with each other. She watches them sometimes when they leave the house, or when they walk away from her across the schoolyard, Nina's hand encircling Stella's wrist, like a bracelet or a manacle. And she watches the other children as her daughters pass by. Groups tighten, turn inwards. Girls says things behind their hands. Boys kick footballs accidentally-on-purpose at them. It makes Francesca want to kill these children, to scream at them, to bang their stupid, ignorant heads together.

Stranded between the two windows, Francesca chews at her thumbnail. She's aware that it's her fault: she is their mother, she is responsible for everything. But she doesn't know what she's done, how she's managed to fail them in this way. Somehow, without meaning to, she has created two distinctly square pegs in a world full of round holes.

She moves towards the back door, looking speculatively at the den. Maybe she should take them a glass of lemonade, tell them lunch won't be long. But she carries on walking, past the fridge, through the kitchen and out of the back door. Her bare feet make no sound in the grass. The sides of the den breathe in the summer air, straining against the stones. Francesca sees the furred flank of the cat brush the taut cotton, then the point of an elbow-bone, close to the ground, and an ankle, high above it.

She knows she's spying, and that it's wrong, but she tells herself, as she crosses the lawn, that she doesn't know what else to do. Hasn't she asked them, again and again, separately and together, is anything wrong at school, do they want to invite anyone over to play, would they like a party for their birthdays, is there anything they want to tell her? The answer is always the same: no, said with an edgy look, a glance passed between the two of them.

Francesca crouches next to the den. If they discover her, she'll say she was just weeding the lawn. On the other side of the cotton the body of one of her daughters shifts and sighs. Stella? Or Nina? Francesca can't tell which. There is a low buzz of voices, like bees in a hive. Francesca leans closer.

'You must try not to think about it,' a voice was saying. Nina's, she thinks. 'When it comes into your head, you must just push it out again. That's what I do.'

The body closest to her shifts again, the juts of bones and joints appearing in the blank canvas of the sheet. It's Stella: Francesca can tell by the length of the limbs.

'But,' Stella whispers, so quietly that Francesca has to strain to hear, 'I can't. It just comes back.'

Francesca tenses, her mind racing. What? What just comes back? Their separation, their isolation? What is it? she wants to beg. Tell me.

Then Nina says: 'No one will ever know it was you, Stel. No one. I'll make sure of it.'

Francesca feels cold suddenly, as if a cloud has passed between her and the sun. She stands and backs away, brushing down her dress with sharp, swift movements. She'll make pizza for lunch. That's what she'll do. They'll like that, and this afternoon, she'll take them to the beach.

In the cool of the house, she shuts the door with a bang and gets down the flour, ready to make the dough.

Stella sits in the empty classroom, drumming the capped

end of her fountain pen against the desk. Today is the final deadline to hand in her university application form. She's been working on it for weeks, filling it in with light pencil – her O Grade and Higher results, her extracurricular activities, her interests, the list of universities she's applying to – rubbing bits out and writing and rewriting them, over and over, until she has it exactly right. She's been spending this free period painstakingly copying over her pencil marks with black ink. She's done the whole form. Except for the list of universities:

1. *Edinburgh*
2. *St Andrews*
3. *Glasgow*
4. *Aberdeen*
5. *London*

She presses the pen into her palm, chews a strand of her hair. Out on the playing-field, the PE teacher is making a straggling crowd of first-years run round and round the hockey pitch. Every ten paces they have to drop to the ground and do press-ups. Stella shudders. She cannot wait to leave school.

'There you are.' Nina is walking through the classroom towards her. 'I've been looking for you everywhere.'

'Oh,' Stella sits up straighter, 'sorry.'

'What are you doing?' Nina slides on to the desk next to her. 'You're not still pissing about with that form, are you?'

'Mmm.'

Nina peers over her shoulder. 'I don't know what you're worried about – you're bound to get in everywhere.'

'I've nearly finished.' Stella eyes her sister. Nina looks flushed and a bit dishevelled. 'Where've you been?'

Nina picks blades of grass off her jumper, swinging her legs. 'Down the pavilion.'

'Alone?'

Nina smirks. 'Of course not. What would be the point in that?'

'I thought you had biology.'

'I did.' She shrugs. 'Couldn't be arsed.'

Stella rolls the pen away from her, then back. 'Neen,' she murmurs.

'What?'

'Don't fail it again.'

'I won't.'

'You might.'

'Oh, don't start with me.' Nina slides off the desk. 'Are you coming?'

'I just have to finish this.' Stella glances at her watch. 'I'll find you at the gate in five minutes.'

'OK.' Nina moves towards the door. 'But hurry up. I want to go into town before the shops shut.'

Stella waits until she's gone, then looks down at the form. Edinburgh, first choice, St Andrews, second, London, last. She and Nina have had it planned for years: she will go to Edinburgh University and Nina to Edinburgh Art College. They'll live at home, sharing the room they've always shared, and in the mornings will walk together to lectures. Perfect.

Stella's never been to London. She doesn't quite know why she's put it there, in the last place. Does anyone ever end up going to their final choice? Stella doubts it. Her teacher told her that what she put fourth and fifth didn't matter. Stella has seen London on television and in films: funny squares with brick houses and trees and black railings, the porcelain-tiled underground railway, street markets, museums, pigeons. She knows it's about four hundred miles from Edinburgh, that it takes four or five hours by train, that it's huge, that it's filled with people talking in jerky voices.

The classroom is chilly, the radiators grumbling. German participles march across the board in chalk and dust motes swirl in the heatless winter sunlight. Outside, the first-years are being instructed to run backwards as the teacher hurls balls at them. Stella pushes her hair back and shuts her eyes.

When she opens them again the sunlight seems brighter, jarring, the walls of the classroom taller than before. She unscrews the cap on her fountain pen, leans over her form and writes in clear, black letters over the pencilled marks reading 'Edinburgh' the word 'London'.

Mel stands at the sink, filling a glass with water. Beyond the window, Jake is in the garden, looking down into the pond she and her father built together when she was about seven. Mel watches the cat crossing the lawn, tail held high, towards Jake. It stops a foot or so from him, looking up at his back, one paw raised. It miaows hope-fully, but Mel knows that its miaows are not as loud as it thinks they are. Jake doesn't hear. The cat waits, tail curled into a question mark. Miaows again. Then, as a last resort, inches forward and rubs its head against Jake's shin.

He jumps and leaps sideways, pulled from whatever reverie he was in. He and the animal regard each other for a moment. Mel holds her breath. Will he touch it? Will he be nice to it? She knows he hates the dog, that he can't bear to be in the same room with it, but will he turn away the cat as well?

She sees him crouch, touch the cat's back, inexpertly run its tail through his fingers. He's never had pets, she knows. 'I don't know much about other species,' he'd said to her once. The cat circles him, surprised by this inept attention, but happy to take whatever it's given.

Jake is not like the other men who have passed through Mel's life. There is something about her that seems to match her with men who buy expensive presents but undress her impatiently, men who pay in restaurants but then drive home too fast. Jake doesn't have a car. She has no idea if he can even drive. She imagines that he would be at an utter loss if she were to ask him where he thought people bought jewellery or lingerie or hand-made chocolates.

Mel smiles. She knows that her family would prefer it if she were with a man who had a good overcoat, a degree, a heated car, a man who knew how to talk about the economy or where to ski or shrubs that grew in the shade or which wine to drink with dinner. Not that her parents or her brothers have ever said anything against Jake. But she's seen the way they look at him sometimes – that wondering, baffled, sidelong glance.

That's the other thing. There's an aloneness, a kind of

completeness to Jake that intrigues her. Other men she's been involved with, and in fact every other person she's ever really known, have all been so enmeshed, so caught up in the criss-crossings of other lives – their families, their old lovers, their colleagues, their friends. The web was endless. But Jake has no family, or hardly any, never speaks about his ex-girlfriends, is private to the point of secrecy, and so elusive that she can never be sure he is really hers. Which only makes Mel more curious, more intrigued, more determined to attach herself to him.

Her own life can sometimes feel too heavy, too over-populated. She adores her family, of course, and all her friends – couldn't do without them. But she is fascinated by the freedom of Jake's existence, the lightness of it.

She rests both hands on the lip of the sink. Her legs shake beneath her, after spending so many months in bed. She should really sit down but she quite wants to stay where she is, watching her strange husband commune with her cat.

'What am I going to do?'

Jake held open the slats of the Venetian blind with his fingertips and peered out. In the acid sunlight, he could see a woman in the building opposite, searching for grey hairs in her bathroom mirror. On the floor above, an old man was putting his poodle out to pee in the window-box.

'Hah?' Hing Tai shouted from the kitchen.

'I said . . .' Jake began, in a loud voice, and then tired of the sentence '. . . oh, never mind.'

He let the blind fall back into place and turned round just as Hing Tai was appearing out of the kitchen with a smoking wok in one hand, tossing his *chow fan* with the circular wrist movement that Mrs Yee had taught them both, years ago, making them practise with a damp cloth standing in for the rice.

'What did you say?' Hing Tai said. 'Can't hear you with the fan on.'

Hing Tai lived on Kowloon side these days, in a tiny apartment in Mong Kok. Much to the horror of all four parents concerned, he had, as soon as he'd got a job at the big broadcasting station, moved out of the family apartment and in with his girlfriend, Mui. Every time Mrs Yee saw Jake, she attempted to get him to talk Hing Tai into either moving back or at least marrying the girl (not that she particularly approved of Mui, who didn't fit Mrs Yee's idea of a good wife – she had a business degree, worked for a record company and spoke four languages, for starters). Jake tried unsuccessfully to avoid the subject whenever possible.

Jake slumped down into a chair. 'Nothing. It doesn't matter.'

'What?' Hing Tai demanded. 'Tell me. You know I hate it when you do that.'

He rubbed the underside of his chin. 'It was nothing.'

'Jik-ah,' Hing Tai said, still vigorously tossing the rice, 'if you don't tell me I'll kick you in the shoulder.'

Jake laughed, despite himself, glancing down at the sling shrouding his left arm. 'Well, in that case, I just said . . . no, moaned, actually . . . what am I going to do?'

Hing Tai regarded him for a moment, his head on one side. 'Hang on,' he said. 'Let me get the food. And the beer. We need sustenance for this conversation.'

Hing Tai clattered and crashed about in the kitchen. Jake got bowls and chopsticks out of the cupboard and put them on the table. He struggled to open the beer with his one good hand, wedging the fridge-cold bottle between his legs.

'Give that to me,' Hing Tai said, as he sat down, reaching out to take the bottle and the opener. 'So,' he said, easing the tops off the bottles, 'how is she?'

'She . . .' Jake watched his friend pushing rice into their bowls '. . . not great. I mean, she's going to be OK but she's very . . . down. Depressed. Panicky. Which . . .' Jake shrugged helplessly '. . . you know . . .'

'. . . is hardly surprising.' Hing Tai finished for him.

Jake nodded.

'What do the doctors say?'

'They say she's incredibly lucky. "Miraculous" is the word they use. It's miraculous that she survived. And that she needs to take everything very slowly. The whole thing of Lucy has made her much, much worse. Of course. They tell me again and again that she mustn't be upset at all, or excited, or . . . or crossed in any way. Which is easy to say, but less easy to put into practice when you're looking after someone who has very nearly died and seen her best friend being killed.'

'Hmm.' Hing Tai upended his chopsticks and began picking out the best bits of prawn and dropping them into Jake's bowl.

'And—' Jake broke off, watching Hing Tai's darting chopsticks, and tried to cover his bowl with his hand. 'Will you stop that?'

Hing Tai pushed his hand away. '*Eiyah*, why so stubborn?' he said, in his mother's voice, making them both laugh. Then he pointed at him. 'You need to get your strength back, man. You look dreadful. Like a fucking corpse.'

'Oh, that's right,' Jake said, grinning, 'come over all racist, why don't you? Hit a man when he's down.'

'Shut up. And tell me—'

'Shut up *and* tell you?'

'Just shut up! And tell me what you were going to say.'

'When?'

'Before. You started saying "and"—'

'And?' Jake thought back. 'And?' He was raising food to his mouth when he remembered. 'Oh, yeah,' he said, lowering his hand, his good mood evaporating as quickly as it had come. 'She . . .' He sighed, cringing away from even saying the words. 'She wants to go home.'

'To her flat?'

'No . . . no . . . to—'

'England?'

'Yeah.'

Hing Tai took a swig of beer. There was a pause. Jake pushed the pink comma of a prawn around his bowl.

'And she wants you to go with her,' Hing Tai said finally.

Jake nodded, without looking up. The fingers of his injured arm protruded out of the white cloth of the sling, pale, stiff and chalky-looking. He flexed the muscles in his lower arm and was almost surprised to see his fingers uncurl in response. It was as if that arm was no longer part of him, just a weight he had to carry, slung about his neck.

'It's such an insane situation,' he muttered, still examining the hand. 'It gets more insane by the day. Sometimes I look at her and think, who are you? what am I doing with you? And then it all comes back – what happened and what I did and—'

'Jake, you had to do it.' Hing Tai was insistent, forceful, the flat of his hand coming down on the table. 'You had no choice. You did what anyone with an ounce of . . . of conscience would have done. She was *dying*.'

Jake looked up at his friend, unconvinced.

'You mustn't be so hard on yourself,' Hing Tai said, more gently.

'But she's so determined to believe we're love's young married dream and the idea makes me want to . . . I mean, I like her.' Jake stopped for a moment and thought. 'I used to like her. I know I did. I don't know what I feel now. Everything's got kind of . . . swept away and . . . and jumbled. But it's just that she's . . . she's . . .' His hand whirled in the air.

'She's not the woman for you.'

'No.' Jake slumped in his seat with relief at having articulated something that had been worming its way around him, unspoken, for weeks. 'Not even close. And I just feel that . . . that there's no way out, that I—'

'At the moment, maybe,' Hing Tai interrupted. 'You can't have this out with her now, obviously. But she will get better.' He gripped Jake's uninjured shoulder and shook it. 'She will. And then you can sort it out, and get back to normal and put it all behind you.'

Jake watched his fingers flex and retract, flex and retract, gripping and releasing empty air. 'You think?'

'Of course.' Hing Tai leant back in his seat, picked up his chopsticks and sucked on them meditatively for a minute. 'And as for going to Britain—'

'Oh, for God's sake,' Jake exploded in English, then went back to Cantonese: 'I have to go, don't I? I can't exactly just pack her on to a plane and wave goodbye.'

'Hmm.' Hing Tai shook his head. 'Not really. What about your job?'

'It would be OK. Chen's in development on a new script, so not a lot will be happening for the next few months. Plus he owes me about a year in holiday time anyway.'

'Well, it sounds like you've made up your mind.'

'Had it made up for me, more like.'

'Whatever,' Hing Tai said dismissively. 'You have to go, one way or another. It'll be fine. You might even enjoy it. Seeing your motherland, and all that.'

Jake grunted. 'I've never really been that curious about the motherland, as you call it.'

'Stop whining,' Hing Tai said, pushing his bowl away from him. 'You deliver her to her parents, you wait until she's better, then you take your leave. *Momantai*. It'll be great. I've always wanted to go to London. You could even go to Scotland.'

Jake looked up. 'What, and see the fatherland?'

'Exactly.' Hing Tai smiled at him.

'It had crossed my mind,' he admitted.

'There you go, then. You can't tell me you've never been curious about that.' Hing Tai looked at his watch. 'I've got to go. I'm going to the movies with Mui. In Yau Ma Tei. Want to come?'

Jake scratched his head, glancing at his own watch. 'I'd love to but I really should get back to—'

'The wife?' Hing Tai shot at him, pulling a simpering face.

'Fuck you.'

'Fuck you too, man.' Hing Tai stood up and stretched lazily. 'Haven't I always warned you about staying away from *gweilo* girls? They're trouble, man, trouble.'

Jake eases open the door and slides into the front room, as noiselessly as he can. The heat hits him like a wave. It's the dry, sucking heat of radiators, sealed windows, unventilated rooms. The dog, from its basket by the wood-burning stove, raises its head, alert, ears cocked, rumbling from its throat. It has never liked Jake. He sticks out his tongue at it. Horrible, stinky animal.

He edges round the side of the sofa but, seeing that Mel is asleep, starts backing away again.

'Jake?' He hears her voice, faint and croaky, just as he reaches the door. 'Is that you?'

He walks round and, sitting down next to her, sees with a sinking dismay that her face is as pale as flour, with delicate lilac hollows under the eyes. 'I thought you were asleep.'

'I was.' She yawns, her mouth stretching so wide that Jake catches a glimpse of the fleshy wet red part of her gullet. 'But I heard you come in.'

'I'm sorry. I didn't mean to wake you.'

'It's fine.' She shifts her weight. The sofa springs give out a long, low twang beneath them, like a harp. 'It's nice to see you.' She reaches out her hand to him; Jake makes himself take it. She starts making high-pitched murmuring sounds to the dog, who responds by thumping its tail on the side of the basket.

'Listen,' Jake begins, 'I wanted to talk to you about something.'

'Really?' Mel carries on with the flow of squeaky nonsense to the dog, who is now whining back to her at the same pitch. The noise is making Jake's ears ache.

'Mel?' He squeezes her hand. 'I had a chat with your parents the other day and—'

'Is this about the wedding?'

'Yes,' he says, surprised. 'How did you—'

'My mother is the worst person in the world at keeping secrets.' Mel smiles at him from her pillows. 'She's a pathological truth-teller. I'm not supposed to know. And Dad's not supposed to know that I know. It's all terribly complicated.' She puts her other hand over his. 'But we can talk about it. If you want.'

'The thing is . . .' he begins, and an image of Mel the morning after they'd first slept together flashes into his mind. He'd taken her for *dim sum*, to a place around the corner from his apartment. They had sat opposite each other and the table was so small that their knees kept interlocking, making it almost overturn, making them both laugh. She'd said she'd always been too scared to come into places like this, and he'd said, scared of what, and she'd said, I don't know, and he'd said, don't be scared. Which is exactly what he'd said to her the night before just as he was about to kiss her. Which made them both laugh again and she'd had to put down her chopsticks. Then she'd said, I'm not scared when I'm with you, and he'd said, good.

'The thing is,' he says again, 'I'm not sure—'

'You're not sure you want to do it.'

Jake stares at her. She looks back at him steadily, both hands wrapped around his. His heart seems to rise in him, like a bubble of air in water. Does she realise? Does she, despite all that's happened, know?

'Mel, I—'

'It's OK, Jake.'

'It is?' he says, barely knowing what he's saying, what this means.

'I know it's not really your style.'

'My style?' he repeats.

'The church, the big wedding, the white dress.' She puts her head on one side, smiling. 'I can't exactly picture you in morning suit.'

Jake doesn't know what morning suit is, but can make a pretty good guess.

'I don't know what we'll do.' She rubs her temple with her knuckle and looks out of the window. 'I didn't tell my mum this, of course. They're only trying to be nice. They think it'll be good for me. Something to look forward to and all that. I don't know what we'll do,' she says again. 'But we don't really have to worry about it now. We might,' she says, in a conspiratorial whisper, raising one eyebrow, 'end up having to do it anyway. Just to please them. You know what parents are like. Could you bear it?'

The airport bus leaves from Hennessey Road. Jake trudges

away from his apartment, his head bent low, as if against wind, his mother's old rucksack on his back and Mel's two suitcases clutched in his right hand. She walks somewhere behind him, making conversation. He knows by now that his silent moments make her nervous, garrulous, make her fill up the gaps. She talks to his back about the traffic, how glad she is to be leaving and how she wants to get to the check-in desk in good time because she wants an aisle seat and is he sure, is he absolutely sure they shouldn't have taken the express train instead of the bus, and she is more than a bit worried about the traffic because even though it's only the middle of the afternoon, there's quite a flow coming from Causeway Bay and is he . . .

He cannot look at her right at the moment, so keeps her just behind him. His shoulder is aching from the straps of the rucksack; his cast covers his lower arm, which swings, pale and heavy, by his side. He hasn't let anyone write or draw on it. There is something about its white, hollow-sounding perfection that he finds oddly pleasing. He is beginning to forget what the arm underneath looks like.

She sits on the suitcase at the bus stop, her face ashen and spent with the effort of walking two blocks. She has lapsed into silence now, giving him the occasional anxious glance. Jake sees the bus coming from a long way off.

Once they are inside, it seems to travel incredibly fast. They are powering along, leaving Wanchai behind them, and he can see the slanting face of the mountains on one side, through the gaps in the buildings, and the flash of sun-scored water in the harbour on the other. The bus rises with the road, above ground, and the streets below them look narrow, the people foreshortened, and Jake can see their bus reflected in the sides of the buildings – fragmented, distorted – and, yes, he can see, for a split second, an image of his own face, staring back at him. Then it's gone.

Mel takes his hand, folding it into hers. Jake thinks that, before, when she was well, he liked the way she used to unbutton his shirts, intently, reverently, like a child unwrapping a parcel, and that perhaps he really does owe this to her, that it's the least he can do. Maybe it will be OK. Maybe he will find that he can love her. Maybe it won't be long until he can come back.

At the last stop before the tunnel a family takes a long time getting on, and just before the doors close, a dark shape flies into the bus with a flitting movement, as if jerked on a string. It swings towards the ceiling then changes direction, zooming towards the windscreen, where it crashes into the glass. Jake stares at it, appalled. It has webbed-leather wings and a short, muscular body. A bat.

A horrified murmur passes through the bus. Mel clutches his hand. The bat flaps away from the windscreen, stunned and disoriented, dropping towards the floor. It gains height again just as it comes towards the rows of passengers and manages to skim over their heads. Mel screams piercingly and ducks, her head slamming into Jake's shoulder so that, for a moment, he is so blinded by pain he doesn't see what happens next.

When he opens his eyes, a young Chinese woman in a beige suit is struggling to her feet, her hands clutched to the sides of her head. She isn't screaming, like lots of other people on the bus, but giving out small, crushed whimpers, tears blurring her makeup. Jake stares at her. Something is writhing and struggling in the silken black of her hair. With its clawed feet, the bat is clutching the strands near her scalp.

Jake starts to his feet. 'Open the window,' he says to Mel.

The woman is sobbing, her hair messed and sticking to her wet face. People are yanking open the windows, air roaring into the bus. Everyone is staring at him, wide-eyed. Mel is holding out a newspaper towards him.

'Use this, Jake,' she is saying. 'Use this.'

He has to hook his arm out of the sling to take it. He unfolds it and places its thick paper width across the woman's head. The action makes his arm ache, his fingers sting. Through the pages, he can feel the quick, feral beating of those leather wings and the clawing scratch of bone-tips.

At that moment, they enter the tunnel, sound and light sucked away. The bus and the swaying passengers are plunged into a lurid yellow-orange gloom. In one movement, Jake clutches the paper around the creature and pulls. The bat writhes and slips from the grasp of the newspaper. Beneath it, the woman sobs silently. He tries again and this time he feels the tiny form between his hands, stiff with panic, and he crumples the paper around it. Jake lifts his arms, pain hammering at his shoulder. Long hanks of the woman's hair fall from the bunched, convulsing newspaper. He turns and a middle-aged man is motioning him towards the window and Jake moves to it and flings the bundle through it.

The wind snatches it away greedily. Sheets of newsprint

separate and float in the wake of the bus, falling gently to the grey Tarmac. Jake watches as a black, winged form rises from them, whipping away into the dark of the tunnel's ceiling.

His mother is doing yoga on the other side of the room. The Sun Salutation. Which means greeting, or saying hello. She spreads her hands out on the mat and her body flexes upward, the length of her hair hanging down, her heels flat on the floor. Sometimes Jake crawls through the arch of her body at this point, making her laugh and collapse on to the mat, but today he doesn't feel like it.

He kicks his heels against the chair legs and leans his elbows on the table. He rolls the black cylinder of a crayon away from him, then towards him, back and forth, back and forth. Outside, the sun is heating up the buildings, the street, the glass in the windows, the tops of the buses. The thermometer outside the kitchen window had said thirty-two when he'd checked it this morning. 'It's going to be a hot one,' his mother said, when he showed her. His mother is Caroline and also Mum. He's always called her Caroline but makes sure he refers to her as 'Mum' at school otherwise people laugh at him.

'What are you up to, Jakey?' Caroline is standing on one leg, her arms raised above her head, hands pointing like an arrow to the ceiling. 'Are you doing a drawing?'

Jake holds the crayon in his fist. If he closes his hand around it, it disappears. No one would know it was there. 'No,' he says.

'Oh. Are you writing a story?'

'No.' He can feel his mother looking at him but he keeps his eyes fixed straight ahead.

She appears opposite him, sitting down at the table. She moves aside the cups from their morning tea and the box of sugar. 'Taikoo', the box says. Jake likes the word.

'Are you writing a letter?'

He puts the crayon in the position Caroline taught him for writing, held slanted and firm between thumb and finger, resting on the muscle of his hand. He nods once.

'To Hing Tai?'

He shakes his head once.

His mother looks at him, puzzled. 'To who, then?' She reaches out and strokes the hair away from his forehead. 'Who are you writing to, love?'

'My father.' The words come out really easily. Just two of them. Jake glances up at his mother, anxious. Will she be upset?

But she is just gazing at him, eyebrows raised. Her hand is frozen in an outstretched position, touching his hair. It feels heavy on his head. He wants to duck out from underneath it but doesn't dare. Then she moves again, starts stroking his fringe. 'Well,' she says, 'that's great, Jakey. How far have you got?'

Jake looks down at the rectangle of paper in front of him: d e r e is written on it in big, black letters. 'I don't know what to call him.'

'What do you mean?' she says quietly.

'Well.' He slides the sharp edge of his thumbnail up the side of the crayon. Tiny worms of wax wriggle out of the black and fall to the page. 'Do I say "Tom" or "Dad"?'

'Um.' She thinks, looking out of the window. 'I think . . . either would be fine, sweetheart.' She reaches for the Taikoo and grips it before her in both hands. 'I think it depends on . . . on how you think of him in your head. Do you think of him as "Tom" or as "Dad"?'

'I . . .' Jake frowns '. . . I don't know. I don't . . . I just think of him . . . as . . . a person. A big person. Who looks like me.'

His mother nods. 'He did . . . he does look like you. A lot like you.' She puts a strand of hair in her mouth. 'Just the same, in fact.'

'So, what do I put, then?' His crayon is poised above the white page.

'Perhaps . . . perhaps "Tom" is best. What do you think?'

'OK.' He is already forming the straight, downward trunk of the *t*.

Caroline sits beside him, handing him the colours he needs and helping him with his spelling when he asks her to: *i wud like to see you*, he writes. Then he draws a picture of their apartment block, stretching up the side of the page: *we liv in hong kong. come soon. if you want. love Jake xoxoxo*. At the bottom he draws a picture of him and Caroline. He does her in her favourite dark pink flares and him in his green hat, although he makes sure that he colours in the hair, so that Tom knows he's got black hair like his.

'Jake, it's splendid,' Caroline says, when he lets her hold it in her hand. 'Really wonderful. I love it. The only problem is,' she says carefully, still examining his drawings, 'that I'm not sure how we're going to post it.'

'I do.' He goes into the kitchen and returns with the empty soy sauce bottle they finished last night with their dinner.

His mother stares at it for a moment, then laughs and claps her hands. 'We have to wash it first,' she says. 'We don't want soy sauce on your lovely drawings.'

They take a bus up and over the humpback of Hong Kong Island, through deep-cut roads with concreted sides, through trees alight with fire-red blossoms, and down to Aberdeen Harbour, the road winding back and back on itself, the stretch of water getting nearer and nearer. The day is close and humid, hazy clouds swollen above them. Caroline haggles with the man over the sampan: she pretends to walk away twice but eventually the man spits into the water and motions for them to get in.

Jake clings to the green-painted side of the sampan with one hand and to the bottle with the other. His mother has to stop him throwing it over when they are two minutes from the harbour.

'Wait,' she says, putting a hand on his shoulder, 'wait till we're out a bit further.'

The dark, choppy water skims underneath the wide bottom of the sampan. The man sits at the tiller, a triangular hat hiding his face. The city looks tiny from here, a collection of uneven, upended boxes, loomed over by huge green peaks. When he's decided it's far enough, Jake holds the neck of the bottle in his fingers, draws back his arm and hurls it towards the blank stretch of the horizon. It travels in an arc and when it hits the glassy surface of the sea it vanishes for a moment. Then Jake sees its red screw top break through to air again and, inside, the white curl of his letter – safe and dry.

Mair had never recovered from rationing. Those government restrictions on food left their stamp on her until the end of her life. She would reach out and seize the wrists of her great-grandchildren as they buttered toast in her kitchen. 'Not too much, mind,' she would say, sliding the earthenware dish out of reach. Her daughters-in-law tittered to each other about the way she hoarded eggs in her pantry until they turned hollow and bad.

She lived in a valley in South Wales, in a town with a name that nobody from across the border could pronounce, their tongues stumbling and tripping over its paired Ls and Ds. And if rationing wasn't enough, Mair was sent evacuees from Swansea and Cardiff, urchin children the government informed her she had to house and feed.

They arrived filthy – the dirtiest things Mair had ever seen. They took her breath away, these three snot-nosed, smirch-faced hobgoblins on her doorstep. Mair stepped back into her hall, calling to her sons who were drawing aeroplanes in the kitchen: 'Upstairs. Both of you. Now this minute.'

When she heard the bedroom door shut, she marched the evacuees through the house, quick quick, to the backyard, where she burnt their clothes, the brown paper they wore instead of underwear, and their hair, which she shaved from their lice-infested heads with a cut-throat razor. She dressed them in her sons' patched pyjamas and lined them up in beds in the attic, head to toe.

Sometimes, when she couldn't sleep – and she often had trouble sleeping – she would hear them crying, a plaintive trickle of misery coming down through the ceiling joists, the plasterwork, the wallpaper put up by Huw on a spring day, several years ago, before this interminable war. But what could you expect? They were godless, these children. On the first night she had suggested they might like to say their prayers now and they'd looked at her as if she had two heads. Within a week, Mair had them kneeling at the side of their beds, stumbling through the Lord's Prayer: *Ein Tad, yr hwn wyt yn y nefoedd, sacteiddier dy enw, deled dy dernas* . . . It was her duty, after all, as a Christian. She had never, in all her life, missed a Sunday at chapel.

She had married Huw at eighteen and her friends' jealousy still gave her stings of secret pleasure. Huw did not, like most of the men in the town, work in the mine but in the mine's administrative office. So while her friends were scrubbing at the coal dust seamed into their husbands' bodies, she was serving dinner on proper china to a husband who wore a clean shirt every day.

Food was a magical thing to Mair, her reason for living, the thing that got her out of bed every morning. The simple alchemy of it never failed to enthrall her: a bag of flour, some eggs, a slab of butter, a dash of milk could be transformed, by her, into a cake or scones or pancakes or anything at all. Her mother had taught her how to make meringues from the viscous whites of eggs in a cooling stove. 'Leave them in until their tops are just beginning to brown,' she would say, as she handed Mair the wooden spoon to lick, 'then whip them out. Quick quick.' And golden sponges so light they were like beaten air. And soda bread, to be eaten with salted curls of butter, and shortbread, fruitcake, apple turnovers, jam tarts, oat biscuits, treacle pudding, steamed suet pudding, queen of puddings, and round, raisin-studded, sugar-dusted Welsh cakes. 'A man can tell your worth by the consistency of your Welsh cakes,' her mother had declared, rubbing clots of butter into the flour that fell from the sieve Mair was holding high above the bowl.

Mair loved eating – but only in secret. It was when she married and got her own house, her own kitchen, that she began to see food as an illicit pleasure, something women could lick or nibble or steal a mouthful of while the men were away. It was the only pleasure she allowed herself, those snatched hidden, private moments with her husband at work and her boys out the back when she could stand in her kitchen and fill her mouth, close her lips around the sweet, yielding mush of marmalade bread, the molten crust of a jam turnover. She found it difficult to eat if anyone else was there. Mair hated being watched, hated the idea that someone might count the number of flapjacks she was consuming or hear the small, constricted noises she made when she swallowed. The thrilling, transgressive secrecy of it was the best thing. If she was interrupted – by a neighbour appearing at the back door or a child coming down the stairs – she would shove whatever it was she was eating behind a handy jar or one of her ornamental teapots.

Huw was perplexed by the half-eaten sandwiches he came across occasionally, greened with mould, stuffed into a drawer of the dresser. He assumed it was one of the children. He would tell his wife and she would tut and fling them into the all-consuming mouth of the stove. He left her to deal with it, to talk to the child concerned: food and the family's consumption of it was her domain. It would never have occurred to him that the person who most often caused this paranoia and subterfuge was himself. As far as he knew, his wife, whose figure even after two children still fitted into the stays that had come into his home when they married, wasn't interested in food. She hardly ate a thing.

The war, though, ruined all this for Mair. Instead of beautiful orange-yellow yolks from the farm up the road, the government gave her powdered egg that she had to mix with water, slivers of butter with which she was supposed to feed her whole family, a mean paper twist of sugar the size of her finger. She was a wife, she was meant to provide, to cook, to feed – but how could she, with this dried, tasteless rubbish? And rationing made it impossible for her to make the extra for her to eat on her own. Even if she'd had a spare tray of scones and all the butter she wished, she could never have eaten them: the house was full of those horrible urchins, moping about in the kitchen all day, getting under her feet. It stole from her her very purpose in life, as well as her only pleasure. She had to put away her mother's beloved utensils. She would not insult them with this muck.

Even at the end of her life, when she was consigned to a chair in an old people's home near the Swansea docks, she could recall the feel of her mother's wooden spoon against her tongue, the grain of that damp, saturated wood, the taste of uncooked dough, the sticky, irresistible mix of egg, flour and water, the dry handle held firm in her fingers. Her mother had given her the things just before she died, almost, Mair always thought, as if she knew. 'My cooking days are over, *cariad*,' she'd said, as she parcelled them up in newspaper and string – the porcelain mixing-bowl with the cracked glaze, the wooden spoon, the brass-handled balloon whisk, the iron sugar cutters, the copper-bottomed milk pan.

From her chair with a view, if you sat up straight, of the restless, grey-brown waters of the Bristol Channel and the empty, shipless docks, Mair would ask her son, when he came to visit, 'What happened to my mother's mixing-bowl? Who has my mother's mixing-bowl?' When he evaded the question, Mair would turn to the daughter-in-law who always kept her coat on and say, 'Do you have it, perhaps? Do you use it? Do you?'

There was one day, when both of them had long since given up replying to this question, when she murmured, 'Perhaps Caroline has it.'

Her son had looked up, astonished, from the brochure of the car he was hoping to buy. His wife gaped her mouth at him in mock shock. Because Caroline's name was never mentioned by his mother – if anyone referred to her, she would make her face empty, rigid. But he was wise enough to leap at the chance. He was sick of hearing about that bloody bowl.

'Yes, yes,' he said hastily, creasing the brochure in his eagerness, 'that's right. Caroline has it.'

Mair sat back in her chair and thought about the mixing-bowl and the way it had a single, flat plane on the bottom for tilting it on its side, and how it was most useful for beating eggs into flour, and Caroline, her youngest child, her sin, her shame.

The clock unwinds. Two a.m. Three a.m. Four a.m. At four thirty, Jake gets up, leaving the bed, easing himself from the mattress so as not to wake Mel. The cold is making him shiver so he drags on a sweater and tiptoes out of the room, closing the door behind him.

The ground floor is freezing, the light blue-edged. The dog rumbles and groans from its wicker bed in the utility room. He checks that the door between him and the dog is shut firm, then he sits down at the table and pulls the phone towards him. The codes are unfamiliar to him from here. It takes him two fumbled attempts at dialling before he hears the click of connection and the miraculous pulse of a ring tone. Please be there, please be there.

'Yes, hello?' His mother's voice, clear and faintly distracted, sounds in his ear.

'It's me,' he says, as he always does. 'Hi.'

'Jakey,' he can hear the smile in her voice, 'I'm so glad it's you. I've been thinking about you all day. How are you?'

'All right. Not bad.'

There is a pause. He listens to the sound of distance, satellites, the vast roll of the Pacific Ocean.

'How's the arm?' It's as if she's shifted position. She seems closer to the mouthpiece. 'Are you still in plaster?'

'No. I had it taken off last week. It's fine now. It gets a bit stiff in the cold here, but it's fine. Almost back to normal.'

'And . . .' he hears her pause, selecting her words '. . . Melanie? How's she?'

'Um, well . . . it's slow progress. She's getting better. But, you know, she's had a much worse time of it than me.'

'Yes.' His mother inhales sharply. 'I still can't believe you were there. When Lionel brought the papers in that morning, I—'

'Caroline, it's OK. I'm fine – remember?'

'I know, I know.' She gives a kind of shuddering laugh. 'I just want to see you, I think. Lay eyes on you.' She laughs again, properly this time. 'Only then will I believe that you're OK. Neurotic, I know.'

Jake picks up one of the medicine bottles on the table and reads the tiny print on it: Twice daily, with meals, M. J. Kildoune. He puts it down. 'How are things with you?'

'We're all great. I'm working lots. Lionel isn't. The cats are well. But, look, I don't want to talk about that. Tell me how the land lies with you.'

'It's kind of . . .' he hesitates '. . . complicated.'

'What kind of complicated?'

'Just complicated.'

He's aware of his mother holding back all the things she wants to say. He pushes the pill bottles into a circle, their labels turned inwards.

'It must be the middle of the night there,' she says.

'It is.'

'Can't you sleep?'

'No. Not really. I can get to sleep OK, I just wake up a lot.' He glances at the clock above the Aga. 'Listen, I should really go. I'm on their phone.' Jake takes a deep breath. 'Caroline, I was thinking . . .' He stops, wondering how to go on.

'Yes?'

'I was thinking about taking a trip. To Scotland. While I'm here. Thought I might as well. You know, have a look around.'

Again, the booming silence of distance, punctuated only by his mother's breathing.

'We-ell,' she says, 'if you feel you want to, Jake. But I don't know . . . I don't know what you'll find there. I mean, I've no idea what's . . . there.'

'I won't know until I try, will I? I just thought if I'm here I'd be mad not to go and look at the place I'm called after. Don't you think?'

'Mmm.' She is reluctant. 'Maybe you're right.'

He's been on eight minutes already. 'I really must go.'

'Jake, call me again soon, won't you?' she says in a rush, trying to fit in as many words as possible at the end. 'Or write. Lionel's getting email. Let me know when you're going. And if you need anything.'

'I will.'

'Anything at all.'

'OK.'

'Do you promise?'

'I promise.'

Francesca and Stella surprise each other in the kitchen. Francesca had thought everyone was out and was about to take a guilty, indulgent mid-afternoon bath – something she does occasionally when she thinks no one else is around.

Stella is standing next to the table, eating a sandwich and, Francesca is mildly disconcerted to see, wearing a floor-length scarlet plastic mackintosh. She has the cat, Max, draped round her shoulders like a fox fur.

'Hello,' Francesca begins pleasantly, trying not to mention or even look at the coat. Nina may be tricksy but Francesca thinks that she knows, that she's always known, where Nina's at, who Nina is. She feels increasingly that she's losing her handle on Stella.

Stella grunts through her food. Max purrs loudly, unscything his claws.

'I thought you and Nina were going for a walk.' Francesca thinks of the tank filled and ready with piping hot water.

'We were,' Stella mumbles.

'Ah.'

'But I came back.'

'So I see.' Francesca moves to the fridge, goes as if to open it, but then changes her mind. 'Why was that?'

Stella says something unintelligible, stroking the striped rings of Max's tail.

'Sorry?'

'I said, Nina wanted to go to the Camera Obscura.'

Francesca frowns. 'But . . . but I thought you loved the Camera Obscura.' When Stella was a child, she had been fascinated by this magical trapping of the city in a wide, porcelain bowl. Francesca can feel herself smiling nostalgically for the small, dense-limbed being, leaning out of the pushchair to see. The mackintosh-clad, twelve-year-old

Stella in front of her is eyeing her, scowling. Francesca makes herself stop smiling.

'I do,' Stella says. 'I just didn't feel like it.'

'Why not?'

Stella shrugs. 'Just didn't.'

'Well.' Francesca puts her hands on her hips, then takes them down again. She doesn't know what to say. 'When will Nina be back?'

'Dunno,' Stella replies automatically, and Francesca feels enraged and shut out by this autonomy of two, the kind of single doubleness, the way they always operate for and with each other – and usually against her. Her daughters changed and made her life. They allowed her to see the point of herself. They made her feel as though she belonged to this land where she had never felt any connection before. But they baffle her, frustrate her, drain her.

'I see.' Then Francesca remembers something. 'Stella, there's something I need to talk to you about.'

Stella twists her head towards her and stops chewing. She's picked up on some seriousness of tone. 'What?'

'I phoned your headmaster the other day and—'

'Mu-um.' Stella is furious already. Not a good sign. 'Why do you keep doing that? No one else's parents are on the phone every bloody day to—'

'Stella!' she shouts. 'Don't swear at me!'

'I'll swear if I bloody well want to,' Stella shouts back. Max flattens his ears to his head and leaps from Stella's shoulders to the floor, where he paces about, vexed and ruffled.

Francesca takes a deep breath and starts to count to ten. She gets as far as six. She had told herself she would try not to get confrontational with Stella any more. 'He suggested, and I agreed,' she continues, managing to keep her voice down, 'that it would be best to put you and Nina in different classes when you go up to the high school.'

Francesca waits, trying not to cringe. She doesn't say what the headmaster had really said: that her daughters never spoke to anyone other than each other, that they had no other friends, that the school was anxious about their extreme isolation.

There is silence in the kitchen. Stella stares at her. The silence stretches and Francesca becomes nervous. This is not what she'd expected. Rages and tears and sulks and explosions, yes. But not this. They've never been able to bear being apart.

'I – I thought it might be better,' Francesca stutters. 'For – for both of you. Before you begin your new school. A new start. For both of you.'

Still no response. Then Stella puts down her plate and shifts to the opposite foot. She looks up at the ceiling. 'You mean . . .' she begins '. . . put Nina back up a year?'

'No, no. She'll still be in the same year as you. Just in a different class.'

Francesca waits, chewing at the skin surrounding her thumbnail. Stella appears to be considering the idea.

'Well, you'll have to tell her,' she says eventually, dumping her plate in the sink, 'because I'm not going to.'

Francesca is so relieved to have avoided a row she starts to gabble: 'Of course, of course I'll tell her. I would never, never expect you to do it. Naturally, your father and I will tell her as soon as she gets in and then maybe we could all sit down and . . .'

Stella has left the room. Francesca lowers herself into a chair. She and Max regard each other. She is amazed. Absolutely amazed. She'd expected a major row, a spectacular battle, floods of tears and rage. Maybe, Francesca thinks, hopefully, she might ask her to get rid of that dreadful coat.

An old jazz song was playing, a woman who died a tragic death crooning about there being no sun up in the sky, the pulse of her voice stretching at the thickened carpet walls of the studio. When this place had been built, someone told Stella once, the architects had been anxious about the noise of traffic in Portland Place and Regent Street being heard on air, so all the studios were buried deep in the centre of the building, like the tiniest figure in a set of Russian dolls.

James was leaning back in his chair, one foot on the table, his headphones slipped down round his neck, chatting to the weather girl. Stella leant over the mike that connected her to the studio. 'Two minutes twenty-five, James.'

Through the glass she saw him sit up and reach for his mike. 'OK. We're ready.'

'Weather first and then we've got some calls lined up for you.' Stella kept her voice even, neutral. 'There's a woman who wants to talk to you about the benefits of kick-boxing.'

She saw him look up, searching for her. It was harder to see through the glass from his side. 'Tell her to go fuck herself.'

She laughed. 'You can tell her yourself. She's on line four. One minute fifty. She took exception to your assertion earlier that sport is bad for you.'

'Bloody cranks,' she heard him mutter.

'One minute forty.'

Stella turned back to the mixing desk. The door whumped open and a man from the production team leant in. 'Call for you, Stella.'

'What?' Stella jerked her head round. 'Not now.'

'It's urgent, apparently.'

'Who is it?'

'I don't know.'

She yanked the chair towards the phone and pressed the flashing line. 'Yes?'

'Stel, it's me.'

Stella raised her eyes to the ceiling. 'Jesus, Nina. I'm right in the middle of a programme. I can't—'

'I know. I heard you.'

'Then why—'

'Listen. I've left Richard.'

Stella sighed, tapping the end of her pen on the desk. 'Neen, is there any way—'

'Can I come and stay?'

'Er . . .'

'I'm at the airport,' Nina said threateningly. 'I'm—'

'Look, can you call back later? I'm – I've got plans for tonight.' The man Stella had been seeing had promised to pick her up from work, drive her home, and then ravish her. Which Stella had been rather looking forward to.

'If you don't want me,' Nina burst out, 'then maybe I'll just have to—'

Above her head, Stella saw the On Air light come on. 'Of course I want you,' she said, distracted. In the studio, the weather girl was reading from a script. Stella glanced at the levels and nudged one up with her knuckle. 'Of course you can come.'

Nina sniffed, slightly mollified. 'OK. I'll see you later. There's a flight that gets in at about quarter past midnight. So I'll get to you about one-ish.'

'Great.'

'I got a late one because I knew you were working.'

'Thanks.'

There was a pattern to Nina's occasional marital crises. Richard committed some misdemeanour (usually obscure and often incredibly minor), they rowed, Nina flounced out, not to return for several days, during which time she threw herself heart and soul into various types of outlandish behaviour – sometimes buying lots of expensive clothes, sometimes sleeping with someone else, or sometimes disappearing on a plane to a far-flung place. Richard either always forgave her or perhaps never knew the full truth, Stella could never tell which. Nina's freak-outs seemed to be part of the fabric of their marriage.

Stella finished the show, ignoring James's on-air digs about his producer always chatting on the phone, called the man to cancel, rushed out just in time to catch the last tube, stopped in at a twenty-four-hour Turkish store to buy supplies because Nina would be hungry after her flight. As the three brothers who ran the shop sat in the doorway on stools, Stella selected polished, bitter-skinned olives, a tub of creamy hummus and pitta bread, flat like shoe-soles.

At home, her answerphone was glowing with a message: 'Stel, it's Nina, just wanted to . . .' a crackling interlude while there was some static and then some giggling '. . . calling on Richard's mobile. I rang him after I'd spoken to you and he came to the airport and got me. So everything's OK. We're in the car right now . . .' more giggling and rustling and the rumble of Richard's voice in the background '. . . not to see you. 'Bye.'

Stella picked up a glass – one of the tall, thick-based ones she loved – and hurled it at the wall.

Nina is sent to nursery. She is made to sit in a circle with the other children, her legs crossed beneath her. She has to speak English here, her mother told her, because they won't understand Italian. Sometimes Nina forgets this and asks for *latte* instead of milk and the teacher stares at her, eyebrows pulled down. They sing songs, play with water and sand, pedal round and round the narrow paths on tricycles, make collages of fish with glue and coloured lentils, and cut pictures out of magazines with scissors. The scissors are Nina's favourite thing. She likes the symmetry of them, the way they slice through the grain of the paper, the way the two identical blades work with each other and against each other.

Nina walks down the path, threading her way through

the tricycles, which the boys have left there. She is wearing her red tights and red kilt. This is her favourite outfit. Granny Gilmore gave it to her, not Granny Iannelli. Granny Iannelli gives her funny things – biscuits in thin, crinkly paper and mechanical wooden toys. Cradled in her hand is the snowman she has made: a toilet roll tube, covered in soft, pillowy cottonwool with a red hat to match Nina's tights. Nina drew the face herself.

When her mother, who's waiting at the gate, sees her, she waves, her arm held aloft. Stella kicks her heels against her pushchair and screams. 'Dat,' she says, pointing at Nina, 'dat!'

Her mother is touching the soft white bulk of the snowman, praising it, telling Nina she is a clever girl, but Nina is not listening. She is looking at Stella. Or, rather, her hair. Instead of being brushed and held in a clip at the side of her head – like her own, like their hair always is – Stella's hair is held in bunches on top of her head in two green ribbons. Green velvet. Nina has never seen them before.

'. . . we'll put it on the mantelpiece when we get home,' her mother is saying. 'It'll be our first Christmas decoration and maybe later—'

'What's happened to Stella's hair?'

Nina sees her mother look down at Stella's head, bisected neatly by the white line of a parting. She sees her mother's face blur and soften in something that looks like delight. Or pride.

'It's great, isn't it?' Her mother laughs as she manoeuvres the pushchair away from the nursery gate and down the pavement. 'I was doing her hair this morning and I suddenly realised that it's long enough to go in bunches. It's very pretty, don't you think?'

Nina looks across at her sister, who is sucking on a pine cone. The bunches and the ribbons bob up and down with the movement of the pushchair. 'Will you do mine like that?'

But her mother shakes her head. 'Oh, *piccola*, I can't. Your hair is too short. You and Stella have very different hair. She has my hair, you see.'

Nina thinks about this for a moment. 'Don't I have your hair too?' she asks.

'No, darling. Yours is more like your father's. Or maybe your grandmother's. Granny Gilmore.'

Nina grips the snowman to her. Granny Gilmore's hair is so white and thin the pink of her scalp gleams through. Nina sees that Stella's hair is black and thick and long. If she drew Stella, she'd have to use the black crayon for her hair. If she drew herself she wouldn't know which crayon to use – the brown or the yellow or the red? Or all three?

She watches as her mother reaches over and twines the length of one of Stella's bunches around her finger.

Francesca is breaking eggs into a bowl for an omelette, stacking the half-shells inside one another, when the phone rings. The girls are playing something in the corner, the running commentary from Nina interrupted by an occasional monosyllabic exclamation from Stella. Francesca goes into the hall and picks up the phone.

It's her mother, intent on detailing some imagined slight from one of Francesca's cousins, involving a letter dated two weeks before the postmark. Francesca half-listens for a few minutes, uttering, 'Mmm,' and 'Oh,' at intervals. She feels like Stella, under a verbal onslaught from Nina. Francesca takes a deep breath and tries to head her mother off: 'I can't talk now. The girls haven't had their lunch yet.'

Her mother scolds her, demands to know why Francesca hadn't told her the *bambine* were hungry and hangs up. Francesca rolls her eyes.

She goes back into the kitchen, but stops on the threshold. Nina is standing in the middle of the room, a curious gleam in her eyes. The floor is covered in uneven dark patches, like a shadow or something spilt. Francesca stops where she is. Has Nina dropped something, some water or juice? She stares and the scene in front of her melds into sense. Scattered all over the lino are thick swatches of hair. Dark, soft, black hair. Just like her own. Francesca puts up a hand to feel it. It's still held away from her neck in a silver clasp.

Then a small figure comes lurching round the side of a kitchen unit. For a moment, Francesca doesn't recognise it – a strange-looking homunculus, it has bristly, tufty hair, shorn close to its wax-white scalp, and stubble all over its clothes. A hair-covered dwarf.

'Gone,' it announces. 'Hair. All gone.'

Francesca looks at Nina. She is clutching a pair of scissors. Her expression is calm, defiant, opaque. Stella bends over and starts foraging about in the strands of fallen hair. She regards Francesca for a moment, then offers her a fistful. 'Mummy,' she says, solicitous, 'hair?'

Francesca sinks to her knees. She accepts the severed lock from Stella and holds it for a moment, stretched between her fingers. She takes a deep breath. 'Nina,' she begins.

It is summer time again. The last, lazy weeks of term. Burst particles of pollen float in through the open window. It is double biology on a Thursday afternoon and the sun is angled high, pouring in through the blindless glass like heated syrup. They are supposed to have started next year's syllabus, but no one, not even the teachers, is taking that seriously. Stella, sucking on the tapering tip of her ballpoint, is choosing to ignore the uniform regulations, wearing instead a flowered dress she bought at a junk shop in the Grassmarket, thick woollen tights and some heavy-soled army boots. She is rather hot, but wouldn't admit it to anyone.

She looks up from her diagram of a human heart, where she is colouring arteries in red and veins in blue, and glances round the room. Louise, sitting at the front bench, is staring out of the window, one hand propping up her head, the other tentatively touching the crinkling skin of the packet of crisps under the desk. Felicity is mouthing something noiselessly and elaborately to her friend Rebecca – something that makes them double up in silent laughter, covering their mouths and leaning over the desk with the forbidden, subversive delight of it. The teacher, Miss Fowkes, sitting at the front, keeps loosening and pinning up her hair, over and over again, as if she can't get it right, or as if she wants to feel its warm, coiled length between her fingers.

There is a sudden knock at the door. The class shifts with interest. Stella takes the pen-end from her mouth. Felicity and Rebecca snap upright, mirth dying in their throats. A distraction. They all like a distraction.

'Come in,' Miss Fowkes calls. Nothing happens. 'Come in!' she shouts louder.

The door creaks open and Nina appears round it. She is wearing a skirt that is held together by an annoying buttonhole which is slightly too big. Stella wears it herself sometimes and she sees now that it's too long on Nina. Nina's hair is held away from her face with clips that Stella recognises as hers. The people who know that Nina is her sister are turning round to look at Stella, to assess – what? Their similarity? Their differences? Stella's reaction? Stella makes her face stony, impassive.

'Yes?' Miss Fowkes demands, and Stella flinches slightly.

'Mr Allen was wondering if you had a pipette.'

'Well, of course we do but we're using it just now.'

Nina glances at the floor then back at Miss Fowkes. 'He was wondering if you had a spare one,' she mutters.

Miss Fowkes sighs theatrically and gets to her feet. 'I'll go and see.' Then, addressing the class, she announces, 'I have to pop out for a minute. I want you to carry on copying the diagram on the board. And when I come back down that corridor I don't want to hear a peep out of you lot. Do you hear? Not a peep.'

She sweeps out, leaving the door open, a new, cool draught flowing through the classroom. There is silence for a moment. Then someone at the back – a boy – says, 'Peep.' Quietly but loud enough for them all to hear. Sniggers explode around him like fireworks.

Stranded at the front of the class, Nina hooks one foot around the back of the other. Her fingers fly to one of the hairclips. Her eyes travel over the class then lock with Stella's. The sisters stare at each other for a moment. Then Nina looks away. They don't acknowledge each other much at school. Stella looks down, looks at the diagram in front of her, at the lopsided shape of the human heart, its twin chambers, at the red and blue passageways flowing through it, seeing for the first time the way your heart is always full of two opposing elements.

'Hey! What's your name?'

The voice, brusque and insistent, comes from behind Stella. She turns. Stuart Robson is leaning forward on his bench, staring at Nina. Stuart is one of the more irritating boys in their year. He bangs against Stella outside classrooms, snaps her bra strap, draws obscene things on her jotters, and spits paperballs into her hair. Once he wrote 'FREAK' on the back of her coat in felt-tip. She and Nina had had to scrub at it for ages to get it out.

'Leave her alone,' Stella says quickly.

Stuart glances at her, then back at Nina. A smile curls his lips. 'Hey, you,' he calls again, 'I asked you a question.'

'Leave her alone, Stuart.' Stella grips her pen, hard.

'Are you Stella's sister?'

Nina doesn't reply in that flint-faced, impenetrable way she and Stella have perfected over the years. Her mouth is clamped shut. You'd never know she was holding anything in. But Stella sees the violet-blue thread pulsing in her temple.

'Are you?' Stuart is on his feet now, sauntering down

the aisle towards her. Nina gives no sign that she's aware of this. 'Is your name Ghoulmore, by any chance?'

A ripple of laughter passes over the class.

'Are you?' Stuart insists. 'Are you a freak-girl? A Ghoulmore?' He makes a whistling ghostie noise, like a child on Hallowe'en. Nina still doesn't react, giving the impression she is absorbed in something beyond the windows, her face turned away, her fingers laced into each other.

'If you're Stella's sister, Stella's older sister,' Stuart says, his face close to Nina's now, 'how come you're in the same year?'

Stella sees Nina swallow.

'Everyone says,' he leans close to her, 'that you're a bit of a spastic.'

Nina looks out of the window as if enjoying the view, her lips pressed together. Stuart reaches out and his fingers close over a hank of Nina's hair. Stella sees pain jag across those features as familiar to her as her own and she is on her feet and striding through the benches separating her from Nina. Her fists are curled and fury is raging through her, through every blood vessel webbed out in her body, and she feels she could do anything, anything at all to this boy who is injuring her sister, that she won't be answerable for the damage she's going to inflict on him.

Stella grabs his jumper and yanks him away from Nina. At fifteen, Stella is tall for her age, taller than Stuart.

'Get off her,' she hisses, through gritted teeth, ramming him up against the wall. There is a dull crack as his head hits brick. 'Touch her again and I'll—'

Stella stops, swallowing the words. Stuart is momentarily

frozen, astonished by Stella's vehemence. Just as Stella sees that Nina is putting out a hand towards her – to help her or restrain her? – Miss Fowkes appears round the door, carrying a pipette. 'What's going on?' she exclaims. 'Get back to your seats.'

Stuart and Stella don't move. Blood is pounding round Stella's body, making her head swim and pulsate. Everything seems too close suddenly – the walls, the people, the desks. She is holding on to Stuart almost for balance now.

'Immediately!' Miss Fowkes squeaks, handing the pipette to Nina.

Stella uncurls her fingers from the bunched wool of Stuart's jumper. Her sister's lips part, as if she wants to speak, but then she turns away.

Later, Stella finds Nina in their usual place in the canteen, right at the back, beside the window, at the table where they stack the spare chairs.

Stella puts down her tray opposite her sister. Nina is covering her nails with fluorescent marker, taking sips out of a can of juice.

'You all right?' Nina says, without looking up.

'Yeah. You?'

'Uh-huh.'

Stella picks up her fork, pokes at the crust of the pie on her plate, puts it down again. She sighs. 'I hate the canteen.'

Nina leans across and paints Stella's thumbnail yellow. 'Me too.' She recaps the yellow and gets out the pink, glancing, as she does so, at something over Stella's shoulder.

Nina clears her throat. 'Have you . . . I was wondering if . . . if you'd seen the new boy?'

There is something about the way she says this – carefully, thoughtfully – that makes Stella look at her.

'What new boy?'

'In the year above.'

'No,' Stella says. 'Why?'

'He's over there.' Nina points with her pen, keeping hold, Stella notices, of her wrist. 'Don't look now.' She checks the room. 'OK. No one's looking.'

Stella turns. There, in the dinner queue, is a tall, hulking boy with red hair. She turns back in her seat, forces herself to look out at the playing fields, at the jagged line where the roofs of the houses meet the glaring blue of the sky.

Nina is watching her, Stella's hand trapped between both of hers. Stella extracts it and folds her arms over her.

'He's not that like him,' Nina says, cautiously, 'is he? I mean—'

'Shut up.'

'He's quite good-looking.'

'Shut *up*.'

Nina puts all the caps back on her marker pens. The smell of the pie in front of Stella is making her feel nauseous.

'I just . . .' Nina tries to take her hand again but Stella won't let her '. . . I only wanted to . . . to warn you.'

'I know.'

'I didn't mean to upset you.'

'I'm not upset,' Stella cries, near to tears. 'I'm not upset at all!'

Nina lines her pens up, then starts rearranging them in a

star shape. Stella wants to leave, to run away. She can't bear the thought of that person, of him, behind her somewhere, but she can't look round either.

'When you think you see him,' Nina whispers, as she moves her pens about, 'what do you see?'

Stella stares at her, appalled.

'What do you see, Stel?'

Stella leaps up, dragging her bag with her, and runs through the canteen towards the door.

The library at school smelt of floor polish and damp paper. The dehumidifiers coughed and hummed from the corners, digesting the wet, mouldering heat of the rainy season. But you could still find circular bursts of grey-white mould on the pages of the books, still find your fingers flecked with spores after a lunchtime spent reading there. The other boys played football in the yard at break-time. Jake would have liked to join them but they all talked about football teams from Britain and Jake didn't know anything about that. He once asked the boy he sat next to how you know which team to support, and the boy had stared at him as if he'd asked what two plus two was. Then he'd turned round and started telling the other boys what Jake had said and they'd all laughed. Jake had puzzled over it for weeks – why was it so obvious to them which team to support and why was it so laughable not to know? – finally deciding that it must be something to do with not having a father. It was easier for him to come in here and pretend that he didn't want to play anyway.

Jake stood near the geography books, gazing up at a map

of the British Isles. His mother never talked about where she came from. He'd asked her the name of the place several times and she would always say it quickly, from the side of her mouth, in an accent Jake didn't recognise as hers. She'd taught him a Welsh song once, all about a river, and drawn him a family tree in an exercise book. But when he went back to the book to find it, to put it somewhere safe, he found the page had been torn out.

His eyes travelled over the two uneven islands. The ragged, battered coastlines. The dog-shape of Ireland and the way you could see how Britain would have once fitted round it, before the tectonic plates shifted, easing Ireland free. The bulge of Wales, straining away from England, as if wanting to follow Ireland out into the water. He saw the way the roads and rails all rushed towards the big red dot of London, like streams of water gushing down a drain. He saw how Cornwall kicked out into the sea and how Scotland made everything look top-heavy, as if the narrow neck of northern England couldn't quite support its weight.

'Are you looking for anything in particular, Jake?' The librarian, a woman who wore her glasses on a chain round her neck, was standing behind him.

'No,' Jake fingered the frayed edge of his school shirt, 'thank you.'

'Are you sure?'

'Um,' he flushed deeply, 'no . . . I mean, yes . . . I was wondering where . . . where Kildoune was.'

'Kildoune?' The librarian looked at him. 'Isn't that . . . ?'

'I'm called after it. It's a place in Scotland.'

'Ah.' Her face broke into a smile. 'I'm from Scotland. Where is it near, do you know?'

'Er . . .' Jake tried to recall the word. 'Avie . . . Avie-something. I think.'

'Aviemore?'

Jake nodded quickly.

'I know it well! My sister has a house there. A beautiful place. Look,' the librarian stretched up above his head, 'it's right here. All the way up here.' Her fingertip rested in the middle of the widest part of Scotland, concealing most of the word. Jake could just make out the A and the V, but no more. He fixed his eyes on the point, willing himself to remember it, to be able to recall it when her finger dropped.

The librarian moved away. 'Now, let's see if we can find that other place you were telling me about. Have you used the atlas before?'

Jake shook his head.

'Well, it's very easy. Let me show you.' She pulled a big, lean book down from the shelves. *Atlas of the World*, it read, in faded gold lettering. 'At the back there's a list of all the places in the whole world, in alphabetical order.' Jake sat at her elbow, transfixed, his hands clenched together. It was almost as if this book might split open to reveal a picture of his father.

'Here are the Ks,' she said, and Jake saw a page crammed with tiny black words. 'K-i-l,' she murmured, as she ran her finger down the column. 'K-i-l, there'll be lots of these in Scotland, K-i-l-d . . . Kildare, Kilden, Kildepo Valley, Kildonan. Oh.' She stopped. 'That's funny.'

'What?' He leant forward, anxious. 'What is it?'

'It's not there.' She turned to look at him, puzzled. 'Are you sure you've got it right?'

Mair's sons had been born in quick succession after her marriage: Alun when she was nineteen, and Geraint three years later. And that, Mair decided, was enough. She'd hated the sweat and the bawling and the blood of birth. It made her unrecognisable to herself: who was making that bellowing noise, she'd asked the midwife, and was disgusted, horrified, when told that it was her. She'd insisted that they clean and wrap the babies in a shawl before she would touch them.

As for that other thing, that other act, she'd never been fussed. It all seemed too base, too animal to her. Sometimes, during it, she had to struggle not to picture herself from the outside – a woman with her knees shoved up into her armpits and a man straining and heaving as he effortfully mined his way into her. After Geraint, the place where they stitched her nipped and ached if she stood too long on the kitchen floor, the cold from the flags travelling up the backs of her legs. When Huw came at her in the night, it was so sore she was certain that seam in her flesh would tear and unknit.

One morning, after a dream where a huge red stain was spreading from her into the white of the sheets, into the flowers of the carpet, out of the door and down the stairs into the street where all the neighbours could see it, she seized the heavy end of the feather bolster and rotated it forty-five degrees. Immediately, she felt better and she spent the rest of the day cleaning out her cupboards. When Huw climbed the stairs that night, he found the swollen weight of the bolster, the thickness of another body, down the middle of the bed, dividing him from the warm, soft flesh of his wife.

It would remain there for the duration of their marriage. Very occasionally, he would manage a successful foray over the Wall, as he privately termed it. Once when he'd particularly praised a pie of russet apples, another time when he brought home a Christmas bonus. Otherwise, the mattress would soak up his seed, like tears. Or he'd been known to release them himself as he stood in the toilet out the back, watching through a gap as his wife hung out the washing, her dress creeping up her body like a tide.

The last time Huw ever made it over the bolster was the evening after Alun's wedding. Mair was forty-one but still slim in a suit she'd made specially, sewing buttonholes with thread she'd had to go all the way to the next town to find. Thinking about the way her calves emerged from the hem of the skirt, Huw ventured a hand over the feather-packed bolster. When it was not pushed firmly back, he ventured a wrist and then an arm. Then he risked his head over the parapet.

Three weeks later, when the usual ache in her back failed to materialise, Mair thought nothing of it. You couldn't get pregnant at forty-one. It couldn't happen. Everyone knew that. Three months later, she was still firm in her conviction, dogged in her denial. It was impossible, completely unheard of. There had never been anyone in this town who had a baby in their forties. It just didn't happen.

It was Mrs Williams from next door who said something first. Maybe she'd noticed that the monthly rags were absent from the washing-line or maybe she'd guessed from looking at her. She came round the back one day and into the kitchen, where Mair was sitting at the table, motionless. She'd been scouring the wood, ready to roll out pastry, when she'd felt a quickening, a flutter, low down in her body.

'When are you going to go to the doctor, now?' Mrs Williams placed her knuckles on the table.

But Mair was defiant. 'Why would I need a doctor?'

Mrs Williams sighed and sat down. 'They say,' she began, covering Mair's hand with her own, 'there's a man down Maesteg who can give you something to . . .' she jerked her head sideways '. . . you know.'

'What?'

'You know,' she said again, and leant forward to whisper: 'Bring it off.'

Her face, when Mair looked at it, was kindly, concerned. Mair drew her hand out from under hers. 'I don't know what you mean,' she said slowly. 'Why don't you get out of my house?'

They never spoke again, even though they lived next door to one another for the next thirty years.

Mair had never been ashamed of anything. Everything she'd ever done, she'd done in the full knowledge that what she was doing was right and good and justified. Yet suddenly here she was, a church-going, God-fearing woman of forty-one with two grown-up sons, and a rounded, full, life-stuffed belly. What would people think? The idea that anyone she walked past in the street could look at her and know that she'd done . . . *that* . . . and *recently* . . . was more than she could bear.

When she started to show, she kept mostly to the

kitchen, the backyard, and occasionally treated herself to a lie down in her front parlour. Anyone who called round was told through the letterbox that she was feeling 'poorly' and couldn't take visitors. When the nurse offered Mair the bundle containing her first daughter, she said, 'Take it away,' and turned her face into the pillow.

Caroline was difficult from the start. Whenever Mair looked at her she just thought of the hot shame of Huw's fingers scuttling over the bolster. The way this baby regarded her was different, unsettling. Eyes round as pebbles, fists curled. Mair had the distinct sensation that the baby didn't believe a word she said. Huw said she was going daft but soon her own words started sounding hollow, even to herself.

'It's a lovely day today,' Mair would attempt, as she lowered the baby into its chair. The baby would glance at her, chewing sceptically on its teething ring. Mair would turn to the window and see that there were in fact sudden spots of rain falling on to her washing.

Caroline perplexed and enraged Mair. She was such a perverse, wilful child. If Mair called that it looked like rain so she should take her wellingtons to school, Caroline would go to the back door, remove the wellingtons she had on anyway and replace them with her leather shoes. If Mair remarked that Caroline should cut her hair, Caroline would spend hours cross-legged on her bed, brushing and brushing it so that it would grow more quickly.

The noise of her in the house set Mair's teeth tingling. The tinny rattle of the transistor radio Geraint bought for her sixteenth birthday, the clunk of those dreadful clogs she wore on the stone kitchen floor, the way she sighed all the time, the jangle of the many silver bangles she strung up her arms, the swish through the air of that long, straggling hair.

And Caroline turned up her nose at food – something Mair could never forgive. She said her potatoes were overcooked, her carrots tasteless, her meat stringy, her gravy fatty. She wouldn't eat puddings, wasn't at all tempted by gooseberry fools, refused all gingerbread, jam tarts, flapjacks, homemade fudge. She starved herself until her bones stuck out through her clothes. It was then that Mair started egg-hoarding. If Caroline wasn't going to eat them, she would wait until there was somebody who would. Then Caroline came home and said she was no longer going to eat meat. Mair threw the skillet at her, which missed and chipped the dresser door.

The waste enraged Mair. That a daughter of hers could consign to the bin an entire meal, a perfectly good meal, was beyond her. You never lived through the war, young lady, Mair would say and find that Caroline, hollow-cheeked, was reciting back to her the rest of the speech. You'll sit there till you eat it, she would shout, but Caroline was already up and out of the front door, hair swooping after her. Huw kept his head down, concentrating on his plate. When Caroline did permit food past her lips it was only in the way a prisoner might consume a meal so as to have the strength to escape the next day.

At eighteen, Caroline leaves. Huw finds the note, tucked into the butter-dish. Mair is inconsolable. She takes to her bed, lying alongside the bolster, crying and wailing into it about her Caro, her baby. After a week of this, Huw, out of his depth and unable to negotiate the kitchen on his own, calls Geraint, who calls the doctor.

When Mair descends the stairs again, she is dressed, her hair done, her sleeves rolled, her apron on, the pills the doctor gave her sporing into her bloodstream. She reads the note through once, then pulls open the stove and hurls it in – it's not alight, so Huw is able to retrieve it later.

'I will never,' Mair announces, 'speak of her again.'

And she doesn't, until that moment in the old people's home when her eye is fixed on a distant tanker, cutting its way through the oily waters of the Bristol Channel, heading for open sea.

Jake, who has no idea that he's inherited his insomnia from his grandmother, knows he won't get back to sleep again. After he puts the phone down from his mother, he wanders around the darkened lower floor of the house. Around the kitchen, out into the hall, through the sitting room, then back again, the half-lit garden disappearing and reappearing at different angles through the windows.

He feels vaguely transgressive, illicit, like a cat burglar or a spy. He eats an apple from the bowl on the kitchen table, he reads the various lists and memos and cuttings pinned to the board in the hall, he peers at all the photos on the window-sill in the living room: Mel at primary school with missing front teeth, Mel with her siblings, her elder brother's wedding at the church down the road.

Jake turns away quickly and finds himself facing a bookcase. Biographies of people he's never heard of – cricketers, politicians – a few novels, lots of gardening books, some self-help manuals, and three atlases. He hooks his fingers into the top of the biggest one, tips it towards him and flips it open.

The mantra is familiar to him now: Kildare, Kilden, Kildepo Valley, Kildonan. Right where it should be, smack between Kildonan in New Zealand and Kilembe in Uganda is nothing. Nothing at all. No trace of this supposed place that he is named after.

He once saw a Hollywood musical with Gene Kelly and Cyd Charisse about a mythical Highland village. Lots of fake Scottish accents, red wigs and extravagant dance numbers. You could only find this village on a certain day once every two hundred years, or something like that. Otherwise it just vanished without a trace. Sometimes he thinks Kildoune is like that and some part of him keeps willing him to check all the atlases he can get his hands on, just in case he's hit on the right day and it will be there right between Kildonan and Kilembe.

But not today.

Jake opens the book at the British page and locates Aviemore, roughly half-way between the fibrillated, fragmented west coast and the clear, sheer lines of the east. He looks at where he is now, then back at Aviemore, then at the dense tangle of London and he sees, rising from its confusion, a distinct black line, bristling with dashes. A railway. The line heads singlemindedly north, right through the centre of England, then along the coast, swerving left along the Firth of Forth, through Edinburgh, then on.

Nina was more than an hour late home from school.

Francesca had been into the bedroom twice, demanding that Stella tell her where her sister was, but Stella had been forced to reply, honestly, that she didn't know.

Stella was lying on her bed reading when Nina burst into their room. She didn't turn round. Behind her, she heard Nina throwing her bag and her coat on to the floor. She felt the bed rock as Nina climbed on.

'Where've you been?' Stella said, to the bedhead.

'Out and about.'

'Did you see Mum? She's on the warpath.'

They lay head to toe, like sardines fitted into a tin. Nina's hand was curled around Stella's foot.

'I told her I had music practice,' Nina said.

'But you didn't.' Stella rolled on to her back but couldn't see her sister's face, just the white tilt of her jaw.

'I know.' Nina removed a clip from her hair with slow exactitude and laid it on the bedside table. 'I've made a decision,' she said, with a smile in her voice.

'What decision?'

Nina tipped her head forward and looked at her down the lengths of their aligned bodies. 'A big decision,' she said, her eyebrows raised teasingly.

Stella sighed. Nina could play these games all night. She fiddled with the silver ring encircling her middle finger, twisting it round and round. It was always looser when she was cold.

'Don't you want to know what it is?'

'Yes,' Stella said, impatient, 'but only if you're going to tell me now. This minute.'

Nina examined the nails on her right hand, almost as if

Stella wasn't there. Stella sighed and slumped back to the bed, bringing her book up to her face.

'You know Chris?' Nina said immediately.

Stella knew exactly whom she meant but, for a reason she couldn't really fathom, made out that she didn't. 'Chris Davis?'

'No. Chris Caffrey.'

'Is he the one with a blue jacket?'

'No.' Nina flicked her nail against the sole of Stella's foot. 'He's got a black coat. Blond hair.'

Stella scowled, scanning the printed blocks of text, pretending to be reading. 'What about him?'

'I've just been for a coffee with him.'

This time Stella dropped the book to her stomach. 'You haven't. Have you? What, just now? Where? How come?'

Nina shrugged with supreme nonchalance. 'I waited for him after school. We went for a walk on the Meadows.'

Stella was aghast. 'Are you serious?'

'Yeah.'

'What, you just went up to him and said, hey, Chris, do you fancy a coffee?'

'More or less. Stel,' Nina leaned forward, as if eager to impart a secret, 'it was really easy.'

Stella stared at her sister. They were silent for a moment. Then she turned on to her side, pressing her face into the pillow. It smelt of the washing powder their mother used, of musty feathers, of shampoo. 'Isn't he . . . I mean, isn't he—'

'The best-looking boy in the school?' Nina tossed her head. 'I know. That's the point. Because I've decided.'

Stella sighed. 'Decided what?'

'I'm going to seduce him.'

She liked saying the word 'seduce', Stella could see that. It pulled her mouth into a perfect bow.

'There has to be some way,' Nina continued, her fists curled, 'we can stop all the shit we have to put up with. And I think this is it.'

'What?' Stella scoffed. 'Shagging Chris Caffrey? Yeah, right, Nina, that's really going to—'

'I'm sick of it, Stel.' Her eyes were glittering. 'I'm sick of being the school weirdo. Aren't you?'

Stella didn't say anything.

'Aren't you?' Nina persisted.

'Yes,' Stella muttered, 'but I don't think that's the way to go about it.'

'Well, I do. Here,' Nina threw something on to the bed, 'have a look at this.'

Despite herself, Stella glanced at the book. *Sex: A How-to Guide*. Stella fanned the pages under her thumb; sketchy pencil drawings of a man and a woman, limbs entwined, in various positions, skimmed past. 'Did you buy this?'

'Nah.' Nina grinned. 'Nicked it.'

'Nina—'

'Don't Nina me. It's fine. I never get caught.'

'You will.'

'I won't. I'm too good.' She grinned again and slapped Stella's leg. 'Don't be a prissy pants. Come on, let's read it.' She lay down on her stomach next to Stella, so that they were side by side, and opened the book between them.

Stella touched the smooth grain of the paper with the

whorled print of her finger. Nine of her fingers had matching, almost identical looped patterns, which slanted off to the side, like sand pulled by tides. The fourth finger on her left hand was whorled in concentric circles. The weakest one. Her wedding finger, Nina had pointed out.

'Oral sex,' Nina was saying. 'Yuk.' She stuck out her tongue. 'Foreplay,' she read. 'Let's start there.'

About the time Caroline begins school, Mair becomes obsessed with death. Not death in general, just her own. She wakes up one morning convinced that she is going to die – and soon. She decides to rouse Huw, reaching over the bolster and clutching his arm.

'Huw, Huw.' She shakes him. 'Huw, wake up.'

He opens his eyes in shock and stares at the ceiling. 'What is it, love?'

'What will happen to Caroline if I die?'

'Eh?'

'If I die,' she repeats urgently, sitting up now. 'What will happen?'

Huw closes his eyes again. 'Go back to sleep,' he says, and turns over.

But Mair can't. She is pinned to the mattress with horror at the vision of this late child left motherless, uncared-for, unreared, a wastrel, a vagabond, a disgrace to her family name. She wouldn't trust either of her daughters-in-law with the task, or her sister, who married a man much beneath her and lives at the other end of the town. There is no one, she realises, that she could ask, no one who gives her peace of mind. She hasn't a minute to lose. Mair rips back the blankets and gets out of bed.

When Caroline gets back from school, her mother calls her upstairs. On the threshold of her parents' bedroom, she stops. Spread on the floor is a tea-towel. Which is unusual in itself. Tea-towels aren't allowed on the floor. And her mother's jewellery is arranged over it. Caroline lifts her eyes to her mother. Mair is standing in the middle of the room, one hand clutched at her throat. Her hair, Caroline sees, has been liberated from its perpetual curlers. Which can mean one of two things: somebody has died or this is in some way a Special Occasion.

'What it is, Mam?' Caroline asks, from the doorway.

'Come here.' Her mother beckons.

'Why?' she asks, unnerved by the spots of high colour on her cheeks, the sight of those tight, regular curls that grip her mother's head like a swimming hat.

'This child is sent to try me,' her mother addresses the ceiling. 'What did I do to deserve this? Don't ask questions,' she is speaking to Caroline again, 'just do as I say. Come here.'

Caroline crosses the room, her satchel clutched at her side. Her mother kneels down in front of her and takes her by both shoulders.

'Now, Caro, this is very important. Are you listening?'

Caroline nods mutely, wanting to pull away. Her mother's fingertips are digging into her skin.

'I want you to look at the jewellery on the tea-towel. Look carefully, mind.'

She and her mother stare at the red-and-white striped

Welsh linen. A brooch in the shape of a swan, a string of yellowing pearls with a gold clasp, her mother's engagement ring with its solitary diamond eye, a jet bracelet, an opal on a tarnished chain, some blue bead earrings that screw on to her lobes. They hurt her ears, Caroline remembers her mother telling her.

'Have you looked?' Mair demands.

'Yes.' One of her school socks is beginning a slow creep down her shin but she daren't stoop to pull it up.

'Properly?'

'Yes.'

'Yes what?'

'Yes, Mam.'

'If I die,' she begins, looking into Caroline's face, her hands still gripping her shoulders, 'and your father marries again, the new wife will try to take my jewellery.' She leans closer. 'I want it to go to you. Do you hear? All of it. It's all yours. You mustn't let her have it. Or either of your aunties. Do you understand?'

Caroline nods, not really understanding at all.

'And the silver cream jug downstairs. That must be yours too. And the wooden love spoon your da gave me. Don't let the new wife get it. In fact,' Mair starts up, pulling her apron straight, 'we'll hide them. That's what we'll do. You and me. And we won't tell anyone, see?'

'Yes, Mam.'

When Huw comes in from work, his daughter is seated at the table with her school books spread out in front of her. The kitchen is freezing, Caroline's lips almost blue with cold.

'What's happening, love?' he asks. 'Isn't the stove lit? Where's your mam?'

'Hiding the jewellery from your new wife.'

Caroline can pinpoint the moment she realised her mother's grasp on the world was imperfect, flawed. After seeing a neighbour pushing a pram up the hill, she had turned from the window and asked how babies came to be born. Caroline watched with curiosity as her mother launched into a sentence, then stopped, began sketches, then scribbled them out, flushed, faltered, stuttered, and then muttered something about God's decree and a mam and a da.

'It's about love,' her mother declared, as if she'd at last lit on what she wanted to say. 'And it's only ever something that happens when you are married.'

Caroline remembers the idea unfurling in her mind, as if it had been there all along but she'd never paid it full attention: you are wrong. Her mother was wrong. About everything.

It was a bad thought, she knew, and not one she should ever say out loud. But she suddenly saw that whatever her mother said wasn't necessarily true, as she'd always thought it was, that what she said only related to a small, closed world that Caroline wanted no part of. She looked as her mother showed her photographs of her brothers in a stiff christening gown, she listened as her mother told her that her babies would one day wear the same gown and, even aged nine, knew for certain that it would never happen.

When Caroline leaves, she eases her mother's jewellery

box out of its hiding place — behind a loose piece of skirting-board in the front parlour. She's going to take something with her, the swan brooch maybe, not because she'll ever wear it but because she wants it.

When it comes to it, though, opening the lid on those jewels she hasn't seen in ten years, something fails her. She can't do it. She can't take even one of those things her mother loves so much she hides them away and never wears them. She snaps the box shut and pushes it back into its secret place. She'll take nothing from this house, nothing from this place. Just herself.

She catches the bus to Cardiff. She cries the whole way, great gulping sobs, so noisy that the bus driver asks if she's all right. By Cardiff, she's stopped crying but she's scared, convinced that her mam will appear any minute, shouting that she's not too old to feel the dap on her backside. But she manages to hitch a lift to London, where she asks for directions to the King's Road. She walks up and down until, miraculously, she falls into conversation with two women who ask if she wants to crash at their place. She's not sure what they mean, but says yes anyway.

She schools herself to round her vowels, clip her Rs, swallow her Ts. She doesn't want to come from anywhere, doesn't want a particular place leaving its mark on her. A phrase that comes back to her again and again, during the discussions they have in their basement commune, is 'child of the universe'. She doesn't speak it aloud to the people around her because it comes from some prayer her mother had framed on the wall in the kitchen. She'd never realised that any of that stuff had embedded itself in her at all. But she remembers it as she maps the streets of the city, the geographies of her new life. 'Strive to be happy,' it ends.

She likes to think she remembers nothing, that it's all been erased from her head – the chapel, the prayers, the dreadful dinners, the steep-streeted town, the dual swirl of language at their table, in the shops, at school. But she finds, in those heightened moments of either extreme pain or extreme love, that it comes out of her, that long-buried vocabulary, her mother tongue: *duw duw* will spring from her mouth if she burns her hand on the gas flame. *Cariad fach*, she murmurs to her baby, as she strokes his sleeping head.

Jake sawed through the pinkish slab of beef on his plate and raised it to his mouth. Mel was helping herself to more roast potatoes and her father was stirring the gravy with a curve-handled spoon. The dog sat with its nose tilted to the smells of the table, long curds of drool hanging from its muzzle.

'. . . and I said to her that I always keep my receipts, always, always . . .' Annabel was saying. 'And she knows I've been going into that shop for over twenty years, so I really don't see what is so outrageous about me wanting to take it back. I mean, I must be one of her most loyal customers.' She shook her head. 'The one time. It had to be the one time I threw out the receipt.'

'But are you sure you threw it out?' Mel said, with infinite patience.

'Well, I don't know what I did with it. All I'm say-ing is—'

'So, Jake, tell me,' Andrew sliced through this conversation to address him, picking up his wine glass, 'what are your plans now, job-wise?'

The food felt suddenly cold and congealed in his mouth, coating his teeth. 'Sorry?' he managed.

'You were involved in film out in Hong Kong, weren't you?'

Jake gripped his cutlery. 'That's right.'

'What was it you did exactly?'

'Well, I used to build sets but now I'm a director's assistant.'

Andrew was looking at him, his face open but bemused. 'And you . . . and you like it?'

'Yes,' Jake nodded. 'Very much.'

'He loves it,' Mel cut in, resting her hand on his leg.

'I don't know much about these things,' Andrew began uncertainly, and Jake became aware of a very fine, almost imperceptible web being spun round him. Had Andrew been put up to this by Mel? Or was he just being paranoid? 'But I do know a lot of it goes on in London.'

'It?'

'Films. Film-making. Soho is . . . Soho is . . .' Andrew floundered, waving his hand in the air. Mel and Annabel concentrated on what was on their plates, assiduously cutting and slicing their food, not looking his way. 'It is what you might call the . . .' He cast a glance at the curtains for inspiration. Jake felt almost sorry for him. '. . . the nerve-centre of the British industry, which is . . . which is one of the oldest and . . . and most renowned in the world.' Andrew took a gulp of wine.

Jake felt he ought to say something to acknowledge this speech and came up with: 'Right.'

'So,' Andrew rallied himself again, 'what I would do if I were you is—'

'Dad,' Mel said gently, 'don't hassle him.' Jake was surprised. Was she not in on this after all?

'I'm not hassling him, darling. I am just trying to help. Maybe he,' Andrew indicated Jake with his knife, 'would like to get stuck into a new job rather than just sit about the house with you women all day.'

'Don't point with your knife, Andrew,' Annabel said.

'He doesn't sit about. He—'

'All I'm saying, Jake,' Andrew appealed to him, 'is that I'd be happy to take you into London at some point if you wanted to drop off your CV to a few people. You know. Network.'

Jake inclined his head. 'Thank you.' He saw Annabel and Andrew exchange a glance and realised that the plot, if he could in fairness call it that, was between them.

'And when the time comes,' Andrew lowered his voice and leant so close that Jake could see an uningested slick of potato on his tongue, 'I'm very happy to help you and this young lady here with a deposit on a flat in London. I know that's where you'll want to be – youngsters like you. So. Just tip me the nod whenever.'

'What are you whispering about, Dad?' Mel asked.

'More beef, Jake?' Annabel proffered a dish, which swam with fat and blood.

'Tip me the nod, eh?' Andrew winked at him, swilling his mouth out with wine.

'Actually,' Jake cleared his throat and put down his fork, 'I meant to say. I'm thinking of going away for a bit. A few days. Maybe a fortnight or so.'

'Really?' Mel was looking at him, puzzled. 'Where?'

'Scotland.'

'You didn't tell me that.'

'Well, it's only a vague plan. So far. I was going to tell you but—'

'But, Jake, I can't go to Scotland. I'm not—'

'No,' he said carefully, aware that Annabel and Andrew were trying not to listen to this interchange. 'No. I thought I'd go on my own.'

Mel put down her cutlery.

'If that's OK with you,' he forced himself to add.

Mel looked dismayed, almost tearful, but was struggling to hide it. 'Why Scotland?' she asked brightly.

'I've always wanted to go there. And . . . I thought now would be a good time.'

'You're right, Jake,' Annabel chimed in. 'He's right, Melanie.' She laid a hand on her daughter's arm. 'It's his first time in England. He should be getting out and seeing the place. No point in sitting about the house, is there?'

'It's very cold up there,' Andrew said. 'Play golf, do you? Marvellous courses they have, marvellous.'

Mel's expression relaxed – slightly. She raised her napkin to dab at her mouth. 'Well, as long as it's not for too long.' She curled her fingers round the back of his neck.

Francesca was the last of her parents' five children, all of whom lived in the flat above the café on the main street of Musselburgh. It was a town stretched along the coast outside Edinburgh with only one other Italian family – the two brothers who ran the barber's shop. Domenico would catch the bus with them up to Edinburgh once a week, to go to the social club for Italian men in Leith to play *scoppa* and drink wine. Francesca and her siblings were sent to Italian language classes in Edinburgh after school on Wednesdays, which, in truth, they didn't really need – their parents never really mastered English so they always spoke Italian at home, among themselves. 'My children are Italian, my family is Italian, my friends are Italian, everyone who works here is Italian – why on earth would I need to learn English?' her mother would shout whenever Francesca, reluctant to translate yet another letter from the council, the taxman, the school, begged her mother to learn.

Francesca's brothers and sisters tried to teach her bits and pieces of the language spoken outside their café before she went to school, but none of it had stuck and on her first day she'd been unable to understand anything anyone said to her, or to stop crying. She'd been called a 'durty wee Tally' by her classmates and people laughed at her accent, her clothes, the food her mother gave her for lunch. Once, she approached one of her sisters in the playground and, forgetting, spoke to her in the language they spoke with their parents. Her sister had turned, her face white and scared, and hissed at Francesca: 'Don't ever speak Italian to me here.'

Her siblings left, one by one. Her elder brother married an Italian girl and went to work in her family's businesses in Edinburgh, her sisters both became nurses and slept most nights at the hospital. Her other brother went to America, married, divorced, married again, and later returned to help run the café.

Francesca drifted out of school, thought about applying to college but never got round to it, worked at the café, rolling the pastel colours of ice-cream into balls, went for long walks. Sometimes along the small, curving beach, or past the private school behind a high grey stone wall to the racetrack where the ground reverberated with thunder-hoofed horses looping round the bend. Sometimes she walked in a repeating figure of eight round and round the town's three bridges, crossing and recrossing the river, stopping on the middle stone bridge to gaze down at the slow-moving brown water and watch the swans that gathered there in the weeds, trying in vain to beat back against the current.

She felt a vague fear all the time. Her world had somehow shrunk around her. She knew nothing and no one, or at least no one outside her parents' sphere of influence. How could she decide what she was to do in the world if she knew nothing about it? Sometimes she was afraid that she would one day have to leave her parents, have to go away from them, and sometimes she was terrified that she would never leave them, never get away from them. She worried that people she passed in the street in Musselburgh were laughing at her: there goes that Italian girl with nothing to do. Soon she stopped leaving the café altogether.

It was her uncle who saved her. He and her father were sitting huddled down in a booth. Francesca served them coffee, then went back behind the counter and stood there, gazing out of the big window, shifting her weight from each foot every sixty seconds. She counted them in her head.

Her father and Uncle Agostino were murmuring in low tones. She saw, out of the corner of her eye, her uncle glance at her, then look away. She thought she caught the word *figlia*. Daughter. Were they talking about her? Francesca wiped the spotless aluminium counter with a heated cloth. When it had dried with the energy of its own heat, she wiped it again.

She liked her uncle, who ran a delicatessen in Leith with his wife who'd never, as her mother put it, 'been blessed with children'. But she didn't like him talking about her. She was running the cloth under the hot tap for a third time when her father called to her. 'Come,' he said, beckoning. 'Sit down beside me here.'

Francesca slid on to the plastic banquette. A hundred slit reflections of her face looked back at her from the mirrored walls. Agostino leant across the melamine table and pinched her cheek.

'You are looking so thin, *cara mia*. What has this brother of mine been feeding you?' He raised the espresso cup, which looked tiny, like a doll's house cup, in his huge hand, to his lips. 'Now. Francesca.' He took her hand. 'Appollonia and I were wondering if you could grant us a favour.'

'Sì, *mio zio, senz'altro*.'

'Well, hear what it is first. Appollonia and I, we are not as young as we were. The shop is big. Our legs are tired. We have one girl helping us sometimes,' he shook his head and laughed, 'a crazy English student girl, but it is not enough. I have asked your father here and he says he can spare you. You see, Appollonia and I were wondering if you would come and work with us for a time. You can live with us above the shop. Maybe you'd like to be in the city for a while. A change of air, perhaps.' He pressed her hand. 'We would be so happy to have you.'

Francesca looked at her father, who smiled at her and nodded. She gripped Agostino's hand in hers and took a deep breath, down to the bottom of her lungs. '*Sì, sì, Zio Agostino, grazie. Mille grazie.*'

On her first day, Appollonia put her behind the counter with the crazy English student girl. Francesca had never seen anyone who looked quite like her: she had false eyelashes, great half-moons of blue eyeshadow and a skirt that barely covered her rear.

'I'm Evie,' said the girl. 'Your hair's amazing.'

'Oh,' said Francesca, thrown, touching the thick plait that hung round her neck like a noose, 'thank you.'

A woman appeared, wanting slices of *prosciutto*. Evie hooked the immense haunch of meat down from the ceiling and crashed it into the slicer. 'Have you ever tried backcombing it?' she continued, over her shoulder.

'Sorry?'

'Your hair.'

'Um,' Francesca glanced down at her hands, 'no.'

'But you should.' In her excitement, Evie took her foot off the pedal for the meat slicer. It whirred plaintively, winding down. 'It would look wonderful in a beehive.'

Francesca gazed at her, perplexed. 'In a beehive?' she repeated.

'I'll do it for you. I've got curlers and spray.'

'Um . . .'

'You don't know what a beehive is, do you?'

'Is it a hairstyle?'

'My God.' Evie snorted, her hands on her hips, abandoning any appearance that she might be cutting the customer's ham. 'Where have you been living, darling? In a bunker? I think—'

'Excuse me.' The woman was rapping the counter with her knuckle.

Evie rounded on her. 'All right, all right, I'll be with you in a minute. I think,' she continued to Francesca, 'you need to come over to my digs.'

'I . . . er . . . I . . .'

'What?'

'I'll have to ask my mother,' Francesca mumbled.

'Your mother?' Evie was astounded. 'What are you – twelve?'

'So, darlings,' Evie exhaled a lungful of smoke into the dim light of the department-store café, 'I hear there's a man on the scene.'

Stella, half-way through a sip of hot chocolate, coughed and choked. The first thing in her head was terror, terror that Nina might think she had told on her. But Nina was banging her fist on the edge of the table, furious. 'How do you know? Has Mum—'

'No, no,' Evie cut across her, 'not your mum. Your dad, actually.'

'Dad?' Stella was surprised. 'I didn't know you and he ever . . . I mean . . .'

Evie looked at her and laughed. 'No, you're right. We don't ever. Not usually. He called me yesterday. Said he'd seen one of you locked in an impassioned clinch. He's in a terrible flap about it, poor man.'

'So that's why you wanted to see us,' Nina said accusingly. 'Because Dad told you to, because—'

'I wanted to see you today because I wanted to see you.' Evie uncrossed and recrossed her legs emphatically. Under a narrow black wool skirt, she was wearing a pair of boots with blade-like heels and criss-crossing laces that pulled the leather close to her legs. Stella wanted some like that so badly it made her feel weak. Could she ever be like that? Adulthood seemed an interminable time away. She didn't know if she could wait that long. 'No one tells me what to do, darling, you know that.'

Stella dipped the curve of a teaspoon in and out of the surface of her hot chocolate. She could kill Nina, who was sitting there trying to cry. That was a special trick of hers. It got her out of everything. Stella knew how she did it – she'd told her once: 'Think really hard about the time Max got run over,' Nina had said, 'really, really hard until you feel the tears. It's easy.'

'What cross faces you have,' Evie exclaimed. She stretched up from the table and waved her hand in the air. The waiter saw her immediately. Evie had always had that knack. 'Let's have some cake and you can tell me all about your paramours.'

She insisted on the sweet trolley being brought to their table and wanted to know the names of each and every cake. The waiter even got her a spoon so she could taste the profiterole sauce, before she rejected it as 'far too rich'. Three Morningside ladies watched, shocked, from the next table. After a close inspection, an éclair, a slice of chocolate gateau and a religieuse were placed before them with a flourish.

'Religieuse, for Chrissake,' Evie said, slightly too loudly, as she spooned a morsel into her mouth, 'I bet those poor bloody French nuns never got to eat anything like this. Mmm,' she placed the spoon back on the plate, 'divine, no? So. Your boys. Come on, tell all.'

'I don't have a . . .' Stella began, infuriated '. . . a . . . boy. It's nothing to do with me.'

Evie surveyed her, eyebrows raised. 'I see. Nina?'

Nina tucked her palms under her legs, her eyes huge and bright with unshed tears. 'I don't know what to say,' she whispered, coy and shy suddenly. 'What do you want to know?'

'His name would be a good start.'

'Chris.'

'As in Christopher?' Evie considered this. 'A good name,' she pronounced. 'What else?'

'Well, he's seventeen. He'd be in the same year as me if it wasn't for . . .' Nina stopped short. Evie nodded. 'Um. He collects LPs. He wants guitar lessons. He's got curly hair—'

'Dark or fair?' Evie interrupted.

'Fair.'

'Blond? Good. Blonds are more dependable, I find. Dark ones break your heart.'

Stella glanced at Evie, wanting to ask more but not knowing how.

'And you like him?' Evie said.

'Yes.'

'Really like him?'

Nina shifted in her seat. 'I think so.'

'Good.' Evie smiled and dabbed at the corners of her mouth with a folded napkin. 'And are you sleeping with him?' she enquired, in the same tone of voice.

Stella turned to look at Nina, interested all of a sudden. Would she tell the truth? That she'd been trying to persuade him but so far he'd refused? Would she tell Evie that she had managed to part Chris from his underpants only twice, and both times his erection had shrivelled and flopped? 'Like this,' Nina had told her, and demonstrated with the limp tassel on her dressing-gown.

Evie was watching them across the table. 'Darlings, don't be embarrassed. I'm not your mother and I'm not going to tell your mother either.'

The sisters were silent, Nina glaring down in the direction of Stella's knees.

'Stella,' Evie appealed to her for the first time, 'you tell me. You must know.'

'Er,' Stella glanced at Nina then back at Evie, 'well—'

'No,' Nina said, through clenched teeth, 'we're not. I can't believe you're interrogating me like this. It's unbelievable. It's really . . . really invading my . . . my life.' The tears came now, perfect and silver, chasing each other down Nina's cheeks. God, she was good. 'I can't believe you don't trust me,' she sobbed, as Stella looked on, half in awe, half in disgust. 'I'm not going to sleep with him. I promise, Evie, I promise.'

'Darling child, don't make promises like that, I beg you.' Evie was utterly unperturbed by Nina's tears. Unlike Francesca would have been. 'Now, listen,' Evie rummaged in her bag, 'this isn't exactly the advice your father was hoping I'd give you but, believe me, this is the kind of advice you need.' She pushed across the table a small, flat, blue-and-white box. Stella looked at it. Evie's nails were blood-crimson, filed to a point. On the box was another one of those sketchy drawings of a man and woman. DUREX, it screamed, DUREX DUREX. Stella looked away, at the Morningside ladies, at the Scott Monument out of the window. When she looked back, Nina had her hand over it, trying to cover it, trying to push it back towards Evie.

'No, no,' Evie was shaking her head, 'you must take them. Really. You must.'

'But—'

'Nina, take them.' Evie gave a violent push and Stella saw Nina make a show of reluctantly giving up. 'And whatever you do, don't tell your mad Catholic mother I gave them to you. If she finds them, it wasn't me. Is that clear?'

Nina nodded. Stella nodded.

'You know how to use them?'

Nina nodded again.

'Make sure he has one on before he comes anywhere near you. Understand? *Anywhere* near you.'

Stella clamped her hands over her face, which was prickling hot. 'Evie,' she pleaded.

'It's important, darling,' Evie said to her. 'It's important that you both know this. Spermatozoa are persistent, devious little devils.'

'Yes,' Stella forced out.

'Are we clear?'

'Yes,' they said in unison.

'Marvellous.' Evie leant back and stubbed out her cigarette. Nina was already gathering up her coat and bag. 'Shopping time, I think,' Evie said. 'Shall we go?'

The day after Archie first takes Francesca for a walk in the Botanical Gardens, he sits in his mother's house watching the dog, Jinty. She is rubbing her flank along the edge of the sofa, her muzzle held close to the packed fabric. His mother is making tea in the kitchen; he can hear the gathering whistle of the kettle, the clatter of china cups. Outside, the afternoon is sinking into evening.

Once a fortnight, his mother baths Jinty in the big square sink in the kitchen. Jinty bears this indignity but not without shivering and sneezing, a mournful look in her brown eyes, and a slight moan escaping her lips, to which Archie's mother replies with a strict 'Shush!' After being wrapped in a towel and dried in front of the fire, always this pantomime: Jinty racing round the room in a frenzy, horrified by her scentlessness, desperately trying to pick up, to borrow, any smell she can. The dank, lanolin odour of the carpet, the pungent wax of the parquet, the animal whiff of the horsehair sofa – anything is better than nothing to Jinty.

Archie watches her wriggling around on the sheepskin rug until he can bear it no more.

'Come here, Jint.' He holds his hand out to her. 'Come on. It's no good, you know.' The dog trots over to him, her tail waving, looking up at him as if he might be able to help her.

Archie lays his hand between the dog's ears. He's been buying hunks of cheese off the black-haired Italian girl for almost three months now. He's been in the delicatessen every lunchtime, despite the scornful snickers of the blonde girl, each time trying a different tactic. The cinema? A coffee? Could he take her to tea? A recital? Francesca had shaken her head, her plait swinging from side to side, her eyes cast down. An exhibition at the art gallery? The theatre? A trip to the sea? A dance? He'd made up his mind to suggest church, even though he was sure she'd be a Roman Catholic and he'd never set foot in a Catholic church in his life and wouldn't know what to do, when she leant over the counter, her cheeks flaming, and said, 'Perhaps a walk.'

She turned up with her mother. And her aunt. The older women were dressed almost identically, in long black skirts and black cardigans buttoned to the throats, with their hair pulled severely away from their faces. Archie had to try very hard not to show his shock at the appearance of these Baba Yagas. They were both tiny, about half Archie's height. He had to bend his knees to shake hands with them. The mother clutched a large, furled umbrella in one hand and looked him up and down with thinly disguised disdain. Neither spoke any English, yattering what sounded like instructions – or maybe criticisms – to Francesca.

He and Francesca walked ahead, with the Baba Yagas arm-in-arm, bringing up the rear. They seemed to enjoy the gardens, pointing and exclaiming at everything, the mother, Signora Iannelli, stopping to sniff the flowers. The rose garden was a big hit, also the lavender banks, but they didn't like the hothouses. '*Troppo caldo*,' they complained, fanning themselves, in their woollen skirts, woollen stockings, woollen cardigans. He asked Francesca questions, in between the incomprehensible shouts from behind, and had to stop himself laughing when she told him she'd been born in Scotland. She barely spoke English, he thought, and even when she did her accent was so strong it was as if she was speaking Italian.

Archie bought them all tea, which seemed to thaw the aunt, at least, who for some reason seemed very taken with the teapot. Francesca sat with her hands in her lap. Signora Iannelli glared at him across the cakes. But Archie was not about to give up easily. He'd grown up the sickly, protected only child of a widowed mother, rarely allowed out of the house, let alone Edinburgh, and Francesca seemed to him a breeze flowing from a new direction. As they'd sat around the tea things, he'd had to resist the urge to lean over and sniff her hair, her skin, to inhale her foreignness, her scent of faraway places, of another world.

Jinty wanders away, her claws clicking on the parquet, and Archie's mother arrives in the room, saying something about the milkman leaving two pints instead of one. Archie wonders for a moment how she'd react if he brought Francesca here. A foreigner, an immigrant, a Catholic, an under-educated shopgirl. She would weep into her handkerchief, invoke his school fees, his dead father, his delicate health as a child.

But, like Jinty, he is bothered by his blandness, his scentlessness. A well-brought-up Presbyterian Edinburgh boy who does his job and lives with his mother, he feels he has nothing to him. At times, walking home in the evening fog, Archie thinks he might very easily fade into invisibility, incorporeality, so insubstantial, so ordinary does he feel. He wants something to give him definition, a smell, an edge, something that sets him apart, so that people might no longer say 'Archie who?' but 'Archie, him that married the Italian.'

In a sense, he falls in love as much with her family as with Francesca herself. He loves the way Valeria carries vats of water or sacks of flour on her head, the way she leaves the tap on in the kitchen because she is still so delighted to have running water. He loves the way cousins, sisters, uncles, brothers are always coming in and out of the café. He has always felt that he and his mother were too small, too confined a unit. He loves the pungent tastes of the food they sit round a crowded table to eat. He thinks of them like drops of oil in water: a distinct, cohesive presence, unchanged by the alien element surrounding them.

Archie goes to night school to learn Italian. His efforts make Francesca smile, and Valeria snort. Valeria has not taken to Archie. She doesn't want this freckled, milk-pale Scot who persists in mangling her language getting his hands on her youngest daughter. She keeps telling Francesca that what she needs is a nice boy – which Francesca knows means a nice Italian boy.

But Domenico intervenes.

'If that is who she loves,' he says to his wife one night, as they lie in bed, 'that is who she loves.'

Valeria pummels her pillow irritably but knows better than to argue with Domenico. He'll only bring up her father and how he didn't want them to marry, and being reminded of that at this precise moment would only annoy her more.

Nina succeeded in deflowering Chris – and herself – on his bedroom floor while his parents sat downstairs watching the news and weather. 'I got rid of my hymen!' she whispered to Stella, across the black space between their beds. 'I felt it go. There was a kind of stretch and then a sort of pop.'

Three weeks after that, she ditched Chris and took up with a boy called Pete Gilliland in sixth year. She dumped him after a week and went out with Scott Miller, then Angus McLaren, then David Lochhead, Kevin Patterson and Patrick Caffrey (Chris's older brother).

Stella watched as her sister shrugged off her old persona and stretched herself into a new one. Nina had been right. As her notoriety spread, the boys all suddenly wanted her, suddenly stopped taunting her or calling her 'Ghoulmore'.

Stella saw that Nina's life at school was easier now, saw that sex was a way of making yourself accepted, with certain people. Mainly boys. She also saw that it gave other people – girls – a different reason for hating you.

Jake gets on the train at smoky, rush-hour-jaded Euston Station. He's been on night trains through China and across Mongolia and the length of Vietnam, so he's surprised by the plushness of the compartment. He's more used to bare mattresses and a floor covered in fruit peel, nutshells, cockroaches and spit.

Jake lies on his stomach on the bunk and peers out of the window. A blackened brick wall, a flash of weak grey sky, rows of houses with identical chimneys, red buses, a playing-field, a block of flats, a huge advertising hoarding with an image of a woman, head tossed back and lips parted, the backs of houses, flitting by with giddying speed – a child at a piano, a woman taking down her washing from a rack, a man at a cooker, a couple embracing, a man with a baby on his lap. It seems extraordinary to him that he is travelling up the spine of the island whose shape he's spent so long gazing at, poring over, thinking about.

Last night, after he'd got into bed, he'd suddenly felt Mel at his back, the mattress bouncing as her body moved close to his. He could feel the cold rush of her exhalation on his shoulder-blades, the round bones of her knees pressing into the back of his thighs. He'd cleared his throat, edging himself fractionally towards the rim of the mattress. But she'd moved forward, draping her arm over him.

Jake had stared at it, dangling over him, the short fingers, the slightly squarish nails. It began stroking his chest in an insistent yet uneven rhythm.

'Mel,' he'd begun.

'Sssh,' her voice had hissed wetly in his ear and her hand dived down and started floundering about in his waistband.

'No.' The word had shot out and he jack-knifed into himself and he was sitting up, away from her, on the edge of the bed. 'No,' he said again.

Mel had been silent for a minute. He felt her gaze on

his back. Then she turned over quickly, tugging the duvet after her.

Jake sighs and slides to the floor, pushes down the tap and rinses water over and over his face. Then he lies back in his bunk and stares out at the blackening world. He can't sleep, his mind churning over like an engine that cannot catch. The blue night-light buzzes. He hears a woman on the other side of the partition coughing, the shuffle of the guard down the corridor, the train groaning and creaking beneath him, pulling him sideways through the night, clanking through stations he will never visit.

Stella has cleared away the breakfast mess, set the huge dishwasher in motion, polished the tables and taken the hiking details of another guest before he vanishes up into the mist shrouding the Laire Ghru.

In the kitchen behind her, Pearl is energetically banging pots down from the shelves. Stella likes Pearl – a woman in her fifties who does a night shift at an old people's home before coming in to work mornings at the hotel. Pearl sleeps in the afternoons, then gets up in time to make dinner for her children and grandchildren, most of whom seem still to live with her. Years before, her husband had 'buggered off with the town bicycle'. When Stella asked her how many children she had, Pearl replied, 'Six or seven, hen, six or seven,' then laughed so much she made herself wheeze and had to reach for her inhaler.

Stella stretches out her legs under the desk. Outside, the sun is shining down on the trees, which hold green buds at their branch-ends. White alto-stratus clouds race each other across a blue sky. Beside her, the phone bleeps into life. She lifts the receiver. 'Hello, Reception, how may I help you?'

There is a slight pause on the line, then: 'Stella.'

With that single word, the sense of well-being, of calm, slips away from under Stella. It isn't said as a question, just a flat, unequivocal statement. She swallows, gripping the receiver to her ear. 'Hi,' she manages.

'Well,' Nina says, deadly cold, 'are you going to tell me why you're avoiding me?'

Stella twists her fingers in and out of the telephone's springy coil. 'I'm not avoiding you. I—'

'Stella,' Nina interrupts, 'I've left you seven . . . no, eight messages in the last month. I've written you two letters and four cards. You don't reply to any of them. Not one. You vanish into thin air for weeks and I have to find out from Mum where you are.' She takes a gasp from her cigarette. 'What the fuck is going on?'

Stella's face feels tight. 'Nothing. Nothing's going on. I just . . . I've been busy.'

'Busy?' Nina snaps. 'Don't bullshit me, Stel. You may be able to spin Mum and Dad that line, but not me. You chuck in everything in London and just take off, you—'

'I didn't . . .' Stella stammers. 'I didn't chuck it all in, I—'

'You did, so.'

'I did not.'

'Stella. I phoned your work. They told me you left without giving notice.'

'Oh, did you now?' Stella decides the best course of action is to go on the attack. 'I can't believe you, poking your nose into my business. For your information, my contract was coming to an end and—'

'Mum tells me you're near Kincraig.'

It is her trump card and they both know it. Stella is silent. She presses her fingernails into the soft, fleshy parts of her palms. She doesn't know when she last heard Nina say that word.

'What are you doing there?' Nina asks, and the gentleness in her voice panics Stella more than anything.

'Nothing,' she whispers.

There is a pause.

'Stel, please,' Nina says, her voice low, 'what's happened? Why are you there? Please tell me.'

Stella cannot speak. She can hear Nina breathing, but not herself. She must be holding her breath. Nina, don't, she wants to say, don't. Don't do this, please.

'Stel,' Nina says quietly, 'you have to tell me what's going on. I've been going out of my mind. How could you do that? How could you go there, without . . . without telling me? We both know what—' She breaks off, as if someone has come into the room. Stella can hear her scrabbling for her cigarettes. 'Look, I'm coming up to see you. I'll drive up at the weekend. It'll only take a couple of hours and—'

'No, you mustn't!' Stella bursts out. 'I don't think that's – I mean, I'm really busy. I don't have much time off.' She takes a deep breath. 'I have to go now, Neen. Sorry. 'Bye.'

She drops the receiver and bolts from the chair, bursting through the kitchen and out into the corridor. An image of

Pearl, caught in the act of looking up, surprised, is smeared on to her retina. The phone is ringing again as she reaches the back stairs. It rings and rings and rings. There is a tableau stillness about it from here: she can picture the phone in the deserted lobby, the breath of quiet between each ring, the flowers beside it, the overblown petals scattered on the desk surface, the empty, pushed-back chair, the grass and the trees beyond the open door.

Eventually, she hears Pearl go through into Reception and pick it up: 'Hello . . . Yes . . . No, she's not around just now . . . No . . . Sorry . . . Aye, she was here a minute ago, right enough, but she had to pop out . . . That's right . . . Certainly . . . right you are, then. 'Bye now.'

Stella, standing poised on the narrow back stairs, hears Pearl push her way through the kitchen and into the corridor. 'Stella?' she calls.

'Yeah.' Her voice, trapped in the small, enclosed wooden stairwell, bounces back at her, too loud, too soon.

'That was your sister.'

'Uh-huh.'

'She says can you call her.'

'Right. Thanks, Pearl.'

'No bother, hen. Are you away to do the rooms now?'

'Yeah.'

'OK. See you later, then.'

'OK.'

Nina looks across the dark space between their beds, and sees that Stella has gone. The blankets are pulled back, the exposed innards of the bed glowing white in the gloom. Nina sits up. 'Stella?' she says. 'Stel?'

Their bedroom is dark. Furniture crouches at the walls. Their school uniforms lie, limp and ready for tomorrow, on their chairs, cuffs and hems trailing to the carpet.

Something makes Nina look up, makes her heart leap in her chest. A pale figure looms above her in the dark. Nina has to stare at it for a few seconds before she realises what it is. Her sister is standing, poised and motionless, on the spar at the end of her bed, her bare feet curled round the wood.

Nina pulls back the covers and steps out of bed. The dark doesn't scare her. Nothing scares her any more. 'Invincible' is the word for it, Stella told her. She found it in a book. Nina tiptoes across the room.

Stella is perfectly balanced, like a swimmer poised for a dive. She doesn't sway, doesn't falter, doesn't even have to hold out her arms. Nina has no idea how she does it, how she manages to hold herself on this thin bit of wood.

'Stel?' she whispers.

She mustn't wake her. Never wake a sleepwalker. Stella is looking down, as if at a point far in the distance. Nina knows where she is. She can picture the drop of the precipice, the boom of water against rock. She doesn't like it that Stella goes there without her, doesn't like the thought of her sister there, alone.

'Hey,' she says, and reaches out her hand, curling her fingers into her sister's, slowly and carefully. 'It's me,' she says. 'You're dreaming. Come on. Come back to bed.'

Stella clutches at her hand, frowning.

'Come on,' Nina says, and tugs her arm. 'Back to bed. It's just a dream.'

Stella allows herself to be led down. As Nina is pulling the covers back over her, she starts to shake and shiver, her jaw clenched.

'It's all right, Stel,' Nina murmurs, as she tucks the blankets round her. 'It's all right.' Stella's body is stiff and unyielding. Nina sits on the mattress next to her, stroking her hair away from her face, something she's seen her mother do. 'Everything's all right.' But her sister still shudders. Nina crouches down so that she can see right into her sister's sleeping face. She takes Stella's wrist in her fingers and grips it, hard. 'He can't get you now.'

'No, I'm sorry,' the woman has bright lipstick escaping into rivulets around her mouth, 'I don't know of any town around here called that.' As she finishes saying this she gives the stack of leaflets she's holding a smart tap on the desk, as if to punctuate her speech.

Jake is standing in a bookshop in Aviemore, the only place name he knows for sure, the only one he has, his mother's rucksack at his feet. 'How about a village? Or a hamlet . . . or . . .' His hand circles wildly in the air. Is it just him or is this woman being spectacularly unhelpful? '. . . anything?'

She creases up her face, giving a short show of pretending to think, then shakes her head. 'I don't know of anywhere called that.'

Jake pulls his face into a smile as a way of stopping himself reaching over the desk and shaking her. 'OK.' He is not going to be downcast, he is not, he is not. He had known this would be difficult. Did he really think that by coming here it would magically materialise? 'I'll take this, please.' He lays the map on the counter and hands her a note picked at random from his wallet. She hands back two different notes and some coins with a sniff.

Outside, he struggles to unfold the map in the stiff wind. He's going to scour it for anything he recognises. It has to be here somewhere. He can't give up now he's got this close. It must exist: there was no possible reason why Tom would have lied about it to his mother. Maybe it wasn't the name of a town, like he and his mother had always thought – maybe it was a mountain or a valley or a river or whatever. Who knows what makes people give things names in this place?

The wind is too strong. The map flaps and strains for escape in his hands. The air is thin and icy clear. He needs to find somewhere to stay. But first he needs to find somewhere to have breakfast. Then he can lay out the map on the table and examine it properly – he will find it, he will, he will. And bugger Mrs Bookshop.

Jake looks up, along the street, and sees, for the first time, the peaks of mountains, denting the sky.

The windows are full of weather. Rain flings itself at the glass and clings on desperately as it slides down, buffeted by snatching grabs of wind. Stella sits on a stool behind the counter of the Buttercup Tea Room, her hands propping up her chin. She's driven into town for the puff pastry for tonight's beef Wellington. Pearl's cullen skink to start, the beef for the main course, and a choice of two desserts to finish. Passing the tea room, she'd been hailed by the Australian waitress, Moira, who'd asked her if she'd mind the place for ten minutes.

Cars plough up and down the length of the town, stretched like a ribbon along the main street. People cloaked in primary-coloured rainwear hurry along the pavements. The tea room isn't busy: a couple of tweed-swathed ladies bent in close conference over a scone, a blank-eyed woman with a baby in a bunny-covered high-chair, and a young guy. Black hair, plastered upright into spikes with rain, the shoulders of his jacket dark with water. An empty, crumb-studded plate sits on his table. A rucksack, battered and ancient, is propped on the floor next to him. He doesn't look like the kind of person this town usually attracts. He stands out. His clothes aren't right. Too impractical. They're not tweed or Gore-Tex or wool. They smack too much of the city. He looks like an urbanite, Stella decides, looks like he's landed here by accident.

He is sifting through coins, picking them up one by one and examining them as if he's never seen them before. Must be foreign. American, maybe? No, Stella doesn't think so. He looks European. French, perhaps. He's hard to pin down. There's something about him she likes, though. The way he sits on the chair. It's a rather sissy-looking chair with a padded floral seat and an upright back, but he lounges on it as if it were a bed – his legs splayed and stretched out, one arm dangling loose by his side, his shoulders rolled back. He looks very . . . post-coital. Stella smiles to herself. It's not every day you get someone like him to look at, especially round here.

As she surveys him from her vantage-point on the stool, his head jerks up, as if he's sensed her gaze. His eyes roam round the tea room until they meet hers. Stella blinks, unmoving. Is she still smiling? She's not sure. She has a horrible feeling that there's the ghost of a grin on her face. They stare at each other for a second. Then he drops his coins on to the table and shifts himself upright in the chair. 'Could I have another tea, please?' he asks.

Stella slides off the stool. 'Sure.'

She looks at the Gaggia machine next to her, which is sighing and shuddering like someone on the verge of tears. It's similar to the one in her grandparents' café. She finds a cup and a teabag on the shelf above her. She runs her hands over the Gaggia levers, then eases one down. Boiling water jets into the cup, billowing the air with steam. His voice was odd. Accentless. He's a Brit, definitely. He's certainly not Scottish but he doesn't really sound English either.

She tips a milk-jug into the cup and white unribbons in the dark water.

The waitress walks towards him through the scattered tables of the tea room, a steaming cup held in her hand. Sunlight glows into the room briefly, the windows flaring with light. Jake glances out to the street. A sudden burst of sun is illuminating the wet buildings, the car windscreens. The weather seems so unpredictable here. It had been sunny and clear when he got off the train but then a squall had appeared, soaking him in seconds. His skin is clammy and chilled and sticks to his clothes.

He turns back to the table, to the strange coins lying

there, to his empty cup and plate, to the tea room, to the woman walking across the room towards him with his name written across her breast. Kildoune, the starched cotton of her dress reads, Kildoune.

Jake stares at her. She has smooth black hair, which lies in a slant across her cheekbones, green eyes and skin so delicate he can see the blue thread of a vein travelling up her neck. Her colours assault his mind: the dark, the green, the blue, the white, the red of her mouth. And his name on her chest. Kildoune. In black, cursive letters.

'Your tea,' she says to him, and places the cup down on the table. He goes to move the coins out of her way and the back of his hand brushes against the soft, mushroom-pale skin of her inner arm, and as they touch there is a kind of humming vibration, like two messages meeting on a wire.

'What is that?' Jake blurts.

The waitress glances at him, his empty plate held in one hand, a slight frown dipping her brow. 'What?'

'That.' He points at her breast, the word written there. 'That,' he says again. 'What is it?'

She touches it, the raised embroidery. 'Kildoune?' she says, and Jake wants to shout, clap his hands, seize her by the shoulders, kiss her on the mouth that just uttered his name. 'It's a hotel.'

'A hotel? Where?'

She gestures in a direction behind her. 'Over that way. Beyond Kincraig.'

'Show me.' He struggles about inside his bag for the Ordnance Survey map. It refuses to behave, to open properly, to lie straight in his hands, its origami interleaves resisting separation. He is terrified that this woman – the only woman seemingly who knows where or what Kildoune is – will vanish into thin air. He has to stop himself grabbing her by the arm and handcuffing her to him. 'Show me exactly,' he insists. 'I have to go there.'

She is staring at him as if he's quite mad. Which is a pretty fair assessment at the moment. She shifts the plate into her other hand, throws a glance over her shoulder. 'It's quite . . .' She stops, her eyes straying over his battered rucksack. '. . . posh,' she finishes uncertainly.

'No, no.' Jake flattens the map to the table. He feels crumbs crunching under his touch. 'I don't want to stay there, I just want to . . .' He trails away, seeing the faint alarm in her eyes. Deep green eyes with long, curving lashes. She doesn't really need to know all this. Appear normal, he wills himself, take a deep breath. 'I just want to . . . see it.'

'Oh.' She leans over the map and Jake sees a warning in the neck of her overall: KEEP AWAY FROM FIRE. He gazes at it, at the knuckles of her spine disappearing down into the white folds. 'Right,' she says, the tip of her finger hovering over the map, 'well—'

At that moment the bell on the door dings. The first waitress, a small woman with reddened cheeks, hurries in. 'Stella, you're a star!' she exclaims. 'Thanks so much. Phew.' She comes to a standstill in front of them. Looks from Stella to Jake and back again. 'Was everything all right?'

'I was just showing this guy,' Stella gestures at him, 'where Kildoune is.'

'Oh.' The Australian girl elbows Stella out of the

way. 'I can show you.' She beams at him, her face too close.

Jake doesn't look at where she is pointing on the map, but watches the girl. Stella. She crosses the room, away from him, towards the counter. She picks up a coat and moves towards the door.

'Do you work there, then?' he asks, as she passes by him, close enough for him to reach out and touch her. He can't think of anything else to say. He wants to detain her, delay her, keep her with him. He doesn't want her to disappear out of the door and into the outside world, never to be seen again.

She fixes him with her clear, green stare. Is she smiling at him? No.

'Yes,' she says, 'I do.' Then she turns to the Australian girl, who is talking about bus times and the possibilities of hitching. 'I've got to run, Moira, see you later.'

At the door, she puts her hood up over her hair and turns to close the door after her. Just as it is about to shut, she looks up, straight at him. They stare at each other for a split second. Then she pulls the door to and is obscured by rain and the condensation swarming up the windows.

Stella made a tent with her bedclothes, balancing a mallet from their croquet set in the middle of her bed – the lower bunk, because Nina always had the top – and she dived down into it, delighted. Where she slept prostrate and stretched out every night was suddenly a secret peaked space, with tapering, sloping walls, the light glowing red through the crocheted blankets.

It was early. Too early for her parents to be awake – they weren't allowed to go in to them before eight at a weekend. Nina was still asleep.

Stella wriggled out, feet first, and roamed the flattened carpet of the room, collecting armfuls of bears with non-plussed faces, dolls with eyes that rattled inside their hollow plastic craniums. These, she bundled into the tent and lined up in rows, straightening any that dared to lean drunkenly on their neighbour.

'This is our tent,' she announced to them, lying on her stomach. Her legs stuck out at the end of the blankets, but what did that matter? Most of her was in here, in this new, private space. 'Our secret tent.' The toys looked unimpressed.

After a while, she got bored with arranging and rearranging them, and her arm was tired of holding the croquet mallet upright. She emerged, hair mussed and static, let the tent collapse and it became just a blanket-covered mattress, lumped with the mysterious shapes of toys. Stella could make out a padded leg and the grasping, outstretched hand of a doll. She tipped back her head and looked speculatively at the swollen sag of the mattress above her. Nina couldn't still be asleep, could she?

Stella reached up and, slipping her fingers between the sharp wire meshing, pressed her hand up into her sister. Nothing. She did it again. Still nothing. She threw herself down on her back and, putting her feet against the hard metal knots of the mesh, pushed up. The weight of Nina's body rose and fell back. Stella waited, puzzled. Then she heard something, a soft, unintelligible noise.

Stella slid out of bed and climbed the wooden ladder, the creases falling out of her pyjama knees. She hooked her elbows into the edge of the bunk and looked at her sister.

Nina was lying on her side. Her eyes moved under her lids.

'What did you say?' Stella asked.

Nina's lids lifted, then fell again.

'Did you say something?' Stella whispered, breathing hard into Nina's face. 'Are you awake? Neen? Are you awake? I made a tent. Do you want to see? It's really good. There's room for both of us. Sort of.'

Nina mumbled something.

'What?' Stella leant closer.

Nina opened her eyes. 'Don't feel well,' she muttered.

Stella pushed at her parents' door, hearing it hiss against the carpet. The room was still and fugged with warmth. Sunlight cut in around the edges of the curtains. The carpet had dark blotches of flowers, twining into each other, all connected, and Stella stepped from one bloom to another until she'd reached her father's prone form. Half of his face was obliterated by the pillow. One arm was stretched back behind him, to touch the curve of her mother's hip. Tiny hairs were pushing out of his skin – millions of them. *By the hairs on my chinny-chin-chin.* Stella leant over, fascinated.

'Dad,' she whispered. 'Daddy.'

'Go back to bed, Stella.' His voice was clear and firm. Almost as if he was awake. But his eyes were closed.

Stella turned and walked back to the door on the petal clusters. In her room, she dragged a stool to the cupboard, stood on it and reached up to pull down their doctors and nurses set. She snapped the elastic of the hat with the red cross about her chin and climbed up the ladder again.

'Now, patient,' she said, as she knelt on the bed, 'I'm going to have to listen to your heart.'

Nina gazed at her, listless and inert, as Stella fitted the plastic stethoscope into her ears and pressed the disc to Nina's nightie. She could hear nothing at first, then the tubing picked up a distant, irregular thud, slow as the clock in their grandparents' sitting room. Stella whipped the stethoscope out of her ears.

'And now for your temperature.'

She inserted the thermometer into Nina's mouth. Nina's eyes closed and her head slid sideways. Maybe she wants to be left alone, Stella thought.

She spent a while unpacking and repacking the things into their case, her legs crooked at right angles over Nina's. She listened to the endless swish-swash of her own heart for a bit. She unravelled a crêpe bandage and rewound it into an even cylinder. Then a strange, gurgling sound came from Nina. Stella squashed the bandage into the case, snapped down its locks and crawled towards her sister.

Nina's eyes were shut. She'd gone back to sleep. The plastic thermometer with its inked red line drooped from her lips, which were pale and bloodless. Her hair was sticking to her scalp like seaweed. Stella leant closer and saw that her eyes were in fact half open and her eyeballs were turned upwards so that only the whites showed. Her breathing didn't sound as it always did when Stella woke in the night – it was too fast and shallow.

'Neen,' she began. She touched her hand. It felt damp and burning hot. 'Nina?' Stella gripped Nina's wrist and gave it a shake. The arm fell away to hang loose and slack off the side of the bed.

Stella climbed back down the ladder, through the room, across the landing to her parents' door. This time she didn't use the stepping-stone flowers.

'Daddy.'

'Mmm.'

'Dad.'

'Stella, I've told you—'

'Dad, there's something wrong with Nina.' Stella didn't realise she was frightened until she heard her voice, which was high-pitched and shrill. It made her burst into surprising tears. 'Please wake up,' she wailed.

Her father's eyes sprang open. He looked at his younger daughter for a few seconds, then swung his legs out of the bed and went into their room. Stella trailed behind.

'She – she said she didn't feel well,' Stella spoke through her sobs, 'and then – and then she went back to sleep and then—'

Her father looked at Nina, laid a hand on her forehead. 'Christ,' he muttered, then his voice rose to a shout, 'Francesca! Francesca!'

In the lobby, Stella shakes the wet from her hair and peels away the waterproof from her damp clothes. She is thinking that she must change her uniform because this one is damp and that the duck ornaments could do with a dust and that she should take the pastry straight to the kitchen, when Mrs

Draper bustles past. She stops when she sees Stella standing there, dripping water on to the mat.

'Stella, there you are. Come with me. I want you to meet someone. A new member of staff. Remember I told you we needed some outdoor work doing – maintenance, painting, that kind of thing? Someone to help you when everything gets busy over the summer. I'm sure you could do with a hand . . .'

In Mrs Draper's office, a man stands at the window, his back to Stella. He turns round when they come in.

Stella hadn't realised how tall he was. She has to look up at him to meet his gaze. She is still holding the wet slick of the waterproof in her hands.

'Hello again,' he says to her, and smiles.

part | three

Stella wakes with a jolt, her heart loud and urgent in the cave of her ribs. She is face down, blind, the linen of the pillow pressed to her mouth and nose.

She turns round and sits up in one jerked movement. The caravan is empty, the early-morning air arctic-cold against her skin, the tree tap-tapping on the roof. She can see all the way through to the door. Nothing. It's all right, she tells herself, it's all right. But her heart continues to pound.

She'd been dreaming she was a child again, standing near an edge where brackish dark water falls away to thunder against rocks out of sight.

She scrambles from the bed, fighting off the bedclothes, which clutch and cling to her, and goes to the mirror. The reflection that meets her there is adult. Definitely adult. Stella scans it. Skin imprinted with fabric folds, lips pale, the black of the pupils wide, depthless. It's all right. It was years ago. Years and years. But somehow it doesn't always feel it.

Stella turns away from herself. The light behind the slatted blinds is a dull white. It's early. She goes back to the bedroom, wincing at the cold of the carpet under the bare balls of her feet, and picks up her clock. 6.45 a.m. She won't sleep again so she drags her uniform over her head and pulls two sweaters over it.

The dog joins her as she is trudging to the old stables for firewood. It dives out of its kennel, straight as an arrow, tail waving, high-pitched yips escaping from its throat. Stella sleeks the fur between its ears before they set off again, together, the dog with its nose held to the ground.

Passing the old, renovated pigpen near the stables, Stella is momentarily surprised to see the curtains shut. She passes the wood-basket into her other hand.

'We'd forgotten about him,' she says to the dog, 'hadn't we?'

The dog stops and looks up, attentive, ears raised, scanning her speech for sound patterns it might recognise.

Jake is reluctant to enter the kitchen on his first morning. Mrs Draper had told him to come down for breakfast after nine when the biggest rush would be over. But he loiters in the lobby, his hands wedged into his pockets. From behind the swing door into the kitchen comes the sound of laughter, a brief shout, a radio playing and the banging of plates and cutlery – the noise of people used to working together.

The door is pushed open and he sees the girl from the café emerge. Stella. She has her hair held back from her face in a wide band. She vanishes up the long, thin corridor and into a room at the end.

Jake waits uncertainly at the bottom of the stairs. He feels a bit overwrought, a bit wired. He didn't sleep a wink last night but lay awake watching the night count down on the luminous face of his digital watch, repeating to himself, over and over, you're in Kildoune, you're in Kildoune. It seems extraordinary to him. The proximity of it all, the physical connection with Tom, is overwhelming, unbelievable. Everywhere he looks he sees objects – the banister, the light switch, that stone threshold, the fireplace – which might have been touched by the hand of his father.

From the kitchen comes a burst of hoarse singing, then a clatter, then a curse. He looks down: the trailing, complex pattern of vines in the carpet twists around his feet, as if willing him to trip and fall. He looks up: the stairs wind up to the next floor, and he is just able to glimpse a pair of forked antlers, hanging right above him.

'Do you want some breakfast?' a voice says. Stella is standing at the swing door, a pile of used plates in her hands.

'Yes.' Jake moves towards her. He can feel himself smiling. Is he smiling too much? Maybe. She isn't smiling at all. 'That would be great.' He takes his hands from his pockets and gestures at the plates. 'Can I give you a hand?'

Stella shakes her head, holding the door open for him with her foot. 'I'm fine. Go through.'

The kitchen is hot, cramped, overlit, and full of steam and the smell of ground coffee. At the sink is a small, stumpy-looking woman with a mouthful of broken teeth, and a man in chef's whites stands at the stove, a long, spiked implement in one hand. A pan spits and sparks on the hob, slivers of bacon shrivelling in fat.

Stella slides the stack of plates on to the surface and flicks open a pad of paper. 'Venison sausages for two,' she says, very fast over the noise, 'one with mushrooms, the other without, the one without with scrambled, the one with with fried, OK?'

The chef nods without turning round. 'Got it.'

'This is Jake,' she announces, 'who'd like some breakfast.'

'Got it,' the chef says again.

The woman at the sink is in front of Jake, flipping a sodden dish-towel over her shoulder. 'I'm Peril,' she says to him.

'Sorry?' Jake leans over the counter anxiously. She can't be called 'Peril', can she?

'Peril,' she insists, again.

Stella, standing at the toaster, glances at him, then back at the woman. 'Peeuurrllll,' she explains, flattening the vowels. 'Peuurl.'

'Ah.' The mists clear for Jake. 'Pearl.'

'Ha,' Pearl guffaws, 'Peurl. Peril. Peurl.'

They both laugh. Even the chef turns round and bares his teeth.

'Pearl,' Stella says, 'could you show Jake where all the paint and ladders and stuff are kept? Mrs D told me she wants him to start painting the windows today.'

Pearl staggers off down a passageway, still giggling. 'Come with me, laddie.'

By midday, the air is motionless and humid, the sky heavy with unfallen rain. Jake peels off his T-shirt and works in just his jeans, a blowtorch held in one hand. He is pleased to have something to do, a definite task to perform. Otherwise he'd probably just wander about in a daze. The paint blisters under the roaring jet of heat, pulling away from the window-frames and falling to the ground in shards. Sweat blooms on his forehead and itches at his scalp. He scrapes at the stubborn streaks with a metal spatula.

The rooms of the house are dark and fathomless from the outside, like looking down into a lake. Jake circles the building, hefting the ladder against the lumped stone walls, counting up the windows, calculating how much paint he'll need, checking for any rot. When Mrs Draper asked about his experience of painting windows, he hadn't mentioned that he'd only ever painted windows on film sets, windows that opened on to fake scenery, to digital hallucinations, to nothing. But he didn't think it mattered – how different could it be?

As he is turning the searing blast of the torch on to the dining room windows, he sees Stella inside, the pale oval of her face floating up to the surface.

Of course Jake didn't really expect his father still to be here. He hadn't pictured him standing at the gate of this mystic place called Kildoune with open arms, waiting to welcome him into his life. But there was also, of course, that small, disruptive part of him that kept whispering, he might be there, what if he's there, he could be there. No matter how logically he tried to think about it, no matter how convinced he was that there was no way he'd find him by finding Kildoune – he was still disappointed.

Jake hadn't realised how much he'd wanted to find him until he got there. He'd always told himself that it hadn't mattered, that his mother had been enough for him, that she had made up for any lack he ever felt. But here, standing in front of Kildoune, which is full of unfamiliar strangers, he can't tell that lie to himself any more. Motherhood is a clear, prescribed thing. Those nine months you spend with another being pocketed inside you are a lifelong, unwritten contract that can't ever be cancelled. But fatherhood is nebulous, undefined, and can be almost nothing, a mere tailed cell shot out into the void.

He doesn't know what he expected. He expected nothing and everything. He's thought about Kildoune all his life, imagining and reimagining it, building it and tearing it down in his mind. But he'd never expected this: a grand house in grey stone, a thicket of dank fir trees, a huge sky piled with clouds, and a long-necked woman who watches him with the grave, impenetrable gaze of a cat.

Stella comes out of the front door of the hotel, a plate in one hand with a sandwich on it. She has to shade her eyes against the glare – the sun has broken through and burned away the cloud. The air is filled with the sweetish, steamy scent of hot bracken and peat.

She looks about her, then sees, beyond the gravel and the curve of lawn, the right-angled triangle of a ladder against the house. The new guy, Jake, is perched at the top of a hypotenuse, energetically scraping at the paint on an upper window, his T-shirt draped over his head, Beau Geste-style.

'I made you a sandwich,' Stella calls, as she reaches the bottom of the ladder, holding up the plate to show him. 'I'll leave it here.'

'No,' he puts down the scraper and yanks the T-shirt off his head, 'wait a sec. I'll come down.' The ladder judders and rocks as he descends the rungs. Stella puts out a hand to steady it. 'Thanks.' He grins as he leaps the final three to the ground. 'Fantastic,' he says, taking the plate. 'I'm starving.'

Stella forces herself to look away from him as he pulls on the T-shirt. The ground around her feet is littered with hard, dry paint curls. She waits for him to speak. Didn't he want to ask her something? He says nothing, though, just smiles at her as he lifts the sandwich to his mouth. It is an oddly personal smile – the corners of his mouth curving upwards with an easy slowness as his eyes skim over her face, her hair, her throat.

'How are you getting on?' she asks abruptly.

He nods as he chews and swallows. 'Not bad. Some of the windows are in a bit of a state, a bit rotten, but Mrs Draper says she's going to get someone proper in to fix those.'

'Proper?'

'Yeah. Not like me.'

'Why? Are you not proper?' she says, then immediately regrets it.

He eyes her, and smiles again. 'No, not really. Are you?'

Stella decides to ignore that. 'Whereabouts are you from?' she asks instead.

'Hong Kong.'

She laughs. 'Hong Kong?'

'Why's that funny?'

'I don't know.' She has to stop herself laughing again. 'It's just not what I was expecting you to say.'

'Why? What were you expecting?'

'Er . . . I'm not sure. I don't know – London, maybe.'

He shakes his head and grimaces. 'No way. I've spent all of maybe forty minutes there. Didn't think much of it.' He fixes her with his blue eyes. 'What about you?'

'What about me?'

'You're not from round here either, are you?'

'How can you tell?'

He shrugs, as he pushes the last of his sandwich into his mouth. 'I just can.'

'How?' she demands, although she knows she should really be ending the conversation at this moment and walking away.

He takes a step back and pretends to survey her from head to foot. Stella flushes hot under her clothes. 'Your haircut,' he ticks off on his fingers, 'those shoes, your accent—'

'My accent?' Stella scoffs. 'And what would you know about that, Mr Ex-pat?'

'Not much. But I can understand you,' he touches the centre of her thorax, 'which is more than I can say for most people around here.' He shrugs again. 'You just don't say Invernessshire to me.'

Stella glares at him. She feels obscurely and inexplicably furious. She's been here, alone and undisturbed, for months, and then this guy turns up from nowhere and starts asking her personal questions. Why are you here, she wants to say, why have you come?

'So are you going to tell me where you're from?' he says. 'Or is it a secret?'

'It's a secret!' she snaps.

'OK.' He seems unperturbed. 'Whatever.'

Stella turns on her heel, the gravel crunching under her, and walks away, fast.

'Hey!' he calls after her receding figure. 'Can you tell me something?'

'What?' She doesn't stop but flings the word over her shoulder. He's made her angry but he's not sure why.

'How long has this place been a hotel?'

This makes her stop, he notices, and half turn. In the bright sun, her shadow is a poised black shape at her feet, crouched and ready for her next move. 'Twenty-five years, I think,' she says. 'Something like that.'

Jake lays this mentally next to his own lifespan, like two tape-measures unrolled side by side. That leaves four years over for Tom to go to India, meet his mother, conceive him and – what? What else could he have done in that blank stretch of time? God only knows. Come back here to his commune? The house seems an unlikely venue for a commune – too big, too grand. Did he go elsewhere? Move on? He's not here now, Jake's sure of that, but the possibility that Tom might still be in the area, in another commune, maybe, or leading a straight life in a semi, makes the fine hairs on the back of his neck rise and bristle. He wonders for a moment how Tom might react if he were to turn a corner and find an image of his youth, his past self, his doppelgänger, walking towards him.

'Twenty-five years?' he repeats.

'Yeah.' Stella has turned fully towards him now, her shadow double shifting with her. 'Why do you ask?'

He won't tell her. He won't. 'Nothing, I—' And then he changes his mind. 'Well.' He thinks. 'Someone . . . I know might have . . . lived here once. A long time ago. A . . . a relative.'

'Oh,' Stella nods, 'right. You should ask Pearl. She knows everything.'

'OK. I will.' Jake gives her a small wave as he mounts the ladder again. 'Thanks.'

Stella doesn't go in the ambulance with Nina and her mother. She watches as the two men belt her sister to the wheeled stretcher. Nina's head is turned to one side and they have strapped something that looks like a plastic mask to her face. The elastic holding it there yanks her hair into a peak on the top of her head. Stella wants to smooth it straight. She is sure that Nina wouldn't like the feel of her hair pulled in that way.

Their mother is wearing trousers under her nightdress and has a coat of Archie's round her shoulders. Her feet are bare on the Tarmac of the road. Lots of people have come out of their tenement and the surrounding ones to watch the Gilmore girl being taken away. Stella wishes they couldn't see her mother like this. Francesca steps into the ambulance before the stretcher so she is waiting there as Nina is lifted in. Stella is glad about this. She wouldn't like to be alone in that dark space, hung with wires and straps and tubes. Then the men slam the doors closed.

Stella and her father follow the wail of the ambulance. Stella's place is behind her father, who always sits in the driver's seat. It seems wrong that half of the car is empty. She looks over at the vacant seats where her mother and Nina ought to be and worries that, without the ballast of them, the car might unbalance, tip over.

At the hospital, her mother, still barefoot and in her nightdress, clutches her hand without looking at her and tells her, over and over again, that everything is going to be all right. Stella is put on a chair that wobbles when she moves.

Her father disappears first, then her mother, then both of them. A nurse comes by and leaves a basket of brightly coloured toys that Stella is too old for. Stella rocks the chair back and forth under her, looks at how the light from a window in the corridor ceiling gushes in to pool on the polished linoleum, and counts the number of noises she can hear. She gets to forty-two and gives up. She realises she is very hungry but doesn't know who to tell. She pulls both laces from her shoes, ties them together and starts playing cat's cradle, which is what she and Nina always do when they're bored. But there's no one to insert their fingers into the beautiful symmetry of the criss-crossing joins and lift it away from her and she can't remember what comes after the third move, and when she tries to make it up the skeins knot and tangle around her hands and eventually she drops it into her lap.

Her grandparents appear when the light from the ceiling window has slanted enough almost to touch her on the leg. Stella is surprised to see them. Her grandmother kisses her forehead a lot and squeezes her to her overall. Her grandfather disappears, then her grandmother, and then they reappear with her parents.

The four of them stand in the corridor and a great discussion goes on above Stella's head. The adults can't stop touching her – on the hair, the shoulder, the arm. Stella doesn't like this and wants to wriggle away. But then she looks up at her father's face and she can see that it's wet. His eyes are blurred, the lashes stuck into spikes. Her father's been crying. This horrifies Stella. Her father never cries. Never. Fathers don't. She knows that. She looks to her mother and sees that she, too, is red-eyed and clutching damp tissues in her hand.

Stella begins to weep, very quietly at first, tears rising up out of her eyes and spilling down her face. She holds the thick tangle of laces to her face and sniffs into it. She looks again at her parents' faces and panic surges through her body like an electric shock. She takes a deep, shuddering breath.

'WHERE'S NINA?' she roars. 'WHERE IS SHE? WHERE'S NINA?'

Within seconds, it seems, she is in the café at Musselburgh. She is sitting on the counter, her legs dangling over the side. Her grandmother is feeding her ice-cream with a long silver spoon and talking to her in soothing, soft Italian. The windows are steamed up but she can just make out the rain falling, beyond them. Her laces, strangely, are back in her shoes – not in the way she likes them, slanting over each other, but pulled in straight lines. Her grandfather is on the phone in the corner, a cigarette held in the same hand that holds the receiver. Stella wants to remind him that it's there because he seems to have forgotten it, ash falling in drifts down his waistcoat.

'Where's Nina?' she says.

Her grandmother's brown eyes regard her. 'You know where she is. I told you. Remember?'

'*Dov'è Nina?*' Stella tries Italian.

'You remember the hospital,' her grandmother says gently, and then says more things Stella can't quite understand. She can see her grandmother's lips moving and she can hear the sound but she doesn't seem to be able to separate it into words.

'Where's Nina?' she says again. '*Dov'è Nina?* Where's Nina?'

Stella had what Nina referred to as her 'flip-out' the summer she was nineteen. They had been out of school, and apart, for the best part of a year – Stella at university in London and Nina, initially, at art college in Edinburgh. Nina had lasted half a term: when the tutor had told her she was to spend four weeks building a loom on which she would spend next term weaving her own tweed, she told him he could go fuck himself.

She spent weeks mooching in her bedroom, listening to music, plucking her eyebrows, dyeing her hair different colours and writing Stella long, indignant letters, until Francesca marched her along to a secretarial college. Armed with a 'competent pass' in touch-typing (Nina had only managed this by bribing the girl on the next desk to do hers) she got a temping position at a GP's surgery. The young but ambitious doctor who ran the place was shocked at the state of her typing but decided he wanted to marry her anyway.

Stella returned from her secret new life in London to a house full of wedding brochures, dress patterns, seating plans, present lists, colour swatches and caterers' catalogues. Her mother was so tense the tendons in her neck stuck out under the skin. Her father hid at the office all day. In the place of her art-student sister, who wore paint-spattered dresses, chased boys, drank too many vodkas and forgot her medication, was someone who had manicures, talked to estate agents, discussed fabric for bridesmaids' dresses, and wore tailored skirts, high heels and silk scarves knotted at her throat. And every day for dinner there was this stranger in a suit who addressed her sister as 'My Tempting Temp'.

Stella went into town, withdrew everything she had in her savings account, accumulated from summers of waitressing for her grandparents, and walked along Princes Street to a travel agent where she bought a train timetable for Europe, a rail pass and a guidebook.

She left mid-morning, while Francesca and Nina were out having a fitting at the dressmaker, pulling out her bag from under her bed. Her handwriting was scrawled and unrecognisable as she wrote the note, 'Gone to Europe, I'll be back for the wedding', and she couldn't stop looking over her shoulder as she hurried down Arden Street to the bus stop, as she waited on the platform at Waverley for the train that would take her away to liberty, freedom, peace. She only relaxed when she was on the rolling, pitching night ferry to Calais, surrounded by drunk, snoring men, tartrazine-fuelled children, the smell of petrol and reheated food, and gangs of people with sleeping-bags. Stella had never been abroad before.

She caught a series of trains through France. She bought a tray of white-fleshed peaches in Paris and ate them, one by one, as she sped through maize fields and vineyards with the windows open, the scented, warm air swirling into the carriage. Reaching the south in the dead of night, she climbed quickly on to another train that said 'Marseille → Roma' on the side.

She arrived in the early morning, the muscles in her arms aching from clasping the bag to her as she dozed. She stumbled down the train steps and walked through the station, towards the sunlight. She asked directions in the language her mother had taught her, unsure that it would work. But these strangers not only understood her but spoke back. It seemed unbelievable to her, magical almost, that anyone outside the microcosm of her family used these words, this grammar, this syntax.

In the wide, snag-toothed sweep of the Colosseum, she ate her last peach, a map of the city spread on her lap. She went to the pink-walled house where the famous young poet died, climbed up and down the Spanish Steps, soaked her feet in a fountain shaped like a boat. She kept wanting to stop passers-by, to hold them by the arm and peer into their faces. Everywhere she looked there were people with her jawline, her cheekbones, her brow. Don't you recognise me, she wanted to ask them, surely I must know you.

She was possessed by an urge to see everything. She went deeper into the country, catching more trains, climbed the spiralling steps up a striped *campanile*, went to a town that had been buried deep in volcanic ash for thousands of years, swam in the blue Adriatic, ate *stracciatelli* in tiled *gelaterie*, the taste of it so recognisable it made her smile.

In a town whose name she knew from her grandfather's stories about how he came to Scotland, she got on a bus that the man in the ticket kiosk told her would take her to her grandparents' region. It wasn't easy to get to their village. No one, the ticket man said, ever really went there. She changed buses in Agnone, then had to hitch a ride with a family who said they could take her close to where she wanted to go. Stella sat in the back, wedged between their children, her bag on her lap. Their car climbed higher and higher, the air thinning, crags of mountains looming above the road.

The family dropped her on the verge and she had to walk the path her grandfather had taken, sixty years before, in the opposite direction. When she turned the last hairpin bend and saw the village up ahead, Stella realised she'd never really believed that the place they came from, the place they'd told her about, was real and actual and had continued to exist without them.

She sat for an hour on the double-arched bridge above the split in the stream, and took a secret pleasure in buying a round tin of aniseed sweets at the chemist's shop. She walked around the empty cobbled streets, looking at the piles of neatly chopped wood, the geranium pots, the chickens scratching at the ground, the water fountain with its worn lip. She looked at the blank windows of the buildings that were abandoned, tumbledown, and wondered which one had been Valeria's. An old man coming slowly up the hill saw her in the doorway of a crumbling stone house and mumbled, 'Scozia,' as he passed, 'they've all gone to Scozia.' Stella thought about running after him and asking if he remembered Valeria and Domenico – he was roughly their age, he must have known them – but she stayed where she was. She wanted to remain anonymous, not leave any mark.

She stood in a phonebox in the square, considering the way the light splintered on the water and where on earth she might sleep tonight and how noisy motorbikes were and what she should buy for lunch.

Nina answered on the second ring. 'You are in so much trouble,' she said.

'I know,' Stella replied. She kicked off her shoes and hoisted herself up to sit on the metal stand. Her body was warm to the core in this country, her joints pliable, loose. She might have felt more Scottish here than she'd ever done before but it was as if the very molecules of her being were responding, recognising the climate. In the café in Musselburgh she could hear her mother screeching, 'Is that her? Is that her?'

Stella hung up. She looked again at the trickling water of the streams, at the splintering and re-forming reflection of the sun, at the hazy shapes of the mountains. Jumping down, she discovered that someone had reached under the glass and stolen her shoes. She walked barefoot through the church, the frescoes casting gold and blue light on to her skin.

It seemed to have been agreed without anyone telling her that Stella would live with her grandparents while Nina was in hospital. She was given the back room and the bed her mother had shared with her sisters. It was a double, with a headboard so polished that it threw back a shadowed, indistinct version of your face, and a dipped sag in the middle of the mattress. If Nina had been in it with her, they would have rolled towards each other in the night.

Stella spent several weeks in what her father called a 'dwarm'. She sat on a chair in the kitchen, beside her grandfather as he cooked chips and peas and fish for the *scozzesi*, gazing into space, her legs dangling over the lino. She couldn't speak, wouldn't say anything, except for questions: where's Nina? when's she coming back? is she going to die? when am I going to see her? Without her, Stella had no idea how to behave, how to live her life, what to say, what to do all day.

Her grandfather made her favourite dish – curls of potato *gnocchi* – and fed them to her himself, as if she was a baby. The tears dripped from her face into the *pomodoro* sauce and Domenico stirred them in, calling them seasoning. Her mother came to see her once a week, took her for walks round the bridges of the town, holding her hand too tightly, weeping into her handkerchief.

Valeria came back to the café one day with a navy apron, just like theirs but in a child's size, and tied it over Stella's clothes. It was the summer holidays, she explained to Stella, so the café was extra busy and they needed her help. Stella carried glasses of lemonade to customers, and was allowed to squirt the sauce on to sundaes. She translated the more elaborate requests of the customers so that her grandparents could understand. She sat up on the counter, telling her grandmother who had finished and who was still eating and who might like some more coffee. 'What would we do without you?' her uncle Giancarlo said, often several times a day. Then Stella only cried at night, when the room around her seemed empty and large.

It seemed as if she had been in Musselburgh for months, for years, by the time Valeria took her to see Nina in hospital. Stella was surprised. She had been asking to see Nina for weeks and her grandparents kept saying no, but why don't you write her a letter instead? Stella didn't know why her grandmother had suddenly changed her mind.

'Why can we go now?' she asked, as they sat on the bus.

Valeria pretended not to hear, fussing with tickets and putting the change back into her purse.

'Why am I allowed to go now,' Stella persisted, 'but not before?'

Valeria sighed. 'Just because,' she said, and Stella watched her turn away quickly and blow her nose.

Her grandmother held her hand in both of hers as they trudged through corridor after corridor, went up some stairs, along a glass walkway. They passed abandoned wheelchairs, shut doors, nurses with squealing shoes, people walking along in dressing-gowns, doctors with stethoscopes, a man holding two inverted bunches of orange flowers, a woman with no hair. Before they went through two heavy swing doors, her grandmother stopped to straighten Stella's collar.

'*Sei pronto?*' she said, touching Stella's cheek. '*Andiamo.*'

They were in a long corridor, one side of which was windows, the other a wall of sickly yellowish-green paint.

It was very quiet. Stella suddenly thought she needed the loo but the set look on her grandmother's face told her she shouldn't ask. They came to a stop near the end.

Valeria bent down and hoisted Stella up. There before her, beyond the glass, as if on a television screen, were her parents, her mother sitting in a chair beside a bed, her father standing beside her, and on the bed was a stick-figure with hollow eyes and a shaven head, looking straight at her. Stella saw that it was dressed in a flowered nightgown like the one she had.

'Smile,' her grandmother was whispering, 'give her a smile.'

Stella pulled her face into a smile. The air in the hospital made her teeth feel dry and cold. She lifted her arm and waved.

'That's it,' Valeria encouraged. '*Brava ragazza.*'

Stella asked, 'Why isn't Nina waving back?'

'She can't move, my darling.'

Stella waved and waved. In the scene on the other side of the glass, her mother waved back and so did her father. The three of them waved frantically, as if something terrible might happen if they were to stop.

'Take a good look at her, won't you?' her grandmother whispered, so quietly that Stella wasn't sure if she heard right. 'So you can remember.'

The ceiling above her is a patchy grey-white. Nina knows off by heart the pattern of frail cracks that runs through it like rivers through mountains, seen from a plane.

Nina's never been on an aeroplane. But it's how she

imagines it might be if she were flying high above the earth, just below the white wisps of cloud. She would look down and see the puckered earth passing far beneath her and the flickering shadow of the plane, printed there by the sun.

She moves her eyes inside their sockets. It seems to take a great deal of effort, as if they are weighted or as if a machine inside her is slowly cranking down.

The room is dark, the blinds lowered. The slats have been tilted towards the floor, but from where Nina is lying she can see the black slits of night reaching into the room. She is puzzled. Weren't her parents here just a minute ago? Or was that a long time before? She can't remember. She has a slight recollection of Stella. With their grandmother in the corridor, looking in at her. But maybe that never happened. She can't remember when she last saw her sister.

She lifts her eyes to the clock on the wall opposite the bed. She can see the second hand jerk and stop, jerk and stop, but when she tries to focus on the thicker arms they dissolve and jitter before her.

To her right, she is surprised to see, is a nurse. Sitting in a chair beside her. Eyes bright as mercury through the gloom. Nina doesn't know why there is always a nurse in her room these days, watching her. There never used to be.

Nina looks away, looks down the length of her body, draped in the hospital blanket. She could have sworn that her arms were folded over her, fingers tucked into the elbow creases of the opposite arm. But now she sees that they have been placed by her sides. Her feet fall away from each other in a symmetrical V, the blanket peaked over them.

Beyond the room, beyond the grimacing faces of cartoon

characters daubed on the windows in colours that hurt her head, is a noise. Someone running down the corridor. Feet snap-snapping against the lino. Nina knows that lino. She remembers its dark red, pocked surface, the grainy, uneven feel of it under her slipper soles. On the last day that she'd been able to walk, she'd moved along it. All by herself. All the way to the bathroom. She wouldn't let them carry her, no she would not. She'd shaken and lurched and had to cling to the wall by the last joints of her fingers and it had taken her a long time and it had hurt. But she'd done it.

A small figure whizzes past. A boy from the ward down the corridor. Nina's seen him before. He came into her room at one point and asked her what her name was. Before she could answer, the nurse in the room shooed him away. He is running, pulling a drip-stand behind him like a train on a string. His laughter is torn off as he passes her open door.

Then she hears something else. Feet coming after him. Heavy feet with a broad sound. Adult feet. A nurse.

'Come back,' the nurse calls. 'I mean it.'

'You can't catch me!' the boy cries, and his voice sounds distant as if he's turned a corner. Nina thinks that there is a corner that way, beyond her room, turning off into a larger corridor. She used to see it when she used to leave the room.

Then the nurse outside hisses in a low voice, 'Be quiet.' *Be quiet*. Nina will hear it again later in her head. 'There's a little girl dying in there.'

For a split second, Nina feels sorry for the little girl and is wondering how old she might be, what age you need to be to die, and whether the little girl is frightened and if she will be lonely over there on the other side and Nina is turning her eyes on the nurse beside the bed to see if she is sorry too. But the nurse is looking cross and strangely ashamed. She is darting up out of the chair and slamming the door and making sure it's shut firm.

When she comes back to sit down again she won't look Nina in the eye. Nina stares at her, stares and stares. But she won't look up. And then Nina understands.

Pearl has been ordered to soak twenty-five electroplated nickel silver candlesticks in a vat of scalding water with a touch of ammonia. If there's one thing that gets Mrs Draper going it's globs of wax on her candlesticks. Not to mention grubby skirting-boards, dusty pelmets, old soap, scentless pot-pourri, scratches on table surfaces, cracked plates, crooked rugs, shoe scuffs on chair rungs.

The ammonia sweats from the steam, making Pearl's eyes smart. Hot, griefless tears streak down her face. Her hands are red and livid under the water as she chips off the wax-glue with her fingernails. Under her breath, she remembers the song her youngest grandson had been singing when she dropped him off at school this morning: 'He grew whiskers on his chinny-gan, the wind came out and blew them in again, poor old—'

'Pearl?'

A voice close behind her makes her jump, makes the candlesticks jolt together under the water. 'Christ!' she exclaims at Jake, one hand pressed to her chest. 'You scared the life out of me.'

'Sorry,' he says. He has paint in his hair. Which is a

shame because it's nice hair. Lots of boys his age seem to be cutting it off these days, like her son, shaving it close to their skulls, but he wears his quite long and kind of messy-looking.

'Here,' she says, 'you'll need some white spirit for that.' She points at his head.

Jake raises his hand and fingers the stiffened white strands. 'Oh. Didn't know I'd done that.'

'In the cupboard there.' She hustles him towards it. 'At the back. You'll find a rag over there.'

Jake spills a stinking pool on to a scrap of old towel and checks in the reflection of the door-glass as he pulls his hair through it. 'Er, Stella mentioned . . .' he mumbles '. . . um . . . I was wondering . . .'

Pearl looks up from smearing a candlestick in chalky silver cleaner. 'Uh-huh?'

'Do you remember a commune here?'

'A what?'

'A commune. Like . . . like a house of people all living together. Young people, maybe. About twenty-five, thirty years ago.'

Pearl buffs the frilled lip of the candlestick, puzzled. 'Ehm . . .'

'It was here in Kildoune, I think.'

'A commune, you say?' She sees her lips say this new word in the polished silver shaft and then it falls into place. 'Oh, you mean the hippies.'

'Yes.' Jake starts towards her as if he's going to embrace her. 'Yes,' he says again, gripping the rag in one hand, 'the hippies.'

'Aye,' she says cautiously. The stench of white spirit is wafting off him.

'You remember them?'

'Aye.' She nods. 'Of course.' She laughs briefly. 'They were kind of hard to miss.'

He is staring at her now, his eyes large and intent. 'They lived here?'

'Aye. Well, not in the big house – out the back.'

'Right. Do you . . . I mean, what do you remember about them?'

'Well . . .' she begins.

His intensity is making her uneasy and, as if he senses this, he speaks again: 'You see, a relative of mine lived there,' he gabbles. 'Here, I mean. In the commune. And I'm just trying to – to find out more about . . . him.'

Pearl frowns, thinking, then intones all she can recall, like she remembers having to do at school, a long time ago: 'The old boy, Mr Grant, he let them stay in the bothy out the back. They were here for quite a while. Four, maybe five years. Something like that. I was working for him then – cooking and cleaning but, frankly, it was a thankless task. The cleaning, that is.'

'And you used to see them? Talk to them?'

'Oh, aye. They were nice enough. Very young, most of them. Wore funny clothes, you know. Lots of folk up the town used to complain about them. But I always said they were harmless.'

'Can you show me where? The – the bothy, did you say?'

Pearl and Jake walk through the woods. Her hands are

easier now, out of the ammonia. Jake keeps close by her, adjusting his step to whatever direction she takes.

'There you go,' she says, and points, where the trees thin out, to a long, low stone building. The corrugated-iron roof has part-collapsed, one of the windows gone. A tall, waving plant sprouts from the chimney. As they look, the empty hole in the roof explodes with birds, their wings whirring.

'It was an old clearance cottage that someone put a roof on at some point. The hippies dug a garden all round it, grew vegetables and the like. But it'll have all overgrown since.'

They reach the door and Jake vanishes inside.

'Haven't been up here for ages,' she calls after him, staying outside with her arms crossed. She doesn't like going into disused houses, especially clearance houses. Makes her feel a bit spooked. 'Mrs Draper keeps talking about renovating it. You know, putting in heating and all sorts, to rent out as a holiday home. But she hasn't got round to it yet. I'll believe it when I see it, personally. Is there anything much in there? Any furniture?'

'Er . . .' Jake sounds far away, distracted. 'A bit.' There is a pause. A complete, still silence. The wood around her rustles and sighs, sunlight appearing and vanishing in patches on the ground.

'What like?' Pearl says, just to keep talking. She doesn't like this wood particularly, either, and certainly doesn't like standing about in it, waiting to be got by whatever it is that gets you in a wood.

'Sorry?' Jake says eventually.

'What like?' she shouts. 'Furniture.'

'Um, there's . . . there's an old sofa.' His voice, through

the thick stone walls, comes near her then fades away. He's having a good look, obviously. 'And . . . and a bed frame and . . . a mattress. But it's all rotted.'

Pearl is straightening her apron when he comes out of the door again. He has to duck his head and he puts up his hand to touch the lintel as if to judge the space, or protect his head, or just for the sensation of having the cold grain of stone against his fingers, she doesn't know but, as he does, everything – what they are doing here, what he is doing here, who he is, why he came – is suddenly clear to her. She has seen someone else do that very same thing in that very same spot in the very same way, someone who looked like him. Someone who, all those years ago, looked just like he does now. She'd forgotten all about him but when she sees Jake touch the lintel like that, a shutter somewhere in her memory opens. Pearl stares at Jake as they stand together outside the bothy in a clearing in the wood and she sees, she knows, she comprehends.

'What happened to them, do you know?' he is asking.

She clears her throat. 'They left, son, they all left. When she bought the place, Mrs Draper—' She breaks off, thinking that perhaps he might not want to hear that.

'Threw them out?' he finishes.

Pearl nods.

'You don't know where they went?'

She shakes her head.

'Any of them?'

'No. Sorry.'

As they walk back over the springy, needle-covered turf

towards the big house, Pearl touches his shoulder, lightly, just once.

Stella is doodling, her feet balanced on a drawer of the desk, scoring the corner of a newspaper with intricate squares and triangles. She's on late duty, which means she has to hang about in Reception until after midnight, answering the phone and dealing with anything the guests might want. She doesn't mind it. What she hates is the walk back to the caravan through the black wood, which rustles and moves around her, and how, at night, at a certain point on the path, you can hear the river in the distance, rushing through the earth.

She is pulling her jumper sleeves down over her hands when she realises with a start that someone is standing behind her. She twists round. It's the new guy. Stella stares up at him, speechless, fingers still gripping her pen. He seems as surprised to see her as she is to see him, standing there with one hand raised, his mouth half open.

Stella rallies herself. Why is she staring at him? Why is he staring at her?

'Hi,' she says, taking her feet off the desk and laying down the newspaper. 'You OK?'

'Yeah,' he says, but doesn't sound as if he means it.

He looks a bit freaked, as if he's seen a ghost, his hair standing on end, his eyes wide. In his hand, she notices, he is clutching a twenty-pound note. Stella has to resist an urge to giggle. 'Is that for me?'

'What?'

'That.' She points at the note.

'Oh.' His face relaxes. 'Well, sort of. I was wondering if I could have some change. For the phone.'

'Sure.' Stella bends over and rummages about in the desk drawer for the petty-cash box. Jake stands close by her, she notices. A little too close. She allows the chair wheel to edge sideways, to clash against his foot. He lets out a small noise of pain and steps back.

'Oh, sorry.' She hooks a strand of hair behind her ear, suppressing a smile, and, from the top of the small heap of assorted notes in the box, picks up a scribbled note in Mrs Draper's handwriting: *£20 to Jake Kildoune as pre-wage float.*

Stella frowns and reads it again. Jake Kildoune? That's his name? He's called Kildoune? She turns to look at him, still holding the bit of paper.

'Is there a problem?' he asks. 'Because I can always—'

'No, no,' she says quickly. 'No problem. I was just . . .' She trails away. Jake Kildoune. It really isn't any of her business. She turns back to look at the piles of change and notes. 'I was just wondering how much you needed.' Stella starts counting out twenty-pence pieces. 'I can give you one . . . no, wait a minute . . . two pounds in twenties and fifties, and—'

'I'm phoning long-distance,' he says.

'Oh.' She shakes her head. 'Of course, I— Right.'

Their eyes meet once as she pours the coins into his cupped hands. He is the first to look away. She points out the phone, hidden behind a dried-flower arrangement in the hallway, and she has just picked up the newspaper and started on a new pattern of interlocked squares when she hears money clunking through the phone and Jake saying: 'Caroline, it's me.'

Stella skims an article about a cabinet reshuffle. Caroline? Must be his girlfriend. She twitches the jumper sleeves down her wrists again and shivers. It's freezing in here. She starts again with her squares, colouring in every second one. She isn't listening, she really isn't. It's a private conversation and, anyway, she's reading the newspaper.

She turns it over and stares at an advert for a memory aid. Jake is telling Caroline something about an overnight train and arriving in Scotland early in the morning.

'I found it, Caroline. I found it. I'm *here*.' His voice seems to strain and waver, and the sound of it makes Stella lift her head. 'No, no,' Jake is saying quickly. 'He's gone. Long gone, by the sounds of it . . . Yeah . . . Yeah . . . I know . . .' Stella hears him take a deep, shaken breath. 'It's a hotel . . . No . . . He was in one of the outbuildings . . . Yeah, today, this afternoon. I got someone to show me, someone who remembers them . . . Yes . . . It was so weird, much weirder than I thought it would be . . .'

Stella is hunched over her doodle, horrified. Whatever this is, she really should not be hearing it. She looks about her wildly. She is hemmed in on four sides by the desk, the filing cabinet, the electric heater and a heap of files. She cannot leave without him hearing her. She knows the door will squeal on its hinges, the chair springs will twang, that she cannot step over the files without moving the heater, which will make a crashing noise like a cymbal, and he will realise just how close she is and that she's heard everything. And all the time things are knitting themselves together in her head: the relative he mentioned, the relative who once lived here, that surname of his written on the petty-cash slip, seeing from an upper window him and Pearl walking out towards the bothy in the woods, the way he is talking is not the way you talk to a girlfriend, it's the way you talk to a parent, a mother, the incredulity on his face when he read the word on her uniform in that Aviemore tea room. Stella feels opened out with sadness for him. She doesn't know what she will say when he crosses the hall after this conversation, she doesn't know what to say at all because what can you say when you've overheard—

A loud, shrill noise makes her jump, makes her drop her pen. It's the hotel phone and Mrs Draper telling her something about a consignment of doilies arriving tomorrow and is Stella sure, is Stella absolutely sure, the cupboard was cleared out and dusted today because if it isn't, come eleven a.m. she's going to have a lot of trouble on her hands, three thousand paper doilies and nowhere to put them.

Caroline sits for a moment beside the phone, one hand still resting on the receiver. She turns her neck and looks out of the window. She thinks idly that she must clear the pumpkin bed, must dead-head the roses, should really mash some fertiliser into the soil around the peas. That's the thing about gardening, there's always something to do, you're only ever just catching up with yourself.

It's almost noon, the sun level, the ground shadowless. Thousands of miles away, her son is still in yesterday. *I found it*, he'd said. He had gone searching for it, just as she had always known he would, and he had found it.

She feels as though she ought to do something to mark this moment – make a note of the date and time, perhaps, get out a photograph of her son, burst into tears. But she feels no particular urge to do any of those. The moments that affect you are only ever the ones you're not expecting. The ones you know will arrive, the ones you've been waiting for, have almost an unreal, rehearsed air about them, because you've imagined them so many times.

There are things she never told Jake: that at Kathmandu she'd turned round and gone back to Delhi. That she'd gone about the city, fatigued but hopeful, asking at every ashram for a tall Scottish man called Tom. That she'd pinned notes to three motorbikes like the one he had. That she had felt overwhelmingly that he should know, and that as long as he didn't she'd feel deceitful, a thief. That she spent four days weeping in a room before getting up the strength to leave. That after Jake was born, she'd sent letters to Kildoune, near Aviemore, Invernessshire, but nothing ever came back.

Caroline gets up, pushes her feet into her clogs, gets her gardening gloves down from a shelf. She thinks, not for the first time, about that single, singular, single-minded spermatozoon propelling itself through her, spiralling upwards. It strikes her again as unaccountable that this thing took place while she was busy doing something else – sleeping, walking about, fucking, riding on the motorbike, talking to Tom. It seems mad, perverse, that something as momentous as the beginning of her son could go unheard, unfelt. You'd think there would be some immediate outward sign, that your eyes would change colour or your skin darken or the blood race hot through your veins. You'd think you'd at least hear the moment of impact – a boom, that collision.

Caroline thinks about this as she pushes her way out of her house in Auckland, swinging open the back door, coming down the steps in her clogs.

Jake knows he should phone Mel, that he really must, but he still spends five minutes fiddling with coins and change and another ten minutes or so sitting beside the payphone in the hallway, thinking about what he's going to say, how he should get some waterproof shoes from somewhere, the taste of venison as compared to beef, the way someone has painted half of the ceiling in the hall with a slightly different shade of white from the other half, how light British money feels in the hand, Stella's eyes, the sight of the rusted bed skeleton out in the bothy, how he'd quite like to murder Mrs Draper, the feel of the reflected, radiated heat of a blowtorch, the family whose luggage he carried up earlier, how Hing Tai won't have woken up yet but his mother will be eating lunch soon, the rounded swell of bunions at the sides of Pearl's feet and how she's had to cut slits in the sides of her shoes for them.

He picks up the receiver and holds the low buzz to his ear. He feeds in coins one after another. The machine immediately regurgitates them into a too-small metal cup and Jake has to get down on his hands and knees to retrieve some of them from under the stool. He starts again, hears the ringing but doesn't manage to get the money in quickly enough. The connection dies. The machine eats and digests a fifty-pence piece anyway; Jake hears it passing like a bolus through its system.

He presses his fingertips to his forehead, takes a deep breath and tries again.

'Hello?' Andrew.

'Hi, it's Jake.'

'Jake!' Andrew pronounces his name with delight, which must be feigned because there's a pause while Jake hears him trying to think of what to say next. 'How's the . . . ah . . . golf?'

'Er, well, I haven't really—'

'Must be wonderful. Having a good time, are you?'

'Yes, it's—'

'How's the weather? Awful, is it? Can be dreadful. Rained the entire time I went to Scotland.'

'Yes.' Jake stares at the small grey screen on the phone where his money is being counted down. He doesn't have that much change left – the call to New Zealand made the machine very hungry indeed. A light perspiration is breaking out on his brow. 'Is—'

'Well, I'm sure you don't want to be chatting to me like this. I'll get Melanie for you. Hold on.' Andrew puts down the phone with a clunk.

'Thanks,' Jake says, to nobody.

'Jake?' He hears the pleasure in her voice and it gives him a falling sensation in his stomach.

'Hi. How are you? How are you feeling?'

'OK,' she says. 'Missing you, though.'

'Oh.' He hears himself emit a nervous laugh. 'Um, what have you been up to?' He starts scratching his head and once he starts he finds he somehow cannot stop. It's a rough, grating feeling that he likes, the rasp of fingernail against scalp.

'I'm fine. I saw the specialist yesterday and he said I'm doing really well.'

'That's great, Mel. It's wonderful. I'm so pleased.' And he is.

'How are you?' she says quickly. 'I mean, are you OK?'

'Yeah.'

'You sound a bit . . .'

'A bit what?'

'A bit funny.'

'No, no, I'm . . . everything is . . . fine.'

She drops her voice. 'Mum's been putting on the pressure.'

'The pressure?'

'You know. For us to set a date.'

He is having trouble understanding what this means, and when it does percolate through to him he has to scratch his head even harder.

'I said we could leave it for a bit, couldn't we, but she seems to think that all the good dates get booked up in advance.'

'The good dates? Are there such things?' It occurs to him when he says this that he might be going mad. 'Ha ha ha,' he says.

'Well, apparently,' she says. 'Anyway, let's not talk about this now. Are you having a lovely time? Tell me where you are and what you've seen.'

'I'm in a hotel,' he blurts.

'Whereabouts?'

'Kildoune.' There seems to be a problem with the synapse that filters internal thought from actual physical speech. Where has it gone? He needs it back.

'Kildoune?' she repeats. 'But . . . but that's—'

'My name!' he says manically. 'I know!'

There is a pause in Norfolk. He knows the doubtful expression she'll have on her face. 'Is that why you went there?' she says finally.

'Yes,' he says. He sits up straighter. Maybe that will help. Blood supply from the spine to the brain. Or something.

'Oh.'

Another pause.

'Listen, I'm going to be here for a bit—'

'In the hotel?'

'Yes. I'm doing some work for them and—'

'Work? What kind of work?'

'Er, I'm painting the woodwork—'

'Painting the woodwork?' she repeats, as if he's said *making a porn movie*. 'You're a guest in a hotel and you've offered to—'

'No, no, I'm not a guest. I'm a . . .' He has to stop and think. What is he? At this precise moment, he has absolutely no idea. 'I'm doing some work for them,' he finishes lamely. He has a feeling he's said that sentence very recently but can't be sure.

'But, Jake—'

There is a sudden and bossy bleeping on the line and she vanishes, abruptly, blissfully, as if some telecommunication fairy decided to intervene and whisk her away from him. Jake sits, still holding the receiver to his ear, staring at the grey screen, which is flashing '00' at him.

When Stella is finally allowed into Nina's hospital room, summer has leaked away and vanished down a hole. Stella is back at school but her grandmother made her change out of her uniform into a dress, and her legs are cold.

Stella doesn't look at Nina as she is ushered in by Domenico. She doesn't look as she steps over the square lino tiles – she only walks on the black ones, sideways like a crab, but doesn't do it obviously so that her mother notices because Stella knows her mother wouldn't approve and might tell her off later. She only looks when she's right up beside the bed and her hand is touching the crackle of the sheet.

Close up, Nina is shrunken, worn away like soap. Her hair is shaved close to a colourless scalp and the bones of her face stick up under the skin. It's her eyes that Stella recognises. They're the same as they've always been, the same as hers.

'We're getting a kitten,' Stella says.

Nina doesn't reply, just stares at her as if she's never seen her before. Stella is surprised. She and Nina have campaigned for a kitten for ages and ages.

'He's stripy,' Stella adds. She looks round at her grand-father. Domenico nods at her encouragingly and pushes her closer so that her elbows are pressed up against the bed. Why is Nina looking at her like that? Stella has an urge to wriggle out from between the bed and her grandfather's hand on her shoulder and run out through the door of this room that smells funny and away down the corridor. She doesn't like it in here. She doesn't like the way her sister, or this person they tell her is her sister, is looking at her.

Stella jiggles up and down on one leg. 'We can't have him yet because he's got to be able to lap up milk on his own.'

She sees Nina taking in the coat she's wearing. She remembers that it used to be Nina's, before. She tries again. 'What shall we call him?'

'Max,' Nina says.

'OK.'

She can feel the adults around them, watching them, listening to them, as if she and Nina are on a stage. She wonders what she should say next. Everyone seems to be waiting for her. She runs through the things her mother told her: remember she can't walk, remember she can't move, she's got a virus in her brain, a virus is an illness, and don't talk about school because it might make her sad.

She looks at Nina's arms, lying alongside her. They don't seem connected to her any more and look brittle, as if they might snap like glass rods. The skin on the inside sockets of the elbows is dark with purple-black bruises.

Nina sees her looking. 'They take blood out of my arms every day,' she whispers.

'Do they?' Stella is horrified. 'How?'

'With a needle. And a syringe. And sometimes the blood comes out in a gush and won't stop afterwards but keeps on coming out, and sometimes the needle misses the vein and they have to pull it out and do it again.'

'Does it hurt?'

'Yes,' Nina says, and her eyes spark, 'and sometimes—'

'Why don't you show Nina the book you brought her?' Francesca has appeared beside them.

The book is about a family of creatures living in Finland, which, Domenico told her, is very cold and very far away. Her uncle's been reading it to her. Stella is just disentangling it from her pocket, when Nina asks a question. 'How's Miranda?'

Miranda is Nina's friend from school. Her best friend. She has lots of yellow hair that her mother does in ringlets. Stella glances quickly at Francesca, then back at her sister. Nina's head is propped upright by two pillows. Only her eyes move. How can Stella tell her that Miranda goes about with Karen now and hasn't asked about Nina for a long time, and that no one plays skipping any more – the game Nina was best in the whole school at – and that Nina's year have been on a trip to the Botanical Gardens and that Nina's gymnastics team are winning all their medals without her?

'Fine,' Stella says.

She thinks about all the veins branching out through Nina's body and how they must be empty and dried out like the bed of a river they saw once on holiday in the Borders. She reaches out and touches Nina's fingers, just to be sure she's real, to be sure she's the same. They feel stiff and clammy, and they twitch.

'When you do that,' Nina addresses her with her eyes shut, 'I feel it in the other arm.'

Stella finds this fascinating. She lets go of Nina's hand, darts to the end of the bed and grips Nina's right foot. 'Keep your eyes closed,' she says. 'Don't peep. Which foot am I touching?'

Nina screws up her face, thinking. 'Um . . . left?'

'No!' Stella squeals.

Nina opens her eyes. They both giggle. 'Again,' she says. 'Try again.'

Behind them, the grown-ups scrape their chairs against the floor and start to talk. Nina closes her eyes against the white glare of the tube-lighting and Stella reaches out to grip Nina's right knee.

Stella steers her car up the winding driveway of the hotel with one hand. With the other, she holds a half-eaten apple and fiddles with the tape machine, which, for no apparent reason, has died.

She's going for a drive. She would never admit it to anyone but she loves driving – not in London or Edinburgh, where driving is all about edging your car between the gaps left by other people and waiting at traffic lights. Here you can bowl along roads through forests, over rivers, around crags, branches lashing at your windows, sharp clean air filling the car.

Stella stabs at the tape-machine buttons but then gives up, sighing. She gives the steering-wheel a twist at the top of the drive, pulling the car out into the road. She's wearing her pink-lensed sunglasses and the scene bobs before her, lush, weird and purple-skied.

She hasn't driven half a mile when she sees a figure walking along the verge, where trees with peeling silver trunks crowd in next to the road. From far away she knows it's him, and as the gap between them telescopes down, she is debating whether to stop or not. Why should she, she hardly knows him, what is he to her anyway, just a wave would be fine, why should she stop, there's no point, she's not going to stop, she's not, she's not, she's just going to wave.

But the tyres screech against the asphalt and the car comes to a halt, flinging her forward then back against the seat. She looks down, amazed. She appears to have her foot down hard on the brake. From the other side of the window, Jake is looking at her expectantly.

She leans forward and winds it down. 'Hi,' she says, in her best attempt at indifference, tossing her hair out of her eyes. Again, he's standing too close. 'Have you been for a walk?'

He nods. 'What are those?' he asks, grinning at her in that way he has. 'Your rose-tinted spectacles?'

Stella laughs. She's never thought of that. 'They might be.'

'And how does the world look from behind them?'

'Rosy.' She makes sure she meets his eye straight on. 'How do you think?'

There is a pause, during which he conducts a full and detailed examination of her face, as if he's about to draw it. 'Where are you off to, then?' he asks.

'Just driving.'

He looks past her into the car. 'Got room for a passenger?'

Without waiting for an answer, he is straightening up and making his way round to the other door. Stella is horrified. She doesn't want him in her car, doesn't want him anywhere near her. As he passes in front of it, she is seized with an urge to lean across and slam down the lock so he can't get in.

But it's too late. He's there, right inside, leaning in, his shoulders filling the space, hefting the detritus on the passenger seat – shoes, a book, several maps, bottles of water, an umbrella – to the back seat. 'It's so beautiful here,' he is saying. 'But that's not really the right word, is it? It's wilder than beautiful. More violent, more extreme.'

Stella sees that his hair is almost as black as hers, that the backs of his hands are speckled with paint, that he has at some point chipped one of his incisors, that the cuffs of his shirt are slightly frayed. He folds himself down to fit through the door, then stretches out his legs and feels about under the seat for the lever to push it back, saying something about how he came to a river he wasn't able to cross.

'Seatbelt,' she says, because she has to say something. He seems to bring out in her a curious pitch, the way a tuning-fork can only be heard when set against a table.

'All right, all right,' he mutters, as he reaches behind him, 'keep your hair on.'

Stella lets off the handbrake and they slide into movement. The road curves round a field filled with bent-necked cows, a huge beech tree, a sign for bed-and-breakfast. A car coming in the other direction makes Stella slow and steer more carefully.

'So,' he says.

She glances over at him, then back at the road. He is looking at her, his head on one side.

'What?' she says.

'Tell me things.'

'What things?'

'Everything. Anything.'

'What do you mean?' She jabs her glasses further up her nose.

'Er . . . how long have you been here? Let's start with that.'

'Are you always this nosy?'

'Yeah,' he is shifting about now, adjusting the headrest, opening and closing the glovebox, 'probably.'

Stella winds down the window with jerky movements, about to throw out the remains of her apple, which has turned brown and floury. 'Well—'

'Wait, wait.' He lays a hand on her arm. 'I'll eat that.'

'Really?' She jolts against him as they round a bend in the road.

'Yeah. Pass it over.' He takes the apple from her fingers, careful not to let it drop into the space between them, and she hears the scrunch as he sinks his teeth into it. It seems a strangely intimate thing for him to do, to press his mouth to where hers has been. 'So,' he says, through his mouthful, 'where were we?'

'You were interrogating me,' Stella says, 'and—'

'And you were being uncooperative.'

She smiles. 'That's right.'

'So, are you going to tell me how long you've been here?'

'No.'

'Why not?'

'I don't feel like it.'

'Why?'

'I don't know. I just don't.'

'You'd make a great spy, you know that? Do you ever give anything away?'

'No.'

'To anyone?'

'Not really.'

'Wow,' he murmurs, looking out at the passing scenery. 'A woman of mystery.'

The car mounts a hill, then begins running down an incline, freewheeling. Stella feels suddenly foolish. There isn't really a reason why she can't tell him how long she's been here. 'I've been here since February,' she says meekly.

He turns to her in his seat. 'And where were you before?'

'London.'

'Working in a hotel?'

'No. I was . . . I'm a radio producer.'

'Really?' He sounds surprised and has to take a moment to digest this piece of information. 'So . . . if you don't mind me asking — which you probably will — what the hell are you doing here?'

Stella looks over at him, eyes narrowed. 'What do you mean?'

'Well, you're a radio producer and you're cleaning toilets for a living.' Jake shrugs amiably as he devours the apple. 'How does that work?'

'Work?'

'I mean, are you not just a bit over-qualified? And why

here? This isn't exactly the kind of place you end up in by accident.'

'I don't really want to talk about it,' she says, checking her rear-view mirror. 'And anyway,' she counters, 'I could say the same thing to you. You were a film director, you said to Mrs Draper, and now—'

'A film director's assistant.'

'Whatever. How come you're painting windows?'

Jake scratches his head. 'I don't really want to talk about it,' he says, with a grin.

'Fair enough.' Stella indicates and swings into a left turn. 'We're quits, then.'

She drives him down a tree-lined track, at the end of which, stretched out between them and a steep, rocky incline, is a lake. The Lochans, she calls it. It is a silent place, hidden from the road by dense forest. If you didn't know it was there, you'd never find it. The water, sheer and glassy, is almost black with peat, the ground soft and layered with pine-needles, which have been pulled into neat, uniform directions by the water, like nails drawn by a magnet.

The sky is high and blue above them as they walk along the labyrinth of mesh-covered duckboards. Small, brown-winged birds arrow up, screeching, from the heather, as they pass. He asks her questions – more general questions – and, after a bit more wrangling, he gets out of her that she grew up in Edinburgh, that she likes working in radio, likes the idea of an invisible world out there, listening, that she's never been to Hong Kong, that she once trod on a sea-urchin in the South China Sea and had to sit in the sand for hours, tears running down her face, pulling out the spines, one by one.

He asks her what the phrase 'clearance cottage' means and the question makes her stop in her tracks ahead of him, turn round and stare at him. You really don't know what the clearances are, she says. She is wearing a blue T-shirt and as she gives him a lesson in Scottish history, he notices she keeps pulling at the neckline to knead at a point in her neck.

It fills him with a curious, dragging sympathy, seeing her press her knuckle to this sore spot in her body. It makes him want to reach out, take her hand away and put his where hers had been. He imagines her skin would be warm and taut under his touch and, as he listens to her talking about mass emigration, he finds himself wondering what kind of scent it would leave on his fingers.

When the hospital had relinquished Nina to the outside world again, their father carried her in from the car. Stella watched from the front window, saw her father hoist the blanket-swathed form into his arms and down the front path. She looked so much smaller than she used to.

Stella had been so excited about Nina coming home that she hadn't really thought about what it would be like when she did. She hadn't realised that Nina would still be ill. She'd imagined that everything would be like it used to be. But her parents tiptoed about, and instructed her to do the same. Her mother carried trays in and out of the sitting room, and Nina lay motionless on the sofa, looking out at the street.

Twice a day, Francesca lifted Nina to the floor and did the stretching exercises the physiotherapists set. These hurt

Nina so much they always made her cry; and Francesca, hating them as much as Nina did, cried too, but only when Nina couldn't see. Ever since Nina got ill, their mother had wept all the time – in the bath, in the kitchen with her back to the room, in the garden, in her bedroom, on the street when she and Stella met a kind, enquiring neighbour. But never in front of Nina. Stella kept tissues in her pockets to hand out to her mother whenever she needed them.

When Stella got back from school, she would turn the pages of books for Nina, sit with her while they watched TV, tell her what she'd done in class that day, and, once, when Nina asked her to, fetched the pair of shoes Nina had before she was ill. Stella had to rummage for ages at the back of their cupboard to find them.

'Here,' she whispered, because without saying anything they both understood that this was something they needed to do in secret, something difficult to explain to the mind of an adult, 'I found them.'

Stella placed the shoes on the blanket covering Nina. They were blue leather with punctured holes in the shapes of flowers, small brass buckles and a bar across the foot in the shape of a T. Francesca bought them both new shoes every spring, so these had had enough wear to hold the contours of Nina's feet, to be scuffed on the toe, to be eroded down on the heel, for the leather to be creased and scarred.

'Turn them over,' Nina said.

Stella pushed a hand into each, feeling the empty, inverted shape of her sister's feet, and turned them upside-down. She watched Nina's face as she examined the way the soles were smooth as pebbles, worn down by walking, by running, by the constant moving over pavements, over paths, over grass.

Stella turned them back and, as she did so, a trickle of sand emptied from the inside of one on to the blanket. She and Nina looked at it – a miniature sandcastle. Stella remembered that the day before Nina got ill, Granny Gilmore had taken them to the beach at Portobello and they had run together along the shore, trailing seaweed behind them like tails and their grandmother had shouted at them to watch out for the tide or the sea will ruin those shoes of yours.

Nina looked away, stared hard at the piled fabric of the sofa.

'Shall I take them away?' Stella asked.

Nina nodded.

The virus that Stella's sister caught, a virus so rare that medical books mentioned it only in passing, ate into her brain, making lace of her synapses, leaving her paralysed and immobile for months.

Nina had to learn again how to walk, write, climb stairs, swim, catch a ball, use cutlery, sit up, ride a bike, balance, skip, climb trees, hop, dance, stand, play the piano, feed herself, raise a cup to her lips, run, push buttons through fabric, dress herself, buckle her shoes, grip a pen or a fork or a knife in her fingers, butter bread, open jars, slide a key into a lock, brush her own teeth, comb her hair. Elementary stuff, but then most people only have to learn it once.

The school took one look at her – a shaking, stumbling,

ghost-faced girl – and decided they didn't want her back. They said she belonged in a place for the handicapped. In short, they wanted her to be someone else's problem. Francesca and Archie, uncharacteristically, argued about this with the education authority, the council, the school, the obstinate headmaster, their MP. At the start of the new school year, they maintained, their daughter would be well enough and able enough for her old primary school: they would make sure of it. They were not going to shut her away in an institution and forget about her. At this point, Francesca stopped crying. Just like that. And Stella was determined that nothing should ever make her cry again.

When the school were finally forced to re-enrol Nina, they put her back a year, in a class of children almost two years younger than her. This was Stella's class.

Everyone is wearing a new jumper, has a new pencil case or a new pen. They're going to start writing in ink this year. Stella can see the sharp, boxy creases in the boys' shop-fresh shirts, the reflection of the high windows in the polished, scratchless toes of her shoes. A few people look different after the long holiday – Lydia's skin is brown, her hair yellow (she was going to Florida on holiday, Stella remembers her telling them all last year) and Anthony Cusk is suddenly taller.

Stella glances across at her friend Rebecca. Rebecca is the girl Stella has sat next to since Primary One – her best friend. Stella hasn't seen her all summer. Rebecca is now sharing a desk with Felicity and the two of them are bent over something together. Stella lengthens her back, straining to see. A book? A comic? She can't make it out.

She can feel Nina next to her. Nina has her hands planted in her lap. Stella knows that this is so they won't shake. Nina is wearing the green gingham dress Stella wore last year and staring down at the surface of the desk, scarred with compass marks and ink spillages. Her hair has grown back, but in uneven tufts that make their mother bite her lip as she tries to brush it.

Miss Saunders claps her hands together at the front of the class. 'Now,' she cries, 'everyone!' She smiles at them in an unfocused way, looking over their heads at the back wall. 'We're going to be writing about What We Did in Our Summer Holidays this morning. But first I want you all to give a big welcome to Nina Gilmore.'

The sound of her name makes Nina jump, Stella notices. Her right leg starts to shake involuntarily and Stella sees her grip it with her hand, trying to still it.

'Nina has been very ill, in hospital, with brain damage,' Miss Saunders announces from the front, 'and has been off school for a whole year. So we're all very pleased to have her back and we'll all be giving her any help she needs, won't we?'

All faces swivel to look at them. Under the desk, Stella puts her hand over Nina's, feels the judder of unbiddable muscle and nerve, and presses down with all her might. The leg stops. Nina is trying not to cry, Stella sees, glaring down, her mouth pressed together. She grips her fingers. Don't cry, she wills, sending the message down her arm and into Nina's, please don't.

'Now,' Miss Saunders swings round to the blackboards, 'take out your jotters and on a new page, in nice, neat handwriting, write—'

Stella is distracted by Anthony Cusk turning round and staring at her. Or is it at Nina? She can't be sure. Her eyes flick back to Miss Saunders, trying to rejoin whatever it is she is telling them to do, but he is mouthing something now, his lips opening over his yellowish teeth. What is he saying? Stella tries not to look at him but she can't help it. He is mouthing something, pointing at Nina, then pointing at his temple. Stella recognises the word 'brain'.

She looks away, looks straight ahead of her. Has Nina seen? She can't be sure. Her sister is picking up her pen and starting to form letters in her uneven, jagged handwriting. Stella makes a grab for her own pen but she can't not slip one more glance at Anthony. Why is he saying that? He is making horrible faces now, twisting his features into grotesque, warped expressions, puffing out his bottom lip with his tongue. Miss Saunders is saying something about paragraphs and nice, clear sentences, and Stella is anxious because she's missed the whole explanation and doesn't know what it is she's supposed to be doing and hasn't had Miss Saunders as a teacher long enough to know if she'll get cross if Stella asks her to say it again and why is Anthony Cusk mouthing horrible things about her sister?

Something comes whizzing through the air and strikes Stella sharply on the cheek, making her jump and gasp. It falls to the floor. A balled-up piece of paper, torn from a jotter. The fact that Stella jumped has made Nina jump and her writing arm is shaking, her pen rattling against the desk, a repetitive, persistent noise in the concentrated quiet of the classroom.

Nina drops her pen and grips her arm with her other hand. People are turning round to look at them, and Stella sees Felicity glance at her, then turn away to whisper something in Rebecca's ear and a titter is passing through the room like a breeze.

'Quiet!' shrills Miss Saunders. 'All of you!' She glares round the class. Then she says, in a different, patient voice: 'Nina, do you need anything?'

At break-time, Nina walks next to her, her head bent. She doesn't see the girls from her old class staring at her across the playground, she doesn't see people pointing at her, urging others to look, she doesn't see people laughing behind their hands, she doesn't see Miranda turn quickly away. Stella sees it all, though. Nina walks like someone with their ankles tied together – uneven, lurching, tentative.

Behind the shelter, Stella's friends are playing Grandmother's Footsteps, Rebecca with her face to the green-slimed stone wall, the others in various stages behind her, frozen in position. Stella stops at the edge of their game, bending to yank at her knee-socks.

'OK,' Rebecca is saying, 'you take four scissor jumps!'

Felicity is on her second when she stops, legs splayed like blades. 'Do you want to play?' she calls to Stella.

Stella glances at her sister then back at her classmates who, she sees, are all regarding her with new, guarded expressions. 'Yes,' she says, clearing her throat. 'Yes, please.'

Felicity abandons her marker and crosses the yard

towards them, her hands on her hips. Stella watches her come, watches the bracelet on her wrist as it mirrors a bright sliver of sun, the way her eyes flutter half closed when they meet Stella's, the clean, shining bounce of her hair. She comes to a stop in front of them and looks from one to the other, thinking, considering. Then she opens her thin mouth, hardly at all but just enough to say, 'Well, you can play, but she can't.' And she points at Nina, her finger jabbing the air between them.

Fury flares up in Stella. 'If she's not playing then I'm not playing.'

'Fine.' Felicity flounces round, back to the game. 'See if we care.'

Stella turns to look at Rebecca. But Felicity is linking her arm through Rebecca's and the two of them are facing Stella. Even though Rebecca won't look up but stares down at the ground, her cheeks a scorching red, it is enough.

Stella takes Nina's hand. 'We didn't want to play anyway,' she mutters. 'Come on, Neen.' She turns, pulling her sister after her.

When Jake comes down to the hotel, dinner has been served and the guests are all on their coffee, the girl doing the washing-up tells him.

The monosyllabic chef bangs a plate of risotto in front of him and the girl finds him a fork. For a few minutes there is peace, as the three of them eat. The oven ticks as it cools, the dishwasher swish-swashes and rumbles, and Jake eats quickly. All this fresh air makes him starving. He is slightly dismayed to see no sign of Stella anywhere. He thinks about starting up a conversation, then decides against it. The chef scares him.

'God,' the girl exclaims, glancing at her watch, 'is she still on the phone?'

The chef shrugs and makes an unintelligible noise. He arranges another plate of food, Jake notices, with more care this time.

'She must be,' the girl answers her own question.

'Who?' Jake asks.

'Take this through, would you?' She hands Jake the plate and indicates the door to Reception. 'She'll be starving to death out there. Don't let Mrs D see you.'

Jake pushes the door and it opens, magically it seems to him, on Stella, sitting at a desk, saying 'Mmm . . . mmm,' into the phone. Her face lights up when she sees him – or perhaps it's just the food. She motions for him to put the plate out of sight behind a vase. Jake hands her the fork. He wonders if he should go back to the kitchen but something makes him want to stay.

'Maybe I could suggest . . .' she begins, but the voice at the other end of the line rises, querulous, insistent. 'I see,' Stella says, rolling her eyes at Jake. 'I see. Well, perhaps the answer would be to—'

Again she is interrupted. She pushes a forkful of risotto into her mouth and chews. She mimes someone chatting with her hand, then has to swallow hastily. 'As I said, there are no twin rooms available for that particular weekend. I do appreciate your problem. But perhaps—'

The man has more to say about his problem. Jake shifts from foot to foot, glances round the desk, at the stacks of brochures, price lists, the vase of outsized daisies, the way Stella's fingers are drumming on the cover of a large diary.

'Well, as long as your wife doesn't mind sleeping on a camp bed, then . . .' She shakes her head as the voice twitters on and on. 'If a double bed really is out of the question, then maybe I could suggest a—'

Divorce? Jake scribbles on a piece of paper and holds it up. Stella has to turn away and hold her hand over her mouth.

'OK. Fine.' The conversation finally seems to be winding up. 'No problem at all. Stella,' she says, 'my name's Stella. Thank you. Yes. Thanks so much. Goodbye, yes, 'bye.'

She slams down the phone and buries her face in her hands. 'Oh, God,' she groans, 'I don't want him here! He's evil! Can you imagine being married to him? Do you think the wife was in the background, listening to him telling a complete stranger that he could not, under any circumstances, sleep in the same bed as his wife, even for one night?'

'Maybe she was busy plotting her escape,' Jake says. 'Tying the bedsheets together. Or lacing his food with arsenic.'

'Let's hope.' Stella tucks into her risotto, ravenously. 'I'm starving. I thought I was going to expire from low blood sugar. Imagine if I'd died. The last thing I would have heard was his voice.'

'Asking you for a camp bed for his wife.'

Stella giggles. 'Marriage,' she says, and shudders.

Jake looks down, passing a hand through his hair. She has kicked off her shoes, he sees, her feet bare, her toenails painted the red of newly oxygenated blood. He imagines her doing it, crouched over in that caravan of hers, loading a brush with caramelising, liquid lacquer and daubing it on in careful, straight strokes.

She is eyeing him, her face puzzled, slightly suspicious. Has she seen him staring at her feet? Possibly.

'I can tell a lot about you from your feet,' he says quickly, so that she doesn't think he's a perverted foot-fetishist.

'Really?'

'You see this?' Jake crouches in front of her and points at her second toe. 'My mother's reflexologist boyfriend told me that—'

'Wait a minute,' she interrupts. 'Your mother has a reflexologist for a boyfriend?'

'Had.' Jake grins. 'Among others.'

'Oh.' He can see her making some mental adjustment about him or about his mother or something.

'Anyway,' he continues, still in a kneeling position, 'I can reveal to you that you have Roman ancestors.'

She laughs and he feels the movement of it on his face. He tries to stop himself from thinking that she is within arm's reach. If he wanted to, or dared to, he could raise himself up and kiss her, in one single, swift movement.

What was he saying? Jake tries to focus his mind. 'At some point . . .' he launches off again, uncertainly '. . . a relative of yours consorted with the enemy and—'

He breaks off because she is still laughing, more hysterically than is strictly necessary. 'What's so funny?'

'I have Roman ancestors? Well, thanks for letting me know.'

'You knew already?' he says, a bit crestfallen.

'Er, yeah.' She finishes her final mouthful and puts down her fork. 'My mother's name was Iannelli.'

'Ah.'

'Her parents emigrated here in the 1930s. She's a fully paid-up member of the Hyphenated People. And so am I.'

'The Hyphenated People?' Jake repeats, sitting back on his haunches.

'My mother's phrase. You know, Scottish-Italian. Anglo-Irish. British-Chinese or . . . or British-Asian or . . . whatever it is you are.'

'The Hyphenated People.' Jake tries it out. 'I like that.'

There is a pause. They stare at each other.

'So, tell me about my Roman feet, then,' she says abruptly.

'Well, Tang told me—'

'Tang?'

'The ex-boyfriend. One of.' As he says this, Jake is wondering how she might react if he touched her. Could he do it?

'He told me . . .' he begins, and then he does it. He sees his right hand reach out and curve around Stella's ankle, where veins pulse near to almost translucent skin. He sees a look of doubt, of panic almost, pass over her face and he's certain she's going to pull away. But she doesn't. She allows him to lift her foot to his knee. He feels the bones of it adjust and curve around his kneecap. Her skin is surprisingly warm under his hand.

'Tang told me,' he says again, and he's aware that his

voice sounds slightly different, slightly lower, 'that having second and third toes as long or longer than your big toe is a typically Roman trait.' Jake touches each toe, to demonstrate, feeling the hard surface of that scarlet varnish. 'And those dastardly centurions went about spreading their seed all over the world. Giving lots of people defective feet.'

'Defective?' She pounces on the word.

'Yeah. I'm afraid so. Having extra-long second toes makes you roll sideways on the balls of your feet, damaging, in the long term, the tendons and nerves.'

Stella is quiet for a moment. All he can think is that he has her ankle wedged between both of his palms.

'That's interesting,' she says, her head on one side. 'But obviously bollocks.'

Jake feigns outrage. 'How can you say that?'

'You're trying to tell me that a race of people who conquered a huge empire and had armies marching all over it on foot had congenital foot disorders?' She withdraws her foot and stands up, lifting her plate. 'It's bollocks,' she says again. 'And anyway,' she says, as she passes through into the kitchen, 'there's nothing wrong with my feet.'

Stella and Nina stand in the big assembly hall. Every morning the entire school comes in here and sits in cross-legged rows to sing hymns and watch the children in trouble being dragged to the front. But now it's empty – just their class waits in a snaking line, dressed in shorts and plimsolls, and Miss Saunders, in starch-white plimsolls herself, under her long, flowered skirt, is busy arranging a long line of rubber mats to lead them, one by one, to the gym-horse.

Stella likes the gym-horse. It's solid, packed with wiry hair, covered in leather worn smooth in patches. When you leap over it, just your hands come into contact with it, your feet vanish and, just for a split second, as you clear it and reach the other side, you can see what it would be like to be able to fly. Stella would like to put her arms round it and hug it.

Behind her comes the sound of stifled, snorting giggling. Stella strains her ears but doesn't turn round. She hears someone – Felicity? Emma? – whisper something about butterflies. Stella's mother sewed a patch in the shape of a butterfly on to her shorts after Stella climbed some railings she shouldn't have. Her mother brought the patch back from one of her days out shopping with Evie, and Stella loved it the moment she saw it – its wings are purple and orange and it has deep blue antennae. And now they are all laughing at it.

Stella doesn't care. She lifts her chin to show them she doesn't care. There is the sound of shuffling and more giggling behind her and there is a cold, clammy hand in contact with her arm and she is turning round to see that Anthony Cusk is pressing the flat of his hand to her skin.

Anthony turns round to the people behind him, brandishing his palm at them. 'Gilmore germs!' he shouts. They duck and shriek and dart away from his reach. They are playing their favourite game, a game that Anthony always instigates: a kind of tag with the supposed infection you got from touching either her or Nina.

Stella hates Anthony Cusk more than anything else in the universe. Her grandmother says that hate is a very strong word and that it's wrong to hate people, but Stella hates Anthony. She imagines her hate like a ball of black tar, lodged in her chest. Last week she went to the toilet during break and when she'd come back to the yard she'd found a circle of children around Nina, who was sprawled on the ground. Anthony Cusk had been pushing her back to the ground every time she tried to get up, with just his finger. It didn't take much to overbalance Nina – sometimes Stella thought the wind might blow her down. Stella had burst into the circle and smashed her hand into Anthony Cusk's face and it had hurt her knuckle and Anthony's nose bloomed roses that dripped petals to the floor, and Stella had been in trouble and had to go and sit outside the headmaster's office all afternoon.

'Nina, dear,' Miss Saunders is calling from her position beside the horse, 'you should probably sit this out.'

Stella watches her sister shuffle to the side of the room, almost unable to bear her being that far away from her, and Stella is alone in the line with laughing enemies on both sides.

'I'm not standing next to her,' someone says. Stella doesn't see who because she's staring down at the interlapped parquet that screeches if you rub your plimsoll along it. People are peeling away from the line around her, running round to the back, just so as not to stand near her, and suddenly she is stranded at the front of the queue.

'Come on, Stella,' Miss Saunders calls, 'you first. Stop messing about, you lot,' she says to the children behind her, who are jostling and fighting and laughing.

Stella sees the long runway of mats, laid end to end,

stretching to the hulking mass of the horse. She sees Miss Saunders with her arms held out, ready to help her over. She feels the back of the room, the crowd of their tormentors, fall away from her as she runs. Her legs move under her and she can hear the tugging crinkle of her clothes.

As the orange-brown flanks of the horse loom closer, something falters in her stomach. But she makes herself do it. She can't stop in her tracks, can't fail, not with those people behind her. She pushes herself up, springs forward, but as soon as her palms are pressed against the worn leather, she knows something is wrong. The floor wheels up too soon, too acutely and she feels herself dropping, feels the room twist around her and she is wondering if this is what it's like to be Nina when her forehead and shoulder hit the stinking rubber of the mat.

Miss Saunders is scolding her, saying she's done this lots of times and that she must get straight up and do it again, and her head is throbbing, pulsing with pain. She can hear far-off gales of laughter and Miss Saunders shouting at them to be quiet. Stella doesn't think she can do it again, doesn't want to do it again. She wants more than anything to be curled up somewhere dark and still, somewhere far away from here, because she just feels so tired, so unbelievably tired. She has to press her hands together to distract herself, stop herself crying and maybe Miss Saunders sees this because the next moment she is pulling her up by her arm and telling her to go and sit with Nina and, as Stella walks across the acres and acres of squeaking parquet, she touches the butterfly that Evie and Francesca chose for her, just once.

Jake doesn't see Stella for days. She's always out or having a day off or elsewhere in the hotel, doing the rooms or cleaning or seeing to difficult guests. Occasionally, Jake hears her tread, catches a few snatched syllables of her voice, sees her shape through an upper window, finds a piece of paper scored with her handwriting – a shopping list, a drinks order – but nothing more. If he goes in pursuit of her, he finds only empty corridors, deserted rooms, but with doors swinging shut, curtains moving in the breeze, as if she's always just out of reach.

It makes him impatient, he notices. He catches himself thinking about the red scarf she uses to tie her hair back, how she presses her teeth into her bottom lip when she's concentrating and the sound her shoes make when she walks. A girl from Aviemore does several evening shifts in a row and she slaps Jake's dinner on to a plate with a brusque swivel of her wrist.

He goes to the bothy most days. He walks the rooms, touching the door handles, the rusted window catches, the stone mantelpieces, looks up at the sky through the collapsed roof, gazes out of the windows. If he looks hard enough, he reckons, he should be able to memorise the view from each window. He wants to imprint himself with this place, with this dilapidated house, so he can remember it, keep a reserve of it, for a time when he's no longer here.

Jake is aware that coming here and being here aren't enough. Since arriving, he's realised that he carries within himself a lack, a vacuum, a vacancy. That he always has carried it, and always will. But if he feels it rising inside him, expanding like gas, he has to tell himself what he's gained by coming to Kildoune. Jake cannot get over the fact that he is living among people who have spoken to Tom, interacted with him, had contact with him, known him. Just by being here, Jake is at only one degree, one remove from his father. Whenever he feels that desolation, that lack threatening to engulf him, he has to remind himself of this.

The weather splits and cracks open, and the rain comes down. It is soft, feathering wet, not like the downpours in Hong Kong. This rain is almost invisible and seems to drift sideways. Jake has to leave painting Kildoune's windows for fairer weather. He digs the vegetable garden, taking the iron prongs of the fork to the dense clods of soil, ripping out the snaking, gripping weeds by their roots, driving in stakes for the peas to hook themselves round as they grow.

He gets filthy, his palms mapped out in dirt, his boots heavy with mud. But he likes the work, enjoys the heated sweat it brings, learns how a landscape that appears empty is, when you look from the corner of your eye, teeming – rab- bits, foxes, blackbirds, sheep, pheasant. The ground and the forest rustle and shiver with life. Sometimes Jake puts down his fork and looks round, thinking something or someone is there, but finds nothing, just bracken waving in the wind.

Stella pushes the head of the vacuum-cleaner around her in big, wide arches. She hums as she works and the virulent pattern of the hall carpet bristles and stands to attention under the suction. Two guests pass; the wife nods at her. She ate mushrooms and toast for breakfast, Stella thinks, drank two kirs last night, wears nylon slips and beside the bed has a book about how to time ovulation.

Suddenly, and without warning, the vacuum-cleaner cuts out, the dual pitch of its engine winding down into silence. Stella turns and looks at it, squat and round on the carpet, its neck held in her hands. She gives it an experimental kick – her usual method with wayward machinery – but nothing happens. She reaches down and shakes it. Still nothing.

Sighing and cursing under her breath, Stella follows the extension lead to where she's plugged it in. Maybe the plug's come loose from the socket. She's just about to turn in to the lounge when the vacuum starts up again, behind her.

Stella turns round and goes back. She has picked up the neck and has pushed it away from her once across the carpet, when it dies on her again. She throws it down, cross. 'What is the matter with you?' she demands, and stomps again towards the socket in the lounge. 'Stupid, useless thing,' she mutters.

Again, just as she reaches the door, it quivers into life. This time Stella stands motionless, her head cocked to one side. The sound of stifled laughter is coming from somewhere. She pushes at the door with her hand and moves into the room.

Jake is crouched by the socket and when he sees her says, 'Do you often talk to household appliances?'

She looks at him, amazed, her hands on her hips.

'Was that you doing that?' she asks. She hasn't seen him for days. She has, she half admits to herself now, been avoiding him.

'You should see the look on your face.' He collapses into laughter.

Infuriated, Stella seizes a cushion from a sofa. 'You

bastard,' she says, laughing herself now. 'You horrible, horrible man.'

She makes for him, across the room, the cushion held before her. She thinks of the satisfaction of those stuffed, packed feathers glancing off his shoulders, his head. But as she reaches him, he grabs at the cushion and wrenches it effortlessly from her grasp. She is left weaponless, unarmed, her hands empty. His shirt is half unbuttoned, she suddenly notices, loose, and he smells of the outside, of the rain earlier, wet leaves, the soil he's been digging, and there is something about the way he is looking at her that gives her the sensation he can see right into her.

Stella turns on her heel and crosses the room.

Pearl is in the kitchen, top-and-tailing gooseberries, when Stella bursts in.

'All right, hen?' Pearl says.

Stella makes a small noise but doesn't stop, running through the kitchen and out of the opposite door. Pearl hears her footsteps crunching away through the courtyard.

A micro-second later, the boy Jake appears. 'Did you see Stella?'

'When?'

'Just now.' Jake dashes to the window and peers out. 'Did she come through here? Which way did she go?'

Pearl examines him. He looks peculiar, a bit panicked, and has a cushion clutched in one hand. She points in the opposite direction to the one in which Stella had gone.

'Thanks,' Jake says, and vanishes.

Pearl brushes the minuscule sharp hairs from her fingers

and tips the fruit into a dish. 'Whatever next?' she says to the air, as she reaches for the ball of pastry.

But, dusting the rolling-pin with flour, she shakes her head. She knows exactly what comes next.

Jake is mowing the grass according to Mrs Draper's instructions – in even, level, contrary-motion strips – when the postvan crunches on the gravel. The postman doesn't get out, just hurls the bundle, held together by elastic bands, into the open doorway of the hotel. 'Post,' he yells at Jake, turning his van in an arc and disappearing off down the drive.

Jake switches off the lawnmower, the abrupt stop of the noise creating a momentary stasis. He walks over to the bundle, bends to pick it up and, stretching off the elastic bands, shuffles through it. Some catering magazines, mail-order uniform firms, one or two booking letters, a few for Mrs Draper, a couple of letters for Stella, redirected from an address in London, and a postcard. For Stella. Jake doesn't mean to read it but it's in huge, red capital letters: CALL ME OR DIE. Jake frowns. No name. No return address.

Leaving the rest of the post on the front desk, Jake sprints up the stairs two at a time. The landing is quiet. Sunlight lies in oblong patches on the carpet. He strains his ears, turning his head one way then the other. 'Stella?' he calls.

Nothing.

He walks towards the north turret. The rooms are all shut and silent. The corridor carpet moves under his feet. The severed heads of deer stare down at him from the walls; a stiffened, balding grouse stands, poised for flight, wired to a branch. Call me or die. Who on earth would send such a thing?

Where the corridor splits, turning off towards the laundry cupboard and more rooms or the steep staircase to the north turret, Jake stops. 'Stella?' he calls again.

Still nothing. He listens out for anything – footfalls, the whine of a vacuum-cleaner, the crack of bedsheets. Nothing. He is turning to go back the other way when he hears a noise, a shifting of the building, a creaking of a floorboard or a wainscot, nothing more. He turns back.

'Stella?' he calls. 'Is that you?' He climbs the last few steps towards the thick oak door and shoves at it with his shoulder.

The room is filled with a blazing white light, all the furniture and carpets and objects leached of colour and dimension. Jake instinctively brings a hand up to shade his eyes. He's never been in this room before. All the windows are open, the curtains writhing into the room. The sheets and counterpane and pillows have been ripped from the bed and thrown to the floor. Dead flowers are splayed, up-ended, in the bin. A fox crouches, glaring, in a glass box. Stella stands in the encircling curve of the turret, her back to him, looking out to the glen.

'Stella,' he says again.

She turns and blinks, as if surprised to see him. 'Hi, Jake,' she says. She touches the stone wall with one hand; the other is pressed to her neck.

They stare at each other for a moment across the bright, wrecked room. Jake can't think what it was he came here for. His mind is filled with the idea that she is there, in front of him, six paces from him. All he would have to do to reach her is step through the churned-up sheets and pillows and then he'd be standing next to her.

A cloud must be passing over the sun because the brightness of the room fades suddenly, acquiring dimension, depth. Objects around them rise up like images into photographic paper. Jake clears his throat. 'I brought up your post.' He is stepping through the mess of sheets and towels on the floor but when he nears her she has her hand out. He puts the letters into it and without them his fingers feel empty and stiff.

'Thanks,' she is saying and shuffles through them. Jake watches her face as she comes to the postcard. CALL ME OR DIE. Her eyes flick over the red ink, scored into the cream-white card, then to the address, written in a rounded disjointed hand, then back to the capital letters. She moves it to the back and looks instead at one of the forwarded letters. The second makes her grimace. 'Oh, God,' she says.

'What?'

She sighs as she lifts the envelope flap. 'It's just this—' She breaks off, scanning the closely spaced words on the page. She laughs, briefly, then moves to the bed and sits down. 'Oh, for God's sake,' she mutters, reading on.

'What is it?' Jake lowers himself next to her and lies back, his hands clasped behind his head. 'Bad news?'

'Not really. It's from this guy . . .'

'Your boyfriend?' Jake says this quick as a flash.

'No, no, this guy I used to work for.'

'Ah.' Jake stares at the four-poster canopy above him and tries not to smile.

'He wants to know if I'm coming back.' Stella gives a short, impatient sigh and shoves the pages back into their envelope. 'Can't be arsed to read it now.' She tosses the scrumpled envelope on to the bed between them and lies back. Jake grins to himself. The mattress bounces slightly as she comes to rest beside him.

'I'm really tired today,' she murmurs.

He glances down at the letters, then back at her. Her eyes are closed, her chin tilted towards the ceiling. He's never realised before how long her eyelashes are. He can see the rise and fall of her ribcage as she breathes, and the swell of her breasts beneath her uniform. He sees how close they are, lying together on this huge four-poster bed. He feels the magnitude of the house, the glen, the country around them. If he were to stretch out his arm, he could touch her brow, her cheek, her shoulder. It would be so easy, so natural. He imagines the heat of her mouth under his, the feel of those breasts crushed against him.

He reaches up and rubs his face instead. This is terrible. He wants to kiss her so badly. How would she react? Would it really be a good idea, under the circumstances?

Jake decides, in a split second, that he doesn't care. He doesn't care about the circumstances. He doesn't care whether it's a good idea. He doesn't care about anything at all. He just has this overwhelming, towering feeling that he should, he must, he has to kiss her right now, and that if he doesn't he might never get the chance again. He rests his hand on the bed between them to brace himself as he leans over.

Stella pulls herself upright, into a sitting position. She is humming, pushing her hair behind her ear. 'If I lie here any longer,' she is saying, 'I'm going to fall asleep.' She kicks her legs against the end of the bed, picking up her letters.

No, Jake wants to shout, no, come back. He rolls over on to his stomach, wanting to punch the bed, the pillows, anything. In the effort of not doing so, he accidentally emits a small moan.

Her head snaps round and she looks at him, a slight frown on her face. He has to say something, he has to. Otherwise she's going to think he's a weirdo. Quick. Say something. Anything. Anything at all. Something normal. Jake racks his brain for things to say but it only comes up with things like, kiss me, come here, I want you. For God's sake. Think, man, think.

'Who was the card from?' It comes out in a garbled rush, a burst of inspiration.

Luckily she has understood. She gives a short laugh. 'You saw it, then?'

'Sorry, I didn't mean to, I—'

'It's OK. It's kind of hard to miss.'

'Who's it from?' Jake asks again.

'My sister.'

'I didn't know you had a sister,' Jake says, mildly outraged by the omission of this information.

'Well.' She shrugs, unapologetic. 'I do.'

She gets up and starts unfolding the new sheets, her back to him. Jake raises his head to look at her. What did he do? He's got the distinct feeling that he's said something wrong. Stella has done that thing she does sometimes, and closed herself up like a fan.

'What's she like?'

She shrugs again, still facing away from him.

'Is she older or younger?'

'Older.'

'How much?'

'Two years.'

'What's she like?'

'I don't know.' She shakes out a sheet, which cracks against the air like a whip. 'She's . . . like herself. Any further questions? Or have you finished now?'

Jake gets up and wrestles the soft, swollen bulk of a pillow into a new case, stiff with washing. 'So . . . er . . . how come she's sending you death threats?'

Stella looks at him, the bed between them. 'It's a long story,' she says, and bends over to pick up the box of cleaning things, 'a very long story.' And she heads for the bathroom.

A rap on the door made Stella raise her head from the pillow. She tightened her arm round Sam's shoulder as she eased herself up, so as not to push him off the narrow, unyielding university-issue mattress. He was asleep, his face buried in her shoulder, his leg thrown across her ankles, pinning them to the bed.

'Who is it?' she called.

Suddenly, unbelievably, her sister was in the room, right there, standing beside the rust-stained washbasin, the lower half of her caught in a slanting beam of light, wearing a coat that had been Evie's. The lavender suede, Evie called it.

Stella stared at her, astonished. It seemed so unaccountable, so strange to see Nina here, in this context, in her London room that it took a moment for her brain to catch up, for her to convince herself that she wasn't imagining things. Nina here? It just didn't fit.

'Hi,' Nina said, and she looked round the box of a room, over the desk, the floor littered with clothes, the posters on the walls, the books lined up against the wall, toppled like dominoes, and down the length of Sam's naked, sleeping body, entwined with Stella's.

Stella watched, paralysed, as Nina took in the life Stella had made, away from her. 'What are you doing here?' she managed.

'I've left art college.'

'Left?' Stella struggled upright, easing her arm out from underneath Sam, who was stirring now and turning over.

'Dropped out.' Nina pointed at the body wedged into the bed. 'Who's he?'

'He's . . . er . . .'

Sam chose this moment to come fully to life. Realising someone was in the room with them, he thrashed around – an impossible thing to do in a single bed. He slid away from her, alarm filling his newly awakened eyes. Stella made a grab for him but she was too slow, and he fell to the floor with a thud.

'Fuck,' he said. 'Ow.' Then he looked up at Nina. 'Oh.'

'Hello,' she said, making no attempt to hide that she was having a good look at his naked form. 'I'm Nina. Stella's sister.'

She was even offering him her hand, for heaven's sake, when Stella leapt out of bed, dragging the sheet from the mattress and dropping it over him. 'Nina meet Sam, Sam meet Nina,' she gabbled, as she collected what clothes she could find on the floor and yanked them on. As Sam staggered upright, Nina sat down in the chair beside the desk.

'It's very nice to meet you,' Nina said. 'Stella didn't tell me she was . . .' Nina picked a hair off her coat '. . . seeing anyone.'

'Really?' Sam shot Stella a surprised look.

'I . . .' Stella began, 'I hadn't . . . had the chance . . . I . . .' She ground to a halt, stared at the ground and, seeing a used condom reclining, slug-like, beside a book, kicked it under the bed.

'She's so secretive,' Nina said. 'Don't you find, Sam?'

He was standing in the middle of the room, draped in a sheet like a Roman statue, his face unsure. Stella wanted one of them to leave. At that precise moment, she would have given anything for that. But him or her? She didn't know. All she knew was that both in the room together made her light-headed, dizzy, as if there wasn't enough oxygen in there for all three of them.

'Let's go and have breakfast,' she said.

They walked down the road, an awkward threesome. Sam, as usual, took her hand and Stella saw Nina looking sideways at this, and it made her feel uncomfortable because the only person she ever held hands with was Nina and here she was, walking along beside her, but holding hands with someone else. Stella, under the guise of scratching her nose, extracted her fingers from Sam's. Which made her feel so guilty she couldn't look him in the eye.

When they set out she was between them, but she found this position too oversignificant, too much. So as they passed the bus-stop, she skipped round to be next to Nina. But this made her see how, after almost eighteen years of walking along together, she and Nina were in perfect, rhythmic step, whereas Sam was hopelessly out of kilter, his feet hitting the pavement at irregular intervals between their precise, metronome strides. Which was bizarre because she could have sworn that when she and Sam walked together normally, they were in exact synchrony. How could that be?

The café was run by a Greek family, and cheap. When they arrived, there were several people Stella knew at a table and more chairs were brought, then another smaller table, so they could all eat together. Nina sat between two students from Stella's eighteenth-century seminar group. Two boys, Graham and Neil. Nina didn't order any food for herself but, as she regaled them with a story about a life-drawing class, she reached over, in turn, to take chips from their plates.

'. . . and he had the smallest, and I mean the smallest, cock you have ever seen . . .' she was saying, as Stella watched her pierce the perfect yellow eye of Neil's fried egg, yolk drooling out over the plate into the nest of chips. 'It was like this.' She held up the chip. 'No, wait,' she bit off the end, 'it was like this.'

They were bowled over by her, Stella could see, the two of them gazing at her as if they'd never seen such an exotic, wonderful creature. Stella saw the way she played them off against each other, taking food first from Graham's plate until he felt secure, assured, then turning to Neil and, after just the right amount of time, turning back.

'Hey, Stel,' Nina leant over the table and addressed her in Italian, 'you don't have that kind of problem with him, do you?' She jabbed the truncated chip in Sam's direction.

'What did she say?' Sam said, anxious, laying his hand on Stella's thigh.

'Nothing,' Stella muttered. 'Doesn't matter.'

'So you speak Italian?' Graham was saying, keen to get Nina's attention back.

'Yeah.' She looked at him, puzzled, then glanced over at Stella. 'Didn't she tell you?' She looked round them all. 'We speak Italian at home.'

'I didn't know that,' Graham said, looking from her to Stella as if they were interesting specimens. 'Did you, Sam?'

Sam had both his hands clutched around his empty mug. 'No,' he said. 'No, I didn't.'

Stella pushed back her chair with a scrape and went to the counter. She stared at the rows and rows of cans, the boxes of sauces in bright, full sachets, the heap of wooden forks, the stripes on the apron of the Greek woman. She would buy . . . something. Another cup of tea. Or a glass of water. Or some chocolate? She didn't know what she wanted. All she really wanted was to slip through the door of the café, start running and not look back. This collision of her worlds made her feel insubstantial, weakened, unsure of who she was supposed to be, how she was meant to behave. She had the sensation, when she got close to Nina, that her sister exuded a force like gravity, pulling her back to Edinburgh, to her parents' flat, to everything she thought she'd left behind.

Suddenly Sam was there beside her, his hand in the small of her back. 'Are you OK?'

His face was flushed, unsure, when she turned to face him. 'Yeah. I'm fine.'

'Your sister . . .' he began.

'What?'

'She's really . . .' he looked over at the table '. . . really weird . . . and mad.'

Stella closed her eyes and had a vision of herself hurtling down towards earth, like a skydiver, and laid out in front of her were two fields, in one of which was Sam, his head tilted back to watch her descent. In the other was Nina. Whose field would she choose to guide herself towards? There was no choice to make, of course. It would always be Nina.

'Don't say that.' Stella pulled away from him. 'Ever.'

Jake grips the pitchfork, hooks the chair through the rotted netting of its seat and heaves it to the top of the bonfire. The fire spits out a firmament of sparks, then claims the chair rapidly, flames curling round its structure.

He's clearing out the smallest barn. Mrs Draper has been down here all morning, a mac over her clothes, a handkerchief over her nose, directing him as he disentangled ancient Lloyd Loom chairs from the embraces they'd been in for years, disinterred collapsed chests of drawers, an old showerhead, stacks of mildewed and stinking curtains.

She ordered him to burn everything. The fire took a long

time to catch, smouldering at him sullenly, refusing to burn until Jake splashed it with paraffin, and it exploded, roaring, sucking at the air around it.

He's found a couple of treasures. An old storm lantern, which he thinks he might give to Stella for her night walks back to her caravan, and a bicycle, chain arthritic with rust and tyres flaccid, but it's a good one. It has an iron frame, a sprung saddle and solid, spoked wheels. There's something about it he likes, the way the wheels tick-tick when they move, the arch of the upright handlebars, like a pair of antlers, the bell still gripped to the metal.

With one eye on the fire, Jake rubs down the bicycle with an old rag, groom-style, and pumps up the tyres. He upturns it, working the pedals first one way, then the other, easing oil into the links of the chain, into any part where metal works against metal, the wheel whirring in space.

He is cycling round and round the yard in a circle when he hears a voice, close to his head.

'That belonged to the hippies, you know.' Pearl has appeared from nowhere, like a genie, her hands wrapped into her apron.

Jake puts a foot against the ground. 'The bike?'

'Uh-huh. Find it in the barn, did you?' She looks him up and down, as if considering buying him. 'There was one in particular used to ride it. All the time. Young guy. About your height, your colouring.'

She moves off towards the vegetable plot, vanishing as quickly as she came, leaving Jake staring after her.

When the bonfire has burned out, consumed itself to a smoking heap of ash, Jake rides his father's bike down the track. This simple act fills him with such unadulterated delight that he has to stop himself laughing out loud, or pounding his fist against the handlebars. This seat, these pedals, this rusted bell – all touched by Tom. He feels as though the single degree of separation between them has collapsed. He feels he never wants to get off it, never wants to be parted from it, that he'd like to just cycle off and never stop.

Jake has always wondered if it would have been easier if his father had abandoned them, moved on, run off with someone else. There would have been a clarity, a finality to it. He has never been able to get over the fact that his father doesn't know, that he has no inkling of there being an offspring of his out there in the world. Jake feels a kind of sympathy for him sometimes. He has always felt that he knows enough of Tom to be sure that Tom would have wanted to meet him, to see him. It's a peculiar cruelty that his father slipped out of their world, like Alice through the mirror. This bike is the closest he has ever got – the closest he'll probably ever get. And that, in itself, should be celebrated.

He passes some guests and has to turn the wheel to avoid a collision with them. He is always surprised to encounter guests, as if he forgets that's what Kildoune is for. They stare at him – a cinder-flecked man on a bicycle – as if he's dropped from Mars. Do you know who this bike belonged to, he wants to yell at them, do you have any idea?

He is thinking that there is something wrong with the steering, some imbalance, or that the handlebars are misaligned when he curves round a bend in the drive and suddenly Stella is there in front of him, next to a rhododendron weighty with red-black blossoms.

Jake squeezes the one and only brake. Nothing happens. He careens past her and comes to a stop only when the front wheel hits the ditch at the side of the drive. He topples over, into the wet bank of flowers, banging his forehead on a branch, crushing petals and leaves beneath him.

'Are you OK?' She sounds anxious, Jake is pleased to hear.

'Yeah.' He rubs his forehead, picking himself and the bike out of the ditch. 'I think so.'

'Where did you get that?'

She is dressed in jeans and a black sweater, and looks more as he imagines she does when she's not at the hotel – in that other life of hers to which Jake has no access.

'I found it.' Jake pulls burrs and twigs out of his clothes. 'And resurrected it.'

He grins at her, unspeakably delighted. She looks from him to the bike and back again, puzzled.

'Come for a ride,' he says, on impulse.

'Er, no, thanks. It's clearly not been a very successful resurrection.'

'Come on.' He reaches out and seizes her by the wrist. 'It's strong enough for two.'

She tries to pull away from him. 'There's no way you're getting me on that thing.'

Jake manoeuvres her round to the front of the bike. 'Jump up,' he says. 'It'll be like that film – what's it called?'

He sees her think about it, survey the bike, then relent.

'What film?' she says, as she levers herself up on to the handlebars.

Jake pushes off with his foot. 'You know, it's really famous. It's got Paul Newman and—' The bike wobbles and lurches to one side. Stella screams and leaps off, stumbling to her knees on the driveway.

'Sorry,' he says, concerned. 'Are you hurt?'

'No. But no thanks to you.'

'Let's try again.' He holds out his hand to her. 'Come on.'

She considers him and the bike, brushing off her knees. 'I'll sit at the back,' she says, 'on the pannier thingy. It looks safer. You set off and I'll jump on.'

'Will that work?'

'Yes. My sister and I used to do it all the time. Go on,' she motions with her hand, 'off you go.'

Jake presses the pedal and the bike cranks into motion. The rhododendrons shake their red fists at him and he hears Stella's footfalls crunching on the gravel and then he feels her weight hit the bike, which swerves slightly, but it's easy to keep the wheel steady and then her arms are passing round his body and he looks down to see her feet dangling over one side, skimming along above the ground.

'Whole families travel like this in China,' he says, directing his voice under his arm.

'Really?'

He seems to feel the vibration of her voice through her touch.

'Which way?' he asks, as they reach the top of the drive.

'Right . . . no, left.'

He pushes down on the pedals, hard, as the ground rises.

'Come on,' she says, and slaps him between the shoulders, 'put your back into it.'

They clear the slope and they are moving fast, past silver birches, horses behind a fence, a stone house where a woman is swinging a child round and round. Stella is shrieking and laughing, shouting about the brake, but all Jake is conscious of is her arms round him – the world they are rushing through is indistinct and blurred, as if the two of them are the only real, breathing, sensory beings within it.

He steers the bike along the curves of the grey road, but they seem to fly above it. A car passes, dragging at their hair and clothes, and Stella is saying something about the place she learnt to ride a bike for the first time and how she thought her uncle was still holding on to the saddle, but then she looked round and saw him standing, arms folded, a long way behind her and she was so shocked she fell off.

The road dips again and they are rushing down towards a wide stone bridge straddling a gully. As soon as he sees it he knows he wants to stand there with Stella, that it is the kind of place where things happen, where things begin. He wants to stand with the river below them and the sky above them, with her, on the bridge. Jake puts his foot down, feels the road scraping the underside of his sneaker, and grit flies up, clattering against the bike's machinery.

They come to an abrupt and unbalanced stop. Jake leans the bike against the bridge wall and peers over the edge.

Raging black water boils through striated rocks, whitening and frothing.

'My God,' he says, spray coating his face. 'What river is this, do you know?'

'The Feshie,' she mutters.

Jake turns to look at her and he sees that it's happened again. Her face is closed, set, her hands clenched together.

'Are you all right?'

'Of course.' She won't look at him.

He stares down again at the churning river. Its roar reaches up to them, bouncing off the gully's stone sides. 'It's amazing,' he says, hoping to draw her out of her mood. 'We could walk along it, if you like. There's a path.'

'No. I don't want to.' She sounds desperate, almost childlike.

'Really?'

'No.' She shakes her head. 'Let's go. Please.'

'OK.' Jake follows her, mystified, back to the bike.

'Anyway, so I said—' Francesca broke off and turned her head, listening. There was the sound of the front door opening, the draught excluder swishing against the tiles. 'Here come the silent twins. I'll tell you later.'

'Why do you call them that?' Evie ground her cigarette butt into a convenient teacup (a dreadful thing, garlanded with tartan bows and something that looked like sheaves of wheat – probably some clan heirloom from Archie's family).

'Sssh.' Francesca held a finger to her lips and twisted round in her seat. 'Hello!' she called.

Nina appeared around the kitchen door. She was looking better all the time, Evie thought, more colour in her cheeks, more flesh on her bones. She would never win any more gymnastic medals, but her balance and mobility were improving. She could almost pass for normal, Evie decided, if you didn't know.

She watched Nina embrace Francesca, then Nina moved to link those thin, wasted arms round Evie's neck. Evie pressed her cheek to Nina's head and inhaled. Evie loved the smell of children: not any children, just these two, she didn't like any others. They smelt of soap and air and innocence. There was a hint of school today – pencil shavings, floor polish, the blunt scent of ink – but she could still detect it. There was, she thought again, very little of the Gilmore in them. The Iannelli genes had emerged triumphant both times, especially in Stella.

Stella was lurking in the background, grave-faced. No kisses from her today. Evie surveyed her. Something was up. She could tell. She looked from Nina, seated now at the table with a glass of milk, to Stella and back again. There was something new about them, a kind of consciousness, an archness, as if they were pretending somehow, covering up. They were behaving not like schoolgirls but like two people acting being schoolgirls.

'Cesca, you're not still cutting their hair, are you?' she asked, raising a new cigarette to her lips.

Francesca nodded, her hand flying to Nina's curls, which were also beginning to look more normal.

'For crying out loud.' Evie touched the snipped ends of Stella's hair – an excuse to draw her close – and sparked her lighter. 'You two are going to have to come to the salon with me,' she said, cigarette gripped between her lips, 'are we agreed? Take your scissor-happy mother out of the equation.'

Stella gave a wan smile.

'How is the dread Miss Saunders?' Evie hugged Stella's body to hers. 'She's not still wearing those elastic-waisted skirts, is she?'

Nina nodded, not looking up from her milk.

'I still haven't recovered from the one she had on at the Christmas concert,' Evie continued, glancing from one sister to the other, 'the one with poodles on it. Remember?'

Nina nodded again, smiling now.

'Promise me something – both of you. Never wear dogs. Do you hear me? Our Miss Saunders should be arrested for fashion crimes against the young and impressionable, eh, Stella?' Evie turned to look at her, seeing for the first time that the buttons on her school shirt had been ripped away from the material, leaving ragged-edged holes. 'Darling, your shirt's torn,' she exclaimed.

'It's not, is it?' Francesca murmured. 'Oh, Stella, that's the third time this month.' Francesca started pulling the shirt over Stella's head. 'I've told you not to play those rough games. We can't afford a new uniform at the moment, you know that.'

'What's that, sweetie?' Evie pointed with the glowing tip of her cigarette at an aubergine-coloured bruise mottling Stella's inner wrist. She saw the two sisters exchange the briefest of glances and she saw Francesca, bending over the shirt, miss it.

'I fell,' Stella said, without looking at her.

'On to the inside of your wrist?'

'Uh-huh.'

Evie took a draw of her cigarette. 'Must have been quite a fall.'

'It was,' Nina jumped in. 'It . . . was.'

Evie blew the smoke out in rings for Nina, who usually liked to reach up and poke them with a teaspoon. But not today.

'Haven't you two got a letter for me?' Francesca was saying. 'Stella, this shirt is ruined.'

Again, Evie saw them look at each other, then away.

'How do you know about the letter?' Nina murmured, licking out her milk-smeared glass.

'Don't do that, it's disgusting.' Francesca took the glass from her and put it out of reach. 'I was on the phone to Rebecca's mother today and she said she'd had a letter about a school trip.'

'We don't want to go,' blurted Stella, standing in her vest and school skirt, one hand covering her bruise.

'Can I just see the letter, please?'

'We don't want to go.' Stella spoke with real terror in her voice. 'Don't make us go, please.'

'I would like to see the letter,' Francesca repeated, with infinite calm.

The letter was produced, after much scuffling about in the hallway, the unstrapping of satchels and frenzied whispering. Francesca put on her glasses to read it. Evie crossed and uncrossed her legs, reaching down to straighten the back seam of her stocking, thinking of the lover she would be meeting later, her latest conquest. A lawyer. Married, of course, but that was how she preferred them. That way they didn't start interfering and encroaching. She eyed Stella, who was sitting with her head bent over her undrunk milk.

'It sounds lovely,' Francesca said brightly. 'Wouldn't you like to go?'

No response. Stella gripped her glass between two hands, condensation radiating out from her fingers.

'"We will be staying in a residential teaching centre in Kincraig, Invernessshire,"' Francesca read aloud and Evie could see how, in another life, she might have made a teacher. '"The children will have an opportunity over the week to take part in a range of outdoor sports, including canoeing, hiking, orienteering—"'

'Sounds ghastly,' Evie barked. 'I'm with them, Cesca. Don't make them go.'

Stella remembers hearing her mother, a few days later, on the phone in her bedroom: 'Evie, you know I always appreciate your input . . . I know you love them . . . No, no, I don't think so . . .'

Even from where she was, loitering in the hall, noiseless in her socks, she could hear the tinny rattle of Evie trying to persuade her, trying to save them. But it was no use. When their mother made up her mind, there was no changing it.

'. . . Their teacher told Archie that they were having "integration difficulties" . . . That was the exact phrase . . . I don't know what else to do, Evie . . . You know what they're like. They've only ever had eyes for each other . . . The trip might help them to socialise a bit more . . . It's not normal, or healthy, the way they are . . . They'll have fun, I know they will.'

Near Loch Insh, they go over a bump in the road and the chain comes off the bicycle. They spend ages struggling with its oiled, slippery links, their fingers turning black. Jake is dogged, determined that he can mend it, and wrestles with it for three-quarters of an hour before he's ready to admit that they are not going to be able to repair it without tools. It is, Stella tells him, the last time she'll ever go out on a bike with him.

By the time they reach the hotel, dinner is over and everyone gone, the kitchen empty. Stella hadn't realised how late it had got.

'That was good,' Jake says, stretching. He shrugs off his jacket and the buttons rattle on the counter as he puts it down.

Stella stands at the sink, scrubbing the oil off her hands. 'Apart from the bike falling to pieces,' she says, 'and you being a stubborn bastard and us having to walk miles in the dark – yeah, it was great.'

'OK, apart from it being a disaster, it was good, you have to admit.'

'Do I?'

Jake is silent. Then he says, very softly, 'I had a really good time.'

Stella glances at him and sees that he is looking at her. She looks away, scrubs diligently at her fingernails. She feels light-headed and slightly crazed, stretched like a violin string. She doesn't know, cannot see what might happen next.

'Me too,' she attempts to say, but it comes out too loud. The surface of her, in the unnatural glare of the electric light, seems calm and even and white; but the blood, muscle, water and bone of her is blazing, acute.

'We should do it again another day.' He moves as if he's about to come round the sink towards her. 'When I've mended the bike. Don't you think?'

They stare at each other. Stella counts four thuds of her heart, so hard they are almost painful. 'That,' she forces, and her voice comes out as terribly formal, terribly Edinburgh, 'would be nice.'

Jake seems to hesitate, puzzled, examining her face. Whatever it is he sees there makes him cross his arms and look down. 'Right,' he says, reaching for his jacket. 'Well. I'll see you later, then.'

The kitchen door closes behind him, swinging back and forth. She listens to his footsteps recede down the corridor. Then she collapses on to the sink and clutches her head in her hands. 'Oh, God,' she says aloud, to the kitchen. Part of her wants to laugh, with relief that he's gone, that whatever it is between them has been put off, that she doesn't have to deal with it right this minute, but part of her wants to run after him. 'Oh, gggggodddd,' she groans, and, hearing the well of the sink repeating her word back to her, distorted and atonal, she giggles.

She straightens up and looks about the kitchen. Everything looks very stark and hyper-real: the row of knives above the chopping-board, the mixing-bowls fitted inside each other, the cluster of cafetières, a pile of laundered tea-towels, folded into squares, teacups stacked in a toppling tower. A plastic container of indeterminate vegetables lies beside the kettle, smothered in clingfilm. Without really knowing why, she picks it up and goes through into the storeroom. It is dark and moist and insulated. She doesn't snap on the light because she's just going to dump the box on the table and come straight back.

But suddenly Jake is there, right behind her, taking her by the arm and swinging her round. 'Nice?' he is saying. 'That would be *nice*?'

Stella is pushed up against the table-leg. In the soft dark she can just make out the side of his face – the curve of his brow, the indentation of his eye. His breath is hot on her cheek.

'OK.' She pretends to think for a moment. Her body is vibrating, ringing, like a glass played by a fingertip. 'Quite nice,' she manages.

He points at the plastic box. 'Put that down,' he says.

Stella shakes her head without really knowing why, clutching the box to her.

'Put it down,' he says again. And when she still won't, he takes it from her and places it on the table. He moves nearer again and because she is right up against the table there is nowhere for her to go and she can feel his stubble catching in her hair and it is almost more than she can bear.

'Maybe . . .' she begins, addressing the region of his torso. There is something snagging in a deep recess of her mind, a half-remembered thing, a reason why she shouldn't be doing this. 'Maybe . . . this isn't such a good idea . . . I think that . . .'

But with a swift movement his arms are round her

and his shoulder is pressed up against her face. There is really nowhere for her arms to go but round him and it is so simple, yet such a glorious relief, that she cannot think why they haven't stood like this before. She is sure there is something she wanted to say and she opens her lips to speak, but he leans forward and presses his mouth to hers and the kiss seems to explode into her, like the first gasp of air after a long dive. Stella clutches him to her in disbelief. He is filling his hands with her hair and she finds that he touches her as if he understands her skin's Braille.

Suddenly, a sound interrupts them. A loud, persistent shrilling. She knows he hears it too: there is a small jolt in his movements. But he carries on, pretending he's heard nothing, pretending it's not there.

'Jake,' she says.

'Mmm?'

She is arched against him, her fingers tangled in his clothes. She breathes in and the scent of him fills her body. She imagines the molecules of his particular smell pulled deep into her lungs and mingling and dissolving with the blood flowing through the alveoli, then rushed away into her system.

'That's the phone.'

In the dark, she sees his eyes lift, then close. His mouth meets hers again, silencing her.

'Jake,' she pulls away, 'we'd better answer it.'

He holds her to him tight, so tight she can barely draw breath. He is kissing her neck, one palm cupped round her cheek. 'No,' he says.

She runs her hands down his back, her legs twined round him. 'I think we should.'

'No,' he mumbles again, 'we're busy. Very, very busy.'

Something occurs to her and she stiffens. 'Jake, it might be Mrs Draper. She phones from the gate-lodge sometimes.'

He rests his forehead on hers and looks straight into her eyes. 'This may come as a surprise to you,' he says, 'but right now I don't care.'

The ringing continues, sharp, drilling. Jake laces his fingers, one by one, between each of hers. 'For God's sake,' he mutters.

There is another pause.

'It's going to disturb the guests, isn't it?' he says reluctantly.

Stella slides off the table, away from him, disentangling her limbs from his. He kisses her once, twice, three times before letting her go. 'Come back quick,' he calls after her. 'I haven't finished with you yet.'

Stella staggers through the blazing light of the kitchen, pulling her clothes straight, disoriented and giggling. 'If you stop now,' she is muttering at the phone, as she pushes through the door, 'I'm going to kill you.'

She lifts the receiver and the noise that has been dominating the past few minutes of her life stops. For a split second she is so relieved she forgets who she is and what she is doing.

'Um.' Then it comes back to her. 'Kildoune House Hotel, good evening, how may I help you?' Her voice sounds distinctly hysterical and joyous, she notices. Hopefully the person on the other end won't notice.

'Hi.' A female voice. Soft, hesitant. 'Is it possible to speak to Jake Kildoune?'

'Sure,' Stella says. 'I mean, yes.' Come on, get a grip. 'Who shall I say is calling?'

'It's his wife.'

Stella holds the phone away from her ear. The colours of the flowers in front of her seem very bright. She looks down and sees that someone has put all the brochures in the wrong place. They are stacked haphazardly on the shelf where the registration forms should be. She'll have to sort them out. At some point. Not right now, though. She places the receiver on the desk carefully, as if it's made of very fine, thin bone china.

She stands in the stark electric light of the kitchen. 'Jake,' she says. The single syllable of his name sounds explicit and very final, like the slamming of a door.

'Come here,' he shouts, from the storeroom.

'Jake,' she says again. There is a peculiar feeling in her solar plexus, as if it's filled with a heavy, damp gas. She rubs at her lips, her neck, her cheeks with the back of her hand.

'Come here now!'

'It's for you,' she says. She inhales. The air seems very cold. 'It's your wife.'

There is a long silence from the black oblong of the storeroom door. Then Jake appears in it, dishevelled, his hair standing on end, his shirt half hanging out, and one hand clamped to his forehead.

'Stella, listen . . .' His voice is low, appalled.

She drops her gaze to the floor. 'She's on the phone.

For you. In Reception.' She points. Then she remembers that he knows where Reception is. But she still says, 'Through there.'

Jake swears under his breath and steps towards her.

'Don't,' she says, 'just don't.'

He swears again, then bashes his way through the door to Reception. Stella ducks out into the corridor.

'Hello?' she hears him say, hurriedly, then call: 'Stella, wait a sec, would you, just wait.' Then, in a rush: 'Mel, hi, how are— Right . . . Good . . . Listen, can I call you back?' Mel presumably isn't very happy about this because the last thing Stella hears as she runs down the corridor is the electronic buzz of a voice.

She slips through the darkened shapes of furniture in the lounge and out of the French windows. The cold forces itself immediately between her skin and her clothes. She hurries away from the hotel in a straight line, without any sense of where she is going or why, stumbling down the bank and across the lawn. By the time she reaches the flower border, she is shivering convulsively and her teeth are rattling in her skull.

There's a wife? A wife? He's married? Stella clenches her fists. She has strict views about falling in love with married people – you just never do it, never even get close to it, never get embroiled. But him, this one, he doesn't behave like he's married. Not at all. So how was she supposed to tell? She feels edgy, close to tears, deflated, as if someone has skewered her through the chest. She bites her lip, willing herself not to cry. She has an urge to thump something. Really hard. Preferably Jake.

She hears the front door bang open and feet crunching through gravel. The pale of Jake's shirt streaks across the courtyard. 'Stella!' he calls. 'Stella?'

She steps behind a large stone urn. Jakes sprints towards the top of the bank.

'Stella?' he shouts into the dark. 'Are you there?'

She holds her breath, watching as Jake spins round and runs up the side of the hotel, in the direction of her caravan.

Stella turns towards the river, towards the loch, and presses her back to the stone urn, latticed with moss. She sinks down to her heels, huddling herself into a ball, and waits, her jaw set with fury.

They were wrong for this, Stella saw. All wrong. The other girls were dressed in identical outfits, as if they'd all agreed on it beforehand: a towelling tracksuit in some pale, sugary colour, white trainers and a matching backpack. Felicity's was marshmallow pink, Rebecca's sherbet yellow.

Both she and Nina were in the smocks Francesca had made from patterns she sent away for by post, cardigans knitted for them by Valeria and buckled shoes that clattered on the steps of the bus as Stella helped haul Nina aboard. Stella loved the brushed nap of her smock material, the twining pattern that Francesca had made sure met properly at the seams so as to continue without interruption. Nina's was a bit different, with less red in it. They had spent an hour leaning over the catalogue with Francesca, choosing which pattern they would have. That kind of decision their mother took very seriously. She'd said the red would bring out the green of Stella's eyes, and the green would bring out the red of Nina's hair. Stella had liked the inverted symmetry of the idea.

Everyone on the bus was getting out their lunchboxes. Miss Saunders hadn't said they could but she didn't seem to be telling anyone off. Even there, Stella saw by looking round, they were wrong. The girls around them had proper plastic boxes with a carrying handle and a matching flask, filled with crisps, chocolate and white sliced-bread sandwiches with the crusts lopped off. The box Nina was pulling from her bag was an old ice-cream tub from their grandparents' café – it had 'Iannelli Ices' scored into it in swirling script – which would, Stella knew, be filled with a flat, olive-studded ciabatta, some dried apricots and perhaps some of the almond biscuits her mother had made last night. Those she would give to Nina. She didn't like almond; her mother always forgot this. 'I can't remember which one of you dislikes what,' she said, if they complained.

Stella was just reaching down to her bag to get out her own identical box, when out of the corner of her eye, she saw Anthony Cusk coming down the aisle towards them. His crowd of friends was cheering him on. His hair was violent against the floury white of his skin, his eyes sunk deep into the pudge of his face. Stella hated everything about him – his large, fleshy-lobed ears, his clammy, bitten fingers, his pale, colourless lashes.

'Hello,' he said, in his nice voice, which made Stella quail. He was leaning on the back of Nina's seat and Nina was looking straight ahead, out of the window at the bare-topped mountains flashing by. Stella began to fear that letting Nina sit in the aisle had been a mistake, but they were quite close to Miss Saunders's seat so Stella had thought it would be all right.

'What do you want?' Stella hissed. 'Go away.'

'That's not very nice,' he said, leaning closer over her sister. 'I've just come to see how you are. How's the shaky girl getting on?'

Before Stella could do anything to stop him, he reached right over Nina, seized her by the wrist and started shaking her arm. It was a horrible parody of how Nina used to shake.

'Still shaking, I see,' he said, turning to receive and acknowledge the laughter of the rest of the class.

Nina's lunchbox and all its contents flew from her hand. Stella saw the foil-wrapped packet of biscuits skid across the bus floor, far out of reach.

'Let go of her!' Stella leapt up and gripped a handful of Anthony's hair and yanked. He yowled, still shaking Nina who was crying now. Stella tugged harder and she felt Anthony's other hand grab her round the throat and squeeze. The air was trapped in her neck like a cork in a bottle and everybody around them was watching and laughing. She felt her face going red, her lungs full and burning. In recent weeks, what Anthony did to her had been getting worse and worse. What started as taunts and the odd pinch on the arm had, ever since Stella made his nose bleed that time, become headlocks, arm twists, painful kicks in the shin, body-crushing thumps. She had begun to really fear him, to have nightmares about him, to shake if he came near them. She had no idea how far it might go, or where it might end.

Suddenly Miss Saunders was there, holding on to the ceiling rail.

'There's always trouble wherever you are, Anthony. Go back to your seat this minute!'

Stella felt his hand slide from her throat, felt the noise of laughter subside around her.

'Did you drop your lunch, Nina?' Miss Saunders was asking, in the low, melodious voice she always used when she talked to Nina, as if anything louder might injure her. Stella despised that voice. Why couldn't she talk to Nina properly?

Nina nodded, wiping at her tears with the back of her hand.

'Dear dear.' Miss Saunders picked up the Iannelli Ices box and put the half-eaten ciabatta back into it. 'Here you are. Would you like a tissue?'

'No, thank you,' she muttered, without looking up.

'What did she say?' Miss Saunders looked over her, at Stella. 'Would she like a tissue?'

'No,' Stella said. 'She wouldn't.'

The morning is grey and moist. Mist hangs heavy on the chimneys and turrets of Kildoune House, as if the clouds have given up and slumped, exhausted, to earth. The rooks exclaim and groan overhead.

Jake watches the brindled dog trot along the path with its funny sideways gait, distracted now and then by smells. When it sees Jake, standing by the edge of the forest, it flattens its ears to its head and bounds towards him, pushing the wet nub of its nose into his hand, yelping with pleasure at finding someone not only outdoors at this hour of the day but so obviously purposeless. It licks his fingers with a long, hot tongue and looks up at him with yellow eyes.

Jake runs his hand along its sleek body, feeling the rhythm of its ribs, its muscled torso, quivering with warmth. He is folding and unfolding the velvet of its ear when he sees Stella appear through the trees.

She is wearing wellingtons, her uniform held up away from the wet and dirt of the track, shoes clutched in her other hand. The dog gambols towards her, wriggling with pleasure, unable to contain itself at the idea of not one but two people out and about. Jake sees her bend, offer it a hand and murmur some words to it as she marches towards him.

Jake moves down the track to meet her. Her face is set, steely. 'I've been up for ages,' he begins, 'waiting to see you. I wasn't sure if—'

She sidesteps him. 'I know,' she says, without stopping. 'I heard you outside the caravan.'

'Oh.' He hurries after her. 'Right.'

She hasn't looked at him, hasn't lifted her face to his.

'Look, Stella,' Jake tries again, 'I tried to find you last night but—'

'I know,' she says again. She is walking fast, her wellingtons making an empty sucking sound. Jake strides behind her.

'Stella, please. Can you stop for a sec? We need to talk about this. I know I should have told you but—'

'Yeah,' she cuts across him, 'you should have.'

'It's not what it seems, I promise. If you'd just let me—'

'Piss off, Jake,' she snaps, increasing her speed.

'Listen.' He takes her hand, and his touch seems to startle her so much that she whips round.

Their eyes meet briefly and, as she snatches her hand out of his, Jake is appalled to see that she is on the verge of tears. She wheels away from him. Jake stays where he is, fixed to the spot. What has he done? How can he have let this happen?

He watches her shape, receding from him through the trees, and suddenly knows that he cannot let her leave his sight, that for her to go away from him now would cause such a rift, a scar in his life, that it might never heal over.

'Stella, please!' he shouts, and the forest seems to shift, to absorb his words. 'I can explain. Just listen to me, for two sentences. That's all I ask.'

She takes a step, then another step, then stops. She is standing, Jake sees, by the fork where the path splits in two, one half leading up to the bothy. Around them, the trees fill like lungs.

'One sentence,' she says, without turning round.

'One? OK. Done. One sentence.' He bites his lip, seven feet from her, thinking. 'It's meaningless,' he says. 'Meaningless.' His words come out with effort. 'I don't—'

'That was your one sentence!' she interrupts, walking on again. 'That was it!'

Jake ignores her. 'I don't love her,' he says, stumbling after her, 'and I never have. Do you hear me?'

Stella strides on. 'You married her, didn't you?' she retorts over her shoulder.

'I had no choice.' Jake breaks into a sprint. 'You have to believe me.'

Stella gives a short laugh, also starting to run. 'Oh, yeah, right. She forced you, did she? Very convincing, Jake. She—'

Jake and Stella burst out of the thicket of trees at the same moment. The light is very bright and Mrs Draper is standing in front of them, her arms folded and her high heels wobbling on the uneven stones.

'What on earth are you two doing?' She surveys them both, a frown strung over her face. 'Running a race? It's rather early in the day for that. I've been looking for you everywhere, Jake.'

Stella pulls her uniform straight and slips away towards the back door. Jake's body makes an involuntary move towards her, but he recalls himself in time.

Mrs Draper is watching him, eyebrows arched. 'Well, now,' she exclaims. 'I won't ask what's going on. No, I won't.'

There is a pause while she waits for Jake to speak. Which he doesn't. He rubs a hand over his face, watching Stella walk away.

'So,' she snaps. 'I have plans for you today, Jake. I want you to finish clearing out the barn, get rid of all the—'

'I thought I was helping St—' He stops. 'I mean, I thought I was doing the rooms today.'

'No. I want you to do some outdoor work. If that's all right with you,' she adds, pointedly.

Jake swallows. 'Yes. Of course.'

The centre was a cluster of pebble-dashed white buildings on a high piece of heathland. The land around it had been recently deforested, so all you could see from the window were the severed stalks of trees and a steep, forbidding shale-face of a mountain. Even indoors, the air rang with cold.

Stella turned back to their room, to where Nina was sitting on the lower bunk-bed, laying out her clothes. It had six bunks in it, but only two others were taken, by Fiona and Sally. Fiona was a large-limbed girl with eczema and Sally her mostly silent, small and stunted friend. Stella had often wondered if they were real friends, like she and Rebecca had been, or if they just put up with each other because it had fallen, in the great pairing-off that happens early among girls in the same class, that they had both been left without a partner.

Stella was trying not to think about how, if this trip had come a year ago, she would have been sharing a room with Rebecca and Felicity and all that lot, who had been planning midnight feasts all the way up on the coach – who would be invited, whose bed they would be held on, and who would be on look-out. She tried not to think about it at all.

Stella sat down next to Nina on the bed.

'Have you got them?' Nina whispered.

'Yes.' Stella pulled the teddy they had brought with them on to her lap. He had a doleful face, velvet paws and a belly that could be unzipped at the back, for the hiding of secret things. This morning, they had taken both of the brown-glass bottles of Nina's medication from where their mother had put them, in Nina's washbag, and pushed them into this soft, flannel-lined pouch. Stella eased them out, unscrewed the caps, which were childproof and needed an extra shove down before you twisted them, and was about to count out the right number (a pink one three times a day, two yellow ones twice a day, Stella had repeated it over and over in her head the night before as she lay awake) when Nina said: 'Let me do it. I want to do it.'

Stella hesitated. The last time Nina did it she was gripped, as she often was when it mattered most, by a violent spasm that sent the pills flying all over the room. Stella had had to get down on her hands and knees with her father to find them all again, rolled under the table, into the gaps between the floorboards, one in her mother's slipper.

Stella handed over the bottle and watched, nervous, as Nina tipped out the pills. Then she handed her the soda-water bottle Francesca had filled with water and watched her sister's throat constrict as she swallowed down the pills that smelt how Stella imagined gunpowder might.

'What's she doing?'

'Taking her medicine,' Stella answered, so quickly she wasn't sure if it was Fiona or Sally who had asked.

But Sally was watching them from her top bunk opposite, her elf-eyes narrowed, hands laced behind her head. It must have been her.

'I have to take medicine too,' Fiona said, with a shy smile. 'But Miss Saunders has got mine.'

'Oh,' Stella nodded, 'right.' Fiona's washbag stood on the floor between them, stuffed with medicinal-looking bottles.

Sally slid, snake-like, from her bed. 'I'm going to dinner,' she muttered.

Stella and Nina were the last in the queue. Stella took Nina's plates on her tray because she didn't think Nina could manage and she thought how upset she'd be if she dropped anything. She had to walk extra slow, so as not to drop them herself, putting one foot down in front of the other, following Nina, who was carrying their cutlery.

They sat down at the end of a table, leaving a gap of two seats between them and the other girls. But there was a flurry of tray-lifting, giggling, chairs scraping back, and they all left, moving to another table. Fiona was left behind, blinking, red-faced, then she picked up her tray and slunk away, without meeting their eyes.

'We don't want to catch anything, do we?' Stella heard Felicity say.

'You won't,' Stella shouted at her, half standing. 'She's better now!'

Nina was whispering behind her, 'Stella, don't. Don't, Stel, sit down.'

'If she's better,' Felicity met her gaze, calmly, 'how come she's taking medicine?'

Stella looked at Sally, weasel-featured Sally with skinny arms and mottled skin. She was sitting near Felicity, laughing but in a way that was wide-mouthed, too eager, too mirthless.

Stella turned and sat down again. She hooked and unhooked her feet round the chair legs and felt in her pocket for the stone Evie had picked up for her from their garden on Saturday. 'Keep this in your pocket at all times,'

Evie had said to her, as she handed it over. 'And if anyone is ever horrible to you at school, you hold it in your hand and think of me.'

Stella touched it now, the surface worn smooth by the sea, but she couldn't imagine Evie here in this bright-lit canteen that smelt of old food and too many people, she couldn't imagine it at all.

'I want to go home,' Nina muttered, across the table.

Stella thought for a moment about what reply she should give. Should she force cheerfulness? Say that everything was going to be fine? Say that she loved it here?

'So do I,' she said.

'Do you think if we phoned Mum, she'd come and get us?'

'No.'

'What about Dad?'

Stella thought about this. 'Mum wouldn't let him.'

'Evie?'

'I don't know,' Stella said, and she touched the stone again with her thumbprint. 'Maybe. Yes. She probably would.'

'But Mum would be cross with us.'

'Yes.'

At the front of the hall, Miss Saunders, in a blue tracksuit, was clapping her hands: 'In a minute, I want all of you in the main room, where we're going to talk about the orienteering trip tomorrow up the Feshie river. OK?'

Stella is attacking dirt with a vengeance, scouring bathtubs with bleach powder, vacuuming violently, stuffing the faces of the washing machines with soiled linen, sweeping dirty plates into foaming water.

'Heavens,' Pearl remarks, looking at her sideways, 'you're full of energy today.'

Stella doesn't answer, just starts scrubbing at a black hand-mark on the kettle. She's keeping away from Jake. It's a full-time occupation. She's made sure she's been out of the kitchen all day, up in the bedrooms, or in the games room or stocking the bar. She had to hide in a shower cubicle mid-morning, when he'd come upstairs to look for her. It's a perfect building for subterfuge and avoidance – lots of nooks and cupboards, secret stairways hidden behind drapes, rooms leading out of other rooms, trapdoors up into the attic – and she knows it much better than him, knows every route through it.

Late afternoon, she stands in the turreted room, looking down to where he is stacking the skeletons of old sofas, pollarded branches, broken chairs, on to the bier of a bonfire. She can catch the scorched scent of it, or is it just her imagination? The bonfire coughs and sparks and she sees him swat at his sleeve. An early midge? Or did a glowing cinder land on him? She looks at the curve of his neck, the shape of his shoulders as he stands, leaning on his pitchfork.

You should leave, she tells herself. It's time you were going. Or is it? She doesn't know if she can face life elsewhere. Doesn't know if she can shrink herself down to slot into it again. Could she? Can she see herself somewhere else, a city, working on a radio show? It doesn't seem like a life she once had, a life she could ever fit into. Stella doesn't know precisely what it was she came to do; all she knows is that she hasn't done it, it hasn't happened. Why should she let some man drive her away? Bugger him, she thinks, and turns away, trying to pretend that her heart doesn't feel fractured, sore.

That night, she finds a piece of paper folded and pushed under her door.

Stella
You're avoiding me, I know, and I have to say you're quite good at it. Where did you learn to be so devious?
I need to talk to you. If I don't get a chance to explain myself within the next few hours I may go mad. My sanity is in your hands. Come round to my pigpen. Now. Please.
Jake x

His writing isn't how she would have imagined it. She looks at the way he signs his name, the upward stroke of the *J* smaller than the *k*. The single kiss. Stella reads it through twice, then crushes it into a hard pellet and aims it into the rubbish.

A few minutes later she comes out of the bedroom and leans over the bin, looking at it. Then she pulls it out, unpicks it from its dense ball and irons it flat against the wall. She puts it into her pocket.

She is coming down the narrow, low-ceilinged corridor in the oldest part of the house, heading for the farthest room, where she has to do a change.

Suddenly, and without any warning, something leaps

out of a recess where a deerhead hangs impaled on the wallpaper and grabs hold of her. Stella lets out a shriek and falls sideways into an occasional table, sending a china vase flying to the floor. She is being held from behind, an arm firmly round her waist, and she recognises, if not Jake himself, then the scent of him, the density of his body.

She twists and kicks, struggling to free herself. 'What are you doing?' she shrieks. 'Let me go.'

She feels her feet leaving the ground and she is being lifted and carried in the opposite direction to the one she'd been going in.

'Jake,' she batters at his arm, really angry now, 'put me down!' She curls her fist and sends flailing punches behind her. 'Jake!'

'Stop shouting, will you?' he says, close to her ear, as they stagger their way through the corridor. The repeating pattern of the wallpaper slides past Stella's eyes, giddying her. 'You'll deafen me.'

They reach the door to the laundry cupboard, which Jake kicks open with his foot. Stella grips the door jamb as they pass through, hanging on to it, stopping them in their tracks.

'For God's sake,' Jake mutters, as he prises her fingers from the wood, 'you are actually the most bloody-minded woman in the world. Do you know that?' He manages to loosen her grasp and slams the door behind him before putting her down.

The second she is free, Stella launches herself forward, letting out an inarticulate growl, towards the door – and Jake. He catches her, pinning her wrists together with one hand and turning the key with the other.

'It's true what they say about fiery Italians,' he is saying, as he draws the key out of the lock. 'And fiery Celts. Jesus, what a mix.'

Stella thumps him, hard, on the arm. 'Let me out.'

'No.'

'Let me out!' she shouts, enraged.

He shakes his head.

'Give me the key, Jake.' She holds out her hand. 'Give it to me right now or – or I'll scream.'

'Scream away,' he says, 'there's no one around. Mrs Draper's at the cash and carry. Pearl's left for the day.' He slides the key deep into the front pocket of his trousers, right down by his groin. 'If you want this, come and get it.'

Stella kicks a pile of clean sheets, which topple to the floor. 'God,' she grinds her teeth, 'I hate you, I hate you, Jake Kil—'

'OK. Enough about that. I tried to talk to you like a civil human being but you weren't having that. I told you I was on the brink of insanity and you obviously didn't care. So. Desperate times call for desperate measures. This,' he waves his arm round the neat, pale stacks of towels, tablecloths, sheets, pillow cases, 'was my only option.'

Stella stands in front of him, her fists clenched. 'If you think that abducting me and imprisoning me in a laundry cupboard is going to make me forget what a spineless shit you are, I can't—'

Jake smiles at her. 'Spineless shit. I like that. Now listen—'

'No,' Stella says, stepping right up to him, 'you listen. I am not the kind of woman who does the married man thing, OK? And if you think for one minute that you have any chance of changing my mind about that, then—'

'She was dying, Stella.' He says this very quietly and very deliberately. She almost doesn't hear him, but the words reach her, stilling her voice in her throat. 'Right there in front of me.'

Stella frowns. At their close proximity, he can see the dark, liquid pupils of her eyes widen, like the aperture of a camera.

'What do you mean?'

Jake passes his hand through his hair. 'There was this . . . this thing . . . that happened . . . in Hong Kong. A few months ago. At Chinese New Year.' He breathes in then out again. He hasn't spoken to anyone about this for ages, and he's never had to describe it to anyone from the beginning. 'It might have been on the news over here, I don't know. It was—'

'The crush?' Stella says.

He looks at her. 'Yes. How did you—'

She takes a step away from him. 'I read about it in the newspapers.'

'Well.' He takes another deep breath. These words seem to be taking up more oxygen than normal ones. 'I was there and . . . she was there. Her friend, her best friend, died. Was killed, I mean. And Mel . . . Mel was very badly hurt. And she was lying there on this bed in Intensive Care and she said to me that . . .' Jake rubs his face with his palm '. . . it sounds so weird to just say it like this, but she said that she couldn't bear to die without . . . without marrying me.'

Stella eyes him. Is she wondering if he's telling the truth? He can't tell.

'So you married her,' she says.

'Yeah. That night. The whole thing was completely . . . surreal. I'd just been in this terrible, hellish . . . unbelievable thing, the kind of thing you can't even imagine happening, let alone happening to you, and I'd broken my arm and this girl I'd been seeing for a few months is dying and . . . and I knew I didn't love her but all these doctors were saying she wasn't going to last the night and—'

'But she did.'

'Yes.' Jake nods. 'She did. And there I was, married to this girl, this . . . this stranger, practically, and I brought her back here to her parents . . . which is why I'm here, in this country and . . .' he suddenly feels emptied out '. . . that's it. The whole story of . . . of my marriage. My so-called marriage.'

She doesn't say anything, still scanning his face. 'How is she now?' she asks finally.

'She's all right,' he says. 'Better. Much better. She'll be fine. I wanted to tell you this so you'd understand . . . so you'd see that I'm not . . .' he shakes his head, trying to work out what it is he wants to say '. . . I'm not the kind of person who would try it on with someone while I was married.'

'But you did,' she insists. 'You did exactly that.'

'Yes, I know, I—'

'While you were married to someone who was seriously ill.'

'Yes, yes.' Jake sighs. 'I know. And I can't tell you how

much I regret it.' Realising how that sounds, he falls over himself to add: 'Not telling you before, I mean. About my situation. I regret that. Not . . . not what happened.' He looks at her steadily. 'I don't regret that at all.'

Stella seems to have developed an intense interest in the carpet pattern.

'I'm not really married,' he insists. 'You have to see that. Not really. I mean I am, officially, legally or whatever, but I mean not in the sense that I have any kind of—'

'Does Mel know how you feel?' Stella interrupts him, her arms wrapped round her body like chains.

Jake presses his lips together, checked, silenced. Why is it women have an innate ability to cut to the chase? To sniff out the germ of a situation? How do they do it?

'Hmm,' he elects to play for a bit of time, 'not exactly. I mean—'

'Not exactly?' she demands.

'Er,' he decides to be straight, 'no. No, she doesn't.'

'Right.' Stella holds out her hand. 'The key. Give it to me.'

Jake doesn't move.

'Jake! Give me the fucking key.'

'No,' he says, a childish urge flooding him. 'I don't want to, I—'

'I don't give a damn what you want.' She springs at him again and Jake is momentarily stunned into immobility by the feeling of her breasts jouncing against him through the combined material of their clothes. 'You may not think you're married but if the person you're married to thinks you are, then you are.'

They tussle. Stella fights to put her hand down into his pocket, he holds her wrist away from it.

'You're probably right,' he says, feeling the heat coming off her, 'but—'

'There's no but about it,' she says. 'If you think I'm going to have anything to do with you while you have a wife, let alone a sick wife, then . . .' her fingers enter his pocket '. . . you must be mad.' He feels her hand sliding deep into his trousers and he groans involuntarily. She pulls out the key, triumphant, incensed. 'Pervert,' she spits.

'OK,' he says, as she shoves the key into the lock. 'OK. You're right. Of course you're right. I'll deal with it. I promise you. I'll talk to Mel.'

Her eyes flash as she looks at him. 'Don't do anything on my account.' The lock clicks and she yanks open the door. 'Pervert,' she says again, as she slips into the corridor.

As she comes towards him on the platform at Waverley Station, Jake thinks she must know something is wrong. She must.

But maybe not. She is waving at him, her hand high in the air, a wide smile on her face. She is clutching a magazine and her expression is lit up, hopeful. He feels the cruelty he is about to deal out twist inside him, like something he cannot digest.

He'd called her to say he needed to see her and would come down to Norfolk. But she had suggested a weekend in Edinburgh. She was feeling much stronger and could do with a change and Edinburgh was so lovely, they would have a really good time.

She throws her arms about his neck and is kissing him, on the mouth, on the cheeks, on the neck and he cannot put his arms round her, yet he can't not, and all the time she is marking him with traces of herself, her saliva, her lips. Jake has to stop himself flinching away.

They go to a café across a side road from the station and he buys her a coffee and a yellow triangle of shortbread, crusted with sugar. Petticoat shortbread they call it, she tells him, as she sips her coffee, looking round at the leaflets in a rack, the people going into the art gallery next door, a child drinking from a straw by the window.

'Mel,' Jake says. He has to get this over with but has no idea how to begin. How do you say something like this?

She puts down her cup. Looks at him. He sees her examine his face carefully, as if committing it to memory. An image of Stella flashes, unbidden, into his head. Stella cracking an egg with one hand into a basin of flour, her head bent in concentration. He's in Edinburgh. Stella's city.

Jake clasps his fingers together under the table. 'I wanted to see you today because—'

'We could go to the gallery later, if you want,' Mel blurts and Jake sees the tiniest flicker of panic cross her face like lightning. 'You'd like that, wouldn't you?'

'I have something I need—'

'Or the castle!' she exclaims, leaning to touch his arm. 'I haven't been there for years. That would be nice, wouldn't it?' She is almost pleading now, her face creased, as if she might cry.

'Mel, I can't marry you.' He says it very gently. He puts his hand on top of hers. He tells her he is sorry. Somewhere behind them, a waitress clatters cups on to a tray. A door bangs and two men breeze past them, saying something about a lost bus ticket.

She looks sideways and down, towards the empty chair at the table with them. 'But we're already married,' she says.

'I know.' He finds himself staring at the ring she has worn since that night in the hospital. He realises he has no idea where it came from. Someone, one of the nurses, perhaps, produced it from somewhere and he's never thought about it before. 'What I mean is,' he says, 'I can't be married to you.'

She eases her hand out from under his. Tears spring from her eyes almost instantly, as if they were already there, behind her lids, waiting. They spill down her cheeks and she wipes at them quickly with her napkin, her face turned away.

'Please, Mel,' Jake says, anguished. 'Please don't cry.'

He lifts the curtain of hair away from her face, presses his head to hers. She doesn't pull away. People are glancing over now, looking away, then pointing them out to their companions.

'I'm sorry,' he whispers. 'I never . . . I never meant for this to happen . . . for me to . . . to hurt you like this. It just—'

'Can I ask you something?' Her voice shakes slightly.

'Of course. Anything.' He sees that she is clenching her hands together, nails pressing into the flesh around the knuckles.

'Do you . . .' tears start flooding down her face and

she scrubs at them angrily with a sodden napkin '. . . did you . . .' she gets out '. . . did you love me?'

Jake is silent. This conversation eddies and churns around him like dangerous water. What should he say? He knows that truth isn't always the best thing. But is it better in this circumstance than a lie or a half-lie? He has no idea.

'Did you? I need to know.' She gives him a small, brave smile through her tears.

Jake stares down at the fake teak of the table surface. 'I did,' he says carefully, 'at the beginning. Or at least I thought I could.' He looks at her, into her reddened eyes, at her streaked face, and sees that she is trembling with the effort of not sobbing. 'The thing was, it was all still so new and recent by the time we . . . by Chinese New Year. It was such a massive thing to happen to us that it . . . it kind of made it . . .' Jake grinds to a halt. 'It's not that I feel nothing for you and it's not that I regret what . . . what we did that night. I mean, I would do the same again if . . . if . . .'

'If I was dying in a hospital bed,' she supplies. 'Thanks a lot.'

'No,' he says. 'No, no. It's not that. Mel, you mustn't ever think that I did what I did out of pity or . . . or—'

'What are you going to do now?' She is sitting back in her chair, looking at him with narrowed eyes, toying with the tissue, ripping it into shreds.

'What? This afternoon?'

'I mean now in general. Are you going back to Hong Kong?'

'No. I'll go back up to—'

'This hotel place?'

'Yes.'

There is a silence. She is staring at him, raking his face, her mind churning over. Jake is puzzled. As well as discomfited by this sudden change in her.

'Why do you—'

'You've met someone else,' she says. The sentence comes out with a peculiar precision.

Again, Stella makes an unwarranted appearance in his mind – the way she tugs her fingers through the ends of her hair.

'No,' he lies, 'no, not at all.'

'You have.'

'I haven't.'

'You have.' Mel leans over the table, her face contorted with grief. 'It's that girl who answered the phone, isn't it? I can see it. It's written all over your face. You . . . you shit.'

He doesn't see her draw back her arm. All he's aware of is her hand cracking against his face, his head jerking sideways on his neck and a screaming ache in his cheek.

'Jesus, Mel,' he says, bending over the pain, his fingers pressed to his face, and he's amazed at how mild his voice sounds, 'what did you do that for?' He pushes his tongue round his mouth, feeling for loose teeth. Nothing. But when he looks at his fingers, he sees they are touched with blood. She must have caught him with one of her rings.

'You're a shit,' she bursts out, 'a complete and utter shit. All that – that crap you gave me about wanting to see Scotland and all the time you were just on the look-out for—' Mel stands up so quickly her chair crashes to the ground behind her.

'No, no,' he tries to protest, but his mouth feels numb and rubbery.

She whisks her coat off the back of a chair and slams her way out of the café, leaving Jake standing at the table, clutching his face.

Stella is up on the battlements, lying on her stomach in the lee of a chimney-stack. There's a fire-escape that leads here through the attic and up a ladder. No one ever comes apart from her. She loves the jagged teeth of the crenellations, the way the lead warms up in the sun, the way the breeze that snaps and cracks the saltire flag above her can't reach her if she lies low, how everything on the ground – the cars parked in rows along the hotel, the people walking away from them, Pearl making her way across the lawn – looks tiny and miniature as if she could reach down and pick them up in her hand.

It's late afternoon, almost time for her shift, almost time for Jake to be back. But maybe not. Maybe he'll need to stay longer. Maybe he'll decide—

Stella turns resolutely back to her book, reads through a paragraph. Stops. Goes back, reads it again, and then again. She fingers the note from Jake she found that morning, slid into the pocket of the apron she always wears for breakfast, which she is using as a bookmark. She doesn't need to look at it again. She knows it by heart: *Gone to meet Mel. I'll be back tonight. Get ready.*

She closes the book with a slap and sighs. She can't stop thinking about him. Not in any constructive, intelligent, coherent way. But whatever she is doing or supposed to be thinking about, her mind slips sideways and just repeats *Jake, Jake* to her, over and over again. She's never fallen for anyone the way she has fallen for him. It's almost like a disease, an altered, weakened condition. He deprives her of herself, makes her exist in a kind of stupor, a daze, a state of Jakeness.

It's ridiculous, Stella decides. How can it have happened so quickly? How can it have reduced her to such mindless idiocy? This has never happened before. It shouldn't be allowed, she thinks, as she hears the drone of a car in the distance. A taxi, perhaps? From the station?

Stella scrambles to her feet and leans against a battle-ment, looking out along the line of trees where the car will appear. The engine whines on and Stella thinks she catches a flash of red through the trunks but can't be sure. It's Jake, her mind is telling her, it's him, he's here. Is she ready? She doesn't know. Ready for what?

Then the car bursts out into the light, travelling fast, a little too fast for the curves of the track. It sprays grit in its wake. Stella knows the car, recognises it, but it takes her Jake-confused mind a few seconds to catch up. There is a single person in it, sitting at the wheel.

Stella blinks and thinks for a moment how easy it is to shut out the world with your eyelids. She looks down to the ground and it seems miles and miles away, as if she's looking at a satellite image of another planet.

It was inevitable this would happen, she sees that now.

Inevitable. But she'd thought herself safe here, hidden from the world, she thought that nothing could touch her if she cloistered herself away. She turns and sinks to her knees, crouching behind the battlements.

Jake hurries down the back steps. It would be quicker through the lobby but he knows Mrs Draper doesn't like staff using it as a short-cut. It's still early, just before six. Stella will be in the kitchen, preparing whatever vegetables the chef needs that night. He can catch her alone. Maybe drag her into the storeroom again.

Jake bursts into the kitchen, grinning to himself, which makes his injured mouth throb and hammer but doesn't stop him grinning. OK, he doesn't exactly have divorce papers to show her but surely the fact that they—

He stops short. There, in front of him, is a smaller, sharper-faced Stella, looking at him with the dead flicker of non-recognition.

'Jake, hi.'

He looks to his right and sees Stella, the real Stella, his Stella, standing behind the counter. There is something suppressed or agitated about her face, the expression taut, the colour high. She is gesturing to the woman. 'Jake, this is my sister. Nina.'

He doesn't really look at Nina as she takes him by the hand. No one speaks for a few seconds.

Then Nina says, 'I'm visiting.'

Jake nods. There is something strange in the air between the sisters, something close and secret, like the inaudible screech of a bat, something as fine and brittle and twisted as spun sugar. He almost wants to put his nose in the air and sniff to ascertain, seek out its smell.

'Just for tonight. Although,' she turns to look at Stella, 'I might stay longer. Haven't decided yet.'

'Don't you need to get back for work?' Stella says stiffly. Her hand, resting on the counter, is curled into a fist, he notices.

'No.' Nina smiles and takes in Jake, from his feet all the way to his face. 'The joys of freelancing. What do you do here?'

'I . . . um . . . Lots of different things. Maintenance, digging the garden, that kind of thing. Stella?'

'All sounds very manly,' she is saying, as Stella lifts her eyes to his.

'Have you got a minute?' Jake feels he might very easily burst if he doesn't get to talk to her, alone, right now.

'Er,' Stella looks at her watch, then looks back at Nina. 'I think so. I just need to—'

At that moment, the chef bangs open the door. He looks round them all, one by one.

'The fuck's going on here?' he growls. 'Some kind of party?'

They scatter out of his way as he walks through the kitchen.

'Nice for you if you can stand about chatting but we've got eighteen for dinner tonight and if those veg aren't in the roasting tin in, let's say, ten seconds there's going to be trouble. And you two,' he jabs a ladle towards Jake first, then Nina, 'can get lost. I don't know what you think you're doing in my kitchen, this time of night.' He glares at Nina. 'I don't even know you.'

Stella rolls her eyes. 'All right, all right. Jake,' she turns to him and he has to stop himself reaching out to touch her, 'could you show Nina where the caravan is? Neen, I'll come and see you if I get a chance, otherwise I'll be off around ten-ish, I've got to . . .' She trails away, gazing at Jake, her brow creased. 'What happened to your face?'

He shrugs and grins. 'Tell you later.'

'My God,' Nina says, as they step out of the back door, rummaging for something in her bag, 'is he always that charming?'

'Who?'

'The chef.'

'Oh. The chef. Yeah,' Jake says. 'Pretty much.'

As they walk through the yard, Nina puts a cigarette to her lips. At the start of the track into the woods, she stops, as if waiting for something. She looks at him, fixes him with those oddly familiar eyes. 'Do you have a light?' she asks.

'No.'

She rummages again in her bag and brings out a box of matches. She leans away from the breeze as she strikes one. 'Big place,' she says, cradling the flame in her cupped palms. 'Very chi-chi.'

'Yeah. It is.'

'Have you been here long?'

'Couple of weeks.'

'Not as long as Stella, then.'

'No.' Jake points. 'The caravan's just this way. I'll show you — you can't see it from here.'

They set off again, Nina shaking out her match and flinging it into the moss-draped stones. As they walk along together, Jake notices that she moves in a strangely emphatic way, like someone who's learnt to do it by following diagrams in a book.

'Which way is the river?' she asks suddenly.

'Er . . .' Jake has to think about this for a moment. 'That way.' He points beyond the caravan.

Nina takes a deep drag on her cigarette. 'How far?'

'Half a mile or so. Maybe less.'

This information makes her shake her head.

'You know the area?' Jake asks.

'Kind of. No.'

'Kind of no?'

She gives a short laugh. 'Kind of yes.'

There is a pause. Jake waits for her to elucidate. He doesn't know why but he gets the sensation that he is brushing close to something he's wanted to know for a long time.

'We were here once before,' she says, and Jake finds that he is listening to every syllable, afraid he might miss something. But as she says this she seems to pull herself straighter, toss back her head, as if shrugging something off. 'I've just had a big row with my husband,' she confides instead.

'Oh.' Jake is surprised by this admission. Then he laughs. 'So have I, actually. Except not my husband, obviously, my . . . um . . .'

'Wife?' Nina supplies, turning to him.

It is a very simple scenario, almost like the start of a fairytale.

Two sisters are walking beside a river. They are hand in hand, in matching dresses. The path is winding, embracing the curves and bends of the river. The river is dark, deep and fast moving. There are signs, as they walk, that the river has been higher, swollen by flood, swallowing up the verge and the path. But at the moment they are able to walk along, holding on to each other's hands.

The wood breathes and sighs around them. They have been left behind, far behind, by the people they set out with. The taller sister, who's not in fact the elder, helps the smaller sister as the ground becomes steeper, rockier, looser beneath their feet. They don't know exactly what lies ahead, but they are beginning to guess. There is a dimmed roar, a muted thunder, and the water pools out on the far side, fathomless, dangerous.

The taller, younger sister picks up a stone, pulls back her arm and tosses it in an arc into the river. The waters accept it with a gulp.

'Did you hear that?' she says, without looking round.

'What?'

'An echo. Listen.' She bends down for another stone but this time the stone flies further from her hand and hits the deep, slow-moving current on the far side and the river swallows it without a sound.

Not far away, at some parallel point in history, the same sister is in a hot, steam-filled kitchen, slicing carrots along their cortexes and tipping them into a steel dish. She leans up and away from the cutting-board, wiping the inside of her wrist against her forehead just as the other sister is knocking on the low, wooden door of an old pigpen, a stolen bottle of vodka clasped in her hand.

Jake had been so sure it would be Stella at the door that the sister's face is, again, a shock.

'Oh,' he says, stopping in his tracks. She is so strangely like yet unlike Stella. 'Hello.'

'Hi.' She flashes her teeth at him.

'Did you . . . could you not find the caravan?'

'Yeah.' She nods. 'I found it.'

'Right.'

'What are you up to?' she asks, trying to see past him into his room.

'Me?' Jake begins to feel alarmed. What is she doing here? Didn't he just say goodbye to her? 'Not much. You know. Well, actually, I was waiting for—'

'Mind if I come in?'

'Er . . . the thing is—'

'I don't like that caravan much. A bit spooky.'

'Yes.'

'That funny wood.' She shivers, Stella's sister, on his doorstep. 'Don't know how Stella stands it. I'll just come and sit with you for a bit. If you don't mind.'

The thought that he would be refusing Stella's sister company if he were to say no registers in his mind. What would Stella say about that? 'OK,' he relents. 'Sure.'

He steps aside and Nina enters his room, walks to the bed, sits down and kicks off her shoes. 'I brought this,' she says, holding up a bottle swinging with clear liquid.

Stella drops a tray of glasses on her way across the dining room. She's not sure why. It just seems to slide from her grasp, as if she hasn't got it balanced properly, as if one of her arms is weaker than the other.

The glasses splinter and fragment on impact into thousands of tiny blades. She has to get a dustpan and sweep round disapproving feet, then carry the whole crunching, lethal bouquet to the kitchen.

It seems odd to her, this transformation. Two minutes ago they were wine glasses and now they are slivers of clear glass, to be wrapped and wadded in newspaper and thrown away.

'The thing about Richard is,' Nina is saying to him, leaning close and touching his shoulder with the hand that carries a burning cigarette. Jake doesn't like cigarettes. Why is he letting her smoke in his room? He doesn't remember her asking.

'What was I saying?' she says, looking at him intently. She seems very close to him, curled up on his bed. He can smell the nicotine and vodka coming off her.

'Richard,' Jake reminds her. He should stand up. It's very stuffy in here. Maybe he should open the door, get some air in. He struggles away from her, to the edge of the bed. Without the prop of his shoulder, Nina falls forward on to the mattress. She giggles.

Jake hoists himself upright and it is only then that he realises how drunk he is. The pigpen tips and veers around him and his head feels thick and clogged. How can he be drunk? He looks round at the vodka bottle on his bedside table, puzzled. Still half full. Then he remembers the joints Nina had rolled. How many of them were there? She'd been asking him about Mel, all the while crumbling the resin into beds of tobacco. It was stronger than he's used to, he remembers thinking at the time, much stronger.

Isn't glass made from sand? Stella thinks, as she takes down the dessert order for a family from Glasgow. Another weird transformation, that. She breathes in deeply and tries to focus on what the woman at the table is saying to her – something about a dairy allergy. Keep it together, she tells herself, just for now.

He seems to be back on the bed. His head is sunk into a pillow, at any rate, and that appears to be the ceiling above him. Nina's voice goes on and on, like a river. She's talking about her job, about the people she works with, the patients she visits, how weird it is to be back here, how it all looks just the same, and in between there is a lot of stuff about her flat.

Jake wants nothing more than to go to sleep. His face aches dully where Mel hit him. His mind keeps sliding towards drowsiness and just as he is about to drop off, each time, something pulls him back. Some corner of him is aware that there was something important he had to do. Something very important. But right at this moment, he cannot quite recall what it was. All he knows is that it's stopping him sleeping.

Stella is running through a wood at night, the cone of a

torch-beam bobbing and arching around her. She knows the way, but it still scares her.

The caravan had been empty, cold, the lights off. She rounds the grey bulk of the hotel, coming into the car park. Has she left, gone without telling her? No. Nina's car is still there.

Stella turns. Where can she be? She can't be in the hotel because Stella's just come from there. Did she go for a walk? But Nina would never be out at this time of night in the middle of nowhere on her own – she hates the dark.

Stella wants to shout her name at the top of her voice. How could she just disappear on her like this? She's been avoiding her sister for months but right at this moment she would give anything to have her here, next to her.

She has to be somewhere, Stella reasons with herself. She walks round to the other side of the hotel, past the patio, past the pot plants and up towards the barn. The air is full of minuscule circling insects, which adhere to her face, her hair, her hands. She is still walking when she sees the pigpen, the single window with the curtains drawn, the frame of light round the door. Stella stops.

She clasps and unclasps her hands, thinking. Then she tiptoes slowly, slowly up to the door and presses her ear to the grain of the wood.

At first she hears nothing. Just the muted roar of blood in her veins, like the sea trapped in a shell. She is cold, she realises, with just the cotton of her uniform between her and the night air. She'll go back to the caravan and get a cardigan. Then she hears something – a shift, a movement, like fabric against skin. And a sudden drawing-in of air, a quick sigh or an exclamation or a gasp.

Stella flinches away from the door. She turns and walks, ten maybe eleven paces. Then she starts to run, her hands over her ears, stumbling every few steps.

If you share a room with someone for eighteen years, you can recognise every cry, every movement, every breath, every sigh they make. That was her sister. Without a doubt.

Her sister and Jake. The idea is like red heat near a burn.

Jake looks down at himself, vaguely surprised. He is lying half in, half out of the bedcovers. He turns to see the clock and pain splits his head.

'Shit,' he mutters, putting his hand up to it. He eases himself into a sitting position. His eyes are stinging and his mouth is upholstered with fur. 'Oh, God,' he moans, 'I'm dying. I must be dying.'

Just then, he catches sight of a woman's shoe by the door. Black leather. A high heel. He stares at it and the more he stares at it the stranger it seems, as if it's some antiquated object he's never seen before and can't work out its purpose.

He twists round, making the bed – and the body, with its back to him – bounce. There is a woman lying in his bed. His mind informs him of this fact very calmly, as if this is a normal and acceptable state of affairs. For a moment he is unable to compute what has happened. Is it Mel? he thinks, baffled. No. This woman has short brown hair. Who could it be?

Stella. His brain supplies him optimistically with the name. But Jake knows it's not her and just thinking about her makes him remember.

'Oh, fuck.' Jake leaps from the bed as if it's contaminated. 'Fuck, fuck.'

He is so angry with himself, so utterly and purely furious, that he is unable to put on his shoes. He fights and wrestles against himself for a few minutes, trying simultaneously to stamp on himself, injure himself, and to shove his foot into the shoe.

With one lace done up, he bolts through the door. The light slams into his brow like a hammer on an anvil and he shuts one eye as he runs down the track towards the hotel. At the point where the paths intersect, he has to decide. Caravan or hotel? Caravan or hotel? Where will she be? Jake squints at his watch which is, miraculously as it seems at this precise moment, still round his wrist. It's seven something. Can he wake her up? Yes, he decides in a flash, he has to.

'You fucking idiot, you fucking, fucking idiot, what is wrong with you?' he is muttering to himself, as he sprints up the path into the woods. How can that have happened? One minute she was at the door, then she was inside with her vodka and her weed and then—

Jake comes to a standstill, his breath heaving in his chest. Pearl is standing in the middle of the path, arms folded across her apron, blocking his way.

'You won't find her there,' she says.

He feels very cold. 'Why? Where is she?'

'She's gone.'

'Gone?' The word hits Jake like a blow to the stomach.
'Gone where?'

'Gone. Left. Skedaddled.' Pearl comes towards him and
Jake backs away. Pearl is not someone Jake wants to mess
with. He imagines she would know how to smite him with
black arts or whatever you call them. 'And I for one don't
blame her.' She sidesteps him and walks away, surprisingly
fast for someone so small.

'Pearl, wait—' Jake wheels round, tripping on his loose
lace, stumbling to the forest floor. 'Hang on a sec.'

Pearl carries on walking away from him. Jake, hauling
himself from the ground, has to run to catch up with her.

'What did she say, Pearl? What did she tell you?'

She shakes his hand off her arm. 'She said nothing. Didn't
need to.' She turns on him, this woman who is almost half
his height, and she is scaring him more than anything else in
his life. 'I see things. Doesn't take a genius to work things
out, you know.' She shoves her face up close to his. 'You
should be ashamed of yourself, laddie.'

'Listen,' Jake is forced, by the narrowness of the path,
to walk behind her, 'it's not what . . .' He tries to formulate
what it is he wants to say, what he needs to say. 'It's not
what you think,' he finishes lamely.

Pearl snorts.

'Where has she gone? Pearl, please tell me. Please.'

'I don't know.' She stops so abruptly Jake almost falls
into her. 'And even if I did, I wouldn't tell you.'

Jake watches Pearl walk away through the forest, her
shape receding down and down until she's no bigger than
a goblin. He kicks the nearest stone, once, twice, with all

his might. Then he sinks down to sit on it, clutching his foot in his hands. He doesn't think he has ever felt more desperate. What is he going to do?

Suddenly he raises his head. The trees above him writhe and toss, sunlight glowing through the branches. Something, some recollection from last night, is breaking through. He frowns and looks at his hands, spread out on his knees. His foot throbs vaguely. And then he can picture it as if seeing it on a screen: Nina, leaning over him and whispering into his ear, 'She killed someone, you know.'

part | four

As Jake walks away, he tells himself he won't look back. Not until the end of the drive. That's the best view, the one that takes in the sweep of the lawn, most of the house and the trees behind. From there, Kildoune is turned to face the loch, but you can still see its turrets, the opacity of its windows, the battlements, and the track coiling away from it into the forest.

But when he reaches the gate, he can't do it. He can't turn round. He stands for a moment, the house behind him, the road in front of him, gripping the straps of his rucksack. Then he walks on, putting one foot in front of the other, his eyes on the ground.

He walks the cross-section of the valley, along the winding road, past the church, along the bridge, over the loch, under the railway. At the main road, he stands beside his rucksack, edging from foot to foot. He has this image of Stella getting further and further away from him with every passing second, of the thread between them stretching to breaking-point.

He doesn't have to wait long for a ride. A middle-aged couple take him as far as Pitlochry where they are going, they tell him, to buy their daughter a wedding present. They drop him on the A9 and Jake shades his eyes against the sun, looking down the silver-skinned Tarmac, his thumb outstretched.

When a car slows down and the driver, a man with a scorpion tattooed on his forearm, asks, 'Where to?' Jake isn't sure. Edinburgh or London? London? Edinburgh? Where would she go?

'South,' he says. He'll decide on the way.

It's only when he's swung his rucksack into the back seat that he realises he's left the bicycle behind. It gives him almost physical pain, just below his sternum. He has to stop still, leaning out of the car, caught in the act of pulling the door closed. He bites his lip and yanks the door to. He could never have taken it anyway.

'South it is,' Scorpion Man says. 'Anywhere in particular?'

Nina slams into the flat, flinging car keys, bag, coat to various bits of furniture. She pauses to check the answerphone for messages – none – then stamps into the kitchen.

Richard is sitting at the table, a triangle of toast in one hand, a medical journal in the other. 'Sweetheart,' he says, 'you're back!'

'Evidently.' Nina pushes her hair off her face. 'Listen, have you seen Stella?'

'Stella?' he repeats. 'But I thought you were with—'

'I was, I was. I mean today. This morning.'

He blinks, dazed. 'I . . . er—'

'Yes or no?' Nina shrieks. 'It's a simple question.'

'No.'

'Has my mother called?'

'No.'

'My father?'

'No.'

'Grandparents?'

'No. No one.'

'Shit.' Nina holds her hand to her forehead. Her eyes light on a cup sitting on the kitchen surface. She thinks about hurling it to the floor. She imagines the noise of shattering china, the way the pieces would skitter apart on the flagged floor. It would make her feel a lot better but she probably shouldn't do it in front of Richard. She decides against it. 'Shit,' she says again, and sinks into a chair.

Richard puts down his toast and comes towards her. 'What's up?'

Nina can't answer him. She's thinking, furiously turning over options. Where would Stella go?

Richard kneels in front of her. 'What's the escapologist done now?'

Nina laughs, despite herself, then despair overtakes her again. 'Oh, God, Richard.' She allows herself to bury her face in the front of his dressing-gown. His arms fasten round her, as she knew they would, and she inhales the metallic sleep-smell off him.

'What happened?' he murmurs. 'Did the two of you fall out? You can tell me.'

'No.'

'You can't?'

'I can't.'

He strokes a hand up and down her back. 'Well, don't worry. Whatever it is, it will all be fine.'

'I'm not sure it will,' she mumbles.

He pulls away from her, looks at her steadily, his hands round her waist. 'I'm sorry we argued,' he says.

'So am I.'

'I'm glad you're back.'

'Me too.' She smiles at him, then says: 'I need a shower.'

Jake is quite impressed with his sleuthing. He got himself to London, found his way to a phonebook, looked up Gilmore, S., wrote down her address, bought a street map, found the address, navigated his way there on the Tube, and here he is, walking down Stella's street.

As he nears the number of her house, he feels a dizzying mix of excitement and fear. She is there, probably, behind one of those windows. What will she say to him? How will she react? Will this be the second time in two days that he's been hit by a woman?

Her apartment building is a large house with steps up to the front door. Jake stands on the pavement look-ing up at it. He has no idea what will happen once he's inside – if he's allowed inside. But surely turning up like this will persuade her of his . . . his seriousness about her.

Jake shoves the map into his back pocket and takes the steps two at a time. He peers at the array of bells and locates the middle one, which says 'Gilmore', in green ink that's been blurred and dispersed by rain. He presses it. Far off in the building there is a tinkling noise. He strains for the sound of footsteps, of voices, of anything, running over in his head the speech he's prepared.

Nina waits, surveying the cars lined up at the pavement. The door swings open. 'Darling,' Evie says, throwing her arms wide, 'it's about time I had a visit from you. How are you? I was thinking about you only the other day because—'

'I can't stay,' Nina interrupts.

'Oh.'

'I'm looking for Stella.' Nina allows a small pause in which she examines Evie's face. It is blank of all expression, unmoving, eyebrows arched. 'You haven't seen her, have you?'

Evie rests a bangled arm on her hip. 'Not for months, sweetie.'

Nina leans her weight against the stone door jamb. On a wire overhead, two birds fuss and squawk. 'And you haven't heard from her?'

'No.'

'Are you sure?'

The two women look at each other. They are almost equal height.

'As sure as sure can be,' Evie says. 'Why? What's happened?'

'Nothing.' Nina turns. 'Got to go.' She brandishes her mobile. 'Call me if you hear anything.'

Jake presses the bell again, this time for longer. Still nothing.

He shifts from foot to foot and steps back to look at the building. A leaking gutter has spread an orange-brown stain down the wall. A plant leans out, waving, from a window-box.

Maybe she's out. She must be out. Jake lowers himself to the top step, his rucksack beside him, and leans his elbows on his knees. He'll wait.

He scratches a bite on his leg, pulls off his jacket and lays it over his bag. Maybe it's sitting in the warmth of the sun, but he feel a great wave of fatigue hit him. He's also, he realises, incredibly thirsty. Hangovers always do that to him. But he can't risk going to find some water – not now, not when he's come all this way.

Jake leans against the low wall, glancing up and down the street. A child beats a stick against the pavement, a woman wheels a bike along, a car tries to reverse into a too-small space.

Evie climbs the stairs back to her flat. She really must get the entryphone fixed so that she doesn't have to do this unseemly hike every time her doorbell rings. Inside, she snaps the dead heads off some flowers on a table, fiddles with a radiator setting, straightens a cushion.

'That was your sister,' she says, to the person huddled in the armchair.

Francesca is in the kitchen, peeling potatoes into a bowl, when Nina appears at the back door. Francesca jumps then laughs, still holding the peeler as she goes to open it. 'You scared me!' she says, as she hugs her daughter to her. 'Come in, come in. Why are you creeping about like that?'

Nina's body feels limp and her face, when Francesca pulls back to look at it, is paler than normal.

'What?' Francesca says immediately. 'What's wrong?'

Nina puts her bag on the table and grimaces. 'It's Stella,' she says.

'What about her?'

She utters two words: '*E scappata.*'

Francesca raises her eyes to the heavens. 'Again?' she shrieks.

'Yeah.'

'Where?'

'Don't know.'

Francesca sits at the table, banging the peeler down. A second later, she stands again. She has given up trying to decipher the relationship between her daughters, but it can still infuriate her. 'I don't understand,' she says. 'I thought you went to see her.'

'I did.'

'So, why this? Why—'

'I don't know!' Nina cries. 'Don't ask me!'

Francesca crosses her arms. What is wrong with her family that this kind of thing happens again and again? Where did she go wrong? Motherhood, it seems to her, never ends. She gave birth to the child in front of her thirty years ago: long enough, you'd think, for you to be able to stop worrying about them. But no. They still do things, completely out of the blue, to disrupt your life, to surprise you, to make you anxious.

'There's no point in getting cross with me,' Nina continues. 'I was just letting you know. Putting you on the alert.'

Francesca nods, eyeing her daughter.

'I have to go.' Nina jiggles the keys in her pocket.

'OK.'

'I'll tell you if I hear anything.'

'*Sì, sì.*' Francesca waves her away.

She listens to Nina's car starting up, then walks to the phone. As soon as her mother answers, she announces: '*Stella é scappata.*'

From the street below, Stella can hear the rattle of a radio, the sound of someone hurrying along the pavement in high heels. In the corner, the TV screen is blizzarding, a videotape finished. The cat lies on its flank on the hearth, the tip of its tail flicking.

She raises her head, looks out at the blank, indeterminate sky. She's not sure how long she's been here. Days, perhaps. Or maybe just a few hours. She turns on to her side, drawing her knees up. Her body feels dull and heavy with inactivity.

She'd arrived on Evie's doorstep early in the morning, just after dawn. If Evie had been surprised to see her she didn't show it. She took one look at her and pulled her inside. She led her to the sofa, heaped duvets and blankets on top of her, supplied mugs of scalding coffee that Stella suspected were laced with whisky. She brought pyjamas, a hot-water bottle, lavender-scented handkerchiefs. She sliced buttered toast into tiny, crustless pieces and didn't say anything when

Stella let them grow cold, spotted and unappetising. She put a black-and-white film on the video and Stella watched, dumbly, as a pale woman with over-pencilled eyebrows waited for her lover in a railway café, an invisible orchestra surging in the background.

Evie asked only one question: 'Is it a broken head we've got here, darling, or a broken heart?'

'Don't know,' Stella said. 'Heart, maybe.'

'That's good,' Evie had said, drawing an emery board along one side of her nail as the woman on-screen ran down a platform. 'Hearts are easier to mend than heads.'

Evie enters the room, dressed in an apron Stella has never seen before. 'I have broken the habit of a lifetime,' she announces.

Stella raises her head from the cushions. 'Really?'

'I,' Evie continues, handing her a cup of tea, 'have cooked. I made soup!'

Stella struggles to sit upright. 'What brought that on?'

'The sight of your pale little face, darling. I just couldn't bear it. You're going to have to eat it now, you know.'

'I will,' Stella says, blowing on the scalding tea. 'I promise.'

'If you don't, I might have to feed it to you through a piece of rubber tubing, suffragette-style.'

Stella smiles. 'I don't think it'll come to that.'

'I should hope not.'

Evie sits down opposite her. There is a long moment of silence. Evie pulls off the apron and lays it over the sofa arm. The cat leaps up and settles itself on Evie's lap.

'I do have to tell you, darling,' Evie says, kneading the

cat's ears, 'that your entire family is going crazy. And I mean crazy, in the way only they can.'

Stella starts needlessly fiddling with the flex of a lamp next to her.

'I haven't told them you're here,' Evie continues, 'but I think we need to let them know you're OK before your mother starts getting the bishop to say a mass for you and your father hires a private detective.'

Stella doesn't say anything.

'Darling Stella, I'm not saying you have to see them, face a clan gathering or anything like that. Just let them know that you're alive and haven't driven off a cliff-edge somewhere. You don't have to see . . .' Evie pauses, choosing her words '. . . anyone . . . if you don't want to.'

Stella is relieved to hear the ringing of the phone. Evie gets up and goes into the other room to answer it and Stella is left in the room with the cat, who is ruffled and annoyed at being moved off Evie's lap.

Evie returns quite quickly.

'It was Nina,' she says.

Stella puts down her teacup. She seems unable to swallow and, for a moment, thinks she is about to choke. 'What did she say?' she manages.

'She knows you're here.'

'But . . . I thought you said—'

'I didn't tell her. She said she had her suspicions that this was where you might be, and then she drove around the streets today and saw your car.' Evie points a finger at her. 'Remember that next time – hide the car. Anyway, there's a message. I wrote it down.' Evie holds the paper at arm's length. "'I didn't sleep with him,"' she reads expressionlessly, as if reciting a shopping list.

Stella sits motionless, transfixed by the steam wreathing up from her tea.

'Oh,' Evie says, 'and she's at the café in Musselburgh and wants to see you. Shall we go? Your car or mine? I thought we'd drive over. Mine, I think. Yours is probably caked in sheep shit.'

Stella sits opposite her sister in one of their grandparents' booths. They have sat like this so many times Stella gets the strange sensation that she can't be entirely sure what point they are at in their lives. Are they six and seven, with knickerbocker glories in front of them? Or are they teenagers trying to like espresso? Evie perches at the counter conversing with Valeria and Domenico as she always does – in French with an Italian accent. It seems to work somehow.

'Why didn't you tell me, Stel?' Nina is furious. Her default setting for most situations. 'Why didn't you just say?'

'Say what?'

'That you liked him. I wouldn't have gone anywhere near him if you'd said. You know I wouldn't.'

Stella shrugs, looks down at the jeans she's wearing. Evie had produced them, saying some man had left them behind and they were the only things in the flat that would fit Stella.

'Not that it made any difference.' Nina snorts. 'Nothing happened.' She leans over and touches Stella's hand.

'Nothing. He wasn't having any of it. I tried my entire repertoire,' she says, with a grin, 'physical, narcotic, verbal, alcoholic. No joy. You might draw the conclusion,' she says heavily, 'that he was in love with someone else.'

Stella says nothing, avoiding Nina's eye.

'He talked about you in his sleep.'

Stella looks up. 'What did he say?'

'Oh, I don't know.' Nina gestures, smoke wisping after her. 'You can't expect me to remember that. I was off my face. But he was murmuring your name at some point.'

Stella tries not to wince. The thought of them sleeping side by side is still a little too much for her to cope with.

'How's everything with Richard?' she asks.

'Oh, fine. The same. You know.' Nina takes a sip of her coffee. 'So, what are you going to do?'

Stella tugs at the ends of her hair. 'I don't know, Neen, I don't know. I could go back to London and everything, but . . .' she sighs '. . . I just feel—'

'I meant about Jake,' Nina interrupts.

'Oh.' Stella attempts to think, to make her brain operational. What is she going to do about Jake? She has literally no idea. Her brain comes up with nothing, just starts doing that repetitive *Jake, Jake* thing again. Should she ring him? What would she say? She's having trouble keeping up with events. The man she loves is married. Except he isn't. He slept with her sister. Except he didn't. But they still spent the night together. In the same bed, by the sound of it.

'I don't know,' she says again, hating the pathetic edge to her voice. She would like more than anything to be able to wind back time to the point where she was sending Jake to show Nina where the caravan was, where she could reach over the kitchen counter and prise them apart.

'Because . . . um . . .' Nina pulls nervously on her cigarette '. . . there is something I . . . I have to tell you.'

'What?'

Nina is jiggling her leg, picking at the edge of the table. 'There was one thing that happened.'

'I don't want to hear about it,' Stella snaps, afraid now.

'No, no, not like that. I think . . . I think . . .' Nina stops and then the rest of the sentence comes out in a rush: 'I think I might have told him.'

Stella frowns. 'Told him what?'

'It.'

'It?'

'You know. It.' Nina leans across the table. 'The Thing.'

Stella hasn't heard Nina use that expression for so long that for a moment she can't recall what it refers to. But something in her remembers because the scalp shrinks on her skull and a cold sensation spreads through her.

She sits in Evie's lover's clothes and stares at her sister. Sometimes when she looks at her she can see the ghost of herself in her face. But not now. Nina looks weirdly unfamiliar to her, as if she hardly knows her. It's as if she's never looked at this face ever before. She sees a place where her mascara has smudged, the arch of her brows, that she has a few freckles over her nose, the rapid flutter of her eyelids. 'You are not serious,' she hears herself whisper. 'Nina,' she has to gasp to draw breath, 'why?'

'I don't know.' Nina jiggles her leg up and down again,

making the teaspoons shiver against the china. 'It just came out. I – I don't know why. It was an accident.' She rubs her fingers over her brow. 'It was just so weird being there. I'll never understand what made you want to go back. And I – I was drunk.'

'You've been drunk before,' Stella says, and she is getting up from the table, 'and managed to keep it to yourself. So why now? And why him, for God's sake, Nina? Why him?'

I am Stella Gilmore. I am twenty-eight. I have green eyes and black hair. I am five foot ten. I have a sister. I am half Italian. I own a car and a flat. I have lived in eleven different countries. I have never broken a bone in my body but once had pleurisy. When I was eight years old I killed someone.

These are the facts of my life.

Stella bolts through the café. In the mirrors she sees a gallery of Stellas, wild-haired, running towards her. She sees her grandparents, her uncle and Evie turning to stare at her. She yanks at the door and she is out in the street. The air is thin and cold after the warm fug of the café.

Nina is next to her, holding on to her sleeve.

'Where are you going, Stel? Don't go,' her sister is pleading, 'I'm sorry. I'm so sorry. Please don't go. I'm sorry.'

Stella shakes her off. 'I can't believe you've done this,' she manages to get out from between her teeth. 'I can't believe it. You have – you have broken me.' She pushes Nina away from her and staggers further down the pavement.

Her legs feel weak and boneless, the sky above the stone

buildings of Musselburgh too bright, too white, jarring on her retinas. Stella's vision seems to be closing in at the sides, the scene melting and waving like the horizon line in a desert. She told Jake. Jake knows. This she cannot take, she really cannot take. The thing that she has kept secret, folded up small inside her, has been yanked out. That this knowledge could dry out Jake's love for her is unbearable. For what else could it do? He knows. The worst thing. How could he ever bring himself to look at her again?

Putting one foot in front of the other suddenly seems the hardest thing she's ever done. Then she is tripping and falling to the ground and it's a relief because she doesn't have to keep standing upright, and somewhere she can hear Evie's voice saying that she hasn't eaten a thing for days, and Stella is thinking, is it only days since I saw him, and she can hear her sister crying and saying her name over and over. Nina. Before there was anything, there was Nina.

'What will we do if we can't find them again?' Nina was asking.

Stella used the branch of a tree to haul herself up. 'We will,' she said.

They were climbing the steep path up the side of a waterfall. Misted, air-borne spray floated towards them, damping their faces, their hair, their clothes. Stella could taste the river on her lips.

As she turned to help Nina climb the final step of the incline, something whizzed past her ear like a bullet. Whatever it was landed in the gorse next to them. A loose stone? A landslide? Another missile came hurtling through the air and something struck Stella on the arm, sharp as an arrow.

She whipped round. There was a figure standing in front of them, legs straddling the path, next to where the water started tipping and sliding over the drop. Anthony. Flipping stones at them as casually as someone tossing coins. She saw him raise his arm and pull it back behind his head.

'Don't!' she cried. 'Don't! Don't hit her on the head. You mustn't!'

She shielded Nina's cranium, crouching over her. If she got a knock on the head, she relapsed, sometimes for days. It would be awful, unthinkable, if that happened here. The stone landed beside Nina's shoe, then another, further away.

Anthony stood looking at them, his arms folded. The path behind him was empty. Where was the rest of the class? Anthony liked an audience. But it was just him and her and Nina and the trees and the waterfall. She felt Nina's hand creep into hers.

'Where is everyone?' she heard herself say.

He smiled slowly and Stella saw the wolfish yellow of his teeth. 'Gone.' He jerked his thumb. 'Up that way.'

She didn't like the way he was looking at Nina, his eyes small and slitted, his head on one side, she didn't like it at all. Stella edged closer to her sister.

'What do you want?' she said.

'That's not very nice.' He loosened his arms so that they hung by his sides. 'I came back to look for you.'

'Why?'

He didn't answer but lunged towards Nina. Stella saw

it coming. She stepped in front of her just in time, feeling the mass of his body hit hers. She would not let him get Nina, she would not. Fury was filling her head, roaring in her ears like water. Nina was screaming and clinging to her but Stella felt herself wrenched away from her sister, pushed so hard that the world was pitching sideways.

She hit the ground with a dull crack. Pain spread from her back down her legs and she was momentarily winded, her lungs aching with emptiness, her hands muddy, the sun white and glaring above her. Somewhere, she could hear her sister sobbing.

Stella turned her head. Anthony was standing over Nina like an executioner, the collar of her dress bunched in his fingers.

'So I shouldn't hit her on the head,' he was saying. 'Why? What'll happen?' His other hand was raised high in a fist, Nina's head bowed beneath it. 'Let's see, shall we?'

Stella scrambled to her feet. She looked at the precipice and she looked at him. She saw that Anthony's lace was loose, snaking away from his shoe along the ground. It made very simple sense. Stella lifted her foot and stepped on to the lace. She could feel it there, trapped beneath her sole, and she placed her hands against the chest of Anthony Cusk and she pushed.

It was quite deliberate. She will never be able to convince herself otherwise. He was driven back, away from Nina, his hand coming loose from Nina's dress, his arms wheeling for balance, the raised fist uncurling and jerking back. The lace tugged itself free, slid out from under Stella's foot. She and Nina heard his small grunt of shock. They watched him stagger back, crashing into the river, the bed of wet, slimed stones making him slip and lurch. They saw the black waters claim him, swirling round his legs.

He seemed to teeter on the edge for a long time. His eyes were wide, his lips stretched, his face strangely blank. He kept his grip on the earth with one foot, like a dancer or a man seeking flight. Then he tipped, his arms still circling, and fell.

There was a long moment, between him vanishing from the scene and the sound of his body hitting the rocks below, when Stella found herself thinking that maybe it hadn't just happened, that maybe he was playing a trick on them, that he was bound to be holding on to the lip of the waterfall, and any minute now he would reappear, a grinning jack-in-a-box.

But there was the deadened thud, another pause, then a splash as he fell into the water. And she and Nina were alone again.

Miss Saunders sees them coming from a long way off. They run over the expanse of green, which is wavering and brightening in the uncertain light. Something about them makes her stand, makes her shush the child talking to her, makes her strain her eyes into the sun.

The Gilmore girls are running over the glen. Stella is in front, her legs moving, her arms flying loose behind her like wings. Nina is in the distance, trying to keep up, and is it Miss Saunders's imagination or is she screaming?

Miss Saunders looks at the sisters, from one to the other. It will only be a few seconds, a minute maybe, until she finds out what it is, but she cannot bear it. It's the feeling all teachers dread. Nina's screams reach her in staccato bursts, as if by intermittent radio connection.

'What is it?' Miss Saunders shouts, somehow knowing that it's already too late. 'What's happened?'

Stella had looked. Nina hadn't. Stella had inched her way on her stomach right to the very edge – her dress would be soaking later, all down her front, but no one would ask her why – and peered over.

All her life she's wished she hadn't.

He was looking back at her, his eyes clear and open and seeking out hers. There he was, lying under the thick weight of water, staring at her.

Stella is lying on a bed with her sister, head to toe. Nina has made everyone else disappear. For a while there was flapping and fuss and her mother on the phone and people bringing cups of tea and tissues and advice. But Nina had managed to get her out of the café, into the car and back to her flat in what seemed like minutes.

Nina is stroking her ankle and telling her how she and Richard have decided to have a baby. 'He thinks it will calm me down.' She snorts. 'Weigh me down, more like. Stop me going off. What do you think?'

'I think . . .' Stella says, and her voice still sounds a bit funny to her, a bit hollow and far-away. She can't quite comprehend how she arrived here, in Nina's bedroom. It's as if she went to sleep in one life and woke up in another. 'I think if you want a baby, you should have one.'

'But that's the thing, isn't it?' Nina says. 'I don't

know if I do. How can you know, if you've never had one?'

Stella shrugs. It always surprises her, the way rows and schisms with your family can pass over, drain away so quickly. One minute you can be screaming that they have ruined your life and the next you're curled up on a bed together, as if nothing has happened.

'That's the problem with babies,' Nina continues. 'The only way to find out if you want one is to have one. And by then it's too late. You can't just shove it back up, can you? There ought to be a kind of centre where you can—'

'Test-drive motherhood?'

'Exactly.'

Nina presses her hand to the sole of Stella's foot. 'So, what about you?'

'What about me?'

'What are you going to do? Stay in Edinburgh?'

'I don't know. Probably not. I don't really want to be here.'

'You've never really wanted to be here.'

'I know.'

'And Jake?'

Stella pushes herself up and swings her legs off the bed. Her head stutters slightly but clears. Through Nina's bedroom window, she can see a woman with a red umbrella, pushing a leaflet into the letter-slit of a house opposite.

'Jake . . . is a lost cause, I think.' She lowers her head to pick cat hairs off her sweater, letting them float away on the air.

'You don't know that, Stel.'

'I do.'

'You do not.'

'Oh, really?' Stella turns round and faces her sister. 'Would you want someone after you'd found out they—' She stops, biting off the words, remembering Richard is somewhere in the flat.

'You have to at least give him a chance, find out if that's what he thinks, which I don't believe it is. It was so long ago, Stel.' Nina shakes her by the arm. 'Years and years and years. You have to put it behind you.' She chews her lip. 'I have.'

'Nina, you didn't do it,' Stella whispers, her voice hoarse, as if with disuse.

'But it was as much my fault as yours.'

'No, it wasn't.'

'It was,' Nina insists. 'If it hadn't been you, it would have been me.'

Stella turns to look at her. She cannot get over the fact that they are talking about it. The Thing. 'That's not true,' she says. 'And you know it.'

They are silent for a moment. Nina looks away, starts twirling a strand of hair around her fingers. 'You know what your biggest problem is?' she says suddenly.

'No. What?'

'It's not that you can't forget about it,' Nina begins, 'or that you see him everywhere. It's that you don't think you should be allowed to have a normal life, to have the things normal people have, to—'

'Bollocks.' Stella rounds on her sister. 'It's not that at all.'

'It is!' Nina stands up and starts pacing about. 'It's exactly that! I know that's really why you can't face Jake. It's not that you can't bear the fact that he knows. It's that you think you need to be punished for something you weren't punished for – something I made sure you weren't punished for.'

'Nina,' Stella interjects, but her sister talks over her: 'You have some stupid, pig-headed notion that depriving yourself of him is going to absolve you. You know what?' She comes to a stop. 'I may have even done you a favour.'

There is a pause. Stella stares at her, aghast. 'A favour?' she repeats.

'Yeah.' Nina lifts her chin, defiant. 'In telling him. You would never have told him and – and you'd have carried on being all closed up and shut off. This way you're going to see that it won't make any difference to how he feels about you. You might even begin to realise that you are allowed to be happy, that—'

'Oh, spare me the psychoanalysis.'

'I will not. And I will not let you throw a chance like Jake away. Stella, please,' she urges. 'It was an accident. It happened. Get over it.'

Stella picks at a loose thread in the bedcover. 'Look, none of this matters anyway,' she mutters. 'I mean, I don't see him here.' She gestures around the room. 'It's not as if he's exactly desperate to speak to me.'

'He doesn't know where you are,' Nina points out, with sarcastic patience.

'There are ways he could find me. There's . . . well, Mum and Dad are in the phone book for starters . . . and . . . er . . .' She grinds to a halt.

'I didn't even know where you were till this morning.'

'Well, maybe,' Stella says, 'but—'

'Stel, can't you see?' Her sister crouches in front of her suddenly and takes both her hands in hers. 'You've let yourself get stuck. You've got to stop hanging on to this. Jake loves you.' Stella sighs and tries to pull away but Nina tightens her grip. 'Listen to me. He does. He's not going to give a shit about something that happened twenty years ago.'

'You don't know that.'

'I do.'

'You do not.'

'I do so. If you throw this away because you're too scared to move on, to – to let him into your life, then you're a fool. You'll have fucked up for good.'

Stella extracts her hands, stands up and walks to the window. She presses her forehead to the cool of the glass and looks up and down the street for the woman with the leaflets. She's disappeared.

Behind her, Nina throws herself on to the bed with an exasperated noise. 'I don't know why I bother,' she fumes, thrashing about, thumping pillows into shape. 'Might as well talk to the fucking wall. I know what you'll do. I know exactly what you'll do.'

'You do, do you?'

'You're going to run away again. And you'll keep on running away, just like you've always done.'

Stella thinks about this, watching her breath form and fade on the pane. 'Probably.' She nods. 'Yes.'

In the middle of a huge station, Jake pushes his bank card into a machine, shading the screen so that he can make out the green lettering.

He's been staying in a travellers' hostel, a grim place with twelve beds to each windowless cell and where the choking scent of disinfectant doesn't quite cover other, more ingrained smells that Jake doesn't want to think about.

He watches as the machine considers his request. He imagines the coded, electronic information being exchanged between this machine in a London railway station and his bank in Wanchai. Will it let him have it? He needs eighty pounds, minimum – enough to pay his bill at the hostel, where they have his passport held to ransom, and to buy a train ticket to Edinburgh. Jake glances round at the departures board. There's a train leaving in fifteen minutes. If he gets it he'll be in Edinburgh by late afternoon, and by evening, who knows? Stella's house, the café? If he doesn't find her, then he's in real . . . but Jake doesn't want to think about that.

He checked his email yesterday, for the first time in weeks. There were nine messages from Chen, in ascending degrees of panic. The script they'd been working on had suddenly got the green light and he needed Jake back. Now. The most recent one was from Chen's PA, saying that if Jake wasn't coming back, he should let them know because they had found someone to take over Jake's job, if necessary. Jake had sat in the internet café with his head in his hands for minutes on end. Then typed: *Don't give my job away to anyone. I'm coming back. Give me three days – four at the most.*

Jake has exhausted everything he could think of in

London. The woman in her flat wasn't Stella. She was a friend of hers, she said, one hand on the door, she hadn't heard from her in weeks. The girl he'd spoken to at the radio station had had the same peeved tone in her voice: Stella used to work there but not for a while now and, no, she had no idea where she was.

He turns back to the machine. His card is being regurgitated and a message is flashing at him: Request Denied, Insufficient Funds.

'Eighty measly fucking pounds,' he is muttering to himself, as he yanks a second card out of his wallet. 'It's not much to ask.'

He pushes this card into the narrow slot, sending a silent prayer to the god of autotellers. Please, please. Eighty pounds. That's all. I'll pay it back, I promise.

The machine has a long think. Jake shifts from foot to foot, watching the minutes to the Edinburgh train count down on the station clock. Then there is a horrible grinding noise as the machine gulps down his card. Request Denied, Card Confiscated.

'Shit.' Jake bangs his fist against the wall. 'Shit, shit, fuck.'

He closes his eyes for a moment. He finds it hard to fathom, the way his life has become so precarious. He drifted for years through school, through various jobs, various women, with nothing much to surprise or wrong-foot him. And all of a sudden he's almost killed, he's forced into marriage with someone he hardly knows, he moves half-way across the world, he goes in search of the father he never knew but finds a girl instead, he messes up in a shocking variety of ways, the girl leaves, and he runs after her. Which would have been quite enough for several lifetimes. But then someone tells him that this girl, the girl he loves, killed someone.

Jake opens his eyes and surveys the semi-lit chaos of the station: people running for trains, people gazing up at the departures board, people sitting on suitcases, waiting. What Nina told him that night flashes at him intermittently, like the beam of a distant lighthouse. He feels as though he should be more shocked by it, more affected. But he finds he is curiously unsurprised. There is so much about Stella he doesn't understand.

Jake tries to picture Stella at eight. He sees a thin child with an anxious face and small, clenched hands. 'She did it,' Nina had whispered to him, 'for me. Can you imagine?' Jake finds that he can't, he can't imagine it at all. He cannot for a moment even begin to appreciate what must have made her do it – he's not sure he could ever bear to know. The class bully. It makes him furious for her, makes him want to fold her hands in his and take her somewhere far away.

But he has to find her first. He shoves his wallet into his pocket and walks out of the station.

He stands outside a phonebox. People flow past him, on their way to the mouth of the Underground. The sun is hot, much hotter than in Scotland. Men are in their shirtsleeves, jackets held over their arms. The smell of rotting garbage reminds Jake fleetingly of Hong Kong.

He turns away from the phonebox. He walks off. He stops. He comes back. He stands for a moment, chewing his lip. He cannot do this, he cannot. He's nearly thirty years old

– how can he have come to this? But his stomach is growling at him, he's eaten nothing today yet and he has just under a pound in his pocket. He could always hitch, but the massed tentacled roads of London confuse him. He wouldn't know which one to take and, anyway, he'd be scared of being picked up by an urban serial killer.

Jake presses his hands to his temples. What other option does he have? It'll be almost a fortnight until he gets his paycheck. He can't survive that long.

He pulls at the door of the phonebox and steps inside. Hearing her voice saying that of course she'll accept reversed charges from the UK makes him almost lose his nerve and hang up.

'Jake?' his mother is saying. 'Is that you?'

'Yeah. Hi.'

'Are you all right?'

'Yes.' He presses the receiver close to his ear. 'Actually, no. Caro, I need some money.' He hates the sound of his voice as he says it. 'I am so sorry to ask you this. Especially as I know you and Lionel can't exactly—'

'Where are you?' she interrupts.

'London.'

'London?' Caroline is incredulous. 'What are you doing there?

'I can pay you back,' he continues, 'in a couple of weeks. I'll give it all back to you, I promise. I just need enough for a ticket to Scotland.'

He scuffs his sneaker against the filthy metal wall of the phonebox and listens to her thinking.

'What's going on, Jakey?'

Jake takes a deep breath. 'There's this girl. And if I don't get to Edinburgh today or tomorrow, then—'

'How much do you need?' his mother says immediately.

There was never any question about where Stella would be staying. Nina had swept up her bag from Evie's, slammed it into the car and dumped it in her boxroom. 'Towels in the cupboard,' she said, 'clean underwear in my drawers,' and started showing her how the electric blanket worked.

When Nina goes out to meet Richard for lunch, as she does most days, Stella is left in the flat. She has a long bath, half submerging herself in scalding water, watching her skin turn livid pink, the blood leaping close to the surface. She listens to songs on Nina's favourite radio station, stares up at the ceiling, soaps herself with the products arranged along the shelves. Later, she sniffs her skin and finds that she smells of her sister.

When she's dressed, her hair still wet, she wanders the empty rooms, sipping from a mug of tea. Nina's home is curious. Stella has never spent stretches of time alone here. Everywhere she looks are objects she recognises from the house they grew up in – ornaments, cushions, a chest of drawers, a vase, a picture. On the mantelpiece sits not only Nina's silver christening bowl, but hers. Their names are there, engraved inside the rims: Stella Giuditta Gilmore and Nina Maddalena Gilmore. By Nina's bed is one of the matching lamps they had beside their bunk-beds. Its pair, when Stella looks for it, is on the dressing-table. She is surprised by how much Nina has of their parents' house.

She took nothing, kept nothing. Most of these things she'd forgotten about.

In the hallway, Stella sits on the stool next to the phone and gazes at some china mice Valeria once gave them for Christmas. Stella reaches out and picks them up, one in each hand, remembering the instant she touches them the feel of the hard, slippery glaze, their hollow fragility, their roughened bases.

'Hi,' she murmurs, 'remember me?'

The mice look back at her with an intent, preoccupied stare. She wonders what on earth she's doing, talking to china ornaments. She puts them down again quickly, in the same confidential huddle Nina had them in, and slides open the drawer.

Inside, she's amazed to find a cache of ancient things – school jotters, some Nina's, some filled with her own handwriting, ancient, discoloured photographs of the two of them, their old pencil cases, leather dry with disuse, but still filled with half-eroded pencils, compasses, greying rubbers. Stella unpacks the whole drawer and examines everything, running her fingertips over the jotter covers, the inked pages, the pen shafts, photos of them in the garden, outside Evie's flat, leaning against a car. She lays them all out on the floor, in an arc around her, and sits for a while looking at them.

Nina, she realises, is a kind of curator of their joint past. It gives her a peculiar ache in her throat that Nina wants these things. That, even though Stella disregards them, her sister saves them, looks after them, keeps them together.

There will be a time, Jake thinks, when he is not racing

about Britain looking for people. He has to keep promising himself this — that his life will not for ever consist of mad dashes up and down a country in search of people who do not want to be found.

He shifts from one foot to the other and looks again at the café across the road. 'Iannelli's', the sign reads, in square gold letters. It has to be the one. He's walked around the streets, along the river and back again, asking random people where he can find a café run by Italians. A few of them looked him up and down suspiciously and walked on — he's no idea why — but the ones who did reply said there was only one. Iannelli's. On the high street. Stella definitely said Musselburgh was the town. Or perhaps it was something else. Is he sure it was Musselburgh?

Jake pushes himself away from the wall he's leaning on. This is madness. All he has to do is go in and ask. It's very simple. This, after all, is his only lead. He crosses the road in a straight line, his jaw set. It's going to be fine. It'll be easy. He's just going to say he's looking for Stella, and do they happen to know where she might be. Simple.

As he nears the café, something fails him. Through the window, he can see two men, one older than the other, conversing with a customer. They are big, burly and they look like . . . well, extras from a Mafia movie. Oh God, he thinks, you have messed about with not one but two of their family. He is going to end up at the bottom of the river in concrete boots. Or get a horse's head in his bed. His mother will never know what happened to him.

Jake swivels away and walks past, very fast. Then he walks back again. This is ridiculous. He has to stop faffing about. This café is the only link with Stella he has left. It has to work, it will work. He pushes the door and goes in. The men behind the counter nod at him, one smiles. There is an old woman as well, standing at a coffee machine, a cup in her hand. She smiles, too. Jake feels like an informer in the enemy camp. They all seem to be waiting for something.

'Um,' Jake says, 'er . . . I was wondering . . .' Something makes him glance to his right and he sees, behind the counter, also looking at him, the woman Stella will be in twenty years' time. Are all families this identikit, or is it just this one?

'If I could . . .' His nerve fails him. 'Could I have a coffee, please?'

'Francesca?'

Francesca stops and looks at her friend across the counter. 'What?' She is annoyed. She's in the middle of a story about a curtain-maker in Joppa and Evie is craning round, obviously thinking about something else entirely.

'I think that's him,' Evie hisses at her, ducking down.

'Who?' Francesca is mystified by this behaviour.

'Him. You know.'

'I don't know what you're talking about.'

'Yes, you do. *Him.*'

Evie is winking significantly, and the penny drops. Francesca puts down the sundae dishes she's been wiping.

'Him?' She points at the dark-haired boy sitting at the back, hunched over a coffee. She has managed to glean only the vaguest sense of the recent ruction between her

345

daughters but she's sure of one thing: it's all the fault of some boy. 'How do you know?'

'Nina described him to me.'

'But I thought he was, you know . . . Chinese.' Francesca whispers the last word.

'No, no.' Evie shakes her head. 'He's white.'

'Oh.' Francesca peers over Evie's shoulder to have another glance. 'He looks Italian.'

'Do you think?'

'Yes.'

'What? He's registering on your Roman-radar, is he?'

'Definitely.' Francesca has another quick look. 'Part-Italian, at least.'

'Well, he could be, I suppose. I'll tell you this, though,' Evie smirks in a rather lascivious way, 'your daughters have good taste. If you're going to fight over a man, then you might as well make sure he's—'

'Be quiet!' Francesca snaps. 'I'm going over.' She whips off her apron, muttering, 'Give him a piece of my mind.'

'Cesca,' Evie tags behind her, holding on to a corner of her apron as she marches through the café, 'do you think that's a good idea? Perhaps we should—'

'Is your name Jake?' Francesca bellows.

Jake starts, scattering sugar granules across the table, and looks up to see the older Stella woman bearing down on him.

'Yes,' he says, 'yes.' He leaps to his feet and almost salutes. There is another woman standing behind her, as if ready to restrain her. This doesn't look good. It's not quite the discreet chat he'd had in mind. 'Hi. It's very nice to meet you.' Caroline's lessons in manners seem to be asserting themselves. 'Are you—'

'I am Stella's mother,' the woman announces, drawing herself up. 'And Nina's,' she adds pointedly.

'Right. It's nice to meet you,' he says, and wonders why he's repeating himself.

'May I ask what you're doing here?'

'Actually, I'm looking for Stella. You don't happen—'

'Just Stella?' she snaps. 'Or Nina as well?'

'Er . . .' Jake founders. What would be the right answer here? 'Well . . .'

The blonde woman is murmuring, 'Francesca, perhaps we ought to—'

'If you think you can just come in here and start disrupting things between my daughters again, you've got another thing coming.' Francesca is waving her fist at him in what is definitely a threatening manner. 'How dare you slink in here? Haven't you done enough damage? My girls are—'

The people from behind the counter have arrived at the table. The older woman says something to Francesca in Italian and Francesca gives a short reply. Jake has no idea what it was, but it doesn't sound flattering. It contained the word '*brutto*' for a start.

'It's him,' the small blonde woman says, very much in the kind of voice you'd reserve for saying, it's the devil.

The older man speaks and the woman Jake presumes is his wife turns to him to argue. Jake wants to close his eyes. Is this where he gets bundled into a back room? He wants

347

to ask if he can make one last phone call. Is he letting his imagination run away with him? Probably.

'He just wants to know where she is!' the blonde woman is saying. 'That's all! We have to tell him. If she finds out that we—'

'Evie,' Francesca turns on her and starts arguing, saying something about him being unreliable, a game-player, and how they know absolutely nothing about him.

'Well, it doesn't seem to be stopping you making all kinds of judgements about him,' she retorts, and Jake decides that he likes her, that she's wonderful.

The old man is pointing at him, and his wife is nodding. The other man is leaning against the counter, his arms folded, staring at Jake. Jake doesn't like him. Not one bit.

He feels a hand on his arm and he flinches. But it's only the blonde woman, leaning towards him. 'I'd go if I were you,' she whispers.

Jake walks through the café. It's suddenly very long, seems to take him an age to get to the door. He glances one way and sees bits of himself reflected again and again in lots of angled mirrors; he glances the other and sees a collection of postcards pinned to a board behind the counter.

Then he is outside and the noise of their argument stops. He is, he realises, near tears. A woman walks by, glancing back at him, and he has to press the heels of his palms to his eyes. He moves off, without really knowing where he is going.

He has just reached a side street and is about to cross when he hears a voice behind him: 'Hey!'

Jake turns. Stella's grandfather is hurrying towards him in his shirtsleeves.

'Hey,' he says again, and Jake waits for him, nervously. What now?

'Stella?' the old man questions.

'Yes.' Jake starts nodding, like one of those toy dogs people have in their cars. 'Stella, yes.'

He leans close to him and says something. A single word. Jake has no idea what it is.

'Sorry?' Jake says.

The old man says it again. Twice, each time looking closely at Jake to see if he has understood. Jake strains to hear but the accent is thick and not one he is used to.

It begins with a P – that much he can make out. The idea that he is being given a clue but can't comprehend it makes sweat break out on his brow. The old man pronounces the word again and again, slapping one hand against the other, then pointing down the road. Jake looks in that direction, bemused, then looks back. What can it mean and why the hell did he never learn any Italian? The man grips his arm, willing him to understand and, suddenly, something emerges from the run-together sounds.

'Portobello?' Jake seizes on the word. He remembers seeing it on a railway-station sign on the way here, and thinking that it was a strange name for a Scottish town. 'Stella's in Portobello?'

'*Sì, sì.*' The grandfather smiles. 'Portobello. Stella in Portobello.' He has Jake by the elbow and is hustling him towards a bus-stop. '*Capisce?*' He checks as the bus approaches. 'You understand?'

'Yes,' Jake grins, as he climbs on to the bus, 'thank you. Thank you so much.'

Stella's grandfather dismisses his gratitude with a single, short gesture. Jake says the magic word to the driver, pays, gets his ticket and sits down in the front row before he thinks of something. He jumps up and yanks open the window.

'Where in Portobello?' he says.

The grandfather nods and smiles. 'Portobello, *sì*.'

'Yes, but where?'

The bus jerks into movement and the grandfather waves goodbye. Jake asks the driver – twice – to tell him when they reach Portobello, then watches the road spool out before him. The traffic gets denser as they near the city and more people get on: an elderly man, a woman with a dog in a basket, two teenagers who look like they should be at school.

Jake stares out of the window, hands gripping his knees. They are passing through what looks like a suburb. Large, sandy-stone houses with big, sloping gardens, flashes of the sea through the gaps, clipped hedges, white-painted signs for Bed and Breakfast. He sees, moving along the pavement, in step with the bus, two women.

At first it strikes him that they are walking very close together. He sees that their arms are linked and their hands intertwined. They walk together like old biddies who need the support of each other. Then Jake sees that there is something familiar about the nape of the neck of the taller one.

He leaps upright, cracking his head on the ceiling. 'Stella!' he shouts.

Everyone turns to look at him. The woman with the dog jumps and Jake presses himself to the window, banging on it with his knuckles.

'Stella!' he yells. 'Stella!'

People on the pavement stop and turn their faces up towards him. But not Stella or Nina. They are deep in conversation. Stella is saying something to her sister, and Nina is nodding. The bus picks up speed, leaving them behind. Jake bangs on the window once more, then lurches towards the bell. He jangles it, trying to keep the sisters in view.

'Can you stop?' he says. 'Please?'

The driver glances at him in the rear-view mirror but the bus rattles on, houses and people and streets flashing past.

'Please let me off,' Jake begs, jangling the bell again. 'Please.'

The driver utters a curse under his breath but, at the next lights, pulls the lever for the doors.

Jake leaps from the bus and, the second his feet hit the ground, runs in the opposite direction. He sees the faces on the bus swivel to watch him go. He estimates that he should reach them soon – he is running and they are walking in his direction, after all – but there's no sign of them. He glances over the road, in case they've crossed, then over his shoulder, but nothing. At the place where he'd first seen them, he stops, turning first one way then the other. The road stretches out in both directions, but the only figures he can see are lone people: a mother trailing a small child, a man carrying a carpet, a girl pushing a bicycle. No pairs of people walking arm in arm.

They've vanished. Jake's pulse is so fast, his heart beating so hard, he has to put up a hand and lean against a wall. Where can they have gone? Have they disappeared into one of these houses? Did he imagine it? Is he going to have to wait here in the hope of them reappearing? He would, he decides, he'd wait all night, rooted to this spot beside a lamp-post with an outdated flyer for a bring-and-buy sale taped to it, if that was what it took.

He has to resist the urge to shout her name at the top of his voice. He checks the road again, both ways. Still nothing. He looks speculatively at the side-street in front of him. It cuts between two rows of stone houses, and at its end is the sea. Jake looks at the strips of colour facing him: the grey slice of promenade, the ochre of the sand, the green-grey sea, touched with white, the jagged brownish mass of the opposite coast and, on top of it all, stretched right up from the horizon to arch out over where he is standing, the blue sky.

He hurries down the middle of the road. As he rounds the corner on to the promenade, the sea hurls a salt breeze into his face. Jake stops. He is standing outside a big red-brick Victorian swimming-baths. The beach is a huge expanse of pebbled sand, reflecting snatches of the sky. Groynes of blackened wood run along the beach, sinking themselves into water.

Descending some concrete steps to the beach is Nina. Jake sprints towards her. She is struggling to light a cigarette, turning her back to the sea, holding her coat round her lighter.

'Hi,' Jake says, when he's close enough for her to hear him.

She looks up. She takes the cigarette slowly from her lips. She opens her mouth as if she's going to say something but instead she just points, with the cigarette, towards where the concrete lip of the promenade falls away to the beach.

Jake moves to the railings. Stella is ten yards from him, walking along beside the groyne, one hand trailing against the wood. He vaults over the railings and down to the sand in one movement. Pebbles and shells crunch under his shoes. He is sure she'll turn when she hears him but she doesn't. She is looking at something out to sea, her head on one side, and just as he is about to reach her, he hears her say, 'So, do you think we should—'

'Stella?' he says.

She turns. She has a pebble in her hand. Jake can see the emerald filigree of seaweed on it. He doesn't know what to say, where to begin. Her eyes travel down to his feet and back up to his face, as if checking it's really him. The relief at having her there, in front of him, within arm's length, is so great that he realises the tears he fought down earlier are threatening to rise again. Jake panics – what on earth is wrong with him? – and has to stare at the ground, at their feet, which face each other, at the way stones have stencilled patterns on to the sand.

'I want to apologise,' he says. 'For . . . Mel and . . .' He gestures inarticulately behind him. 'I've been an idiot.'

He curls his hands inside his pockets. He's been rehearsing this speech for so long you'd think it would come out better, but just being here with her makes him lose all sense of what it is he needs to say. He'd forgotten that she has that effect on him, draining his head of all rational thought.

'I know . . .' he soldiers on '. . . that there's no excuse . . . that . . . that there's nothing I can say to . . . to . . . The thing is, ever since I met you, I . . . I . . .'

He gazes at her. She is looking at him, a little perplexed, her hands clasped round the pebble. The mobile, angular beauty of her face – he'd forgotten that too. 'What was I saying?' he asks.

'Ever since you met me,' she prompts.

'Ah.' He looks at the horizon for inspiration. 'Yes. Ever since . . .' he hears himself begin again. Then he sighs, his shoulders slump and he takes a step towards her. 'God, Stella,' he says, in his normal voice, 'I've been looking for you everywhere.'

'Have you?'

'Yeah. All over. In London and—'

'You went to London?'

'Yes.'

'But I wasn't there.'

'I know that,' he says, 'now.'

She is silent for a moment. She shifts the stone into her other hand and he is aware of her looking over his shoulder at something. Her sister? Possibly. Jake doesn't turn round to see. 'Look,' he says, 'will you walk down to the sea with me?'

She glances behind him again, just once, but says, 'OK.'

They walk side by side. Every few steps, he feels her sleeve brush against his. He wonders if she's aware of it too. He still can't get over the fact that she is here, that he found her, that they are together on this huge beach under the wide expanse of sky.

'So how long were you in London?' she asks.

'A couple of days.'

'And did you like it any more than last time?' She looks at him sideways.

He smiles. 'Not much. I was staying in a place that stank of bodily fluids and I couldn't find my way about and I ran out of money. And the only person I wanted to see turned out not to be there after all.'

She lifts a hand to brush a few stray strands of hair away from her eyes. The breeze blows them back immediately and she has to turn her face to the wind to get rid of them. Jake stops walking and she stops too, looking at him expectantly.

'Stella,' he says, and he touches her arm, 'it's madness, us not being together.'

She looks up at him, scanning his face. 'I . . .' she begins, then, dropping her eyes, says, 'I think I'm going away.'

'Away?' Jake is exasperated. 'Away where?'

'I don't know,' she murmurs. 'There's this job in Boston that—'

'Fuck Boston. Stella, please. I want . . . I just want . . .' What does he want? He has to think. Then, suddenly, he knows: 'I want you to come back to Hong Kong with me.'

She laughs. 'What?'

'Hong Kong,' he repeats, the idea unfurling in his mind. 'I want you with me, in Hong Kong.'

'You're not serious.'

'I am,' he insists. 'I've never been more serious in my life.'

'You think I'd come to Hong Kong with you just like that?'

'Why not? You just said you're going away anyway. You'll love it. It's like nowhere else you've ever been. It has everything you could possibly want – a city, mountains, beautiful beaches, national parks. Um. What else? The food is the best you'll ever eat. It's not too hot yet, or humid. Er. My best friend works at the big broadcasting station – we can talk to him about getting you a job.'

Stella, staring at him, shakes her head in amazement.

'Are you convinced yet?' he says. 'You can go on day trips to China. There are these great trams. You can go on night-time rides, from one end of the island to the other, to look at all the neon. You'll love it,' he says again. 'And, anyway, you have a moral obligation to come.'

'A moral obligation? How come?'

He shrugs. 'If I'm not back there in two days I won't have a job and I'll get kicked out of my apartment and I can't leave without you. So you'd be saving me from destitution and . . . and disgrace.'

She leans against the salt-saturated wood of the groyne, running her fingertips over the pocked barnacles.

'You have to come,' he says.

She turns her gaze on him. 'Do I?'

'Yes. Because if you don't . . .' Jake moves towards her. Without thinking about what he is doing, he folds his arms round her and there, on Portobello beach, he lifts her off her feet. 'Because if you don't,' he says tightly, into her neck, 'I'm going to have to spend the rest of my life looking for another you. And I don't think there is one.'

She is struggling and laughing and saying his name, saying she can't breathe, but her arms are round him, her fingers laced behind his neck. Jake kisses her cheek, her forehead, her ear, her lips, any part of her he can reach, and his mouth is full of her hair and for a moment he thinks that everything is fixed, that everything will work out.

But she twists in his grasp, turning her face aside, tugging herself away from him. 'There are things,' she says, 'I have to do.'

'What things? There are no things.'

'I promised.' She presses her hand to her cheek, distractedly. 'I promised my grandmother I'd work this week.'

'Fine. We'll go in a week.'

'But you said you have to go in two days.'

'A week, two days, what difference will it make? Just promise me you'll come.'

She looks down, her toe sketching curves in the sand. She shakes her head.

'Promise me,' he urges.

'I can't.' Her voice drops low into her chest. She lifts herself up so that she's sitting on the groyne and covers her face with her hands. 'I can't.'

Jake leans on the wood, a hand either side of her. 'Why not?'

'I just can't. I'm sorry,' she whispers, and she reaches out for him, curls her hands round his neck and pulls him towards her. His face is pressed to hers, resting on hers, her forehead against his cheek. Jake can't say anything. They are both shaking. He feels as though the sand underneath him is live, quick, that he might slide sideways or down. He puts his arms round her and holds on to her, tight. They stay like this for a while, her fingers straying through his hair. He can feel the fluttering thud of her heart through her clothes.

'I'm sorry,' she says, in his ear. 'I'm so sorry. Don't be angry with me.'

'Stella,' he breathes in the smell of her skin, 'tell me why you can't. Is it . . . do you not . . .' He has to force himself to say it. 'Do you not feel . . . anything for me? Is that it?'

'No!' She clutches him to her. 'Don't think that, don't ever think that. I just . . . I just don't think I'm cut out for this.'

'You are,' he insists. 'You definitely are.'

'I'm not. I'd make you miserable.'

'You wouldn't.' He pulls away and cups her face in his hands. 'Quite the opposite. Can't you see I love you?'

Tears spring from her eyes and slip down her face and he rubs them away with his thumb. 'I love you,' he repeats. 'I really do.' Jake thinks of something. 'Stella, does this have anything to do with – with what your sister told me? About . . . what happened when you were young?'

He sees her cheeks flame beneath the tears, her eyes widen, and he cannot believe it. 'If you think for a minute that something like that could change how I feel about you,' he gives her a shake, 'I can't tell you how wrong you are.'

She sniffs, her face agitated, panicked, brushing roughly at her cheeks. 'Really?' she says, almost inaudibly.

'No!' He lets out an incredulous noise. 'Jesus, how could you ever think it would? It's ridiculous, it's almost insulting.'

'But, Jake—'

'Well, how about if it was the other way round? If it was me? Would it have any effect on how you felt about me?'

She is silent.

'Would it?' he persists.

'No,' she says, in a small voice.

'Right.' He slaps his hand against the barnacled wood. 'Thank you. Now, are you coming to Hong Kong with me?'

She shakes her head.

Jake sighs and grits his teeth. 'Are you coming to Hong Kong with me?'

She looks at him, then looks away. 'No.'

'Stella Gilmore, you're driving me mad. Why not?'

She sits hunched, her hands in her lap. There is something about her expression – a resignation, a closedness – that tells him her mind is made up. He knows enough about her to see that nothing he could say will change a thing. She's not coming. Jake pushes himself upright, away from her, and moves off down the beach. The wind tugs and strains at his jacket. Several feet off, he stops. 'I don't know what to say to you,' he yells. 'I don't understand. This is what you want, is it? I go back to Hong Kong and you stay here, and that's that?'

He leans down and picks up a handful of pebbles and hurls them, one by one, into the wind. The sand is patched with pools of water and he throws the pebbles towards them, wanting to shatter the glass-perfect blue.

After a while, Stella appears at his elbow. 'I . . .' she begins, tentative '. . . I could call you. If you want.'

Jake throws another stone, furious, arching his arm back behind him. 'In Hong Kong?'

'Yes.'

'And what would be the point in that?'

She doesn't say anything, just bows her head. Jake sifts pebbles from one hand into the other. He lets one fall and catches it squarely with his toe, kicking it towards a bank of desiccated seaweed.

'Is that,' he says, trying to keep his voice even, 'all you can give me to go on?'

She nods. 'I'm sorry.'

Jake stands in his apartment, looking down into the street. Everything is so exactly the same it's as if he never went away. Or, rather, that he's stepped back in time. In the kitchen, when he arrived, he found a silver bracelet of Mel's, and in the bathroom cabinet, folded up, one of the slings he had for his arm. He feels as though he might, at any moment, turn a corner and bump into the person he was before Chinese New Year.

He unlatches the window and the white, burning heat of summer hits him in the face. Jake smiles. It's thirty-five degrees out there today and he loves it.

He's been back three days. Four if you count today. The haze of jetlag is lifting – he slept for seven solid hours last night – and he's beginning to get back into the mindset of being here. He needs to go to the market, buy some vegetables, should really give the apartment a sweep. He might get the ferry later to Kowloon, meet up with Hing Tai for *dim sum*. Hing Tai said Mui wanted to go for a swim later and did Jake fancy coming too? He spent yesterday in a meeting with Chen and the locations manager, discussing the places they could shoot the opening sequence of the new film, and Chen had wanted him to see various screen tests.

He is surprised by the ease with which you can slot back into a life. People tend to ask him a few questions about 'his trip', as they call it, then move on. Hing Tai had been a bit more insistent. Maybe he'd been talking to Caroline. He'd asked about Mel, then narrowed his eyes and demanded, 'And what else?' Jake had shrugged. They had been at Hing Tai's mother's and the room had been filled with people, relatives, colleagues, and Jake hadn't felt like going into it just then.

Jake closes the window. He'll go to the market now, before getting the ferry. She hasn't called. But it's only three days. Four, if you count today. Which Jake isn't. Yet.

Stella sits at the till, her knees drawn up. Behind her, her grandmother is talking to her uncle. Something about needing to stir the ice-cream in five minutes and how they have to fix a couple of the chairs and something else, in between, about a letter from Italy.

From her vantage-point, she surveys the room. Nina and Richard sit in a booth, the weekend paper between them. The café is full, as it should be on a Saturday in summer. Stella finds it peculiar sometimes: all these people, eating. By the window, at the back, along the wall, tables with people slicing food into pieces, raising it to their mouths, closing their lips round it, chewing and chewing, then swallowing, pushing the food down into their stomachs.

She imagines the hordes who have passed through the café today, spreading out through Musselburgh and Edinburgh and Lothian, going about their business, Iannelli food filtering through their bodies.

A woman approaches the counter and Stella writes down what she wants. A toastie and a cappuccino. She takes the food order through to her uncle, then she gets down the cup to make the cappuccino.

As she stands at the coffee machine, she sees that the sun has come out. The door bangs and someone is entering the café. Nina is putting a cigarette to her lips and pressing down on the lighter. Richard is stirring sugar into his espresso. A young girl is running backwards past the window, laughing, clutching two loaves of bread to her chest.

Stella thinks: there are some things in life that will always be indissoluble, indigestible. The girl outside collides with a man carrying a saddle and she drops one of the loaves, still laughing. The smoke from Nina's cigarette uncurls to the ceiling.

Days later, she is in Nina's car.

'I want to make it quite clear I'm only doing this because I'm your sister,' Nina says.

'OK.'

'I want you to understand that I completely disapprove.'

'OK, OK.'

'That I think it's a stupid, crap, ridiculous idea.'

'All right, Nina, I get it.'

Nina accelerates up the Royal Mile, the tyres snapping

on the cobbles, and soon they are swooping down the curved hill, the New Town laid out before them. Stella almost sighs. It's a shame she can't bring herself to live in this city. Maybe one day.

'I don't agree with what you're doing,' Nina continues, her steering made erratic by the fact that she's unwinding the Cellophane from a packet of cigarettes.

'You've made your point.' Stella flinches as they only narrowly clear a traffic bollard. 'Do you think you could keep both hands on the wheel?'

They wait in line at the lights to cross Princes Street.

'All I'm saying is—'

'Quite a lot,' Stella mutters.

Nina ignores her. 'Call him.'

'No.'

'Just call him.'

'No.' Stella shakes her head.

'Why?'

'I . . .' Stella tries to think of a reason. Then gives up. 'I can't.'

'I'll call him, then.' Nina flashes her a malicious grin. 'I can pretend to be you, easily.'

'Don't.' Stella looks across at her sister.

Nina shrugs and smiles.

'Nina, I mean it.' Stella is fierce. 'You must not.'

'I might. It's for your own good.'

'If you do − I'll − I really will never speak to you again.'

'Yes, you will.'

'No, I won't.'

'You will.' She blows smoke over Stella's face.

Stella winds down the window. 'I will not. Don't you dare.'

Nina sighs and drums her fingers on the steering-wheel. 'Please.' She changes tack, begging.

'No.'

'Please?'

Stella sighs. 'Neen, just drop it, will you?'

'Why not?'

'Because first of all, I don't know what to say, second of all, he's probably still really angry with me, and—'

'Third of all, you don't know that.'

'Well, you don't know that he isn't.'

'I do.'

'You do not.'

'I do. The man adores you. It's obvious. Sisterly intuition.'

'Yeah, right.' She shoots Nina a look. 'Your sisterly intuition's been great recently.'

Nina stubs out her cigarette in the ashtray. 'I thought you weren't going to bring that up again.' She tosses the butt out of the window.

Stella holds up her hands. 'I wasn't. Look, all I'm saying is, it's my life so let me handle it.'

'By running away to America?'

'Just . . . let me be.'

Nina screeches to a halt outside the travel shop, on a double yellow line. 'I'll wait here. Don't be long. We have to be over at Mum's in twenty minutes.'

Stella gets out of the car and runs over the pavement.

She glances at the lists of flights in the window: Madrid, Barcelona, Sydney, Prague, Los Angeles, Miami, New York. Return or one-way. She gets the light-headed feeling she always gets when faced with a world map, that dizzying scope of the possible. She could go anywhere, be anyone, rewrite her life just by getting on a plane. All she has to do is hand over some money. Travel strikes her sometimes as an almost suspiciously easy bargain: a new life in exchange for cash. Surely there should be something more Faustian, more binding about it? How can it be that easy?

She turns and looks at her sister, who is glaring balefully at her through the windscreen, smoke wisping from her mouth like a dragon.

When she comes back, she puts the shiny packet of an air-ticket on to the dashboard. 'Have a look,' she says.

'I don't see why I should.' Nina jams the keys into the ignition. 'As I've said, I completely disapprove of this whole scheme.'

'Just have a look.' Stella jiggles the packet invitingly in front of her sister. 'Go on.'

Nina sighs, flicks it open and scans the close type. Stella sees her frown, lean closer, frown again, then turn to look at her.

'Oh, my God,' Nina says slowly.

Jake has decided that work is the antidote to misery. He's getting to the office before eight and not leaving until about eleven at night. He's involving himself in everything – locations, rewrites, screen tests, rehearsals, costumes. He even sat in on a meeting with the caterers. Chen laid a hand on his shoulder yesterday: 'Slow down,' he said, 'you might crash.'

He's had the phone line tested twice. He got his mother to call him back, just to make sure it worked internationally. He bought a new answerphone, just in case. But it's been two weeks. Just over. Jake is beginning to realise that she might not call.

Maybe he's an idiot, but this scenario had never occurred to him. He doesn't know what to do. He wants to fly back to Britain, or Boston, or wherever it is she's got to, to see her again, to try to persuade her. But he hasn't the money at present and Hing Tai had said that if he heard Jake had so much as made enquiries about air tickets, he would confiscate his passport. Don't chase her, he'd said, let her come to you. But what if she doesn't, Jake had asked, and Hing Tai didn't have an answer to that.

Jake lifts a spoonful of *congee* to his mouth, then puts it down. He's having breakfast in a place near the office. It's a long, overlit room with rows and rows of tables. Steam obscures the windows and a long queue snakes from the counter to the door. The tables are full of people eating and drinking tea. The man behind the counter calls orders through to the kitchen, then shouts at the boy pushing a greyish mop around the tiles. Music spirals out of a radio. Four men sit at Jake's table, crushing him against the wall. One of them is expounding the faults of their boss while the other three listen. In the corner, an ancient woman on a stool picks her teeth.

Jake tunes into the conversation about the boss then, tiring of that, tunes into the one behind him. Two teenagers talking about their mobile phones. He eats some more of his *congee* but his heart's not in it. He wonders what he is doing, coming into the office on a Saturday. He'd told himself there were lots of things he could get done while it was quiet, but now he's here, he can't remember what any of them were.

He sits, his hands resting on the table. People swim past the windows, some glancing in at him. The boy with the mop reaches up and retunes the radio. The traffic on the flyover rumbles and shakes. The men next to him pour and sip tea, still talking. And suddenly Jake is sitting bolt upright.

He can hear Stella's voice.

He tilts his head, disbelieving. It's her. He would swear his life on it.

He twists on his stool to look behind him. Nothing – just tables of people having breakfast. He leaps up, his stool clattering to the floor. It is her. Talking. As if she's there in the restaurant somewhere, or trapped in the walls, or has invaded his head. Jake turns wildly one way, then the other, trying to find the source.

People are staring at him now, the mad *gweilo*, looking about for something or someone, but Jake doesn't care. Where is she? The idea that she is somewhere near to him but he can't find her makes him feel as though he might lose his mind. Is he imagining it? Has she finally robbed him of his reason? He peers out of the window at the people on the pavement. Then he turns and starts weaving his way through the tables.

'Three suspects have been detained today,' she is saying, 'but police have not as yet issued a statement.'

Jake stares at the radio screwed into the wall, a small black and chrome box. Stella is speaking from it, talking to him about a drugs bust. He has to stop himself reaching up and kissing it.

Jake hurtles across the room, towards the phone sitting on the counter. For a moment he can't remember the number. Then it comes back to him. He hears the phone being answered on the first ring.

'*Wai-ee?*'

'It's me, listen—'

'*Jik-ah?*'

'Yeah, yeah. Now—'

'I'm glad you've called,' Hing Tai says chattily, 'because I was having this argument with my brother last night and—'

'Listen, I can't talk now, I—'

'Oh, thanks. Thanks a lot. For ringing me up and then telling me you can't talk. I mean, that's really nice. If I rang you up and—'

'Shut up, shut up a minute. This is really important.'

'What? What's more important than—'

'Hing Tai. I mean it. If you don't shut up and listen to me, my whole life could fall apart.'

'Shit,' Hing Tai says, unmoved. 'You'd better tell me, then.'

'OK.' Jake takes a deep breath. 'Somewhere in your building someone is reading the news.'

Hing Tai makes an impatient noise. 'Is that what you're calling to tell me?' he demands. 'Has your brain gone soft in—'

'I want you,' Jake carries on regardless, 'to do me a huge favour.'

As Stella steps out of the studio, the news pages in her hand, easing the buffered, soundproofed door closed, there is a man standing behind the producer. He is wearing jeans and a large-collared shirt, and the very tips of his hair are bleached white. Stella is wondering how you'd do that when she realises he is speaking to her. 'You are Stella?' he is saying.

'Yes.'

'Come,' he beckons, 'come with me.'

She follows him, puzzled, away from the studio, down a long corridor, through a lift lobby, into a stairwell, down a few flights of stairs. Every few steps, he turns round — to check she's still with him? Stella's not sure. He seems to be assessing her, looking her up and down, considering her.

'Can I ask what this is about?' Stella ventures.

'Come,' he replies, 'follow me, please.'

The building unravels before her. She hasn't got the hang of it yet, can't orientate herself within it. But that goes for the entire city at the moment. They arrive in a room where hundreds of people are sitting in sectioned booths. The man beckons to her again as he steps into a cubicle. When she comes to a stop, he is holding out a phone to her.

'Call for you,' he says.

'For me?' Stella won't take the receiver. 'Who is it?'

The man puts the phone to his ear, grinning to himself, and says something into it in Chinese. Then he holds it out to her again. 'He says you must stop being stubborn and take the phone.'

Stella is so shocked she does as she's told. 'Hello?'

'I've been waiting by the phone for weeks.' Jake's voice is close to her ear.

'Have you?' she says, and she worries for a moment that she won't be able to hear his answer because her pulse is deafening her.

'I can't believe it,' he says. 'I can't believe you didn't call me, and I can't believe you're here.'

'Well,' she says, 'I am.'

'I heard you on the radio.'

'Did you?'

'You were good. I think. Although I'm probably not the best judge right now. But I wanted to kiss it, if that gives you any idea—'

'You wanted to kiss it?' She laughs. 'The radio?'

The man in the cubicle is pretending that he's not listening, she sees, fiddling with his computer, but he's smiling and shaking his head.

'Listen, I'm coming to find you. You're not going to vanish or disappear anywhere, are you?'

'Jake, you don't need to come here. I can always—'

'No, no. Stay exactly where you are. Hing Tai's under strict instructions not to let you out of his sight. Just stand still, don't move and don't go anywhere.'

Jake bursts from the restaurant. Rain has just started to fall, dark circles spotting the pavement. He runs down the road, his sneakers slapping the concrete. As he turns the corner, the rain suddenly doubles, the spots on the ground merging until the whole street is slick and polished like sealskin. Owners of street-side noodle bars pull canopies over their tables and men are holding folded newspapers over their heads and people are dashing into doorways or under trees or into the MTR station.

Jake runs. The muscles in his legs burn and the rain slides in channels down his hair and on to his face. He gasps for air and drops fall into his mouth. He dodges men in suits, a woman dragging a steel cart, a family running in the opposite direction, a man weighed down with a bucket of crustaceans, two girls laughing to each other as they wring out their long ropes of hair.

As he runs, he sees the way the city copes with rain. Water ribbons from pipes and gutters, from roofs, down the sides of buildings, bubbling across the tilting pavements and into the street, where it swirls round and down the drains, to be hurried away under roads, along invisible trenches. Buses and taxis plash through the lakes collecting against the kerbs, throwing tidal waves of water over the pavement, over people's ankles.

The rain is stinging his skin and he pushes himself to speed up, moving into the road, off the crowded pavement, water soaking through his shoes, his jeans, his socks. He goes under a big bridge where crowds of people are sheltering and when he comes out again into the light he can make out the radio station building up ahead and, in the doorway, Hing Tai and, behind him, Stella.

Hing Tai is looking the wrong way, across the road, but Stella sees him. She steps out into the street, into the rain, and raises her hand, like someone shielding their eyes from light, like someone answering a question.

acknowledgements

My thanks to: William Sutcliffe, Victoria Hobbs, Mary-Anne Harrington, Ruth Metzstein, Kate Jones, Beatrice Monti della Corte, The Santa Maddalena Foundation, Bill Swainson, Alessandra Gnecchi-Ruscone, Mary Lewis, Adam Sutcliffe, Dewi Davies, Elizabeth Ingrams, and my family – Patrick, Susan, Catherine and Bridget.

I am indebted to the following books: *Emigration in a South Italian Town: An Anthropological History* by William A. Douglas (Rutgers University Press, New Jersey, 1984) and *Multiculturalism in Practice: Irish, Jewish, Italian and Pakistani Migration to Scotland* by Suzanne Audrey (Ashgate, 2000). Also to Elizabeth Grant's *Memoirs of a Highland Lady* (Canongate, Edinburgh, 1988) – and to my mother, for giving it to me in the first place.